D0835817

THE LOTUS EATERS

In this huge teeming novel, the gold-plated babylon of a Florida pleasure resort is contrasted with the work of a group of archaeologists who are unearthing in the vicinity the remains of a primitive settlement. The novel's two chief characters vividly point the contrast: Tom Sorrento, one-time football hero, a man of humble origin who bewildered his family by becoming an anthropologist; and Ira deKay, the PR man and smart operator, with a hand in every racket, and a rake-off in every deal, the smiler who can "organize" anything and anyone—Ira the pleasure merchant. The clash between these two men provides the theme of the story, made tense and ironic by the fact that both are in love with the same woman.

The Lotus Eaters, with its wide cast of characters, is rich in excitement and comedy, but beneath its scintillating surface Mr. Green has important things to say. In dramatic fashion he explores and contrasts the search for pleasure and the search for truth.

BOOKS BY GERALD GREEN

THE LOTUS EATERS

THE LAST ANGRY MAN

THE SWORD AND THE SUN

HIS MAJESTY O'KEEFE *(with Larry Klingman)*

THE LOTUS EATERS

BY GERALD GREEN

LONGMANS

LONGMANS, GREEN AND CO LTD
6 & 7 CLIFFORD STREET, LONDON W1
THIBAULT HOUSE, THIBAULT SQUARE, CAPE TOWN
605–611 LONSDALE STREET, MELBOURNE C1
443 LOCKHART ROAD, HONG KONG
ACCRA, AUCKLAND, IBADAN
KINGSTON (JAMAICA), KUALA LUMPUR
LAHORE, NAIROBI, SALISBURY (RHODESIA)
LONGMANS, GREEN AND CO INC
119 WEST 40TH STREET, NEW YORK 18
LONGMANS, GREEN AND CO
20 CRANFIELD ROAD, TORONTO 16
ORIENT LONGMANS PRIVATE LTD
CALCUTTA, BOMBAY, MADRAS
DELHI, HYDERABAD, DACCA

First published in this edition 1960

PRINTED IN GREAT BRITAIN
BY BUTLER AND TANNER LTD
FROME AND LONDON

FOR ANNA GREENBERG

I am a great friend to public amusements; for they keep the people from vice.

—Samuel Johnson

. . . a land where all things always seemed the
same!
And round about the keel with faces pale
Dark faces pale against that rosy flame,
The mild-eyed melancholy Lotus-eaters came.

—Tennyson

PART I

1 *Mr. Banjo's Motorcade*

WITH undulant moan of siren and peremptory screech of whistle, the motorcade lurched from the sticky airport tar, onto the boulevard of palms shimmering in midsummer heat, and sped toward the cool white towers of the Beach.

As motorcades went, it was a shabby one. A quincunx of motorcycle cops preceded the mayor's limousine. Behind the black official car were seven multicolored convertibles, each car tenanted by young girls in bathing suits. In the withering sunlight they were a blur of variegated breasts and buttocks. Each automobile bore a banner of welcome:

BLUE PARADISE BAR
WELCOMES MR. BANJO!

GREETINGS TO MR. BANJO
FROM
THE PERUVIANA HOTEL

STATION KMX-TV
SAYS HELLO MR. BANJO!

At the procession's rear, an open panel truck laden with Deke Dawson's Dixieland Dandies shivered the tropic air with "Down in Jungletown." The city's browned residents, inured to celebrities and noise, watched the parade of screeching vehicles with good-natured indifference.

In addition to the chauffeur there were four riders in the mayor's limousine. The mayor himself, occupied with the dedication of a new dredging machine, had sent a deputy, a man named Charles Rasmussen, whose full title was Director of Community Relations. He was a press agent for the Beach. Rasmussen sat on the visiting celebrity's right. On the dignitary's left flank sat his own manager, a thickish young man with abundant sideburns. The fourth rider was slumped low on one jump seat, his legs extended indolently across the adjacent seat. His name was Ira deKay and he had arranged the public rites for the guest.

The visitor—he was a television performer of international fame—maintained a discreet silence regarding the paucity of cheering crowds, the absence of the mayor, the general shoddiness of the reception. His manager was less restrained.

"You shoulda seen Cincinnati," he said petulantly. "They give us the whole town. Four thousand people in Fountain Square and a United States Senator. Birdie Tebbetts give us a bat autographed by all the Cincinnati Reds."

There was a soggy silence, a shifting of moist bodies, an absent gazing through opened windows at gaudy storefronts and motionless palm trees. Through the dilating whine of the sirens, Deke Dawson's brainless music filtered through to them. The band was singing.

Then the big baboon
One night in June
He married them
And very soon . . .

"And Schenectady, New York!" the manager cried. "What a time we had! Everybody came out for Mr. Banjo! They printed little Mr. Banjo buttons for the kids. You know that big corporation there? Well, the president had his picture taken with Mr. Banjo. His wife came around the next day to have hers taken. Them pictures are right in his office."

Ira deKay shifted his long, willowy body. He patted the manager's hand.

"Sweetie, don't get upset," deKay said. "It takes a little time for the folks down here to warm up to a new face. They're kinda used to big TV stars from New York. As soon as we spread the word that Mr. Banjo's here, they'll *love* him. Me and Charlie'll see to that."

"I dunno, Ira," the manager persisted. "Not a single reporter at the airport. And those punk photographers. They missed all the good action. Like when Mr. Banjo lifted the police chief's watch."

Ira deKay raised one foot. It was shod in gold suede, lashed to his ankle with braided leather. The gilt foot poked Charlie Rasmussen gently.

"How about it, Charlie baby?" deKay asked. "Where *were* the reporters? Not even a television columnist?"

"Lay off me, Ira," Rasmussen muttered. He was an undersized man, as bland as the aimless publicity handouts he wrote for the Beach. A lifetime dedicated to worrying about other people's public selves had endowed his hairless head and face with an excess of wrinkles and furrows. These wounds he had effectively camouflaged with a cordovan sunstain and saucer-sized smoked glasses.

"Charlie *sweetie!*" deKay sang. It came out musically, rising and falling. He nudged Rasmussen's knee again. This time the press agent shoved the foot away.

"It's not like Banjo is like any old television name," the manager said. "He's got a following. He's a national figure. He gets a hunnert letters a day. Ira read 'em when he was in New York, dincha Ira?"

"You bet I did, doll. Mr. Banjo is very big."

The motorcade ground to a sweating halt. A moving van, engineering a hazardous U-turn, blocked their progress. The policemen whistled frantically at the driver.

"Some punk parade," the manager grumbled. "In Huntington, West Virginia, they treated us better."

Ira deKay heard neither the manager's whines nor the shrill of the whistles, nor Deke Dawson's serenade. He was squinting through the car window. The object of his scrutiny had jerked him upright from his leisurely sprawl. They were stalled on one of the lush islets on the azure bay that separated the Beach from the city proper, a place of pastel estates, aromatic with sea grape and hibiscus, a congeries of stucco palaces and three-car garages. Between the blacktop roadway and the still waters lay a stretch of undeveloped sandy land, the only barren acreage in sight. It sloped gently from the highway to the bay and was covered with patches of Bermuda grass. Halfway down the incline, deKay saw three Negroes laboring beside a deep trench. Distantly, nearer the water, he imagined he saw a smaller excavation.

The celebrity yawned and scratched his neck. Charlie Rasmussen consulted his wristwatch nervously. DeKay's stunts were always wrecking his meticulous schedules. He had a sneaking suspicion that Ira owned a percentage of the visiting performer —Ira always had something *extra* going for him. Rasmussen glanced covertly at the tall blond man. DeKay, staring at the colored laborers and the pit, moved toward Rasmussen as if to query him, thought better of it, and resumed his slouching position on the jump seats.

The motorcade proceeded. During the delay on the island a few pedestrians had recognized the visitor. They had laughed and had called his name. He had waved back at them.

"See? See what I mean?" the manager cried. "If youda hadda open car, like I asked, Ira, everybody woulda seen Banjo. You know—one of them big research companies asked a lotta people who they knew better, Mr. Banjo or the people in the President's cabinet. Guess what? Except for two guys, *everybody* knew Banjo better. I got the statistics home. It's true."

"You bet it's true, baby," said deKay.

They were streaking down the main street of the resort. On either side of them rose the great white hotels, soaring castles of plaster, glass, tile. From constricted alleys separating the magnificent erections, an effluvia of kitchen odors and sun-heated garbage drifted toward them.

"That lead cop is nuts," Rasmussen grumbled. "He's doin' forty at least and he knows it's illegal ever since that guy got killed last month in the motorcade for General Avilas."

"This is more like it!" the manager shouted. "People are seein' us! G'wan, Mr. Banjo! Wave at 'em! *Wave at 'em!*"

The television performer was pushed across Rasmussen's lap to a window. He looked with humorless eyes at the blurred panorama: browned women, mammoth automobiles, foot-high cheesecake in restaurant windows, everything coated with buttery-yellow sunlight. He waved lazily.

The crash, noiseless amid the din of horns, band and siren, hurled the limousine's occupants forward when the chauffeur slammed his brakes. Ahead of them, they could see the lead motorcycle and its dismounted rider. The bike had grazed a double-parked ice-cream truck, ricocheted onto the lawn of a hotel and come to rest, upended, in the landscaping. Beneath a flowering mimosa, the injured policeman rested on his knees, holding bloodied head in bruised hands.

Rasmussen flew from the official car, rudely shoving the celebrity aside. DeKay and the chauffeur followed. Several dozen people ran from the hotel porch; someone shrieked for a doctor.

"You were doin' forty!" Rasmussen cried. "Don't you know the rules? You tryina make trouble for us?"

The officer groaned. "Oh, Jesus. For a lousy ape."

"You ain't hurt bad," Rasmussen said. "You better *not* be."

DeKay was kneeling at the officer's side.

"Now, baby, just rest easy and don't pay attention to Mr. Rasmussen," he said soothingly. "Ira will see that you get taken care of. You call me tomorrow." He winked at the gory agent of the law—a wink that promised love, money, recompense.

It seemed incredible and repugnant to Rasmussen that these ludicrous words, directed at a man who almost had been killed in a pointless ceremonial, could have acted as a palliative. Yet through blood and dirt, the officer was smiling. His split tongue reached for a loose tooth, and still he smiled at Ira.

"Oh, it's you, Mr. deKay. You bet, sir. I'll call you."

The crowd was now a mob. Hundreds of people in bright sportswear, in cabana suits, tight pants, beach clothing, surged around the halted automobiles. Of the two foci of attention, the celebrity appeared to have drawn the more exhilarated audience. Several dozen bronzed children milled and jostled around the limousine, trying to touch the visitor.

"I saw him! I saw him!"

"So cute! Just like a little boy!"

"Oooh, I could kiss him! He waved at me."

Rasmussen and deKay elbowed their way through the mob and tried to re-enter the limousine.

"Swell, just swell," the Beach press agent muttered. "You and your promotions. I ain't got enough trouble with that shamus gettin' killed last month and now this. I swear, Ira, one of these days you'll push me too far." Rasmussen ran a trembling hand over his burned, hairless pate. "Ira, you don't run this town. You may think you do, but you don't."

"*Charlie.* You're raising your voice."

"You bet I am. Just because you own a piece of this ape. Oh, I'm wise to you, Ira. Every one of your deals works with another deal. What do you have—twenty per cent of the chimp?"

They paused at the black car, the chauffeur holding the door open, trying to repress the laughing, clutching crowd. DeKay frowned. His golden eyebrows arched in confused chagrin. The manager leaned from the open door.

"Just one moment, Mr. Rasmussen," he said precisely. His doughy voice was quivering. "Mr. Banjo is not a chimpanzee. No sir. He is not. He is an *orangutan.* That is what makes him unique in TV. There's all kinds of chimps, but only one Mr. Banjo. And besides, he didn't ask to come down to this place. Mr. deKay begged us to. Right, Ira?"

Rasmussen climbed into the car. He sat down heavily next to Mr. Banjo. DeKay lingered outside.

"*Aaaaaaaaah!*" the press agent screamed. "The son-of-a-bitch bit me!"

Incredulous and terrified, Rasmussen was studying the ruby teeth marks on his right hand. He had recoiled to a corner of the oven-hot car. Mr. Banjo, upset by his victim's wail, was clinging to his manager's neck and shrieking in short, agonized gasps.

"Awright, Ira," Rasmussen said shakily, "I hope you're happy now!" He screamed at the chauffeur. "Come on for Chrissake! Get this thing going! Get in, Ira!"

DeKay threw up his hands. Surrounded by brown, happy children, he looked like a popular camp counselor. "If that's your attitude, doll," he said peevishly, "you don't need me. You handle it. I got other things to do."

"Don't you leave me with him!"

"Ira?" the manager whined. "You leaving us?"

DeKay winked at Rasmussen. "Charlie will take care of you, kids. Right to the Peruviana. The Presidential Suite. Won't you, Charlie?"

DeKay left them, walking to the first convertible.

The car was laden with five semi-nude girls. A sixth woman, an aloof, fully clothed blond, was at the wheel.

"Girls," deKay said firmly, "please pile out. Charlie will take care of you at the Peruviana. Grab a cab and charge it to Ira."

There were a few squeals of protest. A glandular brunette muttered something about Ira's cheap tricks and he tweaked her thigh as she climbed out. DeKay got into the convertible, seating himself next to the blond. She was an extremely pretty woman in her middle twenties—her tan was of such immaculate quality, so rich in texture and lustrous in hue, that it appeared to have been sprayed on. She wore a simple white linen dress. In defiance of the hellish heat, a tan cashmere was thrown over her mocha shoulders.

"Cleo, baby, turn around and head back to the Ellenbogen place," he said evenly. The wild joviality had left his voice. The woman, as passionless and neutral as the high sterile structures surrounding them, wheeled the enormous car around and horned her way through clotting traffic.

The motorcade resumed its erratic journey. Within the limousine, Charlie Rasmussen backed himself against the seat and glared at his guest, attired in gray flannel suit, gray porkpie, pink shirt, black knitted tie.

"Keep that redheaded bastard away from me," he said shakily, "or I'll crack his skull."

2 *Dr. Sorrento and Dr. Ballard*

ALONGSIDE Dave Ballard, the two Negro laborers had the look of Westernized pygmies. Neither of the workmen were small; it was simply that Ballard was one of those giants who shrinks his environment, whose size and bulk is almost oppressive. He suggested a geological cross-section. His dusty GI clodhoppers, size 15-E, were a primordial schist from the paleozoic; these gave way to the gray basalt columns of his legs; the huge gut and chest, in gray workshirt, could have been a recent shale deposit, merging without intervention of neck, to a sandstone head. Ballard's hat, a low-comedy fedora, brim clipped to a half-inch, was a ranger station on the rocky heights.

The laborers were new, despatched that morning by the state employment office. They rested, attentive and respectful, on battered shovels, as Ballard explained their duties.

"See those clotheslines laid out like a big rectangle? The ones tied to the two-by-fours. That's the big trench. Fifty feet long, ten feet wide."

They nodded thoughtfully. One of the workmen was a young man, in his late twenties. Ballard knew him only as "Spots," a reference to the splotchy dark-brown freckles on his beige face. The other was named McIsaac. He was much older and blacker.

"Now this kind of digging is going to be a cinch if you fellows have been used to regular excavation," Ballard continued. "Just make sure your shovel is flush with the sides of the trench. Keep the sidewall as straight as you can. Don't go deeper than eight inches with each shovelful."

Ballard gestured to them to follow him. The three of them moved about twenty paces, to higher ground. "You get a better idea from here," he said. "Every five feet, on either side of the trench, there's a two-by-four dug into the sand, with a nail in it. We stretch lines across them, then slice the whole trench lengthwise with another line. That gives us twenty sections, each five by five feet. We work a section at a time. Get it?"

A gold-and-white convertible had pulled off the blacktop and was bouncing down the dirt access road that separated the site from the pink walls of the Ellenbogen estate. Ballard and the laborers gazed at it; it was all but hidden in explosive bursts of sand. He led them back to the long trench.

"Hit sound easy enough," Spots said slowly. "Whut you want us to do if we find deh bones?"

"Don't worry about that. It's not likely you'll come across anything until we get below sixteen inches. But if you do find something, just holler for one of us. Myself, or Mr. Peltz or Dr. Sorrento."

The automobile bounced to a convulsive halt. Its dusty wake lay behind it, hanging lazily in the midday heat. Ballard, studying the two-tone mobile shrine, noticed that the yellow-white motif had been extended to the upholstery, the steering wheel, the tire walls and even the man and woman inside the vehicle. They, too, were white and gold.

Ballard ignored the visitors and led his diggers to the excavated end of the trench. Four squares of earth had been scooped out to a depth of three feet. Twin pyramids of tawny sand and scree rested on either side of the hole. A man, working with trowel and dust brush, was on his knees in the damp bottom of the pit.

Ballard gazed again at the convertible, then spoke softly to the man in the pit. "Hey, Benny," he said. "Visitors. Should we tell Tom?"

The man ignored him. He worked the trowel deftly around an irregular stone lodged in the moist sand, extricated it, examined it distastefully and tossed it over the side. He was small and wiry, the natural redness of his frizzy hair and wrinkled skin heightened by the fierce sun.

"We shoulda dug in Van Cortlandt Park," he said to Ballard, looking up. "I'm gonna have it out with Tom once an' for all. Two weeks we been here and all we come up with are beer bottles and Canarsie trout."

"Patience, man," Ballard said. "You'll discourage the new men." He winked at the Negro workmen. "You men can start right here. Don't throw any dirt on Mr. Peltz down there in the hole. He's sensitive."

With arrogant roar, the automobile skidded off the dirt road and lumbered toward the excavation. The woman at the wheel, unmoved by Ballard's wave and shouts, braked the laboring car less than ten feet from the pit. In the rising sandstorm, Ballard towered like some primitive god of the mountain—an ancient Yahweh, iracund and vengeful.

"I better get Tom," he said to Ben Peltz.

"Ah, leave Tom alone," Peltz said wearily. "Lose 'em yourself Give 'em Amos and Andy. Tom's got enough to worry about. Why should he have to bother with every gook who shows up?"

The workmen began digging, clearing the surface soil in the five-by-five squares adjacent to the deep hole where Peltz was troweling. A man got out of the automobile and started toward Ballard. His small round head winked with yellow lights; his sports clothes were of metallic fabrics, opalescent and burnished, woven no doubt by captive virgins. He was a long-limbed, relaxed man, and he was grinning.

"Hello up there!" he sang to Ballard. "Aren't you a big one!"

Ballard removed the comedian's hat from his head and clutched it against his chest. His recent outrage at the automobile and its occupants had vanished. He appeared servile and stupid. Moreover, his mode of speech had undergone a startling transformation.

"Y'all mean me, boss?" Ballard asked.

"I don't mean your Uncle Mose," Ira deKay said. "What's your name, pal?"

"Mah name, boss?"

DeKay crinkled his nose. "Yeah, Big Stuff. Your handle. Your monicker." He surveyed Ballard's inordinate figure. "You sure are a lot of pork chops. What do they call you?"

"Dey jes' call me Satch, boss."

"Well, Satch, I'm reet pleased to meet you. You're a vouty character, Satch. Gimme five!" Ira deKay extended his right hand, palm down. The manicured fingernails sparkled like five diamonds.

"Y'all wan' shake mah hand, boss?" Ballard asked. "Down *hyeah?*"

"Why man, I'm from that hip New York City!" laughed Ira. "I don't dig this segregation bit! I'm show biz!"

With false caution, Ballard looked around, catching as he did, the offended stares of Spots and McIsaac. Then he touched palms with Ira deKay.

"Crazy!" deKay shouted. "Hey man, you ever work in show business? Did I ever catch your act at the Apollo Theatre? Or did I just have a nightmare?"

"Could be dat's deh truth, boss. All us *geejee* niggers got deh inborned sense of riddim. Sho' 'nuff, boss."

For a fragile moment, the masquerade skirted exposure. Ira was himself an adept at guises, at frauds and deceits. A practitioner of charlatanism, he usually recognized it in others, and there had been the faintest note of sarcasm in the last words uttered by the immense black man in dirty work clothes. DeKay shaded his eyes and squinted at the long trench; distantly, he saw the smaller excavation, nearer the water.

"Satch baby, what plays here?" he asked. "What's the action?"

"Ah don' b'lieve Ah understands you, suh."

"I mean, what's the plot? What are you guys digging for?"

Ballard stepped back and placed the ragged hat on his mahogany crown. "Ah don' rightly know, boss. Me and dem udder cullud men, we jes' hired to dig deh hole."

A tremor of suspicion agitated deKay—not just regarding the Negro ogre but the over-all scene. It puzzled him that Erwin Ellenbogen, that shrewd operator, would permit his parcel of land to be arbitrarily dug up. It was the last property of its kind in the Beach—priceless, coveted, untouched. Erwin's father-in-law had owned it since the twenties—five acres of bayfront land, enriching itself with age like a prize shell of beef or a cask of brandy.

"Well look here, Big Stuff," Ira said wearily, as Ballard left him to join the other Negroes, "who can I talk to about this deal?"

Ballard plunged the spade into the soft sand. "Ah reckon deh onliest man c'n he'p you is deh doctoh."

"Doctor?"

"Yeah. Doctoh S'rento. He in charge."

"Well where do I find this cat, Satch? Is that him in the hole?" He pointed to Ben Peltz's hunched figure in the pit.

"No suh. Dat ain' him."

Peltz turned his fiery face upward. "Get smart, Show Biz. Beat it."

DeKay walked to the edge of the trench. *"Hello sweetie,"* he sang. "You growing mushrooms down there?"

Peltz rose from his knees. "Whyncha get smart? We don't want any gooks around here. Take that seltzer wagon and get lost."

"It's a regular Friendly Town here, isn't it?" deKay said.

"We're busy," Peltz muttered.

"I see that, *I see that!* I promise you I'll go—just tell me where I can find Doctor Whosis. The Man. He can't be that busy he won't talk to a visitor."

Peltz wiped his forehead. His hand left a thick riband of dark sand on the furrowed skin. He looked hesitantly at Ballard, now laboring with his shovel. The big Negro had dissociated himself from the caller.

"Okay," Peltz said. "He'll throw you out on your ear, so it'll serve you right. He's in the house. Down by the water."

DeKay thanked him and started crossing the precious soil toward the bay. An enormous boathouse, a relic of the twenties, stood at the water's edge. DeKay noted, as he approached it, that its sagging boards had been newly painted white; the green shingled roof appeared to have been recently patched.

When he was out of earshot, Ballard spoke with some annoyance to Peltz. The minstrel-man accents were gone.

"Why'd you send him down there, Benny?" he asked. "Why does Tom have to fuss with that jerk?"

"*You* told him Tom was in charge," Peltz said.

Then, noting the aggrieved stares of the workmen, Ballard rested on his shovel and spoke to them. "Listen. That act I just put on. I wasn't making fun of you. It was to scare off that guy. We don't want anyone nosing around here. I live down in that boathouse with white people. It's nobody's business."

Spots and McIsaac nodded. Then, in some occult manner, they grinned knowingly at each other and resumed digging. Ballard sighed—everything required annotation.

DeKay paused at the smaller excavation—nearer the shoreline. Two heads peeked out at him. A young man and a young woman, both pale of skin and fair of hair, gazed at him timidly from behind steel-rimmed spectacles. Heaps of chalky, fragmented shells surrounded the perimeter of the pit.

"How's the clamming, kids?" Ira asked gaily.

The two heads vanished the instant he spoke. Ira laughed and continued his journey across the sands. Once Cleo honked the horn at him. He ignored her. There was no mistaking the fact that the old Ellenbogen boathouse had been fully refurnished, and was now serving as a dwelling. Some cheap toys—plastic pails and shovels, a rusted dump truck, a few quoits—lay cooking in the sand outside the rear door. In the hot dry air, the fresh paint smelled pungent and clean. He walked up canted wooden steps and knocked politely at the opened door, held in place by a brick. No one responded. After a moment's pause he walked into the room.

A thick blue haze obscured the interior of the boathouse. The miasma was cigar smoke of a rare, heavy strength. A dark man was seated at a table fashioned out of long plywood board and two sawhorses, and was puffing on a pickled black stub. The room was hellishly hot, a circumstance aggravated by the acrid smoke and the appalling clutter of packing cases, digging tools, books and maps with which the place was crammed.

The walls had been resurfaced with fresh plywood, and one of them was covered with a huge map of the island and its surrounding waters. A sign over a precarious stack of corrugated cardboard boxes read KEEP HANDS OFF PLEASE—TOM SORRENTO'S PRIVATE STUFF. On another wall, someone had scrawled the legend *I Have Very Few Answers. All I Can Do Is Raise Questions—Hall Maitland.*

The man at the table ignored Ira's presence. Before him on the makeshift table was a cardboard box (Indian River Grapefruit) and a half-dozen cigar boxes. With great care he would remove what looked to deKay like irregular stones or shells, or hunks of broken bone, from the big carton, and then consult an opened book on the table. When he had apparently matched the item with a picture in the book he would place it in one of the cigar boxes. He never removed the lethal cigar, manipulating it vigorously from one side of his mouth to the other.

Ira walked toward the table, maneuvering his way around a surveyor's tripod, a pile of short stakes similar to the ones that had been driven around the big trench, and several glass carboys.

The man at the table looked up indifferently at him and Ira grinned.

"How do, Doctor," deKay said. "I'm told you're the chappie in charge."

"Who told you that?"

"The big eight-ball outside. Man, where'd you find *him?* He must eat up all the profits. In watermelons alone."

The dark man set the cigar down on the lid of a coffee can. He studied Ira gloomily. "What do you want? You from the newspaper? We haven't found anything yet. You want to promote something? Go see Mr. Ellenbogen. *Va fa a Napoli.*"

"Oh—you're a smartie, you are," Ira said admiringly. "Listen—I'm just curious. I'm a friend of Mr. Ellenbogen's. I'm wondering what you guys are up to here."

"This is the *Boffongool* Athletic Club. We're full up on members, so don't bother applying."

He bent to his chipped stones and bone fragments, and deKay looked at him appraisingly. The "doctor" was in his late thirties, not a big man, but one possessed of the balanced, strong proportions of an athlete. His skin was Neapolitan dark, his head square and topped with a thick black brush-cut, much streaked with gray. The large luminous eyes and the wide mouth, undoubtedly Italian, hinted at ancient infusions of Arab and Moorish blood. It was the oddly shortened nose, its flattened bridge bearing a white scar, that seemed inconsistent. Beneath faded khaki shorts, his thick muscular legs, blanketed with black ringlets, terminated in a pair of wretched scuffed sneakers. He also wore a venerable, sleeveless sweatshirt. Faint stenciled lettering on its chest advertised: UNIVERS TY ATHL TIC ASS IATIO .

Ira sat down on a wooden crate.

"Mind if I rest the feet?" he asked.

"Yeah. You bother me. I don't want anyone around here. You're a friend of Mr. Ellenbogen's, call him." He puffed vigorously on the blackened stub. Ira leaned toward him.

"Doc, baby," deKay said. "You help me out and tell me a few things and I'll get you a lifetime free supply of those El Ropos. I know a little man who manufactures them. They smell even worse than that stinkadora you're chewing."

The man set the cigar down. "This is a dig. An archaeological excavation."

"Aaaah!" Ira cried. "I get the message! The trenches out there—and those pieces of bones! The missing-link bit, right?"

"Sure. Right."

"Ah, come on, Doc. I'm with you."

"Not for long. I don't know what your racket is, but I got problems here. I want no publicity on this. A guy like you will start blabbing and pretty soon we'll have a tourist attraction. We don't want any crowds. No gooks."

"Don't look at me, baby," Ira said, injured. "Scout's honor!"

He extracted an outsized wallet from his gilt trousers and located a calling card. "That's me," he said, handing the card to the man. "Li'l ole Ira deKay. Everybody knows Ira on the Beach."

DeKay watched him a few seconds, sorting and studying his precious collection of junk. Once he squinted at an irregular white stone, then dropped it into a refuse carton under the table.

"A loser in with the winners, hey Doc?" Ira asked. "You know the story about the fellah who brought the twelve petrified poontangs back from Egypt?"

The dark man smiled.

"I caught you! You smiled. Look, I can't keep calling you 'Doc.' What's your name?"

"Sorrento. Tom Sorrento."

"What's the Doctor gag?"

"Ph.D."

"And what's with you and Erwin Ellenbogen, that fine young industrialist?"

Sorrento took a fresh cigar from a tin. He lit it with the charred stub of its predecessor. "Nothing at all. You know Mrs. Ellenbogen?"

"Lila? The greatest. A living doll."

"She was taking summer courses at the University where I teach—last year. I met her at a beer party one night. I found out she and her husband owned part of this island and I got excited. This area came up with some famous archaeological finds back in the thirties. Then the land got built up, developed, and nobody was able to follow up the work."

Ira frowned. "Hmmm. Things you never know. I always figured this town for broads and high life. Who'd ever think people used to dig for bones here?"

"You remember the WPA?" Sorrento asked.

"Do I! My old man lost his store in '35 and went to work building a reservoir!"

"Well, the WPA financed all this digging. They did a great job. It saved American archaeology." He dragged deeply on the fresh cigar, gazing out the window at the trenches, where his associates labored with shovels and trowels. "But most of it got screwed up." He sounded sad for his frustrated predecessors.

"What played, Tommy?"

"You really care?" Sorrento asked. He looked at the card. It read:

IRA DEKAY ASSOCIATES

PUBLIC RELATIONS COUNSELING

"It's my *job* to care, sweetie."

"I'll bet. You'll be selling tickets tomorrow."

"Tommy *baby*. Tell me."

"Well, the WPA had these digs going. There were six of them. One on this island, and five others north of here. The biggest was north of here. High Mound City, they called it. It was an ossuary."

"Stepped in what?"

"A burial mound. About fifty skeletons, beautifully preserved. Lots of grave goods—pottery, animal bones, carvings. One of the richest yields in the history of eastern-seaboard archaeology."

"A gasser." DeKay was grinning. He had only the remotest notion of what the archaeologist was telling him, but any story of success—*any kind of success*—titillated him.

His round, tanned head with its golden fuzz, the humorous blue eyes, suddenly irked Sorrento. He got up quickly from his folding chair and started ushering deKay to the door. The promoter noticed that the dark man's left calf was shrunken and he walked with a slight limp.

"What am I talking to you for?" Sorrento asked. "I'm asking for trouble."

Ira protested. "No, really, Tommy boy, I want to hear the rest. I'm interested. I'm interested in everything that happens on the Beach."

Sorrento shook his head. "Guys like you loused them up on those WPA digs," he said. "Every local jerk with something to promote got in on the act. Real-estate people, grave robbers, the tourist-trap boys, the religious cranks. Even a slob with a gold-finding machine."

"Why not? I mean—a little publicity never hurts."

Sorrento flicked a white chemical ash from his cigar. "They went crazy. Everything was stolen. Skeletons, grave goods, pottery. What the gooks didn't steal, kids smashed. The team working the dig never had a chance to classify anything. What made it hurt was they were really on the verge of a major discovery."

Ira looked grave. "A bad scene, hey Tommy?"

"The WPA ran out of funds. Then this place became the hottest real-estate area in the country. The land was sold, resold, developed. The whole project was abandoned."

"Until you met Lila Ellenbogen in New York, hey? And found out about this?"

"That's it. Now come on, shove off. *Fammi il piacere.* Do me a big favor. Don't go telling anyone about this."

Ira walked down the steps. He paused on the sand and smiled at Sorrento. "I'll tell you what bugs me, Tommy. What's in it for Erwin Ellenbogen? Erwin never got into anything that didn't return at least fifteen per cent. What's he getting out of these holes your people are digging?" He indicated the two trenches—at the long excavation the Negroes continued their rhythmic labor, *crunch* of spades alternating with *whoosh* of falling sand. At the smaller pit, the one surrounded by the shell heap, the blond heads of the two young people occasionally bobbed above the edge.

"You're such buddies with him," Sorrento said. "Go ask him."

"Zotz," Ira said. "You're rough as a cob."

A child's whining and the fatigued, reprimanding voice of a woman drew their attention. A flight of sloping wooden steps led to the upper story of the makeshift residence. A girl of seven and a woman, both barefoot, were descending the baking boards gingerly.

"Tom, we've had our fourth scene today," the woman said. "I can't handle her any more. I'm ready to give up."

The child ran to Sorrento. He sat on the top step and hugged her. "What's a-matter fa-you? You no be nice to mommy, I no buy you *ceci* beans." The girl smiled, wiping a tear with a brown arm.

"Mother was cruel to me," the little girl said. "I was invited to the club by Sheldon and she wouldn't let me go."

"Why didn't you let her go?" Sorrento asked. "She's allowed."

"She's been there three times this week."

"So?"

"I'm very fond of the Ellenbogens, Tom, but I don't think we have to become their wards. We're not charity cases. Abby doesn't have to spend every waking minute with Sheldon and his rich little friends. Agreed?"

"If you say so, honey." He bounced the child on his hairy knees. "Listen, *chooch,* you be good to your old lady. Your cooperation will be deeply appreciated. You can do your little brother a favor and stay home and play with him today. How is he?"

The woman grimaced. "He threw up again. I guess it's one of those twenty-four hour bugs he picked up at the pool. If it weren't so damned close up there—"

She sounded defeated, uncertain—a woman who had had her fill. DeKay was smiling indulgently at her. His unexplained presence did not seem to concern her.

"Nicky ate a worm. That's why he's sick," the little girl said defiantly. "He ate a worm! *He ate a worm!*"

The woman glared at her. "Make her stop saying that, Tom. She almost had him in hysterics before. I'm too exhausted to discipline her."

"You hear your mommy? Be nice. Nice-a leetla gel."

"Good God, Tom, can't you be serious with her for a minute?"

"Only when she puts grated cheese on the clam sauce, because that's a sin." He got up slowly, and deKay noticed the peculiar slimness of the left leg—the rest of him was solid and muscular.

"I got to finish my work," Sorrento said. "Abby, listen to your mother." He looked at his wife. "Hot up there?"

"It's the ninth circle of hell. I don't know whether we'll last the rest of August. It's unbearable."

"I wanna go to the club!" Abby yelled. *"In the pool.* You promised me!"

The parents studied each other helplessly. His round face glowing, Ira deKay was suddenly bending over the crying child.

"*Lover!* Little *lover!*" deKay said. "Why of course you want to go to the club! Why don't you come to Uncle Ira's club? I have a water mattress, and life-preservers, and I'll buy you a great big strawberry soda! Yes! You and your mommy and your daddy! Everybody!"

Abby stopped sobbing. "Can I go, daddy? Can I go to the man's club?"

DeKay straightened up. "Be my pleasure. I'm on my way to the cabana right now. It's no sweat for ole Ira."

"I wanna go," Abby said flatly.

The preposterous intruder, in his white-gold clothing and matey manners, was an offense to Martha Sorrento. She took Abby's hand and began to lead her away. The child resisted.

"I gather you're the doctor's lady," Ira volunteered. "Tommy and I had a nice chat about his work."

The brash boyishness did not move her. She acted not as if she were administering a snub, but as if he had no substantive existence, that someone as outlandish as Ira deKay was beyond perception. Her attitude disturbed deKay because she was unnervingly beautiful, and he had, since his mature teens, enjoyed a proprietary interest in all attractive women. Her camouflage of plainness was a failure. She was barefoot, wore no make-up, and her lean, flat body was clad in a man's trimmed oxford shirt and a pair of gray shorts. Her hair, an unremarkable brown, stained with yellow streaks where the tropic sun had worked on it, was clipped short. The margins of her face—the pointed chin, the faintly protuberant forehead, the irregular brown hair—had an odd, soft quality, a blurring that suggested an artist's delicate smudging of a pastel drawing. Within this exquisite frame, her features tilted upward—the small mouth, the dented nose, the amber eyes and saffron lashes. DeKay, marveling at her beauty, found himself vaguely resentful of the dour, cigar-chewing husband.

"Marty, this is Mr.—what's your name?"

"DeKay. Ira deKay. How do."

"This is my wife. Mrs. Sorrento."

She turned her back on him, shepherding the girl toward the insufferable house.

"*Marty*. That's a fine name. Very zile kai."

She looked over her shoulder. "What did you say?"

"Oh, no offense. Just my own language for anything I dig. Anything that sings. Zile kai. I liked your name."

Sorrento got up from the hot step. "Marty, how about it? Suppose we let Abby go to the club with Mr. deKay? Take her off your hands—"

"It's out of the question. Come along, Abby. We'll read *Mary Poppins*."

"*That* old thing."

The woman and the child ascended the stairs. DeKay stared at her lithe body. It was the kind of figure that would not age. At fifty-five her legs would show no fat, no varicosis. They would retain forever the texture and resilience of youth. He felt happy for her.

"High-class woman, your wife," deKay said appreciatively. "Not the usual kind of broad we get down here."

Sorrento looked curiously at him. "You really make yourself at home, don't you?"

"Don't get mad, Tommy," he said. "I meant it. I can tell she's quality folks."

"Get smart, deKay. You can't help me and I can't help you."

The convertible honked arrogantly. Cleo was waving at Ira.

"The sage calls," deKay sighed. "One thing I can't stand is an impatient sage. You won't lose me so easy, Doc. I'll do you some good before I'm through. Fellow spends his life going through all those old bones, he deserves a break."

"Save your money and buy *scungilli*."

DeKay grinned. "You and the missus want to go out on the town, just buzz me. Everybody goes first class with Ira. I would adore to show you around."

He started to leave, then turned.

"Doc, what's with that big stove-lid out there?" He pointed to Ballard's mammoth figure. "Is he leveling with that Uncle Tom bit?"

Sorrento chewed his unlit cigar. "He's a Ph.D. Like me. You call him 'Doctor' when you go."

Ira walked rapidly across the sandy slope, passing again the shell heap. The two diggers peeked at him for a frightened second and vanished. At the long trench he pointed an accusing finger at Ballard.

"*Naughty!* You made a funny. Making believe you weren't a smart college man!"

Ballard opened his eyes wide. "Me, boss? Not dis poor fiel' han'. I c'n sing 'n' dance, boss. Jes' like a chile." He removed the burlesque hat. "See dat haid, boss? Like a rock. Y'all nevah hit me deah in a fight. Ef'n y'all wan' hurt me, kick me in deh shins. Ain't dat the troof?"

Ira doubled up in helpless laughter. "*Oh—oh—oh*—Big Stuff, you're the most. You're the *living end!*"

This time, Spots and McIsaac, sharing Ballard's secret, smiled with cabalistic approval. When deKay had left, they looked at him admiringly.

"You jes' actin'," Spots said.

They watched the blond man, still hooting and guffawing, climb into the elaborate car. With much wrenching of gears and excessive blasting, the woman backed the automobile toward the dirt road, swung it around furiously, and roared toward the blacktop.

Benjamin Peltz poked his rufous head over the trench. He had knotted a soiled handkerchief around his forehead. He blinked in the sunlight, scowling at the departing car.

"That jerko finally go?"

"Yeah," Ballard said, digging into the sand. "But he'll be back. With photographers next time. Why'd you send him down to see Tom?"

3 *FT-23*

Tom Sorrento dipped probing fingers into the half-filled jar, removed a round red pepper, studied it as if it were a jewel, and popped it neat into his mouth. It was like eating a hot coal. He chewed it energetically until tears filled his eyes, then offered the jar to his wife.

"Thank you, no, dear," Marty said. "I'll stay with the beer."

triumph of my life since I intercepted the pass against Syracuse. They couldn't get me off that bike. I rode nunnies, feetsies, and backwards all over Quantico."

"Now what is that supposed to prove, Tom?" Marty asked.

He stared sullenly at the sailboats, scudding lightly across the bay. "Look at them," he said. "They know all about sailing."

"But they can't hit two sewers, right, Tom?"

Sorrento tossed the empty pepper jar at Peltz. The little red man caught it deftly, tucked it under one arm, and mimicked a halfback's prancing steps. "Ginzo Sorrento! Pride of the Provolone Beavers!"

Tom laughed. "You're all dressed up tonight, Benny. Going out on the town?"

"You look very sporty, Ben," Marty said.

Peltz stopped his dance. "It's the narrow rumpled lapels. I'm taking Oran and Wilma to the movies. The poor kids got clamshells coming outa their ears."

His guests poked tentative heads around the side of the porch. They were the two young people, brother and sister, whom Ira deKay had frightened at the small pit. The young man, Oran, in a navy blue suit clearly the gift of the Salvation Army, was fair and slight. His querulous eyes tried to hide behind dime-store eyeglasses. His sister, Wilma, also bespectacled, was perhaps three inches taller. In the faded cotton dress and white sneakers, she had the mien of a door-to-door distributor of tendentious religious literature. Her arms were long and sun-freckled and she had difficulty controlling her fluttery, man-size hands. They were both graduate students in anthropology.

"Join us, Wilma and Oran," Marty said. "This isn't private."

They advanced shyly. Five feet from the Sorrentos, they halted.

"I'm sorry I didn't get a chance to check you kids on the find today," Sorrento said. "Anything interesting?"

They darted frightened looks at each other. The girl, her eyes moist, spoke. "Oran found what he thinks is a piece of Weeden Island incised . . ."

"I didn't say *that,*" the brother said thinly. "I said it *might* be. Or it looks a little like it. I'm not sure. It . . ."

"Well, we'll look at it tomorrow," Sorrento said. "You seem to have gotten the rough deal. I thought the shell heap would be easy digging. Benny, maybe we should take a workman off the big trench and lend him to Oran?"

"For all the good we're doing, you could take us all off." Peltz extended two blistered hands. "What I got for them blisters, hah? Some old bones and a few hunks a pottery so broke up we ain't even sure what they are."

"Now, now, Ben," Marty said. "We've only been at it two weeks. There's a whole hot, breathless summer ahead of you."

He started guiding Wilma and her brother toward the stairs.

"Sure. Sure, Marty. Whyncha say it? Who'd hire me anyway if Tom didn't?" He reached into the hip pocket of the shapeless seersucker suit. "Oh. I almost forgot. Davey picked up the mail. There's something for you." He walked back to Sorrento, handing him a thick white envelope.

Tom Sorrento took it. He smiled as he noticed the return address of the University and above it the name E. F. ENGSTROM.

"Where's Davey tonight?" Tom asked.

"I dunno . . . He says he's going for ribs in Hilltown. I think all that Uncle Tom business is affecting him. He really thinks he's a low-comedy dinge." Peltz turned again. "And the big clown runs off with the pickup truck, so me and the kids gotta ride the bus."

Martha shook her head wearily. Peltz's perpetual outrage bothered her because it had no gradations, no nuances. He could get as upset over lack of transportation as he could over a lynching.

"Be careful," she called after him. "Don't get the children into any trouble, Ben."

Sorrento knew what was in the envelope. He opened it, unfolding a sheaf of stapled, mimeographed pages, the chatty newsletter *First Downs* that his old football coach, Engstrom, sent out to former players. The coach was an aging, single, friendless man, a variety of national monument. He never lost touch with an athlete. The newsletter was a reminder to sender and recipients that Engstrom still entered and influenced their lives. The poorly mimeo'd sheets, the badly stenciled headings saddened Tom. The shoddiness seemed to him a commentary on the ephemeral status of the college athlete. It was unfair, Tom thought, to expose nineteen-year-old boys to headlines and then, ten years later, reduce them to a few streaked lines in a newsletter. He was almost glad he had never been a star.

"What a thrill," he said. "I made *First Downs*. First time since I got the Bronze Star. That Engstrom. He must have phoned the anthropology department to get this."

"Read it," Marty said. "Considering that he almost had you murdered once, I'd like to hear what he says."

"He didn't mean any harm," Tom said defensively. "Besides, he couldn't hurt me. I could always handle myself."

"I can't be as forgiving as you are. Go on, read it."

" 'Remember Tom Sorrento, '42? Who could forget that fine wingback, Marine officer and current professor of anthropology at our own University? We hear Tom is heading up an archaeological excavation down south. With Tom is his wife Martha, daughter of Dr. Hall Maitland, head of the anthro department, as well as their youngsters, Abby, 7, and Nicky, 3. We hear little Nicky gives promise of backing up the line the way his Daddy did.' "

The gossipy jargon offended her. "Dear God, what a hypocrite," Marty said bitterly. "A cold, vain man who tried to kill you. His own life is so sterile he has to keep reaching out to touch all of you. And I think all of you love it. I've been to those parties where you and Terranova and Doyle and all the others you played with stand around getting drunk and talking about Engstrom. How could anyone so dull—so phony—affect all of you? Especially you, Tom. You were always wise to him."

Tom got up and stretched. "I don't know. There was something about him. He got to you. You hated his guts and yet—"

"If anybody had a right to hate him, you did." She seemed grave and chilled. "Oh, we've talked about it too much. You might have been a different man if he hadn't abused you the way he did. He cauterized or amputated something in you."

"Ah, *finocchi.* I read how Fitzgerald's whole life changed because he didn't make the Princeton football team. So what? *I* made the team." He made a wry grimace—lifting his black eyebrows, shrugging. "I made the *scrubs* anyway. I was captain of them. Is that why I'm earning sixty-five hundred bucks a year as an assistant professor in my father-in-law's department? And because Doyle was varsity halfback he's a big customer's man?"

"I'm only talking about *you,* and what Engstrom did to you."

"*Ma che!* He couldn't hurt me. Poor dumb Swede."

He had his choice of twenty colleges, but he chose the University because of Engstrom. *"I am interested in my boys not only as football players but as men,"* the coach used to say. He told the truth: his athletes became doctors, attorneys, civic leaders. The University had harsh admission requirements, standards that were rarely lowered for a giant tackle or a star fullback. The gravy trains of the big football factories (or the rarefied air of truer Ivy Colleges) were lacking. The undergraduate men's college was perpetually submerged, its identity blurred by the academic ziggurat of the University. But Tom and his parents were captivated by Engstrom. He spoke not of national fame, but of a sound education, preparation for a professional career.

Tom was a distinct prize. He was a unanimous "all-city" fullback—a high school athlete who was "copy."

. . . you take the fancy dans, the heavers and kickers. For our dough the finest college prospect in town is Thomas Vincent Sorrento, the bugle-nosed paisan with the sad eyes who is perhaps the greatest ball carrier ever to wear the Green and Gold. He's one hundred and sixty-five pounds of TNT, this Tomaso, and he backs up the line with the kind of teeth-jarring tackles that should bring smiles even to morose Coach Engstrom. Isn't it nice that a local college landed the Bronx Express . . .

Amidst the blunt-headed, pigeon-toed freshman athletes, he was already a hero. There was always something special about the young football players—acolytes in T shirts and high school sweaters, swaggering around the red-brick, green-roofed campus. Among the blond crew-cuts, Sorrento was a rare bird, with his enormous fleshy nose, his sorrowing eyes, the twin peaks of black curly hair. There was something comical about him—his gargoyle's face aroused mockery and cruel jokes. Tom never resented them. The barbs, instead of inducing anger, made him more of a jokester. The freshman football team, on which he played first-string fullback, respected him. He threw fierce, numbing blocks and was a deadly, reckless tackler. Somehow he infected the other players with a kind of mocking, humorous attitude toward the game that made the arduous practice sessions palatable. When McCabe, the freshman coach, would eat them out, Sorrento would mutter: "What's he so serious about? It's only football."

As a sophomore, he soon sensed that Engstrom was acting strangely toward him. The coach was a national shrine, and what Tom never understood was that a shrine cannot tolerate doubters, jokers or irreverence. He was relegated to the third-string team—not as a fullback, but as a utility defensive back. He got into games when they were well lost or overwhelmingly won. It bothered Tom; he knew he was as good as the varsity fullback. In scrimmage, he outblocked and outran him. And yet Engstrom continued to ignore him. Years later, Tom concluded that it had something to do with his appearance—he had never really *looked* like a football player. Engstrom was an immaculate man who paid two hundred dollars for tailored suits and owned twenty pairs of bench-made shoes. Apparently, he found something distasteful in this slovenly, ugly boy who always seemed to be laughing at him. Once, in scrimmage, when Tom's helmet was shaken loose, Engstrom stared at him dully, and in his flat, toneless voice, told him: "Get that mop of hair clipped, Sorrento, and your helmet will stay on. This is no poolroom."

He got a crew-cut that night, but it didn't help. His jersey was continually in shreds; his yellow overshirt, emblematic of the scrub team, lasted for a half-dozen plays; his shoelaces were usually untied. Engstrom, shaking his small gray head, would watch him ripping adhesive patches from his pants and mutter: "You're a sandlot athlete, Sorrento, sandlot."

Once, in his junior year, he thought he had made it. They had opened the season the last week of September against Brown. It was murderously hot in the small stadium, hotter than most of the vanished summer days. Eleven of Engstrom's varsity players had fainted during the first quarter. Tom was sent in on defense. His frustration at having been ignored so long vented itself on the Brown ball-carriers. He made three vicious tackles in succession, slamming his stocky, muscular body into the opposing backs, glorying in the noisy smack of leather on leather. He was delighted with himself. He knew, too, he was proving something to the unreachable man who had snubbed him. The half was about to end when Brown punted, the ball rolling out inside the ten-yard line. In the sickening heat, two more players had fainted. The haggard, gasping teams started to line up when they saw the referee signaling them back. The Brown kicker had been roughed. The play would have to be run over. Sweaty and breathless, the twenty-two exhausted young men began the mandatory dogtrot back to midfield. Engstrom demanded it: *run all the time.* The idiocy of the order suddenly bothered Tom. *Why run? Why run just to get back to the line of scrimmage? Especially when it was so hot!* He found himself resenting all these stupidly obedient athletes, trotting for no purpose. He had the urge to do something about it. The Brown captain, a white-faced Slav, was alongside him. Tom grabbed him by the elbow and whispered to him.

"Hey, sport," he said. "Tell your guys to *walk* back. *Walk.* The half's almost over. If you guys *walk,* we can walk. *Why run?*"

The player, drenched in sweat, did not understand him. He kept up his aimless dogtrot. A few minutes later the half ended. In the dressing room, Engstrom took Sorrento into a corner.

"What did you say to that fellow?" he asked.

"Who, Mr. Engstrom?"

"The Brown captain. After Degerman roughed the kicker."

Tom grinned. "Oh. I was needling him. I told him to walk back to midfield. If his guys walked, we could walk. It was so darn hot out there."

Engstrom's neat face was impassive. All the man really believed in was the game. The game, and all its attendant ritual and mythology, its written and unwritten laws. You did not joke about the game. You believed, or you were an enemy. Looking at Sorrento's smeared, ugly face, he felt a gratifying justification in his hostile attitude toward the boy.

"Never do that again, Sorrento," Engstrom said slowly. "You'll sit out the rest of this game. On Monday you can take fifteen laps around the track and a half-hour of wind sprints."

He melted into the obscurity of the scrub team after the Brown game. He became the unofficial captain of the third-stringers, the yellow-shirted drudges who scrimmaged the varsity, the nameless boys who could not run fast enough, block hard enough. They respected Tom, for they knew what Engstrom would never admit: Sorrento was as good as any of his varsity players. Still, the gap widened. The coach suspected that Sorrento had the power to infect his whole team—to make all of them unbelievers, enemies of the true church. This suspicion was confirmed one afternoon in late fall, just before the final game of the season. The squad was weary and maimed; they had lost most of their games to bigger, rougher teams. By now, Tom had become the squad clown—an artful mimic, an irreverent critic. The boys were getting into their leathery armor when Doyle, the varsity fullback, dared him to imitate Engstrom. The coast was clear. The coaches were meeting in their office. Tom accepted the dare. He thrust his ungainly head forward and bounced on his toes. Already the imitation was a success—the players laughed appreciatively.

"They are *mere* men," Tom said, in the droning, sterile monotone that Engstrom affected. "They are mere men as you and I. We must hit them harder and faster. They are not your friends. They are your enemies. Doyle, tuck your shirt in."

Their laughter suddenly halted. Tom, jaw-outthrust, surveying them with half-shut eyes, the way the coach did, saw Engstrom and two horrified assistants watching him. Not a word was said as they passed through the locker room. Tom would always remember the back of Engstrom's creased neck and tiny ears: as scarlet as if rouged.

It was cold and dark on the practice field. A November wind whipped across the turf and lights blinked early in the red brick apartment houses surrounding them. The first team was practicing running plays. Tom lined up with the scrubs. They assumed the defensive formation of the team scheduled for that Saturday's game. He took a stance as left line backer and blew on his hands. Perreau, the defensive center, whispered to him: "He *heard* you. He's tear-assed. His voice was shaking when he lined us up."

Tom shrugged. "He can't hate me any more than he does. What did I ever do to him?"

An assistant tossed the ball to the offensive center. The teams faced each other. There was a cold heaviness, a dull resignation in the air. They had had enough football for one year.

"This will be our second-from-last scrimmage," Engstrom said. "But that does not call for any letup. We can never let down. You men must work as hard as you did pre-season. Defensive team—hit hard. Blockers—do the same. Let's start with the FT-23 variation."

The play was a delayed buck lateral. The fullback spun as he hit the line and passed off to the tailback, who followed blockers through the left side of the line. It was the kind of play which called for the interference to obliterate the line-backer. Just removing him from the play was not enough, he had to be run over. Tom knew what was coming. He braced himself, hands on knees, a few feet in back of the tackle. The ball was passed and there was the sudden violent, hysterical smack of bodies and churning of legs. He always had a feeling of imminent disaster when a play began. A blocking back and a guard came at him and he lifted up the first man and smashed him into the second. The ball-carrier crashed futilely against his own men.

"Run it again," Engstrom said.

Again, signals were called, the ball was snapped and the blocking pattern formed in front of the ball-carrier. They came at Sorrento again. Tom smashed furiously into the lead blocker, piling up the play. They hit the icy turf in a heap. The varsity blocking back was gasping.

"For Chrissake, Bugle Nose!" he wheezed. "Are you trying to kill me? You can't make the team this late."

"I know," Tom said. "I'm bucking for a scholarship room."

Engstrom called the play once more. The driving knees, the high, cleated shoes charged in Tom's direction. He plunged his iron head into the blocker's gut. They had yet to gain an inch through him.

"FT-23," Engstrom said.

He sent in a new blocking back, a square, solemn freshman who had a reputation for roughness and brutality. The bridge of his nose was scabbed and scarred. The boy, fresh and strong, was harder to take out. Tom committed himself at the last second, stripping both blockers so that Perreau could make the tackle. When the freshman rolled off him, he tasted blood. The inside of his lip was lacerated. He spit a dark red curve and bounced to his feet.

"Again," Engstrom said.

A new running back was sent in, a long-legged kid—also a freshman. They came roaring at him again before he could catch his breath and this time they made two yards through him. He fell to the icy sod again, drowning under the charging, pointlessly angered bodies, knowing that he had been hurt. His great defenseless nose had been smashed. He touched it and shivered at the pain. The agony spread to his cheeks and his eyes.

"Once more," said Engstrom.

They ran the play at him a dozen times, then a dozen more times. FT-23—the churning arms and pounding legs and hard bodies, four men in concert, dedicated to his annihilation. He refused to dog it, to lay down, to miss his play. He would oblige Engstrom.

In the fading November light he barely saw the varsity as it lined up, shifted smartly on the signals and drove at him. His nose was swelling to twice its size and his mouth was awash with blood. The ridiculous yellow shirt was reduced to a single strand dangling under his left arm. Cockily, he spit blood and lined up behind a tackle. No one spoke to him.

"Come on, stars," Tom called to the embarrassed varsity. "Let's play *salugi*. We'll spot you six points."

No one laughed. When they unpiled, after ploughing over him for ten yards (he had clung, limpet-like, to the runner half the distance), he could see one of the assistant coaches whispering nervously to Engstrom.

The coach nodded negatively. "FT-23," he said. "You men haven't gotten it right yet."

Tom, stupefied and bloodied, tried to upend the lead blocker but the strength was no longer there. He remembered the solemn freshman with the scab on his nose smashing into him, cracking his body against Tom's thighs. When he awakened in the locker room, there was a precise, perfect cleat mark on his forehead, where the ball carrier had branded him. The trainer was manipulating his mutilated nose and he could taste iodine. The man's rude fingers made him scream, and he was suddenly ashamed of himself. He was thankful there was no one else in the fieldhouse to hear his shrieks.

In his senior year, his mother pleaded with him to quit the team. She almost convinced him. Each year he played football the game held less pleasures for him—not just the sport, but the ritualistic locker-room banter, the patronizing alumni, the humiliating subordination of the players before Engstrom's monolithic shrine. But he stayed with the team. Football insured his scholarship, his meal job, gave him a limited kind of status. They all knew him on campus: Sorrento, the laughing boy of the scrub team. He had failed miserably as an athlete. But the University, with its grand variousness, touched him and changed him in other ways. He found himself getting better marks, finding friends not among athletes, but with a seedy group of literary gamblers who divided their time between a bookmaker's room on Amsterdam Avenue and the college reading room, deep in Joyce and Kafka. He read perpetually. Where once he had been a note-borrower, he now began to listen attentively to his lectures. He took Hall Maitland's course in anthropology and joined in the thunderous applause at the end of the semester when Maitland said: "*Gentlemen, let us dedicate ourselves to the next civilization.*"

Feeney, the morose, fat Irishman who edited the undergraduate literary magazine, met him in a saloon on upper Broadway one night. The editor had trouble filling the starved little magazine and was tired of writing everything himself under assumed names. Would Tom help him out? Anything would do—a short story, an article. . . .

He wrote a piece called "Honest Cop"—a reminiscence about his father's periodical visits to East Harlem, where his old hoodlum friends were still offended by his opting to join the police force in defiance of tradition. It was a somewhat pointless story, but the sounds and smells of the Italian ghetto were vivid and accurate. Feeney said it was the best story they had published all year.

A week after the magazine appeared, Tom was surprised to get a call from Engstrom's secretary. The coach was anxious to talk to him. Tom felt he had left football behind forever; Engstrom's intrusiveness bothered him.

The coach's office suggested that the man was already dead. It was one interminable memorial to him—framed cartoons and photographs, citations, plaques, awards—the accumulated memorabilia of a public man. Hesitantly, he asked Tom about his plans, how his studies were coming. At length he held up a copy of the literary quarterly.

"You write this story?" he asked.

"Yes."

"I enjoyed it," Engstrom said. "I didn't know you had literary leanings."

"I haven't really. Feeney, the editor, asked me to do it. I got beered up with him one night."

Engstrom smiled. "I never had a boy who became a writer. I've had forty-five doctors, forty-nine lawyers, thirty-one engineers, and goodness knows how many business executives. But not a single writer."

He was a collector of careers—were Tom to become a writer, it would adorn his display.

"I'm really not sure what I want to do," Tom said uneasily. "I have the Marines to worry about first. I'm going to Quantico after I graduate."

"Any way I can help, Sorrento," Engstrom said. "That's why I'm here. By the way, has Doctor Devore called you?"

"No."

"He will. We are arranging to have your nose straightened at the medical school. I guess we're responsible for smashing it for you, so the least we can do is pretty you up for the Marine Corps. They'll do a good job—fine plastic surgeon up there."

Tom smiled. "Thanks. I'll appreciate it. It is a little unwieldy." He fingered his lumpish, twisted nose.

They said their goodbyes; Tom left. At the door, Engstrom called him. Tom turned. The coach appeared shrunken and lonely. Behind him, the opened window afforded a view of the lovely spring campus. Lavish greens revived the dull academic grays and browns. There was a wonderful atmosphere of purpose, of involvement, about the University, and it seemed to Tom that Engstrom in his ritualistic, hierarchical world, dedicated to sweat, was not a part of it. He was the True Believer, an enemy of skeptics and doubters, a relic in his own museum.

He looked absently at Tom. "I forgot what I was going to say," he said softly. "Never mind, Sorrento. I'll think of it."

What was it? Tom often wondered. Some halting apology about the afternoon he had all but had him killed? An admission that he really had been of varsity stature? A clumsy, cold effort to reach him? He never learned; he was just as happy. Engstrom could never communicate with him. They were victims of a total collapse of language, a failure of custom, of belief, of tradition. Engstrom could never reach a man who joked about football.

Tom folded a paper airplane out of Engstrom's newsletter and sailed it over the railing. It rode gracefully on an errant breath of air, then settled noiselessly on the water.

"What a hot rock, that Engstrom," he said to Marty. "He's mystified by me. He hasn't figured me out yet."

"He's a stupid egomaniac. I tell you this, Tom, I'm sorry he got to you when you were so young. It has a lot to do with what's happened to you since."

"Who cares? Eighteen years ago."

"He humiliated you. He took the confidence out of you."

"You mean I dig for old bones because a Swede once ran the buck lateral series through me? Like those movies where the bad guy says 'My father never loved me. I didn't have a cat when I was little'?"

She laughed. "I can't talk to you. You know I'm not referring to your work. You've done darn well. It's just—other things."

"Yeah. Like why I never became Hemingway."

A small boy's whine issued from the boathouse. Marty got up. "The fifth trip of the night. You'd think all that sun and swimming would knock them out. They're usually awake when *we* go to bed."

"Should I go in?"

"No. You'd have them *both* up."

He watched her walk through the screen door, a graceful, beautiful woman, wondering, as he often did, over the magnificent circumstances of time and place that had brought her to him.

Hall Maitland's daughter. He could hear her, calm and poised, lecturing Nicky, assuring him there were no tigers in the bedroom.

In her absence, he wandered to the side of the balcony and looked out over the site. Bright lights blinked across the bay. The ornate hotel towers appeared to have been pasted on the purple sky. Below him, the two excavations in the sandy earth seemed ridiculous. Cars roared by on the blacktop. From a nearby loggia he heard music and the rising voices of a party. He begrudged nobody their good times. Even the savage Glades people who had once encamped on the beach, had enjoyed their ceremonial dances, the sacrifice of war captives. The exotic environment did not worry Sorrento. He and Marty were impervious to it, Dave Ballard was excluded from it, and the Burleys and Ben Peltz could have their wild flings at a third-run movie. What distressed him was the barrenness of the digging. He had made a thorough study of the WPA digs in the thirties and he had been convinced that the site they were working was a rich one. But thus far they had found nothing exciting. He would have to talk to Dave and Ben about sinking new test holes. The University, of course, expected no great discoveries, but he himself had sold the project to Maitland, and there was always someone ready to suggest nepotism. Marty was not a "mixer" with faculty wives, and he could predict the snide comments about the Sorrentos fixing themselves up with a nice beach vacation on the pretext of digging.

Martha tiptoed out of the house, closing the screen door gently.

"Want to hear the limit?" she asked. "Abby woke up when I came in. She told me she met a little boy named Kermit at the Ellenbogen's yesterday and he told her he won't ever have to work because his daddy is giving him a million dollars."

"She made it up."

"She did *not.* I can believe anything down here. Can you imagine poisoning a child's mind like that?"

"If I had a million bucks I'd want my kids to brag about it. I'd buy up all the imported olive oil and tomato paste and laugh it up." He sang, crooner style, holding his spatulate, hairy hands against the tattered sweatshirt: *"If I were a millionaaaaaaah. . . ."*

"I think it's disgusting for children to talk that way."

He looked at her with concern. "Marty, are you sorry you came down here? With the kids and everything?"

"Of course not. I'll manage. The summer won't last forever."

"I thought this would be ideal for you and the children. A resort town. The beaches. Boats. But it hasn't worked out like that. I have the feeling you made up your mind not to like it."

"It's not my kind of place, Tom."

"It ain't mine either. But I adapt. I try to anyway. Did I ever hate anything as much as the Marines? Never. But I was a good officer. You do the best you can."

"That's you, Tom. I'm thin-blooded. I can't stand extremes. I'm like my cooking—boiled and bland."

"Yeah, but you're learning. A little crushed red pepper, a little oregano. You oughta get into the spirit of things. Paint your toenails. Get one of those fuzzy haircuts with the gold streaks."

"I know it's wrong for me to be bitchy. Especially since the dig is going so badly."

Sorrento lifted her feet and rested them on his knees. He stroked her slender legs. "I tell you something, Marty," he said. "What bothers me is I think you really *hate* this place. You have a working contempt for everything here. Maybe even the Ellenbogens because they're part of it."

"That's not true. I'm fond of Lila and Erwin. They've done so much for you. I just wish they wouldn't try so hard to lower themselves to our pauper's level. They're just dying for some of our honest academic poverty to rub off on them."

"Let 'em! Let 'em do what they want!" he cried. "Besides, if Erwin's got ten million dollars, he worked for it."

"A lot of it is his father-in-law's." She seemed to begrudge him his wealth.

"Yeah, but he keeps it growing." He snapped his fingers. "I better see Erwin tomorrow about that guy in the gold suit."

"Who?"

"That character who was nosing around. He said he was a friend of Erwin's. I want to make sure he stays away. Some kind of publicity jerk."

If she remembered the interlude with Ira deKay, she was not moved to recall it. She bent her head back. In the charged purplish dusk, the edges of her delicate face blurred against the darkening sky. The unseen pastel artist was at work again.

"This *damned* place," she said evenly. "It does make me sick to my stomach. It's too much of everything. Those women. You see them and you think they're movie stars. The hairdos with the glittering phony colors, the expensive clothes and the big behinds, and the phony breasts. You know I read an ad in the paper down here for special padding to build up rear ends?"

Sorrento shrugged. "Who can it hurt? Except the guy who grabs it."

"Then you take a second look at them. And most of them are gross. Not ugly, mind you, but something's missing. There's a kind of prideful vacancy about them. A mouth too slack, a nose off center. That damned look of contentment, like they have it all figured out. Such graceless, uncomfortable people!"

Tom leaped to his feet. "Who isn't graceless?" he cried. "Who isn't ridiculous?"

"Not the way they are."

He picked up the empty pepper jar. "You know what this is? What it does to your mouth and your stomach? You should go to jail if you eat these—or teach other people to eat 'em! My relatives live on 'em! And they call a refrigerator a 'Frigidaire'!"

He paced the narrow balcony. "Oh those ginzos! My glorious brethren! They're so innocent they don't even know enough to cultivate those charming ethnic traits that are supposed to endear them to the Great American *Goy!* My old man hates wine. He likes beer. He never jumped on a grape in his life. He cries when he hears an Irish song, because he was a cop with all the Micks in the East Bronx! Don't ask him the words to 'Faccemii Amore.' My old lady calls spaghetti sauce 'gravy.' *Gravy!* For Chrissake, gravy is what an American puts on his cold-storage turkey! What a ridge-runner spreads on fried mush! *Sauce!* That's what it is, not *gravy!*"

Marty laughed. "I think you're as upset as I am. It's just you can joke about it."

"We're all ridiculous! Who knows what to wear or what to eat any more? It doesn't matter—so long as we don't stuff people into furnaces."

"What in the world has that got to do with what we're discussing?" she asked. "Honestly, Tom, I don't see how you ever give a rational lecture to your classes."

"I crack jokes."

"Well you aren't being terribly amusing now."

"Listen—lay off these people. Who knows what's right? When my old man was on the force, he'd arrest any guys who wore a cap. You wore a cap, you were a wrongo. Today, it's very high class to wear a cap. Faggots, television directors. Who's ahead? I don't know. Everybody wants a little edge. If a man thinks he's got the edge and if it keeps him from kicking someone else, great."

"Well I don't think any of these fat women with purple toenails have an edge on *me*. Quite the contrary."

"Enjoy yourself! You sit right there in your torn pants like a *buffone*. Hall Maitland's daughter. Married to a professor! Let them stay where they are and talk about the beauty-parlor appointment."

"I disapprove of any place where Ye Mermaid Taverne is a delicatessen."

"Ah! A new note is struck! Your old man should hear you talk like that!"

"Stop throwing Hall up to me. I don't mind you being closer to him than I am. But that vaunted tolerance of his—he uses it when it suits him. He once said he never knew a really gifted Negro."

"So what? Maybe he didn't." He peered morosely into the empty jar. His eyes were suffused with sorrow. They were the eyes of a betrayed *Mafioso,* an island rebel who had to be crushed. In old age he would look like the elder who sat at the rear of an Italian restaurant and made change for the waiters.

"I wonder if Hall will get down to look the dig over?" he asked. "It would embarrass the hell out of me if he did." He said it with ill-concealed glee, as if Maitland's presence would right everything.

"I'm being a pest, Tom," Marty said. "I've no right to complain. But the last thing I want is Hall coming down here. You and he would start that damned conspiracy of yours against the rest of the human race, or against women, anyway."

They sat silently for a few minuutes. "I'm glad the crew is making out," he said. "Davey's got something going in Hilltown. And Benny is looking after the Burley kids. I was a little worried when I decided to take them along."

"Always the good shepherd, aren't you?"

"What does that mean?"

"I know how you found Wilma and Oran," Marty said. "You walked into Chock Full o' Nuts one afternoon for a cup of coffee, and there they were—too frightened to order anything."

"Who can blame them? If you were fresh from Decalogue, Missouri, with ten bucks and a scholarship, you'd be scared stiff by a cream-cheese sandwich on nutbread. So I ordered coffee for them."

"And ended up being their guardian. Two more lost souls of

the academic world. Mist-dwellers. I'd like to know who looked after them before you took them in."

"I know all about them. Their old man was one of these screwy dissenting ministers. One of those Trotskyite churches. The Holy Sepulchre of the Divided Host. Or something like that. He spends half his life in the clink for defending people. Anybody. Germans, Jews, Communists, Jehovah's Witnesses. The Reverend DuBridge Burley, D.D. The Fund for the Republic gives him a citation every year."

"I'm surprised you haven't asked *him* to join us. Considering the convocation of lame and halt you've assembled."

"They get the work done."

"Ben—who can't work anywhere. He told the Committee so many lies nobody believes him. And Davey, trying to be brave and comical about his agony. Why you had to bring *him* to a segregated state, I don't know. And Wilma and Oran—cringing when people look at them."

"Go on, and you and me also, hey Marty?"

"No, not you, Tom. You give them something. Someone to lean on. I guess it's because you could have been successful *outside*. None of them could, so they look at their boss and feel fine. You could have made it—but you turned it down to dig."

"What's so terrible, baby?"

"Nothing. Except that I get the feeling I'm just like *them*. A damned University misfit. Leaning on you."

He got up from the canvas chair and hugged her. "You make-a me cry. Cut it out. Let's blow this joint. We'll find a baby-sitter. We'll get drunked up. Go to a night club." He rolled his eyes. "A girlie show."

"Nicky's sick, and Abby keeps waking up."

He searched his khaki shorts and found deKay's card. "I got a great idea! That clown that came here this afternoon—in the gold pants. He said he'd take us out on the town. I'll call him! Why should we pay?"

"Who are you talking about?"

"What's his name? DeKay. The fellah who said he knew Erwin."

"That freak? That idiot? Tom, I wouldn't be in his company for five minutes. Damned boor."

"There you go again!" he cried. "Let him wear his gold pants! What's wrong with a free-load? I'll call him."

"No you won't."

"Why?"

"Because he's everything I hate. He's your enemy, Tom. He's why you're underpaid and ignored. He's not human, he's a syndrome of a wasting disease. He's everything that's cheap and vulgar and hateful. He's this city."

"I only asked. Maybe we'll go out tomorrow, hah? Davey'll get us a sitter—"

She said nothing. Her attitude was grave and distant, as she disengaged his arms. Sorrento walked away from her. Thoughtfully he picked up the empty jar, gripped it as if it were a football and assumed a passer's stance with feet apart. Then he stepped back lightly and tossed it into the water below.

"I never could pass much," he said. "Not even in high school." He said it neither sadly nor nostalgically, but as if this shortcoming had puzzled him for many years.

4 *The Pleasure Agent*

SI MERMELSTEIN could usually *smell* Ira deKay before he saw him. Ira used a special cologne, a rare decoction sent to him, gratis, by a New York haberdasher for whom he had done a favor some years ago. It was pungent and heady, and lingered sweetly on the air, yet it was not a sissy's odor. Rather, it was the scent worn by a man so enamored of all women and their usages that he carried a little bit of them around with him, an olfactory reminder of their delights. Si knew that Ira always took a double dousing of the stuff after he had been with a woman. There had been times when Si, encountering Ira outside a hotel room, would all but swoon at the aroma. Ira would grin with boyish innocence at his associate; the effluvia would rise from his armpits and groin until Si could no longer tolerate it.

"You smell enough of that stuff on Ira," Si confided to Charlie Rasmussen, "and you want to grab the first girl you see and commit unnatural acts. He's the only man I know who gets me excited. It's as if Ira wants you to share in his good luck. He gives you a little smell of it."

Mermelstein was small, chubby and pear-shaped. He had a neat, inconsequential face. The darting black eyes appeared constantly to be seeking approval behind giant eyeglasses the color of licorice. His head was permanently cocked and his midget's mouth worked vigorously around a chipped pipestem. Even in the multicolored splendor of the office of IRA DEKAY ASSOCIATES, he had the look of a newspaper rewrite man, a minor editor who liked ballet. At Ira's bidding Si dressed in a crypto-Ivy style: overblooped Oxford button-down, lazily knotted dark foulard, cordovan loafers.

Si had been in the office since eight that morning, finishing the "presentation" for Ira's crucial meeting. He always postponed his work until the last minute. What Ira had asked of him was so ludicrously simple, so elementary, that he refused to concentrate on it. He wrote his employer's "Presentations," "Surveys," "Stewardship Reports" in clear, concise journalese, never correcting them, never changing a word. Sober and seemingly honest, they were magnificently contrapuntal to Ira's hyperthyroid, theatrical assaults on their clients.

These minimal demands on his talent led him to frequent daydreaming. That morning, he was trying to recall the name of the last Socialist candidate for the Presidency. He knew it wasn't Norman Thomas. Si, who had once distributed pamphlets for the YPSL's and had dreamed of winning a Pulitzer Prize for crusading journalism, had no guilt feelings regarding the twenty thousand dollars a year that Ira paid him. But the forgotten Socialist candidate persisted, and when Helene Schwenk, one of Ira's two secretaries, came in, fussing with coffee containers, and adjusting her seams, he challenged her.

"Hey, Helene," Si said softly. "Who ran for President on the Socialist ticket in 1956?"

"I haven't the vaguest."

"All I can think of is Debs Garms. I got him on my mind."

"*Dopey*. Who?"

"Debs Garms. The only left-handed batter to win the National League batting title named for a defeated Socialist candidate for the Presidency. There's a distinction. Never be another one."

"You goof."

Si shifted his pipe—from mouth, to ashtray, to desk edge—in a ritual rhythm, bantering with Helen and with the second-string girl, Lucille LoPresti, listening to the matutinal noises made by Ira and Cleo in the adjacent apartment. DeKay's office occupied four rooms on the third floor of the Peruviana Hotel. The promoter lived in two of them and ran his business in the others. Although the sliding doors separating the living area from the office were soundproofed, Si always imagined he heard the noises of love within. He was an extremely suggestible man and Ira's enviable talents affected him deeply. He thought about it incessantly with commingled jealousy, admiration and wonder. The sliding door opened and Ira's glowing head appeared.

"Good *morning!*" he sang. "Si, have Lucille fix the coffee."

"How do you want yours?"

"Black, no sugar." Ira yawned luxuriously.

"And the other?"

"Si, baby. You don't have to make believe you don't know who's here. Now how does Cleo have her coffee? Milk, no sugar."

The blond head ducked behind the bleached mahogany panel. Si buzzed Lucille on the intercom, ordered the coffee and settled back in his chair, listening sadly to Ira's high, happy voice, the rush of the needle-point shower, the sloshings and swishings of morning ablutions. He found himself not at all resentful over his employer's good luck. It was the blond, empty-headed woman, in whom pride of the flesh was so deep, who filled him with unease.

He resented very little about Ira. Of course, Ira was far from a friend. Si had read Proust when he was fourteen and had picketed the Fenster Dairy in Woodlawn when he was sixteen. Later, he had taught grammar-school English in the Bronx. Ira, as far as he knew, never read a book, a magazine, or even the newspapers on whose good will so much of his livelihood depended. There was no common ground on which the two men could meet, a circumstance which enabled Si to stand back dispassionately and analyze his employer. He saw Ira as a social phenomenon, a cultural necessity, a reflection of all the desires of a rich, burgeoning civilization. He was the new high priest: *the pleasure agent.* Ira made people happy. He moved freely on all levels. He was acceptable everywhere. He was liked by everyone. He was the grease that lubricated the social machinery of the Beach. And what was the Beach but a pastiche of the larger contemporary scheme? He never ceased to be awed by Ira's *modus operandi.* Before a jury of sleek, hard men in dark suits and white-on-white shirts—the board of a hotel chain perhaps—he would assume his jester's role and win them over in minutes. The round, blond head would wobble wildly on the limber body, the outlandish shirt and feverish pants would evoke laughter and approval. To these masters, Ira was the embodiment of the joys of the world. He symbolized all the beautiful whores, the expensive liquor, the endless laughs, the close association with the celebrity world—indeed, the healing sunlight and pale green ocean of the Beach. And he was more than a mere peddler, a sutler on the fringes of their bivouac. He was a joyous participant, a drunken scoutmaster, grabbing the checks, goosing the vice-president's mistress, shouting the rude stories, enabling them to forget their wives, the tax laws, the son-of-a-bitch up the street who would outbuild them next year. He was the pleasure agent.

Shortly after ten, Ira, redolent of his arch perfume, bounced through the sliding doors. A glimpse of Cleo in her slip made Mermelstein blush. In moments like these, he wanted to shake Ira's hand and congratulate him.

Ira wore a navy blue jacket with the insignia of a restricted yacht club. Neither Jews nor gaudy Beach types like Ira were welcome. However, the previous winter, he had aided them in securing the condemnation of some dwellings adjacent to their clubhouse. He was made a lifetime member. Sprawled on the ochre sofa in the office, he shuffled through Si's notes.

"Very neat, Si baby," Ira said. "A gasser."

"You have enough to work from?" Si asked.

"Plenty. We don't want to tip the whole mitt today. Just get them slobbering a little."

"You want the blueprints and the list of contacts?"

"Nope."

"The financing setup? I could call the accountant."

"Nah. I want to hold the money talk down this morning. Si, sweetie, this crowd owns it all. My only problem is to hook 'em good. The zile kai will follow."

Si removed his eyeglasses. Without them he appeared confused and unprotected. He squinted at Ira, as if the decorator's hues, the beiges, golds and browns, served as protective coloration for his chief.

"Ira, you think maybe this deal is too big for us?"

"Si, *honey*. The town's ready for it."

"Another tourist attraction? Look what happened to Cowboyland. They're still paying off the builder. They're in hock to everyone."

"It had a bad location. Besides this isn't cowboy country. Smart college boys like you should know." He jerked his rubbery body upright and spread his long arms along the nubby, gold-shot top of the sofa. "And don't forget our survey. The deKay poll."

"Some poll," Si sneered. "Lucille and Helene took a Sunday

off and asked fifty people loaded questions. I rigged the whole thing."

"They'll believe it. They'll believe anything I say."

Mermelstein rose and sat on the edge of his desk. He loved his desk. It was long and smooth, and finished in pickled walnut.

"That isn't what worries me, Ira. It's that we'll be in this ourselves. Owners. But you've never owned anything. Everything with us is deals and connections and percentages. If this thing goes bust, we do also."

DeKay tossed an ivory pillow high, caught it and hugged it.

"Stop sweating, baby. It'll work out. It has to work out, because people want it. I have an instinct for this."

"I know you do, but look at it this way. Everything else we do is air. Gas. We're on the edge all the time. I'm not knocking it, Ira. Look what we did for the Poochburger chain. And the hotels you've got off the hook. But we don't have anything you can lay your hand on. Just good will, and your personality, and the way you make connections for people. This is different."

"You're so gloomy today, Si. You look very Gentile in that suit."

Mermelstein shook his undersized head. "I wish I could be like you, Ira."

Ira called to the closed doors. "Oh, Cleo! Come on out and get to work on Si!"

"Ah, come on, Ira," Si muttered. He retreated behind the splendid desk. Why did Ira have to embarrass him? He was trying to be helpful. Why did he have to drag in that maddening whore?

"You'd get tired of it," Ira said soothingly. "It's like anything else, Si. You know the three most overrated things in the world?"

"No."

"Home cooking, home screwing and going on the road with a musical show!" Ira roared. He wanted Si to laugh with him, but the little man could only summon up a weak smile. That was Ira—he could not bear to see anyone unhappy, unrewarded, denied pleasure. Yet Si was sensing something out of key in Ira's rude efforts to comfort him. His minimizing of Cleo's charms was genuine. It was tinged with boredom and uncertainty. The tangled patterns of Ira's life were like the backlash of a reel of monofilament fishing line. Was he tiring of the whole mess?

Cleo emerged. Behind armorial sunglasses, in functional navy blue and oyster, her essential vapidity was marvelously disguised.

In heat she would not rumple or sweat or malfunction. Si gathered his notes and followed Ira and Cleo into the reception room, where Lucille and Helene were opening mail.

"Lucille, call the apartment for me," Cleo asked. "Tell the girl I'll see Robin after lunch."

Lucille nodded her black leonine head. When Cleo and the men had left, she raised masculine eyebrows and murmured to Helene:

"The little mother. Sees the kid three times a week."

"That's her business," Helene said. "The kid's better off with the nigger maid. You like to be brought up by something like her?"

Ira had engaged the Pizarro Suite of the Peruviana for the luncheon meeting. He paid nothing for the use of the lavish rooms, nor for his office. The Peruviana was one of his major clients. Like everything else in his life, the hotel was part of an exasperating maze of contacts and associations. He was more than a press agent for its owners, he was a kind of *eminence grise,* an elder statesman. Ira had proved his worth to them in a curious manner. The hotel had been erected the previous year, a garish, exotic palace, financed by five general partners, enormously wealthy men, all vaguely connected with other industries. One of the quintet, a saturnine and bellicose party named Karger, decided that his percentage of the ownership was not commensurate with his contribution. He had been a disputatious and crude fellow all along, and his close connection with lawless elements in Cleveland was a source of continuing distress to the other four owners. Karger, threatening to haul them into court (or worse), awoke one morning to learn that his associates had bought him out. He was furious. All his life he had craved the status of hotel-owning, the joy of sitting in the lavish lobby, hobnobbing with celebrities, announcing himself as the owner. The income he received from the hotel was of less import than the status he had acquired—Karger was a fat, ugly man with a pitted face.

The discarded partner, swearing bloody vengeance on the other four, was in the process of summoning his enforcers from Cleveland when Ira appeared on the scene. He met with Karger in his private suite, listened to his grievance and solved the whole affair in a matter of minutes. A news release would be sent out stating that the partners had taken him back in—*but nothing of the kind would be done*. Karger looked puzzled. Ira explained. In exchange for making no more financial claims on the owners, Ira said, Karger would be allowed to sit in the lobby as much as he wanted, to keep his suite (at a special discounted rate) and keep telling people he was a partner. It worked admirably. All that the ousted partner had ever wanted was recognition as an owner. The money was secondary. Ira had gone to the heart of the matter. He understood, better than sociologists or motivational researchers, the value of illusion, the strength of the useless accolade, the power of the meaningless award. Karger, who was prepared to order his aides to splatter the Peruviana's lobby with blood and brains, now spent his mornings on a centrally located chartreuse lounge chair, buttonholing guests and advising them that he was the owner. This remarkable feat had put the hotel in Ira's debt forever.

The hotel was thereafter frequently parlayed with other clients of Ira's—such as Mr. Banjo. He kept his accounts in perpetual motion. Ira was candid about his technique.

"I'm like the man from Temple, Texas," he would tell a new client, "and they're like the four sisters."

And he would tell the story of the amazing man from Temple, Texas, the greatest lover in the state. One night he met four sisters, members of a vaudeville acrobatic team. He invited them to his hotel room after the performance. "And you know what?" Ira cried. "He had three of them girls in the air and one on the bed all night! Zile!"

Indeed, on the morning of the meeting, Ira was engaged in these very acrobatics: Mr. Banjo had registered at the Peruviana the previous day and was making "copy," toward the mutual benefit of his own person, the hotel, and deKay. He had gotten drunk in the Cuzco Bar, broken a bottle of gin, and made every feature page in the nation. In addition to local reporters and photographers, a man from a national press association had been assigned to him.

The Pizarro Suite occupied half the top floor of the fifteen-story, cream-colored building. The wall facing the ocean was of glass, tinted the palest green. The remaining walls were of mosaic, depicting scenes from the conquest of Peru. In bits of bright tile, one saw Pizarro drawing the line in the sand on the Isle of Gallo; the seizure of the Atahualpa in Cuzco; his garroting; Pizarro in glory surrounded by the Virgins of the Sun. The furnishings were crypto-Hispanic—scarlet draperies dangled from bronze lances; heraldic crests adorned sofas, chairs and lamps. A fully stocked bar, in spurious granite, molded to suggest Inca walls, occupied one small room. Here Cleo busied herself. Ira discreetly dismissed the hotel barkeep. He wanted the proceedings as clandestine as possible. Moreover, Cleo was good atmosphere. She was not a whore, yet she was of the earth. She could be joked with, tweaked, made party to their conspiracies. Withal, her gelid detachment lent Ira's convocations an indefinable prestigious air.

Si reviewed his notes. Ira would call on him to discuss the "survey." DeKay himself stretched on the sofa, awaiting his guests. Once he called to Si:

"Si, baby, when you get a minute call Charlie Rasmussen. Ask him does he know anything about Erwin's property on the bay. Like if anyone beat us to it."

Three of the guests arrived at noon. Erwin Ellenbogen, swart and enigmatic in a black suit, was the first. The young industrialist settled himself in a brocaded chair. Hiding behind dark prescription lenses, he was unreachable, inviolate. Cleo offered to make a drink for him; he declined politely. His smooth, hexagonal face was a source of distress to Ira. Erwin had always been peculiarly untouched by Ira's buoyancy.

"I'm glad you got here first, Erwin baby," Ira said, forcing a lemonade on his guest. "I wanted to ask you about those people digging up your land."

"Yes. You were there yesterday, Ira."

"Oh?"

"Dr. Sorrento told me this morning. He was a little upset. I'd appreciate it if you stayed away." He turned to Mermelstein. "Si—nothing for the newspapers, either."

"Sweetie!" Ira sang. "I was just being nosey. But I mean—what plays? What's your percentage?"

Ellenbogen folded plump, manicured hands on his lap. "No percentage, Ira. Mrs. Ellenbogen is interested in their work."

Ellenbogen settled back, nursing his lemonade. Mermelstein studied him with admiration. He liked Ellenbogen because the man was completely integrated. His character might assume strange and sudden turns, yet nothing he did or said seemed illogical. For example, Si knew, those soft hands of Erwin's were strong and quick. The pudgy body was deceptive. Erwin was a superb boxer and gymnast. A mutual friend who had been at Fort Bliss with Erwin had once told Si how the future millionaire, in need of petty cash, would fight professionally in Juarez for twenty-five dollars per bout. It was amazing, the friend recalled, how

Erwin (fat around the middle and wearing old tennis shoes) would toy with his troglodytic Mexican or Negro opponents (all muscle and hard head) and then deck them with a few snappy combinations of lefts and rights. Later, they learned that Erwin had been boxing since he was ten. This sureness of purpose, this capacity to see all goals clearly and constantly, was Erwin's greatest asset. There was nothing graceless about him. Money and success came to him easily and naturally. It was true that his father-in-law, old man Schneer, had started the beach-furniture business in the twenties. But it was Erwin, newly married to Lila, and fresh from five years in the army and a graduate degree in business administration, who had built a multi-million-dollar apparatus out of synthetic webbing and aluminum tubing. He was expert in time-and-motion studies, ran a desegregated shop, contributed lavishly to charities, and outproduced and outsold his competitors with disheartening regularity.

Two other invited guests had come together, a few minutes after Erwin's arrival. These men, older, simpler and blunter, offered a richer vein to Ira and his janizaries. They gravitated toward Cleo and she immediately engaged them in meandering, meaningless talk. She said little and most of it was irrelevant, yet somehow it brought the two elephantine visitors into Ira's magic realm. They were changeling princes at the feast.

"I been in this town since nineteen ought nine," one of them said, "and I ain't been swimming once." His name was J. J. Campion. He was bulky, white-haired and badly dressed. He would never be found in a scarlet-and-gold cabana suit, playing gin rummy for a dollar a point. Campion was a primitive.

"You really should try water skiing," Cleo said seriously.

"Fall on my big pratt."

"Oh, no. But if you take lessons, the only one to take them with is Pedro at the Marlin Club."

"Yeah?"

"Yes. In you go. He starts you right off. But not on those rotten British skis they use in Nassau. The narrow ones."

"My kid nephew goes water skiing."

"The thing with Pedro is he won't let you get frightened. He had me on one ski in a week."

"I'd like to have you on one ski for a week."

He laughed, his voice heavy with phlegm. Ira cackled and Erwin managed a minimal smile. Mermelstein, fussing with his papers, suddenly thought of something he had read in

Trotsky's writings—a sampling from the Czar's diary, references to carefree days of country strolls, horseback riding, afternoon teas—and the revolutionist's commentary: *All on the very borderline of physiology. . . .*

Campion was a real-estate operator, a hairy mammoth of early beach days. All over the southern counties one saw his signs—J. J. CAMPION, REALTOR—not on prize acreage or waterfront bonanzas, but on scrubby hunks of filled swamp, abandoned stores, peeling taxpayers and deserted ghostly hotels cracked by the hostile sun. From these ragged bits and pieces he had accumulated a fortune in real wealth.

On Cleo's opposite flank was a rarer bird, a man named Fenton Braud. His stock in trade was twofold: a surname identical with that of a revered moneyed family, and a capacity to develop, promote, sell, and then abandon worthless consumer commodities. He was, in fact, remotely related to the Brauds of Missouri, a congeries of bankers, manufacturers and public servants. This tenuous kinship had served Fenton Braud well in a half-century of umbrageous trade. People always asked: "Are you related to the Kansas City Brauds?" He would wink hooded eyes and gargle: "Kinda the black sheep, you might say."

Braud had made his first million in a deep-tanning sun lotion. An increase in dermatitis among its users had brought on the law. Unscathed, Braud turned up a year later promoting kits to turn salt water fresh. Three years later it was a compound guaranteed to grow luxurious lawns in sand. Si Mermelstein, studying his long, corrupted face (he seemed to be chewing his false teeth into fine pieces which dribbled off the side of his lips), recalled that each venture lasted less than a year. Profits were accumulated, corporations dissolved, creditors and trade commissions left breathless, while Braud vanished, as evanescent as the services his products were alleged to perform. His most recent undertaking was a nasal inhalant that induced sleep.

"Who we waiting on?" Braud asked. "I don't mind playing kneesy with Miss Cooke here, but I'm busy."

"Yeah," Campion added. "What's the story, deKay?"

Erwin Ellenbogen yawned. His Oriental face, an olive-toned hexagon, standing on one flat side, disturbed deKay more than the protests of Campion and Braud.

"It's that Jimmy Nudo," Ira said. "Always late. He's probably checking the receipts from Havana. You fellahs know Jimmy?"

"I heard a him," Braud said. "A hood."

"Jimmy Nudo?" Erwin asked. *"He's* coming?"

"Come on, Erwin!" Ira pleaded. "Jimmy's a public figure."

There was a heavy, meditative silence. Ira leaped to his feet. "Hey!" he cried. "Anyone hear about the rich nigger who bought a cast-iron Jew for his front lawn?"

Campion and Braud guffawed. Erwin did not smile.

"I would take offense from anyone else," Ellenbogen said. "But knowing you as I do, Ira—"

"Yeah! You told me yourself—I'm almost smart enough to be Jewish!"

"I said *almost.*" Erwin sucked at his lemonade. "Really, Ira, I wish you'd get down to cases. I can't speak for Mr. Campion or Mr. Braud, but I have a busy day. I can't understand your secrecy."

In feigned sorrow, Ira's mouth dropped. "How's your golf, Erwin?"

"What has that got to do with anything?"

"Erwin, doll, we might as well discuss your golf if you think I'm wasting your time. How's your golf? You think Ira would ask you here for nothing? Give me a chance."

Ellenbogen was exposed as an ingrate. It was remarkable, Mermelstein thought, how Ira turned occasions to his own purposes with an irrelevancy, a change of voice.

The doorbell rang. Cleo, dutifully, rose from between Braud and Campion and moved noiselessly to the door. Jimmy Nudo entered. He was a miniature of a man, glittering and precise. He had a solemn, dark face and was dressed in black, yet the impression he gave was sportive rather than funereal. Nudo's drab features and shrunken frame appeared to have been put to the services of a magical decorator. He was like a peeling, cramped walkup apartment house in the East Fifties, transmuted into something bright and exciting by a pair of vigorous Young Marrieds, with fey, daring notions. A star sapphire the size of a crow's egg nested on his right pinky. The collars of his creamy-white shirt, rolled artfully around the starved neck, were peculiarly rounded at the tips. His shoes were of some rare saurian hide, compartmented and varnished. Even the sparkling touches of white in his waved, inky hair seemed to have been daubed on by a decorator. Mermelstein envisioned the scene: the tiny racketeer sitting glumly in the chair, the fairy mincing around him with a jar of white grease: *just a little touch more on the temple, don't you think Mr. Nudo?*

Nudo shook hands—one quick jerk of the wrist—with everyone, uttering a muffled "hiya" as he did so. It was not lack of poise that rendered him taciturn, Si felt. Rather it was deep knowledge of command presence. He was a leader, not a follower. He was impressed by no one.

"Mr. Nudo, aren't you the proprietor of the Blue Paradise Bar?" Ellenbogen asked. Erwin ripped a rectangle of silicone paper from a small packet and began polishing his sunglasses. He might have been a village chief of Samarkand or Bokhara querying a visiting Sicilian merchant prince.

"Yes. It happens to be one of my particular enterprises."

"I've been there several times. Very nice."

"We serve an honest drink."

"Honest drink!" Ira sang "Oh, Jim-a-reee! What else you got besides the Blue Paradise Bar? Hah? Tell'em about Havana!"

"Ira, I never discuss my particular business enterprises. I wouldn't presume to ask these gentlemen what they did."

"What's the secret?" Ira said. "Mr. Campion is a leading beach realtor. Mr. Braud's in proprietary drugs and Erwin's the beach-furniture man. No secrets. Four nice, successful fellahs."

In sad concurrence, Nudo nodded his head. He was ensconced in a vast black chair. All that was left of him was the startling white shirt and tie and the grave face.

"Like I always have said," Nudo declared. "There's nothing like a legitimate business."

They awaited further exegesis, but it was not forthcoming. Only Si understood him. Nudo craved legitimacy. The rarity of the honest buck, the difficulty in turning one, made the legitimate desirable. For Jimmy Nudo, the world was populated with wrongos and marks. The fix was the normal state of affairs. He hungered for the lawful, the condoned, the honest, not because it was more profitable, but because it was so damned hard to find.

A platoon of waiters brought in a buffet lunch of glazed hams and burnished turkeys, molded and cosmeticized salads. They ate on crested silver and fine china. Cleo tucked napkins in collars, served wine, brushed her limbs against them with excessive casualness. The luncheon concluded, Ira removed his yachting jacket and his turquoise ascot and perched himself on an end table. He rubbed his hands together and grinned at them.

"I didn't ask you gentlemen here to enjoy the Peruviana's free chow," Ira began. "Or to cop a feel with Miss Cooke or because you're all nice fellahs. I asked you here to get in on the ground floor of one of the biggest enterprises ever to hit the Beach."

Si shifted his legs at the small desk. Ira was poised and glib, off to a splendid start.

"I need money," Ira said. "A lot of money. I need a million bucks. Two hundred grand will start me. Fifty thousand from each of you. I've talked to the banks and they're not interested. They think I'm in a risky project. They're wrong."

Campion agitated his great haunches. "You don't raise that kinda dough any more, deKay," he said. "Not just on your word. Money's hard now. They ain't a big hotel going up this year. Just some little motels up north. There ain't no loose cash left. Not for no hotel."

Braud kept chewing his teeth—or was it a biscuit of some kind? Mermelstein wanted to brush crumbs from his lapels. "Get to the point, deKay," Braud said.

"In a moment, sir," Ira said. "You all know my track record. Why should I be modest? I got American Beauty Homes out of trouble. No one else on the Beach could do it. Si will show you our stewardship report on that if you'd like to check on me."

Mermelstein nodded. *American Beauty Homes:* four hundred wretched warrens built on a filled swamp, houses so patently fraudulent that even the easy Beach economy rejected them. And then Ira had entered the scene. He held an American Beauty Contest; induced some entertainers to dedicate the scabby development, gave free American Beauty roses to women visitors. A scholarship was set up for the teen-ager who wrote the best essay on "Why It's Good Citizenship to Own a Home." A national TV show, visiting the beach, originated a "remote" from the former swamp one morning in an "editorial feature" on "new trends in housing." In two weeks, every cracked and warped dwelling was sold.

"I got a reputation," Ira said. "I stand or fall on my undertakings. I have no measurable wealth like you gents. I have to keep operating."

Si marveled at him. Now he was sincere and humble—a lesser person beseeching their aid.

"Si, honey," Ira said. "Show the gents the sign."

Mermelstein had set up a small wooden easel. On it he now placed a large pink sign. In gilt lettering it proclaimed:

"What the hell's that?" Braud asked. "Sounds like a fire sale."

"You'll find out in a second," Ira said politely. "I'd like to ask you a simple question. What's the most important thing going today?"

"Well, you want me to say it's money, Ira," Erwin said. "But I won't."

"Anyone else?" Ira asked.

Nudo cleared his throat. "You might say," he said solemnly, "that the most important thing is a nangle."

"A what?" Ira asked.

"A nangle, a nangle. Like is the store open. Or is everyone greased. Or do you have the whole thing alone. You know, deKay. You got a nangle in everything you do."

"Jimmy!" Ira laughed—an honest laugh, not his commercial joviality. "You're *my boy!*"

"Kids?" Braud asked. "You sell kids, you got it made."

"Nope." Ira closed his eyes.

"Don't ask me," Campion said. "I ain't read a newspaper since Lindbergh. Come on, deKay, I got work to do."

Ira surveyed them all. He was suddenly serious, dedicated. "Gents, the biggest thing on the national picture today, the sure-fire commodity, is *religion*."

Campion flushed, then started to rise. "I never talk about religion or politics," he said heavily. "It's everyone's private business."

"Who said *no,* Mr. Campion?" Ira cried. "Give me a minute to explain! Hear me out. Religion is the biggest. It's box-office. Everybody wants in. The rock-and-roll singers—they record hymns. A guy wins the hundred-yard dash and he says 'the Lord helped me.' All these top industrialists and statesmen, when they're written up, it has to say 'he is a religious man.' And the beauty part is—nobody knocks it. How can you when it does people good? Look at the big movies—the books. All on the religious kick. And gentlemen, this town is ready for it. The God Bit."

He fell into a chair, enervated by his sermon. "Si, sweetie, take over for me."

Mermelstein handed Cleo four heavy folders. She distributed

them to the guests. He worked at the easel, using a set of brightly colored cards, removing the cryptic legend GOD-O-RAMA.

"Our survey was conducted by Institutional Research, Inc.," Si began, "an opinion-testing firm specializing in consumer preferences. Briefly, they did this: trained interviewers quizzed a representative sample, residents and tourists, with a ratio of four tourists per one resident. They asked two questions. First, what is the most important force for good in the world today, and second, is there a need for more spiritual emphasis in the Beach."

He adjusted his outsized glasses, then placed a new card on the easel. "Eighty-three per cent named religion as the most important force in the world. Answers to the second question were even more astonishing. Ninety-two per cent wanted greater spiritual emphasis."

Ellenbogen flipped the pages in the folder. "I see nothing here about the interviewing technique. Or a breakdown on your sample. I knew a little about these surveys, having studied them in graduate school at NYU. It sounds to me like the questions were loaded."

"I—I—have supplemental data at the office, Mr. Ellenbogen," Si said quickly. "I'll send it to you."

Campion and Braud were holding the folders in their mottled hands as if they were cakes of ice. Jimmy Nudo had placed his on the arm of the chair.

"Gents," Ira said, bounding up, "I'm talking about a tourist attraction. A multi-million-dollar plant. Marginal upkeep. Small overhead. Make the investment back in one year and it's all gravy after that. Nothing but money coming in."

Fenton Braud croaked. "You brought us here for another tourist trap? A lousy Indian village? Tropical Paradise? DeKay, you should know better than that. Underwater World is in receivership. Living Museum closes down next week, boy."

"Besides," Jimmy Nudo said archly. "I don't see a nangle. Like the dogs, or the track, or jai alai. Where's the income?"

"I'm not clear on what you have in mind, Ira," Ellenbogen said reasonably. "Gentlemen, I think we owe Mr. deKay a hearing." His tone implied that once the hearing was granted, Ira could be left for dead, gasping on the silver beach.

"Thank you, Erwin," Ira said. He walked to the easel and put the first card back. "Here it is, gents."

The words stared at them idiotically.

"You must be fooling, Ira. You can't really call it that." Ellenbogen appeared mildly shocked.

"It still sounds like bargain day," Braud said.

"The GOD-O-RAMA is a giant indoor and outdoor panorama of the world's great religions. Man's quest for higher things. From primitive man's search for the stars to our great present-day faiths. Illustrated with models, exhibits, cycloramas—all combined in one massive format. We envision a series of daily performances. The loaves and the fishes. The burning bush. The Crusades."

Mermelstein picked up the flow of ideas. "There are a million kinds of good merchandising gimmicks we can use," Si said. "Tie-ins with schools and churches, of course. And mind you, nothing that's competitive with the actual organized religions. I mean, we're neutral. We inform, educate, excite people about the over-all grand scheme of the spiritual side of man. Non-sectarian, objective—"

"Just one minute, Si," Ellenbogen interrupted. "I have a good deal of experience in interfaith work. And with all due respect to anyone's particular beliefs, I can tell you that you and Ira are stepping into a very complex thing. It is not a matter of hatred, or even jealousies, but a more subtle kind of thing, such as who gets first billing, who gets more time, whose campaigns are more effective. Be very careful."

Si nodded, pursing his small mouth. "We've checked that out, Mr. Ellenbogen," he said. "There'll be an advisory board, of course, of clergymen, representing the major faiths. We shall also have special consultants on groups like the Moslems and Hindus who aren't really represented in our national population."

Braud worked his lips around his crumbling teeth. His shrewd, practical mind had heard nothing to excite him. "It sounds like a museum," he said hoarsely. "No museum makes out."

"DeKay," Campion asked. "What makes you think these church people will cooperate?"

"We have sent questionnaires to fifty top religious authorities," Si said quickly. "The results are gratifying. Only two groups have raised questions."

"May I inquire which ones?" Ellenbogen asked.

Si looked to Ira for approval, then spoke. "Well, the Roman Catholics wanted to know a good deal more about it. Their first concern was that they have a separate building. The Orthodox Jews never answered us. I learned from an outside source that they felt the questions were in the wrong language."

The group lapsed into a pained, abrasive silence. The promotional ping-pong ball that deKay and Mermelstein had been tapping back and forth across the flat green table of their guests' collective minds, now lay motionless and cracked on the gold carpeting. At length Campion spoke.

"I ain't convinced. These tourist deals are rough. Braud is right when he says they have trouble making out."

Ira stretched his arms outward. "Fifty thousands bucks to find out, Mr. Campion. The money won't break you. We've got a sweet financing program for the general partners—*us*. Every tax break in the books."

"Where you gonna get the million you talked about?" Braud asked.

"A stock issue to limited partners," Ira said. "Our friends and families to have first option, of course."

Jimmy Nudo cocked his head. He had somehow remained apart from the give-and-take, an observer rather than a participant.

"You got property to build this on?" Nudo asked. "That's what killed Underwater World, building it way out on Mango Key, where nobody wanted to drive. It hasta be near."

Ira looked quickly at Ellenbogen. "Oh, I have a choice piece of property, Jimmy. It will need some wheeling-and-dealing, but I have it."

Some additional questions were thrown at deKay, but by now he had become secretive and cautious. There would be more meetings, a financial briefing, a lecture from the architect, the consultants. Like a reverse strip tease, Ira would add a piece here, a prop there, until the whole complex scheme stood detailed before them.

Cleo had left the room. Now, the presentation concluded, she returned, advising deKay, "He's here now, Ira."

Through scarlet draperies, pushing a toy supermarket basket, waddled Mr. Banjo. He wore a white Dacron suit, a coconut straw hat with red pugree band, white buckskin shoes. A cigar was clamped between his pendulous, fleshy lips. His manager prodded him gently with an electric wand and the orangutan, bowlegged as a superannuated jockey, walked into their midst. Amid helpless laughter, he scratched his nose, then took his shoes off. His vestigial feet were almost hairless.

"Aaaah!" Campion roared. "Look at him!"

Braud screamed. "You got to see him close up to appreciate him! I never miss him on the television!"

"I hear he gets over a grand a week," Jimmy Nudo whispered. "He must have a nangle."

Mr. Banjo chattered, leaped into his manager's arms. Ira winked at Si. "That ain't all, gents!" deKay cried. "Mr. Banjo brought li'l presents for all of you!"

There were four small boxes in the shopping cart, each wrapped in metallic paper and bright ribbons. There was one for each guest. At Ira's bidding, they opened the presents. In each was a key to a room at the Peruviana.

"Ready and waiting!" Ira shouted. "You go with deKay, you go first class! Why do you think I broke off the questions? Why waste precious time? All aboard for zile kai!"

They clutched the keys like amulets, made their goodbyes. At the door, Ellenbogen returned the key to Ira.

"Very generous of you, Ira," Erwin said. "But thank you, no."

"Come on, Erwin, sweetie. You never?"

"If I did, you would not find out."

"Never mind, Erwin," Ira said consolingly—as if the man's moral strictures were a defect, and his confession called for sympathy. He draped a proprietary arm around the manufacturer's shoulders. "About that piece of land you have, baby," deKay said. "I ain't subtle. You know what I was thinking—"

"I know, Ira. You know what that land is worth."

"I know. *I know.* That's why it should have a real money-maker on it—not just another lousy mansion."

"Ira, I have an obligation to Dr. Sorrento. When he concludes his work, perhaps we can look into it. But these are problems you aren't equal to. Zoning laws and so forth. You have a lot of good ideas, Ira, but I wonder if this project may be a little involved, a little intricate for you. When I have mulled this matter over, I'll contact you." He undraped Ira's arm and left.

Inside the suite, Cleo and Si watched, fascinated, as the manager fed Mr. Banjo scraps from the buffet. The ape munched a turkey leg.

"It's an innaresting thing," the manager explained. "Anthropoid apes are vegetarians. But *not* Mr. Banjo. He loves turkey. Ever since he was special guest at the newsboys' Thanksgiving dinner in Jersey City."

5 *The Old-Timer*

Two days after deKay's visit to the dig, the long trench yielded a major find.

Dave Ballard had been teasing the workmen about the possibility of a skeleton rising from the pit. He had established a tremulous relationship with them, one so charged with nuances, so precariously balancing satire and sympathy, that he often lost track of who was playing what joke on whom. However, his invocation of minstrel dialect was usually the occasion for tolerant smiles on the part of Spots and McIsaac.

"In d'event you locates a skelekon in deah, Mistah Spots," Ballard was saying, working his trowel gently through the unproductive sand, "doan be skeered. Dat is ef'n he doan come up afteh you."

McIsaac, the lay preacher, mopped his face with a soaked handkerchief. It was breathless and still on the parched littoral. Sweat poured freely from their heads, dripped down noses and chins.

"You forget, Mist' Ballard," McIsaac said softly, "I has officiated at many burials. I has workin' experience wit deh departed."

Ballard was silent. Now there it was again—McIsaac calling him *Mister*. He had told them to call him Dave. Was the old black man joking with him? Or did Ballard's education demand a *Mister?* It was too complicated, and it was his own fault, not so much for letting them in on the silly game, but for begging Tom Sorrento to bring him South, back to everything he despised and feared.

"Whut about me?" Spots asked challengingly. The younger man rested on his shovel. "You think these old bones in deh ground scare me? I was in Graves Registration in deh ETO."

"You two biggoty niggers, das what," Ballard said sullenly. "We see how you acks when bones come."

They had unearthed half of the five-by-five sections of the long trench. The two endmost, where Ben Peltz had dug to a depth of three feet, had proved dishearteningly barren. Eight other sections had been cleared to a depth of about sixteen inches. Sorrento had advised Ballard that instead of clearing the remaining ten squares, the first ten were to be fully excavated. If they remained sterile, new test pits would have to be dug, perhaps an entire new digging scheme set up. It would mean several days of surveying, mapping, planning, but it would be mandatory. Sorrento had this for cold comfort: the project would be neither a gigantic success or a total loss. The academic processes, he told himself, were largely additive, operating without criteria of success or failure. If he were to unearth a stone city to rival Machu Picchu (most unlikely in the marginal Glades culture) he might merit an article in the Sunday *Times Magazine*. Sorrento knew it was a fair arrangement. If all the pits he ever dug produced nothing but a few meaningless pottery fragments, he could not be marked as a bankrupt. This capacity of the academic world to render its members faceless, to emasculate them at the expense of the bits of knowledge they added to the grand scheme, he found comforting. There were no bank examiners, no irate sponsors, no stock issues, no depletion allowances, no Nielsen ratings, none of the signs and portents of achievement. There were, of course, hierarchies of position and there were certain coveted academic chairs, awards and fellowships. But these bore no true relationship to the world without. They were like secret honors conferred by conspiratorial terrorist societies, meaningless to anyone but the initiate.

He was musing over these circumstances of the career he had chosen, sitting at his desk in the boathouse, when he heard Ballard summoning him. He walked past the Burleys and Peltz, the three of them puzzling over fragments, and approached the long trench. Dave was kneeling at the edge of the vertical facing, pointing with his trowel.

"The old-timer showed up," he said.

Tom dropped to one knee. The workmen stepped back a few feet.

"You just find him?" Tom asked.

"Yeah," Spots said eagerly. "I was clearin' dis piece heah, like Mist' Ballard tell us. Den I hit somethin' hard. Too big fo' a stone."

In the matrix of yellow sand, the smooth round skull rested peacefully—white-gray, dry, as perfect as a stage prop. Only the parietal area was exposed.

Ballard bowed solemnly. "After you, Professor." He gave Sorrento his trowel. Tom began to chip dirt away from the cranium. He worked quickly and daintily, holding the mason's tool point downward, tapping it lightly against the impacted sand. After every few strokes, he would pick up a soft brush and dust away loose earth. Two eye sockets, ageless and bored, stared at them. A nose cavity appeared. Tom set the trowel down.

"I wanted to see a little more before we open it up," Tom said. "What do you think, Dave?"

"I been wrong before. You take my advice we might wreck the whole thing. Ask Benny."

Peltz, with the Burleys at his rear, had drifted over to the trench.

"I figure it's an extended burial," Ben said. "That's typical of Glades Tradition. Of course, it could be flexed."

"Or semi-flexed," Tom said bitterly.

"Or nothing else there but the skull," Ballard said. "But I think he's flexed. Look at the angle of the head."

Sorrento spit on his hands. *"Avanti!* I don't care if he's flexed, extended, or whether the head's all we got. We'll give him all the room he needs." He took a trowel and stepped into the pit. "Come on, Davey, earn your money." Ballard joined him.

They began clearing earth. They worked in the manner of landscape gardeners digging up the root of a large tree, starting about four feet from the skull and working inward and downward, delicately and slowly, so as not to agitate the precious remains. They used only trowels and brushes, loosening soil, dusting, poking tentatively and lightly in search of the rest of the skeleton.

A feathery hand was exposed; a crumbling rib cage; a scapula as flaky as old paper. They did not attempt to remove any of the bones. The technique called for a clearing of the upper surfaces of the skeleton. Then, measurements and photographs would be made. Anything worth preserving could then be removed. It was the find *in situ* that was important—the nature of the burial, the condition of the skeleton, presence of grave goods. A circular hole more than a foot deep had been cleared around the remains. The new pit had eaten several feet into the north vertical facing of the trench, destroying Ballard's fine geometric pattern of excavated squares.

"There he is," Sorrento said. "Last man to get out of the real-estate panic. Take your hat off, Ballard, you're in the presence of greatness."

Ballard smiled and doffed the comedian's fedora. "Sho' nuff! Preacher, say a few words for our brother in sorrow. You have no doubt officiated at many interrings. Here is your first exterring."

The laborers remained silent. The exposed skeleton seemed to have dampened their enthusiasm for Ballard's game.

"A beauty," Sorrento said. "I love him like I love my cousin Angie deStefano, the policy banker. The same kind of purity. You know something, Dave? This place is full of them. His relatives. They knew a good thing when they saw it. The beach. The sun. Shellfish for free. Benny, run up to the house and get the camera and the measuring tape, and the Krylon. The old boy looks strong enough, but I think we better give him a shot."

Sorrento took a ragged notebook from his hip pocket. With a pencil stub, he wrote:

TRENCH I: SECTION SEVEN

He stopped writing, stared at the heap of fragile bones and spoke to Ballard. "Dave, trowel around the edges. Maybe there was some grave goods."

Sorrento wrote slowly:

encountered our first flexed burial. Skeleton lying on the right side, facing east, curled around a small sand rock. Head turned so that face was skyward but chin was dropped to the body. Arms were flexed and palms of hands folded on shoulders while knees were tucked back of the rock. Grave three feet long, about a foot and one half wide. Topmost bone (parietal) sixteen inches below present surface, but top of grave proper about twelve inches from present surface. . . .

He was about to write "no artifacts found" when he saw Ballard begin working with his hands. He was like a bear scrounging for white grubs.

"Come to papa," Ballard said. "We got company."

"What you got, Davey?" Tom asked.

Ballard cleared a few more scoops of loose sand, probing gently with his fingers. A second skull peeked through the protective earth. A bemused look germinated on Dave's vast face. "Son of a gun," he said. "Son of a gun, he's playing a trick on me."

He kept shaking earth loose, probing, blowing sand, until the new discovery emerged—not another burial, nor even a complete cranium—but only the upper half of a human skull. Ballard turned it upside down and offered it to Sorrento, as he would a bowl, balancing it on his pink fingertips.

"My cup runneth over," he said. "The old chap took his drinking cup with him."

"Are you sure it's a cup?" Sorrento asked.

Ballard stepped ponderously out of the trench. His huge foot sent rills of surface soil spilling into the hole. He rotated the bone in his hand.

"I'm not sure. Just an educated guess. See how the edge is rubbed smooth? And that incised line around it—maybe a design." He beamed at Tom. "We're getting there, boy."

Sorrento took it and balancing it lightly on the fingertips of his right hand, raised it to the level of his lips. Across the smooth-rubbed rim, he saw the causeway, the sleek cars whizzing by, distorted in shimmering heat, bound for the improbable hotels and the great complex of mortal joys. A gap of perhaps a thousand years separated the papery skull from the glistening white towers. The miracle of time, the unfathomable mysteries of the past, thrilled him. The same shivering sense of discovery he had experienced on his first dig, the first plunge of spade into earth, the first mute fragment of pottery. For one irrational second he hoped that the ancient vessel, fashioned (he suspected) from some tribal enemy's severed head, was brimming with whatever potion the dark people of the Glades drank in celebration of their rude gods.

He glanced almost apologetically at the flexed heap of bones in the dusty pit. The damned skeleton, jaw agape as if offended at the intrusion, the arms and legs comfortably circling the yellow rock, the whole attitude one of smugness, moved him to a blurred sorrow. Maitland once warned him that he was a romantic, adding with typical bluntness, *I'm afraid I have never known a really competent social scientist who was an Italian. . . .* Tom had been appalled by Maitland's chauvinism, but now he half believed him. Continually, he found himself forced to discipline his own enthusiasms, his own attachment of value judgments to the evidence of the earth—the measurable, visible bones, shards, refuse. The vanished villages, peopled with brown bodies—chanting, dancing, performing their bloody sacrifices—were fine for the Sunday supplements. For a working anthropologist they were a deadly trap. As soon as you started writing popular articles in which you endowed your primitives with colorful traits, you were headed for the academic ashcan.

The sight of Ballard's old-timer prompted him to recall his first dig. It was the summer of his first year in graduate school and he had been sent to a site in the Mohawk Valley in northern New York State. Their luck had been marvelous: after a few tests pits were dug, postholes began to show, not just random scatterings, but an endless succession of them, in a widening meaningful pattern. They appeared as distinct circles of dark earth, where wooden posts had rotted, unmistakable in the fulvous clay. The round stains were everywhere, and in two weeks they had denuded a hillside, exposing the outlines of an enormous longhouse, an oblong of postholes and carbonized hearths, more than one hundred feet in length.

Tom had been a laborer that first time, and he regarded his role with wry humor. The head of the dig, a dour Canadian named Fiske, worked out a cyclical theory about Sorrento's destinies. "Your grandfather," Fiske told him, "swung a shovel for about a dollar a day when he came to this country. Then your daddy got some education and became a cop. His son goes to college, graduate school, and what's he back to when he gets out? Pick and shovel. For less than a dollar a day, hey, Sorrento?"

One evening they bought a case of beer to celebrate the unearthing of the longhouse. It would become something of an event in the study of Northeast archaic settlements, a rather important contribution to Woodland archaeology. They rested on the moist green hillside. Below them stretched aromatic summer meadows, alive with lightning bugs. Lights winked in a distant farmhouse and at their backs they heard not time's winged chariot but the sorrowing wail of the New York Central's Laurentian, bound north for Montreal. In the restful darkness, Tom suddenly leaped to his feet. His head was pleasantly fuzzy with beer—he felt loose and limber, intoxicated with the past as much as with the upstate Pilsener. He wanted Fiske and the three undergraduates to share his vision. Below them stretched the exposed earth. Dozens of small white stakes had been driven into the ground, one for each posthole, several around each hearth. The shape and size of the long tribal house was unmistakable in the August moonlight. The house had been built on the slope of the hill. About thirty feet below the habitation site there was an irregular cluster of postholes—probably the remnants of a protective palisade, Fiske had theorized.

"Look at it!" Tom shouted. "Look at it! They're down there! All of them—the whole tribe! The fires are burning! The deer is roasting! Here comes the False Face Company! Come on, Fiske, admit it! Admit it! They're down there right now! They're going to sacrifice the white dog!"

Half drunk, he had danced up and down the hillside, waving a bottle of Utica Club. The undergraduates joined him; Fiske smiled indulgently. He attributed Sorrento's outbreak to racial instability. He had fought at Taranto with the British First Airborne Division and had reservations about Italians, particularly southern Italians. Later, Fiske conceded that his assistant's outburst was nothing more than a spasm of joy, a happy convulsion triggered by discovery. You couldn't fault a man for enthusiasm, particularly in a field where the tendency was to play everything down, to avoid the dramatic, to write annotated papers.

"What are you thinking about, boss?" Ballard asked. "Communing with the dead?"

"Watch the birdie," Peltz said. He clicked the shutter, then shouldered the tripod and moved closer to the pit. "Now a close-up," he said, "for the desk in the office."

Sorrento extended the cup to Ballard. "Where'd you ever see one of these, Dave?"

"I know what you want me to say, but I'll be damned if I'll say it."

"Come on, Davey. *Non rompermi coglioni.*"

"Lots of places. Archaic Woodland. Coclé. It's a recurrent trait."

"Arawak?"

"Why not? You want it to be Arawak, sure."

"I know what he's thinking," Peltz said, sighting through his camera. "He finds a skull and right away he's got a new theory of Circum-Caribbean connections."

Sorrento punched Ballard's gut playfully. "Suppose we found a whole big settlement? Another High Mound City. Only it's not pure Glades Tradition, like High Mound City. It's *Arawak!*"

Ballard sighed. "Ben, you better call for Maitland. The son-in-law is waxing romantic. Tom, you keep that up, they'll trade you to the New School for Social Research for an assistant in social psych and a shortstop."

"I got six pictures," Ben said. "Want more?"

"No," Sorrento said. "Give him a squirt of Krylon and save me the skull, the limbs and the pelvis."

"Save the bones for Hennery Jones," Ballard said sadly. "Cause Hennery don't like no unproven theories of cross-cultural contacts."

Peltz knelt at the edge of the pit and started spraying the remains. The odor of the fixative lay on the air for a few seconds. Ben lifted the bones from their ancient abode and Tom sensed a faint revulsion. *Let the dead be dead.* Almost affectionately, Peltz placed the limbs and the skull in a large cardboard box. When he tried to dislodge the fragile pelvis it crumbled into a thousand flaky particles. He looked angrily at his fingers, smudged with venerable gray dust.

"What a way to end up," Peltz said sorrowfully. "Boy do we have a lot to answer for."

Peltz started toward the boathouse with the box.

Tom looked at Ballard. "I think the guys should dig down about sixteen inches—all the way back. Let's clear the lid off."

"You hear that, men?" Ballard asked.

Spots and McIsaac nodded, picked up their shovels and went to work.

"Come on down to the house," Tom said to Dave. "I want to study the charts again. Maybe we should start all over."

"I hear you right?" Ballard asked. "You got a year to work? Boy, we don't have the manpower, the time or the money."

They trooped across the sandy parched land, three oddly assorted men, one bearing a cardboard box of bones on his head. They were the last survivors of a desert patrol in a war movie: a giant Senegalese scout, an Italo-American sergeant, a wisecracking Bronx Jew carrying the amoo. Would the relief column from Tobruk reach them in time?

"Now look, Tom," Ballard said. "One burial doesn't mean High Mound City. You're expecting too much. Let's finish what we got. Two nice modest trenches. Then beat it. You can't dig up five acres."

"I know the history of this place. Ever since 1936 they been digging stuff up around here. Remember what Erwin told us? When they excavated for the foundation for his house? Listen. We might be standing on the first big permanent settlement of Southeast Archaic ever discovered. Dream, Davey, dream!"

"We're going to need more men," Ballard protested.

"We'll get 'em."

"He's blowin' the old *walyo* top," Peltz said. "He likes it here. His kind of place."

"Cheer up, Benny. I'll cook you *pasta-fagioli*. With *ditalini*." Sorrento aimed to kick at Peltz's rear; it grazed the faded shorts.

Sorrento's wife came down the side steps. She was dressed for town, in a sleeveless white blouse, a blue denim skirt. The children—hair downslicked, shiny and tanned in sunsuits—accompanied her.

"I thought I'd shop," she said, shading her eyes from the implacable sun. "I can't bear looking at Abby's behind sticking out of her bathing suit. Nicky needs sneakers."

"Great idea," Sorrento said. "Get him black Keds with the thick bumper guard, so I can teach him one-wall handball. In the schoolyard, like Benny used to play it."

"He wants plaid sneakers." She laughed.

"Plaid sneakers," Sorrento said miserably. "Hear that, Benny? Plaid sneakers. They'd lay me out dead on Tutwiler Avenue in plaid sneakers." He shouted at Peltz. "Hey Benny! Show Marty the boy."

Peltz put the box down. "This is my Uncle Hymie. They buried him on unsanctified ground on account of he married one of Ballard's relatives."

"Wonderful!" Marty said. "First of the season!"

"Skelekon! Skelekon!" Nicky shouted. He danced around the box, shooting an imaginary six-gun at the skull. *"Bang! Bang!"*

Abby looked at the bones, pleasantly horrified. "Can I touch it, Daddy?"

"Eh!" Sorrento cried. "No touch-a da bones!" He looked earnestly at his wife. "A perfect flexed burial. Look what Davey found with him." He held up the half-skull. "It's probably a ceremonial cup."

"Your ever-loving husband is off again," Ballard said. "One find, and he's got a theory. Tell her about all those Arawaks we're going to find. He's talking about sinking new holes. Keep us here right through September."

"Not really, Tom. In this heat?" She looked pained.

Sorrento mopped his face. "I don't know. I'm not sure of anything. I want to go back and check the old surveys. I tell you, Marty, I'm feeling good about this whole thing for the first time."

"Aren't we freaks, though?" Marty said. "All excited over some bones! It's too bad we can't run up and down the beach and tell everyone. Of course—*they'd* never understand."

Ballard and Peltz looked quizzically at her. Some criticism of their life and work seemed implied in her curious comments.

"So what! That's what makes it worth while!" Sorrento cried. "They don't *get* it, but I do!" He made a wide sweep with his hairy forearm. "Who cares what they understand? What they think? It don't bother me. It don't bother Benny here. Or Davey!"

"Well, include me, Tom. I'm not bothered by *them* either."

Sorrento shoved a cigar between his lips. "Right! We'll knock 'em dead. *Acqua fresca, vino puro, fica stretta, cazzo duro!*"

Oran and Wilma Burley poked curious heads over the shell heap. Peltz turned on them fiercely. "Back in the pits, you two! Butt out!"

"I need money, Tom," Marty said.

He reached into his hip pocket and took out a sweaty wad, held together by a paper clip. "Four bills," he said. "I was going to cash a check today. Who figured Nicky needed sneakers? *Plaid* sneakers."

Fiscal matters reduced them to semi-paralysis. It was not the mere lack of cash that upset them, but rather the eternal knowledge that steamfitters and millwrights (whatever *they* were) earned more money than assistant professors of anthropology. The battle could never be won, so it was best to act as if there were no battle. Now and then, surrender was demanded, and they bowed their heads. One of Tom's more successful classmates, an athlete who had made good in advertising, kept inviting them to his home in Rye. Marty did not like him, did not like his wife, did not like his money. When he tendered the fourth invitation, she told him flatly: *I'm sorry, Vince, we can't afford a baby-sitter.* It was only a partial victory; against the demands of new shoes, rising food costs, taxes and the exorbitant rent, they were helpless. They did without; they improvised; they made wry jokes.

"Write a check," Tom said. "Draw on the dig's funds. There isn't enough left in ours to buy a small pizza, without sausage. I'll get the dough back in by the end of the month."

"Are you sure that's all right?" Marty asked.

"What the hell! The University should be glad to stake my kids to sneakers and a bathing suit."

"An' a boat," Nicky said. "Sheldon has a boat."

"Yeah," Tom said to his small son. "But he hasn't got a skeleton like this! One that can dance around in its bones!" He shook the box slightly and the skull wobbled.

"Tom, you'll give them nightmares," Marty said. "Let's go, children."

The little girl and her brother, dark and elusive, skipped off toward the highway. "Look at me, Mother!" Abby cried. "I'm doing the bone dance!"

"Me too!" Nicky squeaked. "I'm deh bone dance!"

"Where do they get the energy?" Marty asked. "I'm ready to pass out, and it's only one o'clock. Tom, can I get you anything in town?"

Sorrento took a step closer to her, touched her elbow. "Look baby, why don't you take the kids to an air-conditioned movie or something? Or a Kiddie-land. Give them a fling this afternoon. Then you and me'll go out. I'll call that guy deKay—"

"It's too deadly hot, Tom," she said, with fatal finality. He recognized the tone, and it bothered him—she had used it on adventuresome college swains, on randy editors in her newspapering days. It not only cut off the advance, it annihilated enthusiasm. It was as emasculating as surgery. She sensed his distress.

"Besides, Tom, you forget," she said. "We're invited to Lila's, and I suspect it will be one of those all-night affairs. If you're going to embark on new excavations, you'll need all the rest you can get."

"Absolutely right," he said.

"I'll see you about five," Marty said. In white high heels, she had no difficulty negotiating the sandy terrain. She walked, Tom noted proudly, with the litheness of a woman adept at all things physical—high diving, horseback riding, water skiing. People always assumed that Marty was good at athletics. The truth of the matter was, she had never enjoyed them. Sports bored her. For this unintentional deception, he loved her all the more.

"Nu?" Peltz said rudely. "You gonna stand here till *Simchas Torah* discussing your social calendar? Dinner with the Ellenbogens. Look out you don't drink from the fingerbowl."

They resumed their journey to the boathouse. "I'll bring home a little chopped liver for you, Benny," Sorrento said. "In a paper bag. Just for being a wiseguy from Southern Boulevard, you can start the new holes tomorrow."

"Man, you goin' to work us to death," Ballard said. "Why don't we open a tourist stand if we're going to be here so long?"

As Ballard joked, Sorrento looked back at the roadway. Martha and the children had just climbed into a green bus. On the edge of the blacktop, a half-dozen curious people—passersby, some teen-agers on bicycles—were staring at the trenches. Perhaps, Tom mused, they had gotten sight of the skeletal remains. Two young boys left their bikes and started sauntering down to the pits.

"See? See what's happening?" Peltz said.

"I'll talk to Erwin," Sorrento said. "We'll put up a fence."

"Ah, let 'em in," Peltz sneered. "Just give me the hot-dog concession."

The gawkers did not really concern any of them; the soil was surrendering its mysteries—that was all that mattered.

6 *A Visit to the "Senimoles"*

EXCESS was abhorrent to Martha Sorrento. She had been raised in a tradition of severely limited materialism, a stern convention which decreed that the world's hoard of pleasures and comforts must constantly be boiled down so as to vaporize the richer ingredients, to reduce fleshly joys to a state of tasteless simplicity. In curiously different ways, her parents had adhered vigorously to this notion, setting examples of denial, practicing a perpetual shrinking of the physical. Her mother had waged the battle dourly and deliberately, with hard Puritan purpose. In Hall Maitland's case, indifference to tailored clothes was the casual disinterest of a man whose geographical and ethnological horizons were limitless. Maitland kept long-range appointments with Sea Dyaks and Naga headhunters. He numbered among his dearest friends anthropophagi, pygmies and tree-dwellers. Whatever appetites he may have had in his youth had long been blunted, if not deracinated, by periodic diets of locust grubs, lizard stew and manioc. The great anthropologist, Martha observed somewhat cynically, was not above utilizing these exotic experiences to reduce his associates of wealth and status. A University trustee, for example, might honor Maitland with estate-bottled sauterne at a Lucullan feast high above Park

Avenue. The anthropologist would repay this largesse with the comment that the wine was delicious, but not unlike the wild-grape toddy distilled by his friends the Kabyles of the Sahara. "It gets its strange bouquet," he would add innocently, "because they use mare's urine to help it ferment."

The New York apartment on the outskirts of the University where the Maitlands had lived for a quarter of a century and the peeling farmhouse in New Hampshire where they summered were monuments of bleakness. The foods they ate were spiceless and bland. The essential step in Mrs. Maitland's kitchen skills was the boiling of water. They dressed indifferently—almost shabbily—and cheerfully ignored the blandishments of the mass media. A ghostly radio in Martha's bedroom was their only concession to the Age of Talk.

For all this, they were marvelously free of envy. In her mother's case, a prim and stolid past served as a blockade against the forays of hedonism, the incursions of jealousy. In the flaking summer home, its interior always pleasantly damp and musty, these ancient sources of strength were exhibited: old prints and books (including a wormy ninth edition of the *Britannica*), stained and faded photographs of ancestral Yalemen, austere, tribal leaders; cryptic preRevolutionary runes on the massive fireplace. A new visitor to the venerable house was invariably shown the frigid root cellar where runaway slaves had been afforded sanctuary.

Maitland's origins were less imposing. He had been the son of a schoolteacher, a starved and dedicated instructor in the natural sciences, at a succession of inferior schools in southern Illinois. Maitland's upbringing had benefited from no center of gravity, no anchorage. His father was an academic gypsy, a confused and frustrated man. The anthropologist, displaying brilliance while yet in high school, had forsaken his fragile family ties early and gone on to a succession of scholarships, traveling fellowships and field trips, creating in the process his own splendid fortifications against Mammon. He had, in his early fifties, arrived at that comforting level of academic achievement (based largely on four superb textbooks and a shelf of trail-blazing field reports) where he moved freely on all levels of American life. He was a genuine intellectual, but also a poised and practical man who gave the lie to the stereotypes about professors. He brimmed with anecdotes with sexy and scatological marginalia, that caused him to be much in demand as a dinner guest, as a speaker. *The damndest thing about these Trukese women, smearing that yellow powder all over themselves. Turmeric. Spend a night with them and you smell like a veal curry. . . .*

Maitland's credentials were impeccable. He had a distinguished combat record in the First World War, important friends in government and industry, and was a frequent contributor of popularized sociology to mass magazines of Republican proclivities. Maitland's colorfulness, his anecdotes, his poise, blinded his lofty associates to the fact that the man was a public menace. They were constantly intrigued with his hilarious stories about the Bontoc-Igorots, tales of his perilous journey across Madagascar with a Moslem missionary. None of them bothered to read the dry, lacklustre papers he submitted to scholarly societies. A recent one bore the lethal title: "The Erosion of Personality in the Profit-Oriented Society."

This duality had always disturbed his daughter. Somehow, Marty entertained grave misgivings about his talent to flit from a meeting of the Commerce and Industry Association (a speech on "My Eskimo Brothers") to a grim seminar room inhabited by five starved disciples of graduate ethnology. It was not that Martha sensed anything dishonest in her father's double standard; it was simply that his agility confounded her. He would wear the same shapeless twenty-dollar suit at both functions, tell the same ribald anecdotes *(a word about subincision among the Hottentots would be sentient here)* and gather the plaudits of both groups—the hard-headed Power Elite and the impecunious seekers of evidence.

Thus her parents confronted the world of pleasures: Mrs. Maitland brandished genealogy and breeding as her shield, while the anthropologist flaunted his free-wheeling, multi-purpose scholarship. If both of these defenses were imbued in Martha at an early age, she had a third, a mechanism more effective and peculiarly her own. She was beautiful. She had always been beautiful. If her shoes were scuffed and her dresses tacky, if her parents' apartment was bleakly inhospitable, if they had never owned a car, she was still a gossamer heroine to the fat neighborhood girls, most of them the children of comfortable middle-class Jews. Indeed, so overwhelming were her delicate, upturned features, her soft, unruly hair, that they served to transmute her parents' comparative poverty, their academic shoddiness into something rarefied and desirable. There was romance, adventure and daring, Sheila Rosenstein and Claire Katz knew, in dining on cold canned corned beef and weak tea in the Maitland's barren kitchen, an elusive quality that their own mother's rich aromatic cooking failed to impart. And what availed their clothes from Saks and Bonwit's if their pudgy, dark faces were unchanged? Marty Maitland, in a hand-me-down coat which her impoverished father (he was then an assistant professor earning thirty-eight hundred dollars a year) had accepted from the head-of-department's wife, still looked like the Girl of the Limberlost.

Bred in the bone, Marty's defenses were actually stronger than her parents'. Her mother had to fight a continual battle against envy; but her standards were culturally instilled, traditions rooted not in the genes, but in cranky New England forebears. Her husband was less an enemy of pleasure than a man indifferent to it. What would his dear friend, Paramount Chief Lingelap on Rongerik Atoll, say if he knew that his blood comrade *Hawr-May-Tran* was hungering for a pair of custom-made alligator shoes? Yet in each parent the pressures had to be resisted. The daughter, resting her case on fragile physical superiority, a child envied and adored, had an easier time.

At least that was the case in childhood and adolescence. When she graduated from the Wheatley School and went on to the women's undergraduate college of the University, she discovered that the rewards of beauty were more complex, more troubling than the vaguely homosexual adoration of the Sheila Rosensteins. Honors and courtship came to her immediately. A quiet, uncommunicative girl, she was elected president of the freshman class by acclamation. As a first-year student, a fragile seventeen, still gawkily slim and poorly attired, she was dated by football players and campus politicians. One night, at a fraternity house, a porkish young man from Princeton, down for the week end, necked feverishly with her, burst into tears and proposed marriage. Friends with summer homes in Easthampton and Far Hills invited her to week ends of brainless racing in convertibles, nauseous inebriation, parties on darkened beaches, with a good deal of soughing and thrashing under sandy blankets. All these rich experiences, the pleasurable immersion in the sensual and the soothing that she had ignored as "beneath" her, or as unnecessary, or as trivial, she now found thrust at her—and for what seemed to her the arbitrary reason that she was beautiful. She became amenable to good times. In the patois of the fraternity house she was "an easy neck." It bothered her that the people in Far Hills had not the faintest idea that her father was the author of *Man's Rise* or was the first white man to visit the Ona Indians of Tierra del Fuego. There was a wide, wide gap between the awed little girls of Riverside Drive and the flat-headed Princeton men of her young womanhood. If her prep-school friends had endowed her with a mystic singularity that grew out of her beauty, her new escorts wanted her in much more practical fashion, as an adornment. Eventually, she realized that her delicate face and lithe body were in the same category as the new tweed coat from Abercrombie & Fitch or the *fabulous* new Chevy convertible. She was a luxury item.

Understanding this, she rebelled, falling back on her father's considerable status, less often on her mother's ancestry. Still, she dated frequently, got drunk, necked, kept her virginity via a kind of bored superiority that reduced her swains to hot-handed wretches. By her sophomore year she was uncomfortably well known along fraternity row. *Marty Maitland? What a dish! Yeah, but you ever try to talk to her for five minutes? She's so goddamn smart she doesn't have to say anything. A little creepy, the way she clams up, just sitting around looking beautiful. I copped a feel one night. She necked okay for a little while and then all of a sudden it was as if I was making love to a scarecrow. I thought I was going to score, the way we got off the ground. Five minutes later—she could have been eating a tangerine the way she ignored me. Who the hell buys her clothes? She looks like a rummage sale. Yeah, but who needs clothes with a kisser like that? She had an offer for a modeling job. She laughed in the guy's face. . . .*

She abandoned them—all the insipid young men in porkpie hats and fingertip raincoats—by her third year. They were, after all, aliens. It comforted her, in saying no once and for all to the last of her fraternity suitors, that they were fringe people at the University. Unlike the situation that prevailed at most doughy out-of-town colleges, where a fraternity house meant power and status, the undergraduate men's college had a peculiar perverseness: eccentrics, oddballs and literary rogues were as much celebrated as were the blameless blonds who stroked the crew. The fraternity-house row had a sad and decaying air. The brownstones were filled with sullen boys from the Middle West who had been sent to the University at the behest of fathers who had gone there when it had "class." Their sons longed for New Haven or Hanover, not the austere, citified atmosphere of the University. These people were not for her, Marty decided.

Her false involvement in an environment that upset her led her to further minimize her appearance, to cultivate traits of character which she felt would prevent a relapse into that mindless, vacant world she had just forsaken. Her attire became more modest. She assured herself that the insular stupidity of beautiful women, the lack of curiosity, the conviction that the world owed them something, would never distort her character. She reacted coldly to comments about her beauty, refused to run for office, resigned from her editorship of the college magazine. She read excessively, and spent long, agitated evenings with a group of seedy, intellectual undergraduates, at the opposite pole from the fraternity men. Still in demand for parties and dances and week ends, she administered cool rebuffs, tilting her fine head slightly and smiling frigidly with her imperturbable mouth.

Her dates were a mixed grill of male studentry: a Eurasian graduate in Oriental languages; a lunatic cartoonist on the humor magazine, a perpetually hung-over young man who drifted, years later, into radical Catholicism; a frail, burning English major, a gifted essayist and poet, with whom she might have fallen in love had he not been expelled for cheating freshmen at bridge. She would remember him forever, in the fading, unspeakably lovely dusk of a New York spring day, standing in the quadrangle, its severe red buildings suddenly soft and soothing, encircled by disciples, and sputtering angrily: *Hart Crane! Hart Crane! Why all this fuss over Hart Crane? Hart Crane is an obscure and impossible fool!*

She loved their company because they were doubters and skeptics. Without the advantage of her beauty (they were by and large a homely lot) they denied the good, full undergraduate world so joyously proclaimed by *Esquire, Charm* and the New York Sunday *Times* advertisements. None of them had ever owned a button-down shirt. In turn, they adored Marty: she had never needed an Ivy League wardrobe to achieve status. Her rejection of honors and plaudits was even more admirable. Increasingly, her feminine classmates resented her independence; they blushed guiltily when she mocked them as they greedily inspected Back-to-School Fashions. Armed with *Axel's Castle,* she laughed at their duffer coats and luxurious sweaters. She made fun of the ritual of shopping for new clothes for the new term. A new pair of moccasins, perhaps a flannel skirt and some cheap rayon underwear, and Marty was all set for another year. The whole concept of exchanging currency for goods had always been something uncomfortable and strange to the Maitlands. A basic shrinking from the conventions of trade made it impossible for her father to purchase a box of cornflakes. Secretly, he believed that food should be hunted, fished for, or gathered, the way most of his friends got by. Her mother was worse. She would lose her voice or forget her mission at the corner drugstore. Mr. Waldinger, the friendly pharmacist, was always patient and understanding. Five minutes of gentle interrogation usually succeeded in unfreezing her. *Oh yes—a bottle of Rhubarb and Soda.* In Marty, this aversion to commerce took even odder forms. Riding along upper Broadway in the bus, she would feel suffocated by the endless array of shops, so many of them dealing in the same products. She would sense a heavy sadness for the proprietors (how in the world could so many of them make a living?) and for the customers (how could they know where to go?). Why seven stores in three blocks—all selling corsets? Why *twelve* food stores? Who were all the people who kept them in business? The excess of the material made her numb, resentful.

The only shopping Marty had ever enjoyed was at their summer home. At Minton's Crossing, there were three stores—all that you really needed. It was almost pleasurable to purchase a pair of cotton underpants at Dailey's; there was only one variety of pants available and the decision was made for you. The errand was a simple, direct transaction, devoid of the confusing richness of the bursting, well-stocked emporia of upper Manhattan.

Walking now, half hypnotically, through the Beach's main shopping section, she thought longingly of Dailey's General Store, of Mr. Wynn's grocery–gas station–post office. The plethora of wares, the garish colors, the crowds of shoppers, propelled by some inner frenzy, all these bemused and disoriented her. The shopping promenade was palm-lined. The wide walks were decorated with islands of Bermuda grass. Under and around the tropic trees, the buyers milled and pushed, all of them happy, noisy, talkative, people in whom the pressures of life had been apparently extirpated forever through adequate purchasing power.

She was amazed by the range of prices, the juxtaposition of the truly luxurious with the cheap and tawdry. A narrow shoe store boasting "marked-down factory rejects," its window cluttered with odd sandals and moccasins, nested alongside a sedate castle of pedal luxury (in whose glass a solitary pair of courtesan's spiked pumps rested on a sea of red velvet). There were adjacencies more appalling: a soft-drink stand (*Passion Punch—Nine Frooty Flavors*) shared the front of an arcade with the local branch of a Fifth Avenue jeweler. She purchased Guava-Colas for the whining children and the three of them sipped the ruby effervescent drink before a display of cultured pearls. Finishing, they continued their pilgrimage, pausing in front of a store dedicated to the perpetuation of the alligator as tribal god. There were stuffed alligators, bleached alligators, cured and dyed alligators; alligators fashioned into pocketbooks, belts, slippers, hats, table lamps, luggage, camera cases and cigarette lighters. An alligator doll dressed in Indian clothes drew Abby's attention. She tugged at her mother's skirt.

"Oh, Mother! I want *that!* Can I have it? *Please?*"

Marty noted the discreet price tags: *$3.50.*

"No, dear," she said firmly. "It's one more toy you'd never play with. Remember those beautiful Kachina dolls Grandpa brought you from the Hopi Indians? You and Nicky wrecked them in one day."

"They were ugly old things. They scared me. Oh, mother, why can't I have the alligator?"

"No."

"I'll take good care of it! I promise."

Nicky refused to be left out of the protest. "Me too! I wanna agalator doll! I want one!"

"Now both of you stop at once. It's out of the question. You've gotten new sneakers and Abby has a bathing suit. And we all had a cold drink and a ride on the bus. That's enough excitement for one day. Maybe when we get back Davey will let you dig for a while."

The onset of hysteria in the seven-year-old girl came like a thunderclap on a hot summer afternoon. Eyes and nose contorted wickedly around her tiny mouth. The latter member widened, enlarging into an enormous and encompassing maw. All that remained of the dark, intense face was the outspread lips and the quivering tongue. She wailed in grating ululations.

"Now stop that, Abby. *Stop-that-at-once!*"

Marty was a calm and logical mother. She answered her children's protests with reasoned explanations. The modulated approach was splendid stuff, she knew, except in the face of the unreasoning hysteria of which Abby was capable. What availed the measured, spaced words, the low-keyed tones, when the child—mercurially, diabolically—reverted to Neapolitan blood? The

Latin explosiveness was overwhelming, a crashing nullification of every soft-spoken word, every logical argument. Marty had spent long nightmarish afternoons in their apartment watching Abby in these feral seizures. The tears would vanish after ten minutes or so, but the breathless convulsion, with its accompanying wheezes, would not abate. Often, the affliction (usually brought on by some vital issue such as what shoes to wear) would prove contagious. The virus of tantrum would infect Nicky, and the boy, normally lethargic, would make it a duet. In the privacy of their home, Marty endured these assaults on her equanimity as one would a staggering migraine headache. Since there was no cure, you rode it out as bravely as possible, waiting fatalistically for the agony to ebb. In public, they were unbearable.

Abby was stretched face down in a grassy square around the base of a palm tree. Her brown arms and legs, as thin as pipe cleaners, pumped rhythmically. Her feet (in sassy plaid sneakers) worked like pistons. She was beginning to give voice to the tortured, choking gasps that Marty dreaded.

"I—want—an—alligator—doll—you—promised—"

"I did not promise you any such thing. Get up, Abby. I hear the bus coming."

Nicky backed himself against the tree trunk and settled for some routine weeping. His spurious sorrow, brought on by his sister, distressed Marty more than Abby's hysterics. He was an amenable, happy child and it seemed dreadfully unfair for him to be involved. He was like someone sobbing at a sad movie.

"You promised," Nicky wailed. "You promised us we could have a doll!"

A plump gray-haired woman, in white baseball cap, paused and clucked in commiseration. "Such a pity," she said. "Such nice children." She bent over, trying to pat Abby's writhing back, then withdrew her hand when the girl's screams soared off at a higher pitch.

"She'll be all right," Marty said weakly. "I'd rather you didn't try to help."

The woman shrugged. "The children today. They have too much. Don't tell me. I have seven grandchildren, God bless them, but to keep them happy it's a full-time job for my daughter." She waddled off.

A half-dozen people were watching them. They looked on with vacant stares, delighted that the predicament was not theirs, impersonally sorry for the helpless woman. Their curious interest agitated Marty. In her book of rules, one had one's tragedies *indoors,* away from public scrutiny. Only the poor died, got sick, gave birth, in the streets. She remembered, irrelevantly, riding through Tom's old neighborhood in East Harlem once in midsummer. An elderly man was having an epileptic seizure in the gutter. Around him milled almost a hundred people—children, vendors, police. It was like a carnival. She felt ashamed for all of them, annoyed with the old man. Why didn't he go into his house to have his obscene fit? The memory chilled her and she wanted to shriek, to crack Abby and Nicky's dark heads together, to run away and leave them to public disgrace. She tried reasoning with her frantic daughter once more and succeeded only in producing a new cycle of screams.

As silently and secretly as a ghost, Ira deKay was kneeling at Abby's side. He was holding an alligator doll in each hand and he was whispering in her ear.

"There's a sweet little girl I know," Ira said, "who wants a dolly. And what do you think? She's got one, only she doesn't know it!"

"Go 'way!" Abby shrieked. "I won't—talk—to—you—"

"Well if you won't, there's a little boy I know who wants an alligator dolly," Ira said, "and he's got one, too!" He extended one of the attired figurines toward Nicky. The boy stopped sobbing at once, looked questioningly at his dazed mother, then took the toy. Miraculously, Nicky began to smile. He rotated the doll, inspecting the bright Seminole Indian costume and showed it to his mother. Marty said nothing. DeKay had descended upon them with such startling suddenness, had resolved the crisis so expertly, that she was speechless. She did not approve of her children accepting gifts from strangers, yet how could she possibly intervene? To her utter confusion, Abby, that unreasonable wretch, was now rising, wiping dirt and grass from her face, and staring at the proffered bait.

"Now isn't that better?" Ira asked. "Isn't that so much better than crying? Go on sweetie, take it."

"Can I, mother?" Abby sniffled. "Is it all right? Nicky took *his.*"

"Yeah! It's an agalator! It's mine!" Nicky shouted.

"Why of course you can, Abby!" deKay cried. "That's what toys are for! For good children who listen to their Mommy! Everybody knows that!"

His intonations, his phrasings, Marty noticed, were not those of a man talking down to children, but rather those of a grownup who, easily and gracefully, entered the world of children and made himself part of it.

"I don't know if it's right," Marty said evenly. "I don't like the children to be spoiled. They were acting terribly."

Her protests were too little and too late. With savage possessiveness, they were clutching their alligator dolls. The Maitland doctrine of denial was surrendering to Ira deKay with not even token resistance.

"Now wasn't that easy?" deKay asked. He got up, bronze and gold in the sun. "Mrs. Sorrento, I do believe. The prettiest unmade-up lady in this town. Am I right?"

Marty shaded her eyes. "I'm sorry. I don't remember your name."

"Mr. deKay. Ira deKay. You remember? I was visiting your husband the other day. Over on the island, where the boys are digging up the sand."

"Of course." In his native environment, the colorful shops and the brightly clad shoppers, he seemed less of a freak. He was wearing a gray silk suit and black suede shoes and was sufficiently reduced in glitter to merit an exchange of civilities. Moreover, Marty was in his debt. He had rescued her from crisis.

"I'm embarrassed by your generosity, Mr. deKay," she said. "I normally object to the children taking gifts from strangers."

"It worked, didn't it? Look how happy they are!"

"Where did you come from so quickly? I didn't see you go in or come out of the leather store."

"Never you mind. That's Uncle Ira. Wasn't it lucky I was passing by?"

The assumptive familiarity grated. However, common courtesy demanded that she show her gratitude. "It was nice of you to help. Thank you." She began shepherding the children toward the bus stop. DeKay strolled alongside them.

"Why run off? If this is shopping day, I can be helpful. I'd like to."

"I've made all my purchases, thank you."

"My alligator is gonna kill your alligator," Abby said to her brother. She jabbed it at his doll. "My alligator has big teeth and will eat yours up."

"He will not!" Nicky cried. "Your agalator is naughty!"

DeKay glanced at her lithe, uncomplicated body. The appalling plainness of her clothing, the fine face, so superior by dint of its uncosmeticized flesh, filled him with baffled excitation. It was the kind of feeling he invariably got on entering a hotel room—any hotel room, anywhere. The promise of sexual adventure was implicit in the simple furnishings.

"You really oughta take advantage of the summer sales here," he said, as they paused at the bus station. "You get better deals here on dresses and shoes than you can in New York. Top names, too. High fashion."

She smiled bleakly, trying to discourage him.

"I don't need any clothes."

"Well, if you do, it won't hurt to use my name. Tell 'em Ira deKay's your friend and you'll get treated right." He inserted a blond-tufted hand inside his breast pocket.

"Don't give me your card, Mr. deKay. You gave my husband one yesterday."

He laughed. "Trapped me, didn't you? I was going to write a little message on it. Just for Miss Marty."

He was like the relentless young men she had necked with so many years ago in the fraternity houses on West 113th Street. He could not be embarrassed, ignored, defeated. She was relieved to see the bus approaching. He had done her a service, he had been duly thanked, they were quits.

"Say goodbye to Mr. deKay," she told the children. "Thank him for the presents."

DeKay squatted next to the children. "You kiddies don't really want to ride that old bus, do you? Would you like to ride in Uncle Ira's big car? With the top down? Would you, Abby?"

"*Yeeeeeeees!*" the girl shouted. "Right now! Oh mother, let's ride in the car! I hate that bus!"

"Yeah," Nicky concurred. "In the car!"

"We will *not*," Marty said. "We're riding back in the bus."

Abby's pinched face distorted. Having, in some mysterious manner, won a complete victory over her mother, she was now prepared to drink delight of battle again. Marty saw the savage lines forming, the tightening of mouth and jaw.

"I'm going to ride in Mr. deKate's car," she announced. "That old bus smells bad."

"Yeah," Nicky said, "it's bad."

She was furious with the blond intruder. He abided by no rules, he left his adversaries nothing. His act of mercy was meaningless. From good Samaritan, he had changed into a corrupter of the youth. The bus stopped, discharged passengers, took some on, departed. DeKay had kept them glued to the sidewalk, grinning at the helpless children, holding their small, eager hands. Marty sensed that means were as important as ends in this rude, absurd man.

"Mr. deKay, I don't appreciate what you're doing. I've half a mind to make the children give back those dolls."

"You *wouldn't,* Miss Marty."

"For God's sake, stop calling me that. You're too damned presumptuous."

Abby clenched her fists. "If you don't let us ride in his car, I'll throw myself down and scream again."

DeKay was contrite. "I'm sorry. I messed you up," he said abjectly. "Honest, I am. I just wanted to help. I'm sorry you missed the bus. Look, I'll have you back at the Ellenbogen place in ten minutes. Then you can chase me away."

She hesitated. "All right," Marty said. "I can't stand another tantrum. I warn you, I don't like being taken advantage of."

"*Yay!*" Nicky shouted. "We're ridin' in the car!"

The Oldsmobile was parked around the corner. The carnal luxury made Marty wince.

"I have a bit going with the local Olds dealer," Ira volunteered. "I don't own this heap, I just use it." He said it almost apologetically, perceiving the woman's revulsion at the vulgar car.

She was perched, legs daintily crossed, against the door, as if refusing to succumb to the motorized palace the way her children had.

"Strictly a custom job," Ira said. The car screeched away from the pavement. "They only make four or five like this a year. Special tires, special carburetors."

"It's a little ornate, isn't it?" she asked. "I mean—even for you?"

He turned his round face toward her, smiling boyishly. "You know me pretty good already, don't you?" he asked. "The dealer loaned this car to Winchell last time he was down here, but it was too much for Walter. Too loud. I don't mind it. It's part of my bit."

"What is a 'bit,' Mr. deKay?"

Ira sailed the car around a double-parked white Cadillac, shouting as he did: "*Move that kosher canoe, Freddie!*" He barely halted at a stop sign, spun noiselessly around a hairpin turn as a light changed, careened down the wrong lane of a two-way street, then wheeled the humming vehicle onto a four-lane highway. In the course of his reckless, jolting journey, he kept waving and shouting to people—a police officer directing traffic, a redheaded woman at the wheel of a low-slung sports car, a white-haired man standing in front of a jewelry store.

"A bit is like an act. A dodge. My bit is I can operate," Ira said cheerfully. "You and your nice honest husband wouldn't understand how I do it, but you're better off for not understanding."

"But what exactly do you do? Did you inherit money? Do you steal?"

He threw his head back, guffawing, exposing fine white teeth. "Oh dear lady! I'm too nervous to steal, and the only thing I inherited was my daddy's old store in Moriah Center, North Dakota." He winked at Marty; when he spoke again, his brash show-biz accents had been replaced by a caricature Midwestern drawl, nasal and oppressive.

"Detzler's store," he said, "coal, coke, ice, hay, grain, feed and seed. That was no place for Ira. Those cornshakers stealing gum when he wasn't looking! Purina Chows. Sweet-Orr. Mail Pouch tobacco. That's life in Moriah Center. The gateway to the Mouse River Valley. *Aaagh*—"

"I never suspected your earthy origins," Marty said. "You still haven't told me what you do for a living."

"*You* changed the subject," he said. "Saying I *stole*."

"I'll tell you something, Mr. deKay. I was brought up to assume that anyone who drives a car like this is suspect. Maybe you're not outside the law, but you've done something illegal to get it. I'm sorry if I've hurt your feelings, but I have a hunch you've survived a lot of insults."

"But it's not *my* car, lady. It's a deal I have."

"That makes you even more dubious."

"You really throw the language around, don't you?" he asked, with frank admiration. "Educated. Ever teach school?"

"I was a newspaperwoman for several years."

Reluctantly she was divulging more about herself than she had intended. The man was so improbable, so many light years removed from her experience, that the situation almost demanded an establishing of credentials. She was like an anthropologist visiting a primitive village. The disparity of cultures required full and free explanations, at an early stage of contact.

"I've got my own little firm," deKay said. "Ira deKay Associates."

"What does that signify?"

"A little of everything. I'm mainly in PR. You were a newsgal. You should know about us poor slobs who send you the handouts you throw out. It's a small business. My writer, a coupla girls. What makes it work are my contacts."

"What besides public relations do you do?"

"Oh—promotions. Little real estate. Getting people together."

"For what purpose?"

"Anything where there's a buck going. I set up meetings. I own some small properties. Piece of a TV show. Some performers. A slice of a night club. Teenyweeny part of the Peruviana. This is a great town for my kind of operation. Everybody wants *in.*"

"In on *what?*" She realized how naïve she sounded.

"Everything. *To get with it.* To be involved. The whole country is getting that way. And what's the Beach but a kind of reflection, a miniature of the whole country?"

"A microcosm?"

"Zetz! Right in the House of David! I gotta remember that. Use it on Erwin Ellenbogen, just to show him he isn't the only educated person around!"

"You were saying—how the whole country wants to be *in* on things. What do you mean?"

"Well, like celebrities. Everybody wants to know 'em, to be part of 'em. They want the big tip on the market. They want to be part of anything successful, colorful, no matter what. I think television did it to 'em. Right in their own house. They're all bright and famous and everyone loves them. Of course they aren't *really,* so that's how I make my living. My job is I get them together, I grease the machinery. Take Mr. Banjo. An ape. He's pretty dumb, even for an ape. But they all want to be part of him —love him, share his fame, kiss him. Why not? He's on the television. He makes over a grand a week."

"And that's how you make your living? Arranging for people to be *in?*"

"Right! Nobody wants to be left out. This is Howdy Doody time! Everyone's entitled to share in it. There isn't a door closed to me down here."

"I gathered that."

"Now, take some of those early settlers up the Beach. The old grumpy families. Cattler, and Tremarque and the Aubusson brothers—you know, the bunch who invested the first money and knocked down the mangroves and filled the swamps with sand. The whole place is artificial, or didn't you know that? Mangrove swamps. Mosquitoes, snakes and raccoons. Even the palm trees and bushes are phony. Old Tremarque had 'em all brought in from the West Indies. There was nothing here except mangroves and malaria fifty years ago. Well all these early money boys, they thought they could snub me. They learned. I run their debutantes' balls now. Work out a tie-in with a charity so it's all deductible. They never thought of it."

"I think I'm getting the idea. What are some other enterprises of yours?"

"Oh, I handle Braud Industries and maybe ten other manufacturers. Bond drives. A chain of motels, the Peruviana. I'm tied in with a network in New York as a kind of regional man. I'm in the middle of a big tourist promotion right now. Million-dollar stuff."

Marty wondered how much of his bragging was truthful. She had known a good many press agents and publicity men in her newspaper days, and by and large, they had seemed a seedy lot. She knew, of course, that in the highest echelons of public relations there were men of great wealth and style, yet she always imagined they were a little ashamed of how they earned their money. DeKay, on the other hand, was infinitely more honest about his work. For all his boorishness, he seemed to relish his occupation, to be completely without guilt, to have no burdensome second thoughts.

They stopped at a red light, a block away from the turn-off to the causeway that led to the bay island. Ira turned from the wheel and pushed his sunglasses up on his unclouded forehead.

"I'll take it through channels this time," he said. "Why don't you let me take you and the kiddies for a ride? I bet they'd love to see the Seminole Indians."

"Just get us home."

"Heck, it's only three-thirty. You go back to that old boathouse and you'll just sweat. The doc is busy pulling bones out of the dirt, and you'll sit around and sulk."

The snide remark about Tom's work did not offend her. Ira said it without malice, without any attempt to exalt his own world of two-tone convertibles at the expense of Sorrento's.

The children, temporarily silenced by the careening ride, were jerked into action at the mention of "Indians."

"Can we go, mother?" Abby cried. "Please can we go?"

"You've done it again, haven't you, Mr. deKay?" she asked. "Can't you just go back to your office and work up some deals?

Arrange a meeting. Let somebody in on something. But please, let me control my children."

"Oops. Sorry. I have to see people happy. Especially kiddies."

"I don't believe you. I have a feeling you never do anything for its own sake. What can you possibly want from us?"

DeKay swung the giant car around. "You didn't say *no,*" he bubbled. "So it's off to the Seminoles!" The children shrieked; Marty gasped. DeKay ignored an onrushing trailer truck, laughing wildly as the driver put on his brakes and cursed them.

He took them on a frantic pilgrimage through backroads and side streets. Once they had left the resort, Marty was surprised to discover how much of the surrounding area was shabby and depressed. It was, after all, deep South, with all the crumbling lassitude, the grass-in-the-sidewalk lethargy of the deep South. They sped madly through a Negro quarter, row after row of peeling shacks with the inevitable sagging porches and rusted furniture, through the inescapable miasma, the universal odor of the Southland—old, tired grease being refried for the hundredth time. It made no difference where you were in the South: in the lobby of a modern hotel, at a functional airport, in the back alleys of niggertown, old South or new South, your nose was assaulted by this culinary affront. She suspected that the grease, some deadly amalgam of fats, was used and re-used and kept simmering, the way chefs keep a soup stock in perpetuity. So pervasive was the stench that she often thought small colored men were employed to keep grease frying—*even when there was no cooking going on.* This ensured the proper atmosphere at all times, even when the kitchens were inoperative.

Leaving the Negro quarter, she wondered vaguely whether this was the section to which Dave Ballard repaired on his recidivistic nocturnal sorties. She wondered what could possibly draw Dave, enlightened and educated, to these decaying streets. She seemed to recall Ben saying something about "ribs."

They sped on to a main highway where Ira kicked the car up to a blinding eighty-five. He talked incessantly, making himself heard over the rush of wind, the engine's hum. His conversation was like the immaterial buzz of a radio one listened to while reading or sewing. You could take it or leave it. If you missed a sentence you never lost the main thread, which concerned Ira and his deeds. It was inoffensive talk, amusing talk, the braggadocio relieved by deKay's willingness to poke fun at himself. They passed a boarded up, flaking drive-in restaurant, and it moved him to recall a recent defeat.

"The only Chinese drive-in restaurant in the state," he said proudly. "My idea. I had a little piece of it, but I got out in time. Terrible time staffing it, and the night air made the egg rolls soggy. We wanted some cute Chinese gals in short skirts to be carhops, but we couldn't find enough down here. I tried sneaking in a few high-yallers, but some sharp-eyed Kluxers caught me. It was a bad scene."

It was a land of dirty sand and savage weeds, a dry and barren littoral, dotted with an endless vista of vulgar, misshapen tourist attractions. Orange and pecan emporia abounded—the fruits and nuts crated, bagged, transformed into confections. There were shacks selling atrocious artifacts fashioned of bone, shell and coral. Others dealt in hideous lawn statuary. Hot-dog stands and frozen-custard booths alternated with driving ranges and batting cages. One stretch of high yellow fencing carried the legend "Chimpville: Land of Apes." Another enclosed compound was labeled "Serpents of the World." A green plywood python, eighty feet long, ogled them with flaming red eyes.

"We're almost there," Ira said, braking the car. "Incidentally, I've got a little deal going with the owner of the place, so let the kids have anything they want. It's freebies."

"Do you ever pay for anything?"

"Honest, I didn't mean for it to happen this way! Most of it comes naturally. Half the time I don't even ask—people just want to *give*. People want to do things for Ira."

He drove into a dirt parking lot, in front of a twenty-foot-high replica of a Seminole Indian. The flaking edifice, concocted of some inferior plaster, stared balefully at them with purple orbs. Its chocolate face and bright robes lent it an air of deliberate insanity, as if some crazed sculptor had created it as a final insult to a world that had never appreciated him. Abby and Nicky, scrambling out of the rear of the car, halted in their headlong rush toward the gate. The statue's cold eyes slowed them to a respectful walk.

A woman in an admission booth nodded at Ira and he ushered Marty and the children around a rusted turnstile. They entered a dusty clearing, dotted with ragged palms and bordered by a series of thatched huts on raised wooden platforms. The Indians lolled about in timeless, hateful ennui. The place swarmed with filthy, snot-smeared children. Their narrow dark eyes and solemn mouths were already imbued with the spurious wisdom of the primitive. A woman sitting in front of the nearest house was making cakes out of corn flour. She patted the cakes into shape, alternating her culinary labor with the care of an infant with a runny nose. Wiping his face, she worked the exudate into the dough, never losing a beat. Three young bucks in frilly Seminole blouses and hot-rod dungarees tossed an indoor baseball about with approximate lacrosse sticks. An elder in bleached buckskins and full headdress squatted outside a souvenir booth. Ira tossed him a five-dollar bill and scooped up head-feathers, tom-toms, braided belts and dolls for the children. Marty had trouble recalling when she had seen them so happy.

They toured the compound, pausing at a forlorn zoo filled with a variety of swamp rodents, mangy wildcats, and tropical monkeys. A scrawny mountain lion dozed in his ammoniated stink and an Everglades fox blinked shrewdly at them. A muddy pen at the end of the clearing was filled with a parliament of alligators, and in a sandy arena beyond it, a young Seminole was engaged in the state's equivalent of the No play: the wrestling of the saurian. A scattering of bored tourists watched in the deadly heat as the drama unfolded. The youth bulldogged the giant lizard, clamped the voracious jaws shut, and stroked it into blissful slumber. Triumphant, the boy got up, took his bows, and picked up a sprinkling of coins. Ira handed him a dollar bill and he grinned. Marty noticed he had an ear missing and she wondered if one of the scaly opponents had once gotten the best of him. She rather liked the idea: *I'll teach that two-legged bastard to stroke my belly—snappp!*

Walking back through the dusty village, they watched a woman in billowing skirts work a primitive loom. The sight moved Ira to a lecture on Seminole folkways.

"A real kick, isn't it?" he said. "I mean, nothing's changed in a coupla thousand years. Here's that lady sitting on the same hunk of dirt, working the same gimmick her ancestors did, right here. Makes you kind of think."

"Yes, doesn't it?" she said cruelly. "It's a shame you aren't equipped to think properly."

"Beg pardon? Who got a contract?"

"Your ignorance is really charming, Mr. deKay."

"Ira to my friends."

"You're much better at keeping people happy than enlightening them. My father and my husband are both anthropologists,

Mr. deKay. It's quite possible I know more about the Seminoles than you do."

"I say something wrong?"

"The Seminoles weren't even formed as a tribe until the middle of the eighteenth century. They were part of the Creeks. They didn't come here until late in the seventeen hundreds. They're no more native here than you are."

"Zile. I asked for it. Open my big mouth."

She shepherded the children away from the old man selling souvenirs. A touch of the rich life, she suspected, was already corrupting them. With all their loot, they were hungering for more. Abby was eying a cheap Indian dress and Nicky was fingering a tomahawk.

"I think we have to go home now," she said. They started toward the gate.

"Hey, tell me more about the Seminoles," Ira said.

"I don't claim to be an expert. Tom knows all about them. Most of these people are part Negro. They've been so acculturated by Negroes and whites that they have almost no culture of their own left. All this nonsense that goes on here was dreamed up by one of your promoters."

"Hah! Lousy job, too. The place is dying. Of course, the problem is there's too many of 'em. There's five Indian villages, all going bust."

"And that poor old man in the war bonnet. He's dressed like a Plains Indian. Plains buckskins, headdress and decorations."

"*Hoo boy!* What a goof! Well, it's his living. If he can sell more tom-toms in a phony war bonnet, why not?"

They helped the children into the rear seat. "I suppose you're right," Marty said. "What's the difference down here? So long as he sells more of these Made-in-Japan curios."

They drove back to the Beach through late afternoon commuters' traffic. The clogged roads failed to impede Ira's progress. He swerved and wheeled the lavish car, heedless of elementary safety precautions. He laughed at the people he cut off and shouted wild greetings to highway police and traffic cops—they all seemed to know him. Nicky dozed in the rear and Abby stood, stiff with excitement.

"Must you carry on like a madman when you drive?" Marty asked, as he veered wildly off the causeway and down the dirt road to the site.

"It's part of my bit. I get my jollies when I drive."

He brought the car to a trembling halt. Across the sandy waste, Marty could see her husband sighting intently through a surveying instrument. It was pointed at the mountainous figure of Ballard, who was unwinding a spool of clothesline from its anchorage on a driven two-by-four. She called to Tom; he waved back distractedly, shouting to Ballard as he did.

"Hold it! Hold it there, Dave! Tie it off. Now get Benny off his butt and let him sink a pit along the new line."

Sorrento walked toward the automobile. His children, staggering under Ira's gifts, crawled out of the car. Both wore their war bonnets.

"We had an adventure," Marty said. "Mr. deKay was our host this afternoon."

Tom recognized the automobile before he remembered the man.

"Hey—my friend, the gook," he said.

"Hello there!" Ira sang. "I met the missus in town. The kids were giving her a bad time so I decided to help out. We took them to see the local Indians."

"Yeah!" Nicky shouted. "Real Senimole Indians! The man rassled an agalator!"

"Mr. deKay ran across us in town. Just as Abby was beginning to eat the pavement. God knows how he did it, but he had them smiling in a few seconds." Marty sounded apologetic.

"And look what he bought me, Daddy!" Abby thrust forward her arms, heavy with fraudulent curios, the alligator doll.

"Madonna!" Tom cried, "you really cleaned up! And Nicky too! That's very sporty of you, deKay. But what's the whole idea? What'd my kids do to deserve this?"

Ira executed a low-comedy bow. "Nary a thing. My pleasure. Old Ira is available for weddings and bar mitzvahs. I want both of you to be my guests."

On the higher ground, Ballard and Peltz were digging again, thrusting their spades into the new, unexcavated earth, along the clothesline boundary. Marty, hearing the *klumppp* of their spades, the *whoosh* of sand falling, turned to watch them.

"What are we up to now?" she asked. "We starting all over?"

"Just about," Sorrento said. "We dug up that single burial and I started wondering maybe the village site lies further back from the water. Benny and I went over the surveys and decided we'd at least make a few more test holes higher up."

"All that work? Tom, we'll never get out of here—"

"Ah, it won't take long. I figured if the burial ground was here"—he indicated the land just above the big trench—"and the refuse heap there"—he pointed with a hairy forearm to the small pit—"then maybe the village site was higher up, if it was like other village sites. Just an idea."

Sorrento pressed a forearm against his soaked forehead. The sweat left a wet oval patch on the black hairs and dark skin.

Ira frowned. "You're really hot on the trail, hey Tommy?" he asked suddenly. "I mean—you figure you'll hit pay dirt pretty soon?"

"Who knows?" Tom asked.

"Will you excuse me?" Marty asked. "The children are exhausted. They're not used to this kind of overstimulation. Thank you for your kindness. I'm sure they had a wonderful time."

"I hope Mommy was amused, also."

"I enjoyed it." She turned to Tom. "What's the schedule?"

"I want to dig a few holes up there myself. Maybe we can sneak in a swim later."

She herded the children down the slope, toward the boathouse.

"Well, don't work too late. The Ellenbogens expect us at eight."

Ira's face glowed. "You people going to be at Erwin's tonight? At the big borefest? Zile kai! That makes it worth my going!"

Martha, with her back to deKay, sighed. There was no escaping the man. She had absorbed all of Ira deKay that day that she could stand. In small doses, he took a lot of digesting; being around him required a concentrated, almost pained, effort on her part to be civil, to accept, if only temporarily, his standards. She had a dread premonition that he fully intended to cling to them for the rest of their sojourn in the resort city.

"See you later, Miss Marty!" he called.

Sorrento started trudging up the incline toward Ballard and Peltz. Ira, undismayed, tagged behind him.

"It would really mean a big score for you if you found a lot of stuff under here, hey, Doc?" he asked.

Tom scowled at him. "Blow, will you, deKay? I know you're promoting something. Now beat it. Ellenbogen told me to be careful when you're around."

"That Erwin. Some friend."

"Look—you took care of my wife and kids for a day. That was nice. Now if you get any idea you're going to work out some screwy deal with me, you're nuttier than you look."

"You won't even *listen.*" DeKay looked about him, anxious that he not be overheard. "There's this local Archaeological Society, see? Amateurs. Schoolteachers, retired people. A few years ago they contacted me about setting up a museum. Early history, Indian stuff. There was no money in it. I figured that out right away. But they took me through an old warehouse of stuff they'd been collecting for maybe thirty years. Bits and pieces."

"What's that got to do with me?" Tom asked. "I know about these amateur diggers. They do more harm lousing up sites. They break pottery, ruin stratification, never keep any records. I'll tell you right now—that junk you looked at is probably unclassifiable."

"So what? I'll figure an angle."

"What are you talking about?"

DeKay's face bloomed. "We'll get the best stuff they have," he half-whispered. "You and me, we'll pick it out, without them knowing, and then we'll bury it here, so you can find it later. Anything you want! Pots, statues, bones—"

Sorrento blinked. Sweat clouded his eyes, and he saw the promoter dimly, as through water. Staring at him, a long-limbed, golden man in a wastefully expensive silk suit, Sorrento understood that he was not joking. His mission was to purvey pleasure, and, if it was his belief that a few odd bones secreted in a trench would make Tom happy, why not do the obvious, the simple? In Ira's scheme of things, the stolen, hidden bones were no different than the white-faced girls sequestered in various rooms of the hospitable Peruviana.

"You're out of your mind," Sorrento said. "You're dumber than I thought. Now stay away from here. You try salting these pits and I'll bury you in one of them."

DeKay smiled innocently. "No offense, Doc—no offense! I just want to help out." He headed for his car. "See you and the wife tonight!" he called. "You stick with Ira and I'll show you where Erwin hides the ten-year-old Scotch!"

Wearily, Sorrento walked up to the taut clothesline, along the edge of which Ballard and Ben Peltz were methodically digging a series of small holes. Tom knelt alongside the first pit and began sifting the earth through his fingers.

"What do you know?" he said. "It's sand. You see anything, Dave?"

"Nope. We're still at the beer-can stage."

"I'm through," Peltz whined. "I had it. I'm goin' back to New York tomorra. I can get a buck and a half an hour for this."

"My heroes," Sorrento said. "I'll take the workmen off the big trench tomorrow and start 'em here. What a great expedition this turned out. Guy wants to salt the pits, maybe I should let him."

Above, an ancient biplane buzzed them. Behind it, a legend sewn on netting read: VISIT CHIMPVILLE LAND OF A THOUSAND APES. Tom shaded his eyes and studied it. "Poor bastard up there," he said. "He's probably got a Distinguished Flying Cross and eighty combat missions behind him. Now he makes a buck advertising a monkey farm. I guess we don't have it so bad, after all, hey, Davey?"

Looking down again, his eyes bleary from the sunlight, he saw Wilma and Oran Burley standing several feet from the clothesline. It occurred to Tom that they had probably been there for some time. They had a habit of just standing by, not speaking, waiting for Tom (or Dave, or Ben) to offer the first exchange of civilities. They had been working on the refuse heap, the pile of shells and bones, since early that morning, probing, digging, separating, patiently examining the assorted junk left by the residents of the beach centuries earlier. They were thoroughly coated with sand. Oran looked for guidance to his sister; she nudged him faintly in the back.

"What's up, kids?" Tom asked. "You look like you've done something naughty and you're afraid to tell me."

Oran stepped forward. His wispy blond hair had been bleached almost white by the merciless sun; great peeling blisters mottled his high, reddened forehead. He was an eternal victim, one of the army of snubbed, maltreated and ridiculed. Oran thrust his hand out at Sorrento. In it was a dusty stone. Tom took it from him.

"When did you find this?" he asked.

"Just now. Wilma really did."

"*You* did," the sister said. "I was going to toss it away, until you saw the markings."

Sorrento rotated it carefully. He dusted it gently with his hand, blew away some loose grains of yellow sand. It was clearly an artifact, a flat triangular stone, about six inches long on its widest side. It was of a dark, greenish cast. Turning it, he saw that one flat side was still rough and relatively unworked. The obverse side was smooth and had been grooved and pitted with a cutting tool. There was an unmistakable series of lines on the smooth side, and despite the stone's eroded state, the suggestions of a face were indicated. There was a blunt, wide-nostriled nose, worked into one point of the triangle. There was a gaping, tortured mouth; there was a single primordial eye.

"Jesus," Tom said. "If it's what I think."

Ballard and Peltz set their spades in the earth and crowded around him.

"Oran found it!" Wilma cried wildly. "By himself!"

"You really did," her brother added.

"What is it?" Ballard asked. "You recognize it?"

"You'll laugh at me if I tell you what I think it is," Tom said. "All of you. Only you and me, hey Oran? We know what it is."

"Do we?" Oran asked. "I don't—"

Sorrento held the triangular stone up for all of them to see. The features had been carved along one edge of the triangle. Beyond what appeared to be a vestigial ear, a series of wavy, parallel grooves had been etched. Did they represent hair? A crown of some kind?

"I'll tell you what I think it is," Tom said. "It's a *zemi*."

"A *zemel*?" Peltz asked. "A *zemel* is a Yiddish word meaning a roll, a bulky, a hard piece of bread usually with seeds. Three for a dime in the corner grocery."

"Shaddap, Benny," Tom said. "*Z-e-m-i*. Davey knows what I'm talking about. He knows Circum-Caribbean."

"Oh man, you're off again," Ballard said softly. "A *zemi*, kids, is Arawak. An Arawak idol, fetish, religious object. They had 'em for everything—in the house, outside the house. The spirits of nature took up residence in them. *Zemi*-worship."

Sorrento held the odd stone at arm's length. "Oh, baby, you're all mine! Dave, we'll build him a little niche, just like the Arawaks did."

"Tom," Ballard said soothingly. "The heat's hurting you. It's just a stone. It could be anything. A fragment from something else."

"I feel great! Tomorrow we block out a whole new excavation! Oran—Wilma! Get back to that junk pile and find me five more!"

Ballard looked at him gravely. "I hear you say that guy deKay wanted to fill the pits with some old stuff he knew about?"

"Yeah. I kissed him off."

"Maybe you were too late," Ballard said.

"What? You mean he's been here already?"

Dave plodded back to his shovel. "Guy like that works fast.

How do you know he didn't send his people around last night and throw that piece in the midden? I wouldn't put it past him. Maybe he tipped the mitt today to see how you'd react."

"He couldn't be that smart."

"That guy's got something going. Why's he keep coming back?"

"I tell you he couldn't be that smart. Where would he find a piece like this?"

The notion of Ira deKay, immaculate in silk suit and suede shoes, prowling around the pits at midnight, and inserting, with manicured hands, old artifacts in the earth, could not be seriously entertained.

7 *In Search of Ribs*

THE sights and smells of his childhood and young manhood evoked in Ballard a blessed sense of relief, a euphoria born of the conviction that he had left all the dirt and degradation behind him forever. But, as always, when he visited a black ghetto, it was a comfort short-lived and doomed by its concomitant guilt pangs. He felt impotent, uncommitted, helpless. Like a man who survives a massacre by hiding under corpses, he would be perpetually disturbed by memories of the dead.

Guiding the pickup truck through Hilltown, with Ben Peltz slumped in silence alongside him, he saw once more in the littered streets the horrors of poverty and caste he believed he had escaped. Dave Ballard was not a sentimental man. An adulthood dedicated to stern academic disciplines had imbued him with what he hoped was true scientific detachment. Yet on this, his first extended visit to the South since his graduation from Boys' Country School in Caterman, Georgia, he found himself lapsing into extended periods of a frustrating, numbing pity. The Uncle Tom performance he affected, Ballard understood, was as much a neurotic symptom of his malaise in the land of his origin as it was humorous protective coloration.

The Negro women distressed him most: grannies in dime-store eyeglasses and ante-bellum handkerchiefs; middle-aged mothers in baggy dresses and scuffed slippers, porting their watermelon breasts with heavy discomfort; young chicks in tight red sweaters and ass-round skirts, pomaded and powdered; incredibly perfect little girls—black, sepia, tan, palest yellow—unaware for a few wispy years of the painful limitations of their lives.

"I loves women," he said to Peltz. "I loves 'em all. I loves deh old ones 'cause dey *been* women so long and I loves deh young ones 'cause dey gonna *be* women so long."

"Knock it off," Peltz said. "Play another record."

Ballard sighed. He knew why he loved them. He loved them for their perpetual warfare with their own men—the black male animals with quick tempers and sharp knives, the "nonrespectables" who snarled at the church and the uplift associations. A race-ridden society, he had long ago learned, created tensions and pressures peculiarly its own, and particularly in the male members. It devolved upon the women to become the safety valves, the escape hatches. It was always the luckless women: doing the odd jobs in tough times, taking care of other people's kids, washing other people's soiled underwear, debasing themselves daily, pressing the new dress for school or church, awaiting the drunken curses and insults in the middle of the night, the flash of knife and shock of fist. *The blessed women,* he thought, forever in solemn league against their men—old ladies heavy with dropsy and eaten by cancer, and all their daughters and granddaughters. How many thousands of them, tens of thousands, there were, deserted by the harsh and lawless man, rearing the children (how? with what?) in peeling shacks, traveling north and west for periodic employment, leaving the young brood with some aged, infirm female relative while they labored to bring home enough for sustenance.

. . . His daddy, he gone. He doan come heah no moh. . . . Dat no-good man run off one night . . . he never write me . . . he say he gon' Chicago make some money, but Ah never see him 'gain. . . .

These reflections inundated him with gloom, and he disposed of them in his usual manner: he restated his thesis in the sterile language of the sociologist. He envisioned a splendid doctorate paper, replete with statistical tables and unreadable footnotes: *Some Aspects of Male Irresponsibility Among Southern Negro Familial Groups. . . .*

Peltz, exhausted from his labors at the dig, shifted his stringy body on the seat. The rattling truck bounced over a great cavity and he jerked upright.

"Where you takin' me, Ballard?" he asked. "Where's this place that serves these great ribs you been talkin' about?"

Dave glanced at him innocently. "You know something,

Benny? I hate ribs. I never eat them. They're greasy. What makes you think I'd eat a rib? Damn liberals."

"*It was your idea!* You been tellin' me about ribs! How you found this place! And don't call me a liberal. I'm nonpolitical."

Cheap neon signs blinked around them. Knots of slouching black men stared at them as Ballard negotiated the wretched truck around wild children, stray dogs, parked cars.

"Ben, my friend, I have a confession. We will not eat a single rib this hot night. I lied. I lied so Tom wouldn't start worrying about me."

"What are you up to? I never shoulda trusted an educated coon."

"Now, you might get some coffee and cookies from the Ladies' Improvement League. All the *respectables* belong. They like coffee and cookies. But no ribs. If you're still hungry later, I will let you off at a kosher delicatessen."

Peltz eyed him coldly. "What are you handin' me? What's this about a Ladies' Improvement League?"

Ballard started slowing down. He shifted gears noiselessly, double-clutching with a facility born of years as a truck driver. He turned the pickup into a dark alley. They were alongside a church, a high brick building, painted a pale yellow. A dozen people gathered on its steps.

"We have arrived, Benjamin. Dismount. We're going to church."

"Stop needling me."

"It'll do you good." Ballard climbed out, walked to the opposite door of the cab and yanked it open. He dragged Peltz from the seat, the way a fisherman would pluck a live killie from a bait box.

"Hey! Lemme go, Dave! I ran away from Hebrew School when I was a kid! I wasn't even allowed in the *schul!*"

"All the more reason to start now," Ballard said in a low voice. "You've tried several orthodoxies and have found them wanting. Try another."

"You're screwy, Ballard."

"Benny, like all of your people, you have a literal mind. We're entering a church, but *not* for a service. This is a civic function. We're going as dispassionate observers."

They walked down the alley, passing a row of mongrel fences—old boards, chicken wire, discarded sheets of linoleum and corrugated metal. A dog snarled at them, a radio blared gospel music.

On the façade of the church, a single yellow bulb burned over a sign:

MOUNT OF OLIVES CHURCH

SHIP OF ZION: NEGRO

REV. F. M. HARKEY, D. D., PASTOR

The people standing on the narrow steps were mostly of middle age. They were neatly dressed and spoke in quiet tones. They were "respectable"—far different from the loungers they had passed on the drive through Hilltown. Through opened white-washed doors they could see the illuminated interior.

"Awright, I give up," Peltz asked. "What's the big deal?"

"My relatives," Ballard said. "I wanted you to meet them."

"Nuts. You said something about a civic affair."

Dave steered him toward a lamppost at the curb. "We have a few minutes before the meeting starts, so I'll enlighten you. If I don't you'll keep asking questions and embarrass me."

People kept arriving, in pairs, singly. Uniformly, they seemed pleasant and sociable, yet there was an odd undercurrent of purposefulness about them. One enormous black woman, aided by a cane and a younger woman, clutched a thick notebook as she waddled up the stairs.

"Now take it easy, Miss Phyllis," the younger woman said. "You're our recording secretary. We need you."

"The Ladies' Uplift Group," Peltz said. "This I had to come to see?"

Ballard waved to a young man. Peltz saw that it was the workman, Spots. He wore a clean sports shirt, neat slacks and a straw fedora.

"Ever hear of a gerrymander, Benny?" Ballard asked.

"What am I—a dope? Sure I know. It's where they divvy up the election districts to *yentz* somebody. To take advantage of the way the population is laid out, or how they vote."

"Correct. This meeting we are about to attend is aimed at organizing a protest, a big protest against just such a—what did you call it? A *yentzing*."

"Explain."

"Well, you know how it is down here. It's South, but it's fairly new South—a lot of it. Just north of the city it's all peckerwoods and crackers, mean as hell, dribbling tobacco juice over their chickeny necks. Now in the city proper and the Beach, just south of here, there's lots of Northern folk, including thousands of liberal-type people. Right here in the middle is Hilltown, the colored section. It's the biggest concentration of Negroes in the county. It's also part of the electoral district that includes the big city with all those emigré Northerners. In the past few years, a good many colored people have been registering and voting. There's about six hundred enfranchised residents of Hilltown today. Compared to none—zero—five years ago. Progress, man. But due mainly to the fact that the city is a freak—more like New York than Brunswick, Georgia."

"Sounds great. What's to protest?"

"Well, the peckerwoods won't let it stay this way. That's what's so nice about hate. Hate sustaineth. It giveth man energy, dedication. Those lazy woolhats won't move off their asses to build a county hospital, but give 'em a little hate to work on, and wow! They got a bill going through the state legislature next week. Hilltown gets detached from the city and becomes part of the election district just north of here—the one run by the crackers. Get it? You ever see those stuffed dummies? *This Nigger Voted.* That's the end of the six hundred enfranchised voters. So now you know why there's a meeting tonight."

Peltz backed away from him. "You're an agitator. You big jerk. You'll get Tom in trouble. And some idea bringing me here. I'm going home. Gimme the truck keys."

The irate little man, ruby red and squint-eyed, extended his calloused hand. "Come on, Dave, I'm getting outa here."

For a moment, Ballard wondered why he had tried to involve Ben Peltz, who had an unenviable history of Party affiliations, of Committee appearances, of informing and reinforming, of avowing and disavowing. The man was a bat's nest of radicalism and counter-radicalism, a charred and cold stick, long ago plucked from the burning. He was so nonpolitical that he now restricted his newspaper reading to the sports pages. Ballard patted the frizzy red hair with an ogre's hand.

"Now, Benny, be a good boy. I'm here strictly as Ballard, Ph.D. An impartial observer. They're talking about a boycott of white merchants as reprisal. I got interested reading about these passive resistance movements. Gandhi—Thoreau—Tolstoy. Here's a rebirth of the idea in our own deep South. Thought maybe I'd make some notes and do a paper on it."

"I don't trust you. Whaddya need me for?"

"I respect your opinion as a social scientist. Scout's honor, friend. That's why I asked you here. That's the whole story."

"Oh, yeah? Then why are you lyin' to Tom? All that stuff about eatin' ribs. I bet you got private pipelines to the N double-A CP. Or worse outfits. You're too clean to suit me!"

"Everything's a conspiracy, hey, Benny? You can't shake the old nonsense."

Gently, he guided the little man away from the curb, up the steps of the church—a giant Nubian retainer escorting a Mamluk princeling.

"Tom's got enough worries," Ballard said. "The dig's got him down. He's got this Arawak bug. He'll become one of those one-theory oddballs if he doesn't straighten out. I worry about our leader. I tell you Ben, he was meant for better things than digging refuse heaps. His wife tells him that, too. So now he's going to make a big, dramatic find and become famous."

They entered the foyer of the church. It smelled of fresh paint, of fruity hair pomades. A young man in a light blue suit shook hands with Ballard and looked inquiringly at Peltz.

"Evening, Dr. Ballard," he said. "You going to use us as your laboratory animals tonight?"

"If you don't mind, Reverend, this is one of my colleagues at the excavation. Benjamin Peltz. Ben—Reverend Franklin Harkey. He's the pastor here."

"How do," Peltz said uneasily. Harkey shook his hand firmly. He was a slim, medium-brown man with tired, humorous eyes. In his lapel a tiny gold cross glittered.

"Let's go in," he said to the visitors. "Attendance is a lot better tonight than I figured."

Ballard and Peltz took seats discreetly at the rear of the congregation. A few of the parishioners noticed the white man, and there was some whispering and turning of heads. Ben, studying the gathering, realized that here was the backbone, the proper middle class of Hilltown. The rowdy, knife-wielding "nonrespectables" were not in evidence. The women wore sedate dresses and stylish hats; the majority of the men were in suits and ties. But for the color of faces and hands, it might have been a meeting of the Bazaar Committee at Holy Family Church in the Bronx.

On the raised stage, four people—evidently church officers—were seated on folding chairs. There was the fat woman with the cane, holding her notebook grimly; a younger woman, schoolmarmish and beige in color; the Reverend Harkey; and, to Peltz's surprise, the other workman from the dig, the old man McIsaac.

A coal-black woman, seated at a small organ, sounded a few chords, and the congregation rose.

"Let's begin our meeting with a hymn," said the Reverend, "to show the world we love those who hate us. Our hearts are so full of love for them, we will sing for their salvation. Love and Prayer will bring us the victory."

There were no shouts of *A-men,* no Holy-Rolling, no theatricals —again, much to Peltz's confusion. The attendants began to sing:

We are climbing
Jacob's ladder . . .

Ballard plucked a ragged hymnal from the rack in front of them and shoved it at Peltz. "Sing, you sinner," he whispered. "Page 104."

Ben held the book as if it were a hot coal. He looked about him apprehensively. "Surrounded by *goyim,*" he said.

8 *An Evening with the Ellenbogens*

THE overblown supercharged dreadnoughts of status jammed the Ellenbogen driveway and spilled out on the causeway. A few late-comers were maneuvering giant cars onto the dirt access road running down to the dig. Two city policemen directed traffic, one handling the normal flow on the roadway, the other functioning as a parking attendant. In the black and breathless night, their flashlights painted sharp yellow cones on the darkness. Scattered swollen raindrops warned of imminent downpour.

Crossing the site with Marty, Tom stopped to talk to one of the cops.

"There's some archaeological digging going on down below," he said to the one working as an attendant. "You better stop the cars at the road. One of those jobs falls in the hole, you guys'll be all night getting it out."

The officer looked at him with the humorless face of the law. "Mist' Ellenbogen told us 'bout it."

The rain hit them as they reached the driveway. On the adjacent highway, parked in the wrong direction next to a fire hydrant, Ira's convertible squatted.

"Wouldn't you know it?" Marty asked. "Does anything faze him?"

"Our buddy," said Tom. "He's probably an honorary cop."

The Ellenbogen home, pale pink, loomed over them. A giant spotlight burned high on the stucco façade. Hibiscus and royal palm, artificially illuminated, had the look of stage greenery; Tom expected a chorus of leggy mulattoes mouthing Calypso to appear from behind the gray trunks. In the white marble foyer, cold as a tomb, Lila Ellenbogen awaited them.

"My two favorite people!" she cried. "You're excused for being late because I know how far you had to come!"

She was a vigorous woman in her early thirties. Burned brown by the sun, attractively plump, her eyes wide and deep violet, she had a lively natural quality, which she had succeeded in falsifying through excessive adornment. Her scarlet gown, too rich in texture and too intense in color, the lacquered and molded crown of black hair, the heavy patina of expensive cosmetics, all these detracted from an essentially exciting woman.

"You two crazy Ivy League types!" she said. "Tommy, I could kiss you in that nutty tweed jacket! With *leather elbows!*"

"Turn it off, will you, Lila?" Tom asked.

"He's sensitive!" she cried.

"Lila dollink, I know you expect this kind of uniform from me, so I overdo it. I was going to buy one of those shiny black suits—"

"You wouldn't dare! We have enough of those!" She embraced Marty with genuine warmth. "And Mrs. Professor! Don't I wish I had your face and schoolgirl figure so I could get away with a navy blue sheath! And no girdle!"

Marty disengaged her arms. "Lila, you can wear anything you please. If you won't stop making apologies about your friends and your clothes, Tom and I are going to leave. Or else we'll get terribly drunk and start insulting people."

They entered the living room. In its draped and carpeted precincts, a 440-yard hurdle race could have been comfortably run. Ornate women and sedate men smiled at them indulgently. Tom had the feeling that he and Marty were on exhibit. A colored butler came at them with champagne cocktails. Other servitors brought trays of hors d'oeuvres, hot, cold, multicolored, in geometric patterns. Soon Lila had them stationed on a gold-flecked oval sofa; it might have served as a marriage bed for an Arab oil prince. They were greeted with a good deal of warmth and enthusiasm. As each guest departed, Lila supplied *sotto voce* footnotes about him; sometimes, it seemed to Tom, while the guests still were within earshot. *He's got every parking lot in town tied up. He keeps the city paid off to keep them from issuing building permits! . . . You heard of John Aubusson? He was one of the first men to develop the Beach. The Dredging King. He sucked up all the sand from the bay and made the Beach . . . and that drunk is his son! . . . The big blond dame with the gold stars in her hair . . . the gold lamé dress . . . she's an heiress! Look at the way her husband holds her hand. Afraid she'll run off somewhere. . . .*

Erwin pulled up a chair and joined them. Behind his tinted glasses he seemed curiously detached from the noisy party.

"I was watching you fellows this afternoon," he said to Tom. "You were really swinging the shovels. Anything interesting?"

"We're getting hot, Erwin," Tom said. "I want to talk to you about it tomorrow. I think we started on the wrong foot, but I know what has to be done now. Some new excavations. Higher up, toward the road."

Erwin nodded. "I see no problem." He leaned toward Marty. "How about that husband of yours? All he wants to do is swing a pick."

A few people laughed. Tom didn't mind Erwin's jibes. He liked Ellenbogen. He was a Bronx boy like Tom; they could converse freely in terms of pickup games in Van Cortlandt Park, ringalevio, hot afternoons in the bleachers at Yankee Stadium.

"It's a living," Tom said. "Now, if I got union scale, like my old man did before he went on the force—"

A handsome woman with white skin and copper hair was looking at him with vague distrust. "Why do you do it?"

"I can't do anything else," he said.

"Oh what a fib!" Lila cried. "He's kidding you. He can do anything, this man. He was a Marine hero—a football star! He does it because he's dedicated."

"Knock it off, Lila," Tom said. "Marty—make her stop."

The woman persisted. "He still hasn't explained anything. Why should a man want to dig up holes to look for old bones? Sure, it's interesting and educational, but what good does it do? I would think a University could spend its money better. With all the people who die of cancer and heart trouble."

A portly man, standing nearby, sipping a drink, nodded in agreement. "I have a kid nephew I want to take into the firm. Brilliant kid. Straight *A*'s at Cornell. What does he want to do? He wants to be an anthropologist, something like that. I tell you, my brother is going crazy. He's like a madman trying to talk the kid out of it."

"I'd talk him out of it," Tom said. "There's too many professors bothering the Indians already. You get down to Central America and there's more anthropologists than Indians. There's a village in Guatemala where the professors have to share the Indians."

"He's *kidding*," Lila explained patiently to her guests. "Don't you see he's *joking* with you?"

"I can't tell with him," a woman said distrustfully.

"No, no, he means it. He's right." The portly man winked at Tom.

Marty shifted her legs on the saggy couch. She did not resent Tom's minimizing of his work. But she was offended by the shameless probing of Lila's friends. In the arch lighting, which the Ellenbogen's decorator had so cunningly installed, her upturned face was stunning.

"Of course, he's fooling," Marty said. "Erwin and Lila know he is. He digs for those bones for a very simple reason."

"Probably he just enjoys it," the heavy man said. "Like a hobby. Nothing wrong with that."

"Oh, sure!" Lila shouted. "Oh, my dear friends! What's the matter, Fred? You think it's like you being gin rummy champion?"

"What are you yelling about?" the man asked.

"What I'm trying to say is this," Marty persisted. "My husband, and the people who work with him, every one in the social sciences, are simply looking for truth."

"*Truth?*" the coppery woman asked.

"From digging holes?" the man queried.

"That's it," Lila said. "Truth always comes in little bits and pieces. Not in big chunks. Is that right, Tom?"

Tom stabbed an aromatic midget weenie encased in flaky pastry. He dipped it into a mustard crock and popped it into his mouth.

"Lila," he said gravely, "these are the best hot dogs since I was a kid on Fordham Road."

"No, I won't give up," the copper-haired woman said. "All

right, so you're finding truth. What good does truth do if it doesn't help? If it doesn't make people better, or cure diseases, or *something?*"

"What is this?" Lila cried. "What's going on? A Henry Wallace rally?"

"I'm yellow," Tom said. "That's my trouble. I tried to help out once and I landed on my duff."

"Tell us about it, Tommy!" said Lila. "He's a riot! It's probably some story he made up!"

"Oh, Tom," Marty said. "I don't think they're interested."

Her intonation indicated her impatience with the curious company. The Oriental mélange of rich fabrics, the rare perfumes, dizzying colors, the soft, palatable foods, were making her queasy. Her low threshold for sensation was being violated.

"No, no! Let's hear about it!" Lila said.

Tom helped himself to a spicy meatball. "I got this grant to work in Santa Rosa," he said bluntly. "In Central America. Professor Maitland recommended me for this survey of an Indian community in the rain forest—"

"That's *Hall* Maitland," Lila interrupted. "Marty's father. One of the great names in American social science."

The uncomprehending faces informed her that her program notes were useless. Tom continued:

"It was an interesting project, because it was financed and supported by the government. Santa Rosa was supposed to be a fairly progressive place. Elections, higher wages. So there were these Tapapa Indians, about four hundred of 'em. Now you probably think I'm going to tell you how sweet and charming they were and how they loved me. The hell they did. They were treacherous and stupid and bad-tempered. They practiced cannibalism when the district officer wasn't looking and they did in a few missionaries and prospectors. I got along with them, I guess, because I'm about the same color they are. At least they never tried to slice me up for pepper stew."

Erwin chuckled. "It sounds like you're making it up, Tom."

"What happened?" Lila asked.

"The idea was I was supposed to study these people and make a report on how to save them."

"From what?" asked Lila. "They seemed happy. Did they want you to make vegetarians out of them?"

"No. The grimy, monkey-eating bastards were dying out. These four hundred Tapapa Indians were the last of their kind. The birth rate was declining. The people were dying younger and younger, which was crazy because they had enough food—fish, monkeys, wild fruits, a little cultivated manioc—and there were no endemic diseases."

"What was causing it?"

"Water pollution. There was a fertilizer factory upriver. It poured all this chemical waste into the river, and was infecting the whole village. I didn't have to be a genius to figure that one out. So I made my report. I spent ten days in the capital, Santa Rosa City, drawing up recommendations. I'm not a sanitary engineer, but I had some pretty good notions. I wanted part of the tribe resettled on the banks of an inland lake. There were two totems—clans—in the tribe and they had been getting pretty nasty with each other. Between the resettlement and a purification plan, or at least a diversion of the waste, the poor buggers would at least have a fighting chance of survival."

"That's what I mean!" Lila said. "See how much good people like Tom can do?"

"Oh, sure," Tom said. "I went before the government commission—the top brains in the country, to present my case. Now these people weren't tyrants or murderers. They were teachers, industrialists, professional government people. They listened to my report. Then they told me to shove it."

"I beg your pardon?" Erwin said.

"Shove it. Lose it. They *wanted* those Indians to die out. Who could blame them? The Indians wouldn't work on the farms or in the factories. Their dietary habits were a source of embarrassment to the Church. The last two padres that visited them ended up stew. So why not? The country's overpopulated anyway—like all those places."

"But why'd they send for you?" Erwin asked. "I've done a little work with our Inter-American Commission here, and I know there's a lot of constructive thinking going on down there. Especially since those people you worked with were a better element than the old-fashioned killers."

"My report *looked* good. It *sounded* good. It made the *American Anthropologist*. The government of Santa Rosa submitted it to the World Health Organization. Then they forgot about it. One of my buddies down there says the Tapapa population is down to about two hundred."

"So that's why you turned to archaeology?" Lila asked. "I never knew that."

"It's easier. They're *all* dead."

"Lila, don't take him seriously," Marty said. "Or any of you. His paper on the Tapapas was a classic."

"I forgot one thing," Tom said. "The government before the one I worked with, it was an old-fashioned machine-gun dictatorship. A pistol local. They had a better way of handling the Indians. They paid them in *snuff* for every pair of infant's ears. I couldn't figure out for a long time why some of the Indians were practicing infanticide—drowning the kids. They figured somebody might start rewarding them with snuff again."

His shocking story seemed to settle a thick guilt over his audience. Marty noted it, and tried to control a smile. She envisioned them, black silk trousers thrust into muddy boots, sun helmets crowning the varnished hairdos, making their way through steaming rain forest to succor the doomed savages. The challenge had been implicit in Tom's narration—or had it? Was the story nothing more than a justification for what seemed to him a sterile life? An apologia, an excuse, for digging into a meaningless past instead of grappling with a provocative present?

"The folks might be interested in your work down here," Lila said after a bleak pause. Who could sip cocktails and eat caviar on wafer-thin pumpernickel when the Indians were drowning their young, snipping off their ears and collecting snuff?

"Ah, it would bore them stiff," he said.

"No, not at all," Erwin ventured.

Tom lit a vinegary butt. It offended Marty. She sensed that he was smoking it as a defense—a malodorous symbol of his impoverished scholar's life. In some dimly understood way, he was getting back at them. She was upset by it. His status and his work should have been sufficient to make them respect him.

"I'll make it brief," Tom said. "I get wound up, I'll bore Lila and she'll throw me off the land."

"Fat chance," Lila said.

"The old Indian cultures down here are generally called the Glades Tradition," Tom said. "Before that there was something called Archaic, but we don't know much about it. The Indians of the Glades Tradition lived here—right here on this island and to the north—from maybe 700 A.D. till the middle or end of the seventeenth century."

"Seminoles?" a woman asked.

"No. The Glades people came long before them. The Seminoles were Creeks, invaders. They got here much later. The last

Glades Indians around here were the Calusa. There aren't any left. The last of them died out about 1725, as near as we can figure."

"You got a knack for people who are always dying out," Erwin laughed. "Everybody here insured?"

"For maybe a thousand years," Tom continued, "there was this culture around the Beach and just north of here along the coast. A thousand years and we don't know anything about it. They ate good. Not as good as Lila feeds us, but good enough. Oysters, scallops, conches, fish. We have a hunch that one of the reasons they never developed any complex civilization was that they had it so good. These Calusas, they could be rough, too. They murdered the Spanish traders, kept them out of here for years. About 1650, something hit them—some kind of weakening agent—and they got weaker and weaker. When the Seminole Creeks descended on them, they had just about disappeared. Just a few little fishing villages. Fifty years later, they were gone, too."

The ghosts of the dead Calusa, the vanished killers of the Glades, hung over the velvet carpeting. In the enchanted draperies, a naked chieftain squatted, sharpening a forked stick on a conch point.

"Well, what exactly do you hope to find?" Erwin asked.

Tom drew on his cigar. "I don't know. We never know for sure when we start. This was a populated Glades area. We might learn more about them. What happened to them. How they lived. Why they vanished. You never know."

Lila asked, "What have you found?"

"Damn little," Tom said. "The first two trenches have been pretty barren. One's a refuse heap. What we call a midden. The other might be a grave site. We got one skeleton but it doesn't tell us much."

"Oh come on!" Lila persisted. "You're not telling it all! I heard you talking about Arawaks the other day with Dr. Ballard! I took Anthropology 101-102 at Ohio State!"

"Ah, the people don't care. Let's play spin-the-bottle." Tom blinked his eyes. Marty had a feeling he was getting drunk.

"The Arawak—" he suppressed a burp. "The Arawak were the *Galitzianers* of the New World."

"Watch out, Tom," Erwin said. "There's some here. They might take offense."

"You know what I mean. They were like Sicilians. Anything

they had was better than anything you had. They were always one-up. A rich, inventive culture."

"In your whole life," Lila asked, "did you ever hear a professor talk like that? His students must love him!"

"The Arawak were all over the Caribbean, the Antilles. Cuba, the Bahamas, Haiti. Now it's just a short run from Cuba or the Bahamas to the mainland here. The Arawak were good navigators. Why wasn't there any contact? They were a pretty advanced people. Complicated religion, social structure, they even played a kind of football. As far as we know, they never settled along here. Except for a legendary settlement called Abaibo that no one knows much about. If I could prove a relationship between the Glades people and Arawak, that would be something."

"What would it prove?" the heavy man asked.

"Oh, I give up, trying to educate you people!" Lila shouted. "It's knowledge! *For its own sake!*"

Erwin nodded, agreeing solemnly. Tom seemed to have concluded his lesson.

"He was wonderful," Lila shouted. "My old professors at State should have been that interesting!"

On the fringe of the puzzled group, Marty heard a familiar, bubbling voice.

"He was the most. That boy could sell storm windows on the television." It was Ira deKay. He had been lingering at the edge of the informal seminar, lustrous in a creamy white suit. The points of his rolled collar seemed to dip halfway down his chest. His announcement touched off raucous greetings and hand pumpings. There were hearty shoulder slaps, winks and nods, a sly goose.

Ira had brought good times into the room with him, serving these bounties off a tray like some of Lila's hot hors d'oeuvres.

"Why, it's ole Tom Sorrento and his lady!" he called.

"You know them?" Lila asked.

"Sweetie," Ira crooned, "can't I have high-class friends like you and Erwin? Didn't I go to Minnesota Tech for a year?"

"Mr. deKay met us at the site a few days ago. He was nice enough to entertain our children this afternoon." Marty made her confession with not a little defiance. Resentful of sleek men and women, she would brandish Ira—the crudest and cheapest of their lot—at them. A hinted friendship with deKay, a caricature of themselves, would, she assured herself, render them bitter and jealous. It did not occur to her that they were unsubtle, uncomplicated people and would miss the point.

"You went back again, Ira?" Erwin asked.

"Not at all, Pops. I met Marty in town, took the kids sightseeing and dropped them off. Baby, you're so suspicious tonight!"

Erwin looked at him bleakly. "Can you see me in my study a few minutes, Ira? And ask Charlie Rasmussen to join us."

DeKay excused himself. He found Rasmussen in a darkened corner, in sullen conclave with Si Mermelstein and Cleo. The woman's blond hair was piled high in a topknot. She wore a kind of tan leather envelope, daringly split at the sides. Most of her dizzying legs were visible.

"Charlie sweetie," Ira called. "Leave the hired help and join me in chapel. They won't tell you anything about me, anyway. I pay 'em too good."

Rasmussen followed him through the crowded room to Erwin's study.

Around the gold settee, the haphazard class in American Indian origins dismissed itself. Lila settled next to Marty and whispered to her.

"You see the one in the corner—with the hair like the cannibal king in the Katzenjammer Kids?" she asked Marty.

"The blond? The nice-looking one?"

"Ira's latest. I'm not a prude or anything, but the way he flaunts her around!"

"I don't know that it's so horrifying, Lila. That's par for the course down here, isn't it?"

Lila arched her plucked brows. "Not my course, Marty! She's got a six-year-old son. His daddy was killed in the Air Force—that's *her* story. *Listen.* Erwin's sales manager remembers when she was getting fifty dollars a night. Suddenly she's high class. Ira's *associate.*"

"I'd like to talk to her."

"You? You—talk to her? What could she possibly tell you?" Lila protested. She shook her molded black hair. Lights dazzled on the veneer. "You think he's any better? Why Erwin has to have dealings with *him*—"

Erwin flicked on a bottle-green table lamp. Light suffused on the walnut paneling of his study, illuminating hunting prints, old maps, crammed bookcases. Ira glowed in the semi-darkness.

Charlie Rasmussen, bald and bleak, retreated to a shadowy corner.

"Lila and I furnished this room ourselves," he said proudly. "Whenever we're up North we cruise around for old gimcracks that aren't worth a darn to dealers. Got this old lamp in Norwich, New York, for all of ten bucks. Amazing, isn't it?"

Ira grinned. Erwin's study had cost five thousand dollars to furnish, but he'd brag endlessly about a ten-dollar lamp he had conned from some antique dealer.

"Ira, I've given some thought to your proposal," Ellenbogen said. "I've read Si's prospectus and I must say, while it is intriguing there are a good many questions raised in my mind."

"Zile." Ira beamed. "You with me, Father?"

"I assume Charlie has been filled in. The city should be working with us at all stages."

Ira turned leisurely in his chair; he reached out and patted Charlie's reluctant knee. "Charlie, sweetie, it's that new tourist attraction I mentioned last week. The *God-O-Rama*. The world's great religions?"

The invisible spring that had coiled inside of Rasmussen took a few more wrenching twists. "You never told me anything about that," he said. "You've just had me working my tail off for Mr. Banjo."

"Didn't I?" Ira said, almost tearfully. "I *meant* to."

Rasmussen snorted nervously. He earned very little from the Beach. Most of his income came from grants-in-aid, scholarships for small favors from wealthy people like Ellenbogen and Fenton Braud.

"Now, Ira," Erwin said calmly, "I like your concept. For the life of me I can't figure out how an irreligious and disrespectful person like yourself thought it up. However, I've done some phoning and I find a good deal of favorful climate for such a venture."

Ira's long form uncoiled. He rose, hiking his pants, and performed a Pat Rooney clog on the deep green carpeting.

"My little Erwin," he crooned. "My li'l ole Erwin with the money . . ." He leaned over Ellenbogen's desk. "If your check is already in the mail, please disregard this notice. If not, may we have it forthwith? Yours truly, the Keester Collection Agency! *Wow! Waaaaah!*"

Erwin indulged him. "Sit down, Ira."

"Yeah man, teacher."

"Ira, I have a few reservations which I should like to outline to you."

"Shoot-a-roo."

"I think it would be inadvisable to include that fellow Nudo. There is sufficient capital available without using the likes of him."

"What do you mean?" Ira cried. "No one's ever got anything on Jimmy. He's clean."

"We can discuss the Nudo problem later. With the other general partners if necessary." He thumbed through the hard-covered brochure. "Another thing. I'm worried about the name *God-O-Rama.* I know you and Si mean well, but it might be considered disrespectful. I mean, we aren't being disrespectful, but people may think we are. We need something tasteful. Oh—something like *Man's Ascent* or *The World of the Spirit.*"

"Whatever you say, Pops. Let's use it as a working title, is all I say. Si thought it up. I kind of disagree with you, Erwin. The religious bit is very show biz today. I mean, you can say things in a sort of half-kidding way and really mean it nicely. There was this rock-'n'-roll kid I was handling a month ago. Remember him? Freddie Spain?"

Erwin nodded.

"Well, I gave him a little bit for the newspapermen. I set it up to have one of them ask him was he a churchgoer and he came right back *'No regular church, man. I dig all religions the most.'* It got printed everywhere. Nobody got mad. He meant it sincerely. Like the cat who did the juggling in front of the Virgin. Same thing."

"Ira," Erwin said, "how far have you progressed in drawing up incorporation papers?"

"Well—I haven't. I was waiting—"

"Good. I'd like my attorney to handle that end. You know—my brother-in-law, Ted Ballison."

"*Sweetie.* Wait a minute, sweetie—"

Ellenbogen spun around in his swivel chair, showing Ira his black silken back. It was a broad, strong back. The Mexican and Negro middleweights who had been matched with Erwin down in Juarez had learned how strong it was.

"Don't interrupt, Ira. Just listen. I will aid you in this venture, but only on my own terms. If you will not accept them, I will drop the whole thing. You may look for financial backing elsewhere."

"Zetz. You're a mean ole man tonight."

"I said not to interrupt me."

"Yeah, for Chrissake, Ira. Let Erwin talk, willya?" It was Rasmussen, suddenly emboldened.

Ellenbogen resumed. "My feeling is that the prime consideration in this rather risky new tourist attraction is the location. It is no secret to any of us that my bay-front acreage is the ideal, indeed the *only* place to locate. I am prepared to contribute it, in lieu of moneys. These should be forthcoming from other general partners when it is learned that the attraction will be on the prize piece of property remaining in the Beach."

"He's a doll," Ira said in a half-whisper. "A living doll."

"Now in exchange for this donation on my part, I shall demand a fifty-one per cent interest and full control of the undertaking."

Ira whistled. "Erwin, baby . . . what'll I tell Braud? And Campion? Not to mention Nudo?"

"Nudo is out."

"Listen—he'll stuff me in concrete if I cross him. Besides, he ain't much worse than your buddies next door. Shoe-box millionaires. In small bills, yet."

"That will be enough, Ira."

DeKay sulked. His smooth, round face drooped. "Ah, you're given' me the business, Erwin. I don't see how it'll go. You want everything."

"I want to make something clear to you, Ira. Part of my interest in this project is financial, true. Another part is, well, personal. I feel that a project such as this can do a good deal toward mutual understanding."

"The other guys won't buy it," Ira whined.

"They will when I explain to them the nature of the burden I am assuming. Even without a profit-making enterprise on that land, the taxes are exorbitant, almost confiscatory. What do you think will happen to the tax rate when the attraction opens and begins to earn?"

"Okay, okay, so you're being a regular prince. What about me? It was my idea."

"You'll be taken care of. I might make you head officer of the corporation. I'll make it attractive. Straight salary, expense account, and of course a liberal piece of the entire thing."

A rare, discomfiting flutter of doubt came to deKay. He recalled Si Mermelstein's warnings—*we're involved ourselves.* A motorcade and a piece of Mr. Banjo were not quite the same as an understanding of tax laws and corporate structure.

"I love you, Erwin," deKay said, rising. "I just love you. My idea. My promotion. And now I'm on your payroll."

"Oh, please," the manufacturer said. "If you're so sensitive, let's drop the whole arrangement."

"Hah! Hah!" Ira cackled. "What else? I'm with you."

At the door, deKay paused. "I figure we should move right away, Erwin. Like ready to open Christmas. It would tie in with the season. But we gotta move fast. You oughta give those bone-diggers notice."

"All right, that's enough, Ira. Now I'd like to talk to Charlie alone."

"Serially, Erwin," deKay pursued, "we oughta start excavating and building the end of August. I got a sweet architect lined up and he's made some sketches."

"Don't concern yourself with that, Ira."

Ellenbogen had had his fill of deKay for the night. He disliked deKay as only a brainy city boy can hate a shrewd rube. He had sat through a thousand GI poker games with Ira deKays: they talked too much at the table, they distracted from the game, they were not above cutting the pot or making wrong change, especially in foreign currency.

DeKay waved and left. Erwin gave his swivel chair a quarter turn and looked solemnly at Charlie.

"We have a lot of work ahead of us, Charlie," Erwin said. "Building permits, clearances, street widening. The zoning laws must be carefully studied and amended if necessary. We had best meet with your superiors."

"You got it. Name the day."

"And by all means let's keep Ira out of City Hall. He'll be selling dirty postcards to the mayor."

Charlie laughed bitterly.

"As I see it, Charlie, the main question to be raised is that of taxes."

"Oh, hell, Erwin, you'll get a break on the assessment—"

Erwin wagged a thick, manicured finger; his class ring glittered. "Not a mere *break,*" he said. "A total exemption. We must get this project, whatever it is called, *God-O-Rama,* or *Man's Ascent,* or what have you, classified an educational institution, a public service. The city and the county must be involved in our work, not only as onlookers but as participants."

Rasmussen's sour face puckered. If it wasn't Ira with his damn wheeling and dealing, it was someone smarter and stronger; they didn't let you live for a minute.

Like the ornate food on the buffet tables, the party had jelled into a series of bland mounds. Marty Sorrento had heard more off-color jokes at faculty parties, seen more drunkenness at the annual anthropology department beer brawl. At one point in the tiresome evening, she had joined a group of women in animated discussion. The substance of their conversation, which lasted a half-hour on the single topic, was a new hairdresser who made capital of his homosexuality. The man's sexual ambivalence seemed to produce a violent hilarity in them; each reference to his foot-stamping, his lisping, his boy friends, was greeted by loud guffaws.

She drifted to a group of elderly men and fared no better. One of them wore an odd, paper-thin wristwatch. It was the focus of considerable discussion.

"A Marmiton, right?"

"Yeah. I picked it up in Curaçao. Duty-free port."

"They list it at two grand."

"I paid twelve hundred."

"That ain't bad at all. You know Frank? Frank from Cleveland? He bought a dozen of them."

"It's a good investment. They only manufacture one a day."

The unfathomable mysteries! Marty thought. Balancing an outsized bone-china plate piled high with tender meats and purple aspic, she found herself posing a dozen unanswered questions about the watch: Who in the world would pay twelve hundred dollars for a watch? Why did Frank have a dozen of them? What does a man do with *twelve* watches valued at two thousand each? Why Curaçao? What did he do in Cleveland?

Wine did nothing to ease her malaise. The old terror of excess, of the dreaded material world, the world of comforts and pleasures, was at work again. The bright gowns, the coiffures, the abundance of food and drink was smothering her. She had arrived that evening, serene and tolerant, but now she sensed a burgeoning despair; the game had been lost before she had had a chance to bat. It was not just their total immersion in pleasures, their capacity to savor them, that oppressed her. What was unendurable was their refusal to recognize *her* world, to accept *her* credentials, to acknowledge Tom's. Nobody knew who her father was. They had heard, vaguely, of the University. (One man mentioned the undergraduate football team and Engstrom; it galled her that the tyrannical coach was the only recognized public symbol of the great castle of learning.) Tom's half-serious lecture on his field work had enjoyed only limited success. As the evening ground on, she realized they were indeed poor relatives, the academic fools in a wealthy family, who had refused to go into business. She excused herself, leaving Lila and the copper-haired woman, now deep in comparisons of the outrageous prices charged by the local obstetrician, and went looking for Tom.

By now she was bothered by the plainness of her dress. Even the authentic copper medallion Tom had brought her from Santa Rosa had failed her. No one—not even the dependable Lila—had commented on it. She found her husband in conversation with the blond woman with the topknot, and a pear-shaped young man hiding behind thick horn-rimmed glasses. Momentarily, she was annoyed with Tom's tweed jacket and black knit tie. Moreover, he seemed to be getting drunk and she knew him to be a bad drunk. He had a tendency to get surly and sick.

"Hey, Marty!" he called. His voice had a gruff, unmodulated quality. "Meet good old Si Mermelstein, from Olmstead Avenue. And this is Miss Cooke. Cleo Cooke. From I don't know where."

Marty smiled helpfully. She understood that, in a sense, these people were *auslanders,* too. Mermelstein had an aggrieved, querulous expression. The woman made a grand failing effort at *sang-froid.*

"They're both with Ira," Tom said.

"He seems to get into everyone's lives," Marty commented.

Si's eyebrows jumped slightly. He shot a glance at Cleo, but she remained insulated.

"Are you enjoying the party, Miss Cooke?" Marty asked.

"It's a drag," Cleo said. "A draggy affair."

"I was telling your husband—Tom—" Mermelstein ventured, "that I remember when he played football in high school."

"Do you?" Marty asked. "You don't look *that* old."

"He was some guy," Mermelstein said. "He was the best high school fullback I ever saw. I was sports editor for our paper. Also campus correspondent for the *Times.* I saw him one Thanksgiving Day—"

"Hey, Si, you're embarrassing me." Tom yawned.

"—no, no kidding, you were great. I think you scored three touchdowns. They couldn't stop you. He'd take three guys over the goal line with him. Who was that other Italian kid who was so great? The passer?"

"Farenga," Tom said. "The only difference was he made it in college and I didn't."

Mermelstein frowned. "I never could figure that. I guess Engstrom goofed. It's funny, as soon as I heard your name I remembered it. But I had trouble recognizing you."

Tom fingered his nose. "The bugle. I had it redone in college. It was busted three times."

"*Right!* Right!" Si cried. "Now I remember! They used to call you Bugle Head! Or Banana Nose!" He turned helpfully to Marty. "Every time we razzed him, he went for another ten yards!"

"Quite a memory you have," Marty commented. It was strange, she thought, how the stereotypes keep turning up with distressing frequency. Si Mermelstein was every sports writer she had ever known: weak-eyed, pot-bellied (or somehow incapable of physical excellence), still haunted by memories of eighty-yard runs and pinch-hit homers, buffs and hangers-on and free-loaders, perpetually enthusiastic about vanished heroes.

"What kind of work do you do for Mr. deKay?" Marty asked.

"I'm his utility infielder," Si laughed. "Writer, idea man, survey chief, head of research. I'm brilliant, Ira says. Ira's idea of brilliant is if you read a book a week. And since I used to teach English at P.S. 178, I'm extra brilliant."

"How about you, Miss Cooke?" Marty asked.

"I give up. How about me?" Cleo responded. She said it not gracelessly or insultingly, but with a candid, self-deprecating smile.

"I'm a little naïve about Mr. deKay's kind of work," Marty said. "It took me the better part of two hours to get any kind of explanation from *him*."

The merest narrowing of Cleo's clear blue eyes suggested her suspicions. What was Ira doing for two hours with this exceedingly good-looking woman—this nervy, flat-voiced broad who didn't wear powder?

"I'm an account executive," Cleo said cryptically. "I service Ira's biggest accounts."

"I'm still in the dark," Marty laughed. "What exactly are your duties? Do you write?"

Cleo's purple lips curled at one corner. She regarded the questions less as a source of embarrassment to herself than a mark of Marty's stupidity.

"Cleo is a kind of good-will ambassador for special clients," Si said helpfully. "She's the front-office glamor and I'm the behind-the-scenes brains."

Lila Ellenbogen, followed by the Negro butler, bearing a telephone on an extension cord and plug, approached them. "Oh, you Sorrentos! Talk to people! Don't act like you're bored with us!"

Tom blinked. The sour wine was scraping against his gut. All the creamy foods he had ingested were clotted into a heavy ball inside of him.

"*Hmmmm* . . . that Tommy," Lila pursued. "Sitting there looking so smart, thinking up sociological jokes about us. In-groups and out-groups."

She grabbed the phone and shoved it at Tom. "A call for you," Lila said.

Marty looked upset. "At one in the morning? Maybe one of the kids isn't well. It must be Wilma."

Tom followed the butler to an alcove, where the Negro plugged it in.

"You sure they asked for me?" he asked.

"Yes, sir."

Tom took the receiver. "Hello. This is Tom Sorrento."

Ben Peltz's irritating voice responded. "Tom? Ben. Listen. Don't get sore. Just don't get sore at me."

"What are you talking about? Where are you?"

"Listen. Dave and me. We got in a little trouble."

"What'd you do? Talk up, Benny."

"Well—we're in jail."

"You're in jail? What for?"

"We were picked up for questioning, 'cause we looked suspicious. It's complicated. Honest, Tom, we didn't do a thing. These dopey cops—"

"Let me talk to Dave. You don't make any sense."

"They said only one of us could make a call. They want you to get down here right away. No charges against us—so far. But they want to talk to the guy we're working for. That's you."

For a disbelieving moment, Sorrento held the receiver away from his ear, studying it, listening to Peltz's hoarse filtered voice, with frustration and gloom. "Benny," he said slowly, "I warned you. If you're getting your feet wet again—"

"My word of honor!" Peltz cried. "I didn't do a thing!"

There was an exchange of muffled obscenities at the other end—curse words that seemed oddly good-natured. Sorrento wobbled slightly. The champagne and the heavy food; the insane call in the night and the imminent crisis; the oppressive weightiness of the Ellenbogen gathering; all these were inundating him with a sense of utter fatigue, the kind of weariness that asks only solitude, retreat.

"Benny, you hear me?" he asked. "What is this all about?"

"There was this meeting," Peltz whined. "In a church, yet. Davey took me along, and they made a Confederate case out of it!"

Another voice was on the phone. "Y'all know this man?" it asked politely.

"Sure. He works with me."

"Well y'all better get down heah at once. Pronto. This is the Hilltown Po-lice Station. Seventh Precinct."

"Can you tell me what happened?"

"Ah will when y'all get yo' ass down heah. If you don't you ain' gonna find out. Hyeah?"

A click of finality terminated the conversation. Tom looked up to see the colored butler awaiting the phone. Tom handed it to him and turned to Marty. He could feel the abrasive sloshing in his stomach.

"What's happened to Ben?" she asked.

"I don't know," he said grimly. "He's in the pokey. He and Dave. They were picked up by the police. Or as that ridge-runner said it, the po-lice."

"Good God. What were they doing?"

"I couldn't get a straight story. Something about going to church." He rested against the back of an overstuffed chair. "They want me down there right away."

"I'll go along. Let's borrow a car from somebody."

He rested against the chair back, immobilized. The shining face of Ira deKay appeared. "I listened in, kids. You need a car? Be my guest—I'm at your service."

Marty ignored him. "That's all Ben said? That they went to church? Maybe it isn't as bad as you think. Just a misunderstanding."

"Aaah, I can smell it. They're in trouble."

Ira put a comforting arm around Tom. "Tommy boy, it can't be that bad. Come on, let's pile into my heap and go see. Us New York boys gotta stick together. Besides, I know the cops."

Sorrento stared at him, confounded. Somehow, this inane, absurd man had reduced the crisis to his own laughable dimensions. Apparently, the world of pain and sorrow, of crisis and friction, could always be envisioned in terms of loot and favors. Once, when a business associate of Ira's was in despair because his wife had suffered a painful miscarriage, deKay had cheered him up by sending him a telegram reading: *Sorry Franny blew the kid bit.*

"You know how to get to Hilltown?" Tom asked. "Is it far?"

Ira winked. "About an hour, except when I drive. Half-hour." He guided Marty and Tom to the door.

Erwin and Lila fought their way through the crowd and hurried to the door. "Can't stand the talk any more?" Lila laughed. "Believe me, I get sick of three-for-one splits and deductions myself. Who can blame you?"

"It's not that, Lila," Marty said. She darted a look at Tom. "Abby woke up with a slight fever and Wilma is worried. It's late anyway, and Tom has a lot of work tomorrow."

Ira, swift and efficient, was already outside, wheeling the giant car around. He honked noisily. Tom guided Marty through the marble foyer, down the pink steps. The rain had ended, but the air remained damp and close. Ira held the door open. No sooner were they in than he lurched off into the tropic night, leaving twin thick rubber streaks on the blacktop.

Cleo watched her employer's frenetic departure, then addressed Si with reasonable civility. Normally she moved around and about him, like a speedy launch avoiding buoys.

"Where did he go running off to?" she asked.

"I couldn't hear," Si said. "You know Ira. Some crazy notion and off he goes. It had to do, I guess, with that call Doc Sorrento got."

"Some doctor. And that washboard-hips wife of his."

"She's a beauty, Cleo, don't deny it."

"Oh yes. I know the kind. She probably wears dirty cotton pants underneath." She laughed. "And wouldn't Ira like to get into them!"

Si frowned. "You're nutty. She isn't his kind. Besides—he'd never stand a chance. He's dreaming up some promotion connected with that dig. I think he wants to tie it in with the *God-O-Rama.* Early religions—that kind of gag. The papers would eat it up."

"Why do you defend him?" she asked.

"I'm not defending him. I just think you jump to conclusions too fast."

"Well I know that look in his eye. He's not after any early religion." Her flat, characterless voice wavered. She touched her topknot reassuringly. Si edged an inch or two closer.

"You want me to take you home? To your place?"

"You know I won't let you in. Robin is fast asleep."

"Listen. If Ira ever dumps you, or gets tired, there's me—" He gulped. "You know how I feel. I watch you in the office and in the apartment all the time. I swear, I know how your skin feels, your hair, even though I've never touched you."

"And you never will. Just shut up, Si, will you please."

She could not be troubled with his schoolboy pantings. Grim portents were on her limited horizon. The terrifying presence of discard loomed. For a dread, alcohol-stained moment she shivered at the thought of falling; of having to start all over from the sloping white frame cottage in Wilmington, North Carolina, the postman father and the seamstress mother, the staleness of lower-middle-class life. Now she had a beach apartment and a charge account at SFA; she would never surrender these.

"Cleo. I want to make love to you. I would really love you, not the way Ira uses you. I'd be a tiger."

"I can't stand a hard-up man."

His face, his neck, turned scarlet. "Goddamn it," he muttered. "What's the matter with me? Am I so awful? How many men have you slept with? More than you like to think of, I bet."

"Is that so? Well I can tell you exactly. I keep count. I remember every place and every time and how good or bad they were."

"How many? How many? You're so damn proud of it, tell me."

She raised her sharp nose. "Twenty-three different men, and maybe a hundred and forty times," she said. "Pretty good considering I'm only twenty-five and did it the first time when I was sixteen."

"Here's your chance to make it an even two dozen," Si choked out. "Give me a break, Cleo. You might even like me." He reached out for her hand; she yanked it away fiercely.

"Now, now. I'm an old-fashioned girl. Only one man at a time, and Ira is the man. Besides, Si, you're too brainy. I don't think you'd know how to enjoy yourself in bed. You couldn't relax."

He fell back against the sofa. "Which of the twenty-three was Robin's father?"

"You leave my son out of it," she said haughtily. "If you must know, he was a naval officer. He was drowned off Korea."

The previous time he had asked her, the mysterious sire had been a Marine major, before that an Air Force captain. There was a splendid consistency about Cleo's vision of her boy's putative father: he was always an officer. Si wondered momentarily whether she was enjoying a joke at his expense. He decided against it. Cleo was humorless; she possessed that adequacy of flesh that freed her of the need for wit, charm or intelligence. Indeed, Si suspected—and he was a sentimental young man, ready to think the best of most people—it liberated her from any moral obligations. She took good care of little Robin, he knew—expensive clothing, a fine school, nurses and sitters. Beyond that, she was immured from the rest of society in her own smooth skin and sublime body. Where, Si wondered, were all the good-hearted, put-upon, well-meaning, high-intentioned whores of fiction? Cleo liked what she was; she *loved* it. In Ira's rewards—material and fleshly—she had found an ecstasy that had successfully nullified the harsh memories of Wilmington, North Carolina. Recalling his own blessed escape from pedagogy, Mermelstein thought better of her.

9 *The Barbarian Camp*

AROUND the speeding car the neon nightmare bloomed. A dazzling blur of primary colors, a floral hell, whizzed by in the sodden dark. On lime and persimmon façades blossomed messages in electric blues and ferrous reds, cuprous greens and sulfurous yellows. As the car raced north, on the trek of realtor and developer, the signs grew larger, assumed free-forms, blinked, ran in schizoid circles, told stories. The predominant motif was African Desert. Plaster camels and zebras, hollow mahouts and painted mukhtars glowered with Levantine stoicism beneath NO VACANCY signs. Colored spotlights played on foreign palms, and a hundred feet away the ocean growled savage disapproval at the legend AIR CONDITIONING IN EVERY ROOM.

Ira whipped the car over bridge and causeway, past restaurants, motels, boatels, spicing his wild ride with an insider's commentary on the resort. He knew every establishment, its owner, his worth, his potential, what each could do for him, and what he could for them. A sprawling, multicolored motel called MICRONESIA reminded him that his friend's children were all entitled to free swimming and diving lessons from a former Olympic champion there. A seafood restaurant, THE BRINY DEEP, moved him to recall his lifetime free supply of fresh stone crabs from the grateful owner. The dog track, he pointed out, kept a reserved box in his name, throughout the season, at no charge. These windfalls, a sampling of his splendid situation, were described to Marty and Tom not with a braggart's orotundity, but with casual grace. Ira deKay was of the Beach and the Beach was part of him. He could not go to heaven because he had already found it on earth, savoring the limitless pleasures of the vacation town. Man and community had been subtly, delicately merged, each giving, each taking, both loving.

His head thrust at the damp night, Tom gulped for air. The undulant surge of the automobile was aggravating his illness. In his pained stomach, a great, agitated lump sent shivers of nausea upward.

"Stop the car," Tom gasped. "I'll ruin your two-tone upholstery if you don't."

Ira guided the car to a halt on a clipped sward of Bermuda grass. A futuristic temple, cantilevered and calsomined, loomed above them. Winking lights, chartreuse and gold, advised them they had reached SIDI-BEL-ABBES. Tom leaned against a palm trunk, and under the glare of a baby spot, retched in great heaving spasms. At once his head cleared. Doubled up in public agony, he dimly saw two elderly people, white-haired, kindly folk, watching him with pity. The woman was clucking in commiseration, the man shaking an Old Testament face sadly. His stomach drained, Tom almost wanted to explain to them: *I'm really a nice boy who hates to drink. It always makes me sick.*

Marty patted his forehead with her handkerchief. He could hear deKay's soothing ministrations: "Get it all up, Tommy baby. You'll feel so good. That Erwin and his cheap booze."

Back on the clothesline road again, Tom felt better. He had always been a poor drinker—headaches, sleepiness, nausea. Even a night of beering it up in college used to make him queasy for a day or two. Marty lapsed into silence after the halt at Sidi-Bel-Abbes. Ira, on the other hand, after making sure Tom was all right, was moved to a discourse on his own limitless capacities for alcohol, the little tricks of drinking he had learned. A shot glass of pure olive oil taken an hour before the evening's frolics, he confided, prevented inebriation or illness. It had to be *pure* olive oil. He got his for nothing from an Italian importer he knew.

The car plunged noiselessly into a stretch of darkness. The bright lettering and gaudy escutcheons vanished. They rode several miles through deserted flatland, and then were in Hilltown. Shacks and crumbling stores were jammed together on either side of the pitted streets. Marty recognized it as the neighborhood they had driven through on the way to the Indian village. Ira had to ask where the station house was located and they sped down a main street toward a tired brick structure, its front illumined by green lamps. Ellenbogen's old pickup was parked outside, wedged between two prowl cars.

Inside, a desk sergeant eyed them with the suspicious eye of the law. He asked them to wait, and they sat on wire-backed chairs, sniffing the eternal disinfected aroma of justice, the tired stink of crime apprehended. In a few minutes, a fair young man in a white sport shirt and gray rayon slacks came out of an inner room. He wore tan shoes, ventilated with myriad holes; a leather sheath holding several automatic pencils and pens was attached to his braided belt. There was a clerkish, prissy quality about him.

"Which of you is"—he consulted a slip of paper—"Dr. Sorrento?"

Tom got up. He was unsteady on his feet. "That's me," he said.

The young man nodded. His face was small and scrubbed. He could not have been more than twenty-seven. He studied Tom with calm, appraising eyes, then, surprisingly, shook hands with him. "How do. I'm Lieutenant Fry. Who are these people with you?"

"That's my wife. Mrs. Sorrento. That's Mr. deKay. He lives down here. We were at a party with him and he drove us over."

Ira grinned impishly at the officer and threw him a snappy highball. Lieutenant Fry did not smile. Tom watched his unchanging face and felt pleased with Fry—not only for resisting Ira, but because he was not a stereotype. He should have been fat and red-necked and foul-mouthed. The young managerial type confronting them probably spoke at Rotary meetings and conducted a children's highway-safety program on television.

"I spoke to Peltz before," Tom said shakily. "I understand

you're holding him and Ballard." Vertigo assailed him. "Can we sit down?"

"By all means," Fry said. He pulled up another wire-backed chair. "Yes. A Benjamin Peltz and a David Ballard. They are your employees?"

"I guess you'd call them that," Tom said. "You see, we're digging at the Beach. Archaeological work. I'm the head of the project and they work with me. They're both archaeologists."

"Archaeological work," Fry repeated slowly. He enunciated each syllable, the way a radio announcer delivers the name of a new ingredient: *hex-a-phil-o-my-a-dent.*

"What is this all about?" Tom asked. His face was umbrous and troubled. "I mean—what's all the mystery? Peltz said he went to a meeting at a church. What's wrong with that?"

Fry rose, walked to the desk and spun the blotter around. For a moment Tom fancied he saw a brief exchange of mocking smiles between the desk sergeant and the lieutenant.

"Your employees," Fry said, "were booked at eleven-oh-seven on a charge of loitering."

"Loitering? In *church?*" Tom shouted.

Fry looked up. "It won't do any good to lose our tempers," he said. "If the men aren't guilty of anything, I'm sure you can explain everything."

He rejoined them. Ira offered the officer a cigarette. The cop accepted it, and deKay leaned forward, lighting it for him. "Lieutenant, how's my buddy Chief Ennis these days?"

"Fine, I suspect. I don't get around much on his level."

"He's a dear, close friend," Ira whispered. "He and the missus were my guests two weeks ago at the Peruviana." He winked.

The officer refused to comment on Ira's gross hint at high connections. He listened to these testimonials with great frequency.

"Now suppose you tell me just what you and these people are working on at the Beach," Fry said to Tom slowly. There was only a trace of a Southern accent in his speech.

"What's the difference?" Tom asked. "You shouldn't be asking me. I should be asking you." He looked suddenly at Marty. "We should have brought a lawyer. Why didn't we talk to Erwin? Why'd you give him that story about the kid getting sick?"

"Really, Tom," she said. "What has that got to do with it?"

"If you haven't anything to hide, you'd better fill me in," Fry persisted.

"Let's stop this nonsense," Marty said curtly. "We're living at the Ellenbogen place. We're working on the land near Mr. Ellenbogen's home. On a grant from the University. That's all there is to it."

"Don't tell him anything," Tom exploded. "He wants to find out, let him release Ben and Davey!"

Fry ignored him. "Mrs. Sorrento, since your husband is so determined to have a chip on his shoulder, maybe you can help. Now tell me—are all these people *officially* connected with the University?"

"Well—my husband's an assistant professor. Mr. Peltz is working on his doctorate."

"What about the Negro?" He pronounced the word correctly. It was not "nigger" or even "nigra."

"Dave? Well, not officially, except that he's working on the dig. He got his doctorate last year and he's waiting for a teaching appointment."

"Ah, tell him the truth," Tom cried. "I'm an agent of the Mafia. The Black Hand. Ballard is Lucky Luciano in blackface and Peltz's real name is Gagliardo. We're digging up uncut heroin and old policy slips on Ellenbogen's place. He's the front man, Vito Vivante."

"Quite a sense of humor, you have," Fry said. "Frankly, Doctor, a man in your position, a scholar, I'd expect you at least to cooperate."

"What do you want?" Tom cried. "A sworn statement?"

"These men of yours," Fry said, "were arrested tonight as they left a meeting of Negroes. We would not have been suspicious except for the presence of this white man, Peltz."

"Hey, Lieutenant," Tom said hoarsely. "You look to me like the *New* South. As opposed to the Old South. You went to college and I don't hear a cracker accent. Why can't a white man go to a colored church? Ballard brought him along for ribs."

"You're either being naïve or you're eager to cover something up," Fry said calmly. "That church was the scene of a meeting aimed at organizing a Negro resistance movement, an organized boycott of white stores and services. Within a week or two the state legislature is going to enact a bill to rezone election districts. It will be the law of our state. The Negroes claim it's a dodge to disfranchise them. Hence this boycott. Frankly, I can't see what the fuss is about. Very few bother to vote when they get the chance. And what's the difference anyway? The major parties down here are *both* in favor of segregation."

His dispassionate summation seemed to settle the issue. Tom breathed deeply; he felt constricted, strangling. The same kind of pointless, frustrated anger he used to feel in boot camp assailed him. *Goddamn it Sorrento you march like a man with a paper asshole . . . I'll show you how to count cadence you New York college wiseguy. . . .*

"Tough," Tom said. "I bleed for you. They want to boycott your stores, you can't stop 'em. Besides—my people aren't connected with it. Ballard went as an observer, he's no secret agent. And he dragged Peltz along to show him."

"I'm not so sure that's the case," Fry said. He was sweatless and immaculate in the breathless room. "I don't think you realize how a total boycott can paralyze a community. The Negroes will realize sooner or later, after a lot of ill will has been aroused, that these acts of resistance don't help them at all. This is a progressive community, Dr. Sorrento. We built the finest Negro high school in the South here last year. Why, their baton-twirling team—all those nice little colored girls—won the Negro state championships."

Ira leaned back. He unloosened the top of his glossy shirt and yanked his tie down a notch. "Lieutenant, people are allowed to go to meetings," he said reasonably.

"Not if they're paid agitators sent down from New York."

"They're diggers!" Tom shouted. "They're looking for bones—not to start any riots!"

"A convenient front," Fry said. "A perfect blind for this kind of activity."

"That's ridiculous," Marty said. She managed a cold smile at Fry, reluctantly trying to use her beauty as a lever. "We've known them for years. They simply aren't involved in any of that."

They were desperate; in the face of Fry's patient logic, neither Tom's sullen anger nor Marty's charm could achieve anything. Ira, yawning, seemed left out of it.

"Tell me this, Pops," Ira said, stretching. "What did these cats tell you when you picked them up?"

"Peltz said they were observing. But the Negro talked like a field hand. That's why I don't believe he *is* a Ph.D. I've known a good many educated colored people. I went to graduate school with a fine Negro lad. But this Ballard—"

"He was needling you," Tom said abruptly. "It's an act."

A grave look clouded Fry's sharp face. "Now what do I make

of that? Doesn't that prove my point? If the man puts on this act, he must be concealing something."

They had reached point of no return. Tom, talked out, slumped in the chair. Marty patted her forehead. Ira looked innocently at the officer.

"Well, Lieutenant, baby, what do we do now?" Ira asked plaintively. "My friends have to get some sleep. You can't hold these people forever. How about turning 'em loose? You know where to find 'em."

"I'm going to have to hold them," Fry said. "Considering Dr. Sorrento's uncooperative attitude, and the whole questionable nature of this affair, I have no choice. We'll check it out tomorrow. I'll have to talk to all of you again. I suggest you get some legal advice."

An internal shudder made Tom wince. The whole dreadful prospect grew hair and teeth. There would be charges, insinuations, publicity, the rehashing of Peltz's old sins, nasty aspersions on himself, on Maitland, on the University. It would burst upon them and spread with a brainless persistence, drowning truth, discoloring everything. The idiocy of the notion horrified him: *Benny Peltz goes to church for the first time in his forty-four years on earth, and gets into trouble.*

Ira unwound his rubbery body and got up. "Officer?" he asked. "May I use the phone?"

"Go right ahead."

Ira winked at Tom. "Stay loose, Tommy boy," he said. He slouched over the desk and dialed a number. As he waited for an answer, he executed a few *cha-cha-cha* steps. Nobody smiled.

"Crazy jerk," Tom muttered to Marty. "Get us all in jail."

Ira's face suffused with joy. "Helloooo out there!" he sang into the phone. "It's two A.M.! Fun and Games time! Is that you, Willie? Is that my Willie boy? Who is this? Who is this, he asks? Why it's Ira! Good ole Ira! Yeah, boy! Yes. Yes. Yes indeedy. Suite nineteen-oh-five at the Peruviana!"

The mention of the hotel room convulsed him in boneless laughter. Evidently the person he was phoning was similarly stricken. As Ira held the phone away, they could hear booming, raucous laughter.

"Aaah—aaaah—aaaah!" Ira gasped. "Oh, God love you Willie boy! Will I ever remember that night? You were—her—her—her—idea of a *gentleman!* Waah! Haaah!" Again, deKay and his correspondent took time out for mutual hysteria. When he addressed the man again, his voice was low and confident, yet a tinge of joviality remained.

"Willie baby, I'm not drunk. No sir, ole Ira is much too sober for two o'clock in the morning. I got a little problem which only you can help with. I'm down at the Hilltown precinct. *Hilltown.* Hell no, Willie, I ain't changing my luck. I'm here with a very nice young lieutenant named Fry. Yes, that's the lad. Arthur Fry? Yep. Well this is all very complicated, like the Peruviana's bookkeeping, so bear with Ira. I have these dear friends down here, archaeologists who are working at the Ellenbogen place. Old bones and stuff, you know. You heard about them? Good-o. Solid. The fellow in charge is a fine Eye-talian boy from New York, an old dear friend. You'd love him, Willie—a big Marine hero . . ."

"Where the hell did he learn that?" Tom said to Marty. She shrugged. DeKay was omnipresent, omniscient.

"Well, he's got two crazy professors working with him, a white fellah and a big stove-lid. A what? A stove-lid. Alligator bait. An eight-ball. A big *dinge,* Willie. So tonight these two jerks, just for kicks, show up at a meeting in the coon church down here. Don't ask me why! Nothing secret about it. They're curious. They're nuts, also. Nah, none of that stuff. Some guys get their jollies skin-diving and you and me get it by another kind of diving, and these jerks go to coon meetings. Willie, they ain't *bright* enough to agitate. I wouldn't let either of 'em sell lottery tickets. Well, baby, as I was saying, these two guys who worked for my Eye-talian friend are leaving the church when some of Fry's cops arrest them for loitering. Fry tells me the dinges are organizing some kind of boycott, on account of they won't be allowed to vote. He figured maybe these New York guys were with it. Nah, not at all, Willie. They went there for kicks, laughs . . ."

"I'd better stop that lunatic," Tom said. He started to get up. Marty restrained him.

"It's too late, now," she said. "Let's take our punishment."

He turned on her bitterly. "It was your idea to ask him along. What is he? Our counselor?"

"*Tom,* stop shouting. I couldn't keep him away."

DeKay was rattling on. ". . . my personal word, Willie. On Ira's word of honor and you know I never short-change anyone. Listen, not to change the subject, but did you ever get those two dozen fancy glasses from the Stockyard Inn? Yeah. A set of highball glasses and a set of Old Fashioned glasses. I ordered 'em just for you. You didn't? *Zile.* I'll send a telegram off to Chicago, Willie. They're the greatest. Great for your rumpus room."

He paused, listening to the unseen recipient of favors, nodding his blond head easily.

"Right. Right-o, Willie. So you'll fix the thing. And you wanna talk to Lieutenat Fry now. Oh, no, nothing like that. He's been a prince." He nestled close to the receiver. "Goodbye, sweetie. And you'll knock the names off the blotter? Like it was all a mistake? *Bye-ee.* Give Cynthia a big wet kiss from Ira!"

He turned, holding the phone toward Fry.

"Chief Ennis would like to talk to you," Ira said. "He is the most darling man I ever knew."

Fry hunched himself over the sergeant's desk, his back to the others. He spoke in a low monotone, fingering the sheathed automatic writing tools at his belt. At length he nodded and hung up.

"Chief Ennis seems to feel that Mr. deKay's word is sufficient not to pursue the matter," Fry said. He looked at Ira. "He seems to think a great deal of you." Ira beamed.

"The chief told me to pass on to you a little advice. Well, more than advice. An *order.* Those two men are to stay out of Hilltown. It'll be up to you, Doctor, to see that they do. The situation here is most tense and we don't want any more misunderstandings. I'll make the usual written report on this, but there'll be no investigation pressed, no interrogation."

"The blotter, Lieutenant?" Ira asked.

"We'll amend it." He gestured to the desk sergeant. "Tell B. J. to let those two out."

The sergeant climbed off his perch and waddled toward the inner rooms. There was a clanking of heavy keys, a rattling of iron doors. Ira walked up to Fry, handing him a calling card.

"Any time you want a big evening on the Beach, Lieutenant," he said. "Look up Ira. I think our cops are entitled to it. I was active in the plot to raise police salaries last year. Did most of the PR for free."

Ballard's soaring figure filled the narrow doorway at the end of the room. He ducked to avoid a dangling electric bulb, then shuffled toward them. A step behind him was Ben, bouncing on the balls of his feet, hitching his belt in schoolyard fashion. A sodden turnkey, an old man with a crimson face, walked alongside Ben. Evidently he and Peltz had become friends.

"B.J., ya nuts," Peltz said. "You talk like a man who don't know second base from a grilled cheese sandwich. That bum

McGee could never hit big-league pitching. Sure, down here in the swamps he hit three-fifty."

"Led the damn' South'n 'ssociation three years," the turnkey whined. "That's pretty good hittin'." He seemed delighted that a white prisoner would deign to converse with him on equal terms; he would have liked to have continued the baseball argument into the night.

"B.J.," Peltz said earnestly, tapping the man's chest, "he coulden hit a curve. I'm sorry to hurt your feelings since McGee was a home-town boy, but face it. He was a bum." He looked up suddenly, seeing the visitors.

"Hah!" Peltz shouted. "Saved!"

Ballard rolled his eyes from Fry to Tom. "Dey lettin' me be a free man, boss? Dey din' even let me be in deh same jail wit' Benny heah."

"Go on outside, Dave," Tom said. "Wait for me."

"You're all cleared," Fry said. "On your own." He squinted coldly at Ballard. The masquerade offended him, as only a logical and fair-minded man can be offended by a deception. Ballard plodded by abjectly and walked out the front door. They could hear the seat in the ancient pickup protesting as he installed his hulking body into the cab.

"You are aces with me, B.J.," Ben said to the jailer. "Next time I get locked up, I'm askin' for you!" He pumped the old man's hand, snubbed Fry and walked out.

"Thank God," Marty said. "*That's* over. Now can we all go quietly?"

"Yeah boy," Ira said. "I'm beat to the socks. I took a Dexadrine five hours ago and I'm way, way down." He seemed enervated, drained, for the first time that evening. "Miss Marty?" he said. "We'll drive you and the doc home."

They all walked out. Fry watched them, hesitated, then walked toward the door. Outside, Marty and Ira got into the convertible. Fry stopped Tom at the top step. In the green light, he seemed even younger, paler, more decent.

"Listen, Doctor," he said earnestly. "You people mean well, but you must stop preaching to us on how to handle our race problems. I don't mind you losing your temper tonight, or saying what you did. A cop gets used to that. But I must tell you, speaking personally and not as an officer, I get kind of fed up with you smart Northerners. Now I'm a reasonable man, and I suspect you are. Why can't you allow us a little bit of justice on our side?"

"What the hell is this?" Tom asked. "A debating society or a police station? I came to get two of my people out. Who's arguing with you about anything else?"

"You New York folks are all alike. Got your minds made up about us, haven't you? None of you really understands the mind of the South. We know the colored people. We know what they really want. Why, this boycott they're planning would never get off the ground if it weren't for a few agitators like that Harkey. And where does he get his idea? From up North."

Tom squinted at his supplicant figure, green and white, poised on the chipped steps of his castle.

"Why they are the most ungrateful people there are," Fry said sorrowfully. "I try to love them, to help them. And now this. I'm no extremist. I'm against that White Citizens' Council myself. I deplore violence."

"Listen," Tom said. "You ever think maybe they don't like getting screwed?"

"Who?"

"The colored people. You ever figure they just don't *like* it? All this crap about how you know what's best and they really have a good deal down here. You know the story about the Chinese cook in the lumber camp?"

Fry's chin shook faintly. "You've got it all wrong, Doctor. You don't know a thing about our traditions. You can only see things in your own narrow terms."

"I don't want to fight with you," Tom said. "I got other problems. I keep you going long enough here, I'll get you to *un*deplore violence."

"I do not believe that. It's you people—you and them in there" —he indicated Ben and Dave, silent, listening in the truck— "who are creating the vicious atmosphere."

"Tom! For goodness sake!" Marty called out. "Let's go!"

He shook hands with Fry—so surprised at seeing the proffered freckled hand that he gripped it firmly—then ran down the steps to Ira's roaring ark. As they pulled away, Fry was still standing there, isolated, misunderstood, grieving.

Wilma and Oran were awake when they returned. The brother, his eyes mangled by distorting lenses, sat on the balcony, reading with the aid of a flashlight. Wilma was inside sewing. Marty learned that the children had been quiet, and sent them to bed.

Tom noticed that Oran was holding the triangular stone in his lap.

"What you doing with the *zemi,* Oran?" he yawned. "You feed him good, he'll take care of you. Money, prestige, a big sex life."

Oran's Adam's apple bobbed. He held the book out toward Tom.

"I found one just like it. In this article on Arawak in an old Smithsonian publication."

He played the flashlight on a line drawing of a three-cornered stone, somewhat similarly incised. Tom read the notation beneath it: *Problematical three-sided stone from Cuba. Late Arawak. Thought to be a zemi, or sacred idol.*

"Great, Oran," Tom said. "We're all out getting in trouble and you're making progress. You're smarter than we are."

Oran ducked his head; a word of praise was like a light blow against his temple. "It's nothing. I mean—anyone would go through the books. . . ." His voice vanished.

"You better go to bed, kid," Tom said. "Big day tomorrow."

The youth gathered up his books, dropped one, retrieved it, tucked the flashlight in the rear pocket of his trousers and walked down the side steps. He had forgotten to turn the torch off, and it cast its muted glow on his starved behind. Tom stumbled into his own room. He was not merely fatigued; he felt beaten, clubbed, worked over. Marty was already stripped down to her sleeping costume: cotton brassiere and rayon briefs. Lean and distressingly energetic, she was wrestling the daybed to double-size, stripping the cover, fluffing pillows. At one end of their living quarters was a rudimentary kitchen: tiny stove, refrigerator, sink. Tom poured himself a glass of cold milk and settled wearily in a canvas Ellenbogen chair—Lila had furnished their rooms with samples from Erwin's showroom. The total functionality of their residence, its barren simplicity, pleased Tom. Below, in the "men's dormitory"—Wilma slept upstairs with the children—they could hear Dave, Ben and Oran conversing in whispers.

Marty stretched out on the bed. "You've got to talk to Dave tomorrow," she said softly. "And Ben, too. I knew they'd get you in trouble."

"Who's in trouble? We're off the hook. Your buddy deKay fixed it."

"A good thing he was there. He may be a vulgar idiot, but I hate to think what might have happened to us if he hadn't been around." She pushed the pillow against the wall and sat up, jackknifing her slender legs. "I warned you about those two, Tom," she said. "If you can figure some way of sending them back, you'd better do it. What have we got here? Another month? Six weeks? Get some diggers from the local University. What's so complicated about trowel work anyway? You don't need a Ph.D. for this kind of stuff." She was talking quite loud.

"Hold it down to a roar, will you baby?" he asked. "They'll hear you."

"I wish they would. Your damned charity ward down there. They'll ruin you, Tom."

"Ah, *scungilli*. With lemon juice and olive oil."

"Tom, you carry tolerance to the point of self-destruction. What kind of judgment can Dave have to go to a meeting like that? And then! Compounding what he's done by taking Ben along. Tom, I'm as liberal as they are. I have no apologies to make. But *those* two. They can't possibly be of any help to the colored people. They're just the kind who'll ruin whatever it is they're planning."

"Dave was making notes. For a paper."

"I'd like to believe that. He's already gotten his doctorate. He knows by now no amount of papers are ever going to help him. If you hadn't hired him this summer, he'd be working for Railway Express again."

"He's a terrific field man."

"And Ben. The no man's land of American anthropology. The only reason you were allowed to hire him was because the funds for this project came from *outside* the University. Reliable Benny. He confessed everything to the Committee and named everybody in the world—how come he didn't include you?—and now he doesn't believe in anything. He's no good to anyone. Except my trusting husband."

"Ben is the best surveyor in the business. I don't listen to him. He's got no more political sense than my Uncle Sal who couldn't sell grapes from a pushcart. He's a *yente,* an old lady. He wants to believe the worst. If he delivers for me, who cares? The poor bastard. Forty-four years old."

She got up swiftly, walked to the refrigerator and found a can of beer. In the moonlight, clad only in briefs and brassiere, she looked nineteen years old, a sorority girl. The panty raid had been repulsed and now the girls of old Kappa Tau would raid the kitchen! Her loveliness seemed a burden to him—as if his own life, his own achievements were unequal to such beauty.

"That's your problem, Tom," she said. "You suffer from an oversupply of compassion. You pity Davey because he's black, you pity Ben because he's ruined his life and you pity the Burleys because they're lost. You absorb their unhappiness, their frustrations, and all you can do is get mad in a limited, choking kind of way. How in God's name you managed to be a Marine officer, in that stupid authoritarian system, with all its idiotic ritual, I don't know. How could you bear to order those poor enlisted men around?"

"I was a rough bastard," he said proudly.

"Oh, I'll bet." She returned to the bed. "I've had my say about your helpers. I think they should be sent back."

"Not a chance," he said. "I told you two days ago—if this upsets you—I don't mean just what happened tonight—but the whole deal, maybe you should go back to New York with the kids."

"I can't be in that hot apartment through August," she said.

"Well, I'm out of suggestions, Marty. I have to get the work done."

Tom wandered out to the balcony. Beyond, the bright neon signs glowed in the city of pleasure. Around them slept the secure, the rich, the arrived: the people who listened to Ira deKay. The insane sequence of events of the evening bothered him—not because of any real danger to himself or the dig, or the University, but because of deKay's dizzying performance. Somewhere in Marty's embittered attack on Dave and Ben was a cynical admiration for deKay and what he had accomplished. It annoyed him not because of ordinary male jealousy; deKay wasn't in that category—he was so outrageous, so alien that you could not conceive of him as a rival. Rather it scraped against his ego—a reminder of his own limited effectiveness. The unexpected reference to his Marine service was the clue: she knew too well he had been a superb officer. Was the reminder necessary?

He walked back into the room, dragging his shrunken leg. The endless hot day and the angry night had been too much for the atrophied calf.

"You'd better get *some* sleep," she called.

"I might try staying awake right through." He got into bed, lying prone alongside her. He stared at the ceiling: masking tape peeled from the plasterboard seams.

"How do you figure that guy deKay?" he asked.

"What about him?"

"The way he took over. That clown. You realize what he did? You understand what he did for us? For me?"

"Be grateful."

"Yeah, I'm jumping up and down. That crazy bastard. You know what it is to do what he did? My old man's a cop. *I* know. And there I was arguing my head off. Nice, logical arguments."

"You weren't *that* logical, Tom. You were getting pretty mad."

"Why shouldn't I? I tell you what. As mad as I got at Fry, I should have been madder at myself. That's what's eating me. We stand around like two freaks. Oran and Wilma, that's us. Then comes deKay. With the dirty jokes and the bribes—not even big bribes, chinchy ones—two dozen glasses! And look what he does. He gets the agitators released. The New York nigger and the Jew Communist. With laughs. *Laughs*. It's all for fun, see?"

She raised herself on one elbow and looked at him intently. "Tom, you're being childish. Has it just dawned on you there are people with influence, everywhere? Fixers? Operators? Of course deKay can get things done. It's his kind of town. My goodness—Bertrand Russell could be living here and he couldn't get arrested. Or maybe he could, and not get released, except if Ira deKay spoke up for him!"

"To hell with him. I'm not sore at him. He did me a favor. Saved my big Italian can. I'm mad at myself."

"It's my fault," Marty said. "When will I learn? I haven't heard you indulge in this kind of self-immolation since you were passed up for the MacIntosh fellowship. Tom, we're on different planets than deKay. What makes you think you have the right to —to—*power* in a place like this?"

"I'm a citizen, ain't I?" he asked. "A red-blooded American boy." He embraced her. "Couldn't even hold my liquor. In the middle of everything I'm throwing up on some guy's lawn. And deKay. He's bouncing around, making jokes."

"You're making me miserable."

"I'm enjoying it. I love every minute of it. What would my old man say to see me stammering in a police station? He always told us when we were kids—you get in trouble tell 'em your daddy is a cop, Frank Sorrento, Forty-second Precinct. I didn't even think of *that*."

"That would have been a *big* help. That really would have carried weight. Now, Tom, please. Go to sleep."

"Inadequate bastard. I can't ice skate."

"We're off. Now tell me about the bicycle."

"Can't roller skate. Or dance. Didn't drive my own car until I was thirty years old. How much of a *buffone* can a grown man be?"

They lay silent, listening to the whoosh of speeding tires on the highway; the occasional sounds of Nicky's adenoidal breathing. He held her; her body had a firm, springy quality. It would never be soft, pliant. It had an independence that had always delighted him.

"Do you want to make love to me?" she asked.

He kissed her ear, her slender neck, the curled edges of her unruly hair. "Nah," he muttered, "I'm not good for anything tonight. You wouldn't enjoy it."

"It might cheer you up."

"You cheered me by suggesting it." With habitual possessiveness, he ran his hands along the thin legs. Then he stretched full length. His legs felt like one of those tortured frog muscles in biology lab, a mass of cells, perpetually agonized by stimuli.

10 *The Return of a Hero*

THAT was the magic time: the summer of 1945. There would never be a time like it again. It had been too promising, too crammed with expectations of success, fame, love. Behind were the years of tortured discipline, of brainless following and imposed leadership, the prospects of death and mutilation. Ahead stretched an endless vista of thick steaks, clean, perfumed girls in silk stockings, expensive whiskey. Each man had his dream—yet they were oddly similar dreams. There was an officer in Tom's company, a fine-featured boy from a wealthy California family, who, after four years of metal messgear, longed only to eat off his mother's fine Rosenthal china. "The only guy I know," Tom said, "who'll be happy with a soup bowl."

It was as good a symbol as you could find, the officers agreed. The fragile china soup bowl (adorned no doubt with fragile floral design) seemed a fair trade for the pitted beaches, the shell-smashed palm trees, the deadly reefs and the unseen, tenacious enemy. All these were gone forever, and the Rosenthal soup bowl awaited.

It was a time of fragile, unbearable anticipation. So much that was abrasive and disgusting had filled the immediate past that the future, even if only mildly rewarding, would be glorious, pleasurable, satisfying, an extended dream of delights. Tom, more than most of the men he served with, was a realist. He sometimes wondered if all the talking might diminish the actual joys of this hungered-for afterlife. It seemed to him they had talked about it from the very first day at Quantico. They discussed it in OCS, at the embarkation points, on the troopships, in combat, at rest centers. They talked about it under fire and in death. The litany developed its own rhythms, its own shibboleths; men said it as they would a catechism. Tom could remember a boy in his company, a BAR man whose name he could not recall, dying one night in the bottom of a wrecked LCI on the beach at Saipan. He was a large-boned, overweight boy, not at all muscular and agile, who had trouble lugging his automatic weapon. He had been something of a malingerer and a cry-baby; a stray mortar burst had torn away part of his chest, and in spite of the morphine that the corpsman had pumped into him, he refused to be quiet. With witless, dedicated persistence, as his life drained from the obscene wounds in his fat body, he recited his canticle. . . . *I'm gonna get me the biggest nicest room in the Fairmont Hotel with the biggest whitest private crapper you ever saw. I'm gonna lay in that warm, warm tub half the day and then take an hour to move my bowels on that white clean john. I'll take an hour to shave in front of the big mirror and use all the hot water I want and then I might just lay in that bed with the white sheets and laugh all afternoon . . . I won't even start on the broads until the next day . . .*

Not a bad testament, at that, Tom thought. If that's what the fellow wanted, why not? In a way the BAR man was lucky. He went out with the dream vivid in his doped, moribund brain. If you lived it, you were bound to be disappointed. The dream was simply too good, too vivid and sensual, too perfect. The real world held no such pleasures. Tom, with a kind of dogged pessimism, understood this. He had no wife, no sweetheart, no career, no money, no ambitions. With the foreknowledge that these desires were ephemeral and untrustworthy, he restricted the area of what-it-will-be-like to two vague, Spartan notions: he would go back to the University for some kind of graduate studies, and he would try to write.

Now, circling his native city in a flatulent MATS DC-3, the volcanic ash of Iwo still in his nostrils, he wondered about the dream. He was already a terribly lucky man: *he had survived.* Four of his college classmates, fellow Marines, had died in the islands. The wounds on his left calf were healed; the Navy medics assured him he would be bothered only with the faintest limp. The plane had puddle-jumped from San Francisco to La Guardia, an interminable Odyssey with a mixed grill of wartime types. There were two civilians in ill-fitting gray suits and Tom, with practiced eye, knew they were ex-cops now in CID. They seemed offended when he told them, and his effort to engage them in casual talk met with cold muteness. The plane dipped a wing over the gray-red desert of Brooklyn. Beyond the tenements and the two-family hutches stretched the sandy beaches, the bays, inlets and brackish marshes of the littoral. It was much like the East Bronx, his home grounds: City Island, Pelham Bay, Castle Hill. . . .

This was the New York to which he belonged: the outlying marshes, the misty transformed wastelands, where the grimy patterns of Manhattan had been transported *en bloc.* It was the city of schoolyards and stickball, of dollar-a-man football on weedy lots, of policy bankers and local boxing heroes. The storybook Manhattan, its towers of status and wealth now peeking through the opposite window of the aircraft, was no more his city than were Paris or Los Angeles. He was as much of an intruder in mid-town Manhattan as were the frigid people lined up outside the Radio City Music Hall in sub-zero weather, hicks and hayseeds waiting stoicly for a glimpse of *The Christmas Story* and the Rockettes. In some cloudy way, his dream had been associated with this *other* New York. He envisioned a moment in a publisher's office, an epiphany, the magic word that he was a "find," a truly creative literary person. . . . The scene blurred and he saw himself in a book-lined apartment, possibly on West 12th Street, the artist engaged. . . .

The city rooftops, rising to meet the plane, dispelled the fantasy. The choked back-streets of Brooklyn gave way to the ragged edge of Queens, a place of harsh names: Elmhurst, Maspeth, Flushing. Beyond, the spires of the great congeries of money and talent filled him with an uneasiness, the sense that even his modest dream was a cheat. It was valid only so long as you were in bondage. Freedom killed the dream because it put the onus on the dreamer's shoulders. With freedom came the nagging realities of the world. And as soon as the DC-3 touched down, these descended on him in the guise of Tom's sobbing, heaving family, all of them waiting at the gate for the returning hero. He could see his father, gesticulating to two strangers, no doubt advising them that his son Tommy (who was a great football player) had showed the Japs a thing or two. His mother was convulsed with tears. She wore a formless deadly black coat and a fearsome black hat; it was her standard costume for weddings, wakes, all public occasions. His two sisters, their skirts short and their hair long, their naturally dark faces surfaced with pale powder, were waving frantically. A trim, antiseptic ensign with whom he had shared some casual conversation, asked him: "Your folks?" and he found that his voice was too clotted with tears for him to answer. He nodded, hastily putting on sunglasses to camouflage his wet eyes. It was bred in them, Tom knew. The amalgam of joy and sorrow: baked into them in the cruel hard hills around Naples, in Lacedonia, in Avellino, in Salerno, in a hundred bitter, impoverished towns, where suffering and back-breaking labor were eternal and essential. By the time Tom had reached them, tugging at him, pulling him, kissing him wetly, with great heaving sobs, he had succumbed to blood. He was bawling.

"Oh, my baby!" his mother shrieked. "Oh, my baby boy! You're not hurt? Look at him! Look at him, Frank! He's so skinny!"

"He looks great, great," his father said. "Leave him alone, willya, Serafina? Watch out for his leg!"

"That's right!" his mother cried. "Angie! Get away from Tommy's leg!"

"Holy smoke, Mom," Tom protested. "I'm here one minute and you're starting already. Why don't you bawl me out for flying? It's so dangerous. I had asthma when I was little. Why didn't I take a train?"

"Tell 'er, Tommy," his father shouted. "You're out there killin' Japs and all she's worried about is do they feed you enough. Your old lady!"

"I *saw* you limping," she said with final authority. "I don't trust those doctors. You'll go to Dr. Bruno tomorrow for a checkup!"

"It's healed," Tom said, his voice rising. "I told you that in my letter. Besides, I get free treatment at the VA hospital. What's the matter, Mom, don't you believe anything I tell you?"

He had just arrived and they were screeching at each other already. It always offended his father. Anyone who yelled too much (like his wife) was a "mountain guinea"—they lived on mountain peaks and had to yell to make themselves heard. Frank punched his son playfully on the chest. He was anxious to divert the welcoming ceremonies from his wife's perpetual worrisome greediness.

"Hey, Tommy, look who else came out here," Frank said. "Grampa. Looks like a kid, doesn't he?"

He had not seen the old man, his father's father, standing to one side. He was a shriveled brown gnome, as hard as stale bread, possessed of all his teeth. He wore his hair in a trim *Umberto* and his mustaches were full and eggshell white. A faint affirmative nodding of his old skull (or was it palsy? Tom wondered) indicated that he knew what it was all about, that no special interpretations were needed for him. He wore an olive-drab shirt, a size too big, and a black, baggy suit that Tom remembered had been his own when he was a teen-ager. Tom hugged the desiccated, wiry body. The limbs and chest had turned to rock after a lifetime of swinging picks and shovels. He kissed his grandfather's cheek, wondering as he did, how much the old man, Savino Sorrento, had absorbed about his complicated, alien grandson—*football, the University, the Marines, the Japs.* How much had his parents been able to explain to this illiterate primitive, a man who could not even read or write his native Italian, who spoke the graceful tongue in the slurred rhythms of Napoli, and who had once lived in a hillside hovel older than Christ? Tom studied the coarse, healthy skin, the living white hair, and marveled at the miracle of change, the unbridgeable gaps that widened and deepened each year of their lives. *Grampa,* as they called him with middle-class American coziness, was not two generations removed from Captain Tom Sorrento, USMCR. He was two thousand years distant, gathering faggots on a limestone cliff above the Bay of Naples.

In the old Chevy they talked incessantly, trying to consume three years of incidents in a half-hour drive, drowning him in trivia and gossip. Esposito, the butcher, was a millionaire, his mother said bitterly. He had made a fortune in black-market meats, taken bribes, cultivated a new wealthy clientele with his steaks and roasts. Albert Lanfranconi had seen a big truck pull up at two in the morning and unload sides of beef at his back door. Esposito—who couldn't write his name and whose brother was in Riker's Island! Tom's older sister, Rita, he was informed, was going steady with Georgie Schultheis (*you know*—Georgie from around the corner). He was a yeoman in the Navy, working at 90 Church Street, and Tom sensed a rising note of pride in Frances' narration of their romance: Georgie was *not* an Italian, a circumstance that seemed to assure her of augmented status on the block. His father, coaxing the sluggish car over the Whitestone Bridge, confided that he had half a mind to retire from the force. He had been walking the beat twenty-six years without a promotion; what deterred him was a rumor that the city was going to raise pensions. It would be a shame if he quit just before pensions were increased. He had his eye on a good local business: an all-night service station on Tremont Avenue, whose owner was looking for a reliable partner to share the long hours. His mother broke in to volunteer a catalogue of misery. She was at her best conveying gloomy news, and in three years' time she had amassed a rich anthology of disaster.

"Your cousin Willie Costanza? You know? Mary Costanza's oldest boy? A *distant* cousin. You used to play with him when you were little. He had red hair. He was the *smart* one in that family. He had a scholarship to Fordham. *He* gets killed. In Germany. And his lousy brothers, they never give Mary anything but heartaches, they stayed in the United States, healthy as can be. It's always the good ones that get killed." She shook her head gravely from side to side. Tom looked at her square face. She had a granite chin; her hard features had once been beautiful. When she smiled (rarely now) her teeth were firm and white. A wispy mustache decked her upper lip and an outsized mole, one she had talked of having cauterized for as long as Tom could remember, nested on one cheek.

"Pete Potenza's little boy died," she continued. "Thirteen years old, from a bad heart. I heard the doctor who operated was responsible. He didn't know what he was doing. Yolande and Charlie Innocente—your father's cousin—they broke up. She ran off with the man she worked for doing embroidery. A Jewish man with a wife and children. The worst is our own neighborhood. I never saw so many spics in my life. They're all over. It's bad enough niggers three blocks away, but now spics."

Tom sighed audibly. She caught his disapproval and suspended her narration of doom. Angie, his little sister, took it up in a minor key.

"And the nerve of the Castle Hill Pool!" she cried. "Twenty-five dollars for a season ticket. Remember Tommy when we used to go the whole summer for five bucks?"

He remembered. And he remembered Tutwiler Avenue, where nothing had changed. Nothing short of razing, he felt as he got out of the car, would ever change that vista of semidetached yellow brick houses, two-story monoliths, boxlike and cheerless, built in the twenties, each with its narrow driveway, and plot of green hedges. Beyond the cement driveways, hutlike garages were visible. Their own home boasted a screened-in porch—a tribute to his father's skill at construction work. With a small shudder (he felt ashamed of himself later) he noticed that his father was flying the American flag to welcome him home. He had bought the flag many years ago at a Police Legion Post rally in Cincinnati. It was displayed at the slightest provocation—Columbus Day, family birthdays, events of national or local significance.

"What's the idea of the colors, Pop?" he asked.

His father took no offense. "Why not? It's *our* flag."

Tom accepted the simple explanation and dropped the matter. He wished he could feel the joy his father did at displaying the flag; he envied him. But he had had his share of flags, parades and loud music.

Across the street stretched a tangled expanse of empty lots; a mile beyond these sloped into a sluggish muddy creek that emptied into Long Island Sound. On the land opposite their home, Tutwiler Avenue's householders had staked out vegetable gardens. Long before the "victory garden" had become a wartime fad, Serafina had cultivated tomatoes and beans, Swiss chard, lettuce and escarole on the Bronx earth. And before that, in his childhood, he could remember his Grandmother Malfitano, his mother's mother, taking him into the weed-choked brush of the "lots" in search of wild *cicoria* and dandelion greens.

"I see you still have the garden, Mom," Tom said.

"Why not? With the prices the way they are? Me and Mrs. Del Balso are sharing it this year. You should have heard your father complain when I asked him to dig the ground up this spring. I swear, you'd think he was an old man."

"Ah!" Frank Sorrento said. "What's this? The old country? We gotta be farmers? She wanted I should start the grapes again!

That whole business with the wine presses. I had enough of that when I was a kid."

"Pop's right," Tom said. "Pressing grapes is for *ciuci.* We're all one hundred per cent Americans here. You can buy wine cheaper in the store."

Old Savino Sorrento, one parchment ear cocked to hear the argument in the alien tongue, unloosed a vigorous flood of Neapolitan. Something had aroused his hibernating temper.

"What did he say, Pop?" Tom asked.

His father laughed. "He said it's our fault the fig tree died. He's blaming me and your mother. He says we didn't bundle it up right, not enough newspapers and blankets and linoleum, so it froze to death. He's still mad about it."

"Good riddance," Serafina said. "It brought worms into the garden, that old thing."

The neighbors peered from windows and assembled on porches. One of the first to pound his back and pump his hand was Leo Mazzochi, nearsighted, dopey Leo, who had played in the same backfield with him in high school. Leo had been 4-F and had socked away plenty, as his mother put it, working in defense plants.

"Hey Tommy, boy!" Leo shouted. "Ya knocked off alla Japs so they let ya home! Boy, getta loada the fruit salad on the guy's chest! This guy's got bronze stars on toppa bronze stars! What's this one?"

"The Navy Cross, Leo. I won it when we had field day. The potato race."

"Getta loada him! Same old Tommy! With the jokes!"

The neighbors studied him as if he were a visiting celebrity. The silent and sour O'Hares, who had been his parents' tenants for twenty years, trooped out to nod their greetings. Looking at these dry and dismal people, Tom often wondered: where were all the jolly, witty, happy Irishmen he read about in books—or saw in movies? Old Mr. O'Hare, stale and bloodless, had the same quality as the bread and cakes he sold from a chain bakery truck. And there was Mr. Palermo, the wily old Sicilian, still porting himself around on crutches, a perpetual reminder (his legs were strong, firm and undamaged) of the ten thousand dollars he had wrenched from the Interborough Rapid Transit Company for damages in a subway crash fourteen years ago. He had won his case by hiding a piece of bleeding beef liver in the bandages around his calf. His hysterical pleas, commingled with the ruby flow on his leg, had frightened the IRT lawyers into settling.

A young woman was waving to him from an upper window and displaying a fat baby. It was Diana Trapani, the last neighborhood girl he had dated—way back in his sophomore year. She had once been the local beauty: clear of skin, black-eyed. Now her hair was undone; large blue circles weighted her eyes. During the war years she had married Ralphie Trapani, who despite prolonged sea duty with the Atlantic Fleet, had taken advantage of his furloughs to endow her with three children.

"What a *doll!*" Diana shouted. "Look at him! A captain already!"

His mother hustled him into the house. He was too precious a prize to suffer these familiarities. On the porch, he noticed Mrs. Santangelo, *La Signora,* still sitting on the stoop, still rocking, still reading her *Daily News.* She had waved white hair and wore pince-nez; a widow of some means, a legend had grown up surrounding her past. She nodded graciously at Tom.

"Hello, Mrs. Santangelo," he said. "You look younger."

"Very nice to see you home," she said quietly.

Serafina favored her with a few words; *La Signora* was always treated with respect. They made it inside the screen door just as old Palermo came hobbling up the steps. The girls made sure it was locked, and ignored the neighbor's attempts to open it. Everyone did that to Palermo: if you didn't cut him off he'd have you by the ear for the next hour, bragging how he cheated the IRT, and how he and his sons used the money to start a machine shop.

"Well, here we are," Serafina said. "Everything's like you left it. I been after your father to paint and wallpaper but he keeps putting it off. If it isn't his feet it's his back."

The familiar cramped rooms, overdecorated and heavily furnished, enveloped him like a gust of steam. The sun-faded maroon drapes, the graceless dark furniture, the spurious Oriental rugs, the gloomy pink wallpaper with its counterfeit Fragonards mincing and bowing—it was not part of the dream. The repeated, vigorous reminders from his parents on how *great* it was to be home, that anything he wanted was his, set him to wondering again about the fantasies of the landing barges and the beaches. How could he ever explain to them that he had slept in the finest hotels in San Francisco, in Los Angeles, in Auckland? That he had been an officer and a gentleman, a man of status, who spent big and lived big? Now, confined to the lower-middle-class dullness of his father's house, tremulous doubts about his future gripped him.

"You go to your room and get washed up and take a rest," his mother said. "I'm making *lasagna.*"

His sisters followed him, worshipful, into his room.

"Leave Tommy alone, willya?" she cried after them—but they were hypnotized by him. His room looked out on a timeless vista of garage, clothesline and faded fence. He had forgotten how small the room was—smaller than the narrow scholarship room he had lived in during his first two years at the University. The girls buzzed and flitted about him, fingering his garrison cap, forcing him to describe every ribbon on the tunic, inspecting his wounded leg with proprietary interest. They rummaged through his Valpak, spilling dirty underwear on the floor, squealing with delight at the squares of brightly colored Japanese silk he had gotten on Saipan for them. With pride, they located the scuffed leather toilet kit they had given him three years ago.

"We saw your picture in the newsreels!" Angie said. She was sixteen and would have been pretty, except for the same abundant nose that her brother once had. "Mama almost fainted when she saw you in front of the barge!"

"You shoulda seen her!" Rita said. "Grabbing people all around her and hollering that was her son! I swear, she made everyone go to that movie three times to see you in the newsreels!"

Angie yanked his trouser leg up. "Can I touch it? Does it hurt?" she asked, with horrified delight.

"Cut it out!" he said. "What is this? Medical inspection?"

"Oooh. It's all white and scaly! Rita, look at it!"

Rita shuddered. *"Ick.* Leave him alone, willya Angie? Honestly, I never saw such a pest. I told her if she got herself some boy friends and worked off all that energy she wouldn't be such a pest."

"I bet it hurts, but he won't admit it," Angie insisted.

"It doesn't hurt," Tom said, "It feels great. It's all healed. Now will you stop rolling my pants up?"

He was back in the unmistakable teasing, badgering rhythms of family life. The change in roles made him momentarily happy: two months ago he was shouting obscene oaths at his young killers, disciplining them, punishing them, making his authority manifest with every order. Now he was reduced to bickering with his sisters. He appreciated the comical manner in which his power had shriveled.

The girls peppered him with endless questions about the war, about Tarawa and Saipan and Iwo. Angie wanted to know if he knew any nice handsome young Marines in the Bronx. He could hear his mother slamming and stomping around the kitchen; she worked with fury. The inevitable groaning meal was in preparation. Leo Mazzochi and his father were matching shots of Imperial, waiting for him to join them.

The girls followed him when he went to wash, lingering in the bathroom door. He studied his face, making mental comparisons with the faded high school football picture he had just seen in his room. They were different men. He was handsome now: the trim blunt nose, the lean contours of the sun-hardened face, the dark sad eyes. Why should he worry about his future? There wasn't anything he couldn't do.

"Whatcha gonna do now, Tommy?" Rita asked.

His face white with lather, he looked up at her accusingly. "Never mind about me. What's this I hear about you quitting Hunter? Pop saved the money just so you could go."

Rita wrinkled her nose; she was a mutation—her hair dusty blond, her eyes metallic gray. "Georgie and I are getting married in September. Who needs college? All those creeps there. I'll probably go to work at Metropolitan for a year or so."

He slapped his face vigorously with hot water. "Big deal. With all the other Italian girls who won't get jobs anywhere else. You're a smart kid. Why don't you stay in college? You could be a schoolteacher. Or at least learn *something*. What's the hurry about getting married?"

Rita pouted. "Georgie's gonna give me a ring. Seven hundred dollars."

Tom gave up; he was a stranger. He knew the pattern: the expensive wedding ring, the big, catered wedding, the honeymoon in Bermuda. By then both participants had cleaned out their savings. They settled down to day-by-day budgeting, never capable of imbuing the practical, functional aspect of marriage with the roseate glow, the fairy-tale joy of engagement and nuptial rites. Tom had made his mind up years ago: he'd get married by the City Clerk.

He brushed his crew-cut vigorously. A Navy Stores wristwatch sparkled on one thick wrist.

"I made Arista," Angie said.

"That's great," Tom said. "Bet your marks are better than mine ever were. I was too busy with sports all the time."

"You're the biggest hero they ever had at high school," Angie said proudly. "Mr. Feigenbaum made a speech about you in Assembly. He asked me if you'd come and speak some Friday. And on the bulletin board outside the principal's office—you know, on the third floor—they tacked up the article about you in the *Bronx Home News*. The time when you captured the eighteen Japs."

"They weren't Japs. They were Korean laborers."

"What a riot he is," Rita said. "He knocks everything he ever does. Everything's a joke to him."

As always, there was too much food, enough to have fed liberally twice as many people. (Was it, Tom wondered, a reminder that not too long ago they never had enough to eat, nor sufficient variety?) It amused Tom that his mother's cooking, while superb, was conditioned largely by what the women's magazines considered the American festive board. There was invariably a stuffed turkey, as irrelevant as the Yankee relishes and vegetables, and the potatoes—both white and sweet. There was, of course, a *pasta*—spaghetti or ravioli, or as on this occasion, *lasagna*—but it was served *after* the soup and *before* the roast. The *lasagna,* Tom felt, was much too good to deserve this secondary billing. His mother made it in cunningly devised layers (Frank said you needed a contractor to set it up), laced with rich *ricotta* and stringy *mozzarella,* spiced with elusive pine nuts, all of it inundated in ruby-red tomato sauce, a thick decoction that had spent half a day simmering on the stove, an amalgam of tomato paste, tomato sauce, whole stewed tomatoes, basil leaf, oregano, and scented Italian sausage and zesty meatballs. (It further upset Tom that his family insisted on calling this glorious sauce *gravy. Gravy,* he explained to them patiently, was a Yankee American *goy* expression. *Gravy* was thick brown tasteless goo that Americans put on fried meat or mashed potatoes to disguise the bad taste. It did no good. *Gravy* it remained). The meal, Tom knew, was a masterpiece of acculturation. Old-country customs lingered, new traditions emerged. For example, after the *lasagna* had been served (it was eaten out of a soup bowl, in great bloody squares) the *gravy* meats were sampled from a separate bowl—the garlicky meatballs and the sausage, fragrant with anise. Here was a true hangover from ancient days of poverty in Naples: pasta was cheap, so you filled everyone up with it, leaving the meat for last. What meats remained could be saved for another meal, another stewpot.

Tom had never been a trencherman, and by the time he had eaten two meatballs from the "gravy," he had little heart left for the turkey, the endless parade of vegetables. In the crowded dining room, he grew impatient with Leo Mazzochi's locker-room banter, the painfully repeated anecdotes about their high school days (serving only to remind Tom how he had failed them in college).

"Hey, Tommy, remember that champeenship game with Evander?" Leo shouted. They were cramped around the narrow table and the room seemed to have shrunk, yet everyone shouted. "Boy, do I remember it! Tommy gettin' his shoulder dislocated on the first play and still stayin' in!"

"I remember that one all right," Frank said. "I got all the clippings still. Wait I'll find 'em—" He started to rise from his high-backed chair at the head of the table. Tom touched his arm. "Forget it, Pop," he said. "Some other time. It'll just remind me how ugly I was."

Everyone laughed. Tom mopped his forehead. A plate of redolent mushrooms, fried black in olive oil, was passed under his nose. The rich, oily smell made him gag. He excused himself and took a five-minute break on the porch.

It occurred to him, after four days of lounging about the house, that he was more of an alien than ever. The fissure that had begun in college was now a widening gap. The tragedy of it, the gnawing pain, was that love and warmth abided. These were things that had always been taken for granted in their noisy, outgoing family. There had always been much hugging and kissing, tears and hysteria; it was honest and deep-rooted, and it held them together. The maddening things were the externals, the nuances of everyday life: these had become the hinges of their relationship. He found himself increasingly, and shamefully, bothered by them. Georgie Schultheis' white-on-white shirt, a cheap imitation of what he imagined to be Broadway high fashion, upset him terribly; he did not have the heart to tell Rita. It bothered him as much as her decision to quit college. His mother, ever the ruling force of the household, kept dropping sly comments about their rich friends in Pelham, the Gagliardos, and the nice daughter they had, who was dying to meet Tommy. With a surge of guilt, Tom envisioned her in his mind's eye: heavily made up and overdressed. It was his father's appeals that pained him the most. He wanted nothing more than to have his son join his American Legion post, to meet the boys over a few beers. Frank had served with the Seventy-seventh New York in World War I; he was a charter member of the police post. He could not understand why Tom refused him this small request. "A great buncha guys," Frank said. "Not just punks like me. Lawyers, judges. Magistrate Fragente is a member. He comes to all the meetings." Tom was unmoved.

What they did not seem to understand (and how explain it?) was that even before his Marine duty, four years at the University had made him a stranger. The petty tyrannies of daily life, the modes of dress and speech, a matter as simple as calling a Negro a "boogie," had thrown a curtain between them. As an undergraduate, he would make the short trip from the University to East Harlem to visit his grandfather. In his brown tweed jacket and gray flannels, his clipped hair, he was as obvious as if he were nude. The boys at the bar, the policy runners and bookies, the funeral-parlor kings and pizzeria owners, knew who he was—Frank Sorrento's kid Tommy, the one who played football. But they studied him as a curio, a freak, a strayer from the proper routines of life. And now he had traveled, commanded men, held the power of life and death over them, killed enemies. His parents' bickering over new wallpaper, the envious comments about the Gagliardos, his father's pathetic complaints about the force (loving it and hating it) all engendered in him a floundering pity, a knowledge that for all his education, and despite the bright captain's bars on his shoulders, he could not aid or comfort them.

His father, on the eight-four trick, would come home in early afternoon, complaining about the desk sergeant, the shoofly, some hoodlums on the beat. He would join Tom on the screened porch and they would sit there sipping beer until dinner time. There were long, aching pauses as they spoke; beyond the marshes and the river, in reddish haze, they could see the jagged New York skyline.

"The good old summertime," his father said. "I rented the cottage up at Cairo again. There's room for you if you wanna come for a week. Rita ain't goin'."

"No thanks, Pop."

"Well, seein' how you have nothin' else to do . . . "

"You worried about me, Pop? The unemployed son?"

"Naah. I was just wonderin'. You gotta decide pretty soon. You never tell me or your mother anything about your plans. Don't get me wrong. I'm not criticizing. We'd just like to help. You know, anything . . ."

Tom laughed. Frank had a long, hard, perpetually unhappy face. He was a good cop, an honest cop. He had spent his life watching people at their ugliest, taking abuse, suffering disappointments, exposing what was essentially a soft and sympathetic nature to the harsh, abrasive dwellers of the slum. He had never shot a man, although the opportunity had presented itself on many occasions. "Give 'em the stick around the arms and the back," he confided once to Tom. "That usually stops 'em. Why should I kill anyone?"

"Your mother and me were wondering. Maybe you could go into business up here. If I retire, I got my eye on that filling station. Mulcahy owns it now. On East Tremont. You and me—we could do good together."

"I'm no businessman. I wonder if you are. We're Neapolitans. We make good civil servants. There'd be some Sicilian around the corner who'd put us out of business in a week."

His father got up creakily and sat on the edge of the porch. He was a big-boned, powerful man, still heavy with strength at forty-eight.

"You think of stayin' in the Marines?" he asked. "It could be worse. A captain already."

"I've had the Marines. Besides, with this bum leg, they wouldn't want me."

His father's tanned face furrowed. "Now don't get sore at me. I got a good suggestion to make. Just don't get sore." He folded his mahogany arms. "You could go on the force."

"Me? A cop?"

"Listen to me, Tommy. A college man like you—with your personality and your war record. You'd get veteran's preference on the exams right off. They're lookin' for smart young guys, educated men. No lunkheads like me. All kinds of special work for them now. Why those exams would be a pipe for you! You'd make Inspector in no time. It could be a great career for you."

Tom, politely as possible, turned his father's third suggestion down. He knew what Frank was thinking. The force was a religion, a passion. He was a man who had not had the advantages of an eighth-grade education. He had sat for hours under a tree in Morningside Park, mastering the mysteries of simple arithmetic so that he could pass the police examination. He had just barely made it, scoring a low grade on the written test. What had cinched the job for him was his superb showing on the physical: the running, jumping and weight-lifting were child's play for him after years of pick-and-shovel work. But in all his years of service, promotion eluded him. He never made sergeant. Tom could remember sitting in the old Ford outside the Delehanty Institute, on wintry nights, waiting for his father, who was inside studying for the sergeants' test. Year after year he attended the special school; just as regularly he would fail the exam. He loved the force the way other men loved women, or wealth or land. It seemed to Tom the ultimate injustice, the vilest of oversights, that Frank never got his stripes. He felt again the choking sadness for him, the tongueless affection.

"Look, Pop," he said. "I could never pound a beat. You know that." Then, seeing the hurt in his father's morose face, he added quickly: "Hell, you know what I mean. Giving people orders, having to be responsible for them. Now you, you're *il patrone*. It comes to you naturally. Those walyos on Van Nest Avenue would never get the *bocce* tournament organized if they didn't have you to do it."

Frank drained his beer. He ran a massive hand through his thinning, almost white hair. "Yeah, I guess you're right. You have to really be interested in your work. Me, I never wanted anything else but to wear the uniform." He looked intently at his son. "I dunno, Tommy, maybe I shouldn't say it, but it's like you don't care about anything."

"What do you mean?"

"I don't know exactly. You don't care. I mean about getting ahead. Not just now, but even in college. Now don't get sore at me, Tommy—it's like I never figured out what you studied for. Now I can understand, Fred Gagliardo's kid, he studied for a doctor. But you—"

"I don't blame you, Pop. It was what they call a liberal-arts course. They don't even know what it is."

His father shrugged. "All them years in college, I'm not knocking it. But at least if you could go to medical school, or be a lawyer..."

"You're right. I guess I just went to college, and that's all."

"Mr. Engstrom would help you," his father said eagerly. "He

used to call here every six months to check up when you was away. You should go see him."

Serafina called from the living room: "Come and get it!" Tom winced: another acculturated trait. The slang of the lumber camp had found a home in the East Bronx. Why didn't his mother say it in Italian?

As he knew he must, he returned to the University. Footloose, disoriented, he discovered he had no friends, no associations on Tutwiler Avenue. There were only his family and Leo, and what could he discuss with them after the old stories had been rehashed? His mother, he soon learned, had taken to investing small sums of money in the stock market, an avocation she worked at constantly and with considerable shrewdness. She had taken some of their savings, and the insurance money she had received when her father died, and had placed it in the market. She read esoteric newsletters and pored over the financial page of the New York *Times* (because of her interest in stocks it had replaced the *News*—much to the grumbling of the girls) and once a week she visited a branch brokerage office on Fordham Road. Tom would see her, her eyes bright and intense behind rimless spectacles, crouched over the latest inside dope from some securities house, making notations with a pencil stub. He marveled at her. In a way, he was pleased with her new dedication. It served to diminish—if not replace—her rapacious proprietary feelings about him, the darling, delicate, favored son.

On the campus, protocol dictated a visit to Engstrom. He found the coach grayer and leaner, but still the same austere, self-created monument who so thoroughly dominated the University's meagre athletic picture. Tom sat again in the holy office and they discussed teammates who had also served in the Marines, many of them now dead or maimed, others still in the Pacific awaiting return. It was amazing the way Engstrom knew where every boy was, what they were doing, what plans he had to assist them when they got back. He assumed the responsibility for the direction of their lives—whether they wanted him to or not.

"I keep busy," Engstrom said to Tom. "I've just arranged for Frank Neal to go to medical school. You know how tough it is. I picked up the phone and discussed it with Dean McAdams. There was no question about Frank going after he makes up a few credits in chemistry. Charlie Karpinski is slated for law school. And so is Ted deVito."

These were not idle boasts on Engstrom's part. A phone call from this lonely, illiterate man could effect miracles of higher education. No boy of his was ever turned down by the severest of medical schools; once they were in, of course, they had to make it on their own. But the difficult problem of admission (particularly since some of them were not quite able to compete on equal terms with the hordes of eager, grinding pre-meds) was overcome with rare ease. In dozens of giant corporations around the country, there were boys of Engstrom's, placed there by the coach. It had always struck Tom as a trifle unfair. He knew, for example, that Frank Neal was a knucklehead. That business about "extra credits" in chemistry meant he had never passed it, had barely got his baccalaureate. But Neal, stupid and undeserving, would go to medical college. Somewhere, Tom felt with growing indignation, there was a slouching, nearsighted, brilliant Jew (probably at CCNY) who would never reach med school because of one of Engstrom's guards or tackles.

The unstated offer to assist Tom was politely acknowledged. He assured the coach that only his own indecision, his own uncertainties prevented him from availing himself of his generosity. They had lunch at the Faculty Club, sitting at a window overlooking the squalor and savagery of Harlem, and talked football. Engstrom knew all about Tom's Marine service; he even knew that Tom had been the first-string fullback on the Quantico team. This was no mean attainment; it was a bruising squad, jeweled with professionals and college stars. Engstrom talked with unaccustomed vigor about Tom's Marine coach, the offensive system they had used. It seemed to Tom a crude, belated apologia for the dreadful humiliation he had inflicted on him five years ago. Soon Engstrom was complaining (almost whining, it appeared) about the drain on his supply of athletes, the consistently bad teams he had fielded. Tom found himself pitying the man. He would forgive Engstrom the past; that was easy. He had a lot more difficulty accepting him in the present. The man's one-track seriousness, his numb worship of a game played by twenty-two men in leather hats and padded pants rendered him unreachable, insulated.

They parted on the street. Engstrom, before leaving, made explicit his desire to assist Tom. What did he want? Law school? Business school? Journalism? No problem at all. A phone call to the Dean. . . . Or maybe Tom didn't want to go back to the University. Was he interested in advertising? Sales? He was well connected with several of the better banks and insurance companies; his boys were always welcome. Come to think of it, old Fred Foster, '22, was in the market for a bright young lad, preferably an ex-officer, to handle his . . . Tom, embarrassed by his own negative responses, thanked him generously. He promised to contact Engstrom when he made up his mind.

He suddenly felt impelled to leave the campus. The pangs of nostalgia, of good times remembered, were more than he could bear. In the fine spring weather, the grim red-brick piles, crowned with their evergreen copper roofs, overwhelmed him with a sense of things lost, irretrievable, never to be experienced and enjoyed again. He had loved the University, unashamedly and frankly, loved the severe buildings and the starved sprinkling of trees, the libraries, the gloomy classrooms, the stark offices of the professors. He wanted to visit the rathole office of the undergraduate literary magazine where he and Feeney had talked about Joyce (only five years ago, yet it seemed a lifetime) and then he remembered that the little quarterly had died without protest in the war years, a victim of the paper shortage. There were a half-dozen professors he wanted to see, but these calls would have to wait. The bright, poignant reminiscences of his undergraduate days could be ingested only in milligrams, with intervals of blandness in between. He was like a liberated concentration-camp inmate suddenly offered a feast; too much rich food might destroy him.

Each austere building, harboring its wealth of knowledge; the cheerless dormitories where he had lived during football season; the satellite stores—bookshops, greasy spoons, drugstores—all these reminded him of a hundred pleasant, tender, meaningless associations. He thought less of the ideas he had absorbed, the excitement of learning, than of the treasured trivia that endow college life with its comforting texture. He would have to come back later; the sights, the noises of the Heights were making him giddy. He turned off a side street and headed toward the curving drive above the park. It was a street he barely knew—a neighborhood of high, dusty apartments where faculty members and graduate students lived. In front of one monolith, evidently assigned to naval trainees, a midshipman in brassard and puttees threw him a snappy highball. Tom smiled and acknowledged the courtesy. He was jubilant, bouncy with freedom: all that was behind him. The ritual, the savagery, the blind obedience, the unlistening superiors, the omnipresent chance of death and mutilation—all this was gone forever. His marvelous good luck astounded him. He had been part of it, made his sacrifice, come through a modest hero. Returning the salute to the pale young boy, he felt a rush of sorrow for him. If you had to go through the nonsense, it was better to do it when it counted.

A tall heavy man and a young woman came out of the adjacent building—a similar Gothic apartment house, but one uncommandeered by the Navy. Tom recognized Hall Maitland at once. The anthropologist was unchanged: the lurching, wobbly gait, the great gut atop broomstick legs, the cropped sandy hair, the face flushed with vascular pressure and alcohol.

"You remember me, Dr. Maitland?" Tom asked. "I took Anthro 1-2 with you. About six years ago."

Maitland appraised the uniform: the captain's bars, the ribbons. He was a social scientist who got on famously with the military, a serious thinker who was ready to admit that not all generals are despots and dolts. He had served with distinction in the Argonne in the First World War, and had, in most unscholarly fashion, liked uniforms and martial honors ever since.

"I think I do," Maitland said. "You were one of Mr. Engstrom's young men. Weren't you on that labor gang he sent up to Armonk the summer I set up the University Field Museum?"

"That's right," Tom laughed. "Strong back, good candidate for an NYA job. I dropped some kind of Peruvian jug and I thought you'd kill me."

"I certainly remember you, Captain. But I'm darned if I know your name."

"Sorrento. Tom Sorrento. I was in the class of '42."

"Of course. Oh, excuse me. This is my daughter, Martha. Martha—Captain Sorrento."

She smiled—a flat noncommittal alteration of her lips. "Hello." She was a slender, graceful girl in her early twenties.

"How do," Tom said. "I was just wandering around—" His voice was suddenly stiff and strained. What was the matter with him? How big a dope could he be? He was twenty-six, a big hero, an officer. Why couldn't he speak up?

"Martha was a novitiate at our woman's college across the tracks," Maitland said. "Perhaps you knew her there?"

"I never dated college girls," Tom said defensively.

"A wise policy," Maitland said. "In my undergraduate days

I favored nurses, Salvation Army girls and employees of the New Jerusalem Dye Works."

"He's bragging again," Martha Maitland said. "Didn't he use that line during his lectures? For goodness sakes, Hall, the man's back on the campus *one day* and you're trying out all the old wheezes on him. Besides, he's an alumnus now. He doesn't *have* to listen."

"Oh, I don't mind. I was going to drop in on Dr. Maitland anyway."

She asked: "Back from the war for good?"

"I hope so. The Marines should spring me soon. I have a game leg—I was thinking of going to graduate school—maybe starting in the summer session, or waiting until fall."

"*Which* school?" Maitland asked challengingly.

"You'll think I'm crazy," Tom said. "But I don't know. I figure since the government'll pay for it, and I've got a disability pension, I might as well. I might learn something. And there's nothing I can earn a living at now anyway."

"Now that's refreshing, isn't it, Hall?" Martha asked the professor. "Here's a man who just wants to learn, no strings attached. No eye on the future, no pet theories, just interested in getting educated. You ought to grab him for the department of old bones and mud huts."

"It's not that refreshing for *me*," Tom protested.

Maitland had barely heard his daughter's denigration of his sphere of knowledge. He was studying Tom closely: the hard, square face, the varicolored tributes to bravery on the forest-green chest.

"What islands did you hit?" he asked.

"Tarawa. Saipan, Iwo. I picked up some mortar shell on Iwo and was sent back."

"Did you get to Palau? I did an interesting turn in Micronesia in the thirties."

"I flew over it a few times. Babel-thorp, the place with the limestone cliffs."

Maitland chuckled: some esoteric recollection of mysterious Palau, some happy memories about the All-Men House, a ritual giveaway, or perhaps merely an evening of quietude, chewing betel nut with his dear friend Chief Bugulroo, evoked the laughter. "Palau," he said. "Dear, dear Palau. I suppose by now my dark friends know all about Rita Hayworth and Coca-Cola."

"I guess so. Those that were left by the time the Nips and our artillery got through with them."

He turned thoughtfully to his daughter. "Remind me to get in touch with Altmeyer in Washington about Micronesia. They'll be needing help there, and I wouldn't mind a quick junket. See some of the old friends."

"You might be disappointed," Tom said. "Lots of those little islands—there just aren't any gooks left."

"Any *what?*" Martha asked.

"Gooks. Wogs. Little people."

She appeared shocked; Maitland laughed. "My daughter, Captain, suffers from exposure to the liberal dogma. She resents the use of the pejorative generic for any ethnic group."

"I guess she's right. I don't particularly like any one calling me a wop."

"But it depends on who does the calling, isn't that the truth, Captain? I'm sure you meant no offense calling the Palauans and the Saipanese gooks. I'm afraid that's what they are. And wogs, for that matter. When the Captain and I use these terms, Martha, we use them with affection."

Maitland started to lurch off. He turned around. "Sorrento, drop in and see me some afternoon. I'm still over in Detering Hall. Just the other side of the diorama of Grand Canyon. I'd like to talk to you about the islands. Maybe I can help you on this notion you have about going back to school!"

He left them. His daughter looked at Tom curiously. "You're in trouble, *now,*" she said. "He'll get his hooks in you and have you putting old pots together."

"What does he do? Run his own recruiting service for the anthropology department?"

She had started walking downtown, and with a naturalness that surprised him, he escorted her. The prospect of strolling the Heights, where once he had studied and known delights, in the company of a beautiful young woman, thrilled him. The uniform was almost (not quite, but almost) as gratifying as the freshman numerals he had once worn; his companion of five years later, he had to admit, was much prettier than any of the student nurses from St. Francis' he had dated.

"My father doesn't think much of most graduate students, and what with the war, he's reduced to old ladies and 4-F boys. He calls the graduate departments the League of Lame and Halt." She looked grave. "I'm sorry—I forgot about your leg."

"Don't feel sorry. It's the cheapest, most satisfying wound a man could get. It's much milder."

"Well, if you don't mind talking about it—I think that's what appealed to Hall. The wound. And the medals. He's like a small boy. His complaint is that most graduate schools are filled with misfits, what he calls *unrelated* people. People who can't make an impression on the world outside the University. That's why he'd like to trap you and get you inside Detering Hall."

She turned the corner. "I'm headed for the subway and my job."

"Job? What kind of job starts at three in the afternoon?"

"Newspaper girl. I write for a press association."

"I'll walk you. May I?"

"I wish you would."

They crossed the street. Around them rose the gloomy caves of learning, starker than modern prisons, built of strong, immortal materials: granite, copper, limestone and hardwoods. On the outdoor running track and athletic field to their left, a company of midshipmen drilled to the inane *hup-toop-threep-forp!* Tom guessed that no one played softball or touch football on the field any more. In his undergraduate days they used to play fierce intramural games there; once he had won the college softball championship for his team (it was managed by Immerman and was called The Royal Cuban Giants) by slamming a mighty home run over the tennis courts. The game had been against the college fraternity champs and the victory had given Tom particular pleasure because the opponents were what he called "blond Aryan Jerks—big crewmen." The memory was so real, so much with him, that he swallowed.

"What class did you say you were in?" Martha Maitland asked. Her upturned face was pale and perfect. Only a careless smudge of lipstick infringed on its inherent loveliness.

"Nineteen forty-two," he said. *"Hoity-toity, Christ o-mighty, who the hell are you? Biff-bam, goddam, we are the boys of forty-two!* Our class cheer. See the things a college education does for you?"

"I'll bet you were a card. Big Man on Campus."

"I was the confused type. What class were you in?"

"I would have been class of forty-five. I'd be over there right now getting fitted for a cap and gown and all that tearful idiocy. But I quit last fall and went to work. I felt useless going to interpretive-dancing classes. It was a dreadful bore, I guess, because we've lived up in this neighborhood as long as I can remember and all our friends have been University people. I wanted to know someone who hadn't passed the doctor's oral, or didn't have a stack pass."

"What did Papa say when you tapped out?"

"He was neutral. He's always neutral. It shocked my mother. She was a leading alumna. She judges the poetry contest every year and advises the Library Committee."

"A real educated family. Nothing but brains."

She laughed. "Not really. I'm only half brainy. My parents are and I'm *not*—like the fellow who claimed he was half Jewish."

A round, beefy boy who had played guard for the freshmen when Tom was a senior, greeted him. He looked with appraising, appreciative eyes at Marty and exchanged small talk with Tom: *Yes, he had seen Engstrom, yes he knew that Frank Sebastiano was killed in Germany, no he had no plans. . . .* When the boy left, Martha studied him, with a small, mocking smile.

"I did guess it. You *were* a Big Man on Campus."

"I was a third-string back. The only football player who got beat running for Student Council. And once I wrote a story for the magazine. I was a carpetbagger from the Bronnix, yet."

"A what?"

"A carpetbagger. A commuter, a home boy. I lived in the dormitory only during the football season. And I never owned a black knitted tie."

She stopped at the newsstand outside the subway station and bought all four afternoon papers, fumbling for change in a scuffed suede bag large enough to tote a child in. "I'm on night rewrite this week," she said. "And because we're a third-rate press association, we have to steal all our news. There's no news like old news. I brief myself on the ride down."

She extended a thin, unmanicured hand to him. He grasped it, sensing as he did a delicious, unearned thrill. The world was good and full and promising, and this exquisite girl, the comforting haven of the University, her famed father—somehow all of them would be involved in the inevitable happy future life of Tom Sorrento.

"Listen," he said. "I want to see you tonight. My time is worth nothing and I have too much terminal leave pay." He was delighted with his own sureness.

"I'd love to see you. But I work until eleven. They don't normally have women on night rewrite, but this is war."

"I'll meet you a little before eleven. At your office. Where is it?"

"The *Record* Building. On East Forty-ninth, over near First Avenue. We're on the sixth floor—*World News*. Or ask any drunk. We can meet in a saloon if you'd prefer."

"No. I'd like to see what the home folks have been saying about us heroes. Maybe you can introduce me to the guy who invented Mom's blueberry pie."

"I can't, but we have a man who hung up when he got the tip on Pearl Harbor. Fellow said to him: 'The Japs bombed Pearl Harbor' and he said: 'Stop kidding me' and hung up."

"And today that boy is Richard Harding Davis, right?"

"I'll see you at eleven. I've forgotten your name."

"Tom. Tom Sorrento. As in the song."

"Fine. I'm Marty."

He watched her disappear through the turnstile and down the dusty steps. The dream was taking form, assuming dimension. The great anticipatory fantasy, the obsessive wishes about what-was-going-to-be, all these were on the verge of realization. This woman had to be his: he had earned her. He was a hero. He had survived. Crossing the campus again, he debated the merits of the uniform against a sports jacket and slacks for the evening. He decided in favor of the Marine greens.

The New York office of World News appalled him. It was not merely dingy and dirty, it had a look of defeat, a neglect growing out of corruption and despair. He walked through a scarred fire door into a long room crammed with sagging desks. At a long table near the front of the dimly lit room (the walls were stained and the plaster cracked) a crosseyed copy boy, puffing a White Owl, was rhythmically inserting carbons into books of yellow onionskin. He had decorated his work table, Tom noticed, with portraits of hockey players, and the inconsistency of it bothered him: why hockey players in late spring? Was there anyone other than Canadians who really liked hockey players?

"Watcha got?" he asked Tom rudely. "Handouts? Leave 'em here."

"I'm looking for Miss Maitland."

"She's allaway at the back. Next to the juice machine."

Tom started down a narrow passageway between a series of desks and a bank of clattering teleprinters. The noise was deafening; nothing had been done in the way of soundproofing to muffle the idiot chatter. Halfway down the passageway, three desks were placed to form a *U*. Opposite these, three teletype transmitters were being operated by men in shirt-sleeves and green eye shades. At each desk in the *U* was an editor, typing furiously, all liberally smeared with carbon. One man had tucked yellow paper in his belt and fashioned paper cuffs to protect himself.

The rear of the office was a clutter of supply cabinets, vending machines, haphazard stacks of old newspapers. Two desks, considerably smaller and filthier than those at the front of the office, were wedged back-to-back in the gloom. A short, fat boy, perhaps eighteen, was seated at one of them, reading copy. He had a mottled rosy face and wore a half-dozen automatic pencils in the pocket of his violet sports shirt. Marty was at the other desk. She was typing vengefully on a rattling upright. A headset was clamped around her short brown hair and she was listening, typing, and asking questions with a febrile speed that astounded Tom.

"He *what?*" she was saying. "He refused to give any other names at present? Yes, I have that. Go on, Phil. Yes, I got that about the two other suspects. . . . Yes Phil, you gave me that. I'll read it back. . . . *Falcone, 34, has a long record of arrests ranging from assault with a deadly weapon to burglary in the night season . . . he was paroled in 1940 and has a wife and three children living in Queens Village.* All of this is from Detective Sergeant Harmon, is that right? One hundred second Precinct? Anything else? Well, Phil, I can't help it . . . Hoag is screaming his head off . . . AP was out with this a half-hour ago. I can't help it if you're the only World News man covering the case . . . you should be used to *that* by now. . . ."

She winked a greeting at Tom, took off the headset and put a fresh book of onionskin into the typewriter. "I'll be just a minute, Tom. I have to knock out a new lead for the desk. They've just picked up a suspect in the Forest Hills Bank robbery. You can talk to Howie while I work, then we'll go. Howie Markowitz . . . Tom Sorrento."

The fat boy shook hands limply. "Just get back?" he asked.

"About a month ago." He looked around the dusty, poorly lit office. "Is this the whole World News Association? Right here?"

"The New York headquarters. The heartbeat. It's poor but dishonest."

"Everything comes out of here? All the news you people cover?"

"*What* cover?" Howie whined. "We steal it. Me and Marty here, we're the brains of the whole operation. We rewrite the dayside report. Then the overnight comes in and rewrites the nightside. And so on. Now and then we steal from the New York *Times*, the *Britannica*, my mother's Hadassah newsletter. Anything in writing, we'll steal."

"Okay, take out the needle."

"No, I'm leveling, Cap. Why not? The readers don't know the difference. The editors and publishers don't even know. How else can we stay in business? All a paper has to get right are the ball scores, anyway."

Marty slammed the trembling typewriter a few times, then yanked the yellow booklet from its nervous roller. She reached for her bag. "Just let me drop this at the desk, Tom, and we're off."

Howie Markowitz looked at her sorrowfully. "You do the piece about the cat wedged in the wall in Jersey City? The one Hoag thought was a cute human-interest story?"

"I left it for you, Howie. You're so much better with that bright, lively material. I have no sense of humor."

"Thanks loads," the boy said glumly. "All I need now is MacArthur should issue another communiqué. I'll be here till one A.M. You like MacArthur, Cap?"

Tom shrugged. "He never did me anything. They used to say no one ever beat him ashore except the photographer."

"Yeh," Markowitz agreed, "and I bet it was a WNA man at that."

Tom helped Marty into her tweed jacket. They proceeded down the aisle to the *U*-shaped group of desks. The man at the center desk took the copy from her without looking up. He read it silently, quickly, made a few angry notations on it with a stylus and then threw it to the Teletype operator on his right.

"Bulletin this," he said sourly. He looked up at Marty as if his mouth were filled with vinegar. "We're dead on that one," he said in a loud, embittered voice. "Biggest goddam city in the world and I can't even get a man assigned to police headquarters permanently. Leave it to those bastards on the *Record,* our sister enterprise, to phone us last."

"You can't blame them, Ed," Marty said. "They don't get a penny extra for calling us when we haven't got our own man on a story."

Tom, standing behind Marty, with his back against a glassed-in private office, was aware that the man was squinting at him with rude curiosity. He was a handsome man of middle age, his sharp features corroded by dyspepsia and cynicism. His coppery skin and tarry hair suggested an Indian done in by cheap whiskey.

"Who's your friend, Maitland?" he asked crossly.

Marty drew her breath in faintly. "This is Tom Sorrento. Tom—Ed Hoag. Mr. Hoag is the fastest two-finger rewrite man and night editor since Walter Burns."

Hoag exposed wide, rapacious teeth. "You a college chum of Miss Maitland's?" he asked.

"Her father was one of my profs."

"You know our guy with the Marines?" Hoag asked nastily.

"Which guy?"

"LeBaron. The WNA correspondent. He made four invasions."

"I'm sorry. I didn't understand you. No, I never met him, but I know some men who did. They thought highly of him. He took a lot of crazy risks he didn't have to. Too bad he was killed. Plane crash, wasn't it?"

"He had the old WNA spirit," Hoag said. "The old pepper. Poor old underpaid LeBaron. He was twenty-seven and couldn't write an English sentence. But he had guts. Know what he was paid? Sixty-five bucks a week. That's the truth. He was getting scale for a three-year man. And no overtime since he was out of the country. But he had the old fire." Hoag stretched his arms, yawning rudely. "Now take Maitland here," he continued. "I wonder about her sometimes. She writes good and she's the best-looking broad in the Guild, but I wonder about her. She hasn't got the old pepper. We can't get her off her duff, Captain. I want to sell her to dayside as a feature writer, but she refused. Try to make her understand she should be on the street more, using those good looks to her advantage. A pretty kisser never hurt a dame in this business. But she says she can't be bothered interviewing a lot of dopes she has no use for. Some attitude."

"Never mind the eulogies, Ed," Marty said. "Where's my merit raise? I was promised that a month ago."

"Hear that?" Hoag said. "Hear what she said? No morale. No *Semper Fidelis* here. They left me here with the college girls and the high school boys. Everyone else became a hero. Got his feet wet. Like you. Or LeBaron."

"Ed's an incurable romantic," Marty said. "The general manager knows there wouldn't be any nightside without him. That's why he didn't let him go overseas."

Hoag said nothing, and spun around, snarling at the Teletype operator. "Chicago come in with that new lead on the hotel fire? What the hell's wrong with Brady?" He reached for a phone; it occurred to Tom that the man was living a role every minute —the tough, cynical newspaper editor. He could not possibly take himself seriously: or was that the biggest joke of all?

Outside the *Record* building, three-star editions were being loaded into a fleet of trucks. The street was effectively blocked by police. The power of the press forbade transit on East Forty-ninth Street. A gang of inky pressmen, union men in paper hats and blackened dungarees, whistled at Marty. One of them, Tom thought, said something to him about a "tin soldier." The eternal boorishness of the American clod, Tom thought. It didn't bother him; he was so much luckier than they were. They dodged a careening truck and started walking west.

He had no idea where to take her. In his college days, the local movie and beer joints were the limits of his socializing. She suggested Greenwich Village, and it seemed a fine idea. They took a cab downtown, ending up at Nick's where they listened to the ear-splitting vigor of Dixieland and laughed when George Brunis sang:

You so ugly
You so ugly
You some ugly chile!

They stopped at the Vanguard to hear a socially conscious trio, with guitar, bass and banjo, chant topical left-wing lyrics to tunes like "The Great Speckled Bird" and "Low and Lonely."

Tom whispered to Marty: "You can't charge money for folk singing."

"Why?"

"Well, anyone can do it. Folk singing is like stickball. Any kid can play stickball. You can't charge people money to watch it. Now, the Yankees you can charge money for. Sinatra or Lily Pons you can charge money for. They sing better than most people. But folk singing is *anybody's* business. There were twelve enlisted men in my company, cornshakers, and they all played guitars and sang like that."

At two in the morning they sat in a minuscule Spanish restaurant, eating chicken *mole*.

"They make the chicken with chocolate sauce," Marty said. "It sounds impossible, but it's delicious."

He studied it suspiciously, then sampled it. "Hey. Not bad. The old Italian ladies make up a dessert with chocolate sauce and pig's blood—"

She opened her eyes in horror.

"No, I'm not kidding. *Sanguinaccia*. They make it at Easter. It's got some bloody religious significance. My old Grandma Malfitano used to bring it around in a paper bag. I'd never touch the stuff and I'd hurt her feelings. Now I'm paying three-fifty a portion and liking it. Chicken with melted Hershey Bars."

"I feel guilty. Making you do something you wouldn't do for your grandmother. And you hurt her feelings."

He looked at her with a schoolboy's longing. "She wasn't as beautiful as you. She wore black all the time and couldn't speak English." He sighed, sorry that he could say no more for the poor, uneducated, dead Italian lady. "She cooked up a mean ravioli, though. She lived on a pension from the sanitation department for twenty years. She bought greens and stuff like brains, tripe, neck bones. It tasted great when she got through with it."

Marty took his hand. "She sounds marvelous. I hope I'm not being patronizing, but I admire Italians. They give out. They *live* all the time."

"Yeah. Tomato paste and the numbers." He picked up the gooey chicken and sucked at it. "Funny thing about my Grandma. When my mother was busy she'd send the old lady to the public school to take me home. I guess I was nine years old. I was ashamed of her because she couldn't speak English. So I'd hide behind the annex. The old lady would walk around twice, three times, calling my name, and me, the dirty little status-conscious bastard that I was, I'd keep hiding. Then when all the kids had gone, I'd sneak out. And she'd be there, patient, forgiving, in her black shapeless dress and the black stockings, waiting for me, never letting on she knew I was hiding because I was ashamed of her." He sounded gloomy. "She died during the war, and I never had a chance to tell her how sorry I was."

"I'll bet she understood."

"I guess so. She was proud of me. She had three pictures on the wall of her room in back of a tailoring shop. Jesus Christ, Vito Marcantonio and me. I was in my college football uniform, looking fierce."

"She covered a lot of ground with that trio."

"She got by. I guess anything was a good deal for her after spending half her life scrubbing diapers for rich ladies in Naples."

They strolled through Washington Square, saturating themselves with the mystic city: the eccentric bookshops, the cubbyhole antique stores, the cellar theatres, the flaking, shuttered houses with spidery nonutilitarian railings. Within these homes, Tom imagined, young men and young women wrote novels and poems, carved statuary and splashed canvases, alternating acts of artistic prowess with fierce sexual engagements. Years later, he would learn that most Greenwich Village houses were tenanted by bright creative guys in public relations and sales executives of corporations. But now he yearned to be of the putative artistic company. The nagging dream was at him again: someday he would write ferociously about his Marine experiences. He would call it *First Wave.*

They climbed wearily to the open deck of a Fifth Avenue bus. The early morning privacy, chill and crisp, drew them together. He put his arm around her. The bus roared away—softly, it seemed, almost in deference to sleeping apartment dwellers on lower Fifth Avenue. She rested her head on his arm.

"Ouch," Marty said. "I think I've gotten my hair tangled in your Good Conduct Ribbon." She straightened up. "You've got a regular briar patch on your chest. I feel like Bre'r Rabbit."

"Should I remove the arm?"

"No, I'm joking." She rested against his shoulder again. Her hair smelled fresh and sweet. He kissed her lightly on the temple. She looked up at him solemnly.

"Your first big night on the town. I hope you enjoyed it."

"The greatest. It was worth it just to visit the World News Association and learn how American Journalism operates."

"I'm sorry you had to be disillusioned. It's terribly embarrassing. Most people don't even know what I'm talking about when I tell them I'm with WNA. They have a vague idea of what AP is, and some of them know UP. But INS and WNA? Probably some leftover New Deal agencies." She laughed. "But

I wanted to be a newspaperwoman, so there I am. I enjoy it though—sometimes."

"Maybe you should have finished college." He made a comical grimace. "Hey, don't I sound like the voice of middle-class righteousness?"

"Maybe I should have. I don't know. I just got fed up with them. It was as if they were play-acting all the time. Make-believe. It might have been different if I had gone out of town. But right here in the city—"

"What did that have to do with it?"

She leaned forward, her sharp chin resting on clasped hands. "Oh, this damned city. There's just too much of it. Too much of everything. It's all right if you can be indifferent to it. I was pretty good at that for a while. Then you feel you've *got* to be in the swim. They should make sections of it off-limits. I tell you, there's this terrible abundance of goodies to contend with all the time. The wonderful jobs, the new plays, the books, the movies, the restaurants, the fancy stores. I hate them, because I sometimes wonder if I can keep myself from wanting everything. Every now and then, I get the feeling I'm losing the battle. That's why I became a newspaper gal. So I could be right in the middle of everything—I thought."

"Yeah, but your boss—that Hoag—he said all you want to do is sit at the desk and rewrite. You refused to go out and meet people, become a big by-line writer."

"That's my defense, Tom. If they won't limit what's around me, I'll limit myself."

He half turned her chin with his hand. "You should have no trouble getting anything you want. *Anything*."

"You think so?"

"Sure. The face. A good-looking woman can write her ticket. If she's got brains, she's *way* ahead of the game. If you want, you can corner the market on *pasta* and starve out my relatives."

"Do you believe that's true?" Marty asked. "I don't. Personally, I think I'm a little skinny and sloppy."

"Go on, knock it, baby. It won't do you any good." He became serious. "Listen, I know. Other things being equal, if you *look good*, you win the duke. I don't want to bore you to death with my heroic football playing, but I swear, if I had looked more like an athlete and acted like one, I would have played first string. But me with my big beak and my uniform that kept coming apart. Ah, what the hell—"

She was studying his blunt, flat nose curiously. "Tom, you don't mind my getting personal, but did you say *big* beak?"

He laughed. "Ah, I forgot to tell you. The University treated me to a nose job. Plastic surgery. The nose had been busted so many times I looked like Bozo the Clown. Besides I couldn't breathe. They were running an earn-while-you-learn program for medical students uptown and I was one of the practice jobs. Not bad though." He turned his head, in the manner of a fashion model. "Except for the itty-bitty scar. They made a regular *goy* out of me."

She touched his nose, running her fingers gently up the contracted, flattened bridge, to the high, dark forehead, the coarse short hair. His face had the character of one of those uniplanar, delicate drawings on ancient Mediterranean vessels—Minoan, or Etruscan. He shivered and they brought their heads together, touching lips. She stroked his cheek with her fingertips and it evoked a little cry from him. He reached for her waist and held her.

"Can't quit now," he gasped. He kissed her again, fully, open-mouthed, exhilarated by her response. She pulled her head back and held him away gently.

"Enough, Tom. Don't make me a 'please Tom' kind of girl. I couldn't help kissing you. You're so damned real."

He slumped in the cramped bus seat. Street lights illuminated his sorrowing black eyes. He looked like a defeated Camorra chief, a deposed king of conspiracies and vendettas.

"There I am patronizing you again, but I mean it. You're valid. You have substance. That's why my father wants to get his academic hooks into you."

"Why don't the two of you adopt me? I don't eat much."

"Now listen to me. Remember what I said about this city and all the bright rewards in it? Well *you're* the one who deserves them. Not me with my alleged beauty. But you. You put your life on the line, didn't you?"

"Oh Jesus, no. They carried me off kicking and screaming."

"Never mind. I can tell a lot about you. You're entitled to the big prizes. I had to kiss you, because it was like—like congratulating you on how marvelous your life is going to be. You'll show 'em—all the wiseguys and fast talkers."

"Ah, *scungilli*. I thought it was blind, hot passion."

"That's easy. You can get that anywhere."

He embraced her again, kissing an ear, her cheek. "I want to make love to you tonight. Let's make believe this is Tom Sorrento Night at Ebbets Field, and I'm getting all those awards, I have a right to you. You know, the Nash convertible—why is it always a Nash?—two hunting dogs, a deepfreeze and a gift certificate for five hundred dollars' worth of clothes at Abe Stark's. Then I say: 'I wish to t'ank everyone who made Tom Sorrento Night necessary' and then I go home with you and take your clothes off and make love to you all night."

"You'll get involved with the Maitlands more than's good for you, Tom."

He looked grave. "I haven't made love under a tree since I was a counselor in the Adirondacks. We're a great pair. You live with your old man and me with my family."

"I live on East 66th Street," she said. "Way over near First Avenue."

"But—"

"My weekly visit to Hall for a lecture and to borrow some money." She patted his knee. "Now look—you're invited up for a drink, but nothing else. I don't want to spoil what's started out so nicely."

"Chicken."

In the East Sixties, opposite the Central Park Zoo, they got off the bus and hailed a cab. She lived in an ancient, clifflike stone house, one filled with internes and nurses from the nearby medical buildings. They hiked four flights to her midget apartment. Inside, it was as functional as a monk's cell. Tom took off his tunic and loosened his tie as soon as they entered. Marty walked into a closet-sized kitchenette and began fumbling with a bottle of gin, a tray of ice cubes. He saw her there—a casual, witheringly beautiful girl, and he knew he must make love to her. He grasped her arm and guided her into the apartment.

"To hell with that," he said shakily. "I've got to make love. Don't say no. Just don't say no."

"All right," she said. "All right. But please don't be disappointed."

They rested, nude and drained, on the narrow studio bed. He had gone at her with a voracious boyishness. He kept telling himself *stop acting like it's your first piece. . . .* He had been too wound up. Her straight, lean limbs, her trim body, the lovely, half-sleeping face—it was more than he could bear.

"You are disappointed, aren't you?" she asked.

"Me? I'm the goof-off. I ruined the whole thing. I didn't give you a chance. Big Wheel Sorrento. Big Marine hero."

"It's not that important. I enjoyed it."

"The story of my life. I get so wound up beforehand I can't take advantage of my good luck. I leave my fight in the dressing room. I ever tell you how I fought in the Golden Gloves?"

"Tell me." She turned sideways, pressing her limbs against his body. He gasped involuntarily, embracing her. "Oh, Marty," he sighed. "You're too much for me, too good. You have no right to be so good to me." He felt drugged; her presence disoriented him, endowed him with pleasurable vagueness. She, on the other hand, was remarkably calm: the passion in her gracile body had been carefully hoarded and then discharged (with a violence that surprised Tom) during climax. He started kissing her neck, her ears, the half-smiling face, and she restrained him gently.

"Slow down. You were going to tell me about the Golden Gloves."

"I guess I better. Get my mind off how I loused up the detail."

"Will you please stop talking like that?"

He sat up in bed, looking down at her restful face.

"You're too good for me. Too rich for my blood. What right do you have to be so generous? You know I never wanted anything more in my whole life than to sleep with you? 'When Boyhood Dreams Come True.' You know that story? James T. Farrell."

"The Golden Gloves," she persisted.

"Oh. Another Sorrento fiasco. I was sixteen. In high school. These two pals of mine from the block, Leo Mazzochi and Allie Cooperstein, they decided I could win in the novice class, welterweight. So they enter my name without telling me. I never had a boxing lesson in my life. I never had gloves on. I hated to fight. We're playing punchball one night in the schoolyard, and Allie drives up in his brother's vegetable truck. Come on, he says, we're going for a ride."

"Poor Tom," she said. "The trusting soul."

"That's me. The original *ciuco.* So they take me down to the CYO gym off Bruckner Boulevard. Before I know it, they're taping my hands and fitting me for a jockstrap. They have great plans for me. I'm going to be the next welterweight champ. And besides, the novice class is nothing but kids who've never fought.

And I'm the strongest sixteen-year-old on the block. They get me in the ring, and I see the guy I'm supposed to fight. It says on his bathrobe 'Sal Testa,' but I know he isn't Sal Testa. His name's Sal Messina and he and his four brothers are all professional fighters. So I complain to Leo and Allie—what's the big idea? This is a *novice* fight. I'm a *novice*. This guy fighting under an assumed name is a pro. *Sssh,* Allie says, the Golden Gloves are *all* pros. They all fight under different names. I started to climb out of the ring, but it was too late."

"What happened?"

"I decked him the first shot. I figured it was him or me, and I didn't know anything about boxing. So I flew right at him and belted him on the nose. He went down, bounced right up and then knocked me down eleven times."

"*Eleven?*"

"The rules were different then. Funny thing was he wasn't hurting me. He'd belt me and down I'd go. It was a three-round fight and he couldn't knock me out. I'd keep bouncing—off the canvas, off the ropes, off the posts. It wasn't tragic, it was ridiculous. I remember Messina's face. It was all scarred and lumped. Some novice. I was madder about his being a pro than I was about getting knocked down."

"You've got a talent for laughing at yourself. I wish I could console myself with a sense of humor."

"Yeah, I'm a million laughs. My old lady didn't laugh so hard when she saw my picture in the *Daily News* the next morning. They got me just as I hit the bottom rope. There I am—sitting on it, my legs doubled up, my mouth open, and that wise guy Messina, that phony, walking away like the pro he was."

"What did your mother do?"

"She belted me once more for good luck. I was sixteen, still her baby. She'd show me. After the way they were saving money so I could go to college—and here I turn out a bum, a tramp."

"You say your mother *hit* you?"

"Why not? My mother's got a jaw like Randolph Scott. Of course, it was the last time she slapped me. I guess she felt a little guilty about it." He laughed. "Sal Messina. Of the Fighting Messina brothers. He drives a laundry truck now."

"Serves him right," Marty said consolingly. "I'll bet if you had a few lessons you could have beaten him."

"I don't think so. I'm a born loser."

"You are not. You've got some need to keep telling yourself that."

"You know, I wonder how the Marines did it. I mean, how they won with me on their side. Oh, I'm a loser all right. Especially with women. Wanna hear?"

"No. Now stop talking this way."

He hugged her, his hands trying to reach and stroke all of her. "All right. You've encouraged me. You gave me yourself. No nonsense. No games. You gave me your body. All of it. No one's ever been that good to me. I'm the original foul ball. The All American out! More broads have said no to me—"

She touched his lips with her fingers to silence him; firmly he took her hand away. "I've gotten less for a man my age than anyone I know. Not that I haven't tried. It eludes me. In college, there was this nurse, everybody's lay. The whole football team. They fixed me up with her one night. She wouldn't. I reminded her of her *brother*. Can you believe it? In the Corps, whenever we went on the prowl, I'd always end up with the girl who wanted to talk about literature. And me, I'd oblige her. I'd tell myself it didn't matter that much and then I'd cry, listening to the guy in the next room getting his. Plenty of times I've had the chance and just couldn't manage it myself. Anticipation. The big letdown. I don't know. I've always had some kid's notion that women hate sex. That it pains them and dirties them, that only the man enjoys it. Why should any woman want to sleep with me? I never pushed it. When a dame said no, that was it. I wouldn't even try again. How do you figure that?"

"Tom, I only know you one day. I wouldn't presume to analyze you. You ought to stop doing it to yourself."

"All the books I used to read. It was so *easy*. Where were all those women who were putting out? I was lucky if I got a good-night kiss. Back in the dorms listening to those guys tell how they made out. Every now and then I'd make up a lie so I could be in on the post-mortems. I think they knew I was lying."

She raised herself on an elbow and looked at him thoughtfully. "I had no idea I was performing such a good deed," she said. "You make me very happy. But really—I can't believe you were *that* unlucky."

"I was. And I am. A loser."

"Well maybe this is a good omen. Your conquest. You could become terribly lucky from now on." She kissed him delicately. "I hope you do."

They held each other lovingly in the darkness. The telephone's invasive shrill made them jump.

"Who the devil is that?" Marty asked. "At *three* in the morning?"

She took the phone off its hook. "Yes?" she asked. In the darkness, Tom could see her frowning. "Oh, for God's sake," she said with annoyance, "you have no right to be calling me now. You're darn right I'm mad." There was a long pause as she listened; the strained tones of a man's voice issued from the phone.

Marty tried to terminate the conversation. The caller seemed adamant. At length she said: "All right. All right, Ed, now that's enough. Yes, he *is* here. And it's none of your business." She hung up. Angrily, she got up, lit a cigarette and sat in a slip-covered armchair across the tiny apartment. The rude call had severed the intimate web between them. She remained silent, drawing vigorously on the cigarette.

"Was that Hoag?" Tom asked.

"Yes."

"Pretty possessive fellah. I got the feeling up at the office he was casing me and didn't like the whole idea."

"He can go to hell," she said quietly.

Tom tried to find her face in the gloom—the delicate features, the soft hair. She had turned her head away and was staring vacantly at First Avenue below.

"You've been having an affair with him, haven't you?"

She said nothing.

"Well, haven't you?"

"Tom, this isn't something for us to discuss. I don't want to talk about it. You hardly know me."

"But you *are,* aren't you? I can tell. No guy calls a dame at three in the morning unless it's to check up. How long you been sleeping with him? Or is he only one of the gang?"

"What was that cute expression you used before? Everybody's lay? Is that what you think I am?"

"I just asked. I have a right to know. You're his mistress."

She rested her forehead in her palm. "You have no right to know. But I'll tell you. I've been sleeping with him. Are you happy now? He's married and has three kids and a mortgaged house in Great Neck. He's miserable and unhappy and I thought I was in love with him. Are you satisfied?"

"No." He got up from the bed and knelt in front of her. "Listen. I don't want you to have affairs with other guys. Just me. Only me. I'm in love with you. I don't want you giving your body away. Kissing other men. I know I sound like a wild man. I haven't even known you twelve hours. But I have to have you. For myself. You understand?"

"Tom—don't expect too much of me."

"You were good to me tonight. You made me feel like I could do anything. I'm not a loser any more. If I could sneak back into college I'd make first string."

"Just letting you sleep with me—it did all that?"

"That's why you can't sleep with anyone else." He looked at her appealingly. "Why'd you do it? What right did that bastard Hoag, that make-believe editor, have to sleep with you? Who does he think he is?"

"Now *stop*. You've no right to moralize. You can't make demands like that. You know—we may decide tomorrow we never want to see each other again. Why carry on like that about Ed Hoag?"

"But I have to know. How long? When was the first time?"

"You're impossible. Do you want me to really shock you? I slept with him originally because I thought it would get me a promotion. That makes it even worse, doesn't it? He dangled that as bait. Then I started feeling sorry for him, so miserably frustrated. Poor man spends his life watching AP beat him."

Tom got up and walked back to the bed. "So that's it. Okay." He started getting dressed. "You did it to get a promotion. Oh, boy."

"Yes. And shall I tell you something else? When I had the chance for a promotion I turned it down. I wouldn't take it on those terms. You heard Hoag tonight—how he wanted to make me a feature writer. Well that was my reward. But I refused it. By then—"

"By then you were sleeping with him regularly and you both liked it. Ah, I should have known better." He started looking for his tunic. Walking by her chair, she seized his wrist and drew him down.

"Don't go, Tom. I want you to stay."

A street lamp, peeking through the drawn blind, touched her skin with slender bars of light.

"You can't leave me now," she said. "Do you think I slept with you just for laughs? So we could have our little spasms and then never see each other? Maybe *you* were being generous.

Maybe I needed something you had to give. Would you admit that?"

He knelt, resting his head on her slim thighs. He began to cry. "How did it happen?" he asked. "How did something so good happen to me?"

He could never remember being happier.

PART II

1 *The Stone*

Two encouraging things happened at the digging site the day following the Hilltown episode. A second flexed burial was discovered just north of the first, and one of the new test holes led them to a curious rock formation. The second skeleton, as papery as its predecessor, was curled comfortably in the same embryonic manner. Ballard, poking gently at the edges of the first grave, had discovered its supplicant hand, then unearthed an arm, a rib cage, the remainder. The two graves had destroyed the neat geometrical pattern of the trench; Tom decided to abandon the remaining unexcavated five-by-five squares, and merely start digging north and east, in the hope that the site was a large burial ground. A circular area, roughly fifteen feet in diameter, was described, and the workmen, under Ballard's supervision, began clearing the upper levels of dirt.

The discovery of the test hole was even more intriguing. Ben Peltz had been working on a line parallel to the highway, digging about two feet down at intervals of four feet, and examining the fill for any evidence. He had found a few bone splinters —probably deer or raccoon—and the usual quota of shells. At the fourth hole, his spade hit something hard. Peltz widened the hole, and probing with a trowel, discovered that a flat stone of considerable size lay at the base. It did not have the look of native rock: the area was dotted with yellow sand rocks, none of them much more than eight inches in diameter. This, on the other hand, was a whitish calcite, hard, and almost flat. It was about two and a half feet wide, roughly circular, and about six inches high. Ben summoned Tom and they studied it, both of them puzzled.

"Clear about three feet around it and see where it takes us," Tom said.

Ballard plodded up the slope from the grave site, dragging his spade. "Want some help, Ben?" he asked. He ran his sleeve across his black forehead. It was early afternoon: the sun hung above them in a cottony haze.

"Nah, I wanna suffer. I'll do it myself."

Tom and Ballard squatted on the inhospitable, baking sand. They watched Peltz with grudging admiration. He was older than either of them, a wiry, undersized, slum-bred man, filled with bitterness and frustrations, a mass of ancient grudges and bad will. Yet there was something admirable about Ben when he worked. He dug faster and harder, he had an instinct for the arts of the spade that amazed Tom. He had been in archaeology longer than either of them—as a common laborer in the days of the WPA, later as an undergraduate. Now he was a perpetual graduate student, a man forever in search of the Ph.D. At seventy, Tom suspected, he would still be spending his summers helping out on digs *(Asawampsett Pond Site II: Some Evidences of Early Woodland Settlement Patterns),* his winters hanging around graduate schools that didn't want him.

"Where's he get the jizzim?" Ballard asked. "After last night's outing, I'm beat to the socks."

Tom shifted his legs. He reached in his hip pocket for a half-burned stub and lit it. "I want to talk to you about that," he said. He studied Ballard's great ebony face. "I'm no good at chewing out." Tom said. "I always let my platoon sergeant do it."

"Go on. I deserve it," Dave said.

"You shouldn't have taken Ben with you, that's all. Nothing would have happened if he hadn't been there."

"You're right, Tom. I won't do it again."

Ballard's contrition embarrassed Tom. For all of Dave's comic antics, he was, like most educated Negroes Tom had known, insular and secretive. Who could blame them? They spent years of preparation, subscribing to whatever their liberal white peers expected of them, cultivating industry, sobriety, the modes of dress, speech and manners demanded by the University world and then discovered that their diligence was rarely rewarded. Ballard had made the mistake (or was it deliberate, Tom wondered) of choosing a field that always seemed overstocked with eager young people. Maitland had told Ballard when he first had come to the University for graduate work: *there are too many of us measuring skulls, interviewing Indians, digging up old bones. Other things being equal,* he had informed Ballard in his usual blunt and almost callous manner, *you will not get an appointment if you are colored.* He advised Ballard that many social scientists would rather resent a Negro getting in on their act: colored peoples, whether in grass huts in Bechuanaland, or in Harlem, were the quarry, the meat-and-potatoes of the anthropologist and social worker. To reverse the hunter-and-hunted relationship (particularly with someone so obvious as Dave, so big, so black and so overwhelming) would be a little hard for them to take.

"Now if you were to daub yourself with red ochre and turmeric," Maitland had said, not insultingly, "and take up residence among the Kikuyu, learn the dialect, and acquire some skill with the spear-thrower, you'd be quite a celebrity in our circles. But to have you go out and *do* the interrogating . . . it's against all the rules. . . ."

Looking now at Ballard's melon-sized head, Tom realized how little he knew about him, how successful Dave had been with his masquerade, his defensive banter, his knack for suffocating his personality in his giant's body. Tom had met him four years ago, when Dave was working for his doctorate. Ballard was all but penniless; his GI Bill of Rights money had run out the previous year, when he had gotten his master's degree in Ohio. He lived in a hall bedroom, sharing a malodorous bathroom with three other tenants, in a Harlem rooming house directly below the University. He worked from midnight to eight in the morning in a garage below the elevated on West 125th Street, washing cars, parking, going out on emergency calls. In addition to carrying a full load of credits toward his Ph.D., he worked as Maitland's assistant in class. He took attendance, marked test papers, and ran errands for Maitland. The class was the basic undergraduate course in anthropology and was conducted in a lecture hall. Ever since Maitland had begun the course, it had been one of the most popular in the curriculum. The anthropologist's remarkable skill as a lecturer, his fund of ribald stories, his tolerance in grading (Maitland's theory was that since none of the students knew very much, it was just as easy to give them all A's and B's) drew well over a hundred men to Anthro 1-2. Ballard would sit in the first row, first seat, at the base of the amphitheatre, his soaring black form suggesting some kind of tribal guardian of the shrine, a dark monolith who called the roll and brought in maps and charts. Twice during the semester, Tom had filled in for Maitland. On both occasions, he had found himself distracted from his lecture notes by Ballard's impassive, almost somnolent figure. It was almost as if the Negro had deliberately cultivated his size, his obviousness, his choice of profession, and had, through some primitive wizardry, sought out the front seat in the first row, to remind all of them (the class was all white except for a Chinese exchange student) that something was terribly wrong, that all their palaver about siblings and totems and culture patterns was rather inconsequential in view of the ancient injustices done Ballard and his fellow blacks. When Tom got to know Dave, later in the school year, he understood that Ballard never viewed himself as a symbol, that the burdensome problems of race rarely infringed on his conversation, that if there was self-pity in him, he camouflaged it with humor.

Once he had come across Ballard sitting in the archaeology lab. It was late afternoon of a winter's day. The room's gray walls and long gray tables were coated in academic gloom. Ballard sat by himself at a sink, washing a collection of broken pots, arrowheads, and bone fragments that some amateur group in upstate New York had sent to Maitland for classification. He would wash the odd pieces, dry them, squirt them with Krylon, and lay them on a plywood board. While he worked he yawned prodigiously, and his great head wobbled occasionally in semi-surrender to fatigue. He seemed curiously at peace in the bleak chamber. Outside, traffic on Amsterdam Avenue squished by on December's slush; horns honked and whistles screeched. Tom, watching Ballard yawning, washing, inspecting bits of refuse left by vanished Mohawks, envied him his happiness, or whatever substitute for happiness it was he had cultivated. He engaged the Negro in conversation and learned about his back-breaking schedule, his hopes for getting the doctorate the following year, his gratitude toward Maitland. Tom wanted to know when he slept, and Ballard, with no show of martyrdom, told him: "When I can." And he resumed washing his fluted points and incised shards, his privacy inviolate. Tom rarely talked to him after that interlude in the lab. He found that something in Ballard inundated him with a wrenching pity. Ballard didn't ask for pity, nor did he cry about his hard luck and wretched life. Perhaps, Tom suspected, it was just his size that bothered him, that evoked in him a clutching compassion. He wanted to grab Ballard by his threadbare lapels and scream at him: *Do something! Get mad, you big bastard! Don't just sit there making believe you're satisfied with those damn pieces of clay!*

"Pretty chicken of me, hey?" Tom asked.

"No. Not at all," Ballard said. He indicated the old man McIsaac, swinging a pick at the extension of the long trench. "The old man told me about it. I got curious, so I went to a couple of meetings. Don't ask me why I took Ben along." He squinted at Tom. "Maybe to convince *myself* it was all for social science and that I didn't give a damn whether they had their boycott or not."

"You convince yourself?"

Ballard laughed. "Not hardly." He shaded his eyes to study a passing monoplane. Behind it flew a legend on netting:

VISIT THE DOG TRACK:

TEN RACES A NIGHT: QUINIELAS

"All earthly pleasures do here abide," Ballard said softly. "Quinielas at the dog track. Why don't they all go to the dog track and let those people in Hilltown vote? You'd think with all the distractions around here they'd forget about us."

The *us* jarred Tom. Ballard's identification with Harkey's congregation was unexpected. Dave might keep lying to himself that he was a neutral observer (should he have had a white jeep with "UN" on the roof?) but he was evidently bound to them tighter than he would admit.

Across the site, Tom could see his son Nicky struggling up the incline. He was brown and round; he looked like the gingerbread man.

"I don't know," Ballard said. "Maybe I did the wrong thing, coming down here."

"Why? I got no kicks."

"No. From my own standpoint. I once said, after I got out of the Army, I'd never go South again. Never. But I did. I guess I figured this community would be different. But it's here. Everything I escaped."

"It's got you down, hey, Dave?"

"Got me wondering what right I have to feel sorry for myself. To be hanging around graduate schools and digging for artifacts." He picked up a flat stone and sailed it delicately toward Peltz. It ricocheted off Ben's shovel.

"Cah-man," Peltz whined. "That's all you're good for? You wanna dig, I'll go sit down."

"You're doing great, Benny," Tom said.

"Like the people in the church," Ballard continued. "The respectables. Like my own folks in Caterman, Georgia. You know what the basic division is in a Negro community in the South?"

"Nope."

"Respectables and non respectables. The respectables go to

church. The ladies have Helpful Groups. The Negro lawyer, doctor if there is one, always the undertaker and the beauticians. And all the domestics. Like my folks. My old man was a handyman for Judge Campbell. My mother was his cook. Then there's the nonrespectables. Raise hell on Saturday night. The cut-and-shoot crowd. Those two groups, they hate each other more than they do the crackers." He sighed. "And there they were. All the respectables in that church. All the God-fearing, duty-doin' miserable, humiliated people. And I tell you what got me excited, Tom." He turned and looked intently at Sorrento. "They were using *Jesus* to get justice."

"Why not?" Tom asked. "That's part of His job, isn't it?"

"You think so? Why, I can remember my old lady coming home, beat and weary. Then she'd start to sing and look happy. 'The white folks has their money and cars and big houses,' she used to shout, 'but I don't envy 'em. Das 'cause I has my Jesus!' "

"I'm no expert on this," Tom said. "I quit going to Holy Family after my confirmation. I didn't like the way the Irish ran the church and made all the Italians feel like poor relatives. My old man agreed with me. He felt the same way about the police force."

Ballard grinned. "You walked out on Jesus, my old lady would have said. But these people at Mount of Olives. My friend Reverend Harkey. They learned something. Jesus is a weapon. He gets results. You know what they preach now? Love. Love me. Love my color. I love you. God is love. Love is God. Jesus loves me. I love Jesus. Love, love, love. We love you white bastards who are humiliating us. We love all the lies you've told, and the sneaky way you've made virtue out of your sins. We love you and pray for you, for all the crap you put out about honor and the Southern way of life, and your poor lost dream. We love you because this is a big lovin', religious, sweet-talking country. And all we have to do is keep loving and praying and getting on our knees and invoking Jesus. My old lady had it all wrong. All she needed was her Jesus to laugh her troubles away. Well, it's changed, man. They got Jesus, but they're puttin' him to work. Every time the night riders throw a bomb, you know what that shrewd Harkey does? He holds a prayer meeting. He loves 'em up a little more. He throws Jesus at them!"

Tom studied him, disturbed by Ballard's meticulously controlled outburst. Beneath his comic peroration he detected hysteria. "You think it's going to work?"

Ballard shrugged. "Who knows? The thing is, the white folks may get *sick* of being loved so much. You can take only so much of this praying and kissing. Just like the colored people down here got sick of being told how much the whites love *them*. You know—*I love those nigra people so long as they keep their place*. So people like Harkey, they said, nuts with them lovin' us, we'll start lovin' *them*—and in public, all the time, especially when there's newsreel cameras and reporters around."

Nicky plodded toward them. He was barefoot and wore only a pair of surrealist trunks. He carried a ragged, coverless children's book, which he thrust at Tom.

"Read a 'tory, daddy."

"Where's Mommy?" Tom asked.

"Sleepin'."

"Where's Abby?"

"She went to Sheldon's pool."

"Why didn't you go?"

"I don't like him." Nicky squatted on the baking sands. He located a shell and started digging with it. "I don't like no one and no one likes me. I just like myself."

"Hear that, Davey?" Tom asked. "There's a man after my heart. No togetherness for this fellah." He tweaked Nicky's neck. It was dark brown and velvet. The little boy's ears seemed to have been glued on to the perfect round head as an afterthought. Tom often fancied they were detachable, that Nicky took them off at night and hid them under his pillow. There were times like this, studying the brown, immaculate body, a tiny replica of his own, that he found his love for the child unbearable. The notion that the boy would grow up to know sorrows and disappointments, would have to leave the comforting safety of childhood, edged his paternal rapture with a gray gloom. His daughter never affected him this way—she was an intense, burning child, constantly at war, perpetually making treaties. Nicky, on the other hand, made the best of everything: he was the kind of child who would have to be hurt someday, and seeing him now, content with a broken shell, Tom wanted to hug and protect him.

"A prince among men," Tom said. "Nicky here, he's what it's all about, Davey." And saying it, he noticed a fleeting pain on Ballard's face. Ballard was unmarried, unbound, uncommitted. Tom could guess why—what joy would Dave get out of raising children, educating them, teaching them right and wrong, and then seeing them humiliated and confined? Tom often had to answer his own children's puzzled questions: *Why are colored people poor? How come they all work as maids?* How infinitely more hurtful, he thought, must be the questions from a Negro child when the inequities of the world became apparent to him.

Ballard struggled to his feet. He dusted clouds of yellow sand from his columnar limbs and picked up his shovel. "I been reading on the history of slavery in this country," he said slowly. "Know anything about it?"

Tom shook his head negatively.

"The whole thing was a lie. It was invented just for *this* country, just for the South. The thing about any kind of bondage in Europe, or Asia, for that matter, was that it ended some time. Manumission was inevitable for most slaves. It had limits. Not *here*. About the middle of the seventeenth century the colonies started putting it into law. Slavery was deemed hereditary. Colored people were chattels—now that was something new right there. All this crap about it being in the Bible, and traditional, and something that everyone practiced. I tell you, Tom, it was *legislated* between the middle of the seventeenth century and the end of the eighteenth. But that wasn't enough. People like Jefferson got worried about the rights of man. So what's next? You legislate to prove that the Negro isn't a man. He's less than a man. A different species. And what was really behind it? A soft life, that's what. The glorious vanished dream, like that novelist is always yapping about. The dream was a series of carefully legislated and plotted lies. That's why the bastards are so mad. That's why they've been mad ever since the Civil War."

"What do you mean?"

"If they had been *right,* they wouldn't be so mad. They wouldn't want to keep sitting on us and reminding us we're dirt. But they were wrong. They made up lies. They justified lies for two centuries to keep the easy life going. When they got beat, it didn't reform them. It just made 'em madder. There's nothing a man'll fight harder for than a fraud he's invented to prove he's right. Read the history of slave laws in the colonies. They just didn't *happen* because of plantation economy or a way of life. They were planned. Deliberate. No wonder they're still mad. After all that work."

Ballard plodded down the incline toward Peltz, calling to him: "Take ten, Ben. I'll relieve you."

Peltz tapped the edge of his shovel on something hard at the base of the pit. It clanked noisily and he looked up at Ballard. His red face was twisted and sand-daubed. "Another stone," he said. "A big baby, just like this."

Ballard peered into the hole. "Crazy, man," he said. "Side by side, and glorified. Just like they were put there. Get this, Tom."

Sorrento swung his son over his head and placed the fat brown legs around his neck. The child giggled. He limped down the slope to the edge of the new trench. The stones rested less than three feet below the surface line, embedded in darker subsoil. Like its mate, the rock was whitish and more or less flat, irregularly shaped.

"Don't ask me," Tom said. "Could be just rocks. I never heard of any of these people building with stones." He disengaged Nicky from his shoulders and climbed into the pit. On one knee he inspected the surface of the two stones. "Beats the hell out of me, Lieutenant," he said.

From her bedroom window, Lila had a fine view of the diggings. High in the air-conditioned sleeping chamber, she could look out and feel that she was part of the educational process going on below.

Struggling valiantly into her new pure-silk Silfskin girdle (Lila fought a losing battle against weight; she rationalized her defeats with the excuse that Erwin appreciated her, as he put it, "rounded off at the end"), she peered down at the site, infusing herself with the mystique of the Sorrentos and their diggers. It would make her afternoon of canasta (a game she hated) more bearable if in the midst of tiresome conversation (with women she disliked) she could remind herself of Tom Sorrento, Ph.D., and his band of truth seekers. While she was gartering her stockings, Erwin, in immaculate tennis dress, entered the frigid room, espied a peek of white flesh above the stocking, and favored her with a lecherous tweak. He would never tire of his wife's charms. He panted for her as much now, after twelve years of marriage, as he had when he courted her in Manhattan. He did not delude himself: Lila, while quite attractive, was really no match for the plethora of sexy vessels who infested the Beach. Erwin, in his esteemed post, might have availed himself of a rousing variety of women. He could have emulated Ira deKay. But it was the "extra" that Lila gave him, beyond love and beyond lust. Lila knew about all the things he didn't really understand. She read books; she understood politics; she knew classical music; she could converse intelligently with writers, poets, statesmen and analysts. All these were things for which Erwin had never found time. His life had followed a straight and true course, and he had no regrets. But how wonderful to have a wife who could function in the areas he had neglected! In a sense, this gratitude colored his sexual hunger for her. His love-making was a kind of tribute, a propitiation, a thank-offering for the way in which she had led him toward what were undoubtedly the better things of life, but things he had regrettably overlooked. His frequent passionate encounters with her were always accompanied by a comforting "money-in-the-bank" feeling. When the more basic appetites were appeased (all too soon) Lila could brief him on the Camus she had just read, or furnish him a digest of a new theory of geriatrics.

Erwin dropped to his knees and embraced his wife's encapsulated form. The sight of her made him dizzy, inarticulate, the opposite of everything his business associates and competitors saw in him. Her full body, semi-clad, reduced him to childish limpness, a tallowy state that evoked memories of the perfumy odor in his mother's dress closet.

"*Stop,*" she whined. "What is it with you? Twelve years married and he still gets the hots at eleven-thirty in the morning."

"I can't stop. You're too much for me." He kissed the ribbon of soft tan flesh between the cruel white binders. She shoved him away gently.

"You get worse every year, Erwin. Go work some of the energy off playing tennis."

Sheepishly, he got up. Lila negotiated her way into a magnificent cotton dress—a dusky gray flecked with silver. In the full-length bedroom mirror, Erwin paused to admire his tennis outfit. It was of a richness and a texture that suggested he played with a golden racket on a marble court. The cable-stitched sweater was draped lovingly over his thick torso; the shorts, fractionally precise in length and cut, were of lustrous white; the woolly socks appeared to have been squirted around his ankles from a whipped-cream dispenser; the snowy canvas shoes were delicately molded to Erwin's small feet—custom jobs, hand-stitched at a special shop in New York City. The immaculate uniform, somehow unrelated to Erwin's pudgy, hexagonal body, hinted at a masquerade. Indeed, Ira deKay, once viewing Erwin in costume at the local country club, had muttered to Si: "Look at him—the Outdoor Jew!" But the joke was on Ira, and on anyone else who suspected that the chubby, dark man, so solemn behind his rimless prescription glasses, was unequal to the clothing or the forty-dollar racquet. Erwin was a murderous tennis player. His form was impeccable, his strength unlimited, his speed confounding. In the tropic heat, his opponents would gasp and sweat and stagger. Ellenbogen, swart and silent, would calmly wipe his spectacles, toe the baseline and blast his high, twisting serve past them. He never smiled when he played and he rarely talked.

"Tommy's opening some new holes, I see," Erwin said. He paused at the window, chuckling. "I hope he finds something. Poor guy, working all summer in this heat."

Lila joined him. Slyly, he tried to sneak a quick hand under the flounced skirt. She smacked him heartily.

"I'm glad we asked him down here," Lila said. "It is a relief to talk to *different* people."

"I like Tommy fine," Erwin said. "That wife of his, though. She's got problems."

"Why do you say that? Marty's a *doll.*"

"Oh, I don't know." Erwin squinted across his vacant acreage, the Naboth's vineyard of the Beach. Sorrento, the Negro and Peltz were huddled around a new trench. It amazed him that people could get so involved, so committed to something that was valueless. Yet he accepted Lila's judgment: if she said so, their work must be important. He shook his head. "Anyone as good-looking as she is," he said carefully, "who's got so little to show for it, must have problems."

"Listen to him. Family counselor. I'll tell *you* something. She's very happy. She isn't the kind who needs beach clubs and convertibles. She's got a wonderful man, that's enough."

"That makes it worse for her, I think," Erwin said pedantically. "You can't tell me she isn't bitter that her husband earns so little. Especially when she sees all the dopes in the world doing so well. I can sense these things." He put an arm around her gently. "I'll tell you something else. I don't think she likes you and me particularly—"

"Oh, Erwin, you're seeing things—"

"No, I think I understand her. Tommy's different. I can talk to him. He's a Bronx boy, like me. But she's something else. I think once she had the idea she was something special. Or maybe she was afraid to be. With her looks she could have had *anything* if she played it right. Or at least a lot more than she has now. I have a feeling she resents what we're doing for Tom."

"You're dreaming," Lila said. "I like her."

"Why'd they go running off like that last night? She said the kid was sick, but I didn't believe her." Erwin frowned. "I think she couldn't stand us any longer. It really shouldn't bother me, a woman like that, with all kinds of false notions about how great she is—but sweetie, I don't like seeing *you* treated that way, after the interest you took in these people."

Sorrento and his colleagues were still in the excavation. The archaeologist's small boy, Erwin noticed, was digging his own hole with a shell.

"Lila sweetie," he said. "I'd like to take the Sorrentos out to dinner this week end."

"Anything special?" The casualness of his request put her on guard.

Erwin frowned. He removed his eyeglasses and began polishing them furiously with a square of silicone paper. "I don't think I told you, but I'm thinking of developing the site. DeKay came to me with a remarkable idea, a kind of educational museum. A panorama of the world's religions. It can be an enormous success, and as far as I'm concerned, a great force for good will down here. So I thought—"

"So you thought you'd kick Tom off, so that phony deKay can make a buck out of a tourist trap?" Her voice took on a harsh, agitated quality. Erwin flinched.

"That's not it at all. You know I wouldn't countenance anything in bad taste. DeKay may be an operator, but this idea of his is a magnificent one. Besides, do you think I'd ever let him run something as big as this—something as important as—as—religion."

"Well, just so it doesn't interfere with Tom. He gets first call on that precious five acres of dirt of yours."

"Of course, of course. I just want to make sure he's got enough time. Maybe he can hire some more laborers to speed it up. Ira feels we should have the ground-breaking in a month to be ready for the winter season."

Lila picked up a straw handbag. It was the size of a wine cask and was surmounted with a formal garden.

"Ground-breaking?" she asked, wrinkling her nose comically. "Erwin. I really think you're making a mistake tying in with deKay. He's all right to get your furniture shown on NBC for free, but who said he can do anything else?"

"Darling," he called after, as she left the bedroom for the hallway, "you let me be the businessman."

Catching up with her, he made another grasp for her rear end.

"Erwin!" she cried. "Play tennis!"

Tom and Dave gave Peltz a breather. Tireless, the little red man wandered off to work with Wilma and Oran Burley at the midden. In the sandy subsoil, they were troweling out breccia, agglomerate deposits of refuse—shell and bone fragments, odd bits of stone. Ben squatted alongside them, tapping the chunks of ancient detritus with the wooden handle of a short hoe, separating the accumulated junk. At the new pit Tom and Dave, working at opposite ends of the exposed earth, shoveled furiously, eager to learn whether the curious white stones were a geological freak—which seemed unlikely—or part of a deliberate structure. What could it have been? Pyramid? A ceremonial platform? Tom, dripping with sweat as he plunged the spade into the sand, tried to recall everything he had read about Glades Tradition. Nothing relevant came to him. The dwellings of the primitive peoples of the area were not known. Most of the sites had not even yielded postholes, let alone floor plans or building stones. It was generally surmised that the Glades people lived in simple huts of cut and trimmed wood, covered with leaves and bark. The use of stones for construction was out of keeping with everything known about the culture.

He saw deKay's gaudy ark turn off the blacktop and park on the access road. The intrusion did not bother him; he was thrilled by imminent discovery. He found himself glorying in the fellowship of manual labor, vying with Ballard, whose mammoth figure, wielding the long-handled shovel, as if it were a garden tool, challenged him. He hoped that in the search for the white flat stones, Ballard might divest himself of his misery.

DeKay was not in the car. Cleo Cooke was driving. Si Mermelstein and a middle-aged man lugging a leather camera case got out and trudged up the slope toward the new excavation. DeKay's assistant waved heartily at Tom. His attempt to approximate Ira's joyous greetings failed. He sounded halfhearted and apologetic.

"Hi, Tommy!" Si called. "We're gonna bother you a minute or so!"

Ballard, without interrupting his labors, muttered, "You deh mos' popular man 'round heah, Mistuh Tom."

Mermelstein was lugging a cardboard box. The photographer, surly and sweat-stained, labored behind him. He appeared to be cursing. At the edge of the pit, Mermelstein set his burden down and smiled weakly.

"Gee, Tommy, I'm real sorry to be annoying you," he said. "But Ira wants a few pictures and a little story."

Tom rested on his shovel. "What for?"

Mermelstein flicked his glasses a half-inch upward on his snub nose. "Ira thinks there's a good story here. Oh—this is Barney Field, from the *Register*. He works for us, also. Barney is gonna take some pictures and I'll get a story. We'll release it to the locals and the press association. It can't hurt."

Barney spit savagely into the pit. The oyster landed on the surface of the exposed flat stone. The photographer exhibited the characteristic nastiness of people who develop a limited skill, one protected by hereditary unionism. Tom knew from his discussions with Marty that a chimpanzee could learn to be a news photographer. It therefore became mandatory to invest the infantile work with a *mystique*. In addition, its practitioners were required to cultivate a barbaric rudeness to discourage aspirants to their holy trade. Tom had noticed the same kind of boorishness in drill sergeants (again, a limited skill that could be learned in a few hours), plumbers and automobile mechanics.

"Hey," Tom called to him. "What was that for? I wouldn't spit in *your* hole."

"Wiseguy," Barney mumbled. "Let's go, Mermelstein. DeKay ain't payin' me no overtime and it's hot."

Tom glared at Mermelstein. "Just because you saw me play football in high school doesn't mean you got an in with me. I don't want to be in the papers. That's the worse thing that could happen. Every jerk in the Beach will be here tomorrow."

"Ira promises they won't." Mermelstein sounded petulant.

"No. No pictures. *Va fa a Napoli,* Si."

Cleo honked the horn. She appeared to be smiling frigidly at Mermelstein's discomfort. For a confused moment, Si looked around him, then said to Tom: "Can I talk to you privately? By ourselves?"

Tom plunged the shovel into the sand. "Okay. But no pictures."

They walked a few yards away from the trench and Mermelstein, folding his arms, spoke in a low, tense voice.

"Look. This is my job," he said. "I know you don't want

people lousing you up, but take Ira's word for it. He'll keep 'em away. He'll get a police guard if you want. I gotta get it for him. I *gotta.* He's going to build some tourist thing here this fall and he figures this is a great tie-in—you know, the site of an old Indian village, or whatever. Please. Let me have the story. Ira's word of honor—you won't be bothered."

Tom studied his immature pasty face. Like many permanent residents of the Beach, he apparently never availed himself of sunlight. Or was Mermelstein the kind of troubled man whose aggrieved features could never be brightened—by sunshine, good luck, or sexual fulfillment?

"You sell almost as hard as your boss," Tom said.

"I know, I know, I overdo it. I'll level with you. I think you're that kind of guy. I get twenty grand a year and an expense account. I used to teach English composition in the Bronx at P.S. 178 for three thousand a year. You know what it is to explain a gerund to a class of kids big enough to kill you? Kids who can't read—and you're telling them about *Ivanhoe?* I went crazy. It wasn't the three thousand bucks salary. It was the terror of going in front of those big kids every day. *Ivanhoe.*" His voice cracked on this final invocation of Sir Walter Scott. Either he was a magnificent actor or he was genuinely terrorized by the recollection of his dreadful past. Tom found himself smiling—not critically, but sympathetically—at the supplicant.

"All right, Si dollink," he said. "You probably had some of my relatives in that English class. Anyone named Del Balso? Colangelo? Never mind. I owe you something. I know what P.S. 178 is like. I got three stitches in my head there one day. Go ahead, take your pictures. Then we'll go down to the house and I'll show you what we've found."

Mermelstein's face regained composure. "Thanks," he said, sighing. "I knew I could count on you. I swear, I knew it when I met you last night."

They walked back to the trench. Tom noticed the cardboard box that Si had brought. He kicked it. "What's that? Lunch?"

Mermelstein laughed. "Now don't get sore at me. It wasn't my idea. Ira figured if you didn't have enough stuff for the photographs, I should bring some. So I dropped in at the archaeological society this morning and borrowed some junk they didn't need."

Tom knelt alongside the box and opened it. A dozen odd pieces littered the bottom. He scowled at them, then began picking them up and identifying them.

"Want to learn something, Si?" he asked. "This hunk of pottery is Weeden Island Incised—from up north, on the Gulf side. This is Weeden Island Punctuated. This is a fluted stone. This is Carabelle Incised, maybe two hundred miles from here. This is a bone projectile, probably from a deer antler, could be Glades, I'm not sure. This is a small dagger, probably alligator bone, could be from anywhere in the state. This is Glades Plain and this is Glades Plain with fluted lips. You know what you have here? A blivit. Six pounds of oatmeal in a two-pound bag."

"I'm sorry. It was Ira's idea. Say, you really know this stuff."

Tom got up wearily. "Level with me, Mermelstein. Has deKay sent you around salting the pits? He could screw us up forever with a pile of unclassified junk like this."

"Oh no! Ira wouldn't. He wants to *help* you. I mean—this box here. You don't have to use it."

The twenty minutes that followed were characterized by a kind of orderly inanity that confounded Sorrento. There was Barney, cursing and lurching across the hot sand; there was Mermelstein, justifying his twenty thousand dollars a year with creative notions that would intrigue photo editors everywhere *(Hey Tom! How about you leaning over the trench and making believe you just found that hunka white stuff).* And there were Tom's own people, resentful or embarrassed by the sudden impact of fame, their unexpected initiation into the celebrity complex. Peltz refused to have his picture taken. "I'm wanted in five states for stealing from the *pushky,*" he told Si viciously. "No pictures." Wilma and Oran, blinking and flinching, and reacting to Barney's camera as if it were about to squirt acid on them, consented to pose with their leader. Ballard loomed in the background in several shots. Tom joined in his conspiracy—he identified Dave to Mermelstein as "a workman."

As they plodded up the slope after a few photographs inside the boathouse, Tom found himself intrigued by Mermelstein's buoyancy. Si's goal had been achieved; his salary justified; the terrors of P.S. 178 eliminated. All over the country, Tom mused, there were thousands of Si Mermelsteins, purveyors of trivia, dispensers of minor journalistic *gaseosa,* winning small victories, getting the stick of type in the newspaper, the picture in the magazine, the mention on the radio, the plug on the television, thousands of petty pilot fish, sucking along the mainstream of mass communications. It was not the mere desire to increase sales or to achieve fame for someone or to further a cause that impelled so many bright creative guys like Si into the field. Rather it was a basic, deep-rooted national trait of character—a craving to be seen and heard, to be a part of the celebrity complex, that had erected the airy superstructure. The Si Mermelsteins of the nation were instruments of the whole people, mechanics who had arisen because the culture *demanded* them. The only society in the history of the world, Tom theorized, in which every member wants to know everything about every other member; a society of rubbernecks, Peeping Toms, exhibitionists and Nosey Parkers.

Si pumped Tom's hand damply. "Boy, what a pal," he said. "I promise—you won't be bothered any more."

They walked toward the parked car with Mermelstein.

"We're late," Cleo said nasally. "You know we have a two o'clock meeting with Ira."

"How do, Miss Cooke," Tom said.

She did not answer him. She smiled with her mouth alone. The inviolate smooth face, the clear eyes and high straight brow remained immobile. She was, Tom sensed, like the All-American football players from Midwestern universities he had known. Total physical perfection afforded them special privileges. Pride of the flesh decreed that they need not observe common courtesies, evince interest in anyone, or permit their own splendid physical selves to be touched. One summer Tom had worked as a counselor at a boy's camp in the Adirondacks. One of his colleagues was a Polish boy who had achieved considerable fame as a halfback at Michigan. The campers, most of them overfed little Jewish boys from New York City, adored Uncle Frank. Yet Tom could recall this Slavic clod, this hero, looking dully and distractedly down the dining-room table while his worshipful campers attempted to reach his glorious soul. *Uncle Frank, how 'bout when you ran eighty yards 'gainst Ohio State? . . . Uncle Frank, who caught that pass for the touchdown when you beat Illinois?* And Uncle Frank Stefanowski would slump gloomily in his chair, his violet eyes faintly hooded, and mutter, "Feldman, pass da soup."

Studying Cleo's indifferent face, Tom saw that she was blood sister to Uncle Frank Stefanowski. His athlete's skill and her pale beauty permitted them rudeness, grossness and a comforting sense of getting theirs first. Brainless physicality had inundated them with other people's adoration—why should they give anything in return?

"What did you say about a tourist camp?" Tom asked Si. "What's deKay going to do? Put up a motel?"

"Oh, nothing like that," Si said. "It's an interesting notion. A kind of educational thing. Sort of a museum. He'd like to talk to you about it. You know much about primitive religions?"

"Tell him to buy a copy of *The Golden Bough*."

Cleo backed the car viciously up the dirt path. Si cautioned her to hold up. He waved to Tom. Sorrento walked toward the car.

"Ira would kill me. I almost forgot. These are for you and Mrs. Sorrento." He handed Tom two embossed cards. They read:

COURTESY CARD

PERUVIANA CABANA CLUB

"What's this?" Tom asked.

"Ira figured any time you and your wife and the kids want to use the Peruviana pool, just go ahead. It doesn't cost him anything. It's real nice. They have a special kiddie pool with a girl to look after them. Ira says if you want any drinks or lunch there, just sign his name."

He heard Ballard calling him.

"Hey, Tommy," Dave shouted. "Number three. There's nothing but stones here. Come on over."

He walked toward the new pits. A third flat white stone, irregular in shape, but of the same dimensions as its companions, nested in the subsoil. The three boulders appeared deliberately to have been set in line.

"I don't know," Tom said. "It's probably historical. An old Spanish ruin of some kind. Maybe even more recent. You know you can't tell a thing from the strata here, with the waters washing over this place all the time."

"Want me to dig one out?" Ballard asked. "So we can look it over? If it's historical there might be inscriptions on it."

"No. Let's leave 'em. Get the workmen to give you a hand and just keep extending the trench east and west. Let's see how far it goes. I'd better call Maitland and see what he thinks."

He left Ballard, gathered up Nicky and headed for the boathouse. It was early afternoon and he had not seen Marty since arising. He found her looking pale and distracted. The mad chase and the interlude in the station house of the previous night had drained her. Normally she was resilient and tireless—her talent for noninvolvement spared her. Abby, in a wet bathing suit, was reluctantly munching a Swiss cheese sandwich and sipping chocolate milk. Nicky demanded an identical lunch; Marty obliged him.

"We found something exciting today," Tom said eagerly. "Some big rocks up near the highway."

"That's wonderful," she said. "Have you any idea what they are?"

"I'm lost. I figured I'd give Hall a ring."

She said nothing. It bothered him that the merest reference to her father induced these sullen silences.

"You don't feel so hot today, Marty?"

"I'm a little knocked out. About three in the morning I took a sleeping pill. I shouldn't have. They always make me dopey."

He hugged her. "Come on, baby, smile it up. It isn't that bad. Aren't you happy about my new rocks?"

"I am. I'll be all right as soon as the barbiturate wears off."

"*Mother!*" Abby cried frantically. "I was telling you about the car wash at Sheldon's! You aren't even listening!"

"Tell *me*," Tom said. "I wanna hear."

The little girl's face tightened with tremulous ecstasy. What she had to relate was almost too much for her nervous system. "*Well*," she said, "the teen-agers were having this car wash for charity. Twenty-five cents a car. Sheldon and I were helping. Sheldon's cousin, Francine, was the chairman of the committee for the car wash. And there was one girl there, Sandra, *who didn't wear blue jeans!*"

"Wow," Tom said. "What a thing to do. Not to wear blue jeans."

"They kicked her out of the club," Abby said tensely. "She was wearing silk stockings and a red dress! And the club had voted they all had to wear jeans! So they said she couldn't wash cars. She has red hair and the other girls said she wore a dress because she knew boys would be there! But now she *isn't even in the club any more.*"

"Boy," Tom said. "that's some story. Well, I guess when you're supposed to wear blue jeans you better wear 'em."

"When I grow up," Abby announced, "I want to change my name to Sandra."

There was a lesson somewhere in his seven-year-old daughter's report on charitable endeavors by the daughters of Beach millionaires, but it eluded him. Where had he been living for the past thirty-eight years? On Mars? In the Belgian Congo?

"You missed the scene," Marty said. "We had a little discussion, your daughter and myself, about car washes, just before you came in. She wanted me to run the pickup truck over so the club could wash it. She was quite upset that she had no car to contribute. I tried explaining that it isn't *our* truck and it doesn't need washing anyway."

Abby's lower lip fluttered. "I was the only one who didn't bring a car. That's why I didn't stay."

Marty started cleaning off the diminutive formica table. Her swift movements betrayed a burgeoning disgust, a repugnance toward the environment and what it was doing to her family.

The children, distressingly tireless in the heat, grabbed rusted pails and shovels after lunch (they seemed to eat with only half their small behinds on the chairs—one leg dangled toward the door awaiting the last gulp of food) and darted out the back to dig.

"Want a bite?" Marty asked.

"Only if it's *ceci* beans," he said. "*Ceci* beans with a little olive oil and garlic, maybe some oregano and basil. Cold. It's better than anything. They sell 'em hot in Jewish neighborhoods. *Haisa arbis*. In Mexico they call 'em *garbanzos*. Do Anglo-Saxons have a name for *ceci* beans?"

"Chick-peas. I'm fresh out."

He pulled her into his lap. "Ah, I'm needling you. I can't eat. I'm too excited about that pile of stones outside. I feel great. I wish you did."

She touched her fingers lightly to the back of his neck. "Tom darling, please don't worry about me. You make me feel guilty. I wish you wouldn't be so noble."

"I can't help it. I'm a big noble dog. How can you have bags under your eyes, and your skin is all sweaty and still be gorgeous? Hah?"

She rested her head against his chest. The heat-laden air enveloped them like a hot bath. "I wish I wasn't such a drag, Tom," she said.

"You're not. It wouldn't be any fun without you." Aware that he had not rallied her, he tried another tack. "Hey, I had a talk with Davey. He admitted he was wrong last night. He isn't going to bother with that Hilltown business any more. We're in great shape."

"I'm glad."

"Yeah, this is the day we give babies away!" He reached in the hip pocket of his shorts. "Look! Free coupons!" He gave her the pass cards that Mermelstein had left with him.

"What are these?"

"Passes. To a beach club. DeKay sent them over. His man Si wanted some pictures of the dig and I guess this is how he showed his gratitude. Look. Grab the kids and get into a taxi and go to the Peruviana Hotel. Live a little. Now that the kids have new bathing suits and their asses are covered, why shouldn't they live it up?"

She studied the embossed cards distrustfully. DeKay's generosity had become a rhythmic interval in their lives, like breakfasting, showering, paying bills. She had seen the Peruviana from the outside—a high, coruscating palace of multicolored tiles, glistening white plaster and curving tinted glass.

"Why don't *you* come, Tom," Marty pleaded. "After last night's nonsense it would do you good to swim and sit around in the sun."

"I'm up to my navel in rocks. I want to call Hall. If I get wound up early I might drop by. Here, take some dough and grab a cab—"

"A bus will do," she said firmly. She got up from his lap and walked to the door, summoning her children.

He stroked her bare thighs gently. "I love you," he said. "You know what? Ever since ninteen forty-five when Ed Hoag, that bastard, called you in the middle of the night."

He hopped down the steps and trotted toward Ballard. Spots and McIsaac had joined Dave, and the sight of the three Negroes, working their shovels in the hot sand, reassured him of his mission.

2 *Our Heritage*

THE urgent matter of launching the *God-O-Rama* had caused Ira deKay to neglect another of his enterprises. Ever since the halting motorcade, four days ago, the promoter had lost track of the honored guest of the Beach, Mr. Banjo. As Charlie Rasmussen had suspected, Ira owned twenty per cent of the orangutan.

Nothing Ira did was ever without its hidden facets, its subtle unseen values. The red ape now earned eleven hundred and fifty dollars a week as a network television performer. Moreover, he picked up an additional twenty thousand per annum for guest appearances, endorsements and the like. One-fifth of this total of roughly seventy thousand dollars a year accrued to Ira. His interest in the welfare of the orang was thus not merely a matter of publicizing another visitor. It was a matter of cash in Ira's pocket. Recently, some officials of the network had voiced doubts as to whether an orangutan (a stupid orangutan at that) was really worth in excess of a thousand dollars a week. An ill-timed publicity story about Mr. Banjo's earnings had deluged the network with angry letters from school teachers, PTA's and the National Education Association. It was suggested that Mr. Banjo take a short vacation at the Beach, while the public furor ebbed. The protests, they felt, would be short-lived. The fact of the matter was, that aside from the cranky pedagogues (whose letters, Ira insisted, had the earmarks of a write-in campaign) the bulk of the network's viewers *approved* of Mr. Banjo's high earnings. It was argued that nothing could be more in the American tradition of equal opportunity for all than the capacity of a rufous Malayan ape to earn fifty thousand dollars annually. Besides, how could anyone get angry with someone as cute as Mr. Banjo?

In overlooking the animal's welfare, Ira experienced a slight stab of guilt. His relationship to the orangutan and to his manager, Walt Kapustka, was an old and honored one, a partnership that had left a rare mark on American mass communications. Some five years ago the network had started a program called *Our Heritage*. It was to be, in the words of an executive, *A Window on American Culture*—an hour of the finest in music, drama, literature and all the arts, telecast from noon to one every weekday for the culture-starved housewife. In an hour's time, the weary home-maker in Des Moines might rest in her living room and hear Robert Frost read his own poems; listen to a lecture on Botticelli by a man from the Metropolitan; be introduced to modern dance; learn about Ashanti carvings. The program was an abysmal failure. It competed with a cozy variety show, whose MC specialized in double-entendres. It could not possibly succeed. There was less of a demand for poetry and chamber music than was dreamed of in the executive's philosophies. *Our Heritage,* sponsorless and unwatched, was destined for early oblivion. At the time of its struggles, Ira was employed at the network in the press department. He was a kind of free-wheeling, "special assignment" publicity man, earning more money than the vice-president in charge of the department, a solemn, worried man who used to head the United Press radio desk. Ira, virtually illiterate, and given to spending his afternoons buying drinks for the boys at Shor's, operated as a commando, doing special work for the network's top stars, placating irate television critics, using the corporation's lavish expense accounts to keep the free-loading press in a state of snarling toleration.

Our Heritage was hardly Ira's dish of tea. Indeed, the program's producers, all of them Harvard Club types with impeccable tastes in wine and possessors of charge accounts at J. Press, regarded the brash, blond man as a boorish freak. Yet through some mixup in memoranda, Ira found himself invited to a high-level meeting at which the fate of the network's ambitious, money-losing cultural compote would be decided. The fact that three vice-presidents were attending the sombre conclave did not prevent Ira from arriving a half-hour late. He had been entertaining a visiting lady television columnist from the prairie in the Sherry-Netherland, and had implanted in her a reservoir of good will that would last until her next exciting visit to New York City. On the way to the executive chambers, deKay passed an office where such odds-and-ends as children, animals and "specialty acts" applied for casting. His curiosity was aroused by the sight of a pink, hairy, baby ape, dressed in yellow cap and yellow trundle-bundle and wrapped in a yellow blanket. A thickset young man with lush sideburns was feeding it formula from a bottle. Ira was irresistibly drawn to the infant. Introducing himself, he borrowed the infant orangutan and proceeded to the gloomy deliberations in re *Our Heritage*. The effect was instantaneous and overwhelming. Except for one of the Harvard Club fellows, the vote for Mr. Banjo (as Ira named him) was unanimous. He would be the needed "humanizing" element on *Our Heritage,* a mascot, a companion for the program's genial master of ceremonies (*Cultural Guide* the network called him), Hal Justice. What ensued made history in the annals of broadcasting. An ignored, ridiculed, unsponsored program became a massive success. *Our Heritage* still dealt stubbornly in terms of the Fine Arts Quartet of Minneapolis and the newest way to hang mobiles. But now there was Mr. Banjo—always looking on with his adorable quizzical grin, stealing Hal Justice's fountain pen, eating the script, trying to play the recorder when Pro Musica Antiqua gave its weekly recital. Culture, the jobs of two vice-presidents and two producers, and the cause of daytime television, were all saved by a baby ape. Publicly, the officials of the network would not admit this. They commented: "*Our Heritage* proves that the American people crave the finer things on TV. They want more art shows and classical music. Statistics show that more people attend concerts than go to baseball games." But in their heart of hearts, they knew what Ira deKay knew—that Mr. Banjo had triumphed where Botticelli had botched. In time, the ape took his lofty place in the national celebrity complex. Fan clubs blossomed; women offered him love and money; invitations poured in daily—to civic fetes, athletic events, resorts, corporations. Everyone wanted to know Mr. Banjo, to have his picture taken with him, to be touched by his clammy hands. Behind the new public hero, the adorable little fellow who now had a wardrobe of two hundred outfits designed by Sarah d'Alois, stood Ira, owning a neat twenty per cent and as he put it, "laughin' and scratchin' and havin' a ball." When, two years later, with Mr. Banjo firmly established, Ira left the network for the brighter horizons of the Beach, his furtive ownership of the orang continued. Ira saw to that. He impressed upon Walt, the manager, his powerful associations with network hierarchy; he refused to be bought out and had the arrangement formalized in a severe contract.

Mr. Banjo's current sojourn in the Beach had a twofold purpose. First, it was considered politic to remove him from the program while the brouhaha over his earnings continued. Mr. Banjo was also the opening wedge in a campaign to bring *Our Heritage* to the Beach for a week of telecasting. Mr. Banjo was an advance party for the network. To aid him in surveying the Beach, the network had despatched a young lady from the staff of *Our Heritage*. Her name was Kitty Schmitt and she was currently Ira's guest at a meeting in the Peruviana. Miss Schmitt's assignment was to determine whether the Beach was a good locale for a week of *Our Heritage* and, more importantly, whether Ira could raise enough money to help finance the costly business of transporting and provisioning a staff of forty people.

She was the kind of young woman who gravitates toward the rougher jobs in mass communications as naturally as a paramecium will wiggle toward light. Ira had known dozens like her. He understood Kitty Schmitt, appreciated her, found himself in rapport with her from the moment she burst upon him in his office in the hotel. Cleo and Si watched her narrowly: she was, after all, from New York, from a network, from a big program. They both felt a grudging admiration for this hyperthyroid, attractive girl with orange hair and pale powdered skin. When Mr. Banjo and his manager joined the meeting, she scooped him up with athletic arms and bussed him furiously. He whimpered joyfully, and the manager, jealous of Miss Schmitt's proprietary onslaughts, reprimanded her.

"Ah, cut it out, Kitty,'" Walt Kapustka whined. "You know the vet says you upset him. It's your perfume, or something. I can never get him to sleep after you love him up like that."

Kitty guffawed. "*Crazy!* You hear that, Ira? The monkey's got hot pants for me!"

"I often wondered about that, Walt," Ira said, grinning. "How does Banjo get his jollies? All these years you've never let on."

The manager blushed. "He's too young. The vet says they don't mate until they're eight years old. Banjo isn't six yet."

"Two years to go," Ira said. "Got anyone in mind?"

"Don't look at me!" Kitty shrieked. "My date book is filled up until New Year's Eve 1960! *Waah!*"

There were additional references to Banjo's sexual habits. Only Cleo remained aloof from what she regarded as a crude subject. Soon Ira directed the conversation toward the business at hand. He discussed in perfervid terms the Beach's emergence as the Cultural Mecca of the New South, the variety of program elements that could be arranged. He spoke lavishly of the *God-O-Rama,* suggesting that *Our Heritage* should originate its first telecast from the new tourist attraction. For the rest of the week, the Peruviana would be an admirable home base. As for the matter of the moneys needed to defray the expenses, Ira was convinced he could raise whatever was needed. His word was his bond along the Beach. Everyone would want to get in on the act. By simply plugging a half-dozen local enterprises and industries they could raise the money in a week. As for transportation, billeting and meals, he would work out a deal with an airline and with the Hotel Association. Shrewdly, he made the problems appear a little more difficult than they actually were. Miss Schmitt was there on a mission. To minimize what she was after would be to do her a disservice.

Mr. Banjo was due to make an appearance in the toy section of a department store. The visit had been hastily arranged by Si to appease Walt, who noted that a second-rate lightweight boxer was getting more space in the newspapers than Mr. Banjo. Ira, anxious to be rid of the ape, suggested that the task force proceed to Erlenmyer's Toy Department immediately. The manager, still complaining that his principal was being slighted, guided Mr. Banjo (trig in Navy whites, a gift from the officers and men of the U.S.S. *Hannebrink*) toward the outer office. Si followed. The women remained seated, bronze by gold, ignoring each other like two wary three-year-olds in a nursery.

Ira uncoiled his legs and walked across the room. He peered indifferently down at the cabanas, baking below. "Cleo, sweetie," he said. "You better go along and help out. The Erlenmyer people are clients. We oughta give them the grade-A treatment."

"If you say so," she said. She started for the door.

"I guess I should go also," Miss Schmitt cried. "I mean—I *am* supposed to keep an eye on our hairy friend. Don't you—"

"Oh, *never,* doll," Ira crooned. "You're the *guest.* We'll handle Mr. Banjo. I want to check you on this *Our Heritage* bit. Besides, I haven't talked to a network type in months. I'm achin' to hear all the old gossip. Who's doin' what to whom and with what."

Kitty Schmitt bellowed. Her laughter was rich with echoes of lumberjack camps and tramp steamers. She and Cleo flashed startling white teeth at each other in lying smiles.

" 'Bye," Cleo said.

" 'Bye-ee," Kitty answered.

As soon as Cleo was in the outer office—weathering with crimsoned neck the arch winks and nods of Helene and Lucille—Ira glided toward the sliding doors and locked them. Kitty touched her cuprous hair lovingly. It billowed and dipped about her white face. Across the air-conditioned atmosphere, an arcane aroma drifted from the television girl's arms. Ira appreciated the odor. He knew it was expensive stuff, probably freebies—an elixir that Miss Schmitt in her post as a strong-arm girl had mulcted from some manufacturer's representative. It had the smell of loot.

Ira sat next to her on the sofa. "So what's new at the factory?" he asked. "Sometimes I almost miss the old place. Oh, those crazy expense accounts!" He leaned closer. "I'm the only man in the history of that company to put in for a urinalysis!"

Miss Schmitt could laugh almost as loud as Ira. She joined freely in appreciation of his past exploits. The raucous howling suggested a convention of gag-writers, all sworn to indulge in convulsive laughter at each other's wit.

"Oh, I heard all about you before I came down," Miss Schmitt said. "I was warned."

"Zile," Ira said. "What they say about me?"

"What *didn't* they! You're a legend there." She suppressed another bellow. It seeped out of the sides of her wide, red mouth in driblets. "You know that big couch in Hubert Fassnacht's office? The one you used to have?"

Ira leaned his yellow head on the back of the sofa. The memory of the couch was too much. "*That* couch. Kitty, sweetie, stop—"

"Well," she bubbled, "that's known as deKay's Castle. They claim you and your friends rubbed it smooth. And that recording!"

"What recording?" He touched her knee considerately. His hand moved gently up a thick thigh.

"*You* know, don't play cute. The tape they made with the hidden microphone the day you had that actress in your office. Oh, I almost split a gut when I heard that the first time. They play it every Monday at the programming meeting. What I never could figure out is why you didn't say anything—letting her do all the talking and moaning. It's the craziest!"

Ira nodded; the remembrance of old victories stirred him. "Yeah, that was some caper. I was young, strong and foolish then. Kitty doll, you're lookin' at a shell of that man. This tropic living is wearing Ira down."

His hand had reached bare flesh, and there it rested. She placed her own hand on top of his, a gesture of encouragement rather than deterrence.

"I haven't noticed it," she said. "I've known you one half-hour, and you're living up to the advance."

Here was the enviable, unimprovable, magnificently compartmented situation: the locked, isolated hotel suite (what matter if Ira's secretaries sat ten feet away), the available woman—preferably a new woman, the pleasing atmosphere of self-sufficiency, of insularity, of imminent success. The odors, the small noises, the sense of freedom, all these were marvelously familiar to Ira. He spoke of these pleasures with a hint that he wished he could share them with unfortunates like Si. This was his attitude towards his bed partners—how many there had been! How various and how deliciously remembered! The important thing was for *them* to have a good time. Ira got more than he could handle, he confessed modestly. It was the woman who needed happiness, whose pleasures were important. He told this to all of them, and invariably it helped break down resistance and intensify pleasure.

Kitty Schmitt had been engineered into a reclining position. Ira sat at her side. He was in no hurry and he was rather enjoying the ambling conversation about his days of glory at the network.

"Everyone still flips over the way you worked both sides of the street," the television girl said.

"Who would *ever* say that about me?"

"Only everyone. I nearly died when they told me how you worked it. You know—being a big wheel at the network where you could get anything plugged on the big shows, and also having your own public-relations outfit on the side! What an idea! No wonder you made out."

It was true. During Ira's last year with the corporation he had met Si, a penniless but creative press agent. The association was made in heaven: Si thought up the gags, the copy, the gimmicks and Ira got them on the air. At first, a good deal of secrecy surrounded the relationship. No one knew that Ira, employed at high salary to publicize television performers, was running his own business on the side. The firm, predecessor of Ira deKay Associates, was called simply Public Service Counselors. But there were no secrets in the industry. In time it became common knowledge that the network's top publicity man was in business for *himself* feeding his clients to network programs. The network was run with Puritan firmness, and everyone anticipated that Ira's downfall was imminent: men had been summarily discharged for far less imprudent actions. Yet Ira survived. Indeed the reaction of network officials was to laugh the whole thing off. *Good old Ira! That deKay—anything for a laugh! You have to admire the son-of-a-bitch's nerve!*

"Good old Ira!" Kitty cawed. "That's what they say about you! I almost split a gut when I heard how you had Hal Justice giving free plugs for Victory Outboard Motors, who were *your* client. And Ferguson Motors are paying *Our Heritage* seven thousand bucks a commercial. The network lost that account, didn't they?"

"Yeah. A bad scene." Ira looked sheepish. "I couldn't keep everyone swinging." He seemed to melt in the middle. His tallowy figure bent over her. He kissed her wide, wet mouth; his hands deftly lifted her skirt.

"Hey," Kitty whispered. "What is this? Field Day?"

The bus dropped Marty and the children two blocks from the Peruviana. They walked in a sun-flooded canyon. The walls were of plaster and glass; at its base flowed a river of acromegalic cars. The children seemed happily oblivious. They knew they were going to a club, just like Sheldon Ellenbogen did every day. Marty envied them their simple acceptance of the Beach. As on the day when deKay had rescued her in front of the alligator store, she sensed the uncomfortable disorientation, the feeling of not-belonging and not-understanding. The endless vista of high white towers staggered her. Where did all these people come from? How could they all afford vacations? In her innocence she did not understand that secretaries and shipping clerks made up a good part of Beach clientele. She, who worried about paying the baby-sitter, could not comprehend coach flights, packaged one-week holidays (free mambo lessons) and the Modified American Plan. She did not understand that pleasure was now served in a great public trough; that the Ira deKays had opened wide the gates.

Pizarro, ten feet tall and bearing a suspicious resemblance to Robert Taylor, saluted them in front of the Peruviana. In spurious stone, he sat astride his charger, raising the sword of conquest. Horse and rider were set in a little island of greenery, bordered by sidewalk and broad asphalt driveway. The terror of the Andes, the murderer of Atahualpa, stared with sightless stone eyes at the banner:

ANNUAL GIN RUMMY TOURNAMENT!

WELCOME PLAYERS!

Marty smiled. She envisioned Pizarro in scarlet cabana suit and hand-rolled Havana double claro, shuffling a fresh deck and casting a dour eye on the score pad. She wondered if perhaps Pizarro might have been less the bloody, greedy bastard that he was, had he known how to play gin rummy.

The lobby suggested a wing of the Armoria Real in Madrid. Memories of the conquest and of the Inca Empire abounded—in mammoth tapestries, in suits of armor, in pasteboard weapons. Urns, benches and desks were fashioned of a curious brown-gray imitation stone, cunning approximations of the boulders which the Indians had used to build Cuzco. She halted at the threshold, overwhelmed by the vista. A bellhop noticed her dazed condition. He imagined her to be a lost governess—the plain cotton dress and the unvarnished face belonged to a guardian of wealthy children rather than a paying guest.

"Can I help you?" he asked.

"Yes. I'm looking for the cabanas. The pool."

"You'll have to go 'round the side. No bathing suits in the lobby—even *children* in bathing suits." He winked with vulgar familiarity. He was convinced she was hired help—a working stiff like himself.

Marty ignoring him, reaching in her bag for the passes deKay had given them. "I'm Mr. deKay's guest. He's supposed to have reserved a cabana for us."

The bellhop glanced at the pasteboard rectangles. These, and the mention of deKay, effected a miraculous change. The matey coziness was gone. He was back in line. "Oh. Friend of Mr. deKay's. Sure. Go right through the back, down the steps. Forget about the kids' bathing suits."

She guided the children through the lobby, to an enormous patio on which people were lunching, down a flight of marble steps, to a turnstile where an enameled blond checked credentials. Marty flashed the cards again.

"I'm Mrs. Sorrento," she said. "We're Mr. deKay's guests."

The woman reacted. "Of course! Mr. deKay said we should expect you. He'll be down later." She tapped a desk bell, and in answer to her summons a muscular water-god appeared. He was blond, tanned and fuzzy; his face as vacuous as a grapefruit. Around his thick neck hung a whistle on a lanyard and he carried a clipboard under one arm. What seemed to be a faded insignia (Olympic Team? Red Cross?) had been sewed to his trim yellow trunks; he had no behind.

"Shep," the blond said, "this is Mrs. Sorrento, Mr. deKay's guest. Did you get Number Two ready for her?"

He beamed. "You betcha. Right this way."

Marty and the children followed him through a maze of small tables, chaises, beach chairs. A score of gin rummy games were in progress. The players were largely men of middle age, most of them with a kind of stooped, round-shouldered weariness. Shep, the water-god, moved among them like a eunuch slave among the Ottoman Turks. At the center of the patio was a small bar, set beneath a thatched roof. A half-dozen bathers lounged at it, sipping tall drinks. The pool itself was immense, free-form and empty. The guests of the Peruviana seemed more intent on card games and sun-bathing. Marty asked Shep why no one was swimming.

"They had a live porpoise in the pool yesterday," he laughed. "A promotion stunt for one of Mr. deKay's accounts. I spent all morning scrubbing and vacuuming the pool, but everyone's still a little nervous. I don't know why. There isn't a cleaner animal in the world than a porpoise."

The cabana was at the edge of the beach. Shep opened the door with a master key. The interior of the beach locker was dazzling, its walls painted with red-and-white peppermint stripes. There was a full-length mirror, a private sink, toilet and shower, a radio-TV set, a selection of modern beach furniture. A closet was stocked with snowy towels and bath mats. The water-god fumbled in a medicine cabinet and brought out a selection of oils, unguents and creams.

"You don't look like you've had much sun," he said solicitously. "Want me to grease you up a little?"

"No thank you," Marty said. "I'll manage."

He bustled about, arranging chaises, spreading towels, checking the plumbing. Marty, mildly self-conscious, undid her cotton dress, beneath which she wore an old white bathing suit, a relic of their summers in New Hampshire. She shaded her eyes from the fierce sun. Shep was upon her with a pair of expensive smoked glasses. Distantly, across the giant pool, she could see a brightly painted children's playground—swings, sliding ponds, Jungle Jims—and a smaller pool. Dozens of noisy children shrieked and raced around its rim.

A dark young woman with the massive thighs of a swimmer walked toward Marty. "Mrs. Sorrento?" she asked.

"Yes."

"I'm Florrie, the swimming instructor. Mr. deKay suggested I take the youngsters off your hands. Would they like to come over to the kiddie pool? There's lots of children there today."

Nicky and Abby, awed by the splendor, hung back in the interior of the cabana.

"If they'd like to—" Marty said hesitantly. "The little girl can swim, but Nicky's rather shy in the water."

Florrie smiled. "Mr. deKay left life preservers with me, and brand new shovels and pails. Come on, Abby. You too, Nicky."

They inched out of the protective walls, surveyed the heavy-legged temptress and were won over. They waited for the approving nod from their mother and followed her across the duckboards.

"You're on your own," Shep said cheerfully. He gave the beach mattress a few housewifely pats. "That's Mr. Braud in number three. *Fenton* Braud. You know? The Kansas City people?"

"I'm afraid I don't."

"Well, that's him. Wonderful nice man. Looks like he's in the gin rummy tournament. Would you like a drink?"

"No thank you. I'll just rest here."

"Okay. You want anything ring the buzzer." He half turned and eyed her again, with an odd, probing gaze that bordered on effrontery. "You an account of Mr. deKay's?"

"I beg your pardon?"

"Does he represent you?"

"No." She looked the other way, and the water-god bounced off. Marty stretched out on the chaise. She had a splendid view of the pale green surf, the snowy bubbling breakers. The sun, a dispiriting enemy inside the hot boathouse, was now possessed of a comforting, strengthening quality. She rubbed a fine patina of aromatic oil on her limbs, and looking up, saw Fenton Braud turn from his gin rummy game to leer at her with randy humor. He offered no greeting. In his venal mind, she could only be one thing—especially when she came as deKay's guest.

She relaxed. Sweating pleasantly, absorbing sunlight, she appreciated the absence of the children. To be free of Abby's abrasive whinings and Nick's moodiness was more of a boon than she had imagined. Bound to the children incessantly, she had forgotten the guilty joy of losing them for a while. Around her rose the dull hum of card games, of aimless conversation, the sputter of speedboats. She was part of it, yet comfortably isolated from it.

Exhaustion drained from her limbs; her mind became splendidly free of worries. Withal, she conceived a fine distinction between her surroundings and her state of comfort. She could still ignore (or, if she chose, abhor,) fat men in tangerine cabana suits and one-dollar cigars; over-blond women in pink wedge shoes; all the vulgarity that she imagined the Peruviana and the Beach, and deKay for that matter, exemplified. Yet she could still avail herself of the simpler pleasures of rest, freedom from her children, change from the horrid boathouse and her husband's crew of misfits. For the first time since their arrival in the vacation community, she felt at ease. It delighted her that no one around the amoeba-shaped pool knew her, that the water-god's nosiness had gone unrewarded, that Fenton Braud's lewd wink had been as ill advised as the black silk half-hose and black patent-leather slippers he favored for beachwear. Distantly, a Latin-American orchestra played; the repetitious phrases, suggestive of wiggling behinds, drifted across the littoral. Marty closed her eyes and rested. Sun-warmed and brain-washed, she dozed.

3 *The Treadway Viking*

THERE was no telephone in the boathouse. In mid-afternoon Tom had tried to reach Maitland, using the phone in the Ellenbogen foyer. Neither Lila nor Erwin were at home, but the colored butler, aware of Dr. Sorrento's esteemed position with his employers, had welcomed the archaeologist. Maitland was not in his office, and Tom left word with the switchboard operator at the University to have him return the call. An hour and a half later the butler summoned Tom from the site; the call was being completed.

In his sandy shorts, shirtless, Tom felt ill at ease in the Ellenbogen mansion. He kept thinking of the story of the old man who was ashamed to use the toilet in his rich friend's house: *I took it out and it looked so shabby I went outside and made peepee on Lefkowitz's lawn. . . .*

Maitland's high-pitched voice with its undercurrent of amusement came to him after a few seconds. He could see his father-in-law in his mind's eye: the gluttonous torso, the ridiculous skinny legs, the small, well-shaped head. He was probably sitting at his desk in the cramped office in Detering Hall, surrounded by remembrances of his years among the primitive peoples of the world. There was the Malagasy war mask over the filing cabinet . . . the Mandan blanket . . . the stone money from Yap . . . the batik cloths from the Celebes. . . .

"Hall?" Tom asked. "That you?"

"That's right. What's the matter, Tom? Anything wrong down there?"

"No. I just need some advice. I don't know what we've got here—a big bust or a gold mine."

"Lucky you got me. I just flew in from Canada this morning and I'm leaving for Guatemala in a few days."

"What were you doing in Canada?" Tom asked, smiling. Maitland was always being summoned to adjudicate ethnological arguments, to pronounce his benediction over a new fossil, to observe, honor, participate and in some manner underscore what his hosts conceived to be another major discovery in the quest for man. Tom understood that before he could raise any of his problems regarding the dig, Maitland had to be "on."

"Do you know anything about the Treadway Viking?" Maitland asked.

"It sounds like a Sherlock Holmes case. 'The Treadway Viking' —a story for which the world is not yet prepared."

"It does indeed," Maitland said. "I've just had the assignment of destroying the poor chap. It'll be a long time before I'll be invited to Ontario again."

"Hall, you once warned me to stay out of Viking controversies. How'd you get hooked?"

"Oh, I owed the Canadian Archaeological Society a favor. They did me a few good turns when I lived with the Haida back in 1928. So I agreed."

"What was all the hollering about?" asked Tom.

"An unusually severe case of virulent *Vikingitis*. A little mining village named Treadway above Port Prudence. Ever since the iron mines gave out, the chamber of commerce has been trying to remake the community into a tourist mecca. There's a heavy Scandinavian population in Treadway, and it was decided that a local history of Norse settlements was in order. I needn't remind you that *every* Viking claim ever made in North America has been proven fraudulent. But they keep cropping up. In this instance, the ancient Norse tradition was based on a handful of old artifacts—two alleged halberds and a broken sword turned up by an old sourdough named 'Liar' Bruce."

"*Liar* Bruce?"

"Yes. A tribute to his credibility. Yet the city fathers were ready to accept this old rascal's handful of junk as irrefutable proof of the prior existence of a colony ruled by Lief the Unlucky. It took me about a day and a half to throw Mr. Bruce's artifacts into the ashcan. I had the halberds scraped down and the cleaned metal revealed the ancient runic inscription: 'Souvenir of the Keen Blade Tobacco Company 1895.' They were souvenir tobacco cutters, about as Norse as the stuff you're digging up. And the broken sword—well, it was genuine Viking, but it was from Lars Ulfmann's collection in Oslo. I recognized the insignia of his private museum after we'd scraped it down. Somehow it had found its way to Canada. So much for the Treadway Viking."

"I guess they voted you man of the year in Ontario," Tom laughed.

"Hardly. I was practically run out of town. The local Norse's asses were all for lynching me. You see, I'd destroyed the dream. The Treadway Viking already is in a new textbook and he's been widely discussed on television. He'd become so famous that rival groups are claiming he isn't a Viking at all but a Norman knight. The local French-Canadians are damned if those Swedes will out-ancestor them!"

It was a pure Maitland adventure, the kind of escapade in which the anthropologist delighted. Indeed, it appeared to Tom, it was what he seemed to live for in his autumn years. Maitland rejoiced as much in the *rejection* of his findings as he did in the search for evidence. If the Treadway Chamber of Commerce had accepted his judgment, he would have been miserable.

"How's *your* work progressing?" Maitland asked.

"That's why I called. I need counsel."

"I'm no expert in Southeastern prehistory, but I'll try. What have you found so far? Have you been digging according to the plan we worked out?"

"I started with it, but I'm way off in left field now. The stratification is all screwed up. Even Ballard can't figure it out. There's a white sand surface soil, then a yellow subsoil, and it's interlaced with accretions of muck. Davey figures the muck was used in association with the burials."

"Burials? Then you've found skeletal remains."

"Two of 'em. Usual flexed burials. And a skull trophy cup with one of them. If the ossuary follows the usual pattern, the rest of the bodies should be north and south of the two we found. I'm stopping the excavation of the provenience sections and extending the pit around the gravesites. Okay?"

"You're there, Tom. You know better than I do."

"Well, the kitchen midden is what we expected. Lots of shells and some small animal bones and a lot of pot shards. The usual Glades pattern—incised, fluted, so on. Haven't found any fancy wood work. A few Busycon picks and one shell scraper. Everything would indicate a Calusa settlement, late Glades. The way the strata are loused up, I guess the place was occupied and reoccupied from time to time."

"That doesn't sound particularly confusing," Maitland said. "Why do you need my advice? You're doing as well as can be expected."

"I'm coming to the zinger. The other day the midden turned up a triangular stone with a face carved on one side. We checked it with the published material and it looked an awful lot like an Arawak piece."

"*Arawak?*"

"That's it. Hall, it was almost a ringer for the picture in the book. It was identified as a problematical stone, maybe an Arawak *zemi* or idol."

There was a heavy, breathless pause. Tom stretched his legs out; his dirty sneakers, almost toeless, looked ludicrous on Lila's velvet carpeting.

Maitland cogitated. "Another Treadway Viking in the making. Be careful, Tom, very careful. You know I'm wary of Sunday supplement theories. They've been talking about Arawak culture in the Southeast for years and they've never found a bloody thing to substantiate it. Oh, those old stories about Abaibo—but no proof. As a matter of principle I'm against that kind of unproven nonsense."

"Sure, Hall. But I still got a *zemi*. The book says it could be an Arawak idol."

"You want my advice?"

"That's why I called."

"Keep the thing out of sight until you're back in New York and we've had a chance to classify everything. It's probably a freak of some kind and has no more to do with that simple little Glades settlement than the Treadway Viking. It's probably a piece of trade goods. It might be as recent as Spanish historical, for that matter."

"One other nutty thing, Hall," Tom said. "I started sinking test pits east of the baseline this morning, after I decided to abandon the sections. We were working about twenty feet from the highway and we didn't find a thing all day yesterday. I figured that meant the land had been excavated already and pretty much disturbed. But this morning Ballard hit a big white stone—a kind of calcite—not the usual sand rocks you find here.

It was about a foot high—maybe two and a half feet wide. Dave thought it had been worked. We extended the pit east and west, and we found two more white stones—irregularly shaped, but placed as if to mark something off."

Maitland waited a good five seconds before responding. "What are you planning to do now?" he asked.

"I don't know. I wish I knew what I'm digging. I'm just going to keep extending the trench and see how far the thing runs. What do you make of it?"

"I would guess—and this is just a guess—that they're historical. They could be the remains of an old Spanish fort or retaining wall. Or even more recent. Have you checked the history of the area?"

"I'm going to have Peltz do that tomorrow. I left the stones *in situ,* so I don't know if there are any inscriptions on them."

"Tom—will you hang on just a moment?" he asked. "I want to look at one of my books."

Sorrento rested the phone (it was chartreuse—matching the foyer's decor) in the crook of his neck and shoulder, and lit a cigar. As he looked for an ashtray, Lila materialized. She smiled warmly at him and brought an onyx platter to the marble-topped table.

"I'm awful," she whispered. "I was eavesdropping. I was *fascinated.* How do you know so much?"

"Be my guest, Lila. No secrets."

Pleased, she sat down opposite him. The dull afternoon of canasta, of aimless babble about hairdressers and pediatricians, the chattering nonsense about what things cost, and what you could pay and what you could get, vanished.

"Give my regards to Professor Maitland," she said quietly. "Tell him he's more than welcome to visit us. He could stay here. But warn him—if he does, he's got to speak at the Women's Club."

"He'd love it. Just feed him good and make sure the wine is iced."

He heard a shuffling of papers and then Maitland again. "I'll be damned if I want to get into this can of worms," the anthropologist said, "but what do you know about the ball court?"

"*Ball court?*"

"The way you describe those stones—I wish I could see them—they might conceivably be the *seats* around an arena. You recall anything about the game?"

"Little bit. The courts were rectangular, weren't they? About two hundred feet long and half as wide? It was a kind of Indian *salugi*—wasn't it mostly a Mayan and Aztec game? But the Arawak played a simpler version of it."

"Oh, yes. They found a beautiful court in Puerto Rico some years ago, neat as a football field. On either side there were stone seats for the spectators—a kind of early Shibe Park."

"Suppose it is a ball court?"

"Tom, all the caveats I mentioned earlier still hold. This is only a vague guess. My personal feeling is, you've unearthed an old Spanish ruin. But we've got to take any possibility into account. Don't talk about a ball court—not even to Peltz or Ballard. It's the kind of notion that will titillate every idiot reporter and half-witted feature editor in the country. It has the same kind of identifiable quality as that Egyptian Ship of the Dead—or the Dead Sea Scrolls. It's what my friends in Journalism School would call a natural for the split page, whatever that is."

"I'll keep my mouth shut and keep digging."

"Keep extending your trench along the axis of the unearthed stones. Let's see how long the thing runs. If it is an arena, there should be a parallel row of stones either north or south of the line you're working on. Where would that take you?"

"Let's see. Fifty feet north, we're dead. We're on the highway. I don't think the city would let us dig it up."

"What's in the other direction?"

"That's fine. We go fifty feet south, we're beyond the big trench—the burial ground."

"I'd suggest you start sinking some test holes immediately. Of course, the fifty-foot figure is variable. I seem to recall that's an approximate size. I'll check the literature." He paused. "You know—you may end up having to clear the whole area to find it."

Tom whistled. "Five acres of sand? Two and a half feet down? How can we?"

"I'll tell you this, Tom—and it's only for your ears. If you've hit on an Arawak community in the Southeast, you've found something of enormous importance. All our notions about Circum-Caribbean cultures will have to be reappraised."

"What you're saying is I better do this as thoroughly as I can. But hell, I'm short-handed, and it's the middle of August. Take me another six weeks to clear that place—I'd need heavy equipment, trucks to haul the fill away, and workmen. We're still fooling around with a small shell-heap and an ossuary. We figured the funds out to the last three cents. Where's it going to come from?"

"I'll worry about that. I'll come up with some foundation. You do what's necessary. Make arrangements with your friends—what's their name?"

"Ellenbogen."

"Yes, Mrs. Ellenbogen. Tell her you may be there through the end of September or later. I'm sure her husband will advance you some money. I'll get it to you within a week."

"What about my class? School starts September 23."

"I'll have Grafmyer sit in for you." Maitland paused. "I'm supposed to be in Guatemala in a few days," he said slowly. "I might . . ."

"What's in Guatemala?" Tom asked.

"Oh, another jurisdictional fight. The country is oversupplied with anthropologists. I've been warning them to leave the Indians alone—the miserable people are so busy answering questions and staging ceremonies, they don't have time to tend their fields. There's a little upland village—Chacatenango—with about fifty Maya-Quiche in it. Two rival gangs of anthropologists descended on them this summer, and the economy's been paralyzed. There are a dozen of our colleagues from the Institute for Creative Social Science, and a like number from Yale. That's about one anthropologist for every two Indians. That's a bad ratio, and besides, the intergroup squabbling has become disruptive of native life. You know the kind of thing—bribing the elders for recollections of the good old days, stealing artifacts. The Maya-Quiche don't particularly mind—the price of a photograph has gone up to three pesos, and if you want to see the Jaguar Dance, you've got to keep the whole town in beer for a week. But the local officials want those maize fields harvested, and my job is to decide which group has prior rights."

"You're having a great summer."

"I'm rather enjoying it," Maitland said.

Tom knew that he was: his wife, a drab and unresponsive woman, had been dead five years and he was not the kind of father who had to immerse himself in children and grandchildren, using them as selfish reminders of his immortality. He and Marty observed a cool, formalized relationship. Apparently they both wanted it that way. For Maitland, life was at its richest when he was racing for a plane or a train, off to Timor, or British Honduras, or even a prosaic meeting of the Southwest Ethnological Association at Taos.

"I tell you what's occurred to me," Maitland said. "On my way down to Central America, why don't I drop off and look at the work? A day or two would be sufficient."

"Great!" Tom cried. "We'll be glad to see you! Wait till I tell Marty—and the kids!"

"Fine, fine," Maitland said. "I'll wire you when I get my reservations. Looking forward to it, Tom."

They said their goodbyes. Hanging up the pastel phone, Tom mused over Maitland's indifference to his daughter, to Nicky and Abby. He had not asked about them, he had not indulged in sloppy sentiments about how much he missed his darling grandchildren. Tom wasn't shocked by it—in his own family you were perpetually inundated in affection. His parents slobbered and wallowed in their estate as grandparents. There were always gifts, wet kisses, hugs, sighs and squeals. The children didn't particularly appreciate it, and Tom could remember as a child rather objecting to these moist displays of love by his grandparents. If Hall Maitland chose to be casual about the biological process that had prolonged his line another generation, why criticize him? It was refreshing, Tom felt. Wasn't most parental and grandparental affection *self-love*? An assurance that your own special essence was extended after death? He was sure Maitland *liked* the kids, *liked* Marty, valued the fact that they were a happy, integrated family. What more was he supposed to do? Sing "Baby Shoes"?

"Is Professor Maitland coming down?" Lila asked. "I'd love to see him! And he *must* stay with us!"

"Looks that way. He's excited about what we're digging up. Hey, Lila, you weren't supposed to hear. You're in on the secret now. The ball court. Maitland doesn't want any speculation about it until we establish what it is."

She rolled her eyes. "Not a word! Not even to Erwin!"

"That's my girl." He got up, aching. Lack of sleep and the day's digging had enervated him. He started toward the door, limping pronouncedly.

"Where are you running off to?" she called. "Rest a while. How about a drink? Have you had lunch?"

Was he the young Thomas Wolfe? Fussed over and made love to by glowing Jewish women? Seeing Lila, dark and round and eager, offering him food, he dismissed the comparison. Lila merely wanted him to enjoy a nice glass of root beer, to munch on a tunafish-salad sandwich. Where did these romantic notions about women originate?

"I'll take you up on it," he said. "Considering the luck I've had today."

Her kitchen was the kind that endowed a visitor with a feeling of helpless inadequacy. It was endless, tiled, compartmented. The eight-burner stove was an island entire of itself, located in the middle of the terrazzo floor. There was no true refrigerator: rather an entire wall had been given over to a series of cold lockers suggesting a merchant ship's storehouse. Coppery pots and pans, almost too decorative and lustrous to be dirtied with sauces, hung in patterns like a group of mobiles. There was a built-in Dutch oven, wide and high enough for a haunch of venison, and there were burnished cabinets, cupboards and storage areas sufficient to hoard comestibles and potables for an extended siege. Withal, it was a strangely sterile kitchen. No food was in sight, no smells intruded, nothing seemed to have been used. Tom suspected that Lila's grandmother's kitchen smelled better. All he could discern was a pine-scented deodorant, as appetizing as a broom closet.

"What a setup!" Tom whistled. "Boy, you could cook *linguini* with white clam sauce for the whole Beach here!"

"You'll have to settle for a corned-beef sandwich," she said apologetically.

She bustled about authoritatively, served him a massive sandwich and a glass of beer and then watched him eat with a quiet pride.

"I feel guilty, already. Leaving poor Ballard out there by himself."

"You deserve a breather. Erwin and I were watching you this morning."

"You learn anything?"

"Stop teasing. I love to listen to you talk anthropology. The way you just did with your father-in-law. I like it because it hasn't anything to do with making money. It's all for its own sake."

Tom sputtered. "Hey, Lila! You think I wouldn't like to make money? My trouble is I've never known *how*. I have a kind of built-in resistance. For one thing, I'm a Neapolitan and they're lousy business people. No *Yiddishe kopf*—"

"Where did you learn all that Yiddish?"

"I used to be *Shabbes Goy* on Tutwiler Avenue. No kidding.

Lila, as long as I can remember, I was always the guy who couldn't earn a nickel. I had a *Bronx Home News* route once. What happened? They tore down all the houses on my route for a Sanitation Department Garage. In college, I used to get jobs from the Employment Office. The worst jobs. One year I was an usher at Forest Hills—the tennis matches. Every other usher was making out like mad—quarters, half-dollars! Me? I got three dimes and a thank-you. Maybe I didn't look like the Forest Hills type. Naturally I ended up teaching. Where else could I get paid so little for being so smart?"

"Oh, sure. I guess you don't love the work, do you? How about how excited you were talking to Professor Maitland?"

"Sure I like it. Sometimes I wish I could do better by Marty and the kids. I'm thirty-seven and still an assistant professor. Maitland won't let me leave the department because he says I'm too valuable a lecturer, and he's reluctant to promote me because he's related to me. Besides, I'm lazy. He'd get an argument from the University if he tried to upgrade me—I haven't written a paper in two years and I'm a slow reader—can't keep up with the literature."

She leaned over the gleaming kitchen table conspiratorially.

"But the ball court—won't that make a difference?" she asked. "What a paper that'll make! A *book!*"

"Who knows?"

She was looking at him intently. Her round black eyes were something more than motherly. He was her discovery, her protégé, her gift to the Beach. "Where's Marty?" she asked.

"She went to some hotel. DeKay's stooge—that little guy, Mermelstein—came around with some passes. So she took the kids for the day."

Marty's recent spurning of Lila's own hospitality (she was welcome any day, at any time to the Ellenbogen pool) distressed her.

"He certainly is latching on to you people. You know, I didn't think of him as your type. How does Marty stand him?"

"She doesn't have to talk to him. He's done us some favors."

For a moment he wondered whether he should tell her about the misadventures of the previous night—the mad ride to Hilltown, the encounter with the law and Ira's magical intervention. But he said nothing.

"I envy you and Marty," Lila said. "I know I'll put my foot in it—whatever I say—but you do so beautifully without any of the external nonsense we put up with. It's like—like the two of you have done away with paper work."

"Marty's a good girl. To put up with me, she's got to be."

"Don't knock yourself, Tom. It's both of you. You're so wonderful with each other—understanding, in a casual way."

"Are we? I never noticed."

"Well you wouldn't, Tommy, because you have that kind of offhand *grace*. Marty, too. It seems all the married people I know, all of Erwin's friends, they go around advertising publicly what hot stuff they are. The women all *tsatskied* up and the men puffing and huffing. They're saying, look at us! *We're married and we go to bed every night and we're secure!* Chances are he's sleeping with his secretary, and she's had a premature climacteric. I can't stand people showing off how happy they are with each other! It should be unsaid, *unadvertised*."

"You think Marty and I have some kind of special touch? Why? Because my kids' behinds stick through the trunks? Because one of Erwin's assistant foremen gets more money than I do? You know better than that, Lila."

She frowned. Solemn, her face was prettier than when it was distorted by humorous outbursts. Her mouth needed repose to look its best. "I never meant that. It's as if there's some kind of unspoken goodness between you and Marty. Respect—a balance—an appreciation of really valuable things. It's something the two of you share. Of course you'd like more money. But it's so wonderful how the two of you ignore that. Honestly, Tom, you're teaching me a lesson just being here—what it's all about."

"When you find out, tell me," he said sourly. He drained his beer. She had served it to him in a frosty copper mug.

"You know—you're a terribly attractive man," she said. When she delivered judgment her voice was a trifle too high.

"A beauty. Enzo the Ginzo."

"No, you are. It would be like you to knock everything about yourself."

"Now what brings this on, Lila?" he asked. He sensed that their bland and semi-jocular conversation was veering off the paved highway into a jungle trail.

"Well—as we used to say when we were kids in Manhattan—*don't hit*. I think you're terrific. Not in any suggestive way, but just as a kind of neutral observer. That's my opinion. You're some man. Your work—your humor—that gladiator face with the sad eyes."

He got up. "Enough. Lila, you're too rich for my blood."

"Go ahead, have a joke at my expense. I deserve it. Me with my sneaky compliments because I happen to like you." The last two words she uttered seemed to droop and falter—as if she were fearful of uttering them, then managed to overcome her embarrassment.

"I think you're neat," Tom said. "The beer and the corned beef was great. I'm going out and I'm going to dig like a wild man. Listen—if you want to, grab a shovel, put on a pair of old shorts and come out some day. There's no union and it's your land."

"Could I really?"

"*Any* day. On second thought you better wear loose slacks instead of shorts. The crew will be falling into the holes."

"Aren't you sweet! Erwin likes me this way." She jokingly slapped one jeweled hand against her high, round rump. It responded with a rich, live noise. The gesture was a humorous one, Tom was certain, yet the hint of flesh was unmistakable—and unnerving.

They walked to the door.

"I almost forgot—Erwin wants to take you and Marty out to dinner this Saturday night. Can you make it?"

"You and Erwin don't have to go escorting us around," he complained. "You aren't under any obligation to us."

"You aren't being very gracious," Lila said. "Besides, Erwin wants to talk to you about something. Some ridiculous thing he and deKay cooked up. I don't know how it concerns you."

"You twisted my arm. I'll ask Marty."

He opened the enormous door. The exterior heat rushed in like a blast from an open hearth furnace. "What I said before—about how much I like you," she said quietly. "That's between us, isn't it?"

"*Ma shoo*. You're allowed to."

"I mean, I felt a little stupid after I said it. After all, I'm thirty-three and married, with a child."

"What are you going to do? Feel guilty for a week? I'll see you at the big trench. Wear old clothes."

When he had left, she went up to her bedroom and watched the diggers for a while. It filled her with a wondering admiration that these poor people could work so hard, so long and with such dedication for something that had no relevance to the goals she had been taught to respect. She marveled at Tom and his father-in-law (one of the great names in social science) bubbling with schoolboy enthusiasm over a row of white stones. She began to undress, unlayering her canasta uniform, releasing her soft body from the confining straps and rubber and hooks that it suffered for public display. During the disrobing process she made wry comparisons between Erwin, whom she loved and respected, and Tom Sorrento's ragged friends below her window. The difference, she suspected, was that Erwin *related* to his environment; he understood it and thus could control it, or, when it contested him, meet it on its own terms. Tom Sorrento—and his wife, for that matter—were on the fringes of the culture pattern. Nothing they were involved in related to the well-oiled, operative mechanism of the economy, of the social structure, of the intricate tables of status and role.

Freed of the binding encumbrances of high fashion, she put on a lounging robe and sat at the window. She stationed herself at an angle, fearful of being discovered in her clandestine observance of the diggers. Tom had rejoined Ballard at the new trench they had started. Peltz walked over to them, and all three were studying the white stones at the bottom of the pit. They seemed in high spirits, and she loved all of them for it. The older she got, the harder she found it to laugh, or to enjoy herself or be diverted without an expenditure of money. She began to smile, sharing their boyish pleasures; she could never tell Erwin how she felt.

Tom lowered himself into the trench. He took a trowel from Ballard and began loosening earth around one of the stones. He worked quickly and deftly, changing the positioning of the tool in his hand as he cleared loose earth. After a few minutes of intense work, he placed his hands on either side of the stone and with a slow, deliberate motion, using his muscled back and shoulders, raised it from its ancient bed. He straightened up, in the manner of a weight-lifter, and held the pale rock aloft to Ballard and Peltz. They applauded his heroics, with appropriate mock enthusiasm. All three now bent over the stone, turning it, examining it, touching its aged surface.

Lila, observing it, trembled with compassion for Tom Sorrento. She scrutinized, with poorly suppressed longing, his almost nude body, hard, brown and black-fuzzed, his square cropped head with its blunted profile, and she wanted desperately to protect him, to help him, to be mother and lover and sister and all women to him. Perhaps the world had no use for him and his works. If that were the case, Lila was convinced, they didn't know what they were missing. Of course, he wasn't much of a help to himself. Why couldn't he at least wear a decent pair of shorts and sneakers without holes in them?

4 *Detzler's Rise*

MISS KITTY SCHMITT, having fulfilled her initial assignment for *Our Heritage*—securing the enthusiastic cooperation of Ira deKay Associates in the plot to telecast the program from the Beach—was efficiently despatched to an ocean-front suite with a few fatherly pats from her host. Ira had lived up to all notices, professionally and socially. When she got to her room, she shrieked joyously on discovering a white silk Baby Doll from SFA on her bed, with a scrawled note reading: *Live a little—Ira.*

As soon as the television girl had left (Ira found her noise a trifle unsettling) he showered, splashed armpits and chest with his post-lust cologne, and garbed himself in a rakish cabana set—a lemon-yellow terry-cloth item, figured with green sailfish. He strolled, scrubbed and perfumed, through the outer office, advising Helene and Lucille: "No calls, kids. I'm going to the cabana to rest it."

They giggled, and resumed collating Si's questionnaires. Ira never shocked them. Everything he did was so *funny,* so *crazy,* how could you get sore at him?

Marty saw him strolling through the crowded patio. He waved to friends, pinched an elderly woman's arm, kissed a bald man's head, sampled a stranger's rum punch at the bar.

Ira crossed the duckboards and waved at Marty. She smiled indifferently at him.

"Hello *there!*" he sang. "Aren't we relaxed!"

Fenton Braud made a half-turn and stared insolently at Marty again. Ira introduced them; they exchanged greetings with cool civility. From the manufacturer's standpoint, she was a high-priced whore; in turn, Marty regarded the old man as a brainless lecher indulging in a child's game. They had no time for each other.

Ira sat on the edge of a padded chaise. He took off his yellow jacket. His skin was tanned, hairless and baby-smooth. For a few seconds he indulged in the cosmetic arts, moving with the luxurious sloth of a woman at her toilet. He squirted fine golden spray on his limbs and his chest, rubbing the oily liquid into his skin with adoring strokes. He dabbed his button nose with a white salve; he adjusted a pair of sunglasses on his eyes; he fiddled with the adjustable reclining chair until he had achieved the angle most delicately suited for his long body. Then he settled back and grinned at Marty.

"Position is everything, I always say," he said. "What do you always say?"

"At the moment I'm having trouble saying anything. Someone's using some disgusting perfume and it's making me nauseous."

Ira could not be offended. He sat up quickly. "You don't like my Rome Mist? I send all the way to New York for it."

"Is that smell on *you?*" she asked.

He vaulted from the chaise, trotted to the empty pool, and dived in. In a few seconds, dripping, he was back. "That should help," he said. "The sun and the chlorine should get it off. Most women go *wild* for it. I guess you have special tastes."

"As a general rule I don't like perfume on anyone. Myself—or men."

"Zile. Are you putting me on?"

"I don't understand you." A conversation with deKay required simultaneous translation. "Putting you on *what?*"

"*Oops.* I have to remember you're strictly Squaresville. I meant are you kidding me, pulling the leg. It's musician talk. To put someone on is to slip 'em the needle."

"I wouldn't try to kid you, Ira."

"I'm never too sure when I'm chatting with you. Or your husband for that matter. I got a feeling you both know too much. Not my kind of knowledge—but something you've worked out up there in the big University."

"We're not that complicated."

"*Heeeell* you're not." He looked at her askance, narrowing his eyes behind the green glasses. "I'm the type chappie who can reach anyone. I can do my act in front of Senators and corporation presidents and they love it. But not you and old Tom. You don't buy me."

"Let's say we wouldn't know what to do with you if we did." Marty sat up, letting an ocean breeze strike her warmed face. She saw deKay staring at her—not with his customary brashness, but with what seemed genuine puzzlement. She felt she owed him more than polite detours and prim restraints.

"I guess I'm being something of an ingrate," she said.

"It's all right. I ask for it."

"No, I don't mean it that way. You've been very generous. I'm enjoying it here. Honestly. It's the first relaxation I've had since we came here. It's cool, and it's private, and to be frank, it's a delight getting the children off my neck. It's wonderful the way they look after them. My two are among the world's champion complainers—but I haven't seen or heard them for two hours. I can't believe my good luck."

He half turned, resting on one elbow. "Why that's peachy. That's what I want. For *you* to get a break. That's all."

"I wonder. You've always got some motive, haven't you? I mean—there I go insulting you again. I'm sorry."

"No, no. Go on. You think I mind insults? I eat 'em up. The president of the biggest ad agency in New York once called me a four-flushing, mother-loving, conniving son-of-a-bitch. You know what I did? I sent him a case of champagne with a note that said 'Congratulations. You are the One-Thousandth Person to call Ira deKay a son-of-a-bitch and therefore you win this.' Go on—what were you going to say about my motives?"

"Just that all the attention you're paying to us—to Tom and myself—can't be out of the warmth in your heart. I suspect you think you can make some money out of the dig. Disabuse yourself. Nobody cares about old Indian bones."

He lit two cigarettes, expertly shielding them from the ocean breeze, and handed her one. He was wearing what appeared to be an outsized fraternity ring on his pinky and it confused her—it was inconceivable that deKay had ever gone to college.

"Since we're getting chummy," he said, settling back on the chaise (he did so with an exquisite languor that suggested he had access to every chaise in the world), "I'll open up the discussion. You know why I've been hunking for you and your old man?"

"I've no idea."

"Oh, you play it cool, doll." He wrinkled his nose, then looked grave. "I can't shake you. I can't lose that first crazy vision of you walking across Ellenbogen's land, barefoot and beautiful, with that flat, private can of yours in washed-out shorts."

She drew her breath in. "You're damned rude."

"You wanted to know about motives. Who told you to have that kind of skinny rear-end? And that smudgy, no make-up face, all by itself. Why you didn't even *look* at me! I was *hurt*."

"I wonder why I'm bothering to look at you, or have anything to do with you now." She turned her head. All he could see was the unruly, short brown hair, gold-flecked from the burning sun; he wanted to touch his mouth to it.

"I thought this was Fun and Games time," Ira said. "We started out so nice." She ignored him. "I promise I won't mention your fanny again. But that won't stop me from thinking about it. Or staring at it."

To get up and leave would have been, in a sense, a surrender to him. On the other hand, subjecting herself to his undergraduate sexual forays was barely worth the sun, the breeze, the invigorating absence of the children.

"You know," he went on, "I don't suffer for a lack of broads. They're in oversupply in this town. Inventories are way, way up. The last thing in the world I thought was that I'd start getting weak-knees over a married woman with skinny legs. I guess maybe it was because you cut me short. It was the old challenge again. Trouble around here is it's all too easy. For *me,* anyway."

"Be quiet," Marty said. "I *am* enjoying it here, and I'm grateful to you, but you sound like those Porky Pig boys from Princeton I used to date many years ago."

He bounced up and sat on the edge of the chaise, confronting her, resting his chin on his clasped hands. Gold and blond, yellow and tan, he exuded health, comfort, joy unbounded.

"How old are you, Marty?"

"Thirty-three. Why?"

"You ever cheated on your husband?"

"No, and shut up."

"Why?"

"Because I've never felt the desire to."

"Hmmm. You know what the man with the survey said. What's his name?"

She despaired of his ignorance, his intrepid gall, his cavalier assumption that you had to meet him on his own terms. Yet, curiously, his physical presence did not trouble her. He was like a bullfight poster in a rumpus room: out of place and nonfunctional, but decorative and in some measure, exciting.

"Kinsey."

"Yeah, that's the cat. He says twenty-six per cent of all married women have cheated. But he's way, way off. It's at least twice that. And you know what? The others, maybe they've never given in, but they'd just love to."

"How do you know so much?"

"It's my specialty. That's what it's all about. More and better love. If you don't believe that, you're lying to yourself. Most people can't manage it. That's where I'm different. I admit that's what I want. I go after it. I get it."

"I can't take you seriously for one minute, Ira," Marty said, trying to staunch the flow of self-adoration. "If you think you're getting me excited, you couldn't be wronger. You don't know a damn thing about me." She smiled. "All that boasting makes me suspect you're a suppressed homosexual."

Ira patted the white ointment on his nose affectionately.

"You're making it *rough* for old Ira," he half sang, his voice rising musically, on the word *rough*.

"Old Ira will get much much older before it gets any smoother for him."

"What's with you? Don't you crave adventure? Change? With that head—and that limber body? Who you kiddin'?"

She looked at him soberly. "I'll be damned if I know how I've come this far with you, but I'd better put an end to it right away. Ira, I know all about sex. You can see the baboons doing it in Central Park Zoo if it's the right season. All the importance that people like you attach to it—you'd think it was terribly, terribly hard to do. Since you're so bloody interested, I had a few affairs before I got married. I rather enjoyed them. And I slept with Tom before *we* were married. I like it. It's pleasant. It's necessary. But I married Tom not just because of a series of athletic contests on a mattress. I respected him, and admired him, and wanted him. Now as for this much-publicized cheating you recommend, what about it? Isn't one adventure pretty much like the next? The same clumsy shedding of clothes, the embarrassed peeks and the ridiculous opening grabs and tumbles? And the uncoordinated mingling of arms and legs, the mechanical procedures that any Hottentot is capable of, the fumbling, and the positions that hurt your back and tire your legs? Is that what your life is dedicated to?"

"Go on, go on, sweetie," he said admiringly. "I'm dizzy."

"I had some of that when I was single, and very young," Marty said. "It was all right. Fun and games, as you put it. But how much of it do you really need? Why strain a marriage by indulging in this kind of four-footed copulation? Why ruin your life for a sweaty afternoon in a hotel room? I seem to recall you never got around to getting all your clothes off. Or the chambermaid walked in at the wrong time."

She lay back, proud of her declamation. Ira's thoughtful silence indicated she had made an impression on him. He stood up, stretching lazily. "Like a drink?" he asked. "Old Freddie over there whips up a cool thing called a Conquistador. Three kinds of rum and four fruit juices."

"I'd love one."

He ambled off, exchanging humorous banter with Braud, with a glandular blond woman in a Bikini, with the bartender. He returned with two long, frosted glasses: peppermint-striped straws and a gardenia decorated each icy tumbler. She sipped the decoction gratefully.

"All I can say at this crucial moment," Ira said, "is you just knew all the wrong men. Let's see—you're thirty-three and you been married how long?"

"About nine years."

"*Zotz.* So you were just a girl when you had those affairs. With older men, I bet, who were sick of their wives. Goof-offs. I wouldn't expect you to appreciate a Rembrandt now, if the only pictures you ever saw when you were a kid were Mickey Mouse and Popeye. Rembrandt's an acquired taste."

"Will you do me a favor and drop the subject?" Marty asked, with evident annoyance. "Class is over. I can only stay here another half-hour and I want it to be as relaxing as it was before you showed up with your Hygiene Lecture. If I'm being ungrateful, I mean to be."

Ira was not hurt. "Right. I don't know you that well. Good-o. What do you want to talk about?"

She adjusted the chaise into a full horizontal position and lay back, closing her eyes, hoping to discourage him.

"Oh, I don't care. I'm talked out. Tell me about your life, Ira. Somebody like you just doesn't happen. How'd the elephant get its trunk?"

"Kiss my what?"

"You boor. I was being literary. That was Kipling."

Her request, tendered half jokingly, was promptly honored. Ira began talking about himself. He discussed his rise to eminence with a good deal of wild humor, with flashes of shrewd self-analysis. Marty appreciated that. He confessed that he was largely a fraud, but what difference did that make? He was in step with the times, with his environment, with what people wanted. And how could anyone get mad at Ira? If he picked your pocket, you laughed while he did it.

His real name was Detzler, a rather common German name in the Dakotas. DeKay was something he had dreamed up for his first job—demonstrating waterless cookers for housewives in St. Paul. It had a nice, classy sound, and he had it changed legally some years later when he left the Army. He had once read a paper-bound novel (he couldn't remember the title or the author) about this poor kid from the Middle West who tries to crash high society on Long Island, who changes his name, and becomes a big boot-legger, but is very sad because they never really accept him and he finally gets killed by mistake. Ira was confused by the book. It was very close to his own story: the humble prairie origins, the change of name, the striving for a higher social level. Ira could not see what the cat was so miserable about. He, deKay, could move anywhere, see anybody, get any broad. Everyone laughed at his jokes and invited him back. Why, there was this crazy Cotillion that the old social families asked him to promote last year, and before the thing was over he had two of those sweet little girls. . . .

Marty halted him, reminding him the subject was off bounds. She thought for a moment of offering him a condensed course in American Lit., beginning with the lecture on "The Ordeal of F. Scott Fitzgerald," but she felt that Ira, in his one-dimensional way, had offered a fairly good critique of Gatsby. What was so terrible? What was there to shed tears about? Who in the story was worth it?

Ira's father, he told her, had operated a store in Moriah Center, North Dakota. There were no farmers in the family. All of their relatives were merchants of some kind, supplying goods and services to the agricultural community surrounding them.

As long as he could remember, he hated Moriah Center, hated North Dakota, hated most of the people with whom he was forced to associate. He hated the flatness, the bone-chilling winters, the gasping, breathless summers. "They got the fastest dogs in the world in North Dakota," he told Marty, "because the trees are so far apart." Yet despite the bleak surroundings, Ira managed to "live it up"—to the extent that one could live it up in Moriah Center, pop. 3,401 (Gateway to the Mouse River Valley). During the depression Detzler's Store was closed half the time; his father worked for the WPA; his uncle Walt, they said, died of a broken heart when his jewelry store went into bankruptcy. It seemed to Ira that in these years—he was in high school then—the men in his family seemed to shrink and pale. Their shoulders drooped, their flesh sagged, they became moody and given to sitting quietly for hours, wondering perhaps what had happened to their splendid, sure-fire world of trade. They even lost interest in baseball, which in many ways was the closest thing to True Faith among the merchants of Moriah Center. The local semi-pro team went out of business; six of its star athletes, including "No-Hit" Hansen, were in the C's—the Civilian Conservation Corps. In time, there was even very little discussion about the Chicago Cubs. Hack Wilson's batting average suddenly became unimportant, unworthy of prolonged debate, in the face of three new foreclosures in Clark County. His mother, Ira remembered, a long-faced woman, taller than his father and as flat and hard as an old barnside, sustained herself through these years of poverty with the River Brethren. He could never remember her wearing make-up, looking pretty, offering anything in the way of romantic excitement to her husband or any other man. Many years later, Ira heard about the theories of human behavior which contended that you were supposed to be secretly in love with your mother; he had himself a good laugh over that. His mother was all right, he supposed, for darning socks and baking cakes that had no taste, but she was about as sexy as yesterday's cold mashed spuds.

Ira had always been a "card." The people of Moriah Center began talking about Hank Detzler's funny kid from the day he took part in the fourth-grade poetry recital. Ira, decked out in navy blue suit and boiled white shirt, was supposed to recite *I Wandered Lonely as a Cloud.* Mrs. Burmeister had rehearsed him for a week until Wordsworth was coming out his ears. Then, in the crowded Assembly Hall, before the eager parents, Ira bowed and, grinning impishly, recited:

When Washington was President
As cool as any icicle
He never on a railroad went
But always on a bicycle!

Mrs. Burmeister was furious, but everyone roared and applauded, and asked for more. Ira's declamation was a welcome relief after a hot afternoon of Shelley and Longfellow, what with the horseflies eating people alive in the crumbling auditorium. From that moment of glory (public opinion saved Ira from disgrace) Ira was marked as a joker, a funny guy, a kid who always had something snappy to say or something crazy up his sleeve. Ira soon learned that he could make his clownishness pay off. He had his big chance when the *Bismarck Journal-Register,* in an effort to boost circulation in the outlying farm areas, began to distribute cartoon buttons to children. The buttons were of white enamel with a pin on the back. On their faces was the picture of one of the *Journal-Register*'s cartoon favorites—Boob McNutt, Der Captain, Etta Kett, Castor Oil, Barney Google. Above the likeness was a five-digit number. Every day, the newspaper, above each comic strip, would print twenty such five-digit numbers. If a child were lucky enough to get a button with both the published number and the cartoon character, he then mailed it to Bismarck and received a cash prize—anywhere from a dime to a dollar depending on a code at the bottom of the cartoon page. The kids in Moriah Center went wild over the buttons. Even without the incentive of cash prizes, the buttons were the most exciting thing that had happened to the children of the dusty, baking town since the Mouse River had dried out, leaving its muddy bed alive with leaping crappies and buffalo-heads. Oddly, although the *Journal's* circulation jumped noticeably, very few youngsters could be found who had ever had a winning button. Indeed, in all of Moriah Center, only Freddie Meinicke got a button with the magic digits. He mailed it in and received his twenty cents in a thick yellow envelope. One evening, when a dozen children were loafing on the loading platform of the Moriah Center Cold Storage Plant, Ira, for laughs more than anything else, invented an intriguing story. He created a fictitious relative—his uncle Bert Detzler—who held an important position with the *Journal-Register.* In fact, he helped set type for the newspaper and was in a position to control the numbers above the comic strips. Ira had been talking to his Uncle Bert that very week end, and his uncle had allowed as he'd be very happy to include a few numbers from buttons owned by Ira and his pals. However, he'd need the figures two days in advance—plus five cents per number, because it involved changing type. Ira told the story with such brilliance and with such complete believability that his friends inundated him with buttons and nickels. He collected a dollar and thirty-five cents before the prairie sky had darkened. The children wanted to believe; they yearned for the shimmering promise of Free Money. Ira continued his magnificent stories about Uncle Bert for something less than a month. He collected close to twenty dollars, and not *once* did a winning number appear in the newspaper. Dutifully, he kept accepting buttons (once, he even staged a mock mailing at the Moriah Center Post Office—despatching a fat envelope loaded with buttons to the mythical uncle) and regaling his worshipful audience with tales of his uncle's imminent fulfillment of all their dreams. As the weeks went by, and the boys became uneasy over the failure of their numbers to appear, Ira began inventing excuses. For a twelve-year-old, his performance was dazzling. He did not merely lie, he created cliff-hangers that kept his donors spellbound. The reasons for Uncle Bert's negligence were so glorious that the boys would leave Ira almost delighted that the distant agent of happiness had *not* been able to gratify them. On one occasion, Uncle Bert had been enlisted by G-men to track down a notorious killer; he had lost the buttons during a mad chase across the state line. Another time, just as Uncle Bert was about to insert the Moriah Center figures in the newspaper, the publisher caught him in the act; they had a bloody fist-fight, and the plan was delayed. On another afternoon, Ira's uncle had been forced single-handed to remake the entire newspaper because the editorial staff had called a strike. For several days Uncle Bert alone put out the *Journal-Register,* and obviously he could not be bothered with cartoon numbers. After six weeks of breathless anticipation—few parents in Moriah Center got to read the newspaper before the kids tore it apart to scan the comic pages—Ira called his friends together for some sad intelligence. *Uncle Bert had died.* He had been feeling poorly that morning, but in the great tradition of newspaper work, he had gone to the office, determined, *that very day,* to get every single number that Ira had sent him into the newspaper. There were, Ira revealed to his drooling audience, five one-dollar winners, ten fifty-cent winners, and many, many twenty-five, ten- and five-cent winners. He was starting to set type when a terrible pain seized him around the heart and he fell stone dead. It was suspected in Bismarck, Ira whispered, that cronies of the killer whom Uncle Bert had helped the G-men apprehend had poisoned him. Not a single childish voice of protest was raised when Ira had finished his story; not a single boy bothered to check up on him; not a single benefactor asked for his money back. The truth of the matter was, that in picking their pockets, he had given them a darned good time. The daily search for numbers, the ritual of giving Ira the buttons and the accompanying money and, best of all, Ira's serialized story-telling about the Adventures of Uncle Bert were well worth the thirty-three dollars and eighty cents that young Detzler had earned through his imagination and glibness. The experience taught Ira that it is wrong to work hard; that it is easy to make money; and that people like to be had.

Ira had laughed his way through high school, learning little beyond a working knowledge of the saxophone, which he played in the marching band. He was a good athlete, but he hated the discipline of competitive sports. Besides, he was better off running the hot-dog and soft-drink concession during football season (and making more money out of it than anyone before or after him) than getting his head cracked by gigantic Swedes and Finns.

His parents sent him to Minnesota Tech to take a business course. He had already advised them he had no intention of standing behind the sagging counter at Detzler's (Coal, Coke, Ice —Hay, Grain, Feed & Seed) and letting the surly, tight-fisted farmers eat his heart out by running up huge bills they never paid, and then going to the chain store that had opened across the tracks. *Nerts to that,* Ira told his parents. His father nodded and accepted his only son's decision—he never could talk to Ira, largely because he didn't understand the words Ira used. His mother was horrified; it seemed that all Ira cared about was dance bands, girls and clothes. He spent all his money ordering new suits and shoes and shirts from Monkey Ward, and there wasn't a pretty girl in town who wasn't crazy about Ira Detzler—*the funny things he comes out with!* The River Brethren held no attraction for him.

He lasted less than two years at Tech. The dingy college bored him stiff, the courses put him to sleep, the girls were a drag. He organized a five-piece dance band (The Northern Lights) and made enough money to pay his tuition, his board, and leave him a tidy profit each semester. In his last few months at Minnesota Tech, the bulk of the profits went to pay for an abortion for the school nurse, a pulpy blond woman in her late thirties who had an apartment in town, a husband in the Navy, and a yen for Ira's slim, fair body.

By nineteen-forty he was in St. Paul, demonstrating fireless cookers, picking up odd jobs as a sideman with dance bands, hanging around radio stations and vaudeville houses. He was never broke, but he never had quite enough money. He had severed all ties with Moriah Center and his bleak, miserable parents—to send to them for money or advice was unthinkable. There were always women—divorcees, widows, girls on the fringe of show business, waitresses. The vast army of dissatisfied, lonely females of the plains turned to Ira and his jokes, his boyish good looks, his capacity to make them forget, to make them feel enormously important, to inject them with his own exuberance.

The footloose life ended on Pearl Harbor Day. Ira went into service. The circumstances of Ira's entry into the armed forces were remarkable in themselves. A few months before the outbreak of war, Ira had organized a four-piece combo, with girl vocalist, to play at a private party at the home of a Minneapolis industrialist, a vice-president of the Universal Farm Equipment Corporation. Ira had gotten up a little comedy act—a risqué take-off on radio programs that involved much goosing of the singer—and the boys in the band did a few cute novelty numbers. They made a tremendous hit with the Twin Cities' top families. The host and his wife were fascinated by Ira, who, knowing a good thing on sight, ingratiated himself with both of them. He was an honest, straightforward country boy, one who knew all about Universal Tractors and Threshers and Binders—but also knew the latest songs and dropped hints about his good pal Tommy Dorsey. The vice-president would meet Ira for lunch once a week, take him to the exclusive Hide and Hoof Club, introduce him to his rich friends, and in general came to look upon the handsome, blond kid with the snappy dance band as one of the family. Ira reciprocated. He always had a fund of new jokes for the vice-president; he arranged for him to sleep with the vocalist; and he himself seduced the man's wife.

When war came, the Army Ordnance Department, in need of trained mechanics, began to form battalions of technicians from the ranks of private industry. An Ordnance maintenance battalion's entire cadre of officers and noncoms, for example, would be recruited wholesale from a General Motors plant or an International Harvester factory. Commissions would be awarded to correspond with the civilian status of each man. A company vice-president would be a lieutenant-colonel; a section chief a captain; a foreman a master sergeant. The rank-and-file would be drawn from basic-training centers and the entire battalion would then undergo intensive indoctrination as a unit. Ira's friendly vice-president received a major's commission. Nothing would do but that Ira accompany him into Ordnance. Ira liked the idea. The war was a big kick and you had to get with it. It took a little finagling to get Ira his first-lieutenant's bars, but the vice-president made out a convincing argument for young Detzler. The battalion needed a morale, special-service and public-information officer, didn't it? Who better suited than Ira Detzler—college man, musician, entertainer? And so Ira, in elastique blouse and dusty pinks, took his basic training at Aberdeen and then went off to California with the 6028th Ordnance Battalion. They were stationed at Camp Santa Anita, a converted race track. (Ira was credited with first calling the post "Chicken Shit Academy"—a clever play on the initials CSA.) The army routine bored him to distraction. As an officer, you were not required to know anything. The various technical skills of the Ordnance Department—paper work, supply system, maintenance procedures—were all in the domain of master sergeants and tech sergeants. Enlisted personnel knew all the tricks and gimmicks. Officers just stood around and watched, administered, signed reports and enforced discipline. Ira was a much-loved officer. His orientation lectures were a combination vaudeville show and pipe night; his history of the Ordnance Department was highlighted by his reference to the hallowed insignia—the round bomb with its crown of fire—as "the flaming pisspot." Marching his men to and from the endless round of classes (it was always pointed out that in the field everything they learned in class would be thrown out the window), he would lead his men in singing new lyrics to the tune of "Colonel Bogey" which the post loudspeaker system blared at them all day.

Horseshit!
It makes the grass grow green!
Horseshit!
The finest ever seen!
Horseshit!
Oh good old horseshit!
Oh it's just horseshit
And more shit for me!

But there were pleasures beyond the composition of obscene lyrics. The camp was hard by Hollywood and Beverly Hills and it was inevitable that Ira should gravitate toward these tenderloins. As a special-service officer he had access to studios, broadcasting companies, musicians. He bought a Cadillac convertible (one conveniently appropriated by a few sharp operators from Japanese internees who had preceded the

Army at Santa Anita) and lived the high life. He slept with a variety of "starlets," crashed movie parties, enjoyed the pleasures of beach and sun, and became something of a "character." The sophisticates of the entertainment world relished his country-boy charm. "He's really a native American type," one high-priced writer told another. "He's quite impossible, but you can't help admiring that naïve Midwestern vitality." When the 6028th Ordnance Battalion went to the Pacific, Ira Detzler stayed behind as special-service officer for the post. The commanding general had taken a liking to the brash, bouncy young man with the funny stories. Ira sat the war out in a variety of jobs and when CSA closed down he became a liaison man between the networks and the Army. He was never happier. Southern California was like living inside an orchid. It smelled good; it felt good; the women all seemed smoother, and better in bed, and more agreeable. He wondered why anyone was left in the Middle West, and congratulated himself on having discovered a better way of life.

Discharged, he went to work immediately for a small public-relations firm, specializing in entertainment personalities. Captain Ira Detzler became Ira deKay. He didn't last long. Ira was too busy promoting himself, too much of a character in his own right. He seemed to appear in the gossip columns more frequently than the firm's clients. *Lunching at Lucey's: Brilliant young PR exec Ira deKay and starlet Vivianne Kent.* Asked to resign, he gravitated toward the network's coast headquarters, accepting a minor job in the press department, where his contacts with newspapermen stood him in good stead. He spent freely, had a marvelous catalogue of phone numbers, and was always ready to do some reporter for a national magazine a good turn. The network didn't mind his getting his own name in print; he delivered. Three years later he was summoned to New York to beef up the publicity department of the home office. In his vulgar clothes and corn-fed accents (California never infringed on his speech) he drew a good deal of scorn and ridicule from the hard-working, underpaid ex-newspapermen who peopled the department; Ira was an illiterate; they had all read Sartre.

His superiors, offended by his garish appearance, his butchery of the language, and his boorishness, nonetheless were appreciative of his handling of the network's stars. One, a comedienne given to hysteria and assorted psychotic problems, would refuse to go on the road unless Ira deKay was in the retinue. He soothed her. His salary was raised; some of the leading performers willingly sweetened the pot, knowing that Ira was only making eighteen thousand a year. Now he owned a Jaguar and rented a neat three-room apartment on Sutton Place. *Lovesville,* he called it. His *sub rosa* association with Si Mermelstein's struggling firm followed, and his income soared. He brought Mr. Banjo into the corporation's ranks of famous artists, and several months later he was instrumental in bringing the first nationwide network television program—*The Jerry Binks Show*—to the Beach. The tropic vacation community and the Midwestern boy fell in love on cutaneous contact. The Beach was created for him, and he had been born thirty-three years ago in that dreadful town in North Dakota for one purpose: to go to the Beach. He and Mermelstein liquidated their New York office and Ira resigned from the network. Ira deKay Associates was created. The firm could not fail—Ira was loved by everyone in the resort city (except possibly Charlie Rasmussen, who figured him for a wise rube). Clients begged him to take them on; leading citizens cultivated him. He never had to solicit business—it fell on him in a warm, loving avalanche.

"I'm too lucky," he told Marty. "The luckier I get, the more they love me."

"Who loves you?" she asked cynically. It was close to five; shadows were lengthening across the patio. Only a corporal's guard of gin rummy players and die-hard children were still around.

Beyond, in the playground, she could see Abby, tireless and yeasty, scrambling on wiry legs through the upper reaches of the Jungle Jim. Nicky, the perpetual loner, was quietly sitting in the filtered white sand—he had been there for better than a half-hour—thinking his own private thoughts. He would never be an Ira deKay.

"Who loves me?" Ira cried. "They all do! I give their lives a little zetz!"

"You mean zest?"

"No! *Zetz!*" He got up, stretching with a kind of proprietary ease. He seemed to be encompassing and absorbing the soaring white towers, the imported palm trees, the blue-green ocean itself.

"I'll give you a for instance," Ira said. "A few months ago I met a fellah named Campion, a big-time real-estate operator.

Only worth about ten million. His old lady barbecues us some steaks for dinner. They were lousy. Hard and stringy and no-taste. One thing I know is good steak. I'm a farm boy. I know beef. I know the cuts. So I took old Campion aside and told him —'Mr. Campion, for all your dough, you should serve good steak. The best steak.' He felt kinda hurt, but I laid it on the line to him. I happened to have a friend in KC, from way back—big meat-packer. So I got Campion a special deal. The best cut is a Kansas City Strip, if the steers have been fed right and the shell is aged enough. So I arranged for my pal to ship Mr. Campion a three months' supply for his freezer. Campion serves the best steaks in the state now. Every three months the Kansas City Strips come in, dressed and frozen. It costs him a little more, but wasn't it worth it? He loves me now."

How wonderfully simple! How much easier than analysis, theology or the National Conference of Christians and Jews! *Three months' supply of Kansas City Strips equals Love.* Ira deKay was the prophet, armed with the new vision—an aged steak.

She found herself unwilling to engage in pointless debate with him; she felt too good. The sun and the dermal lubricant, the brainless relaxation, had infused her with a physical glow. She felt as though she could have played three sets of tournament tennis. Across the patio, now all but emptied of the bright, busy people, she could see the thick figure of the counselor guiding Abby and Nicky toward them. Marty got up, assembling their belongings. She slipped into her cotton dress, unmindful of its tackiness.

"That outfit has to go," Ira said. "I'll get you some decent duds. I have a little deal with Tremerton's in town. Won't cost a—"

"No thanks, Ira. I'm happy to use the cabana, and I'm grateful for the way the children are being taken care of. But I draw the line at charity clothes."

"Sorry. No new clothes, no use-ee cabana. You're a beauty, but I can't have you lounging around with me dressed like a Jehovah's Witness. When you go with Ira, you go first class."

"Maybe we'll just stop going with Ira."

She got up to greet the children. Abby flew at her, bursting with anecdotes about the magnificent day at the Peruviana Kiddy Kamp. She had three new friends; she could swim backstroke; she had a strawberry malted; Florrie would teach her to high-dive. She had had a week's experience in one afternoon. Marty wondered where she had acquired the devastating capacity to be violently and inextricably enmeshed in her environment. Abby's life was a series of tearful crises arising from frustrated plans, disaffected friends, lost toys. Even when overcome with joy—as she now was—there was always an undercurrent of impending tragedy within her.

"Oh *Mother,*" she said—loudly and commandingly, "Mother, we *must* come back tomorrow. Florrie says I'm the *best* pupil she has!"

Marty didn't doubt that she was. Abby learned everything quickly, yet somehow she never stayed with any pursuit long enough to develop true skill at it.

"We'll see," Marty said. She started for the hotel. DeKay escorted her, talking continually and with apparent concern, with the little girl.

"Well, you just bet you'll be here tomorrow," he said. "Uncle Ira will even send the car for you and Mommy! How 'bout it, Nicky, you want to come back?"

The gingerbread man, lagging in the rear, studied the white duckboards. "Dey got cracks in dem," he said.

"Maybe Daddy will come tomorrow!" Abby shouted. "Oh please, mother! Let's bring Daddy!"

"We'll discuss it later, Abby," Marty said.

She thanked Ira for his hospitality and left unanswered his plea for their return—tomorrow, the next day, any day. Leaving via a side exit through a palm-shaded alley, Marty heard the strains of the Latin band. Inside the lavish lobby, couples kicked and short-stepped and wiggled in Afro-Cuban rhythms. Ira executed a few *cha-cha-cha* steps. "It bugs me," he called to Marty. "The way they dig those crazy spic songs."

"Why?" she asked. "They're allowed to."

"Yaaah. Cubans don't dance the hora." He blew her a kiss and, still dancing, entered his castle. She was able to manage a smile as he left. It had been, all things considered, an enormously restful and therapeutic day. The tightness was gone from her neck and she was free of the dread worn feeling she had come to expect at the day's ragged end.

5 *A Reunion*

On saturday night, the Ellenbogens took them to dinner. The restaurant they selected was a venerable one, in the "Old Beach" section of the community. The drive, in Erwin's air-conditioned, noiseless, pale blue Cadillac, took them through streets that evoked in Tom memories of the Bronx, and in Marty an image of Tel Aviv. The hotels were small, cramped and modest, the signs were bilingual, English and Yiddish, the streets and porches filled with old Jews. They moved slowly and quietly, patriarchs and earth mothers, beneath palm trees and under lamplight, descendants of high priests and desert prophets. They passed an Orthodox synagogue. In deference to the summer night the doors were opened and within, a sprinkling of people, in skull caps and shawls, were in prayer.

"*Shabbes* is over," Tom said. "What's happening in there, Erwin?"

"Oh, it's probably the mourners. *Kaddish.* Prayers for the dead."

The ancient ritual, observed within walking distance of the dog track (seven quinielas a night) and two doors from Joe and Sal's Pizzeria, seemed magnificently soothing.

They pulled up to an old mansion at the southernmost end of the Beach. A headwaiter greeted Erwin with evident respect. *Yes, sir, Mr. Ellenbogen.* It differed from the greetings Ira got. With deKay, there was always a hint that the two parties were almost coequal, that Ira would be allowed to go into the kitchen, pinch the salad girl and sample the soup. In Erwin's case, it was a business proposition—an employee's respect for a genuine big-spender and big-tipper, who would brook no familiarities, but had damn well better get the best cut of meat.

The interior of the restaurant was simple. It consisted of one long, high room, the walls much painted, plastered and repaired, and hued a dull gray-green. The ceiling was covered with the kind of figured metal plating, thickly coated with white enamel, that Tom remembered in old barbershops and saloons. Marty, studying the heterogeneous clientele, the innocuous bar at the rear, knew why Lila had chosen the place. In one of the Peruviana's lush rooms, or any of the other hothouse eateries of the Beach, she would have been on guard all night—apologizing, explaining, wallowing in guilt.

The food was superb—the best they had eaten since they had come South. The owner specialized in stone crabs, a delicacy that the Sorrentos had never tasted. The fat claws were served cold, each finger of firm, delicate flesh encased in its shell of ivory, edged with vermilion and black. Pre-cracked, it was necessary only to extract the white, chilled chunk of sweet meat, dip it in lime-laced melted butter and suck the delicacy from its cartilaginous stick. The flavor was subtle, elusive—tangy, evocative of sea spray and cool ocean floors. A high mound of shells grew in front of them. Erwin ordered slender glasses of pale beer and a bowl of fresh green salad. It was the kind of eating that had a spiritual side. It was simple, it touched the heart.

"How's the work proceeding, Tom?" Erwin asked.

"It's brightening up," Tom said. "Two days ago I was ready to pack up and quit. But we've come up with some exciting stuff."

Lila shot him a warning glance. As his confidante of the foyer, she wanted their particular intelligence guarded.

"Really?" Erwin asked. "Like what?"

"Well, it's a little hard to explain."

Marty looked exasperated. "For goodness' sake, Tom, you can tell Erwin."

"Oh, no, he can't!" Lila cried. Splotches of excitement darkened her cosmeticized face.

"What is this?" Erwin laughed. "What kind of conspiracy are you up to?" He seemed enchanted with the notion that his wife was party to some secret knowledge shared with the archaeologist; it enhanced her.

"Ah, the hell with it, Lila, let me tell them," Tom pleaded.

"Don't you dare! You know what your father-in-law said!"

"Hey, not so loud," Tom protested. "What are these people going to think about me—a big goof thirty-seven years old making promises to his father-in-law!"

"Well," said Lila, as loud as ever, "when he's Hall Maitland, it doesn't matter what *they* think."

Marty looked at him questioningly. "What did Hall tell you that was so secret? You didn't mention it to me. You just said he might be coming down."

She had accepted the news of her father's imminent arrival with something less than enthusiasm. Theirs was a father-daughter relationship that no standard text on psychoanalysis could explain. Marty found his company disturbing, an intrusion. He took Tom over completely. There was a surly maleness about Maitland's world, and no wife, daughter or mistress could ever penetrate it. It reeked of charred deer bones and chicken entrails, of betel and valerian. The anthropologist believed firmly that matriarchies are freakish; that priests and kings are, by and large, men; that the average man, when it matters, can beat up the average woman. He and Tom had their private names for the two well-known women anthropologists in the department. One, an authority on the Inca, was "Wafer Ass"; the other, a renowned scholar in ethno-musicology, was "The Water Hen." Marty hated it when they used the terms—the damned male wall was excluding her.

"We found some unusual stones, right off the highway," Tom began. "There's a chance—"

"Shaddap!" Lila shouted.

"Let the man talk, honey," Erwin pleaded. "Really, he's in charge, not you!"

"I heard what Professor Maitland told him!"

Marty patted Lila's soft, jeweled hand. "Lila, don't worry about what my father told him. Hall seems to think that only the elect should be allowed in on his secrets. Not that anyone really cares. Half the things he's discovered don't mean as much as one day's production at Erwin's factory. If he told Tom to keep something quiet, it was for dramatic effect."

The speech unsettled Lila. This was Maitland's daughter speaking, and speaking heresy. She cocked her head, chastised. Lila had a harsh tongue and a fair wit—but you could not engage in this sort of thing with Marty. Martha Sorrento was no canasta player to be put in her place with a riposte.

"This is all very simple," Tom said. "We may be—may be, I say, on the verge of an important find. Remember I told you at the party about the chance of Arawak contacts on the coast? I was half joking. None have ever been found. But a few things have turned up in the last few days that might show that there was some kind of contact with Arawak. Either an Arawak colony—or an Arawak-influenced Glades colony. Or maybe just a parallel development. Hall is cautious because he doesn't want any publicity on something that hasn't been proved. He's spent half his life knocking down phony theories about man."

"What exactly have you found that would substantiate this

theory?" Erwin asked. "You were saying something about unusual stones?"

"We found three of them in a row, about two and a half feet down. They could be just an old Spanish ruin, but they also might be the sidelines and seats of a ball court—an athletic field."

"How long is this job of certifying your discovery going to take?" asked Erwin.

"I can't say for sure."

"Well—an estimate? A guess—you originally figured on being cleaned up the last week of August, as I recall."

"That's right. But we may have trouble locating the other wall of the ball court."

"You'll find it!" Lila cried. "I know you will. Ellenbogen Field—the first stadium in America!" She laughed with warm vigor, and nudged her mate. "Fame, sweetheart, fame! Think how jealous all those people at the club will be! And the publicity!"

Erwin's eyes were half shut. "Suppose I give you some help? Additional laborers, trucks. I could borrow a tractor and a crane."

"It would help, Erwin," Tom said, "but most of the work has to be done by hand. I might as well tell you. Maitland said that we might have to dig up the whole area. That would take a lot of time."

"How much time?" Ellenbogen asked.

"End of September, maybe. Or longer. Depending on what turned up. I can't be sure."

Marty's face flushed. "You didn't tell me this," she said. "You mean we may be stuck here through September? What about school?"

"You and the kids can go back. Hall is going to have someone take my classes."

"Why did you have to call him?" Marty asked. "Why couldn't you work this out yourself? I know why he's coming down. In case you do find something, he wants to be in on the photographs in *Life*. All this nonsense about not telling anyone—that's an excuse so *he* can do the talking!"

Erwin laughed uneasily. "I'm sorry I started this," he said apologetically. "I just wanted to know when Tom could wind up. You see, a little problem has arisen. I thought you'd be through, per our discussions in New York, the last week in August. I was hoping it might even be sooner."

"What's the problem, Erwin?" Tom asked.

"Some problem!" Lila cried. A few patrons turned from their stone crabs as her voice rose. "He's got some scheme going with that charlatan Ira deKay! Isn't that it?"

"Lila, you don't give a man a chance—" Erwin nervously removed his smoked glasses. He called for a check, and continued. "Ira came to me with an interesting notion. A kind of educational museum and exhibit. We'd build it on my land. Something new, unusual, and, to my way of thinking, most beneficial in spreading brotherhood."

"A tourist attraction," Lila sneered. "A tourist *trap*."

Erwin ignored her. "The theme would be the world's great religions. Exhibits, lectures, motion pictures. All in the best of taste and all checked out by the best scholars in the field."

Tom's brow furrowed. "But don't people have churches for that?"

"You misunderstand me. This would be nonsectarian, yet religious in theme. It would be open to one and all."

"Tell 'em what deKay wants to call it," Lila prodded. "Get this—the GOD-O-RAMA."

Marty's eyes widened in disbelief. "The GOD-O-RAMA?"

Erwin appeared increasingly upset by his wife's taunts. "Oh, that's just a working title. I know it sounds ludicrous. I propose to have it changed, when the scholars join us in planning the exhibits. I like something like *The Spirit of Man* or *Man the Magnificent*."

"Don't change it," Marty pleaded. "Oh, please, Erwin, it's too precious, don't change it. The GOD-O-RAMA."

"Yes," Lila laughed. "You could put up signs on the highway *Twenty Miles—Nearer My* GOD-O-RAMA *to Thee*."

"I don't think it's that funny," Erwin said. He signed the check, adding an exorbitant tip.

"When would you start work on this?" Tom asked. "I guess that's why you want us out."

"Frankly, yes," Erwin said, rising. "I hoped we might have the ground-breaking ceremony on Labor Day."

Tom whistled. "Labor Day. Less than three weeks. We'll try, Erwin. I hope we can get it cleaned up. But if we find—"

"There will be no problem," Erwin said. "You tell me what help you need to expedite it. I'll arrange for it."

"Listen," Lila said sharply. "Tom will finish his work. Erwin can have his ground-breaking a month later. There's a holiday every month."

Erwin held his hands out. "But you don't understand—we have to start *building* right after Labor Day to get it up in time for the season—"

From the restaurant, the Ellenbogens drove them to the Blue Paradise Bar. Lila thought the Sorrentos might like it—it was offbeat, featured modern jazz, drew a crowd that was a shade different than the usual run of Beach night spots. Inside the car, the discussion regarding Tom's timetable was terminated. Sated with fine beer and cold stone crabs, Tom puffed contentedly on one of his host's imported Havana double claros; these comforts prevented him from worrying about the ball court and his tantalizing Arawaks.

They passed the Peruviana. Its driveway was jammed with enormous cars. A minked and ensilked mob milled around Mr. Banjo—he was in top hat, tails and ebony cane, presenting a cup to the winner of the Gin Rummy Tournament.

Lila turned her lacquered head. "Tom tells me you and the children were Ira's guests here the other day," she said.

"He's terribly insistent," Marty said. "The children were clamoring to get away and that little man who works for deKay—"

"Si," Lila said.

"Yes. He left Tom these passes. It turned out rather well. DeKay left us alone most of the afternoon. He showed up to say hello but we weren't required to laugh at his abominable jokes." The small lie comforted her. She was on shaky footing with Lila, and the precarious situation demanded a discreet minimizing of deKay's role.

"Personally, he makes me nauseous," Lila said. "The walking Phallus in Wonderland."

"Lila!" Erwin said sharply. "What kind of talk is that?"

"It's true, isn't it? That's his whole life. Propitiation of the Male Accessory. He acts like he invented intercourse."

At the Blue Paradise, a menacing headwaiter was charmed by the Ellenbogen magic—a folded fiver. They were escorted to a doll's table near the edge of a postage-stamp dance floor, hard by a musical trio. The Blue Paradise Bar, belying its name, was a two-tone palace in red and black. The walls were painted in wide alternate vertical stripings—black and scarlet. There were dimmed candelabra, draped valances and plaster pillars, all similarly hued.

The interiors of night clubs always filled Tom with a sense of sad fraudulence. They looked jerry-built in spite of the luxury, thrown up hastily over dirty plaster walls, crumbling bricks and rotten floor boards. You sensed the decay in the malodorous men's rooms, the back alleys where garbage piled high, the sweating kitchen. The papered, painted, emblazoned interior was like the plastic liner of a child's backyard pool. Bright and new, it could be yanked off in seconds, revealing the ugly, barren cage.

"This trio is supposed to be hot stuff," Lila confided.

They listened politely. The band consisted of three young Negroes, as alike as triplets. They were all lean, *café au lait* men, each sporting a tiny beard, horn-rimmed spectacles and a look of snide boredom. It upset Tom. The Negro's search for identity, his desire to escape the stereotype forced on him, was leading only to new conformity. Why wasn't one of the musicians fat? Or as black as Dave Ballard? Why didn't one of them grin? Why did all three cultivate that aloof expression? They attacked their instruments with colossal indifference—a pianist, a bass player, a French-horn man. It was as if they were determined to get as little music as possible out of the recalcitrant machines. The rhythm was elusive, the melody undiscernible, the spirit of the muse smothered.

The patrons were of two minds. Those who had no ear for music conversed and laughed in loud tones. Those who appreciated the niceties of progressive jazz were required to lean forward, ears twitching, to catch an occasional note. Halfway through the trio's first number—an endless version of "Honeysuckle Rose" in which the pleasant melody was triturated and comminuted beyond recognition—there was a stirring in the night club. It began with guests at the rear rising and craning necks. An animated, piqued buzzing indicated the arrival of a celebrity. In a few seconds, all were afoot, peering, gawking, seeking the magic visitor, eager to be part of the thrilling world he represented.

"Who is it?" Lila asked a woman at the adjoining table.

"Henry Tarr!" she cried. "He's down here for the week."

A man, stretching his neck and adjusting his eyeglasses, nodded approvingly. "He looks great for a guy who did a month in stir."

And who was Henry Tarr? Marty and Tom posed the question. Lila enlightened them, with a proper show of disgust.

"Leave it to this town to create a fuss over Henry Tarr," she said. "Honestly, sometimes I get so fed up—"

"It isn't so terrible," Erwin said. "He's a *curiosity*. I don't think people really care about him."

"But who is he?" Marty persisted. "I've never heard of him."

"I'll tell you who he is," Lila said. "He's a second-rate textile importer, a man on the town. A big man at El Morocco with the hundred-dollar-a-night girls."

"That's all?" Marty asked. "And all this excitement when he walks into a night club?"

"That isn't all," Lila said sharply. "He went to jail for a month because they caught him distributing silk handkerchiefs with dirty pictures."

"You're joking," Marty said.

"It's for real," Lila insisted. "It was in the papers. They raided his apartment and found *hundreds* of these silk squares —with positions on them. Sixty-nine different positions."

Mr. Henry Tarr had been seated. A knot of handshakers and greeters gathered around him. Others, less intimate with the celebrity, stared at him, commented on his trim figure in its two hundred and fifty dollar tuxedo, admired the vulpine redhead at his side.

The agitated hum occasioned by Mr. Tarr's entrance subsided. The trio continued their impartial pulverizing of standard tunes. Dimly, in the outer reaches of the Blue Paradise Bar, Jimmy Nudo counted the house, floated easily on tiny feet, communicated softly with headwaiters and bartenders.

"The owner of this place is quite a fellow," Erwin said. "His name is Nudo. He came down here from New York about five years ago. He was broke. Now he owns this place and another one up north and has part of a few hotels. He's supposed to have had a really terrible past. He killed two men in some kind of union fight when he was eighteen, but they never convicted him. You know the kind—arrested twelve times and never a conviction."

"He *is* quite a fellow," Marty agreed.

"Oh, he's changed since he struck it rich," Erwin said. "If he is involved in anything illegal, nobody knows about it. He tries very hard to be an upstanding citizen."

"What's his name?" Tom asked.

"Nudo. Jimmy Nudo." Erwin waved at the small, glittering man.

"I know him," Tom said.

"How would you know him?" Marty asked. "Don't tell me he was a graduate student with you."

"I know him. He's from East Harlem. I know his family. I haven't seen him since I was a kid, but I'll bet it's the same guy."

Erwin stood, and gestured at the proprietor. Mincing on alligator-encased feet, Nudo threaded his way through the tables and joined them.

"Good evening, Mr. Ellenbogen," he said softly. "Mrs. Ellenbogen. I hope everything is all right." He snapped his fingers at a waiter nearby. "Angelo," he said decorously, "a round for these people. And the check is for me."

"Join us," Erwin said. "My guest here thinks he knows you."

The white highlights on Nudo's temples seemed to turn on and off as he reflected on this news. He sat down as Erwin introduced the Sorrentos.

"This is Martha Sorrento and this is Tom Sorrento," Erwin said cheerfully. "Jimmy Nudo."

Nudo studied Tom's face.

"Yeh," Nudo said flatly. "Yeh. You know me. Your old man was the cop. Frank Sorrento. Frank the Cop we called him. Right?"

"Right," Tom said. "Know what else?"

Nudo shook his head negatively. He would acknowledge what had to be acknowledged, but he would volunteer very little. Long hours of interrogation by a variety of lawmen had taught him this: New York City detectives, state troopers (in several states), federal men, Treasury agents, the CID.

"I'll tell you what else," Tom said. "My old man, Frank Sorrento, he was your *compare*."

An approximation of a smile germinated on Nudo's grave features. The small, petulant mouth turned upward, the unrevealing eyes seemed to glow for a fractional moment.

"Yah. You lived upstairs from us on First Avenue. The corner 118th Street. How come you know? If you're Frank Sorrento's kid, you're younger than me. Like five years or six."

Tom nodded. "I remember *your* father. After we got fancy and moved to the Bronx he used to come to play *bocce* with my old man. When your mother died. Didn't you live with your aunt in Lodi, New Jersey? Wait a minute—I got the whole picture. Me and my sisters, we went to visit you there once in my old man's second-hand Chandler. A big red car. It kept getting blowouts every few miles. My sisters were little babies, and I guess I was five or six. There was this farm, or at least a kind of farm. The house had a wooden john in the back and your aunt grew escarole and *cicoria*."

"What a memory," Nudo said. He was smiling generously now. "Frank Sorrento's kid. Tommy. Yeh. You were a husky little guy."

"I know what," Tom said. "You had a BB gun and you shot a bird. Tell me if I'm crazy."

Jimmy Nudo was smiling. "I did? Jeez, how long ago is that? Thirty years? More? I remember Lodi. Couple years later they stuck me in St. Vincent's. Over on Arthur Avenue."

St. Vincent's was a home for bad boys. In Tom's mind was summoned up the fearful image of the institution, with its high red walls crowned with a thick layer of cement, jeweled with broken glass. Sometimes you saw the Fathers taking the boys out for a walk, a ball game, a movie—children with the furtive look of the damned about them. That was why he had never seen Jimmy Nudo after that July day in Lodi. He had difficulty reconciling the memory of St. Vincent's, the ragged line of bad boys in black hand-me-downs, with this shiny, prosperous man sitting with him and buying the expensive drinks. He recalled that Jimmy's father—Joe Nudo—had been a consumptive wretch, who worked for the Sanitation Department until his ravaged body collapsed. Where had he died? When? He could not remember his parents mentioning the Nudo family for years; Jimmy had evidently been the only child, and after his transfer to the home, they had lost track of him.

"Hoddya like that?" Jimmy asked everyone at the table. "His old man was my godfather! Small world, right, Mr. Ellenbogen?"

"It certainly is," Erwin agreed. Lila seemed to be pouting again. Her private image of Tom was offended by the revelation that Nudo, at best a perfumed hoodlum, and at worst, a murderer, had some ancient claim on the archaeologist. Marty, on the other hand, seemed amused. She had the capacity to accept the Jimmy Nudos of the world as curiosa.

"You've done very well since leaving that home," Marty said. "I'd imagine the priests would be very proud of you, Mr. Nudo."

"I made out," he said. "You know. A nangle here, a nangle

there. The best thing is to be legitimate." He looked at Tom. "How 'bout you? You been making out?"

"Just barely, Jimmy," Tom said.

"Yah kiddin'. You legitimate? Excuse me, Mr. Ellenbogen. He's *your* friend, he must be."

Lila suppressed an urge to toss her rum collins in the little man's furtive face. She fairly yelled at him: "Tom's a professor! At a college!"

Nudo took a few seconds to digest this intelligence. The information was light years away from his world of fixes and payoffs, yet its strangeness pleased him. "You mean you *teach?* In a college? You went to school and everything all these years?"

"That's me. The All American student."

"I mean, like, it's nice that you turned out so good. *College! A professor!* You know, Missus Sorrento, it was easy for a kid to turn out bad in East Harlem. The numbers. The ginmills."

Tom was beguiled: even Jimmy Nudo read enough newspapers and watched enough television to realize that environment was ever the handy excuse for an abhorrent life. In his enthusiastic praise of Tom—*the boy who came out good*—there was a corrollary, namely, that you couldn't blame the boys who came out bad, such as himself. It was wonderfully neat. The jargon of the social scientist had become standard equipment for the hoodlum. Trapped, exposed, brought before the bar of justice, the criminal now immediately quoted statistics on crime in slums, pleaded the negligence of his dead parents, blamed everyone but himself.

"You down here on vacation?" Jimmy asked.

"No. I'm an archaeologist," Tom said. Thus identifying himself, he felt asinine. How explain to Jimmy Nudo what he did? Why he did it? The arts of communication were appallingly limited.

"Tom's digging up part of the Beach—Mr. Ellenbogen's land on the bay—looking for remains of some old Indians," Marty explained. "It's part of what he teaches at the University."

"*Indians?*" Jimmy asked incredulously. "They had *Indians* living on your property? I seen them Indians when the racetrack opens, but some guy tole me they're phonies. They're all eight-balls."

"This was a long, long time ago, Jimmy," Tom said. "A thousand years or more."

"I guess it's okay," Nudo said thoughtfully. "You say you

make out, that's okay. And it's legitimate." He leaned forward. "But there must be a nangle. I don't figure it."

"Neither do I, sometimes," Tom said. "Take my word for it, Jimmy. The pay's lousy. But you have to do something. If a man's smart like you, he can do a lot of things. Erwin was telling me about everything you have going for you down here."

"Yeh? Like what?"

"Oh, this place," Erwin said. "And the restaurant. Your hotel interests."

"I got something new going also. A light-heavyweight. I got a big piece of him." For some reason, Nudo now smiled at the women and addressed them. "I always been interested in sports. I like when they call me a sportsman in the newspapers." He turned to Tom. "You remember that kid Farenga, from the old neighborhood? He played pro football after the war?"

"Sure," Tom said. "I played against him in high school."

"That kid was great. I looked him up once with a small proposition. It wouldn't hurt him. He wouldn't have to throw a whole game. Just the points. But he wouldn't talk to me. He got very nasty. All I tried to tell him was, if he was smart, he could make a million bucks. How long could he play football? He was too stupid to make out doing anything else. But he wouldn't listen."

In the horrified silence that followed, Tom marveled at the recurrent subtle and sometimes not-so-subtle liaison between sports and crime. He remembered the rash of basketball scandals —all those upstanding young athletes, selling their "honor"— for what? A hundred dollars a game? Or the cribbing scandals at West Point. When he read about them, he was not surprised. There were curious shadowy similarities between organized athletics and lawlessness: the use of deceit, the absolute necessity of coming out on top, the emphasis on muscle. There had been a football coach (not Engstrom) who enjoyed brief fame because of the diagrams of opposing players he employed to indicate where they had been previously injured—this halfback with a vulnerable knee that could be kicked out of whack; this tackle susceptible to a good punch under the breastbone. Moreover, there was a long tradition of *illegality* associated with the more commercialized sports of the *Lumpenproletariat.* For decades, horse racing and boxing had been outside the law. Now sanctified, the traditions of crime lingered. It mattered not that pari-mutuel betting was supervised by the state or that boxing commissions passed on the fitness of fighters. The likes of Jimmy Nudo continued to control them because of custom, prior right, an ancient lien on these manly contests. And why should he not try to "help out" Vince Farenga, who had once run eighty yards through the whole North Carolina team? Vince had known the secret payoff in the sealed envelope from the interested alumni; he had worked the racket of buying student books from freshmen and reselling the tickets for three times what he had paid; he had enjoyed the rewards of muscle. The miracle was, Tom reflected, that Farenga had the strength of character to turn Jimmy Nudo down, after the way in which his corn-pone Alma Mater had trained him so honorably. In a sense, Jimmy Nudo was the true sportsman; you would never find him making speeches about sportsmanship.

"We'd better be shoving," Erwin said pleasantly. "I have an early tennis date tomorrow."

"Whyncha stay?" Nudo asked. "I hired a swell act in New York last week. A female impersonator. Clever kid. Ya'd swear it was a broad."

Lila got up quickly. "No thanks. Some other time."

Nudo escorted them to the door. He refused Erwin's valiant attempts to pay and invited them all back for dinner *on him.* As they left, they could see the singer make his entrance. In white satin evening gown and platinum wig, he was a vision; more feminine than half the women patrons of the Blue Paradise Bar.

As they awaited Erwin's Cadillac, they could hear the husky, concupiscent voice, braying an old blues. The singer waggled his padded behind and counterfeit breasts with a sensual grace that belied their fraudulence. In his passion he gathered up the audience and made love to them.

All of them were subdued and burdened by Nudo's intrusion. A scent of crime and blood lingered after he had bade them goodbye under the tasseled canopy of the Blue Paradise Bar. In the frigid car, the two couples were silent and ruminative. Tom, particularly, seemed affected by the unexpected reunion. It was almost as if Nudo, gleaming in his hoodlum's finery, had been reviving some old claim on him—a claim redolent of wine pressed in squalid backyards and olive oil sizzling in blackened spiders.

Marty noted his brooding despair. He was slumped on the white leather seat, his laced fingers covering his flattened, abused nose. She was reluctant to examine his morosity, fearful of the distressing conclusion she would reach. Was it conceivable that Tom had made an invidious comparison between his own life and Nudo's? It was undeniable that the racketeer, in terms of rewards and status, had achieved much. Uneducated, maltreated, he had needed neither scholarships nor honorable military careers to succeed. She felt helpless and weak. Impoverished genteelness had its limits and it was possible that Tom was simply fed up with the patterns his life had assumed. With precipitate despair, she was annoyed with Tom for never having pursued his writing. They had talked about it so much before their marriage. It might have been the talisman. Now he was pressing forty and was being treated like a ward of the state by Lila Ellenbogen.

Erwin left them at the dirt road. They could see a dim light in the upper floor of the boathouse where the Burleys were baby-sitting. As they started across the site, Lila called motherly words of encouragement to Tom. *Get enough sleep. The work is more important than getting upset over hoodlums!* Marty wished she would shut up. Halfway across the sandy slope, Tom stopped.

"I want to look at my white stones," he said. He limped up the incline.

"I'll see you at the house," Marty said. "I don't want to keep Wilma up any longer." She left him. She had taken a dozen steps when she heard Tom yelling.

"They're gone!" he shouted. "Stolen! Oh, the bastards! Oh the crooks!"

He came hurtling down the slope. "They stole the stones!" he cried. "I gotta get Davey up. Ben!"

His cries filled her with a watery compassion that could offer him no assurances. It all seemed so desperately ludicrous: a grown man, overeducated and of good heart, crying in the night over some stolen rocks.

6 *Harkey's Way*

BALLARD had reneged on his promise to Tom. He knew he would the moment old McIsaac told him about the meeting at Reverend Harkey's home. But he would be discreet. He would try to camouflage his trip to Hilltown. He would tell none of the diggers, he would proceed by a circuitous route, and with naïve disregard for his bulk he would try to melt into the shadows. As a final mark of his determination to protect Tom, he took along a small loose-leaf notebook and a ball-point pen. He was going as an observer, an interviewer, a sociologist.

Satisfied that he was exercising sufficient prudence, he rode a segregated bus to Hilltown, scrounching down in a rear seat, bent over a newspaper. Then he had a Negro jitney drive him to a point several blocks from Harkey's address. It was dusk and the neighborhood was sparsely populated. There were few street lights and there were long stretches of littered lots between the frame houses. He proceeded on foot, shuffling innocently along the unpaved street, until he found the pastor's dwelling. It was a small green house with the false-brick shingling one associated with the more respectable sections of depressed communities.

Harkey greeted him at the screen door, and led him into a living room crammed with neat, faded furniture, a sagging piano, and a wall covered with diplomas and citations. A dozen Negroes sat in the hot room. If Harkey and his followers were distressed by the possibility of surveillance, they did not show it. There had been no passwords, the lights shone brightly, the shades were raised and the windows were opened wide.

"You all know Dr. Ballard?" Harkey asked. "He's with an archaeological team working at the Beach. He's here strictly as an observer, a social scientist. So please don't ask his advice or his opinions. He's neutral."

Dave mopped his head and sat on a folding chair. It creaked threateningly under his heft. They looked at him with undisguised curiosity. Their mildly hostile gazes suggested a group of Auschwitz survivors about to be interrogated by a helpful young Jewish Ph.D. from Harvard, who had never smelled the smoking furnaces. He recognized McIsaac; the fat woman who played the organ. A handsome tan man was introduced to him as a physician, Dr. Emerson. Harkey's wife was a slender woman of middle age, in a flowered print dress. These were Hilltown's best, he knew. They had spent their lives getting along with white folks, imitating them, cooperating with them, acceding to their laws. What had brought them to this edge of rebellion? What had caused the congregation of these unlikely revolutionaries? The black woman who had played the organ at Mount of Olives Church—what mysterious mechanism had propelled her to a role of conspirator? It mystified Ballard. They were no more honorable than other middle-class people—the doctor probably prescribed placebos and charged for them, McIsaac was a stupid old man, the black woman might have stolen secretly from her white employers. But now they were ennobled, determined to change the world for the better.

Looking at their earnest, sweating faces, he marveled at them. His mother, happy with Jesus, would never understand them. Indeed, they would have scandalized her, and he imagined that there were hundreds in Hilltown who felt that way, who would be happier if Harkey and his committees would just quit. *All that fuss over voting—who cares so long as we git paid regular?*

There was one man in the Reverend's parlor (and it was a true parlor—not a living room, or a family room, but a wall-papered, chandeliered old parlor) whom Ballard knew immediately was of a different cut. He sat apart, on a piano stool, a foot or so removed from the circle of conspirators. He was a short, blockish man, the color of bittersweet chocolate. He sported gold-rimmed glasses, a maroon shirt and a tie embellished with a painting of a sunset over a palm-fringed lagoon. His suit was a yellowish beige and his shoes were white suede. A semicircular scar, pink on the cocoa skin, adorned one cheek. He had large gnarled hands. On each thick pinky a jeweled ring sparkled. He was introduced to Dave as Mr. Shorty Freese, and when Harkey, half smiling, added, "I'm afraid I don't know your first name, Mr. Freese—" the dandy responded, in a hidden voice: "Albert, but I prefers Shorty." There was a nervous giggle from one woman, and a sense of withdrawal on the part of the others. Ballard knew why. Mr. Shorty Freese was a bad nigger. If you asked him where he got his dazzling rings, he would advise you, winking, that he stole them. He was of the moonless world of cheap whiskey and crap games, of razor fights and savage women, of blood feuds and stolen automobiles. Ballard had to hand it to the minister—he was missing no bets. No doubt Mr. Shorty Freese (he had magnificent supra-orbital ridges—almost like an Australian abo's) was a man of some stature among Hilltown's nonrespectables. They were not, Dave knew, a moiety given to accepting disciplines or following strange banners. Mr. Shorty Freese was a Judas sheep: with Harkey's connivance he would lead his flock of black ewes and rams into paths of righteousness.

"Per our custom," Harkey said, "we'll begin our meeting with a prayer." He had a soft, weary voice. Often it seemed tinged with a desperate humor. "Dr. Ballard, since you're just an *observer* you don't have to join in this ecclesiastical exercise. You're not required to do as us Romans do."

"It might be good for me if I did," Dave said. "Not from a religious standpoint, but from a scientific one. You know, we make it a practice to participate in all the ceremonies of the culture we're studying."

"Our pleasure," said Harkey. Decorously, they bowed heads. Harkey spoke in a low, calm voice. It was beginning to bother Ballard. There was a so-what quality, a sense of humorous doom about the man, that was unnerving.

"Sweet Jesus, dear God," Harkey began. "give us the gift of love. Let us love those who hate us, and in so loving, let us, with Thy Divine Guidance and Mercy, change their hate to love, so that all may love each other. Almighty and most merciful Father, we are lost sheep seeking the way. Take our hand, precious Lord, and show us that way, that we may meet our brethren who now despise and chastise us. And grant, most merciful Father, that we may hereafter live Godly, righteous and sober lives to the glory of Thy holy name, Amen."

They responded with subdued *Amens*. Ballard tried to catch a glimpse of Mr. Shorty Freese, but the king of the nonrespectables had retreated behind the piano. The sound of the righteous was an offense to him. He rotated one sparkling ring, and it seemed to Dave it was an act of primitive magic, an amulet to ward off the organized forces of Good.

"As all of you know," Harkey said softly, "the state legislature is still in special session. There's every expectation that the bill to redraw the election districts' boundaries will be voted into law and signed some time next week. That makes our campaign for first-class citizenship more urgent than ever."

The physician raised his hand. "Isn't there a chance the bill might get pigeonholed?" Dr. Emerson asked. "I heard there was a moderate group—two fellows from the Beach—who were trying to hold it up. Something about asking for a state commission to examine voting districts."

"There isn't a chance of that, Dr. Emerson," Harkey said. "Besides, if the bill *is* held up till the next regular session, the board of registrars in Hilltown have been instructed to resign, and refuse any new Negro registrations."

The black woman blinked away the sweat behind her eyeglasses. "When dey gon' get you, dey gon' get you. No matter what."

"How many Negroes vote in Hilltown now?" Ballard asked.

"Six hundred," Harkey said. "That's one of the highest county registrations in the South."

McIsaac leaned forward. "Dat's what hurts. Dey tell us live decent, git educated, git jobs, git homes. And then we lets you *share*—we done that in Hilltown, ain't we, Reverend? And we git to vote. Now what happens? We become good Negroes, but we can't become better Negroes."

"I tell you what I don't understand," Ballard said. "All you people who registered and *have* voted—you're still voting for white candidates. How about the people on the Beach who let you register? Can't they testify that no revolution took place?"

Dr. Emerson responded. "The people down at the Beach are considered interlopers. What the crackers are afraid of is that if more of us vote, we'll elect colored sheriffs or mayors. Maybe even state assemblymen."

"Some chance," Harkey said. "You find me a Negro who'd *want* to run for office."

"Dat's deh truth," the black woman said.

"I'd like to review, if I may, our proposed plan of action, as drawn up at the last committee meeting," Harkey said. He picked up a dog-eared notebook; it might have been his little daughter's third-grade composition book. "The way we discussed it last time, when the gerrymander is signed into law, we will hold a mass prayer meeting in Fountain Square. The emphasis will be on love. We will extend our love to the members of the state legislature and pray for them. Guest pastors from parishes that have had similar problems will appear. Our press committee, headed by Dr. Emerson, will notify newspapers, wire services, television and radio outlets. Once we've gotten off on this constructive religious note of uplift, we get down to serious business."

Ballard marveled at him. Was he being cynical? If that were the case, his flock did not notice it, nor did they seem to object. Franklin M. Harkey, D.D., was no dullard. The new religion was a faith that worked for you; it made you rich, famous, got you elected president, settled your marital problems and solved your neuroses. It was a splendid utilitarian faith, and if Harkey chose to make of his ministry a perfect usufruct, a double-edged tool for the uplift and advancement of his worshipers, who could denounce him? He was more in step with his time than he imagined. Twenty-five years earlier, when Harkey was just learning what his dark skin meant in the way of humiliation and limitation, the jargon of the egregious Left would have been employed by an agitator in the interests of racial justice. A quarter of a century later, *religion-in-general* had elevated Acts and Revelations to the status of social weapons.

A puzzled frown on Ballard's face caught Harkey's attention. "You want to ask something, Dr. Ballard?" Harkey inquired. "You go right ahead. I think our committee is enjoying this friendly observation."

"It's just this," Dave said. "Ah—I'm intrigued by the *devout* basis of your campaign. I was brought up in a little community in Georgia, just as race-ridden—forgive my sociological terminology—as any deep South community. As I remember it, the church was usually a force for keeping the *status quo*. People had their Jesus so they didn't care if they couldn't vote. My recollection of those old ministers and the Helpful Ladies is that they were the *least* aroused of the Negro community."

"Hit done changed," McIsaac said. "Jes' look here."

Harkey laughed, an annoying, self-sufficient laugh, that testified to his own boundless knowledge of the problem at hand. The minister reached for a paper-bound book on his writing table, thumbed through its pages and began to read.

"Listen to this, Dr. Ballard," he said. "I'm quoting. 'Its record indicates clearly that the church is the most segregated major institution in American society. It has lagged behind the Supreme Court as the conscience of the nation on questions of race, and it has fallen far behind trade unions, factories, schools, department stores, athletic gatherings and most other major areas of human association as far as the achievement of integration in its own life is concerned.' "

Harkey located a clipping, inserted it in the book and began to read from it. "Or this. 'Surely this is the most striking irony of the twentieth century: that the church of Jesus Christ has become the primary institution for the perpetuation of segregated life. This is more dramatically, though not exclusively, seen in the South where the Christian church openly represents the greatest bulwark of segregated power. The church will undoubtedly be the last bastion to fall—if, indeed, it ever will fall.' "

The pastor looked challengingly at Ballard. "Now who do you expect made those statements? Left-wingers? NAACP? Commies? Crazy social scientists? You guess, Doctor."

"I haven't the faintest idea. They sound a little extreme to me. I mean, not *all* church groups. . . . That Archbishop in Louisiana."

"These quotes," Harkey said, "are from two white Christian ministers. One's Dean of the Yale Divinity School and the other teaches theology there."

"You never know about Yalemen," Ballard said lightly. The committee laughed. "Assuming what they say is true—and I take it you concur. How does all this relate to your own use of religion as a social *lever?* You don't mind my academic language, do you?"

"Not at all. My point in reading you those revolutionary quotes is this—if the white people's churches have abandoned Jesus, *we'll* find him. We'll use him. There's nothing new in that. Jesus has been enlisted in more battles than He probably knows about. I think we've got Him in an exceptionally worth-while one now. I think this is what His Father sent Him to earth for."

"I never knew what Jesus was 'till Reverend Harkey showed Him to me like dis," the black woman said.

"A-men," said McIsaac.

"And between you and me," Harkey said, "nobody can get mad at you if you go at it this way. Oh, they *can* get mad, but it makes them a little ashamed of themselves. Besides, you can't miss getting a good press with Jesus. He's copy."

"Don't let me hold up your meeting," Dave said. "I'd like to get into this with you later. I stuck my two cents in when you were reading your plan of action." Harkey's ambivalence was making him giddy.

"Now let's see," Harkey said. "The day after we've been disfranchised by legislative act, the boycott goes into effect. It will apply equally and impartially to the entire voting district. All white-owned stores will be boycotted. That applies to services, transportation, recreation—the works. If they want us to stay away from their ballot boxes, we will. We will also stay away from their stores. It won't be easy. Now each of you here will be charged with the job of organizing a boycott team in your own particular field, based on locality. We've broken the district down into four geographical divisions, and there'll be a team leader in each division, reporting to each of you. Dr. Emerson, he's in charge of professionals; Mrs. Defore, housewives and domestics; Mr. McIsaac, working people and craftsmen; Mrs. Harkey, schoolteachers and clerical people."

He continued, identifying each person in the breathless room, and then he got to Freese.

"Mr. Freese, this is the first meeting you've attended, and I've asked you here for a special reason. Do you mind if I be very frank?"

"You ast me heah. It youah house."

"Good. You own the biggest saloon in Hilltown. You run the biggest crap games and you've got other interests, which I won't particularize in deference to the ladies. You're a man of considerable influence. May I call you an unofficial mayor of certain elements? The people I never see on Sunday?"

"You makin' deh speech, Reverend," Mr. Shorty Freese tugged at his ring. Under the beautiful supra-orbital ridges, he was his own man.

"We want you to take over the job of encouraging the boycott among your flock. We want *every* Negro in Hilltown to join in this effort." The minister suddenly became grave. *"'Why eateth your Master with publicans and sinners?'"* Harkey asked Mr. Freese. "I'll tell you why. To help us be better human beings."

"Ah do whut Ah can," Mr. Freese said. The parable may have eluded him, but the lesson did not. "Dey ain't deh easiest people to git o'gnized, but Ah tries."

"That's fine," Harkey said. He turned to the anthropologist. "You've just observed a bit of social history, Mr. Ballard. I hope you're as impressed as I am."

"I am. Intrigued."

"There's something all of you must understand," Harkey said. "This won't be easy. Our estimate is that the Negro-owned stores can support about half of our population. It's our hope to set up two co-ops, run and staffed by our own people."

Dr. Emerson raised his hand. "What can we expect in the way of reprisal?"

"Anything they can get away with. A few of us might get jailed. We can expect a court order asking us to show cause why we shouldn't be stopped from enforcing an illegal boycott. The usual old laws will be dug up. Menacing public health and safety. Conspiracy."

"Whut we gon' do?" Shorty Freese asked.

"Pray, Mr. Freese, pray. For them, for us, and for the United States of America."

Shortly before midnight, Mrs. Harkey served lemonade and cookies. Mr. Freese excused himself. He explained that his place was jumping on Saturday night, and he didn't trust his bartender to make correct change. He shook Harkey's hand, and departed, with what seemed relief. All those good works in one night were a burden to Shorty. The other members left Ballard in isolation with Mrs. Harkey. She asked him about his education, his work on the dig. She had a master's degree in education herself and had once taken summer courses at the University. The pastor joined them.

"I tell you what I miss in my brief examination of this resistance movement," Dave said. "Its *origins.* How did it get started? Who got the idea? There's been four or five of them in the South so far. What is it? Northern agitators? The NAACP? Grass roots? It's so totally out of keeping with the usual character of the race-ridden community."

"I guess it's because we've had our fill," Harkey said. "You can take so much."

"That's hard for me to believe," Ballard said. "Of course, my standard is Georgia piney-woods country, twenty years ago. I just can't see those country people I was raised with doing what you're doing here. Isn't there a good deal of resistance in the colored community?"

"Some," Harkey replied. "It doesn't bother me. There's less and less Uncle Toms every year. I tell you what's really making the change. It's the humiliation. I'm no student of culture like you, Doctor, but I know this. You can steal a man's property, sleep with his wife, burn his house—and he'll take it. But there's one thing he won't stand for. Humiliation. Ridicule. Being told he's less of a man, or an inferior man. That's what's losing Africa and Asia, if I may be global."

"You mean if the British let the Egyptians into their clubs we'd still own the Suez Canal?"

"That's the idea. Human beings don't mind being robbed or cheated. But don't make fun of 'em. They'll never forgive you that."

Mrs. Harkey patted his hand. "Franklin simplifies everything. I'll tell you how these movements *really* got started."

"I'd like to hear. I gather you disagree with him."

"I do. Take my word for it, there's plenty of opposition to what he's doing—from our own people. They're frightened and backward and perfectly willing to go on getting disfranchised and cheated of their rights. You know how this thing got started? My husband started it. Churchill's right. It's the occasional rare man who makes history. Look at every one of these passive-resistance campaigns. There's a *man* in back of each one—someone who isn't afraid, who'll shame everyone else into acting. It's Franklin here. He got all these other people to cooperate."

"Somebody's got to start it," the minister said.

"And you're not afraid of what they might do to you?" Ballard asked.

"No. They wouldn't think of harming me. I'm too valuable in good health. I'm the biggoty nigger who went to school up North and keeps getting citations from all them Communist groups. I'm too good to let get away."

"But where's it all going to get you? The majority of the people are against you and what you're doing. You admit yourself, if there are a few sympathetic whites they'll have no use for you after this boycott."

Harkey sipped his lemonade. "You have to do *something*. You can't just sit around and sing 'Sewanee River.' "

Ballard had the sensation that the man was cursed and doomed and bound to fail. In the long run, he would be left friendless. He would end up in New York City, lecturing to liberal groups who agreed whole-heartedly with him in advance; they would continue to garland him with medals and plaques. The anthropologist could think of no analogous situation. The Negroes who broke the color line in sports had people *inside the cultural pattern* rooting for their success. But Harkey was fighting his battle on completely hostile ground, surrounded by an enemy that would grow stronger and more determined every time he made a move. In time, perhaps his own people would desert him, and he would be isolated and ostracized. Hilltown was a relatively prosperous Negro community. How would they feel about Harkey's imposed economic strangulation? Might they not long for the free-and-easy days—with or without the vote?

"I don't envy you your task," Ballard said. "Makes me glad I'm a neutral. Don't misunderstand me. My sentiments are with you. But I don't think I'd have your guts, if I were living down here." Ballard thought he heard an automobile stopping in front. It did not seem to bother the clergyman or his wife, or anyone else in the room. "You know, as a matter of fact, I shouldn't be here. My boss on the dig put Hilltown off limits to me after Peltz and I got ourselves arrested. But I suppose I'm safe enough. He's out on the town tonight himself, and I figured without Peltz nobody would take notice of me."

"See how easy it is?" Harkey said. "You're taking risks yourself. You and Mr. Shorty Freese. Our two converts."

"Oh, please, Frank," his wife said. "How can you compare Dr. Ballard to that—that delegate from the cut-and-shoot boys?"

Harkey smiled his own secretive smile, and got up, going through the papers on his desk again. He found a clipping and came back to the sofa.

"You seemed interested in those quotes I read you about the churches and integration. You know about Virginia?"

"Aren't they still talking about private schools for white kids?"

"Sure. But that's only part of it. The best part of it is"—he permitted himself a choked chuckle—"the best part is that some *churches* are spearheading the thing. Baptist, Methodist, Presbyterian and Episcopalian—they're going to furnish the space for the private schools. Isn't that a laugh?"

"I think you're being a little rough on the cloth," Dave said. "After all, a church—any church—is by definition segregated. There are ins and there are outs. They've got a head start on that kind of thing, and frankly, I can't blame 'em. What good's the church if it isn't set up that way?" He reflected. "Of course, as you point out, the Roman Catholics are somewhat different. They got ins and outs but they sure want all those *outs* to come *in*. The doors are open wide."

"You telling me?" Harkey asked. "You watch the conversions into the RC church in the next ten years. There's maybe half a million Negro Catholics right now. You're going to see a lot more if these crackers keep gerrymandering voting districts."

Ballard sighed. "Maybe we are getting somewhere, Reverend." The *we* came to him naturally. Harkey noted it. "Twenty years ago you'd be mad about lynching. Now it's over losing the vote."

Harkey stretched. "It's all going to work out. I'll get a turn-around collar and learn the sacraments."

"Lot of jazz musicians up North have another bit," Dave said. "They go Moslem. No fooling. I've seen them. They take Arab names and face East. It's understandable—identification with a big, big group that's got its own sources of power."

"I don't believe *that,*" Mrs. Harkey said.

"Scout's honor. I went to a jam session once where they layed down their horns and picked up their Korans." Dave threw his mammoth head back, shut his eyes and chanted: "*La ilaha illa-'llah!* Crazy, man!"

It was close to midnight. The members were excusing themselves and getting ready to leave. Again, Ballard had the bothersome feeling that they were helpless—isolated and naked people. He thought of the white communities he had known in the allegedly friendly North: except for the corporal's guard of Jewish liberals and Quakers, who really cared? Wasn't any and all progress made by forcing unpopular decisions down the public throat—a public that accepted them through indifference rather than conviction? Could it be that it was all too late anyway? He knew too well the extent of Negro crime in Northern cities, the sickening statistics and the dreadful details, the senseless brutality, the uncontrollable savagery. He had once been horrified by a television broadcast from a prison in Philadelphia. He had assumed it was a Negro prison—there was not a white inmate in evidence. Yet as far as he knew, Pennsylvania didn't practice segregation. He inquired, and learned that seventy-four per cent of the prison population was colored. Ballard would not dare invoke the ghosts of Lombroso and Gobineau. He knew, as surely as he knew anything, that black skin and thick lips did not predispose men toward crimes of violence. But was it possible that the social mechanisms had gone too far? That perpetual humiliation (as Harkey put it), perpetual reminders of inferiority, in a culture where getting-ahead was all that mattered, had turned the Negro community irrevocably toward crime? Were the people of his blood destined to become enclaves of criminals within the bigger social structure—like the villages of thieves and murderers he had heard about in India? *Some Comparisons of Criminal Sub-Groups in Dacoit Villages in India and Harlem. . . .*

"We're meeting on Wednesday," Harkey said, as they moved toward the door. "Try and come. You offered some stimulating ideas tonight, Doctor."

"Please do," Mrs. Harkey said. "Would you mind if I asked some friends who are studying anthropology at the state college? They'd be thrilled to meet you."

She was suddenly on the floor, her limbs in the nonfunctional attitudes of fracture. The room was lopsided and shivering, and the successive blasts—there must have been three or four—deafened them. Dr. Emerson was sprawled on the piano; he seemed to be picking bits of glass from his bloodied forehead, with a curious, detached quality. Mrs. Defore, wavering on large, flat feet, was praying noiselessly. Her gold-rimmed glasses had been smashed into a fine fretwork, the lenses remaining fixed in the frames. They gave her the look of a heathen idol. A choking black smoke drifted in through two smashed windows. Harkey, unhurt, was on his feet.

"The bastards," he muttered. "Probably landed in the garage." He was remarkably calm. "Come on," he said to Dave, "let's have a look."

"Be careful!" Ballard said.

"Why?" the minister asked.

Dave followed him into the night. The street was deserted. No lights had been turned on in the neighboring houses. The residents knew when it was wise to stay indoors, keep mouths shut, look the other way. Harkey's garage was a frame carport, separate from the house. It, and its resident Ford, had been reduced to a smoking ruin. The lumber was burning furiously, the car was blackened and blistered.

"Damn fire bomb," Harkey said. "They're getting inventive. Give me a hand with the hose, Dave."

They attached a garden hose to a spigot on the lawn and started spraying the blaze. It succeeded only in raising great gusts of smoke; Harkey remembered he had stored paint in the garage. In a few seconds the rest of the committee had joined them. A bucket brigade was set up.

"Cowards," Harkey said. "I better call the fire department and the cops. Keep spraying it, Dave."

He walked briskly to his house. Ballard had the feeling he was almost enjoying the shocking incident. Indeed, the committee, now freed of theory, had whipped themselves into an efficient team. Ballard edged up closer to the blaze. What was he doing here in the middle of the night, surrounded by these doomed visionaries, putting up with Harkey's mystical nonsense? He'd left all that jazz behind him. He was *accepted,* big and black as he was, up North, and he had a career in anthropology. And here he was: standing on a darkened street in niggertown, spraying a leaky hose on a crazy minister's burning garage, a shack that would be better off for being burned. Illuminated in the darting flames, he saw the committee members scurrying around, answering the call to arms. He edged up closer to the blaze with his inadequate extinguisher. The *thwoooosh* of a new explosion staggered him. A tongue of flame leaped out—probably touched off by some of Harkey's turpentine or paint remover. The searing orange finger streaked Dave's forearm and he leaped back. Dr. Emerson, standing by with a pail of water, advised him: "You better come on with me. I'll fix that. The firemen'll be here soon." Who needed him? Who needed any of them? He went along with Emerson, less because he wanted his arm treated than out of fear of having his name mentioned in the police reports. He was out of bounds, off limits. Discretion demanded that he get out. His offended left forearm pained him fearfully as he followed Emerson to his car.

7 *The Enlistment of Lila*

SORRENTO was unable to sleep. He was up and dressed while soft mists were rising from the land, foolishly circling the pits, looking for some trace of the vandals who had run off with his white stones. He felt idiotic. Around him, pastel mansions snored in Sunday morning bliss; maids looked after children, bedroom doors were bolted. The sun, hazy behind banks of gossamer clouds, drew wispy fog from the damp beach. Tom squatted alongside the desecrated trench, blaming himself. He should have removed the rocks, numbered them, kept a diagrammatic record of the excavation, then returned them to their bed when the wall was unearthed. From now on, that was the procedure they would follow. He lit a black stub, wincing at the sour taste, enjoying the agony as a form of self-immolation.

Nothing could be left exposed in this bat's nest. He should have learned his lesson from the experiences of the WPA digs in the thirties. At High Mound City, seventy skeletons had been stolen, smashed, three months' yield of grave goods had vanished. The sandy hole had the appearance of part of a giant's mouth—a gaping wound in the gum where some dentist-ogre had yanked out three mighty molars.

Impatient and ill-tempered, he roused his diggers an hour later and called them down to the office. They were horrified to learn of the theft. Wilma cried and fluttered her hands. Oran blinked and turned scarlet.

"Didn't any of you hear anything?" Tom asked impatiently. Maybe Marty was right—you could look after people only so much. Perhaps if he ran across Oran and Wilma next semester, tongue-tied and stricken in Chock Full o' Nuts, he would not succor them from the cream cheese and nut sandwiches.

"Nothing," Oran said. "Wilma and I were up all the time you were away. We didn't hear a sound."

Disgusted, Tom turned to Peltz and Ballard. "How about you, Benny? You hear or see anyone out there? A car? Or a truck?"

"I was out last night," Ben said.

"Out?" Tom asked. "Doing what? With Dave?"

"No, nothing like that. I got some relatives in town."

"Relatives? You?"

"An uncle and an aunt. I ran into them by accident, so they asked me to come over for dinner. What are you lookin' at me for? I'm telling the truth."

Their abjectness infuriated him. He wished they were like his enlisted men in the Marines—sullen, murderous, hating his guts because of his status and the power of life and death he wielded over them. In a pub in Auckland one night he had heard a drunken Marine private bragging—unaware that Tom was sitting around the corner—how he shot his lieutenant in the back during a landing. The braggart was a ridge-runner, with the contemptible elongated speech, the proud stamp of ignorance on his peroration. *He was a damn Jew-boy and he was chicken-shit so I let him have it right between the shoulders . . . three guys seen me do it and ain't one of 'em gonna rat on me. . . .* The chances were he was lying, Tom reflected. If he were telling the truth what would be gained by hauling him to the shore patrol? The lieutenant, if one ever existed, was long buried with honors. The recollection summoned up an idiotic notion: Oran and Wilma cracking him over the head with a mattock and tossing his remains into the midden; one more bawling out and they'd finish him off.

He looked at Ballard's bandaged left arm. It was covered with surgical gauze from the wrist to just below the elbow and it had some kind of medicated grease on it.

"What happened to you?"

"Fryin' pork chops," Ballard said. "The grease splattered all over me. I was with a family I know last night and I was doing the cooking. Someone dropped a mess of sliced onions into the pan—they were wet. The whole thing sizzled up on me."

Tom thought, *Ballard you are lying. You are a big, lying colored man and you were in trouble last night. You hate pork chops and fried food gives you heartburn. What's more, you know I'm wise to you, but you figure I can't be bothered laying the law down.*

"Okay, let's forget it," Tom said heavily. "I don't know what good it would have done if all of us were here all night. Anybody could have pulled a car off the highway and carted off the stones."

"What are you going to do, Tom? Tell the cops?" Ben asked.

"Yeah, that would be great. Imagine the laughs I'd get, asking these shamuses to track down white stones for me. A million laughs."

He walked over to the grid map of the site.

"Three things. First, I want to clear some sections north of the grave and see if there's anything else there. If there isn't, we'll close it up. Benny, you work on that. Davey, you and me, we'll keep working both sides of the white stones, and see how far they go. The workmen can start digging about fifty feet south of the stones, and sink a continuous trench perpendicular to the stones."

"What are you lookin' for?" Peltz asked.

"More rocks." He picked up a shovel and started for the door. "Let's go."

His four excavators trooped out. Ballard lugged a shoulder load of hoes, rakes, picks and shovels. Peltz gathered up an armful of two-by-four stakes and a tangled coil of clothesline. The Burleys waited for Tom at the door.

"What is it?" he asked.

Oran coughed. "Well—I mean—you mentioned everyone. What about me and Wilma?" He lowered his silky head.

"I'm sorry, kids. You keep on with the midden. I didn't mention it, because I assumed you'd continue. Everything else was in the nature of a new project. Okay?"

"Yes, yes!" Wilma cried. "We will!"

Her eyes became water-logged behind the distorting lenses. It was more joy than either of them could stand. They tramped off to the refuse heap, the leavings of vanished savages, as happy as they could ever be.

Upstairs, the morning meeting had awakened the children, and they, in turn, had aroused Marty. Ever since her newspaper days, when she was forced to sleep irregularly, she had never enjoyed enough sleep. If conditions permitted, she could sleep ten hours a night—solid, drugged, lost hours. But they had never enjoyed a maid to organize the children in the morning. With luck, and if Nicky didn't start to cry, she sometimes was able to remain cemented in her bed until nine. But these blessed occasions were rare. More and more, she found herself craving the restful embrace of pillow and mattress. Now, rudely awakened by her husband's restlessness, she felt cheated and faintly sick.

The children had helped themselves to cornflakes and milk. They were accustomed to Marty's frequent derelictions in the morning. Tom brewed some coffee on the midget range. His wife sat on the edge of the bed; she was pale and unsettled.

"Eight in the morning? All I could think of last night was how much I was going to sleep today."

"I'm sorry," Tom said. "I didn't sleep at all. I was up at six."

"Oh. I remember. They stole the ball court last night." She yawned agonizingly. "It must be ninety in here. How do these people get used to the heat?"

After the children had put on sunsuits and raced out to "help" Wilma and Oran, she got into a bathing suit.

"Going swimming?" he asked.

"I thought I'd take the children to the Peruviana today," she said. "It's stifling here."

"You shouldn't have mentioned it to Lila and Erwin," he said.

"What?"

"About using deKay's cabana. After the way you turned your nose up at them. You hurt Lila's feelings. She must have invited you three times to their club."

"Tom, don't burden me with these social nuances."

He poured coffee for them. She was, in all likelihood, the only woman in the world, who, ill tempered, uncosmeticized, half asleep, exhibited the kind of fragile beauty that made argument academic. Her flesh freed her of disputation.

"I'm going over to Erwin's and see about having this place protected. A fence. Or something."

"You won't find *them* up at eight-thirty." She sounded petulant —almost jealous.

"I guess you're right," he said gloomily. "My own fault. I shouldn't have left anything in the trench. I can't think of everything."

"Cheer up. When Hall gets down here, he can do your thinking and planning and give the interviews."

He glared at her. "Now what brought that on? I'm sorry I woke you up, and I'm sorry it's hot. But don't start hollering about your father."

She rested her head in her hands. "I'm a wretch. I don't know why I carry on like this. There's something about this place—it's eroding me, all my defenses. I'm always ready to criticize, or snap at someone, or start blaming. Be patient with me, will you, Tom?"

"Sure, baby." He patted her arm. "Go to the pool and sleep it off. Heist a few brews."

She shuddered. "All these people here. Erwin and Lila. And Ira deKay and Mr. Nudo. They've got it made, haven't they? They don't worry about stolen stones or Arawaks, do they?"

"Hey, knock off." He gulped his coffee and got up.

She grabbed his arm. "Tom, don't listen to me. It's the heat—or something. You know what I told you a few days ago. You're the rock. I lean on you. I'm like Wilma and Oran—or Dave. I can't bear to see you upset, or mad, or confused. I don't show it, but it eats at me, because you're the dependable one. I'm selfish—you know that. I'm a leaner."

He leaned over and kissed her neck. "Okay, okay, you're a leaner. Now just settle down in there. That's what I used to tell Leo Mazzochi when he was pitching for the Webster Avenue Blue Devils. I played third base. *Settle down in there boy. T'run him your hook!*"

She turned her head and kissed him.

"I'll go dig for a couple of hours," he said. "Then I'll visit with our friends across the way. Go kibitz the gin rummy tournament."

She managed a smile. "For your information the gin rummy tournament is over. The Eastern Regional Water Ski Convention starts today."

At midmorning Tom walked over to the Ellenbogen house. No one answered his ringing, so he strolled around the side, through a bower of fragrant shrubs, to the lawn at the rear. The colored butler was walking up a flagstone pathway from the boat dock, bearing two trays of dirty dishes.

"Good mornin', Doctor," he said politely.

"Hi, Freddie," Tom said. "Where are the people?"

"They're having brunch on the boat this morning."

Tom continued down the path. Sheldon Ellenbogen's miniature Thunderbird, with its two-horsepower engine, lay athwart the walk, and he moved it away. Lila was waving to him from the deck of the gleaming mahogany cruiser. It was a sixty-foot custom job: the kind of boat so perfect in line, so meticulous in detail, so burnished, painted, polished and accoutred, that it would have been sinful to take it to sea and dirty it with spray and barnacles. The windows were artfully curtained and the flying bridge thrust its tubular metal bars forward with an air of decorous piracy. The ensign of Erwin's yacht club flew from the rear deck: a second flag, a blue circle with a hole in the middle, dangled from the portside outrigger.

"Hi there!" Lila called. "Want breakfast?"

"No trouble," Erwin said. "Freddie took the dishes, but I'll ring him." He reached for a field telephone.

"I ain't hungry," Tom pleaded. He bounced over the side of the cruiser and settled in a deck chair.

"We do this every now and then on Sundays," Erwin said. "It sounds nutty, just coming on the boat to eat breakfast, but it's a nice change. We don't take it out much. It's really a little excessive—even for us."

"It's a beauty," Tom said. He looked up at the strange banner on the outrigger. "What's that?"

"*That!*" Lila laughed. "My husband's idea of a joke. You know, there's a big business in gag-type flags for pleasure boats. The martini glass if you're having cocktails, the ball and chain if your wife's on board. It's very Gentile, all of it."

"I guessed already," Tom said, squinting at the flag. "That's the bagel banner. Whenever you have brunch on board. For all the world of Christian yachtsmen to look up and be jealous because they don't know about such joys. Right?"

"It's goofy, but I like it," Erwin said. Tom looked at Ellenbogen's hexagonal face and was filled with wondrous admiration for the furniture magnate. His mission had become imbued with a heavy irrelevancy. He felt ashamed for his white stones and his hot trenches.

"I have some bum news," Tom said. "Somebody robbed the rocks."

"Which ones?" Lila cried.

"The big stones in the new pit."

"That's awful! That's terrible!" Lila shouted. "Erwin! You offer a reward! Call the chief of police! We'll get them back, Tom!"

"Now who would ever do something like that?" the industrialist asked. "They have no earthly value, except to you. I can't understand it."

Tom smacked a hand against his forehead. "I just remembered.

I told Mermelstein about them. He took some photographs last week. I was going to call him after I spoke to Maitland and tell him to lay off. Not to print anything about the stones. I forgot. You remember, Lila—the day I told you about it."

"Maybe he didn't send the story out," Lila said. "It wasn't in yesterday's papers."

The three of them reached, almost simultaneously, for a thick Sunday paper on the breakfast table. It was fresh and unopened, and they broke it down into sections, each scanning the pages quickly. Lila found it in the second news section—a full page of photographs and text.

"Here it is," she said angrily. "Our friend Ira deKay did it again."

Tom studied the article silently. An eight-column banner ran across the top of the page:

DIGGERS SEEK MYSTERIOUS BEACH TRIBES

Below it, a subhead proclaimed:

TEAM OF ARCHAEOLOGISTS HOT ON TRAIL OF ANCIENT CIVILIZATION—ARAWAK CONNECTIONS SUSPECTED

Tom read the article aloud. " 'Who were the unknown savages who encamped on Bay Islet thousands of years ago and then vanished as mysteriously as they had come? A team of archaeologists from New York City is laboring this summer in an attempt to unravel the story of the naked Indians who were the Beach's first residents. Head of the scientific survey is Thomas V. Sorrento, Ph.D., a University archaeologist from New York, who in addition to being a leading figure in American anthropology is a Marine war hero (Navy Cross) and an ex-football star (he played under the famed E. F. Engstrom). Dr. Sorrento heads up a five-man team currently unearthing some amazing "finds" on the estate of Erwin Ellenbogen, prominent local industrialist and president of the E & S Furniture Corporation.' "

"I guess deKay wants your business again," Lila said. "The free plug in the Sunday paper. Excuse me, Tom."

"Honey, I didn't even *know* about this," Erwin protested.

"I wonder. Go on, Tommy."

"This Mermelstein," Tom said. "He really writes prose when he gets started. 'It is Dr. Sorrento's belief that a community of some size, different in character than any previous Indian cultures discovered in this part of the state, once dwelt on the land adjacent to the Ellenbogen house. Although Dr. Sorrento was hesitant to say so flatly, he suspects that a culture similar to the famous Arawak Indians of the Caribbean may have occupied the site. His diggers have unearthed a burial mound, a shell heap, and most exciting of all, the remains of an old stone wall. Thus far, three large white boulders have been unearthed. "They're unlike anything ever found down here," Dr. Sorrento says. "Stone-work of this size was unknown to the tribes in this area. This means they are probably the work of a different people." But now the mystery—what people? Dr. Sorrento isn't saying for sure, but he'd bet—if he were a betting man—on the Arawak. To support this belief, he points to a curious three-cornered stone idol found on the shell heap and a drinking cup fashioned of a human skull. Both of these items *could* be Caribbean in origin.' "

He handed the page to Lila. "Take it. I can't go on. That fink Mermelstein. He promised me he wouldn't write about the boulders."

Lila frowned. "If I know deKay, this went to the national press associations and magazines. They'll all run it. Wait—the phone calls will start this afternoon."

She studied the offensive page with personal fury. There were several large photographs accompanying Mermelstein's cozy prose. There was a picture of Tom pointing to the shell heap, with the Burleys and little Nicky chipping away at breccia with trowels. (The caption read: *Dr. Sorrento's son, Nicky, 4, joins professional diggers as proud archaeologist Pop oversees work on shell heap. This unpretentious mound of "junk" has yielded some of the most amazing finds in the history of Southeast archaeology.)*

Another shot showed Dave Ballard carefully replacing one of the flexed skeletons in the burial pit. In the background, McIsaac and Spots looked on. Tom had reluctantly agreed to do this for Mermelstein. Here, the caption stated: *Workmen show how they unearthed first skeleton on Ellenbogen site. After a thousand years of silent burial, ancient bay dweller sees light of day.*

Lila finished the article. "Now!" she cried. "The crusher! Leave it to Ira deKay—my husband's business associate! Get this! 'The Ellenbogen property, in addition to being a major American archaeological site, is destined for further fame. Beach sportsman and publicist Ira deKay has made known that a group of leading business figures plan to erect a giant "living museum of religion" on the site, to be called the *God-O-Rama.* Plans call for a groundbreaking ceremony on Labor Day and a formal opening of the spiritual enterprise some time before Christmas. On learning of the possible discovery of an ancient Indian civilization on the land, Mr. deKay commented: "Dr. Sorrento's discoveries are almost symbolic. They impress upon all of us concerned with *God-O-Rama* man's rise from naked savagery to his present high spiritual estate. We may even reserve part of our exhibit for a section on primitive religions, utilizing the savage idols and remains of human sacrifice now being dug up—if only to illustrate how far we have come." ' " Lila drew in her breath. "How do you like that? Does he miss anything? He has it all in one package!"

"I don't get it," Erwin said. "Why should anyone rob the stones?"

Tom scowled. "Ah, Erwin, this kind of newspaper crap has to lead to that. Anybody could walk off with them. Fraternity boys, teen-age wiseguys, amateur archaeologists."

"The fence goes up tomorrow!" Lila said emphatically. "And tonight, we'll hire some cops. Or Erwin can *shmear* a few of the city police. Right, Erwin?"

Tom's brown face went a shade darker; the large sorrowing eyes were smudged with anger. "That son-of-a-bitch deKay," he said. "I'm going to call him and tell him off. Two-timing bastard."

"There's an outside phone in the cabin," Erwin said.

Tom went inside. He asked the operator for deKay's number and dialed it. The phone rang a half-dozen times. He was about to hang up (remembering it was Sunday and it was Ira's office he was calling) when a woman's thick, harsh voice answered. It was Kitty Schmitt, the strong-arm girl from New York.

"Yeah?" the woman's voice grated. "Don't you know it's Sunday morning?" She sounded drugged.

"Is Ira deKay there?" Tom asked.

"He's sleeping. Can't talk to anyone." Her last words were distorted with an enormous yawn.

"Wake the son-of-a-bitch up," Tom said. "Tell him this is Tom Sorrento calling. He'll talk to me."

"You got a helluva nerve," Miss Schmitt shouted. "Who do you think—"

There was the sound of a man's voice, and then a faint clatter as the phone changed hands. "Hallo," Ira croaked. "Whozzat? Whah you want?"

"This is Tom Sorrento, deKay. The paper has a big story about my dig. I gave it to Mermelstein because he said you'd can him if he didn't get it. Only it's full of manure. Things I never said and things I asked him not to print. Now I've been robbed. Some idiots read that article and ran off with my big stones."

Ira coughed in a racking spasm. "*Baby*. You're in bad shape without stones. I'm sorry."

"Don't give me any of your show-biz crap, deKay. I'm warning you. Stay away from the site. That goes for Si also. All you wanted was to publicize that tourist trap you're opening here."

"*Sweetie,*" Ira sang. "I never meant it that way. Si gets carried away. I never read his copy because I hate to read."

Faintly, Miss Schmitt's harpy accents filtered through. "For Chrissake, Ira, I wanna sleep. . . . What kinda friends you have?"

"But I don't want you to be mad at me, doll," Ira pleaded. "You won't let me help you. People pay me a grand a week for that kind of service. A whole page in the newspaper—I bet *Life* and *Look* will be on your tail next week."

"Go back to your broad," Tom said angrily. "I'm sorry I woke you up."

"Baby—"

Tom hung up rudely. Outside the cabin Tom slumped into a deck chair.

"Well—what did he say?" Lila asked.

"He was sorry. It was a mistake. He blamed Si and I guess Si will blame him." He scowled at them. "Look at me. You think I'm nuts? Am I crazy getting so wound up? Sometimes I wonder if this business of digging holes has softened my brain. It's like I'm some kind of professional screwball. You know. Bacon wrote Shakespeare. The Flying Saucers are Real. The Vikings. Am I that bad?"

"If you ask me you've been working too hard," Erwin said helpfully. "Why don't you and Marty take a trip for a few days? *Relax*. Let that fellow Peltz run the thing—"

"He will *not,*" Lila interrupted. "With the most important archaeological site in the country out there? Tommy, don't judge yourself in terms of this town. Dig holes. Nothing else will be stolen. Erwin will guarantee *that*."

Tom half heard her. The front page of the *Journal* lay in front of him at an angle, and he craned his head to read a headline Then he straightened the newspaper out and, squinting through the glaring sunlight, read:

BOMB EXPLOSION, FIRE WRECK GARAGE OF NEGRO BOYCOTT LEADER

THREE INJURED IN NIGHT ASSAULT ON MEETING

An explosion and fire early today injured three Negro leaders of the proposed "white boycott" and destroyed the garage of the Reverend Franklin M. Harkey, head of the Hilltown Betterment Association.

Police said the blast was probably the result of a homemade bomb, thrown at Harkey's frame garage as a warning. At the time of the explosion and fire, the Hilltown group was holding a strategy meeting in Harkey's home. The force of the blast knocked out three windows in the house, at 3426 East 47th Street, and caused the injuries. Those hurt were:

Dr. Charles P. Emerson, 54, a physician, with offices at 883 Perreau Street;

Mrs. Wilson Defore, 53, organist at Harkey's church, the Mount of Olives;

Mrs. Emmaline Harkey, wife of the minister, 33.

All three suffered cuts from flying glass. None of the injuries was serious. Paint and turpentine stored in the garage made the fire difficult to control, and two engines from the Hilltown firehouse were called out to extinguish the blaze.

Harkey, long a controversial figure because of his outspoken opposition to the proposed Callander bill, which redraws the lines of voting districts in the Hilltown area, was not hurt. The bill is due for passage within the next week. Negro spokesmen contend it is aimed at disfranchising some 600 colored voters. Proponents of the measure deny this.

Harkey claimed the bombing might be the first in a series of incidents aimed at dissuading him from carrying out his boycott. Merchants have predicted total economic strangulation if the shunning of white-owned shops is invoked. The minister, interviewed at the Hilltown station house where he made a full report to Detective Lieutenant Arthur Fry, would say only: "There is no fear in love; but perfect love casteth out fear."

Fry said that every attempt would be made to track down the bomb throwers. "Boycott or no boycott," he said, "the law will be upheld. No bombs will be thrown, no persons or property damaged. The gerrymander bill doesn't concern me. Law and order do."

Some police sources have hinted that Northern agitators, recently arrived in the state, may be working with Harkey to stir up the normally well-behaved Negro community.

"Isn't that awful?" Lila said. "Those detestable crackers. Over here on the Beach in our secure little nests, our false little world that we transplanted from New York, we forget where we are."

"It's very upsetting," Erwin said. "I'm for anything that will help the Negroes. But—"

"But *what?*" Lila asked.

"It's just that I'm against any extremism. The bombings are a disgrace. Of course they are. But that boycott they're dreaming up is no party, either. I heard about it from a few of my retailers. Besides, we're guests here. It's still their state. How long do you think I'd be selling my line if word got out that I favored—as I do—more rights for the colored? I have to keep my mouth shut. You know where my sentiments lie."

Tom climbed onto the dock, then turned. "I could use two or three more workmen, Erwin."

"No problem. I'll send them over in the morning."

Lila uncrossed her legs and got up. She was wearing a crisp, creamy sailor suit—white Jamaica shorts and a white middy, both edged with navy blue piping. "Tom—can I dig with you?"

"Why?" he asked. "What for?"

"I want to. I'm sick of sitting around. I'll get tired right away, but maybe I could just hand you the implements—like a chief nurse in surgery."

Erwin fidgeted in his deck chair. "Now, baby, you must be kidding."

"I'm not, Erwin. Just let me try it. I'll get into old clothes and join you."

"It's ninety-six degrees out there and no shade, Lila," Tom said. "The sand sticks in your nose and your throat. Talk her out of it, Erwin."

"She's fooling," Ellenbogen said. "Every now and then, Tom, she feels she has to justify her existence. Last year it was social work with the reform-school kids, the year before the art show at the county gallery, and now it's archaeology."

"Yes," Lila said tightly. "Yes. Now it's archaeology. Anything to get me out of my happy world of canasta and hair dressers. I'll be with you as soon as I get out of these clothes."

Tom started back to the site.

"Tommy!" Erwin called. "You mind keeping an eye on her? Don't let her work too hard. She gets these ideas every now and then."

The archaeologist winked at Ellenbogen. "She's in good hands, Erwin. Ten minutes with that pick and she'll be back."

"Says you," Lila shouted at him.

8 *Three Christmases*

Marty got to the Peruviana at midmorning and found the pool and cabanas almost deserted. She reminded herself it was Sunday morning; the guests were recuperating from their revels of the night. A handful of children scampered about the playground. The helpful Florrie took Nicky and Abby in tow and she was left alone. The blond water-god opened her cabana, fussed with the chaise and left her, with a marked show of respect. A few minutes later he returned with an armload of boxes, bearing the characteristic striped design of an expensive Beach store. He set them down inside the cabana.

"What's all that?" she asked.

"I don't know, Mrs. Sorrento. Mr. deKay had it sent down early this morning, for me to deliver here. There's a note for you." He handed her a small envelope and returned to sweeping the duckboards. His assless figure glided by, complete and fulfilled in its world of inflated mattresses, naked legs and chlorinated water.

She opened the letter.

> Marty, My Beauty—
>
> All these are yours. Don't worry, they didn't cost me cent one. Lootsville. I expect you to be in some of it when I arrive, so don't disappoint me.
>
> Crazy,
>
> Ira

She would not even open the boxes. But, after fifteen minutes of solitude, lying greased and heated in front of the candy-striped cabana, she overcame her disdain. The whole thing was a nightmare anyway—nothing to be taken seriously or worthy of guilt feelings. It would do no harm to see what Ira's notions of high taste were like. With a wary glance about her (the children were splashing in the kiddie pool) she entered the cabana and started unpacking the boxes. There were a half-dozen swimsuits—all bearing the label of a nationally famous designer of women's clothing. They were not merely bathing suits—they were emblems of status. One was a remarkable paisley, another a brilliant harlequin in red, white and gray, a third a startling knitted affair with irregular vertical striping. They were arresting, yet tasteful. There were four pairs of beach sandals, with labels that spoke of Southampton and Deauville, and there were three beach jackets, the most remarkable of which was a Chinese creation, fingertip in length and embroidered with large green ideograms. She studied her own tacky white suit and shoeless feet. There would be no harm in indulging Ira. She could accommodate him and laugh at him at the same time. The very act of accepting his gifts would be a nose-thumbing act—at him, at the Ellenbogens, at the whole fabric of the Beach, the vulgar superstructure that she detested so thoroughly. If *they* didn't get the joke (the idea! Maitland's daughter, the professor's wife, going in for their idiocies), she certainly would. She bolted the cabin door. In the hot privacy of the beach house, she found herself fondling and caressing the expensive suits. She was momentarily ashamed of herself—a diabetic child turned loose in a candy store. The paisley intrigued her. It was silk—a dull golden silk, shot with subtle greens and dusty reds. The bodice was cunningly gathered and shaped so as to make much of a woman's breasts; there was a built-in waist cincher to give curve and size to the behind. Marty shook her head in amazement—nothing was left to chance, no bets were missed. She struggled out of her faded, streaked suit, suddenly ashamed of its ugliness. In New Hampshire, it was fine. Here, it simply did not have relevance. The reverse snobbery of plainness had not yet reached them and it was doubtful that it ever would. She enjoyed a rare moment of pride, viewing her trim shape in the full-length mirror. *Very good indeed for two children and thirty-three years,* she told herself. The paisley swimsuit seemed to demand something additional. She wiggled her feet into a pair of aquamarine sandals (twenty dollars if they were a dollar) and tried on the Chinese coat, then took it off in deference to the heat. She knew what was needed—a touch of artifice in her face. A full complement of cosmetics (including a jar of royal jelly) rested on the shelf alongside the enameled sink. She surveyed the congeries of pastes, greases and powders and selected a stick of orange lipstick, favoring her small, upturned lips with a modest dab. She honored her unruly hair with a few bursts from a dispenser. There was a minute gold flask, a cunning replica of a strawberry, containing a perfume whose price might have fed a Greek village for a month. She twisted off its top—a spurious leaf—and sniffed the aroma. *That* would have been excessive. She screwed it tight and returned it to the shelf, proud of her denial. The gulf between the women lounging around the Peruviana pool and herself had to be maintained, if only in the rejection of *Fraise,* forty dollars the ounce.

When she had concluded her transformation, she unlatched the door and returned to the chaise. Supine, she sensed a delightful sloth oozing up around her. She imagined that a mudbath in a Fifth Avenue beauty salon had the same soothing, brain-numbing effect. It was only fitfully sunny. The ocean was overhung with a misty pelagic curtain, and a mild breeze intermittently swept soft clouds over the beach. These would obscure the sun momentarily, then hasten westward, permitting the yellow glare to repaint and reheat the ocean. The effect was like that of an immense stage spotlight controlled by a nervous electrician. The glow suffused over the gleaming hotel, pool and patio, then abruptly disappeared, plunging them in shadow.

A few more patrons made their appearance. Several were breakfasting under varicolored umbrellas. Others were lovingly greasing limbs and torsos and turning their faces, like votaries of the Inca, to the elusive sun. Marty found herself taking particular notice of the women. Normally, she was never jealous, not in the least concerned with what other women wore, how they dressed their hair. Now that she had made concession to their rules, some comparison was necessary, if only to assure herself that the gap still existed. The comparison was an invidious one. Pridefully, she told herself that in inching toward them, she only enhanced her own special qualities. There was a lofty woman in a gold lamé bathing suit crossing the dining area directly in front of the hotel, in the company of Fenton Braud. Marty recalled her from the Ellenbogen party—the heiress. She had auburn hair flecked with caramel beige; her mouth was a crimson scar and her hands were chock-a-block with bracelets and jewels. As she sat down with Braud, she fussed with her curls, crossed her legs (thighs too heavy), lit a cigarette, adjusted smoked glasses and vigorously scratched a knee. Each action, Marty felt, stemmed from a sense of not-belonging, an unsettled quality unhelped by gold lamé bathing suits. In her smart paisley suit, courtesy of Ira, she felt infinitely more important, more adjusted, more valid than the heiress. She was of the academic world. She was a good mother and wife. She read books. And still, she could do justice to a fifty-five-dollar bathing suit. Tomorrow she would return to the starved, Spartan role of the professor's wife, none the worse for her brush with High Life, indeed strengthened by it.

Shortly before noon, Ira came slouching down the duckboards. He seemed stuporous and stiff, responding only halfheartedly to cheery greetings from his friends. In spite of his lethargic mien, he still harbored the promise of a brighter day, more fun, a million laughs. Marty could see Braud dig his brunching companion in one rib and point significantly to the promoter. Then they both laughed. Braud had probably communicated some laughable anecdote, some choice gossip about Ira. Now they were both in better frame of mind to attack their cottage-cheese and fruit salads.

Ira halted dramatically a few feet from Marty. "Zile. Zile kai," he said appreciatively. "You're all duded up. There's even a teensy-weensy bit of lipstick on the mouth. I might pass out."

"Don't make me sorry I put this on," Marty said. "Your loot isn't hard to take, Ira, but I can't stomach the program notes."

"Ah, go easy on me, sweetie. I had a rough night and a rougher morning. Tell me you like the presents. Make Ira feel good."

"It's lovely," Marty said. "However, I won't keep any of it. I'm wearing it because I don't want to be out of uniform."

"You'll keep it. I'll send it to New York if you're ashamed to take it back to the boathouse for hubby to see." He sat up suddenly, holding his head. "Your old man's got the mads for me anyhow. Without me dressing his wife in bathing suits."

"What do you mean?"

"Tommy called me this morning. Roused me from deep sleep induced by two blockbusters and a double brandy—" He was going to add "and a crazy broad" but halted himself in time.

"About the stones."

"Everyone blames Ira. I was trying to help him." He looked ruefully at Marty. "He called me some pretty nasty names, that dago husband of yours."

"Don't call him that. I don't like it."

"Why not? I heard him call himself worse when he was half-shot. Guinea. Ginzo."

He waved vigorously for a waiter, asked Marty if she wanted lunch, and when she declined, ordered coffee for them.

"You went out on the town last night," Ira said, beaming.

"How do you know?"

"I know everything. Especially everything that happens after ten o'clock."

"Did I have a good time?"

"With Erwin and Lila? The Ellen-borings. Him counting his money in that square, smart head of his and Lila sitting on that stuck-out keester like it was the Hope diamond. Great company."

"You're quite cruel when you want to be, aren't you?"

"Cruel? I'm hep. Let's see. You did the stone-crab bit. Then you went to the Blue Paradise to watch the faggot singer. Then you went home early."

"You aren't as smart as you think. You missed the best part."

"Yeah?" Ira's puffy eyes widened.

"We met Mr. Nudo, the owner of the Blue Paradise. Apparently he's a man of some stature. Tom discovered they were old friends from East Harlem. In fact, Tom's father—my father-in-law—was Nudo's godfather. Small world department."

Ira was impressed. "That a fact? Just a couple of old spaghetti benders from Naples, hey? They rub garlic on each other?"

"You're being rude again. Every time you do that, you betray your own inferiority. If you think in those terms you'll be less ready to insult people."

He studied her narrowly. The truth of her observation seemed to reach him—by a circuitous route, by way of his ego and his compulsive lechery—but reach him it did.

"That's why you're so *great,*" he said earnestly. "The greatest. The way you nail a guy. I don't mind your having me tabbed first time out, when you made believe you didn't see me. But it's how you think about it and analyze me all the time inside that lovely head." His voice abruptly hoarse and low. "The head by itself would be enough. That smudgy face and the amber eyes. And the flat behind and the legs. But what's *inside* that head—it rocks me. Why do you think I've been playing escort to you and your old man? Because I like archaeology?"

"We have an embargo on this kind of talk. Remember?"

"The hell you say. I know what you're thinking. This is old Ira Q. Bedspring. But it isn't that way when I think about you. Well, it is and it isn't."

She smiled at him. "You'd enjoy what Lila Ellenbogen called you."

"Yeah. I can imagine."

"She called you—" Marty halted, unable to repeat Lila's rude characterization of the promoter.

"She's jealous. She had a price on that little secret of hers. To the highest bidder. And who else but big Erwin? If a strange man ever goosed her she'd faint. She hates me because I'm so immoral.

Can I help it if I'm honest? That I get what everyone wants because I'm not ashamed to go after it? I don't think *you'd* hold it against me. Not anyone as sharp as you. You might dislike me, but you'd have to be tolerant. Or maybe even admire me a little."

"Oh, be still. I'm trying to enjoy the sun—what there is of it."

The beach was clouded over. The breeze had stiffened and a few of the guests were gathering impedimenta and retiring to the roofed area of the patio.

"Erwin talk about me last night?" Ira asked suddenly. "About that deal I got working?"

"You mean the *God-O-Rama?*" Marty asked, smiling. "What a wonderful name! Did you think of that?"

"Si and myself. What did Erwin say?"

"He's very high on it. He wants the name changed. I don't think you should let him, Ira. It's too good."

He squinted at her. "Smarty. How does your husband stand that kind of thing? Doesn't he have a yen to kick you around the house?"

"He isn't as easy to anticipate as you are, Ira. You're terribly simple. You're as predictable as a wire-haired terrier."

The waiter came with a tray loaded with a lavish silver service. There seemed sufficient pots, cups, saucers, silver and napery to furnish a seven-course meal for a finicky family of five. The waiter assembled the accessories and poured the coffee. The ritual revived Ira.

"The guest silver," he advised Marty. He wrinkled his nose at the waiter, but signed no check. "Thanks, Ernie, sweetie. Give my love to Louie."

The waiter winked back at Ira and left. These furtive unspoken bonds between Ira and the laboring classes confounded Marty. She had always been ill at ease with waiters, garage mechanics, soda jerks, the army of faceless servitors, all of them hating their jobs and hating the people they attended. She experienced, in their presence, a deep sorrow and a touchy enmity. But Ira handled them differently. He was of them, yet above them. He hinted, while they waited on him, that he knew all about their trade, their secrets, their problems, that he had doubtless once worked as a waiter, or a mechanic, or a soda jerk. Now that he had arrived, he seemed to be saying, he would never forget them or fail to understand their problems.

It was almost cool. Marty drew the extravagant Chinese jacket around her shoulders. They sipped black coffee in silence. Ira seemed to doze.

"I'm not the old fighting Ira deKay any more," he said suddenly. "I dunno. I have to work harder to get my kicks."

"Is that a fact?"

"It's rough. I can't put my finger on it, but the wheeling and dealing doesn't give me any real zetz. Like this religious bit I got started. I was all hotted up, but now I'm letting Si do the planning. And the money end—Ellenbogen robbed me of that and I didn't even fight back. I still have lotsa clients. Good connections. If I wanted I could go back to the network tomorrow. They haven't had a good press since I quit."

There seemed to be a genuineness to his despair. She never suspected that deKay could experience *Weltschmerz;* the confession had a certain degree of charm.

"Yeah, the old pepper isn't what it used to be," deKay said. "I'm pushing forty. Maybe the trouble is everything's been too easy."

"Maybe you're getting bored because so much of what you do is empty and meaningless. You're an air merchant. You deal in wind."

He jerked himself upright. "That's what I mean about you. You always know where to jab the needle. The long one with the hook on it." He swung his gold-fuzzed legs around and faced her. He was wearing skintight bathing trunks—black satin, hardly bigger than an athletic supporter. His figure was a shade too paunchy for the abbreviated costume.

"I know what's got me in Gloomsville. It's you and your damned faraway face and that do-me-something voice. I think I got a case for you, and that's something that hasn't happened to me since I was nineteen."

"Don't flatter me," she said indifferently. "And don't blame me for your misery."

"Go on, turn the knife," deKay said. "I oughta know better. I oughta stay where I belong. You see that big dame there with Braud? She's gonna get twelve million dollars some day. She's stupid and ashamed of herself and she looks like a giraffe. But still, she's twelve million bucks. She *cries* for me. I did her a favor once and she'll never get over it. Any of these broads here—they're all a bunch of pop flies. They read me. They get my message."

"I read you, Ira," Marty said. "But I haven't enjoyed dirty

books since I was thirteen. One of the girls in private school used to smuggle them in. You know—Harold Teen, Tillie the Toiler. She was expelled."

"There you go!" Ira shouted.

"Really, do you expect anything kinder from me? Anyone with the slightest discernment can figure you out."

"Yeah? How come I just landed the PR account for the Beach University? No class? Just because I put on the clown act and play cornball doesn't mean I can't *think*." She was still smiling at him, certain that they had come full circle—that he was on the defensive, and in large measure, incapable of handling her colossal indifference, her humorous contempt.

"I'd expect that from a University here. I can imagine the curriculum. Water Skiing 101-102. Sun Bathing, 3-4, two graduate credits."

"I wish you were fat and ugly. Then it wouldn't matter. I'd laugh you off."

"You'd better start chuckling, Ira."

"No. Not yet." He leaned forward. "I haven't had a yen for someone like I have for you—*ever*."

"I believe the word is *lech*."

"No. You won't buy what I have to tell you. But it's above and beyond what that body and that smudgy face do to me. I got bodies and faces I haven't used yet. That much is *lech*. It's your attitude. You're up there all by yourself snickering at us. At this town, at the Ellenbogens, and especially at me. We're amusing the hell out of you, but you won't let us in on the joke."

"It would be hard for *you* to see the joke." He was, after all, a country boy. "You're the joke, Ira. Oh, you're not bad *per se*. I guess you mean well and you're good-natured and you really want to make people happy."

"What's wrong with that?" he asked.

"What's wrong is that you're—you're a syndrome of everything rotten in this country."

"Stepped in what? I know you're educated, Marty, but not here. It doesn't play. Give it to me in short words."

These were his home grounds, his ball park. In denigrating him and his environment, she was constrained to abide by his rules. "I'll give you an example," she said. "That little man who works for you. What's his name? Mammalstein?"

"Mermelstein. Little Si."

"Tom told me that little Si was once an English teacher in the

Bronx, and probably a good teacher. So what do you do? You treble his salary and have him distributing small lies and petty deceits for you, none of them serving any purpose. He might still be teaching English to a bunch of kids who need it."

"Zotz! I'm glad you brought that up!" Ira sat up vigorously. "You know something? Si is ninety times better off working my side of the street. Why, those tough dagoes and stove-lids almost cockalized him! They took his pants off in the men's room and threatened to finish off what the rabbi started. He was so scared he never went back to the lousy school. And you're criticizing me for saving him from *that?* He was so shaken up, he couldn't even make a go of that rinky-dink PR firm until I showed him how to do it. I saved the guy's life—and you bug me for it!"

"I used him as an example. If he's happier with you, that's indicative of his own weakness. It isn't hard to corrupt people. What makes it so repugnant is that you corrupt them to *little* things —petty sin without ecstasy. Foot-high cheesecake. Paisley bathing suits."

He nodded his fuzzed head solemnly. "If I read you, sweetie, you're saying it would be better to be corrupted in spades. Big Sins. Ecstasy. Zile, you make it sound good. I'm gonna have trouble standing up any minute."

"You're disgusting."

"Who isn't?" He surveyed her oiled, browning flesh, the trim figure. "If only you were homely," he said. "It would help. I could bear it. I'd ignore the way you act as if you're wise to everything, especially me. No dame has a right to be that sharp. I resent it."

"I had no idea you were that sensitive," Marty said. "I have the feeling you might cry."

"Yes, and wouldn't you love that. So you could chuckle at me some more. I tell you what it is. Since I've been escorting you around, it's like I've missed something. Normally, I never look back. I never worry about what I've done. But there you were. In those raggedy shorts and that torn Oxford shirt. And that poor, beat-up husband who gets his jollies digging for bones."

"Tom doesn't need your sympathy. He manages."

"Just barely. Why are you so impatient with him?"

"Why do you say that?"

"That night we were in Hilltown, like. Other things. You seem to be waiting for him to do something. Maybe stop smoking those wop cigars. Or fill in those holes and open a pizzeria. I think you could use a change of pace."

"Is that the best you can do? Ira, I've been propositioned more expertly by college boys. You must be tired."

"Yeah, I'm beat." He flattened out on the chaise. "I had a rough night. I think sometimes I'm running down. The old motor is still good. It's just the driver is bored."

She felt a voyeur's interest in his exploits. "Who was it? Miss Cooke?"

"Nah. Cleo's hired help. The utility infielder."

"Was it anyone I know?" She tried to inhibit the eagerness in her voice.

"Nope. It was a business thing. When you combine them, it's never good."

"But Ira—that's your whole life. Business is pleasure. Faith is pleasure. Everything's a good time, isn't it?"

"Yeah. Everything's a kick." He turned on his side and looked at her earnestly. "Why'd I get you those duds? That sneaky bathing suit. The crazy Chinee coat. It's bad enough I have to listen to you abuse me, I have to dress you for the occasion. Big-hearted Ira. Go on, baby, laugh it up."

"I like you better when you're being nasty and foul-mouthed. When you start feeling sorry for yourself, you're *unnatural*."

With no warning, fat raindrops splashed on them. The sky was thickly layered with dark lacerated clouds, and the ocean was now a turbid gray. The pool and patio were emptying rapidly. Marty squinted toward the playground. The children and their counselor had vanished.

"It's coming down hard," she said. "I wonder if the children are all right?"

"No sweat. They got a nursery room inside. It's all taken care of."

She sensed again the delightful easement of motherly apprehensions. It was most exhilarating: *the children were taken care of*.

"We'd better go inside," Marty said, getting up. "Are we allowed to sit around the lobby like this?"

"Go inside the cabana. If it rains in I'll close the door."

She hesitated. "It's ridiculous. You shouldn't frighten me and you don't. I'm just not up to a wrestling match."

He shrugged. "Get wet, sweetie. Ira never forces people to do what they don't want to do." He wheeled in the chaises and she joined him inside the striped interior. For a moment she stood in the middle of the small, hot room, indecisive, and wary of him. Then she realized that for all his crudeness and his announced intention of seducing her, the circumstances were improbable and her indifference was an infallible deterrent. So long as she could keep laughing at him he presented no menace. The swollen rain, driven by the sea wind, drenched the front of the cabana. Ira closed the louvered doors. He beamed at her, suffusing a saffron light.

"Cozy, isn't it?" he asked. He wrinkled his nose.

"Keep your distance and we'll be friends," she said.

In deKay's suite, Kitty Schmitt's late-morning shower was interrupted by the telephone. Soaked and nude, she bounced out of the tile-and-glass enclosure, and in muscular strides, flew to the phone. She was a woman assembled in large white slabs and chunks, a pile of fleshy rectangles and cubes.

"It's your dime!" she yelled into the phone.

"Oh. Oh. I beg pardon. Is Mr. deKay there?"

"Whosis? Who wants him?"

"Who is this?"

"This is his Aunt Miriam. The fat one from Omaha. *Yaaah!* This is his unofficial secretary, Katherine L. Schmitt. I dropped in to finish up some letters this morning. And all I'm doing is answering his phone."

"Good morning, Kitty. This is Cleo. Cleo Cooke."

"*Cleo.* Cleo *honey*. Where'd you run off to last night?"

"It got a little noisy for me," Cleo said frigidly.

"Serves me right, baby. I can't help it if I have a big laugh. Up in New York everyone's used to it. I never figured the Beach for such a fancy town. I guess Ira's the only one allowed to make noise."

"No offense, Kitty," Cleo said. "I thought it was priceless when you grabbed the band leader's clarinet and started to play. It was the hit of the evening."

"Yeah, anything to liven the joint up. All those lard-ass cloak and suiters began to numb me. You didn't think I could play the licorice stick didja? Well, I was first clarinet at St. Brigid's two years running."

Cleo laughed demurely. Although she and Kitty Schmitt were now sisters united by way of Ira's charms, it was obligatory that some distinction between them be maintained. But what? Cleo was prettier than Kitty and, as far as most men were concerned, it would be no contest. But now that Ira had bedded down with the strong-arm girl, Cleo was left very little in the way of vital edge. She understood that once she lost the competitive battle of the mattress, she was only another handsome blond woman with a six-year-old son and no husband. She was in oversupply.

"Where's Ira?" Cleo asked. "I wanted to check him out on some odds and ends."

"Like who was here last night?" Kitty howled. Cleo remained silent. "Cleo, hon, when I got here about eleven this morning, he was just checking out in his bathing trunks. I guess he's down at the pool." She lied effortlessly, knowing that Cleo was not fooled.

"Could I bother you to take a peep out the window?" Cleo asked. "He's got the end cabana. You can't miss it. If he's there, I could ring him."

"Sure 'nough." Kitty barreled across the bedroom, leaving moist footprints in the furry carpeting—a set of Friday's feet followed her to the glass wall. She peered down at the pool. It was enshadowed and windy, and she reconciled herself to a long day's drinking.

Peeking through the Venetian blinds, she saw Ira sprawled on a chaise. A woman—a slim, lovely woman—was on the adjacent beach chair. It had just begun to rain, and the two of them got up and began moving furniture indoors. They were out of sight now. She had to hand it to Ira; the man never quit. Who the delicate brunette was, she did not know, but she bespoke class, and Kitty was happy for Ira.

She smiled in approval and thwacked her bare, square buttocks. "What a man!" she said. "The *greatest*."

She imparted this intelligence to Cleo Cooke.

"Cleo, honey, he's there all right. Operating like crazy."

"Really? What are you referring to?"

"There's some dame with him. I didn't recognize her, but she looked like real stuff."

"Kind of skinny? With mousy brown hair?"

"Well, from where I stood, she looked better than *that*. It started to rain and they went into the cabana."

"I know who that is. The dopey professor's wife."

"I got to admire that boss of yours," Kitty opined. "He's perpetual motion." She could not resist taunting Cleo, whose prior claims on deKay rankled. "You remember *A Christmas Carol* by Dickens, Cleo?"

"I don't believe I do."

"Well anyway, there were three Christmases—Past, Present and Future. That's us. You're Christmas Past, I'm Christmas Present, and that broad in the cabana with Ira right now—she may not *know* it—but she's Christmas Future!"

Cleo's voice was icy. "I'm afraid I don't appreciate your remarks, Kitty. I haven't the vaguest notion of what you mean." It bothered Cleo, not so much that this noisy woman had slept with Ira, but that she was not quite as common as she had hoped. She had been to St. Brigid's and now she was quoting famous authors.

"Well, skip it. Should I switch you over to Ira? I'll tinkle the hotel operator."

"No. Don't bother. I'll catch him later."

In her immaculate, chintzy-modern, air-conditioned apartment north of the Beach, Cleo replaced the phone. Her son was seated at the kitchen table, crayoning a drawing of a pony cart in a fat coloring book. He was a beautiful child, fine-boned and clear-skinned, as lovely as his mother. His flesh was honey-brown and his hair was almost white. He wore a fragile one-piece sunsuit, a delicate seersucker garment more appropriate for a two-year-old. His tiny feet were encased in scarlet anklets and adorable white shoes. He was a solemn, furtive child, wary of his mother, and adept at deceiving nurses and baby-sitters. He seemed an intrinsic part of the trig, efficient apartment with its blocky, brightly hued furniture—the couches that became beds, the closets that expanded and held secret caches of expensive clothes, the medical bathroom. Cleo looked upon him in those terms—a gratifying possession. Her pride in the boy made Ira's defections extremely hard to bear. Ira had rescued her from an existence just a hair-breadth from prostitution. She was a girl on the town, a sleeper-out, available for conventions and top-echelon visitors. Now she had status and income. Little Robin went to a private school and wore nothing but SFA's finest. Even the aggravating truth that he had no substantive father—she herself was not certain when the accident had occurred and who had been responsible, although the boy's delicacy led her to suspect a certain ensign—was considerably mitigated by Ira's largesse. She could do without Ira's passion—such appetites she had indulged early and often. But the apartment, the governess, the private school, little Robin's clothes—under no circumstances did she want these endangered. The likes of Kitty Schmitt were no threat. They arrived, they departed, passing in and out of Ira's life like old baseball score cards. Martha Sorrento was different, and Cleo knew this. She recalled something about the digging ending in August, and she comforted herself with the knowledge that the professor's wife, that dirty bitch with no hips and no make-up, would go back to her libraries and faculty teas in a few weeks. But the reassurance was only transitory. The gnawing fear would not abate. The child, apparently intent on his coloring, had listened with purposeful attentiveness to her phone conversation.

"Aren't we going to see Uncle Ira today?" Robin asked.

"I don't think so, darling."

"He was going to take me fishing."

"Uncle Ira's busy, sweetheart. He'll take you next week."

"Will you take me fishing?"

Cleo walked across the compact, ingenious kitchenette (it held so much in so small an area!) and kissed his platinum head. "Darling, the weather isn't terribly nice. It's starting to rain. I'll call Mrs. Braverman and she'll take you to the movies. All right?"

Robin nodded. He always agreed. He was a remarkably uncomplicated and satisfied child. Mrs. Braverman was fat and gray and bowlegged and was scared stiff of him. He could eat candy and popcorn all afternoon and she would never argue with him. If she tried to discipline him he would hold his breath.

His mother began dialing Mrs. Braverman. Two dollars an hour was cheap enough to be unencumbered, to indulge her concern over Ira and his unsettling behavior. She could expect a call from Si Mermelstein (the only one she knew who was unhappier than herself) and she looked forward to insulting him.

9 *Events of a Rainy Afternoon*

Lila kept good her promise. In tight dungarees, white blouse and kerchief, she joined the diggers shortly after eleven. She wore a pair of new gardening gloves and laughed good-naturedly when Tom wolf-whistled at her.

"Listen!" she said exuberantly. "Down heah in Dixie you can get into real trouble for that!" She clapped a gloved hand over her mouth, noting Ballard, about fifty feet away, slamming his pick into the surface soil. He had unearthed another white boulder, and he seemed to be attacking the sand with personal fury. He made no show of having heard her inappropriate jest. He was in a private, sweaty world of his own; his massive body, the pick, the soil. It seemed to Tom he was doing penance of some kind.

"Where do I start, Professor?" Lila asked.

"Grab a shovel and dig a hole. Anywhere. You'll get tired in five minutes and leave me alone."

"Tom! I'll chase you off tomorrow if you don't let me help."

"Come on over to the shell heap. You can fool around there and you won't get into trouble. Here's a trowel." He gave her a long-hafted gardening tool and she inspected it as if it were a diamond brooch. "*This?* You do it all with *this?*"

"That's why the pay is so bad," Tom said. "Anybody can do it."

They walked down the slope, passing Ballard's towering black form.

"Hi, Dr. Ballard!" Lila called.

The Negro brought his pick down mightily, then rested on it. "How do, Mrs. Ellenbogen," he said. "Are you joining us?"

"If you don't mind."

"Heck, I just work here. The boss needs help—he's going to dig up every inch of ground here, he says."

"I know. He told me about it this morning."

Ballard half laughed, half grunted and, abandoning his pick, took up a shovel and began clearing loosened dirt. A neat pile of yellow sand bordered the big trench—the area from which the stones had been stolen.

"He's powerful, isn't he?" Lila asked, as they walked toward the midden. "Why is his arm bandaged like that? Did he hurt himself out here?"

"Pork chops. He got burned by grease."

The notion offended her. She did not associate David Ballard, Ph.D., with pork chops.

"It's none of my business, so I deserve a nutty answer," she said.

At the shell heap, he introduced her to the Burleys. They shrank to the outer edge of the pit, fearful that she had come to devour them.

"Kids," Tom said patiently, "You know Mrs. Ellenbogen, don't you? Remember when we came down, she met us at the airport? And had the nice tea for us?"

They nodded dumbly.

"Mrs. Ellenbogen is going to help out. She's an amateur, so be patient. Why don't you let her work the rear section, while you two continue up front. Wilma, you make sure Mrs. E. doesn't chuck away any incised shards or ceremonial stones. And just kind of coach her in how to handle the trowel."

"I'm honored, really I am," Lila effused. "Tom thinks so highly of the two of you. Let's see—I think I remember your names—you're Omar and you're Wilma. Right?"

"Oran," Wilma said huskily. "His name is *O-ran*."

"I'm sorry. I wish you'd call me Lila."

Oran gulped. His sun-reddened face turned a deeper scarlet. "Yes. Yes. We'll help you, won't we, Wilma?" His sister blinked behind the torturing lenses.

"Go on," Tom said. "Hop in. You'll be wallowing in clam shells pretty soon."

"Funny boy," she said. "Just start in? That's all there is?"

"Don't ask me, ask them," Tom said, departing.

The Burleys backed away. It was *their* midden, *their* garbage heap, their very own pile of shells. Ben Peltz had willed it to them when he started sinking the new pits. What right had she in there with them?

Lila compared herself to the Scub, a horrible, mythical animal she had read about once in a children's version of Noah's Ark. The Scub, a latecomer to the mercy ship, according to the chronicler, was responsible for corrupting the innocent beasts. There were also, in this version of the Bible legend, two timid furry animals aboard—Tiddley-winks, or Tridgets or something like that—who lived in mortal terror of the slithery evil Scub, and finally left the Ark in a barrel to escape him forever—and presumably to drown at sea. Studying the Burleys' querulous faces, she wondered if they might not abruptly vault out of the trench and set out across the bay in an orange crate. She began chipping hesitantly at the white shells embedded in the dry muck.

Peltz came trudging up the slope, pushing a battered wheelbarrow. Tom's plan was to extract the new stones and keep them in the boathouse. Inside the barrow, Ben had his camera, his tripod and a measuring tape. Tom grabbed one handle of the wheelbarrow and helped him push it up the hill.

"You should have seen my Uncle Pete do this," Tom said. "He was five feet tall and couldn't speak English, but he sure could wrestle a wheelbarrow. He helped lay the foundation for the Empire State Building."

Ben kept pace with him. "You aren't mad at me any more?" he asked. "I mean, last night—"

"It wasn't your fault. I'm just getting a slow red-ass in general. I'm wondering whether we'll be able to finish."

"So long as you're not sore. I was visiting my aunt and my uncle."

"I believe you." Their need for perpetual approbation made him fidget. The role of peerless leader had its drawbacks.

Tom started digging alongside Ballard. In a few minutes a hard surface was struck and they began troweling around one more of the ubiquitous white boulders. If Ballard's scorched left forearm was hurting, he betrayed no pain.

"Your friend Harkey—that minister," Tom said. "He had a little trouble last night."

"No kidding?" Ballard did not look at him.

"He got bombed. It was on the front page. His garage went up in smoke. Three people were hurt."

"That's rough. Man, this is a big one. How'd they ever transport these rocks?"

"Maybe you were frying your pork chops at Harkey's."

Ballard set his trowel down and looked sheepishly at Tom. "I can't lie to you. I was there. But don't worry, I beat it before the cops showed. Harkey and me have an understanding—I'm never there."

"Who treated your arm?"

"Colored doctor. Emerson. He's on the committee. He took me to his office, then I came back here." He resumed digging around the boulder. "I'm sorry, Tom. I couldn't stay away. The call of the wild, I guess."

Tom looked across the site, toward the bay. The waters were a dark, roiled slate-blue and the sky was clouding. "You make me feel like a heel, Dave. I'm on your side. How can I not be? But we're guests of the natives here. You get hauled into the pokey again, and we'll all be in trouble."

"I know. I don't belong there. It's their fight."

"That's not what I mean. You want to make it your fight, go ahead. You got a right to. But not while we have the dig to finish."

"I was thinking," Dave said. "Maybe I could work extra hard this week, or the next ten days, then get off your hands. Go it alone, like England."

"You're of age. Do what you want. I was hoping you'd stay with me till we're cleaned up. We might be digging here through September."

"I owe you plenty. I'd be loading freight cars this summer if you hadn't taken me. Or marking papers in General Studies, which is worse."

The new stone, unearthed, stared at them with alarming whiteness.

"You ought to think of this, too," Tom said. "Maitland promised you a teaching job at that college in Vermont. Next time they invite him for a guest lecture he's making *you* the condition."

Ballard rested. "The only thing is, I'm hooked. That damn Harkey. Tom, you wouldn't believe it. He acts like it's a joke. He smiles. They spit in his eye and he prays for them. You know how they're going to kick off their boycott? With prayers. They're going to have the biggest love feast this state has ever seen. If anyone throws a bomb, they'll pray harder."

"You sound like you want to go to church right now."

"No. I'm still the onlooker. The thing that flips me is they're convinced they're going to make it work. Not with facts and sociology and all the stuff you and I have been breaking our backs over—Maitland and the others—but with good old irrational faith. The *mystique*."

Peltz set up his tripod and took three pictures from different angles. When he had finished, they dug out the new rock and dumped it in the wheelbarrow. Ben waddled off with his prize. His bandy legs appeared to be chasing a runaway pig as the barrow, heavily weighted, rolled down the slope. With an abrupt rush of wind, the rain, splashed on them with refreshing suddenness.

"What do we do now? Is the game called?" Lila called.

"Go down to the boathouse," Tom said.

Ballard hacked away at the sand. "Mrs. Ellenbogen picked a bad day to get educated."

"It's her neurosis, so she can do what she wants," Tom said. "We're getting a fence tomorrow and more laborers." He sounded on the defensive—as if Ballard's innocent comment about Lila required explanation.

"I think it's great," Dave said. "Woman like that—with all her advantages, wanting to learn how slobs like us live."

Tom shouldered his shovel and started to leave. "Aren't you knocking off? You going to get soaked?"

"I can stand it a little while more. I'll clear this last one and then quit."

Tom walked down the slope. At the shell heap, the Burleys, their backs turned on the intruder in dungarees, kept at their pecking and chipping. Tom helped Lila out.

"Oran, where's the stuff you got the last two days?" Sorrento asked. "Now's a good time for me to try to classify some of it. Mrs. Ellenbogen wants a lesson."

"In—in—the b-b-big orange crate," Oran stammered. "Under your table. There are some empty cigar boxes on my bed."

"Good. Why don't you two characters get dry?"

They flashed their timorous faces at him, offered no answer, and continued to work. Tom shrugged; he could not shepherd them eternally. If they were going to get soaked, that was their business.

At the boathouse, he located the crate, a few paper-bound publications and the cigar boxes and suggested to Lila they go upstairs. In the upper room, he dumped the contents of the orange crate on his bed, set the cigar boxes to one side, and lit a fresh cigar. Lila, patting her wet face with a handkerchief, watched him admiringly. He opened one of the ragged publications and squinted at it.

"Is everything all right in there?" she asked. "Are you comfortable? Now that you may be here longer, maybe you need more furniture, or something."

"No, it's dandy, Lila."

"Isn't it crowded? You know, I sometimes think I should have let you and Marty and the kids sleep at *our* place. We have extra rooms that are never used, and it would have been a good excuse to keep my in-laws away this summer."

"How would you explain it to your friends? Me in my sneakers and old sweatshirt carrying dirty shovels into your living room."

"Tom, you don't understand me, do you? At least you don't try to."

He started breaking down the pile of dusty junk into bone splinters, pot shards, worked stones, and shells. He held up a large pointed shell.

"That's something like *scungilli.* Busycon."

"Is that worth saving? Some Indian's lunch?"

"It's a *pick.* See the way the edge has been worked? A typical culture trait along the coast."

"What are all those little bits and pieces over there?"

"*That's* lunch. Mostly animal bones—raccoon, rabbit, possum. We ship this stuff up to a zoologist at the University and let him sweat over it."

"You're changing the subject. Why do you make fun of me?"

"Ma che!" he cried. "All I said was I'd track up your carpeting with my old sneakers, and you got offended! What would the canasta club think?"

"There! You did it again!"

"Lila, don't be so sensitive." He held up a piece of pottery. "Now that's a beauty. A perfect piece of Weeden Island Punctuated." He dropped it into a cigar box.

"I don't see what's so funny about you and Marty moving in with us. You could still do it. It must be terrible here on hot nights. And so crowded! You and Marty and the kids up here and all the others—"

"They manage. They don't know any better. The guys sleep together and Wilma stays with the kids now." He looked up, smiling. "That's some idea—this collection of hole-in-the-ass grifters in *your* place."

"Why do you have to be such a clod?"

He exhaled the fumes from the black stem. "I guess because you're rich and beautiful and Jewish. You're a prize. Deep down in my dark Neapolitan heart I'd like to be married to a rich girl so I could sit on my duff and write. How does that sound?"

"I never know when you're kidding or not. I give up."

"Yeah. I'm full of jokes."

Lila got up and strolled around the barren room. She was vaguely jealous of it. Her mind turned guiltily to Thoreau: *Simplify, simplify!* The dark, cryptic man, sprawled on the army cot, sorting out the leftovers of an Indian village, bothered her. He seemed to be *in precarium,* and yet she was not certain why. He had his job, his security, a beautiful wife and handsome children. Was it the blunted nose or the shrunken leg that aroused some ancestral sorrow in her? The feeling that he was alien to her world and her values, an everlasting outsider, a fellow resolutely out of step? It distressed her that he did not seem to *care*—not even about his own profession. His references to anthropology, to digging, to the social sciences, even to the high vision of the University, were usually denigrating. There was in Tom Sorrento, she surmised, a morose insularity, a displacement that he tried to screen with humor and ribaldry and infusions of Neapolitan dialect.

"What do you really *care* about, Tom?" she asked challengingly. "I mean—does anything move you or excite you?"

"Yeah, white clam sauce."

"That's what I mean! Try to get you to talk seriously!"

"What am I supposed to do? Sing 'Baby Shoes?'"

She sighed and sat down in one of her husband's tricky canvas chairs (Three-way Lounger, $10.98). Outside the rain rattled intimately on the shingled roof. The bay's slate surface was prickly with gooseflesh.

"I think I know your trouble," Lila said.

"Sure. Put it in triplicate and send it to the Del' Assunta Society on East 116th Street. I'm behind in my dues."

She ignored him. "You have insight, Tom. I guess you were born with some of it, but you got a lot of it the hardest way. Street fights with tough kids in Harlem. Football—all that grinding, rugged contact. And the Marines, where you killed people. Admit it, you did. It all gave you a look at people at their worst, what they're capable of. But at the same time, you have compassion. As bad as they are, you have to worry about them. I know it's true. I can see it."

"Lila, *non rompermi coglioni*. You don't know me at all."

"That sounds dirty, so don't translate it."

"You've been reading too many of these war novels, where the hero learns all about life because he kills or almost gets killed. Like all that bullfighting crap. Blood and death and balls. It's supposed to redeem you and invigorate you and be the most important thing. Lila, baby, that doesn't do *anything* for a man. It does something for the guys who write the books, that's all. I got brains splattered on me and I had men die in my arms, and I was scared stiff all the time. I suppose that gives me special credentials, a stack pass to the public library, and a working knowledge of Greek. Like hell it does. The same goes for football. It's great for kids. Every year I played I disliked it more."

She looked at him archly. "You could have stayed out of the service," she said. "Why'd you go in? And the Marines—of all things!"

He dropped a fluted-stem point into a box and looked up sourly. "Where'd you hear that?"

"I have my sources, wiseguy."

"Where'd you hear that?" he insisted.

"Your father-in-law told me. At the beer party last February."

She was reveling in her dishonorably gained knowledge of him.

"Maitland said you were rejected by the Marines the first time you took the physical. They said you had an athletic heart—enlarged from too much exercise when you were a boy. Then you went back the second time and threatened to punch the medical officer in the nose if he didn't pass you. You got some Marine captain who had played football with you to intercede. So they let you in, even with an athletic heart."

"Hiiii," Tom sighed. "So what? Lots of guys cheated on the medical. Friend of mine memorized the eye chart. He was so blind they had to lead him to the rifle range."

"Why did you do it? You could have stayed out. It was a big chance to get ahead with all the men going off. Think of it—you would have had *five-year start* on everyone. No—don't tell me. You did it because you had nothing else to do."

"You guessed it. What was I going to do? Coach high school football?"

"You did it because you're noble, that's why."

He clapped a hand to his forehead. "I give up. I was a spy for the American Student Union."

"Like fun. I knew plenty of ASU types, not to mention Young Communist League types—and you're none of them!"

"That's right. I was nonpolitical. Just stupid. I'll tell you something else. After I got down to Quantico, I wished I had taken their advice and flunked the physical. That athletic heart was the best friend I ever had and I was too dumb to know it. I hated the Marines."

"You could have gotten out. All you needed was another chest X-ray."

He puffed his cigar thoughtfully. "I had nothing to get out for. My family? They didn't need me. No wife. No kids. No girl. No job. Nothing that even interested me. Why should I get out?" He lay back against the plasterboard wall, tossing in his hand a bone pin, as perfect as if it had been machined. "It used to frost my rear end in college. All those guys who had their lives figured out. They had it licked. You'd see them in their freshman year dating girls they were *bound* to marry when they graduated. They'd take the same girls to every dance, all the football week ends, and they'd dance looking into each other's eyes like they had it made. It bothered me. I was jealous. I didn't have anything made. I used to take Diana Trapani to the dances—the Tutwiler Avenue Hedy Lamarr—and I never even kissed her goodnight. I didn't like her. Who were all these guys who knew just what they wanted from the day they entered college? They knew they were going to be doctors, or lawyers, or engineers or go into the old man's firm; they knew the girl they'd marry; where they'd live; what their kids would be like. All laid out. Me? I didn't know from one day to the next what my major was. I started off as a pre-med, but I quit the day I almost blew up the chemistry lab."

She stretched back in the three-way chair. Her matronly breasts, encapsulated in deceitful elastique, stretched her white shirt deliciously. "I think you reach me, Tom, because I'm like those boys in college you knew who had it all figured out. My whole life—a betrothed child bride. Everything was planned, thought out, worked out, happened just the way it was supposed to."

"What are you kicking about? You got a good deal." He held up a pottery fragment and looked at it distastefully. "This beats me. It isn't in any of the books I have here. We'll call it Ellenbogen Incised."

"*Listen* to me. Can't you even let me indulge my two-bit neuroses?"

"It's your boathouse."

"It sure is. Everything's mine. Or at least in my name. Another of Erwin's precautions."

"You're an officer of the corporation, aren't you?" he asked.

"What else? Now don't you dare misunderstand me. I love Erwin. I love him very much. It's just that—he's one of those men who's eliminated risk from his life and from the lives of everyone around him."

"Why shouldn't he? I wish I could."

"He's fantastic. When he started dating me, it was as if he'd been laying in wait for me, knowing I was just right, like a man spending years shopping for the perfect kind of diamond. That sounds awful, doesn't it?"

"No."

"Well, there he was, out of service, with a little money of his own, and his mind made up that he could run a business—any business—better than anyone in the world. So he met me, and he learned about my father's dinky aluminum-extruding firm. Apex Extruders, Inc. Samuel Schneer, President. That was my father. If I say so myself, I was a dish. I'm still not exactly a slob. Nothing like your wife, of course—"

"Miss West End Avenue of 1937."

"I ignore you, boor. Oh, I had fellows—more than I could handle. Doctors, lawyers, fine up-and-coming business types. But Erwin simply *assumed* I would have to marry him. I could dress—just right, you know, not overdressed like most young women of my type, and I was smart as a whip. I graduated cum laude from Ohio State. Did you know that? I read a lot—museums, the ballet, social work. That's just the area where Erwin was weak. Do you want to die? Every time I read a book I have to write up a précis for him and read it to him. You'd be surprised how he digests it so beautifully. Then he asks me questions about it, and as far as he's concerned, he's read the book."

"You must have had a hell of a time with *Finnegans Wake*."

"That's one we skipped. But I bet you've read it."

"Nope."

"Now in addition to all these wonderful attributes that drew Erwin to me, I should say, ended his search—there was the Apex Extruders, Inc. My poor father never really got over what Erwin did for that miserable little firm. Just moving it down here! And the new concepts in beach furniture he pioneered!"

"How'd he learn about furniture?"

"There's nothing my husband can't learn. Or do. Or figure out. He says he feels guilty the way he abuses his competitors. He's thinking two years ahead of them. He doesn't have to be dishonest to succeed. He just out-thinks them."

"I'm lost Lila," Tom said wearily. "I'm somewhere else. What's your beef, lady?"

"I have none, I guess." She frowned, and her sensuous face betrayed harsh, anxious lines. "But no one should have everything figured out so minutely. There's nothing, absolutely *nothing,* that Erwin hasn't figured out in advance. Our lives are as satisfying as a fifty-thousand-dollar order from Macy's."

Tom looked sadly at his fragments. "Knock it off, Lila," he said. "I can't cry for you, because weren't you always used to that kind of treatment? Hasn't the whole thing always been set up for you—by somebody? If not Erwin, your parents, or your grandparents."

"That's true. But it's a matter of degree. Or maybe it's just getting more acute as I get older. The need for risk. Or some kind of marginal danger." She laughed loudly. "Last summer, Erwin decided we needed that kind of thing, so we took up deep-sea fishing. He even looked up the records to see on what days the biggest fish were caught. Naturally, he got the best guide, the most expensive tackle, the fastest boat. Oh, he wouldn't use our own boat. He took a customer along, so the whole outing was a deduction. Would you believe it? He caught a two-hundred-pound blue marlin first time out, and I landed a small sailfish. And it was so easy! The skipper and the mate and the boat do all the work. Some thrill! I felt so sorry for those poor stupid fish. Their eyes were all glassy and tortured."

Tom set his ragged reference publication down. He looked questioningly at his hostess, who was reclining on the tubular chair. Something was expected of him, but he had no idea what—nor was he certain that Lila knew what her rambling discourse meant. Perhaps she was just a woman who needed a good audience; she had no real wants, and hence had to synthesize them.

"Lila, if you want me to commiserate with you because of your good luck, don't wait too long. Sometimes I can't afford a baby-sitter and I never go to the theatre. I get an implication from you that Marty and I lead some kind of idyllic University life. We float around in a wispy, blue haze of Grand Ideas and Intelligent People. Boy, do you have the wrong number."

"I don't want to be *poor*. I didn't say that. I just want to be—to be stimulated, to be more alive that I am."

"Don't look at me. I can't even get an associate professorship."

"You will. You'll be a big man in your field someday."

He laughed. "There's nothing as political as a University. Erwin—he'd make out up there. He'd be a few steps ahead of them. My trouble is I won't cooperate. I won't serve on Community Committees and I don't write enough for the journals. I can't even keep up with my reading. I'm slow. I was a remedial reader."

"You were like fun."

"I was. I was a dope in high school. A dumb athlete. I didn't start studying in college until my junior year—and then in subjects you really don't need any brains for—English Lit, Psych, Sociology. All the gassy subjects, where there are no absolute truths and nothing is really terribly hard. I knocked off a few *A*'s, but I was still really a *C*-plus boy."

She lunged forward, changing the angle of the cunning chair. "Say! Why don't I volunteer to be your reader? Just like I do for Erwin! I'll read the new texts and papers and give you summaries of them—then you'd be up on all the theorists." She grinned, delighted with a notion as tantalizing as it was ridiculous. "I guess Marty does a lot of that for you, doesn't she? With her background—"

"Marty? She can't stand that stuff. *Space and Time in Eastern Woodland Archaeology. Some Aspects of Sibling Relationship among the Hill Dyaks. A New View of the Dunger River Remains. Linguistic Parallels in Five Celebes Dialects.* She was brought up on that." He furrowed his forehead. "Come to think of it, she doesn't much care about anything around the University. You know what it is to raise kids in an old apartment in New York City?"

"Is she unhappy?" Lila asked cautiously.

"No. It's just—just that she got used to being a working girl. And a few years we had no children and the money seemed to stretch. My disability and the GI bill, and her salary at WNA. It was a kind of easy freedom we had then. The postwar glow. I guess the adjustment's been hard for her."

"You're married this long? And she's still adjusting?" Lila blushed.

"It's easy for some dames and not so easy for others. You—you were a natural. You were groomed for this deal."

Lila gazed through the soaked screen door. She could see the edge of her pink-stucco mansion. It reminded her of her enviable security. The house, the boat, the surrounding grounds were like Erwin—they left nothing to chance. They were hurricane-proof and termite-resistant.

"It depresses me," she said, "I've missed something." She darted a proper matron's look at him. "And I don't mean sex. Or maybe that would just be a tiny part of it. If you must know, Erwin drives me crazy. He's the most adoring man in the world. He acts as if we're on our honeymoon."

"I didn't ask," Tom said. "But now that you mention it, let me be the first to congratulate Erwin." He was staring at an irregular ring, carved of bone by some rude hand. As he rotated it, a blurred, eroded figure on one side became evident. Tom rubbed some loose sand from it. The faintest suggestion of a human figure was evident—two starved legs, two flattened arms, a head the size of a shrunken pea, a pimple between the legs to hint at genitalia. "Look at this," he said.

"What is it?" Lila asked.

"It's a pendant."

"Ooh. There's a figure carved on it! It's almost worn off, but you can see it!"

Tom turned it thoughtfully. "It's Arawak. I don't care if I'm crazy, that's what it is. They find these things in Cuba and Haiti."

The thrill of discovery made Lila's blood pump faster; even the ludicrous nodule of sex on the archaic ring excited her. She dropped to her knees alongside Tom, better to inspect the miraculous pendant.

"It's fascinating! Just fascinating!"

She touched the ancient ring, her warm arms brushing his knees. Her breasts pushed against his legs as she examined the amulet. Her body's fine odor—compounded of health, good food, expensive toilet water—stirred the archaeologist. In the humid, heavy air, she was as sensual as an odalisque. Beneath the white shirt and the blue dungarees was the round, secret flesh that Erwin worshiped, the magic that defeated him, the only master of that infallible man. Sorrento could understand his adoration. The book reports were all right as far as they went—but there was a good deal more to love and honor in Lila than a built-in subscription to the *Saturday Review*. She was still on her knees, ogling the primitive circlet, her Levantine head inches from Tom's. He eased her away and got up.

"Don't get so close to me," he said. "I'm a nervous Italian boy and I never know what to do with women anyway."

"What gave you that idea?" she asked. She stretched her brown arms out. "Help me up." He complied, disengaging her as soon as she was standing. She touched his arm. "Why do I act this way around you?"

Brusquely, he picked up the crate, dumped the boxes and the publications into it, and started for the door. He puffed strenuously on his cigar, hopeful that the noxious fumes would discourage her, that it would deaden the piquant spark in his loins, the involuntary lightness of his limbs.

"Lila, baby, let's dig. The rain's over. Don't unsettle me."

Leaving, she fussed with the kerchief around her black hair, and examined her lips and eyebrows in a mirror on the plasterboard wall. They were the automatic acts of a woman leaving a room of sin. Yet what had they done? The nudging of hair and the touching of features, he supposed, were Lila's unconscious substitutes for the unpracticed—the remote, impossible—acts of profane love. He sprinted down the steps.

It was cozy inside the cabana, and again Ira found himself —willy-nilly—in the circumstance of life he enjoyed more than anything. Here was the locked, private room, as warm and self-sufficient as an egg's interior; here was the desirable woman—more desirable than he had imagined a woman could be. In recent years he had tended to generalize them. A Cleo Cooke, a Kitty Schmitt, the newspaper editor's wife the previous winter—they had a tendency to reduce themselves to blurs of legs and breasts, of slack faces and pleasurable moans. "The kicks are harder for me," Ira confessed to Si, "I guess I've had too much."

But the thin woman now sitting near him—so contemptuous of him and his paper world—was worth any effort, any humiliation. She might cut him with her snotty superiority, but he was convinced the ultimate weapon was his.

To a neutral, observant man, a man of average tastes and sensibilities, Ira's technique and the ease with which it achieved its purpose, could only invoke disbelief and repugnance. Informed of Ira's "track record," his series of unbroken victories, this observant man could only conclude that women were asinine and transparent, and that deKay, understanding this, and giving them no credit for much beyond a need for flattery and small attentions, had solved the problem on its simplest terms. A case in point, and one that had drawn much praise for Ira in his network days, involved a prim, schoolmarmish woman in the Educational Television Department. She was in her late thirties; a virginal type, full of breast and long of thigh, with rather ordinary flat features, but wondrous lucent skin and straight hennaed hair which she wore in a tantalizing bob. She was over-educated and insular and had a knack for reducing all men to slavering, rutting slobs. Her attitude was not only defensive, but downright rude. Her departmental superior, like numerous male associates, was excited by her very prissiness, but had become wary of even offering her a "good morning." This innocuous greeting would be the trigger for a sneer, a snort, a lowering of eyes, a twisting of thin, unlicked lips, and an over-all suggestion that the miserable man (a former deacon of the Lutheran church) had suggested an assignation at the nearest cheap hotel. In time, the men who worked with her gave her ground. She held the fortress of her executive desk against all comers, and soon there were none. But what of Ira? He saw her one day at a program meeting. The flat, virginal face, so marvelously balanced at the top of the heavy, ripe body demanded his attention. He took to stopping by the Educational Television Department more often. He would pull a chair up to her desk, and looking deeply into her wary eyes would intone: *Aren't we pretty today!*

Yes indeedy, it's the new shade of lipstick! Hmmm . . . you wear those shirtwaist dresses better'n anyone around here! She reddened, but the acerb comment, the snarl of disfavor, were not invoked. Her distraught superior, at the adjacent desk, brimmed with hot hate: as much for deKay, a congenital enemy, as for the redheaded temptress who succumbed with such abandon to the press agent's illiterate, obscene palaver. In time he was patting her freckled hand and pinching her neck. Lunches followed at cozy restaurants, and the great adventure was inevitable. Long after Ira had left her for new sport, she mooned for him and soughed gently when he bounced by in the corridors on crepe-soled Chukka boots. Once more, she became queen of the dirty look and the suspicious sneer. Her boss gave up. He could not under any circumstances imitate deKay, and there were things more honorable, more treasured, than lust.

These remembrances of good things past stirred deKay. Inside the warm cabana, he surveyed Martha Maitland Sorrento, found her good, and sniffed defeat. He eased off his chaise and sat down alongside her. His rear brushed her thigh and she moved her legs fractionally, creating a tender gap between their bodies.

"Here we are," Ira said. "And I'm so happy for us."

"Get back on your roost, Ira. I'll leave."

"You would not. You're having a peachy time. You like it when we talk dirty."

She barely smiled and he noticed it. "You *laughed!* There! You did! You're having a great time! Marty, baby, you're encouraging me."

"You're a lout. With all your bragging about the women you've had, I can't believe that it's your technique that got them for you. You must pay for it. Or else you just make these stories up. I can't take you seriously, not for one minute, so how could I possibly have an affair with you?"

"You have to be serious about this?" he cackled. "Zotz! And Zile! Lady, this is Fun and Games! Howdy Doody time!" He stroked her leg, starting at the delicate ankle and working up to the nude thigh.

Marty did not move her leg. She was too old for catch-as-catch-can wrestling, and she suspected that any athletics on her part would inflame him.

"Don't move a muscle," Ira said softly. His voice took on a low, undulant quality. Was he serious? Marty wondered. Could he really mean to be sexy and suggestive with that low-comedy throb? A male observer, peeking through the louvered door, could only kick himself in the pants. How did this technique elude him?

"I'll move when your hands get sweaty," Marty said. He continued, slithering his palm and fingers from ankle, to knee, to thigh, and stopping a few inches below the secret delta, triangulated in paisley.

"Why do you fight it?" deKay whispered. "How do you know you won't like unless you try it?"

"I'd be laughing at you. I can't have an affair with someone who is unbelievable. You're a fiction, Ira."

"Maybe I am. But it's a pretty good show, you have to admit."

"No. It's dreadful." She halted the probing hand, and deposited it firmly in his lap. "That's enough for one rainy day. If you think that aroused me, you're terribly wrong. You're about as stimulating as a split-level house in a development in Syosset, Long Island."

"That's because you won't give a little. This has to be a two-way street. If you'd only tippy-toe into the surf, Marty, you'd be soaked in no time. Drenched. Under the waves."

"Will you please stop that idiotic low-register mumble? If you did happen to say something intelligent, I might want to hear it. I can't, with you gasping like that."

"I can't help it," deKay said. He raised his golden eyebrows, hurt. "It's for real. I get this way in any locked room with any woman."

"Well, I'm not your therapist. Call Miss Cooke. How does she phrase it? Your *associate.*"

"That's what I'm trying to tell you, but you won't listen. I've had my share of the Cleo Cookes. I've done that bit, and it's nothing. Cream of Nowhere Soup. Nothingball Pancakes." He leaned forward, his aureate head a few inches from hers. "Why can't I reach you?"

"Because you're ludicrous."

"Well, I just got a bulletin for you. Maybe I make you laugh and maybe I'm not educated like you or your husband. But I'm the world's best authority on sack. I will guarantee you this, beauty. Try me and you won't regret it. Every second counts. A surprise a minute. From the tippy top of your curly head to the ends of those long sexy toes. I can't discuss the International Geo-Whoosis Year, but I'm the original expert of love. You can't say no to me. I won't allow it. I'll have the city pass an ordinance putting you in bed with me."

His voice had grown progressively hoarse and fainter. For all the bravura of his sales talk, he seemed to be losing control. He kissed Marty delicately on the lips, and his hairless smooth chest, pressed close to her, appeared to be fluttering.

"Nowhere," he gasped, "I didn't score a point. Didn't make a yard. What's the matter with you?" He pulled his head back. His buttery skin was suffused with a ruddy glow; he appeared to be turning a slow, even, red, as if warmed by a bed of slow-burning briquets within his willowy torso.

"You can't, Ira," she said. "You just *can't.*"

"Listen—You got to listen! Could it be I want you for more than just a quick romp? Did that occur to you? Could it be I'm sick of the kind of goofy life I've had? Maybe I need some class. Or just to catch my breath and get off the merry-go-round. Do I make sense?" He lowered his golden head in his hands. "What's eating me? I haven't blabbed like this since I was sixteen. I day-dream about you in the office. I haven't done that since I had a crush on Celia Underdahl." The memory of old victories aroused him. "What a keester. Took me three weeks to make out, but I did."

"There—you see, Ira?" Marty laughed. "You almost had me feeling sorry for you. I might have patted that fuzzy head. But Celia Underdahl ruined everything. You can't be so miserable if the memory of her backside can change your mood."

He crinkled his tiny nose. "You got to admit. It was a good try."

Marty got up from the chaise and peeked through the slats. "It's just about quit. I think I'll take the children home. It's not much of a beach day."

"Stay for lunch! We'll do the champagne-in-the-afternoon bit!"

"No. I'm crawling with guilt feelings. I wonder why I came back here."

Ira gathered up the gift boxes. "Don't forget your loot. You didn't earn it, but I won't be chinchy."

"No. What I'm wearing will do me fine."

"You're gonna be a little on the take, you might as well take big. Baby, when I handed in an expense account at the network, it was enough to finance the foreign-aid program to Nicaragua. It was the guys who were afraid to *really* lie, the dopes who put in five bucks for lunch, who got in trouble. Who'd ever question it when I wrote down one hundred and sixty dollars—cocktail party for the whole Rochester Chamber of Commerce?" He offered the striped boxes to her again. "Take. Yours. And more to come."

"I can't Ira. We'll compromise. Leave them here, and I'll wear them when I visit."

He set them down. As she peered again through the louvers, he came behind her, embracing her waist, pressing against her. She turned around, not resisting, still essaying aloofness, but it worked no magic. He held her gently and enclosing each gluteal cheek in his hands, kissed her again, this time probing with facile tongue the inner wet redness of her mouth. A tremor, the faintest convulsive motion, seemed to have gripped him, and she wondered if he were feigning it. She jerked her head away and disengaged his kneading hands, but not before she returned his kiss in miniature.

His eyes were moist and he gasped to locate his voice. "Ah. Ah. The greatest. Better than a whole night with the others. . . ."

She opened the door and walked onto the wet duckboards. Guests were emerging from the loggia and from under the canvas umbrellas—confident people, blinking appreciatively at the burning avatar of the tropic sky. Guiltless, she sought her children. She had merely returned deKay's generosity, keeping the balance intact. One bathing suit, one pair of sandals, one beach coat—one gelid kiss. She had no trouble assuring herself that this was the substantive case. That she had thoroughly enjoyed the hour of banter inside the cabana was immaterial. It had been fun insulting him.

Marty glanced over her shoulder at him. He was the old fighting Ira deKay again. He had just whispered something to a distressingly white, shriveled man and a stout redhead in starched white uniform, presumably the oldster's nurse. They both reacted appropriately. The ancient wheezed and tapped an ebony cane on the duckboards; the woman jounced her stiff white bosom in rhythmic appreciation. Ira winked at them and skipped away, catching up with Marty at the loggia.

"Was that some snide reference to what happened inside your love house?" she asked quietly. "I'd expect better of you."

"Sweetie. I don't broadcast my winnings. Old man Speer's a

client. I cheered him up with a little zetz. I asked him did he know that Jewish Lesbians make the best husbands."

"And did he?" she asked, missing the joke.

Ira frowned. "I just might give you up altogether. Either you are so square you don't dig me, or you hate me so much you won't let me perform."

He watched her walk off in search of the children, marveling at the unreachable limbs, the decorous hollow of the slender back, the slight inviting bulge of buttocks. He sang happily: *"Someday, sweetheart . . . you will be sorreeee. . . ."*

10 A Call to Duty

From his office window on the third floor of Detering Hall, Maitland, somnolent, ruminative, puffing a postprandial pipe, gazed at a green corner of the campus. It was a time of the University year that he liked best: the ragged end of August. Summer session was over, the regular academic year was a month away. There was a sense of preparation, of new faces and new problems. *Dry August and warm does Harvest no harm.* It was pleasingly hot in his cramped office. He liked the heat. The Mandan had honored him with the tribal name *Fears-No-Heat.* He had outsweated their sturdiest braves in the rock-steam baths, squatting cross-legged, his round white belly dripping, inside the fogged longhouse. He missed the Mandan. It had been twenty-two years since he had lived with them and he suspected that by now they had been overstudied. The old tribal leaders probably got a fixed rate for recounting legends, and the rock-steam bath was no doubt available, in diluted form, to any tourist who had two dollars to spare.

Outside, beneath shimmery elms and oaks, thick with late summer leaf, his beloved University people passed by. At times they exasperated him and more often they bored him, but even after a half-century of close association with variegated teachers and students, he still loved the ragged devotees of knowledge. For the past ten years Maitland had sniffed a new obscurantism rising on the wind and he knew that his University people would have to lead the fight against its challenge. It seemed to the anthropologist that the new obscurantism (peddled to a great extent by ex-Communists) was altogether appealing in many ways. It held, for example, that any and all attempts by man to alter his estate—particularly any trifling with property—were damned, doomed and headed for ultimate corruption. It took the species back one step, to the rear of his good friend Inifel, paramount shaman of Yap Island, who could make the taro crop grow by disemboweling a young pig. He had been jotting down, on a ruled pad, manifestations of the new obscurantists and had listed *tauromachy, angry young men, fraudulent religiosos, ex-bolos,* when it occurred to him that *all* of them were simply latter-day Doukhobors. *The Doukhobors!* How he had applauded and laughed the day they disrobed for him and burned their homes and barns (to the distress of the Royal Canadian Mounted Police). For what were the new nay-sayers, the scoffers at laws and institutions, than Doukhobors—shedding the garments of reason and consigning to the torch the *shelter,* man's first shield against grumpy nature?

He nudged his corpulent bulk forward in the creaky chair. Below, on the pocketed turf (the University fought a losing battle against predatory birds and gasoline fumes), he could see two students pushing a wheeled typewriting table. Maitland gauged them as workers for graduate degrees in one of the *hoo-hoo* faculties—fine arts, or philosophy, or comparative literature. The wobbly aluminum table bore a rubber plant in a bronze pot, a stack of musty academic journals, and a chipped plaster bust of some minor Greek or Roman. They were girl and boy, the engineers of the table, the youth lean as a naked cornstalk, hay-blond and chinless. Maitland imagined he was from the Great Plains. The girl was an Oriental, perhaps a Filipino or a Malayan, with a strong infusion of Chinese in her indelicate body. She was not the fragile Eastern beauty so recently glamorized in show business, but a physical type the anthropologist knew to be infinitely more abundant. She was thick in the leg and wide-hipped, and her lank black hair flopped over one ear. He guessed she was an exchange student of some kind—the University had many such. Now they were conjoined in transporting some professor's dowdy treasures—she from Haiphong or Jakarta, he from Hastings or Wichita, two seminarians in the austere temple.

Maitland was not a sentimental man, but the sight of these displaced children, dappled with late afternoon sunlight, gratified him. He knocked the dottle from his pipe, using as ashtray a splendid stone bowl given him by Tu-cu-man, chief of the Tupinamba Indians, and followed their pilgrimage across the checkered shade.

On his desk was a letter from Canada addressed not to him, but to the president of the University. It had gone to the provost's office and been forwarded to him with the scrawled notation:

HALL—

What the devil is this all about? Please write an answer for the President and forward it to me. Sorry to bother you.

FRED

The letterhead, bold and brash, was an immediate challenge.

TREADWAY CHAMBER OF COMMERCE

TREADWAY, ONTARIO

HOME OF THE "TREADWAY VIKING"

At one side was a thumbnail drawing of the fictional Norseman, hirsute and mail-clad, brandishing his double-edged sword and holding his buckler high. It was a bad printing job and the blue ink had run, blurring the Treadway Viking's hairy legs.

The contents were predictable.

. . . would not take this extreme step of notifying you, knowing how busy you must be, were it not for Dr. Maitland's insulting behavior. He insisted on consorting with the lowest elements in Treadway, spending most of his evenings at a tavern frequented by drunkards and other undesirables. We are, Mr. President, a God-fearing and moral community and this example set by a distinguished visitor from your University was hardly what we expected.

In the matter of examining the Treadway relics, Dr. Maitland was perfunctory and opinionated. He was heard, at this same tavern, to refer to Mr. Bjornsen as a "Norse's Ass." I ask you, Mr. President, is this the kind of language one expects from a Professor?

We feel these matters should be brought to your attention. Moreover, the Treadway Chamber of Commerce, of which I have the honor to be the Chairman, intends to discredit and discard Dr. Maitland's findings. . . .

Maitland read no more. He was getting too old to get involved in the internecine bloodlettings of True Believers. What had once been sportive and enjoyable had now become grim business. True Believing had become commercial. Now that it had real value, the fun had gone out of it. He had no one but himself to blame for getting involved in the Treadway affair. Once he had learned that the villagers intended to develop tourism around the fake Scandinavian, he should have bowed out.

There was also a letter from his son-in-law. It was five days since he had talked to Tom. He was eager to learn how the work was going.

Dear Hall—

The news is good and bad. It's good because we are still digging and getting results. It's bad because we may get kicked off the site in a week or so. That's why I am looking forward to your visit. You might be able to prevail on Ellenbogen to let us stay here through September or however long it will take to clear the area.

I have goofed a couple of things. The day after I talked to you, the first three white boulders were stolen. It was my fault because I gave a story to a local public-relations gook and he blew it up, so the stones sounded valuable.

Yesterday, Ellenbogen had his men put up a high plank fence, the kind they use around construction work. It should help. I guess we should pay him for it, but he's going to need the fence anyway when he starts his own project, but I'm getting ahead of myself. He and some other local types plan to break ground here on Labor Day for a tourist attraction called the *God-O-Rama,* believe it or not. An exhibit of the world's religions—everybody invited. That's why he wants us off, and who can blame him? So far, Mrs. E., Lila, has been on our side, but I can't get a straight answer from the man himself and I feel guilty pleading with him since he has been so generous. How can I argue with him?

Which leads me to the work. Since I talked to you, this progress:

1. The site where we dug out the two skeletons is a major burial mound. In two days of hard digging, the workmen have unearthed five more, including a child. All are flexed interments. I have put Peltz on sorting out the grave goods.

2. We're still piddling around the shell heap. A few more Arawak-type artifacts have shown, notably a pair of circular pendants with stylized figures carved on one side. These, with our three-cornered *zemi* and the drinking-cup skull, at least give a working basis for any theory.

3. The big news: we are still finding those crazy white limestone boulders. We have excavated a trench thirty feet long, two feet deep and about three feet wide, and now have an uninterrupted irregular row of stones. They run about two feet by a foot and a half by six inches and in spite of Ballard's feeling they have been worked, I think they were transported here as is.

I have had Peltz check the archives and there's no record of any kind of construction that would utilize these stones in historical times—either American or Spanish, or Seminole Creek. We contacted the road builder who put the causeway in and he says they did not use fill of that type.

Now then, what about the other walls? I'm having the workmen dig a test trench, perpendicular to our stones, all the way down to the beach. I checked the literature and I find that the dimensions of these ball courts varied. Some were squares, about 100 x 100, others 100 x 200, some 100 x 20. So who knows? If the opposite wall is south of here and we're lucky (that is, if it ain't under the highway) we might hit it with this right-angle trench.

I have a feeling if you were here, you could convince Ellenbogen how important this is. If we clear a whole Arawak ball court (what a dream!) he can stage athletic contests here, games of skill and muscle, and charge admission. This might be a better attraction than his *God-O-Rama,* and he could have pari-mutuels.

Looking forward to seeing the Maitland corpus, well fed and well oiled; I have put in a supply of hot cherry peppers. Mrs. Ellenbogen promises you excessive rich food and wine, and demands you stay with them. Take them up on it, Hall. They know how to live. I would appreciate your bringing with you (if you are still planning the visit) the Academy of Human Sciences series on the Caribbean, which has a good account of Arawak ball-court excavations. Volume 17, I think.

Give my good wishes to the Water Hen and to Wafer-Ass. If Grafmyer is going to take my classes in September, he'd better write to me.

TOM

Sorrento's report roused him from the morosity engendered by the Treadway letter. It would be a great coup for Tom if the ball court materialized, a much-needed prod to his quiescent career. The University was no less subject to the pressures of the Age of Talk than was the commercial world. An anthropologist who discovered such a curiosity would become a mild celebrity, and the trustees were inclined to like celebrities. An obscure assistant professor of botany who became something of a national figure because of his skill on a television panel program *(Guess What:*

a TV Game For All Ages) was forthwith promoted to associate professor and had his novel accepted by a publisher. The Arawak ball court might give Tom the needed nudge. Maitland had a few moments of hesitancy. Martha would not welcome him. It was quite possible that his presence at the dig would result in the usual snide remarks—*there goes Maitland making it easy for his son-in-law*. He would make it a short visit—give Tom a few suggestions, do what he could about getting them an extension of time, then leave for Guatemala.

A few preparatory phone calls were indicated. First, he would contact the Foundation, brief them on the Bay Islet work, and arrange for more funds. That would be no problem. They were a small foundation and had trouble finding deserved beneficiaries. Glancing again at Sorrento's missive, he reread the reference to the *God-O-Rama*—"an exhibit of the world's religions, everybody invited." He dialed the University operator.

"Hello, my dear," Maitland said. "This is Dr. Maitland. Will you place a call for me to Kiowa Agency, Oklahoma?"

"Beg pardon, Dr. Maitland?"

"Kiowa Agency. That's an Indian community. When you get the operator ask for Mr. John Throws Knife."

"How is that, sir? John—"

"*John Throws Knife*. Three words."

"Do you have a phone number or address, Dr. Maitland?"

"Everyone in Kiowa Agency knows John Throws Knife. He's the leading citizen. While I'm waiting you may get me the Allerup Foundation. Thank you."

He restoked and relit his pipe and settled back, gazing out on the citified campus, warm and hazy in late August's glow. He felt himself once again involved in mankind, and he was pleased. Between the search for the ball court and the imminent conversation with Mr. John Throws Knife, he would revive his flagging spirits.

Invigorated, he began scrawling a note for the provost in re the Treadway Viking. *Dear Fred,* he wrote, *I'm deucedly sorry for giving the University a bad turn in the hinterlands. But then, I am a farm boy and I lack the capacity to genuflect before and bestow flattery upon our country cousins, skills that city folk are required to master before venturing west of Trenton, New Jersey. Now, sir, the facts concerning that spurious Norseman are as follows ...*

11 The Peyote Eater

WITH charming ease, Erwin had taken over. In a series of deft moves, he had incorporated the enterprise (Educational Projects, Inc.), had rented generous offices downtown, and had laid the foundation for a sound financial operation. Ira deKay, dazzled by the young manufacturer's speed, was content to sit back and let him operate. In a sense, Si Mermelstein had been right. The tourist attraction was too big for the likes of Ira. The publicist grudgingly admitted this, and listened attentively as Erwin read the letter of the law to him.

"From your viewpoint, Ira," Ellenbogen told him, preparatory to a meeting of the general partners, "You may feel bilked. But in your heart you know that we are in extremely delicate territory. What worries me is the talent you have for mixing up your clients and interests. Wouldn't it be a bit odd if an orangutan dressed as a little boy showed up at this ceremony? Do you remember what happened to that morning television show when they allowed a chimpanzee to participate in the Coronation? That's what I want to avoid. For that very reason I have been forced to make you drop negotiations with Jimmy Nudo. He is not the type of individual we want associated with us. Thanks to my efforts and my good name, we already have enough money raised from general partners of impeccable background. We do not need the Jimmy Nudos. And while I give you full credit, you and Si, for coming up with this proposal, I have never liked the name *God-O-Rama.* It sounds as if someone is making an irreverent joke. I suggest, and I propose we adopt, *The Spirit of Man* as the title of our exhibition. In that way we need not be wholly ecclesiastical in nature. Perhaps a bow in the direction of great *nonreligious* thinkers . . . Newton, Einstein, Freud. . . . I think on examination we would discover that these men were basically religious in nature. . . ."

Ira nodded and yawned, scratching at an adolescent skin rash that had sprayed his neck with red welts. It was the kind of thing he suffered from periodically, in moments of stress. Mermelstein, noting his employer's ailment and his lackadaisical attitude toward Erwin's confiscatory moves, worried about him. A lot of the spark seemed to have gone out of Ira. Mermelstein, shrewd and observant, guessed that Martha Sorrento had something to do with it. Each afternoon Ira, neglecting his phone calls and visitors, would visit with the archaeologist's wife at the cabana. The offices in the Peruviana, divested of his glowing exuberance, were strangely quiet. Helene Schwenk and Lucille LoPresti played scrabble every afternoon. Cleo took to leaving early to spend a little time with darling Robin. She seemed friendlier to Si. Her master's snubs appeared to breed in her a grudging need for communication. She permitted Si to buy her lunch twice and she would sometimes kibitz the girls' scrabble game.

For all of Erwin's vigorous pursuit of the undertaking, he had delayed several days on the matter of the ground-breaking. He was, in truth, fearful of Lila's opposition. Eventually, Erwin knew, the matter of prior rights to the bayfront land would have to be faced. At a meeting of the general partners, about ten days following deKay's first presentation at the Peruviana, the issue came up. Unanimously, the participants agreed that construction had to begin early in September to guarantee a grand opening for the season. Campion, the old realtor and builder, understood this better than any of them.

"You know what labor costs now?" the old elephant said. "You know how tough it is to get jiggs? There's two motels and a block of stores going up this fall and they ain't got enough carpenters and electricians."

Charlie Rasmussen, representing the mayor and the Chamber of Commerce, added further urgency to the matter.

"The boys feel this way," Charlie said dolefully. "We got a lot of bad publicity on the gambling stink last season. Also, the long-range weather forecast is for another rotten winter. The Beach is nothing new any more. Also the recession. All in all, they would like this thing to be ready for the season. Even if it don't bring in too many customers, it'll be good for lots of space."

Ira bobbed his head. "Reet, Daddy-o," he said. "Charlie and his friends are with it. The sooner the better."

He bounced out of his chair and circled the barren office, threading his way in between Campion, Braud, a few new financial faces.

"I have just had a message," Ira said. He stopped, holding pointed palms over his forehead. "The message is that if we go with this dedication on Labor Day, I personally will guarantee the appearance of Hal Justice and the *Our Heritage* program."

A respectful hum greeted Ira's reference to the Celebrity

World. Rasmussen wriggled in his seat. "Wait a minute, Ira," Rasmussen sneered. "You told me you were angling for that TV show for a free week in *January*. How come you made me write all them letters to the network?"

"Charlie, *sweetie*. We can have it both ways. I'll get ole Hal down here with the kids just for a one-day stand, like a preview."

"Doesn't that monkey appear on that show?" Erwin asked.

"Does he? Where you been, Erwin?" Ira cried. "He's their little mascot!"

"The monkey is out, Ira. Ab-so-lutely out. I will not have that orangutan associated with *The Spirit of Man*. I mean that, Ira."

"Spoilsport," Ira slumped into a chair and sulked. He studied his wristwatch. Martha Sorrento would be stretching her legs, now turning a rich brown, outside the cabana. Perhaps she was wearing the knitted suit—the one with the wild stripes. He was a man rarely given to anticipation, living confidently in the present. But the vagrant thought of her—calm, contained, taking his measure and enjoying her secret laughter at his expense—excited him.

There was a vigorous rapping at an outside door. The office was as yet unmanned and unequipped with a buzzer system. Ira's head jerked around at the sound and, asserting his captaincy over Mermelstein, he said wearily:

"Just don't sit there, Si, sweetie, answer the door."

Si flushed, set his outsized briefcase on the floor and went to the door. The knocking got louder, and when Mermelstein opened the door, the caller, in the act of slamming a large fist against the glass panel, all but fell in his arms.

"Can I help you?" Si asked. "Who are you looking for?"

The visitor smiled. "*God-O-Rama?*" he asked.

"Who do you want?"

"The fellow in charge of the *God-O-Rama*. The head man."

"In reference to what? I'm associated with it." Mermelstein laughed nervously. "We've changed the name. It's *The Spirit of Man*."

The caller nodded. He carried under his arm a bulging ragged envelope, the color of dried blood, held together with black string. Grinning, he set the envelope down and untied the string, then began rummaging in the interior. He appeared to be selecting samplings of hortatory literature from the envelope, and Si imagined this was a variety of religious crank who had learned of the exhibit. He suspected they would be bothered by these nuts for some time. Yet Si was not certain. Something about the man seemed genuine. There was a candor and innocence about him that did not suggest the crackpot visionaries who rang doorbells and played revelationary recordings—supplementary data awarded their prophets long after the normal inventories of miracles were exhausted.

The visitor was a bowlegged man in his fifties. His hair was white and brush-cut, rising from a long, wooden face. His features were large and heavy—a fleshy nose and black hooded eyes. His skin was a ruddy brown, and when he looked up at Si, thrusting a handful of pamphlets and paper-bound books at him, Mermelstein realized that he was an American Indian, truer to the classic Indian type than any of the local Seminoles.

"I am John Throws Knife," he said cheerfully. "I'm executive officer of the True American Church. This stuff I gave you—it tells all about us. The fastest-growing Indian church in the country. I have been authorized by my people to request recognition in your exhibit of religions."

"I've never heard of your church," Si said. "What'd you say it's called?"

"The True American Church. Headquarters at Kiowa Agency, Oklahoma."

Mr. John Throws Knife had apparently come for a long siege. In addition to the bloody envelope, he carried an ancient, rope-bound Saratoga trunk and an army duffel bag. As Si studied the baggage, John Throws Knife disclosed more of his pedigree. "Second Infantry Division. I was a scout. Silver Star and Bronze Star."

He spoke English perfectly, with neither *ughs* nor *hows,* and the only accent Si discerned was a corn-fed Oklahoma drawl. He reached in the pocket of his tacky double-breasted pin-striped gray suit (worn with open-throated white shirt) and, locating some small object, extended his thumb and forefinger to Mermelstein.

"Take it. The sign of our friendship. *And God said, behold, I have given you every herb.*"

Si stepped back cautiously.

"Don't be afraid," John Throws Knife said. "It's only our peyote. You don't have to eat it. Just take it. *Even as the green herb, have I given you all things.*"

Si held his hand out. The Indian dropped a small hard round bean on his palm. It was the size of a dime, gray-green in color. "I don't get it. What's it for?"

"Peyote. Mescal bean. The basis of our religion. God gave the Indians peyote because he was sorry for them. Poor, ignorant, helpless people. It's the incarnation."

Si backed away. "Who sent you here? How'd you find out about us?"

"Maitland told me. You know Doc Maitland? He really could eat peyote! Four beans was nothing for him! And never vomit, not once! We appointed him Cedar Chief last time."

The executive officer of the True American Church followed Mermelstein into the inner office, hugging his envelope and dragging his abraded trunk and duffel bag with its blurred memorabilia of the Second Infantry Division.

Si, preceding the aborigine, walked up to Erwin's desk. The executive officer lingered on the threshold. He smiled inclusively, neither embarrassed nor abject. He had the true dignity of clergy.

"Erwin, this gentleman says he represents something called the True American Church. An Indian church. He wants to be included in *The Spirit of Man*."

Ellenbogen and the others studied John Throws Knife. His large coppery head, crowned with coarse white roach, nodded in friendly fashion as each face made communion with him.

"I bring the good wishes of my people," the Indian said. Then he took a small deerskin bag from the pocket of his blue suit and began a tour of the group, depositing in each pair of manicured, nourished hands a mescal bean.

Erwin whispered to Si. "What is this all about? Is he a nut?"

"I don't think so. I remember something about Indians chewing these beans. They're narcotics, I think. But I never knew it was a religion."

Erwin looked suspiciously at the bronzed, burly man. He had come to Fenton Braud, the last man in the grouping around Ellenbogen's desk. That venal peddler of nonfunctional commodities, perhaps in the mistaken belief that the Indian was a commercial counterpart, recoiled. John Throws Knife held out one corded brown hand, the thick thumb and forefinger rotating the precious bean. "Go on, friend," he said. "Peyote has much to teach. You can use peyote all your life, and never learn all about it."

Braud, his blue silken back pressed against the chair, took the bean. He held it at arm's length as if it might detonate in his hand.

Ira rescued them. He slipped off the windowsill, more than

ready to abandon the confining atmosphere. Erwin had a tendency to blow soft, hot air into his meetings, to deaden the senses and blunt Ira's operative faculties. "Mr. Knife, baby," Ira said. "I got a friend who digs your kind of medicine. Si, get the Olds and we'll all cut out for Tommy Sorrento. He'll give us the straight dope."

DeKay guided the Indian church officer out, winking at Erwin. "If he's legit, Tommy would know about it," Ira said buoyantly. "What I figure is, it might be a colorful addition. The way you got this thing set up it's about as exciting as Sunday-afternoon television. We could use some Indians for a little zetz." Then, turning to the group at large, he added, "I'd go easy on those crazy beans, men. Might turn all of you into Wah-hoo birds."

Fenton Braud rose to the bait. "What's a *Wah-hoo* bird, Ira?"

"Eats all year but craps only once," deKay confided. "But when he does, *Wah-hooooo!*" He helped Mr. John Throws Knife with his luggage, invigorated by the new challenge.

With Ira's departure, the meeting turned to the dull, pragmatic problems of financing the new Beach attraction. Each member holding his mescal bean like some devilish amulet, they listened respectfully to Ellenbogen's dry recital of amortization, tax benefits, interest rates and all the abstract, complex matters he knew so well and had mastered so thoroughly. But even as Erwin spoke, his mind turned unhappily to the imminent struggle with Lila. The best he could hope for was that Sorrento, aided by more workers and heavy gear, would complete his excavation in a week and permit them to go ahead with the ceremonies. Why should Lila be so stubborn? As much as Erwin respected Tom Sorrento and his search for Indian communities, how could one possibly decide in favor of his aimless digging, as against a noble effort to increase understanding?

12 *The Male Conspiracy*

MAITLAND had not intended to arrive simultaneously with John Throws Knife. He did not envision a pincer movement when he had informed the executive officer of the True American Church of the intriguing panorama of faith being planned in the vacation city. Indeed, he did not expect that his old Kiowa friend would act so swiftly in the matter of securing recognition for his flock. Arriving at the airport in late afternoon, he was surprised to find himself met by his son-in-law, looking surly and burned black by the fierce sun; John Throws Knife; and a third man, a tall, blond chap in an improbable wine-red shirt and lavender pants.

Ira had sped out to the excavation with the Indian. He found Sorrento digging frantically, sweating gallons in the deadly heat, driving his team, which was now augmented by five new laborers and Lila Ellenbogen, her round behind tightly sheathed in dungarees. A high fence protected the digging area from access from the highway. It could be reached only by entering the Ellenbogen grounds and passing through a latched gate. Sorrento, spying the promoter undoing the lock, dropped his shovel and walked to the wire fence.

"Off limits, Ira," Tom called.

"*Baby!* I got a friend here to see you!" He shoved John Throws Knife through the gate, noticing as he did, Sorrento's exhausted mien. He looked bent and dried out. The black mattress on his athlete's chest was soaked with perspiration.

Inside the fence, John Throws Knife, smiling at Cedar Chief's hairy son-in-law, untied a buckskin bag from around his neck and took from it a particularly large and beautiful bean. He gave it to Tom. "For Dr. Maitland's son-in-law, I reserve one Peyote Chief," he said.

Sorrento looked at it. "Mescal bean. Who are you?"

"*He causeth the grass to grow for the cattle and the herb for the service of Man,*" John Throws Knife declared. "Psalms 104.14."

"He's got his own Indian-type church," Ira said. "A bean church. He walked into a meeting at Ellenbogen's and wanted space. I figured we could use Indians. He says your father-in-law tipped him off. Is he legit?"

"He's legit," Sorrento said. "What tribe?"

"Kiowa. Kiowa Agency, Oklahoma. John Throws Knife. I'm an old friend of Doc Maitland. We sure miss him. I never knew a white man could eat peyote the way he could. And sing and shake the rattle all night."

"Great," Tom said. "You can see Maitland in a few hours. He's due down later this afternoon."

"Zile!" Ira cried. "We'll go out and give him the big hello!"

In his fertile mind he envisioned a page-one story: Maitland coming to the beach not only to oversee the dig, but to act as unofficial adviser on Indian religions, on the True American Church. How else explain the double presence of the executive officer and the great anthropologist? *And that crazy business of eating the bean! The singing and the rattling!* They'd have to stage one of them for the press—as a prelude to *The Spirit of Man.* It would be magnificent. Later, it could be a regular part of the daily demonstration. Zotz!

"What you digging for?" John Throws Knife asked. "Indian villages?"

"What we call Glades culture. Maybe a thousand years old, maybe less. Nothing like Plains Indians. No buffalo hunting, no horses. Mostly shell-gathering people."

The Kiowa leaned forward. "They have peyote?"

"No. Mescal-bean eating never got this far east."

The executive officer clucked. "Too bad."

"That's the way it goes," Tom said. "Some got it and some haven't. I never tried mescal myself." He tapped his stomach. "Weak stomach, John. I probably couldn't handle it the way Maitland does."

John Throws Knife disagreed. "You'd learn. *Let not him which eateth not, judge him that eateth.* Romans 14. 1-3."

Traveling with foundation money, Maitland had availed himself of a luxury flight. This was apparent to Tom as he saw his father-in-law's preternaturally red face, a certain sign that he had just overindulged in rich food and liquor. He wobbled ungracefully down the steps, nodding politely to two brittle stewardesses (did the girls exchange critical glances?), and crossed the sticky airport tar to where the committee of three awaited. Sorrento noticed he was wearing a winter-weight wool suit, the color of cooked oatmeal. It was of supposedly dashing cut, favored for a brief period in the early thirties—wide-bottomed trousers, a double-breasted jacket, with a false half-belt in back, bisected by three useless pleats. The late Mrs. Maitland had bought three identical suits for her young professorial husband, at a fire sale in the Midwestern university town in which they were spending the summer. The suits had survived like granite over the academic years, and Maitland wore them in rotation to his classes: one oatmeal, one green-blue, one a purplish brown. It was a whispered canard among his students that the anthropologist owned only *one* suit—there could be only one suit in the world tailored in such an odd manner. Its chameleon qualities they attributed to the fact that Mrs. Maitland, that poor, gray woman, spent her nights dying the suit, drying it and pressing it for the next day's lectures. Long after she had died, the undergraduate myth persisted. Knowing the professor to be widowed, the story now was that Maitland *himself* did the dyeing. A waggish writer for the college humor magazine claimed that whenever you visited Maitland in his apartment, you were greeted by the portly social scientist in rubber apron and gloves, piebald with purplish dye. Acrid fumes roiled the air in the small flat, and his words of welcome were invariably: "Do come in, Fineschreiber. I was just in the process of dyeing my suit. . . . It's a murderous job getting it back to oatmeal after that purple-brown, but I still have a few hours left before morning—"

"Magnificent flight," Maitland said, after greeting his son-in-law and his friend of the peyote ritual. "Something called a Hunt Club Supper was served. Lamb chops and tenderloin of beef and all the champagne a man could handle. My traveling companion was a teetotaling lady and she willingly replenished her glass for me."

He looked blankly at deKay. Tom made the necessary introductions.

"Hall, this is Ira deKay. A local operator. Don't ask me what he does, because I haven't figured it out yet."

"We are honored to have you in our big ole city," Ira beamed. "You here to help Tommy finish up?"

Maitland squinted at the blond man. "I take it you're one of the promoters of the *God-O-Rama?* And that John got in touch with you?"

"That's me. We've changed the name to *The Spirit of Man.*"

"A shame," Maitland said. "I liked the other name."

"Well, Doc, you know how it is. We got some squares on the committee who thought it was a little jazzy."

They waited for Maitland's baggage, and when Ira excused himself to find the photographers who covered the airport, the anthropologist queried Tom about him.

"He adopted us a few weeks ago," Tom said. "I can't shake him. He ran that piece in the Sunday paper about the dig, and right after that the place was robbed. He figures he can cash in on what we're doing—tie it in with this tourist heaven."

Maitland chuckled. "Splendid. And you, John? Any converts?"

John Throws Knife grinned. "They never believe me first time around. I bet if we were still persecuted they'd believe me. Ever since we incorporated, they all think we're fooling." He smiled. "Doc—did you know you can send peyote through the mails now?"

"Really?" Maitland asked. "We've come a long way, haven't we, John? I can recall when we were regularly raided as corrupters of the youth."

The Indian shook his oblong head. "No more. We're respectable. Oh, they still try. You know—they say peyote is a drug, a narcotic, an intoxicant. The missions don't like us and the Bureau is kind of sorry about the way we're growing. But they're still looking for the first case of peyote addiction. Not a one, all these years."

Ira returned with a photographer. Tom recognized him as the surly Barney, the gnome who had taken the pictures at the site. He carried a sixteen-millimeter motion-picture camera as well as the still camera.

"Let's get the three of you all together," Ira said. "Mr. Knife, you hold up the bag of beans. Everybody smile."

Tom took Maitland's arm. "Maybe we better not, Hall. The last time I let this gook take pictures we got in trouble."

Maitland blinked his eyes a few times. John Throws Knife had already made his mind up. By Peyote, he would be in the newspapers and he would get the True American Church full representation in any pantheon.

"No harm in it, Tom," Maitland said. "We want to help John, don't we?"

Barney squinted through the motion-picture camera finder and cursed them all indiscriminately.

Ira left Maitland and Tom at the excavation, then found an inexpensive room fòr John Throws Knife. He had big plans for the Oklahoma visitor. The project was rolling now and he sniffed the charged air, reinvigorated. This was his meat—free space in the press, free time on the air, the uninterrupted flow of useless information, the relation of disparate elements, the incessant attack on the public eye and ear. The Indian was a windfall. The tourist job had been dragging its heels. Now they had copy, color, something to make the clods open their eyes. And he had Martha's old man to thank for it! He wondered, as he sped off to the Peruviana, for one more attempt to entrap the wary beauty, why she had not met him with the children. She rarely spoke of her old man, Ira reflected, and when she did, it was with the same nonchalance she used in discussing people like the Ellenbogens. That was her business. What went on between Maitland and his daughter was strictly their hassle. He, Ira deKay, still had his mission and these failings of togetherness didn't concern him. He tapped the accelerator, and the car responded with a thick undulant groan, as gratifying to Ira as the splendid way in which the tourist exhibit was maturing.

Maitland was made at home in a guest apartment of the Ellenbogen mansion. Lila, taking a break in her trowel work, ushered him in and Freddie, the efficient butler, made him welcome. The anthropologist was anxious to tour the site with Tom and offer any suggestions that might prove helpful. As he prepared to leave the magnificently cold chambers, he paused. He was still wearing his oatmeal suit, his black oxfords. While it was true they were digging in the midst of a cosmopolitan center, certain amenities of the field had to be observed. Ritual was important to Maitland, as important to him as it was to his friend John Throws Knife. The rites of the field demanded proper costume. So reasoning, he changed to some rough clothes he had packed for the Guatemala junket. These included high, laced prospector's boots, scuffed and stained with years of heavy duty in jungle and desert, eroded whipcord breeches, reinforced with yellowing leather, a khaki shirt, its armpits rimmed with dry sweat, and a shapeless felt hat, banded with a frayed leather braid, a gift from Wovokasi, shaman of the Havasupai Indians of the Grand Canyon. He selected as appropriate accessory a corncob pipe, stuffed with Keen Blade tobacco. Thus fortified, he left the freezing air of the mansion and joined the dig.

Ballard shook his hand happily. Ben Peltz joined them, and the Negro laborers, apprised that the boss digger from New York was with them, studied Maitland's bloated form curiously. Tom started his tour at the edge of the asphalt, where Erwin had put up the fence. He and Ballard had uncovered a continuous stretch of white stones, forty feet long. Fifteen boulders had been removed from the trench, three of them by thieves, twelve by the diggers themselves for safekeeping.

"We're leaving them in the ground now," Tom said. "It's too much work to dig 'em out. Dave and I broke our humps lifting them. We figured nobody would want any more of them. Besides, they'd have to climb the fence. Ellenbogen's tipped the cops extra to check here every hour, so I guess we're safe."

Maitland stroked the irregular surface of the rock. "They resemble the stones used at the ball court at Tanagua, Cuba. And they're similar to the complex of ball courts at Capa in Puerto Rico. There, of course, they also found giant monoliths, six feet tall and bigger. But the stones were *native* to that region. These must have been transported here."

"Maybe by canoe?" Tom asked. "Litters?"

"They have the look of river stones. Conceivably they were dragged here. I'll tell you this. I disagree with Dave. There's no indication of masonry. No working of any kind." Maitland climbed out and surveyed the barren littoral. "The damned thing is," he said, "we have no true pattern for these courts. If this were Mayan, I'd have no hesitation about where to dig. But if it's Arawak, the other wall could lie just about anywhere. The courts varied in dimension, you know. Some of the courts at Capa were long and narrow—some square—some with rounded ends. The courts were usually excavated a few feet down. That is to say—these stones represent a raised level, seats or a wall. The common pattern was for a flat stone like this, at right angles to a second stone, pointed downward. This created a sort of shelf. Below the vertical row of stones was the floor of the playing area. It was often a different kind of soil—a foreign clay they'd bring in to give them a better surface."

"You mean, if we go a few feet below, we might hit a different strata—an artificial one?" Tom asked.

"A possibility," Maitland said.

"But hell, we've been as deep as four feet in the midden and in the burial ground. And we've found nothing like that." Tom pointed to the widening pit where the skeletons had been unearthed. "The ossuary there—it's laced with dark muck, but it's irregular, as if the earth was put in with the bones."

Maitland pushed the ragged hat back on his head. "The proximity of the graves may be a clue. These courts, the *juegos de bola* as the Spaniards called them, were not only recreational in nature. They had religious and social meanings. You've read about the Mayan ball games, of course—elaborate rituals, allied with the religion. The Arawak games were simpler, but I'm sure the ecclesiastical element was present."

Tom pointed to the Negro laborers, digging a second perpendicular test trench, in search of the southern wall. "Well, we haven't found any sign of the other wall. That's the second trench I've had them dig, starting thirty feet below us. Nothing yet."

Ballard was troweling inside the burial mound. What had started as a neat rectangular excavation—twenty neat squares, five by five—had become a gigantic circular gouge in the soil. Inside the widening pit, additional skeletons were coming to light; a perfect flexed corpse rested comfortably at Ballard's feet. He fussed and chipped around it, exposing the rib cage, the pale gray limbs, the brachycephalic skull.

"What number is he?" Tom asked.

"Number fourteen," Ballard said. "And lots more where he came from. You want to save any of him?"

"The usual. The skull and the limbs. Squirt him up and add him to the collection."

They paused at the shell heap, where the Burleys stammered unintelligible greetings. "You remember Wilma and Oran Burley, don't you, Hall?" Tom asked. "They're getting their masters' this February."

"Of course I do," Maitland said. "Their father wrote to me about them in July."

Wilma adjusted her eyeglasses. "Oran found the *zemi!*" She cried out the news, as if to justify their arduous, hand-bruising summer amid the refuse—to advise Maitland that they were not merely scavenging the village dump.

Inside the house, Tom unboxed the major finds—the pottery, the miscellaneous stone pieces, the remains of the skeletons. He did not bother with the animal bones or the odd unidentified bits. Maitland and he sat opposite each other at the sawhorse table, both of them squinting in the dusky light.

Maitland did not look well. With cavalier disregard for cholesterol and calories, he had indulged the inner man too frequently. His neck and lower cheeks were splotched with liverish freckles. The short trek across the digging site had left him puffing stertorously. Now, at the makeshift desk, he wheezed and grunted as he studied Tom's assortment of artifacts, as if even the nonathletic effort of recognizing and interpreting the material was wearisome. Sixteen years ago, when Tom was an undergraduate, and had sat in Detering Hall, the anthropologist had been perhaps thirty pounds thinner. Then his high, almost womanish voice had a vigor and a grace that was lacking now. He still had the effortless speech of a good lecturer—but it was edged with fatigue. There had always been a boyish quality about

Maitland, an eagerness and a humor. The spirit of the chase colored his remarkable field work—inhabitants of Kaffir kraals and Amazonian barracas were never dull siblings or pallid moieties in his lexicon—they were friends, drinking cronies, the *dramatis personae* of his rich, turbulent life. Now, all that was left of the old adventurer, Tom could not help feeling, was the shoddy prospector's getup—the hat that had baked under the Andean sun and been soaked with Congolese rain; the shirt he had washed in the Ganges; the corded trousers that had protected his ample rear and protuberant gut from the underbrush of the Celebes; the laced, scuffed boots—veterans of Yap, Palau and Nan Matal. It occurred to Tom, with something of a jolt, that his father-in-law was past sixty. Watching him now, soughing and puffing over bits of stone, his lumpish body surrounded by an aureole of dusty summer haze, Sorrento recalled Maitland's final lecture of the school year to the undergraduate anthropology class. It was one of those rare moments of illumination and of recognition that bejewel the University year. Tom could almost see him and hear him, pacing behind the lectern, the jacket of his purplish-brown boxy suit opened to reveal a vast frontage of rumpled white shirt.

. . . We have set ourselves a goal that implies disappointment, unenviable labor, attack from many quarters. But none of us doubt the worth of our mission—an understanding of the nature of man and the forces that function in human society. These forces are now imperfectly understood. Social science is young; it has succeeded in raising innumerable questions, but has supplied very few answers. The current planners of society are like civil engineers drawing up plans for a massive suspension bridge, but having no idea of the width of the river they must cross, or the nature of the materials they must utilize. We would do well to heed the example of the ancient Greeks. In Greece, for the first time in man's history, the human mind was freed—if only for a brief period. Thought was disciplined, the search for truth organized along lines of logic and reason. But this freedom was short-lived; soon men turned their energies to matters that were safe, because they were trivial. We stand today, in our studies of man and society, where the Greeks did in their probings of nature. A lode of untapped knowledge lies before us. Yet I would caution all of you that the path to this knowledge grows rockier and steeper each day. It may soon become impassable, and the

social scientist, unable to progress, will vanish as did the Greek philosopher. Freedom is shrinking. The totalitarian state—of any variety, of any coloration—cannot abide the social scientist. The study of society cannot help but be anathema to its leaders, for it demands a questioning of the existing order. But the techniques are with us. The goals are understood. Free minds may be suppressed, but they have a gratifying resiliency. . . .

"Well, I'll be damned," Maitland said quietly. He held up the triangular *zemi*. "It's Arawak. There's absolutely nothing in Eastern archaeology like it."

"How about the others?" Tom asked.

"The pendants are very likely Arawak. The skull drinking cup—" He raised it high, as if toasting the vanished hunters of the Glades. "I can't be sure. It's a rather common trait, the trophy cup." He set it down and returned to the three-cornered idol. "But this dandy little thing!"

Maitland leaned back. The table edge pressed hard against his belly, digging a ridge in his shirt. "I tell you my feelings, Tom. We should clear every inch of ground here. If this is an Arawak-style village, or even a temporary settlement of Arawaks—it will be one of the most revolutionary sites in recent archaeological work. When can we talk to Ellenbogen about it?"

"We're all invited for dinner tonight. You can bring it up then." He paused. "I don't know, Hall. He has his heart set on that tourist deal. I feel guilty asking him."

Maitland did not seem to hear him. "What this will do to our cozy theories about the Southeast!" he said softly. "Take the business of the ball-court configuration! We know it came up through Mexico and Guatemala—the complex games of the Aztec and the Maya. And we know about the simpler games of the Caribbean area, notably the Arawak. *But on the mainland of North America!*"

He seemed in reverie, fondling the *zemi* as if the pagan idol might impart new intelligence to him. He heard his daughter's voice and turned weightily in his seat, seeing her framed in the oblong of saffron light of the doorway. His grandchildren, as brown as if they had been dyed, and looking aggressively healthy, trailed behind her.

"Hello, Hall," she said. She entered the bleak office. Maitland got up with what seemed an extra effort to maneuver his abdomen.

"Hello, Martha," he said. "You look splendid. As if you've adapted admirably."

"Do I?"

"Oh, yes. Not at all the professor's wife. The magnificent bathing suit. The exotic sandals. And that fantastic coat. I believe those are genuine ideographs. I used to be able to read Mandarin. Hmmmm . . ." He shaded his eyes, trying to decipher the embroidered legends on deKay's loot coat. His skill at Mandarin had long vanished; he gave up the effort.

"What the hell's the matter with you Anglo-Saxons?" Tom asked gruffly. "Don't daughters kiss papas in your particular in-group? If it was one of *my* sisters meeting my old man, they'd be slobbering and hollering by now."

"Please, Tom," Marty said. She turned around. "Nicky! Abby! Come on in and say hello to your grandfather."

They slunk in, browned and furtive, each bearing more of deKay's gifts. The boy clutched an inflated ocean liner and Abby bore a child's parasol.

"Go and kiss your grandfather," Martha said. "You haven't seen him for a long time."

They shuffled forward, smelling of sea water and sand, and deposited reluctant busses on the anthropologist's liverish cheek. Maitland patted them dutifully on their firm behinds; they retreated. He was not a Grampa of presents and tricks, of whirls above the head and visits to the zoo. Abby suspected he was not a grandfather at all—just her Mother's Daddy.

"The children appear to be blooming," Maitland said. "They tan magnificently. They've got their father's fine melanochroid pigmentation, I suppose. Makes it easier for them."

The youngsters backed away suspiciously. They preferred grandparents like their daddy's parents, who came with bubble gum and Mars Bars and chocolate cigars.

Marty dismissed them, sending them upstairs to wash for supper. She sat on a packing crate. Her Peruviana finery dazzled against the plasterboard walls, the crates and digging tools encrusted with dirt.

"I hear you got here just in time for the newsreels," Marty said lightly. "Ira dropped by at the club and told me he had films made of you, with some Indian you brought along."

"You're doing great," Tom said. "You've seen your old man three minutes and you've got the needle out."

Maitland chuckled, stroked his corncob and studied his daughter. Their antagonism was not a source of distress to him. It seemed to intensify with the years, to develop a stringent quality, so out of sorts with her soft beauty.

"I *asked* Hall to come down here," Tom said. "We're sitting on a revolution. I need help. I figured you'd be in a better mood—with the beach club and the kids off your neck. Now let's have a truce between you two. Marty, you wear deKay's free bathing suits—and Hall and me, we'll dig up the rest of the land. With luck, we'll be wound up at the end of September. You don't like it here, you can go back to New York any time. Abby's school starts in September so you'll have to go anyway."

His voice was heavy and mandatory. Some of the old crackle of his Marine days had crept into it, and his wife was aware of it. Yet she did not bridle at his unexpected incisiveness, the rude references to Ira's hospitality. Rather, she envisioned her father as the villain, the intruder. He had descended on them in his outdated field clothes, looking for all the world like a scout for Teddy Roosevelt's Rough Riders, and had suddenly endowed Tom with his rank, gruff maleness. He seemed to her, particularly in the Beach milieu, a reminder of the life he had bewitched Tom into. The shaman's spell he had cast over the young Marine officer she had loved twelve years ago still rankled. In a sense, she and Maitland had competed for him.

"This may shock you," she said. "But I'm beginning to enjoy myself. The children love it. I'll stay as long as I like."

"Great!" Tom cried. "What are we arguing for? This sounds like my family getting ready for a poker game. There's always twenty minutes of screaming about what the chips are worth."

She got up and started for the door. "Hall," she said, "will you do me one little favor?"

"My dear, I don't know that I'm *capable* of anything that will please you any more."

"You can manage this. Go easy on the dirty stories tonight at the Ellenbogens. Lila will be honored enough feeding you. You won't have to regale them with obscene ceremonies among the Haida or what the Eskimo women do inside the sleeping bag." She left.

Maitland puffed strenuously on his pipe. "I don't know, Tom. I don't know whether I should have joined you. I act as an abrasive on the girl. I've always felt that neutral parenthood was wise, particularly with a child as indifferent and as self-sufficient as Martha was. But why should she be any different? Naturally, her parents were to blame. Be prepared, Tom. Fifteen years from now Nicky will hate you every time he's frustrated. God help you if he turns to a life of crime. You'll be more at fault than the fellow who gave him the gun to hold up the filling station."

13 *Memoirs of An Ethnologist*

MARTHA's admonition did no good. Maitland brimmed with anecdotes and half-serious theorizing, responding with florid loquacity to Lila's lavish cuisine. The anthropologist ate enormous quantities of rich food and downed two bottles of wine—a fine Orvieto and a dark Beaujolais—by himself.

Martha watched him with concealed annoyance. Tom knew her feelings and resented them. She believed that Maitland was like a performing animal. He was at his best, exuding wild reminiscences, when he was rewarded with finely prepared food and vintage wines. He loved to be entertained, and in return he willingly imparted his experiences among the Ashanti and the Nez Percé. It all seemed a little indecent to her.

With the *coupe marron,* Maitland began recalling his work in Australia among the Dieri. Martha knew what was coming and raised one eyebrow. He ignored it and she tried to deter him. "Really, Hall! Is that the kind of story to tell at the table?" she asked. "Maybe Lila and Erwin aren't up to—"

But Lila, vivacious and bellicose, intervened. "Oh, Marty! What kind of prudes do you think we are?" she cried. "I haven't been so intrigued in years! Dr. Maitland, go right ahead! The more risqué, the better!"

It bothered Marty not only that Lila had fallen so thoroughly under her father's incantations, but that she looked alarmingly attractive. In deference to the University guests, she was dressed somberly in trim, tailored black. Her dark hair was soft and unlacquered and she had limited her cosmetics to a streak of scarlet lipstick. Moreover, Marty noted with annoyance, her hands sported a selection of flesh-colored Band-Aids, scars of battle from her enlistment in the ranks of diggers.

Maitland sniffed his Courvoisier and blinked approvingly.

"What about the Australians?" Lila insisted. "Now that Marty's made it sound so dreadful. I can't wait to hear!"

"Your husband's mention of the dry summer made me think of it," Maitland said. "The fact that it hasn't rained in some six weeks. I had a narrow escape among the Dieri because of a similar drought. The invocation of rain is a paramount function of the Dieri medicine man. And one of the sure-fire methods of making rain involves the use of old foreskins."

Lila gulped on her *coupe marron*. "What? Did I hear you correctly?"

Behind his tinted lenses, Erwin seemed to color slightly.

"I'm *fascinated!*" Lila said. "Go on, Dr. Maitland."

"Well, there really isn't much to the story. The tribe keeps a supply of dried foreskins handy as defense against drought. The snippets of skin are concealed in a wrapping made of feathers and glued together with the fat of the wild dog—you remember yellow dog Dingo—and the carpet snake. This parcel, I assure you, was one of the most sacred items in the shaman's possession. No woman dare look at its contents. When the lack of rain is prolonged, and all other magical means have been exhausted, the packet of foreskins is employed. They are utilized one at a time, in a ceremony of propitiation that's too involved to detail. When the rites are concluded, the men of the Dieri bury the foreskin, since its potency has been exhausted. Back in 1933, when I lived with the Dieri on a grant from New South Wales University, the drought was particularly severe. All of central Australia was affected by it, and the shaman of my particular village was having a run of bad luck. The fact of the matter was, that by the seventh week of drought, he had used up all his foreskins. There were no imminent male additions to the tribe, so naturally the search for the magical wherewithal to invoke rain turned upon us. There were three of us in the ethnological team living with the Dieri. One was a Jewish lad, Schneider or Snider, I believe his name was. Naturally, he had nothing to donate. The other fellow, McMasters, was a Scotsman, the son of a physician who believed in preventive medicine and had accordingly performed a nonreligious circumcision on his son. That left me, the only intact male within a hundred miles, the sole possessor of the magic accoutrement. Naturally, I was reluctant. Modesty and pride of the flesh made it difficult for me to appreciate their need for rain. Moreover, I had witnessed mutilatory ceremonies practiced by the Australian abos, and I confess to a certain ethnocentricity where antisepsis and anaesthesia are concerned."

Maitland availed himself of a cigar, offered to him from an enormous humidor by Freddie. It seemed a foot long, of pale, luminous green, as smooth and as sweet as a Swiss chocolate bar. He lit it with the flame of a silver candelabra and scrutinized its glowing tip. It seemed appropriate to his tale.

"The shamans told me I was their only hope of salvation. There was little I could offer by way of rebuttal. You see, the other chaps and myself had taken blood oaths as members of the Dieri tribe. We were not merely foreign observers, we were kin to them. In the dark of the moon, we had sliced our arms below the elbow and mingled our blood with that of the other men of the tribe. Nonetheless, I suggested a variety of alternate magical procedures. The shamans had tried everything. Only a foreskin could save them. To this end—mine, I realized—they had sharpened their knives and built a stone catafalque on which the truncation of my person was to take place. I had Schneider and McMasters prepare sterile bandages and stand by with our morphine. I might add we were a week's trek from any white community where medical aid might be obtained. At dawn, amid much chanting and beating of drums, I was led to my slab, as naked as my accompanying tribesmen. Prone on the cold altar, I awaited the magician's surgery. He had anointed me with the fat of the wild dog and powdered me with red sand, when suddenly there was a heavenly crackling in the east: a jagged scar of lightning cut the morning sky and seconds later came a rolling peal of thunder, the most delightful noise I have ever heard. The operation was canceled. The wizards held a consultation and decided that rain being imminent, it would be insulting to the deities if another foreskin were offered them. They theorized that the gods were oversupplied with the magical objects, and had hence suspended rain. The hot lightning and the noisy thunder they took as a warning to stop offering them shriveled prepuces. It was a case of too much of a good thing. Indeed, my shaman advised me that I had in some measure brought the rain on, even if I had not made the supreme sacrifice. He felt that the sight of my strange white skin, and the prospect of one more thank-offering was what clinched the deal. So it all ended pleasantly."

"Well I never in my life—" Lila said. "It's incredible!"

"That's quite a story," Erwin agreed. He had fidgeted and

fussed throughout Maitland's tale of adventure in the Australian outback, putting on a brave front of enjoying it. Tom, observing his guarded approval, realized the story was a little gamey for the Ellenbogens. Normally, when told to academic audiences, at graduate-school smokers and department beer parties, it was greeted with guffaws and wild interruptions. Lila and Erwin, perhaps awed by Maitland's status, had listened like hypnotized freshmen. They acted as if they expected to be quizzed afterwards.

They retired to the living room, Maitland confiscating the brandy, availing himself of a second cigar. He launched into a lively lecture on Moslem nomenclature, concluding that the reason the Arabs lost the war to Israel was their grievous shortage of names. "The fact is," Maitland explained, settling himself into a leather chair, "All Arabs are named either Ali or Mohammed. Now picture the Fifteenth Syrian Light Infantry, about to storm Tulkarm. The commanding officer orders Private Ali and Corporal Mohammed to deploy as scouts. And what happens? One hundred and forty-three Arabs move out and are cut down by enfilading Israeli fire. The only ones saved are a handful named Abdul."

Erwin laughed. "I'll have to remember that one. It'll go fine at the next UJA meeting." He flicked a remote-control gadget and turned on a giant television. "I hope nobody minds," Erwin said. "DeKay told me *The Spirit of Man* is getting some pictures on the late news. I think some of our guests are included."

They gathered around the gray rectangular eye. Erwin tuned the set artfully, by pressing a variety of buttons on the small control box.

A television variety program was concluding. Four singers and a comedian, all of them reasonably well known, were gathered around a piano and singing informally. The piano player was a famous composer. They were vocalizing some original lyrics to "Schnitzel-bank," the gist of which was what wonderful people they all were. They sang exuberantly and without discipline and the effect was that of a mildly drunken neighborhood party. It was as if all these talented people were deliberately minimizing their skills. The homemade words to the song were rich echoes of the senior class play.

> Is that good old Harry Blair?
> Yes, that's good old Harry Blair!
> Harry Blair, debonair, walks on air . . .

"This be over in a minute," Lila said apologetically. "The news comes right after it."

This will be over in a minute: This was the phrase you heard most frequently around television sets, Tom realized. *It won't hurt long.* Sorrento, watching the five handsome people singing artlessly around the piano, had the notion that the blandness was intentional, the shoddiness of performance cunningly conceived. It made the viewer feel he was in the gang; it reduced all the talented participants to just folks; it barely impinged on the public eye and ear—one could do a crossword puzzle or read while enjoying (or at least undergoing) the new "Schnitzel-bank."

A frenetic series of commercials followed the community sing on the television set. Then, with much fanfare, and a montage of old newsreels (a rocket being launched, an ocean liner, troops advancing under fire) a handsome young man behind a desk appeared. He seemed to be part of the desk, a mock-up nailed to a piece of cardboard furniture.

The announcer read a few bulletins, narrated a clip of shadowy film and then turned to local news.

"And here in the Southland," he said, in rich tones, "preparations are under way for the most exciting new enterprise to come to the Beach in many years. It's *The Spirit of Man,* a gigantic panorama of Man's Faith, which will be erected on Bay Islet. A public-spirited group of citizens headed by industrialist and philanthropist Erwin Ellenbogen . . ."

Everyone leaned forward as the announcer's chiaroscuro head dissolved to a large filmed close-up of Erwin, looking nervous and self-conscious. As the narrator continued, the camera moved erratically around the offices of *The Spirit of Man,* picking up Campion, Braud, Ira deKay, Charlie Rasmussen and the others who had attended the afternoon meeting. Each man tried to appear at ease, but the muddy, indistinct sixteen-millimeter film succeeded in reducing all of them to witless, uncomfortable boobs.

"...Backers of the group hope to hold an impressive groundbreaking ceremony for *The Spirit of Man* on Labor Day week end. Ira daKay, well-known beach publicist and sportsman, tells us that the coast-to-coast television program *Our Heritage* may broadcast from the site of *The Spirit of Man* on Labor day. Here's a look-see at the location...."

Abruptly, the fogged film switched from a close-up of Ira,

beaming and pointing at a map of the city, to a jiggly aerial view of the islet and the surrounding waters.

"...The choicest piece of Beach property still available for development. Plans call for a mammoth parking lot, and a huge, parklike setting for the exhibits and demonstrations. A small theatre equipped for motion pictures or theatrical presentations is included in the educational attraction, as well as full television and radio facilities. Mr. Ellenbogen and his associates stress that *The Spirit of Man* is nonsectarian and has no point of view, other than prompting good will among all people. You'll note the deep trenches marking sections of the Bay Islet site. Those represent important archaeological excavations now taking place there. A team of topnotch archaeologists under Dr. Thomas V. Sorrento are searching for an ancient Indian civilization that could prove as important as the Incas of Peru. Some of the excavation findings, Ira deKay says, will be used in a special museum of primitive religion...."

The wobbly aerial view vanished and in their place, some water-marked and contrasty films of Maitland, Sorrento and John Throws Knife were projected. The cameraman and the film editor appeared anxious to go to the bathroom. The film, a simple recording of three men, one holding a small bag of beans, bobbed and skipped nervously, jumped from one face to another, from close-ups to three-shots, to a tight picture of the bean bag.

"...At Beach Airport, two distinguished arrivals connected with the work on the Ellenbogen estate. On the left, Dr. Hall Maitland, famous anthropologist and author, arrives to oversee the digging. He is greeted by Dr. Sorrento, on the left. The gentleman in the middle, holding the bag, is Mr. John Throws Knife, executive officer of the True American Church, an Indian faith with headquarters in Oklahoma, which will be represented at *The Spirit of Man*. Mr. Knife came to the Beach at the urging of Dr. Maitland, an old friend of the Indians. That little bean you see Mr. Knife holding—oops, there it is—that little bean is called 'peyote' and is the basis of their religion, which teaches..."

Erwin pressed a button and the telecast vanished. Lila looked puzzled.

"Dr. Maitland, isn't peyote a narcotic?" she asked.

Maitland suppressed a belch. "There's a good deal of argument over that. There are no cases on record of peyote addiction. I suspect one reason is because it's so abominable to take. Its use is entirely ritual—as sacrament, or as a catholicon, or as an amulet. Our friend John, you noticed, wears his around his neck. White missionaries, and other groups aimed at uplifting the Indians, claim it's ruining them—poisoning their bodies and destroying their souls. Actually, the Bureau of Indian Affairs, after long efforts to suppress the eating of mescal beans, now permits it. There are state laws against it, but they're regularly broken."

Tom joined the discussion. "Hall, as I remember the Bureau's ruling in 1934, peyote eating was permitted under Constitutional guarantees of freedom of religion. They're still catching hell for sanctioning peyote."

"That's right," Maitland said. "I'm not a little proud that I was active in fighting the anti-peyotists. I've eaten as many mescal beans as any white man, and I can tell you they are not harmful at all—if you can get them down."

"But what do they *do* to you?" Lila asked breathlessly. "I'm dying to try one!"

"It produces visions—revelations," Maitland said matter-of-factly. "You can see or hear the spirit, or both. The Indian generally sees God, or Jesus or some other identifiable spirit. Or he may see a departed relative or friend. With the vision comes guidance for some current problem, or in some cases reproach for doing or thinking evil. In my own case, I kept conjuring up visions of William Jennings Bryan. I heard him speak once, as a boy, and I suppose he represented some childish confusion with the Godhead. I'm sorry to relate that the Boy Orator of the Platte had very little to tell me."

"You just don't eat the beans," Tom explained. "There's a ceremony."

"And a lovely one it is," Maitland said. "Generally a peyote ritual runs from eight on Saturday night to eight the next morning. It's held in a special tepee. The worshipers sit on the earth. There's a leader, but he's not properly a minister or priest—he doesn't intercede between God and the laymen. He's like the impartial chairman of the garment industry."

"I'm somewhat confused," Erwin said. "Is this *really* a religion? I mean, is it a Christian religion?"

"To the Indians, unquestionably," replied Maitland. "There is doctrine, ethics, eschatology and ritual. It's one of the finest examples of accommodation in modern cultures. Originally, the eating of peyote was a nativistic Indian cult. Mescal-bean eaters were common throughout the southern Plains. They were savagely suppressed by white authorities—the Bureau of Indian Affairs led the hue and cry against peyote. Whipping up the antis were the uplift people, the organized churches. So the Indians achieved a marvelous synthesis. They combined the peyote ritual with Christianity and came up with a new Christian religion."

"If you can't lick 'em, join 'em," Tom said. "Didn't you hear John Throws Knife quoting Scripture?"

"Exactly," Maitland said. "For example, peyotists believe in the Trinity. God is the same as the Great Indian Spirit. Jesus plays several roles, sometimes the culture hero who gave peyote to the Indians. Elsewhere he's a guardian spirit, who was murdered by the whites and now looks after the rejected Indians. They recognize the Holy Ghost, but they have the same difficulties that we have in explaining it."

"But is there any ethical content to this kind of thing?" Erwin asked, perplexed. "It sounds like a hash—a little of this and a little of that."

"Ethics, Mr. Ellenbogen, are the easiest part of any religion. They're substantially the same in all faiths, and equally admirable in all. If you haven't got any, you can borrow some from the fellow down the block. It's the ingenious *ritual* that's hard to develop. The peyote ethical code is estimable. Brotherly love, care of family, self-reliance, avoidance of alcohol. Beyond these simple precepts, the believer gets further guidance from eating peyote. Contemplation under peyote is deep and thrilling; the eater is sensitized and his powers of thought concentrated. He sees his errors, confesses, learns God's way from the bean. The bean comes from a small cactus—*Lophophora williamsii*—and its properties are alkaloid. A biochemist could tell you better than myself the effect of alkaloids on the central nervous system, but therein lies the magic."

Erwin seemed puzzled. In his mind were germinating grave doubts about including this barbaric nonsense in his benign panorama of faith. He had not chosen to embrace the executive officer of the True American Church. It was deKay's frenzied operating that had plunked the Indian in their midst. Somehow the vision of the tepee filled with brown men munching nauseating beans, drumming, chanting and summoning up visions did not mesh with Ellenbogen's notions of faith—any faith.

"You know what does fascinate me," Lila said, "is the sense I get of a lot of bitterness on the part of the Indians. It's almost as if they're making *fun* of the whites. Oh, not exactly, but kind of cynically joining them, but insisting that their old tribal ways are really better."

"You've phrased it most accurately," Maitland said.

"They got a right to be mad," Tom added. "They were done in."

Maitland relit the cigar. "Yes, but most Indians are realistic about it. Rubin Brown Bear once stopped me when I started to commiserate with him. 'You won,' he said, 'so you do what you want to us. If *we* had won, it would have been much worse for *you.*'"

"That doesn't make it right," Lila said. "I can't help it if I'm a do-good liberal. Erwin, didn't we contribute to save the Navajos one year?"

"I guess so." He could not get the image of the smoking, malodorous tepee out of his head: the Seminoles were Indians enough for the tourists.

"Hall's kidding about the Indians being realists," Tom said. "At least I think he is."

"Let me put it this way," Maitland said. "I think their bitterness diminishes every year. They're convinced by now they won't get the land back. The buffalo have long gone. The watersheds are irrigating lettuce fields. Whatever you may think of the Indian mentality, they are not prone to self-deception, as are, for example, the Arabs."

"Listen," Tom said, "as late as the 1940's the Plains Indians were convinced that a big wind was rising that would kill all the whites and any Indian who imitated whites, and only the traditionalists would be saved to take the land over. How do you figure that?"

"Old dreams recur, Tom," Maitland said. "I can't deny that. I can tell you a better one. About the same time I was visiting the Sac and Fox and one of the old men told me, in total confidence, since this was intelligence that was being carefully hidden from whites, that *Christ was to be reborn as an Indian savior.*"

"I never!" Lila cried. "That's just incredible!"

Freddie moved among them, emptying ashtrays, offering mints and cigars, an efficacious and faceless black man. Tom studied him, white-jacketed, soft-voiced, and wondered what dreams of revenge and murder ravaged his mind in the night. John Throws Knife had his beans; surely Freddie had some amulet—the numbers, or the booze, or his Jesus. *His Jesus:* The Reverend Harkey's version, Tom imagined.

"I suppose I tend to be biased in favor of the peyotists," Maitland was saying. "Apart from my natural bent toward primitives —most of them are dirty and treacherous, I might add—I was elected an officer of the True American Church in 1940. Henry Yellow Ski, a Menominee, and myself, were co-secretaries of the faith that year. You see there another remarkable example of acculturation. Our obsession with organization, with officers, committees and commissions has probably made more headway among primitive peoples than contraception."

"Look what happened to me in Santa Rosa," Tom said. "I was vice-chairman of the Government Commission to Save the Tapapa Indians. It's always better when you have a commission."

"What's better?" Lila asked.

"The bad deal you give somebody later. The Commission on the Indians was set up to exterminate them. The idea was to talk about them a lot, study them, make recommendations, get the word in the newspapers and newsreels, and then let 'em die. It's beautiful. Invoke the liberal ethic and take a strong moral stand. Then don't do anything."

Marty yawned. "You've enlightened Lila and Erwin about Santa Rosa already. It wasn't your fault that the government didn't have any money. That was the *real* reason they threw the report out."

"The causes were deeper than that, my dear," Maitland said.

"Were they?" asked Marty.

"Tom's splendid work on Santa Rosa—it's still one of our best papers on Meso-American subsistence communities—was rejected by the government because of what I call the shock of potentiality. It's only been in the past fifty years that the notion that we can manipulate society for good has gained any credence. Look what had to happen before there was a Securities and Exchange Commission! And our society of the twenties, please note, was a highly complex and advanced one, rich in moral overtones and abundantly Christian. The poor people of Santa Rosa, governors or governed, or for that matter the Arab fellaheen or the Ashanti—how can we expect them to work up any enthusiasm on behalf of the commonweal? The notion that you can improve human conduct is infinitely harder to fathom than the simple matter of making rain by burning a foreskin."

Marty stretched and got up. Since her visits to the Peruviana, her arms and face had turned a lustrous tan; there was an attractive pinkish peeling on her trim nose. "Tom, I think we'd better head for bed," she said.

"But things aren't that gloomy, are they, Dr. Maitland?" Lila pursued, rising, tugging at her fierce girdle, as her food-heavy guests assembled themselves for departure. "I mean—people do understand each other a little better as a result of all the work people like you have done? Oh, I know human behavior doesn't improve overnight, but there are reasons to be hopeful—"

Maitland patted her taped hand. "My dear Mrs. Ellenbogen, there is always hope. At the time I was completing my report on Auschwitz I was prepared to surrender. The scientific savagery, the descent into hell, the murky abyss with its glib and righteous justifications—all these, while as suffocating as the smoke from the crematoriums, were endurable. But the colossal *indifference* of mankind to what went on there, our superb talent for forgetting about it, for committing it to oblivion—these I found hard to ingest. I was ready to take a job as communications consultant for a firm manufacturing ball-point pens. But I suppose someone has to make the reports on Auschwitz and on the Tapapa Indians."

The Ellenbogens, sobered, followed Marty, Tom and Maitland to the marble foyer. Erwin had lost some distant relatives to the mechanics of Oranienburg, obscure Lithuanian Jews, known to him only as retouched faces on a New Year's card his mother had once received. There had been a message in Yiddish scrawled on the back. Maitland's reference to the terror was like a sudden onslaught of nausea.

"About people forgetting the concentration camps," Erwin said. "Is that true? How can anyone ever forget what happened there?"

"The enormity of the crime demands a lapse of memory," Maitland said. "An analogy is the influenza epidemic of 1918. This was one of the worst scourges ever to ravage mankind. Yet the literature, medical and popular, is curiously devoid of references to it. Very little research has been done on it. It's as if there's been a conspiracy to make believe it never happened. The same thing is now taking place regarding Nazi Europe. And I say *Europe* advisedly. Would it horrify you if I told you the greater part of Europe *approved* of what happened to the Jews? That the only regret they have is that Hitler didn't have time to finish the job? I see you look distressed. You have a right to be. You know, of course, about the learned professor, the global thinker, who feels—and this is just about an exact quote—that the Nazi crime against the Jews was *not* the tortures and executions visited on them, but rather that these atrocities caused the surviving Jews to *stumble.* By this he means the extremism of certain Zionist factions. This is no gutter hoodlum speaking, Mr. Ellenbogen. This chap is called one of our great historians. A man totally without cultural perspective, I might add."

"But he can't really mean—" Lila started.

"He means every word of it. I suspect, too, that the West is secretly delighted with the horrors of Soviet Communism. We profess to hate them and what they stand for, but in a way we're grateful they're around, because they serve to assure us that there is something worse than the Nazis—a point I'm prepared to argue. I will take second place to no one in my distaste for the Soviet system. I was crucified a hundred times by campus Communists in the thirties. But must I be forever reminded that Communism is the vilest form of tyranny *ever* visited on man? You know the obvious corollary that's intended: *the Nazis weren't so bad after all.* Cruder interpreters of the international scene, usually educated Europeans, will say so in so many words. Isn't that really what we seek in our studies of Soviet Russia? A reminder that the Nazis were not such a bad lot?"

Marty noticed how pale and shaken the Ellenbogens appeared. In the midst of their smug, secure lives, her father had cruelly injected the ancient fears and hates, the memories of the knout.

"Don't pay any attention to Hall," Marty said soothingly. "He seems to feel these lectures are necessary to repay his hosts."

"I don't think so, Marty," Lila said gravely. "I think you do your father an injustice."

"It's been a marvelous evening, Lila," Marty said. "We won't get into any arguments about Hall's eccentricities. The squab was delicious."

They said their goodbyes; Lila promised to join Tom for more digging at midmorning.

Leaving, they could hear Erwin trying to elicit from Maitland the admission that many people did care about what happened in the concentration camps. "I know from my own work with interfaith groups, Dr. Maitland," he was saying, "that there's a great reservoir of good will among the different persuasions. That's why I'm so interested in this exhibit—"

"Yes, yes, of course," Maitland said. "Anything to blunt the old murderous lusts! I'm in favor of *anything* that replaces the craving for blood, anybody's blood—"

Outside, Marty looked at the arched doorway, hearing the voices diminish as the Ellenbogens led their guest to his quarters.

"Damn him," she said. *"Damn him."*

Tom looked at her intensely. "Why are you so sore at him? Lila and Erwin expected the lecture. It's better than two summers in the School of General Studies."

"Don't you understand?" she said wearily. "That was his special speech for wealthy Jews. To upset them. To convince them he knows more about their problems than they do."

"He does. Marty, I can't help it if Hall liked the Yaps and the Haidas better than he liked you and your mother. Maybe he had a right to."

Inside the stifling bedroom, they dismissed Wilma. She was mending Oran's wardrobe, a collection of clothes that any self-respecting Negro domestic would have diplomatically rejected if offered by an employer. When she had left, Tom began fumbling in the refrigerator.

"I need a cherry pepper to settle my stomach," he explained. "Burn a hole through all that rich stuff Lila served up. How about that crazy broccoli? With almonds and mushrooms."

He located the hot panacea, and popped it whole into his mouth. *"Wow,"* he said. "They're better when you let 'em age a little. The big mistake is people throw away the seeds. They have the real jizzim in them."

Marty, undressed and in bed, sensed a rebellious swagger in him. The doubts and vexations that had burdened him a few days ago were gone. Maitland had instilled in him the spirit of the chase, had revived his waning excitement over the dig. She had seen Tom swinging the pick and shovel since Hall's arrival. He was working with a fervor and frenzy that belied his thirty-seven years and his shriveled leg. His athlete's torso, blackened and hairy, was responding to the stimulus of Maitland's presence with a vigor that unsettled her. In a hazy way, she used to believe that it was a wife's job to propel a man into action; yet she had never been capable of egging Tom on. Aware of her own deficiency, she was irked by her father's capacity to succeed where she had failed.

"Tom?" she asked softly, touching his rocklike back. "Am I being difficult?"

"No," he yawned. "I'm glad to see you gingered up. I couldn't stand when you sat around feeling miserable because you were so superior to all these rich people down here. Have your laughs."

"I was thinking. You really should try writing again. All your experiences—you had no right to let that lapse."

"Right. Anything you say. The *Tom Sorrento Books for Boys. Meet Tom Sorrento. Tom Sorrento, Sandlot Shortstop. Tom Sorrento, Bench-Warmer. Tom Sorrento, Leatherneck; Tom Sorrento, Officer, or Short-Arm Becomes You.* I'd clean up. I don't write because I don't have anything to say. We went through all this eight years ago."

"You stopped writing because *Hall* didn't want you to. It interfered with your field work."

"You got your mind made up the old man did me in. You hate to admit my own failings, because you still have an idea I missed the boat. So you blame it on Hall."

She rested on one elbow, looking down at his blockish, dark body, the edges luminous with moonlight. "One of these days you'll admit it, Tom. He got his hooks in you for some cabalistic, obscure reason—to relive his own youth maybe, or to make you a substitute for the son he never had, or for something darker and dirtier than that."

Tom spun around in the bed; it creaked loudly.

"For Chrissake, Marty, knock it off!" he stage-whispered. "You've been reading those novels! You started this with me once before and you made me sick for three days. Why is any relationship between two men suspect? If it'll make you any happier, your old man never tried to grope me. Besides, he isn't my type. If I was going to be queer I'd like 'em like Ira deKay—all yellow and smooth. That answer the question?"

"You're the eternal innocent."

"Why? Because I don't like being told my father-in-law's got the hots for me? Hall ever show these symptoms before? Your old lady have any kicks aside from the fact he used to chew betel nut?"

"That isn't the point."

"What is?"

"His interest in you—all those years you spent in graduate school—as if he wanted to *keep* you there, under his wing, where he could see you and influence you and—oh, why do you make me say it?"

He sat up suddenly. "I'm sick of this middle-brow nonsense

about queers. Guy can't talk to another guy unless he's queer. I respected Hall. I admit it. He opened my eyes, he gave me direction. He's the smartest man I've ever known, and when they start re-examining social science twenty-five years from now, they'll discover just how important he was. Why should I have to tell you this? You're his daughter. You're supposed to know it. Sure, he's getting old and erratic, and he forgets sometimes whether it was a Tlingit chief or a Kwakiutl who gave him the copper medallion, but he's still wise to what's going on."

"We're not talking about the same thing. I won't deny Hall's brilliance. I know how you've always revered him. But that begs the question." She sounded oddly triumphant. "I think Hall has always had a homosexual attachment toward you. I mean it. It would never be overt and it probably hasn't ever occurred to him. But it's there; I sense it."

"Va fa a Napoli!" he cried. "That's what I love about you people. It could never be overt and he doesn't know it's there, and I don't know it's there, and he never made a pass at me—but because it suits some notion of yours, some need you have to drag Hall down, it's *there*. If my Aunt Teresa had *cologni* he'd be my Uncle Vince."

"I can't discuss it with you. You're incapable of objectivity where he's concerned."

Nicky whined. They waited tensely, hopeful that his blurred complaint would evanesce. When the whines became whimpers, and these gave way to modest screams, Marty roused herself. She opened the refrigerator, located a fresh plastic bottle and filled it from a cardboard milk container.

"Almost four and still sucking a bottle," she yawned. "What does he need it for?"

"Because his old man's queer, I guess," Tom said. "I don't have enough problems, you have to start *that*."

"That isn't funny," she said. "Let's drop the whole thing."

In the inner bedroom, the child's cries vanished in the presence of the liquid comforter. Dozing, Tom heard the boy murmuring something about a lost pail and shovel, and Marty's assurance that he would get new ones tomorrow.

Her concern for the child moved him. When she returned, he stroked her thigh. "It's been a long time," he said. "I'm not the terror of the mattress any more."

"You know how I feel. As much or as little as you want."

"I want it, but I can't seem to get around to it any more. Why is it never so good after you're married? I used to shiver and shake and get the schoolboy flutters. That cold, cold room you had on East 66th Street. I never loved any place so much in my life."

"You're right. It's never the same."

"I used to ride down on the Fifth Avenue bus—they had the open double-deckers then—with my books under my arm like I was a freshman—and all I could think of was your legs and your belly and the secret you had for me. Oh, it was a secret all right. I used to get so excited I wanted to fly off the top of the bus. Flap my wings over upper Fifth Avenue. Fly right by Flower Hospital and the Museum of the City of New York and the Heye Foundation. Shedding clothes as I went. I couldn't bear it. By the time I ran down East 66th Street I was in a cold sweat."

She smiled. "I know. You were a good lover."

"Past tense. That long-distance affair we had, Marty, it was too good for either of us. We should have known it could never be as frantic after two kids and nine years of not-enough-money. We should have taken courses in husband-and-wife ceramics. Or learned to play recorders. Or whatever married people are supposed to do to maintain healthful mutual interests above and beyond the sack."

"Shhh. Go to sleep, Tom."

He faced her, marveling at her delicate beauty. "You know what it was? It was all tied together. Sleeping with you, and going back to the University, and getting out of service. And learning from Hall. It was a cultural configuration, like the boys would say. That's what made it all so good—the interaction."

"Don't worry about it. Sex was never that important to me."

"It was to me, considering you were the first woman I ever met who gave it to me so willingly. Why was I always a loser? I was ugly, but uglier guys than me made out. Like Doyle, that dumb Irishman. You know what he said when he was drafted?"

She yawned mightily. "Something brilliant, I'm sure."

"For Doyle it was pretty good. He said, 'They can't draft me, I'm getting too much.' "

"Tom, go to sleep. In a minute I'll be hearing about how Engstrom really loved you."

He stared at the moon-streaked plasterboard walls, listening to her settle her weightless body on the bed. Despite fatigue, he could not sleep. His mind brimmed with the detailed, linear clarity of insomnia and he began to think about his years as a graduate student, of the extended and comforting love affair he had enjoyed with the University and its people.

14 *Summer of Hope*

HE could recall the day he had sat in Maitland's stuffy office in Detering Hall and made the decision to return to school. It had been a curious inquisition that the anthropologist had subjected him to—Maitland appearing more concerned with his military career than his academic qualifications. It seemed odd also that no mention passed between them of Marty. Tom had been sleeping with her for three months; if Maitland suspected this, or if it concerned him, he gave no evidence of fatherly apprehensions.

Maitland advised the young man (still in forest greens and bright with ribbons) that his vague and airy undergraduate curriculum—*hoo-hoo* courses he called them—would mean a full year of catching up on natural sciences before he could essay advanced work in anthropology. "You'll need two semesters of chemistry, zoology, botany, geology and physics before you can get into social science," he said heavily. "That means a good five years of work all told before you get your doctorate—if you can stick it out."

He then began interrogating Tom—with almost childlike eagerness—about his war experiences. He was particularly moved when Sorrento told him how he lied his way into the Corps to cover up his "athletic heart." For a moment, Maitland's face abandoned its quiet indifference; he appeared ready to spring to attention and salute the visitor. They argued, Tom remembered, about the effects of combat on personality, the anthropologist insisting that these were salubrious and invigorating—assuming the combatant survived. Tom disagreed fervently with him. He wished that Maitland would talk about something else. It seemed to Tom a waste of the man's talents for him to be so intrigued wih martial nonsense.

At length Maitland advised him to see his assistant, a Mr. Peltz, whom he could find in the archaeology workroom. He reminded the novitiate that he was in for long years of penury and study, and wished him well. Sorrento located Peltz in a gloomy utility room at the end of the corridor. The assistant was hunched over a slate-topped work table, reading from a journal of archaeology. Alongside him, a battered slide projector aimed its blind eye on a furled screen. Peltz made some sneering references to Tom's uniform, then fumbled in one of the desks and located a sheaf of forms.

"I heard the whole idea on those beach invasions was to protect British money," he said uncivilly. "The copra trade and that kinda thing?"

"You bet," Tom said. "First thing we did after landing was secure the General Motors Building."

"Wiseguy. I tried to enlist but I was 4-F. Double hernia."

"I didn't ask to see your discharge," Tom said. He began filling out the forms. Peltz read his entries, upside down.

"See anything interesting?" Tom asked.

"College boy," the redheaded man snarled. "From the Ivy League undergraduate school. You won't last."

"Thanks for the encouragement."

"You'll need it. Know how long I been knocking around here? I can't even get my master's. I quit every year or so and go drive a truck. Of course, I ain't had the advantage of being a football player or a hero. I'm just a slob from CCNY night school. Took me seven years to get the baccalaureate, but I got it."

"Congratulations. Does Maitland keep you around just to discourage everyone else?"

"No. It's my own idea." Peltz looked at him narrowly, moving his wiry head sideways as he did. "I can't figure you out. Marines. All that fascist crap they taught you. Why do you want to come here? Don't tell me. I bet Maitland yanked you off the campus. He's a sucker for a uniform. He's sore they wouldn't take him in the army this time—hypertension and incipient diabetes. I guess he can live the whole war over with you."

When he left Detering Hall he walked across the campus, pausing at the great flight of steps leading to the administration offices. He sat on a stone bench, blinking in the sunshine, absorbing the aura of the University, comfortable in the presence of reason and experiment, of probing and skepticism, the only religious experience he had ever known. He knew why he had fallen so easily into Maitland's entrapment; he *wanted* to be caught. He wanted nothing more than to come back to the University, to spend his life on the campus, learning, teaching, being part of the grand continual process. It comforted him that while he had been away, strait-jacketed in the military ritual, learning nothing (in spite of the *mystique* which assured him that killing and death were rich, rewarding experiences), the University continued. Each year the initiates came, the books were opened, the knowledge imparted. He now regretted the lack of direction of his undergraduate years. He had pitched and rolled haphazardly through the undergraduate curriculum, grabbing at odd bits of English literature, philosophy, the social studies. Nothing had been synthesized. Perhaps now Maitland could do that for him. Sorrento had never been a hero-worshiper; he did not envision the anthropologist as a visionary prophet, a leader who would open his eyes. He liked Maitland's cynicism, his refusal to be typed, his insights into "human bastardy." In a curious way, the anthropologist's awareness of brutality, his preoccupation with man's infinite readiness to torture and humiliate his neighbor, reminded him of his father's stern moralism. Frank Sorrento was a born cop—he suspected everyone and he was always prepared for the worst. He had been on the force only two weeks when he suffered a fearful drubbing at the hands of a pack of Irish galoots on San Juan Hill. They had been engaged in a harmless prank—baiting a Jew vegetable peddler. (The jolly Irish! What fun! Hoorah!) Patrolman Sorrento, in shiny new uniform, came upon them as they were gleefully hurling his crates of cabbages to the pavement. Two bhoyos were unharnessing the spavined nag, and two others were tugging at the old kike's whiskers. Frank waded in, wary of using his billy or gun, and was rewarded with a black eye and bloody nose. The Celts beat him to the pavement, and when he tried to bring his club into action, they disarmed it and used it freely on him. He had the satisfaction of nailing two of them after a five-block chase—Frank could always run, and his legs were like springy steel after years of pick-and-shovel labor. He enlisted the lasting love of the Jew, and a year's supply of fresh greens. But in the Hibernian precincts of the Hill, where aboriginal Corkonians and Sligomen reigned, enjoying the winks and nods of their brethren on the force, he was forever in trouble. Wedger McMann, the local soccer hero, drunk and ugly one New Year's Eve, took him on in a saloon and kicked the young cop purple and black around the legs and groin until Frank unlimbered the billy. His old man, Tom concluded, had to end up a policeman. When all the bad jokes had been made, all the snide references to corruption and lack of courage, there remained something valiant about his father's insistence on justice—at least a *little* justice. Frank knew all about human wickedness; he needed no lectures in Ethics or The Behavioral Sciences. If Maitland were trying to understand these disturbing manifestations in scientific terms, his father would have made a good witness for the anthropologist. He had lived it. The gap between the jovial drubbing of a Jewish vendor of soupengreens and genocide was perhaps not so wide, after all. Tom was pleased that, in this manner, he had been able to erect a bridge between the two men. He knew his family would never understand what had impelled him to return to five more years of University life—an impecunious, nonprestigious waste of time as far as they were concerned. Their standards were as demandingly American as those of the Kiwanis. They knew all about the big houses in Pelham where the successful second generation lived. They knew that an Oldsmobile was to be preferred to a Chevy, provided it was bought for cash, not on time, and was not driven by a colored man. Now, in finding common ground for Hall Maitland and his father, he justified his option in favor of the University.

He walked toward the subway convinced he had made a good decision. At the corner of Broadway he turned, delighting in the vista of the enduring buildings. They seemed more eternal than any mountains or oceans he had ever seen. They reassured him that wisdom was everlasting, that there existed fields of endeavor in which there were no measurable rewards. No one got rich researching Village Settlement Patterns in the Southern Andes, or New Concepts of Neutron Imbalance, or even Aspects of Business Arithmetic. Somewhere between the highly charged competitive nonsense of college football—*kill 'em before they kill you*—and the abrasive dogma of the Marines he had lost all zest for the murderous game. He wanted to be left alone, to read books, to be part of the accretive advance of knowledge.

On his way back to the Bronx that evening—through some tropism he dimly understood—he stopped at the football practice field to see Engstrom. The gatekeeper greeted him with disconcerting joviality. The man was an alumnus of the college—Van Dyke Oberst, Class of '16—a crippled wreck who had come out of World War I barely alive, and had been pensioned by his Alma Mater as a minor functionary at athletic events. In the winter Mr. Oberst sat at a desk outside the gymnasium and checked bursar's receipts. A small black-and-gold sign at his desk read V. D. OBERST '16. It was as dignified as the sign on the Dean's office.

Oberst spoke to him in convulsive gasps. Tom deciphered an effusive welcome, accompanied by much grimacing and wobbling. He shook Van Dyke Oberst's trembling hand, immediately making an invidious comparison. Was he a mental and spiritual counterpart of the ruined inspector of bursar's receipts? Was he to become a pensioner of Alma Mater, living on fellowships and grants—leavings from the commercial world for the starvelings of *Academia?* He had difficulty ridding himself of the greeter. The distorted words dribbled after him as he waved goodbye and walked toward the field.

He could hear the cracks and thuds of a scrimmage, the peremptory whistle of one of the assistants, and Engstrom's flat voice. At the edge of the field he paused, unable to go any further. No one could recognize him from that distance and what could he possibly tell Engstrom? *I'm going to be an anthropologist.* He doubted that the coach knew what it meant. Engstrom would have understood it if Tom were going into business —*any* business; or a profession—*any* profession. To get involved in a doomed exchange of pleasantries was meaningless. He satisfied himself with watching the team run off plays for a few minutes. The savage impact of hard bodies, the almost sexual smacking and crunching, the noises of leather and plastic and rigid young muscle in combat, filled him with a rising sense of superiority. Half aloud he muttered: "Why don't you guys grow up?"—and turned and left the field.

The feeling that he had isolated himself intensified at home. He found his mother poring over a brokerage-house newsletter. She had the financial page of the *Times* spread out on the kitchen table, and was annotating the cryptic figures with a variety of colored pencils. Tom sat down and watched her for a few minutes. She confounded him. Ten years ago she was doing embroidering at home to fatten the family budget. Now she understood margin and dividends and two-for-one splits and apparently made money. Tom felt abject before her arcane knowledge—he still wasn't quite sure of the difference between common and preferred stock.

"Where'd you learn all that, Mom?" he asked.

"It's not hard. Mrs. d'Amato started me."

"Yeah, but she's loaded. Didn't Joe leave her a pile? How can you do what she does?"

"Oh, I don't. I play it very cautious, just with little amounts. I do all right. Your father has no complaints."

She adjusted severe gold-rimmed glasses on her nose. Her craggy jaw moved forward fractionally as she squinted at the columns. *The Triumph of American Capitalism,* Tom thought. It had been one of his undergraduate texts. He even remembered the author: Louis M. Hacker.

"You go to the University again today?" she asked, not looking up.

"Yes, I went to see Dr. Maitland."

"That's *her* father."

Tom shifted in the kitchen chair, moving his legs with a show of annoyance. He yanked a sprig of grapes from the cut-glass bowl. "What's that all about? *Her* father. Sure, he's Marty's father. He's also one of the most famous professors in the country."

"I didn't say anything. You're very touchy."

"Ah, come on, Mom, knock it off. I went to see Dr. Maitland because I'm going back to school. I registered for graduate school today."

She looked up. "Back to school? What are you studying for?"

He almost choked getting the word out. "Anthropology. What Dr. Maitland teaches."

The notion offended her. "What's that? How do you make a living out of something like that?"

"It's—it's—the study of man in society. Mostly in primitive societies. You know—Indians, Africans. I might have to go live with some of them."

Her lips twisted into a wry grimace. "Who pays you for all this? I mean—how do you live?"

He bounded out of the chair—it was shabby modern, tubular black steel and frigid green plastic, an enemy to the spicy red sauces his mother brewed. "Don't worry, Mom, I won't be a strain on you and Pop, I get my tuition and books on the GI bill plus ninety bucks a month living expenses and my disability. And I've saved all my dough from the Corps. I'll chip in."

"How long?" she asked suspiciously. "How long do you have to study for this kind of thing—so you can go live with cannibals and get eaten?"

"Oh, Jesus." He noticed that she had set three frozen chicken pies on the stove to thaw out. The synthetic food offended him; armed with frozen pies and the stock market, Serafina had entered the bright postwar era with the vigor and sureness of a Scarsdale Matron. Meals had always been an occasion in their home. You ate on time and everyone attended; there were no excuses. Even with his father burdened with the irregular hours of police work, they had their evening meal at 6:30. And there were no pallid cream-gravy chicken pies served. "How come you can get away with giving Pop this junk?" he asked.

"They're delicious," his mother said. "Arthur Godfrey advertises them on the radio. They have vitamins. Besides, your father is on the night trick this week. He don't get home till one o'clock. And with the girls working, and Rita getting married next month, and you never home half the time, why should I break my back making *lasagna?* Who's here to eat it?"

She made some notations on a small pad and nodded her head, satisfied with her calculations.

"You didn't tell me," she persisted. "How long do you have to go to school for this work?"

"Maybe five years. Or more. I have to make up a lot of courses I missed. Then I study for a master's degree, then a doctorate. After I get the master's I might get a teaching job, so I could study and make a little dough at the same time."

"All right. The five years are up and what do you do then?"

"I'm a full-time teacher. If I'm smart I become a professor of anthropology. I don't get much money when I start—maybe four thousand a year—but I can live on it. I'm interested in the work. I want to go back to the University."

Serafina's square, handsome face bobbed in disapprobation. "Five years. *Five years* of hard work for four thousand dollars a year? Tommy, the Palermo brothers next door, they aren't half the man you are and already they're making twelve thousand dollars a year! *Each!* At least if you'd become a doctor—a lawyer—anything! But to go live with Africans who'll chop your head off?" She sighed. "I don't know what happened to you. Since you came home. It's like nothing we say is right any more. Nothing means anything to you."

"That isn't true, Mom. You know I love you and Pop. It's my own fault. You know me. I never could make my mind up. It's a good thing I could play football. I never would have gone to college at all."

"Well, that's what parents are for, to help out. You're my only boy, Tommy. You're the oldest, but you're the baby. The girls—they can manage for themselves. Thank God, Rita found a nice boy, and pretty soon Angie will be off our hands. And—"

"And me. I'll be on your hands five years, is that it, Mom?"

"Tommy, I never said that. Anything you want to do is all right with us." Her hard black eye caught something in the minuscule columns and she bent to her magic figures. "Hmm. What do you thinka that? I had that Canadian Mutual Fund—just a couple of shares? Mr. Callaghan at the brokerage told me it had to go up, I shouldn't sell. I sold anyway, because I didn't like the way it was acting. And what do you think?"

"I give up, Mom. What happened?"

"Down two points since I sold three weeks ago! I figured it out all along!" Her voice rose triumphantly. Was it possible, Tom wondered, that the market had become the substitute for the three children, now fleeing her iron discipline, her compulsion to master them? Was the Canadian Mutual Fund the substitute for a son who no longer obeyed her—or a daughter who married the first neighborhood swain who asked her?

"You amaze me, Mom," Tom said. "How you learned so much—"

"I got to do something," Serafina said flatly. "Your father away half the time with those terrible hours. And when he's home all he does is complain how he should have made sergeant. He says he's going to retire in five years if he can find a good business."

"What would he do off the force? He loves it."

"Not so much any more. Since the spics moved in, it's very hard. He might not do nothing. We'd sell this place and get a small house in Jersey. By then you and the girls'll be on your own."

On your own. Off our neck. Whether she had intended it as a barb or not, the reference made him wince. On ninety dollars a month he would be a big help. A big galoot of a football player living with his parents and studying God-knows-what because he liked the way Maitland talked, and because he had been sleeping with the man's daughter. It seemed desperately unfair to his parents, particularly his father. Since his return from service, he found himself in almost perpetual misery about Frank.

Tom kept wishing he could *do* something for him—buy him the sergeant's stripes, join the force and become a captain, help him retire to a pastoral existence of truck gardening and *bocce* in New Jersey. But the truth of the matter was he could do nothing at all—for any of them. Stripped of the uniform and the ribbons he was an unemployed ex-Marine, unprepared for any career, no good at business, disinterested and uncommitted. It occurred to him, with a jolt, that he couldn't even drive an automobile.

"I don't know," his mother sighed. "I guess I don't understand you any more. All the things you could be."

"Don't talk about it. I'm going back to school. If I'm a dope, or if I don't like it, I'll go into the contracting business."

"Go on, joke about it. The Gagliardo family was dying for you to meet their daughter. They'd take you into the business. Next to Colonial Sand and Stone they're one of the biggest! I kept telling Mrs. Gagliardo about my son, the Marine officer. The college man. The daughter saw your picture in the Bronx Home News. But you—you're too busy running off wherever it is you run all the time—"

"Cut it out, Mom."

"Oh, I know plenty. I don't talk to you about it, because you don't listen any more. You're a stranger."

"Well, I know a couple of things, too. Sally Gagliardo is one of those fancy Italian girls. She went to Sacred Heart Academy for two years. A peroxide blond with the blackest eyes and the muddiest skin I ever saw. Why'd she dye her hair blond? A *Napolitan'* like that. I think she wears falsies. Not that I ever got that interested."

"There's nothing wrong with marrying your own kind," Serafina said firmly. "I notice all your college friends, all the educated Italian boys, they couldn't wait to marry some Irish or Swedish girl. With no hips and yellow hair, the kind who cook with boiling water. Oh, I'm on to them. What's so great about Irish girls, that all those college friends of yours married them?"

"How many choruses of 'Baby Shoes' does that call for?" Tom asked. "I can't help what Terranova and de Vito did. It's none of your business anyway. They married Catholics, didn't they?"

"That has nothing to do with it."

"What about Rita? She's getting hitched to Georgie Schultheis and I don't smell any garlic on his breath. Nineteen years old and quitting college because she can't wait—*can't wait* to see what it's like to climb into bed with a man. That's the only reason. He's the first guy who asked her, so she said yes. And he's no Italian either."

"I don't like that kind of talk in the house. I don't care how big an officer you were." Serafina thrust her magnificent jaw forward.

"It's true, isn't it? She'd never admit it, but that's what that marriage is. Two dopey kids who can't wait to see what it's all about. They'll find out soon enough. And she's so happy because he's not a ginzo. Well, luck to both of them. Thank you, Stan Lomax, and lots of luck on your western road trip, Leo Durocher."

"I suppose you know everything about those things—marriage and what's between men and women. I don't know how you got so smart in twenty-five years."

"I don't care what Rita does. That's her affair. I've seen too many kids in my outfit who got married like that and got into trouble. They're not ready for any kind of responsibility. All they know is the sack. They got to get it regular. Right away. Now. All they can get. To hell with any kind of understanding, or economics, or mutual respect. Just, *let's go, now, right away!*"

Serafina did not particularly like Georgie Schultheis and she cared less for his cold German family around the corner. Moreover, she objected to the marriage on the basis of status: Rita had two years of college and might even go back; Georgie was a yeoman in the Navy and something of a dope. Of course, Rita was no beauty, and the best thing you could do with girls was get rid of them in a hurry. . . . The logic of Tom's argument tormented her, but she refused to agree with him. It seemed to Serafina that as she got older there were more family arguments, more tears on the part of the daughters, more sullenness on the part of her husband, more tension and unhappiness in the house. It had been so simple when the children were little: *she gave them orders and they obeyed.* Now they all had their own ideas and the ideas seemed to be in perpetual disagreement with her own notions. The girls—she could take or leave their antagonisms. But Tom was different; he was her vision of glory, her hero, the first and only male child. She had kept the scrapbooks and sent him packages during the war; she had prayed for him and lit candles—even though the family had been drifting farther away from the Church with each passing year. And now he sat in her stuffy kitchen, on a late summer afternoon, arguing with her, acting as if she had never meant anything to him. He had been a fat and shy little boy—before his pudginess hardened into athlete's muscle—and she had spent many hours protecting him from hoodlums. Years later, when he was strong and tough, and could defend himself with quick fists, she would still come charging out of the house, her tomato-splotched apron flying, in defense of her baby Tommy. *Fa Pete's sake Mom, g'wan back in—I gave the guy a bloody nose and haddim down before you come buttin' in. . . .*

"Well, you have no right to talk about Rita this way," she said.

"Why not? I'll tell you something else. I don't like that big fancy wedding you dreamed up. Spend all of Pop's money—for what? So we can eat *goy* food at Rupprecht's Villa? At least if it was a *real* Italian wedding—but we'll get mashed potatoes and roast capon. Asparagus. Why don't you just give the money to Rita?"

"You aren't that smart, so just stop it. The whole idea of the big wedding is for the people who are invited to give *a-boost*. Money. If there's no big wedding, there's no presents."

"Wait a minute," Tom said. "I remember it all. At cousin Celia's wedding before the war. The bride carries a white silk bag for the money. Right? All the dough goes into the white bag."

"What's wrong?"

"Rita will carry no white satin bag, if I'm going to that wedding. Now I get it! The big wedding, to invite everyone, and make the money back. Tell me this, Mom—do they really make out? Suppose no one comes across? I mean—all of Georgie's squarehead relatives, they don't know about *a-boost*. Rita might go in the red."

"Never mind. I told Mrs. Schultheis. When Louise de Fillipo got married last year they made three hundred dollars, after everything was paid off including the waiters' tips."

He unloosened his suntan tunic and yanked his tie open. He suddenly had an urge to be in San Francisco—on the prowl, flaunting his ribbons at the Top of the Mark or La Ronde in the Fairmont. *A vodka gimlet on the rocks please—and one for that lonesome redhead across the way. . . .*

"Okay, but no white satin bag," he said.

Serafina appeared to suck in her breath, to set her lips. She doodled on the margin of the *Times* financial page.

"If I were you, Tom," she said slowly, "I wouldn't be so free and easy to talk about people's weddings, or things connected with them."

"Rita's my sister, isn't she? I'm allowed to get something off my chest here. What am I? A Sicilian?"

"You know what I'm referring to."

"I told you why I think they're getting married. They got big ideas about how marvelous it is. They'll find out. Wait till the bills come in."

His mother tapped her pencil on the table. "All right. All right. Suppose that *is* why they're getting married. But at least it's a nicer way to live than what you're doing right now."

"What's that supposed to be? A call for a confessional on my part?"

"Don't be so innocent. I know what's going on between you and *her*. All those nights you never come home. I know she has an apartment of her own."

Tom's olive skin darkened and he lowered his head, as if ducking a blow. "What I do is my business. You don't run my life any more."

"Don't sound so important. You're going to hang around the University five more years we'll have to support you. I have a right to my opinions. I'm your mother. I know what you're doing with the girl. For over three months now like that. And how many times have I seen her? Once. One time. She did us a favor and came here and didn't say a word to anybody."

He shivered. "I don't want to talk about Marty. How the hell did we get onto that subject? All I wanted to tell you was I was going back to school."

"It's all tied together!" Serafina shouted. "With her, now with her father! What kind of girl is she for you? Lives by herself—she never bothered to graduate from college with all her advantages! And lets you sleep with her like that for three months! And you're not engaged or serious even! What if she gets a baby?"

"Where would she get it?" he asked sardonically. "You mean what if she becomes pregnant? Don't worry, Mom, the Marines taught me all about that."

"And how come she never calls you? You, always you have to be making phone calls to *her*. Who does she think she is? She's never phoned you once. Always you, having to beg her, can I see you now? You free tonight? Can I come down now? Oh, I see what's happening."

"Does it occur to you she works? She works hard. She doesn't have time to be calling me." He spun around, furious. "Now goddammit, stop talking about Marty. It's too bad you can't get your hooks out of me. You're like every Italian mother I know. You worship your sons so much you'll strangle them to death with love before you'll let them have their independence. I'm warning you, I won't stand for it. Now stop trying to suffocate me. I'll see Marty as much as I want, and I'll do anything I want. It's too bad I'm your only darling, beloved, delicate, gentle, brilliant son, but that's the way it goes. You understand?"

She gasped, caught her breath and settled back in the kitchen chair.

"All right, Tommy. But at least let her come have a meal with us now and then," Serafina said.

Tom shrugged: there it was—the resolution of all human problems with *food*. You solved the world's sorrows, you bridged all the chasms with a plate of soup. He shuddered, recalling Marty's last and only visit. It had been for Rita's engagement party. She had insisted on coming, and she made a brave try at mixing, praising Mrs. Sorrento's magnificent display of food (there was that food again!) and exchanging police stories with Frank with much charm and vivacity. Marty had covered police headquarters for a month and she had a newspaperwoman's familiarity with the jargon of the cop. But with the girls—with Rita and Angie and all the other tropic birds, she was lost. The girls fluttered and bangled around her, chirpy and loud, uncertain of her, jealous, secretly hating her for her beauty and her education and the apparent grip she had on their beloved hero brother.

His mother got up, folding her newspapers and leaflets on the kitchen table into a neat stack. She tucked some notes she had made on a scrap of paper into an apron pocket and walked to the stove.

"You be home for supper tonight?" she asked.

"Sure."

"I don't know. Maybe I should make something better. Frozen chicken pies. They're supposed to be very tasty. But with your father on nights this week, and the girls and you flying around—"

She busied herself at the stove, working with a speed and a vigor that had always impressed him. He remembered one Christmas Day, when she had awakened at five-thirty to prepare an interminable feast for hordes of hungry relatives. He recalled leaving for a visit after dinner (or was it a high school basketball tournament at the Garden?) and coming home that night to find her angrily shoveling snow with the strength of a middleweight.

He watched her at the stove for a few seconds and then it occurred to him she was crying. She had begun imperceptibly, nursing an apologetic sniffle, dabbing at her eyes behind the prim spectacles. Soon she was weeping with gasping regularity. He could tell that the tears were involuntary. Serafina Sorrento was not one to seek pity through ancient womanly tricks. Generations before her had learned that life is *duro*. You accepted it and cried only at the ultimate tragedies. Anything short of death could be solved by argumentation, preferably at the top of one's lungs.

Tom walked over to her and held her in his arms. He kissed her cheek. "Stop crying, Mom," he said. "What'd I do to make you start sobbing like this? You stop. Or I'll be bawling also."

"It's nothing. Nothing, Tommy. I just worry about you, that's all. You don't seem to know what to do with yourself. Maybe your father and I, maybe it's our trouble. We're not educated."

"Educated!" he cried. "The biggest *ciuci* I know are educated." He patted her eyes with his handkerchief and she smiled grudgingly.

"I'm a big boy now, Mom. I learned to ride a bicycle in the Marines."

She snorted heartily. The prospect of argumentation revived her. "Why do you have to start that again?" she asked. "You'd think 'cause I wouldn't let you ride a bike or roller skate I ruined your life."

"Almost, Mom."

Serafina's mouth formed in a tight line. "You had weak ankles," she said.

"Sure, Mom. Whatever you say. I made all-city fullback with weak ankles two years in a row."

"I'm talking about when you were a baby."

"Some baby. Have it your way. I had weak ankles."

"It's the truth. I had to buy you arch-supporters, special shoes. And don't think the extra money for them was easy when your father was just on the force, and the girls little babies. Oh, you forget so easy, the way we worried about you and looked after you—"

"And you'd like to still be doing it? Well, you can make me a meatball sandwich to take to graduate school every day. If that doesn't get me a Ph.D. in five years, I'll go into the roofing business."

He walked into his dim bedroom and took off his blouse, heavy with ribbons and sharpshooting medals—honors and citations no longer relevant. He was annoyed with himself for still wearing it. In a cardboard box in his closet he found some of his old notebooks and texts. He emptied it onto his bed: books, looseleaf binders, fat manila envelopes. The second-hand Everyman and Modern Library editions he had read in freshman humanities were shabby and dog-eared. Thucydides had come out of his binding and Rabelais was not much better off. It jarred him to think it was only seven years ago that he had bought them, neatly bound with penny string, in a crumbling bookshop on Amsterdam Avenue. Most freshmen sold their humanities books at the end of the year; his were so disreputable that they weren't worth anything.

He settled happily in the pile of papers and books, sampling them—as if in preparation for his return to the learning process. The pages of looseleaf paper, narrow-lined and triple-holed, crammed with his somewhat childish scrawl, summoned up comforting memories of long hours in the college reading room. The room was high-ceilinged and flooded with natural light from lofty mullioned windows. You could sit there for hours—reading, taking notes, daydreaming, wallowing in the gratifying association with fresh ideas, new concepts, a thousand facts unknown before the precious book had been opened. He realized now how much he had missed the college. He had been plunged into the violence of war so suddenly, he had not been permitted the pleasures of nostalgia. Now the old books brought it back to him, a hundred revelations and illuminations, as inspiring as any sighting of angels.

A scrawled note he had made at one of Maitland's lectures, underlined in red pencil, reminded him . . . *in most societies a perpetual struggle rages between the furtive agent and the fiduciary, or holder of the public trust. The battle is usually imperfectly understood by members of the society and the roles often become blurred. On its simplest level, a policeman who accepts bribes is operating in both roles. . . .*

On the cover of one of his notebooks, Immerman, the frantic pre-med and horse-player, who had sat next to him in Economics of Totalitarianism had written a verse extempore about their professor, the austere Benjamin Kotzkov, who one puzzling semester showed up with his name Americanized to Basil Carter.

Benny changed his name to Basil
Now he owns an English Castle
Kotzkov's Carter, fan my brow
The Russian is a Limey now!

He itched to get back to classes, back to the orderly routine of lectures, reading assignments, research, note-taking—the exhilarating anticipation of the new fact, the new scrap of knowledge, the odd bits and pieces that, wondrously, at the end of the year bloomed into a broader and more reassuring view of the world. In his last two years at college he had even loved the examinations. *Discuss the major differences between the characters of Ben Jonson and those of Shakespeare, using at least six examples from each playwright.* He had written a good essay on that one, pulling down a straight *A*. He rummaged through the sinister blue leaflets that were used for final examinations and found it, reveling in his ancient conquest, more pleasing to him than the varsity letter he was finally awarded for staying with the football squad for four years.

. . . the characters of Ben Jonson are comparable to Wimpy. Wimpy likes hamburgers. That trait of character—perhaps quirk is a better word—dominates his behavior. He sees the world in terms of hamburgers. Ground meat—any kind of meat is his be-all and end-all. Similarly, Jonson's people are motivated by a single overwhelming characteristic. If they are avaricious, avarice directs their every word and move; if they are brutes, depend on them to be brutal in all circumstances. . . .

Idly, he wondered if the graduate faculty of English might have been a better choice. He shuddered at the thought of a year of botany and zoology, as Maitland had decreed. No matter; the important thing was getting into the routine again, immersing himself in the academic life. He could not wait to tell Marty about his decision. They had discussed what direction his life should take, but they had settled nothing. They were, after all, uncommitted to each other beyond the exquisite pleasures of the bed.

Tom flicked on the bedlamp and settled back with a ragged edition of *The Chief Elizabethan Dramatists Other Than Shakespeare.* He turned to *'Tis Pity She's a Whore,* recalling that Immerman used to refer to it as *'Tis Pity There's a War,* and had read a few minutes when his mother appeared in the doorway. With the soft light of the kitchen in back of her, she looked gentle and agreeable; the dealer in debentures and options had given way to a worried, aging housewife.

"Tommy," she said querulously, "are you going to marry her?"

He clapped the book down on his chest. "Who said anything about marrying her?"

"Well, you know, Tommy—any girl you wanted—we'd want her too. Whatever you want to be happy, Tom, that's all."

"I'll tell you when I get married. I got no plans."

"Ninety dollars a month," she said. "And going to school all those years not making a living. You couldn't do it—"

"Hey, Mom, do me a favor. I was peeking in the Frigidaire before and I saw some nice bloody hot sausage you must have got at Venturi's. How 'bout frying me some with green peppers instead of that Anglo-Saxon food, huh?"

"Sure, Tommy. You'd like that better." She turned and left for the kitchen—home grounds, where doubts and fears never assailed her.

"And cook it good!" Tom called after her. "No trichinosis!"

How could the world be bad? There was always hot sausage with peppers; the University; his lover of the slender legs and pliant body. He settled back with his book.

The following day he called for Marty at the World News office. He had become a hanger-on at the press association and had struck up a friendship with Howie Markowitz, Marty's colleague of the night trick. Hoag, the night editor, favored him with a sour nod. Walking by Hoag's soiled desk, Tom invariably had a feeling of revulsion. How many times had this paunchy, sodden man shared Marty's bed? His mind conjured up disgusting pictures of Hoag *impassionata;* the only way he could dispel his loathing was by tempering it with pity. After all, he, Tom Sorrento, USMCR, had won the great competitive race for sexual honors. In the shabby confines of WNA, Marty was prized above all women; by rights she was the editor's. It seemed to Tom that since his displacement of Hoag, the man had grown seedier and redder. The fruity odor of cheap whisky hovered about Hoag's desk, piled high with smudged onionskin and wire baskets. Around the journalist the idiot teleprinters clattered incessantly, sending the ephemeral commodity called "news" to thousands of newspapers, radio stations, TV stations. Tom never visited the inhospitable offices without the feeling that something was terribly wrong; that the likes of Hoag had no right to be in such a crucial job; that all the speeches about Freedom of the Press were a mockery. In his bias, he was sustained and goaded by Howie

Markowitz, the fat boy stationed at the rearmost desk in the WNA office.

Tom removed a stack of dusty papers from a swivel chair and dumped them on a desk.

"Hey, be careful, walyo," Howie said. "That's this week's New York *Times*. That's where the cable department steals the foreign report."

"Sorry. Where's Martha Maitland?"

Howie winked. "Peek through the general manager's door. She's getting the Big Word from the overseas manager, who just flew into town."

Tom turned and peered across the hallway at the row of enclosed executive offices. He could see Marty through an opened door, legs crossed like Rosalind Russell and cigarette a-tilt in the manner of Claudette Colbert (or whoever it was always played girl reporters), talking with a middle-aged man.

"That's Frederick M. Ainsworth, foreign correspondent," Howie said. "How do you like the haircut and the suit?"

"He's kidding. He has to be kidding."

He was witnessing the American Dream in a black pin-stripe suit—the magnificent triumph of the stereotype. Ainsworth, the great foreign correspondent, was a handsome fellow. His honey-colored hair had been oddly barbered. It suggested a thick blond wig, the hairs at the side of his blockish poll lustrous and layered. It appeared that his head, if sliced in cross-section, would be of that rich, hairy yellowness through and through.

His face was pained and poised—a man who had seen too much and done too much. He wore a choking blue shirt and a frazzled light blue tie. Both articles of haberdashery spoke of Old Bond Street or the Burlington Arcade. A black Homburg rested on the desk—as holy as any *yarmulka* or mitre. There was a belligerent quality of self-invention and self-perpetuation about the man that Tom found admirable. He had known officers in the Marines who had that talent—the skill of self-dramatization down to the most minute detail of dress, of behavior, of speech. There was a colonel Tom had served under who lovingly rolled his pants into his combat boots with graceful, soft folds, as beautiful as a decolletage; a major whose webbed equipment glowed with a pale lustre that could only have come from repetitive bleachings with lye. Similarly, Mr. Frederick M. Ainsworth had mastered the externals of his trade. Surely a stained trench coat hung in his locker, companion to a bumbershoot of impeccable ancestry. A discerning motion-picture director, observing the journalist as potential talent to play *himself* in a film, would have thrown him off the set as a fraud. He was too good.

"He was plain Freddie Ainsworth when he started here before the war," Howie whispered. "A corn-fed boy from Madison, Indiana. He used to wear black shoes with brown tweed suits, so you can figure him."

"Where did he get the fancy handle?"

"Made it up out of his own head. In by-line it's always F. M. Ainsworth. I filled in on cables this summer. Every thing that guy files is *Exclusive*. If he gets the time of day off Big Ben, it's exclusive."

"Doesn't he always get the big interviews?"

"Yeah. His stable of regulars. Lady Astor. Pierre Laval. Franco. All the unemployed kings. I got into a big scrap with him this summer and that was the end of my merit raise." Howie did not seem particularly wroth with Ainsworth. He accepted his bad luck as part of the deal at WNA.

"What happened?" Tom asked. Marty seemed vivacious and unusually talkative in the office; the correspondent was enjoying her company.

"Oh, he filed one of his exclusives. You know—like the Russians are Communists, or Churchill likes booze. I forget what the story was—something about Allied Occupation Plans for Austria, which he got exclusive, from a Grand Duke who runs a tie store in Paris. One of his Reliable Sources. So I read the cable and it rings a bell. Then I remember. I read it in the *Times* last week. Same story with a London dateline. So I changed his lead, knocked the exclusive off it, and ran it as a short news piece about the occupation of Austria. He blew his top."

"But you were right. Didn't your boss go to bat for you?"

"Nah. The general manager told me anything with an Ainsworth by-line gets priority and I should have run it exclusive."

"But the *Times* had it a week ago!"

"So what? Who remembers? Who do you think this is, walyo, an Uplift Society? Boy, everything's exclusive here. Bulletin. Flash. First Lead. Special to WNA. Written Specially for WNA. A Special Service for WNA clients."

"Howie, you're ruining me. I used to go out on those night patrols on Tarawa and Saipan and say, thank goodness, the press is reporting the truth about me."

"Those guys *were,* I guess. It's the whole picture that bothers me."

"What do you mean?" Tom slumped into Marty's chair. He could see her laughing and chatting with Ainsworth and he wished she'd hurry up.

"Well—like where does it all come from?" Howie asked plaintively. "Who decides what news is? What news goes out? How it's reported? Forget the New York *Times.* There's nothing they can't do. But take this operation. You know what our great far-flung foreign service is, what it really is?"

"F. M. Ainsworth."

"Nah, he's the window dressing. I guess he has to be showy and dramatic like that—to make up for the missing parts. To begin with, most of our correspondents are *nationals* of the country they're in. So we pay 'em in *yen* or *zlotys,* just enough to buy rice and a piece of fish. They work at other things—usually a local paper—to make out. Then we got a bunch of American kids, getting maybe sixty-five bucks a week. And a coupla pros like Ainsworth."

"That's the whole group?"

"Except for one thing. We buy complete rights to stuff like Reuters, the Latin American News Service, West Europe Press—stuff prepared and put out just like us by *other* agencies. So we have the right to rerun on *our* teleprinter anything they put out. We only credit them if we're worried it ain't true. It's like a cow's stomach. They digest it once and vomit it up, and we eat it again, and put it out. The whole news business is like that. Everyone eats on everyone else. Except the *Times.* They put out their own and check yours. Half the time our foreign report isn't even *our* news—we bought it from some outfit like Asiatic News Association—mistakes and all. Oh, we add some mistakes of our own to spice it up, and a few lines from the *Britannica* for background, but that's it. A volcano blew up in Peru one night and we hadn't had a man in Peru in seventeen years. But we ran four thousand words of copy for the newspapers—all borrowed or stolen."

"Howie, my dollink boy," Tom said. "You're very bad for me. Marty keeps telling me what a great career I could have in journalism."

Howie Markowitz pointed to a creased photograph tacked to the wall adjacent to his desk. "See him?" he asked Tom. "That's the overseas press corps." The photo was of a young Chinese or Japanese, his hair brush-cut, wearing a military blouse. He was slightly cross-eyed.

"Should I know him?" Tom asked.

"Maybe his by-line. That's Harlan Goon. Late lamented Chinese correspondent for WNA. He covered Chiang Kai-shek for us until the Japs caught up with him. Then he sold out in three minutes. Started filing stuff about the glorious conquering troops of the Greater East Asia Co-Prosperity Sphere. Natch, he was canned. However, WNA owed him six hundred bucks back pay. That, I might add, was over a year's salary. They paid Goon in cigarettes and chocolate, mostly."

"Where's he now?"

"He sold out again. He joined the Chinese Communists. Escaped from the Japs and put the blocks to WNA. Only man ever to get the edge on this outfit. He kept screaming for his six hundred bucks and the home office here kept telling him he was a traitor. But they forgot one thing. They had bought him a jeep. They kept hollering at him to surrender the jeep and he kept asking for his six bills. Finally he fixed *them*. He sold the jeep for seven hundred dollars—*their* jeep. That was just before he decided he could make a better deal with Mao. I kind of admire him. I always pictured him in my mind as a coolie rickshaw boy—pulling his cab around downtown Shanghai and stopping every now and then to take a photograph or interview someone. But he had guts, all right."

The phone rang and Markowitz picked it up, cradling it expertly under one ear. "Hallo, WNA," he mumbled. "Whah? A fire in a saloon in Bayonne? How many stiffs? Two? Nah, we can't use it. Thanks anyway, George." He hung up. "That's a domestic Harlan Goon. Jersey stringer. He gets three bucks if we use the piece. You heard me tell him—it wasn't morbid enough. Gotta be at least four dead to make the national wire this late at night."

Marty came out of the office, her audience with the foreign correspondent concluded. She looked joylessly at the spike of unwritten dayside stories on her desk.

"Howie's telling me about Harlan Goon," Tom said.

"He is? He embroiders it every time he does. It's his revenge on American journalism."

Markowitz chewed on a yellow pencil. "What you spendin' all that time in there with Ainsworth for?" he asked. "Still angling for the overseas job?"

"What's this about an overseas job?" Tom asked. "What—"

"Shhh," Marty said. "Not so loud. I'll tell you in a minute. We'll stop in at Charlie's for a drink."

She made a hasty deal with Howie for him to finish her rewrite. Tom got the notion that she sloughed work off on the fat boy regularly; he didn't seem to mind. Leaving, they walked quickly by Hoag's scarred desk, down the aisle of stuttering teleprinters, and into the elevator.

Charlie's bar was dark and inhospitable. In contrast to alleged "newspapermen's bars" in the neighborhood which charged seven dollars for steak, and consequently were off limits to newspapermen, it was an honest Third Avenue rathole where reporters and rewrite men ate and drank. Whisky was thirty-five cents the shot, and the clientele was stimulating—winos, fairies and colored porters from Grand Central.

They sat in a rear booth, holding hands. He had slept with her for three months, yet her presence never failed to induce a delicious pounding in his chest, a euphoria that dispelled all doubts. If he, loser Sorrento, a fellow who had trouble kissing girls goodnight four years ago, could make it with Martha Maitland, there was nothing too rugged for him, no ascents too steep, no problems insoluble.

"Why didn't we go right to your place?" he asked impatiently.

"Because I can never talk to you there."

"Who wants to talk?"

"*I* want to sometimes, but you're so wound up. The way you throw yourself at me and start mumbling and fussing. Not that I don't appreciate it, but it makes discussion impossible."

"It's your fault." He kissed her ear, letting his tongue explore her cheek and neck. She smelled of perfumed soap; his hand shook involuntarily as he stroked her knee.

"Tom! What's the matter with you? You make me feel as though I'm fifteen. Out on my first neck."

He let his lips rest in the hollow of her neck. "I love you. That's it. I don't want anything else, ever. Let's go to your place."

"No. Let's have a drink and talk."

"Okay. I'm this anxious because I'm trying to make up for everything I missed in the way of dames. Sometimes I worry you'll wake up one morning and just as I'm ready to make love to you again, you'll tell me it's all over. Fini. Kaput. You've had enough of me and my Latin passion. I bet I'm the first man ever cried in bed with you."

"You are. Now can we talk about something else?"

"What was going on with you and Herbert Marshall in there—the foreign correspondent from Madison, Indiana?"

"I was asking him about my chances for an overseas assignment."

"Overseas? What about me—I mean us—"

"Will you give me a chance, Tom?"

A furtive waiter brought them hefty double-shot glasses of bourbon.

"Ainsworth said there was a possibility they might be needing a smart news gal in the London bureau. It's not certain, but they have big postwar expansion plans for WNA—a new foreign feature service. He seemed to think I might fit in. He's going to talk to the general manager about it."

Tom scowled into the liquor. "What does that do to me? Where am I in this plot to send you out of the country?"

"Well, I couldn't very well get into *that* with him. It's not as if we're married—or even engaged. What was I to say? Mr. Ainsworth, do you have a job for the fellow I sleep with?"

He grasped her forearm. "You can't go. I won't let you. No."

"I'm not going anywhere yet. The job isn't definite. Besides—why couldn't you come along? If you still have that notion about doing graduate work, you could do it in England—or France—or anywhere else for that matter."

"Yeah. With my luck they'll assign you to the Naples Bureau. I can go to barber college with my relatives."

"Tom, it would be a wonderful opportunity for me—an overseas assignment. I'd love it."

"Howie was telling me what those WNA overseas jobs are like."

"*Howie.* He's bitter about everything."

"Sixty-five bucks a week, and you work twelve hours a day, six days a week and you're on call Sundays. And when they can you, you really get canned—no severance or anything. I heard all about Harlan Goon."

"I think he made that story up."

"Maybe he did, but that whole WNA setup bothers me. It's rotten. They steal news. I don't mind anybody stealing, but if you do it, stop posing as the savior of the human race and the true defender of democracy. If newspapers would only stop loving themselves up in public all the time, I might respect them.

Every time I read a paper, some editor or publisher is reminding me I'd be in jail or dead from cancer or illiterate if it wasn't for his half-ass rag. They can't be that important. All I can remember about newspapers since I was thirteen is that they hated Roosevelt."

"Aren't you the caustic fellow!"

"Marty—I'm going back to the University. I registered yesterday. I spoke to your father, and I'm going into the Graduate Department of Anthropology."

She took a deep breath and said nothing, then took a draught of the harsh whisky. "When did you make your mind up about that?"

"I don't know. I just got sick of sitting on my duff listening to my mother complain. I beat it down to school and filled out the forms."

"What makes you think you'll like it? Head-measuring and linguistics . . ."

"I'm not sure I will. I know this. I like your old man. He's the opposite of those cruds who write newspaper editorials telling the world how great they are. He's wise to them. He's wise to a lot of things. It's the difference between crap and truth. The older and dumber I get, I know one thing. There's an awful lot of fraud getting sold. More now than before the war, I think. A big business in blivits. I want to learn more and I want to learn it from somebody like Maitland." He leaned forward. "I was looking through some lecture notes from your father's undergraduate course—and it was as if I had never left school. I want to pick up where I stopped in 1942."

"Don't start quoting his lectures to me." She cocked her head and intoned: "*The forces through which society changes men and is itself changed are still imperfectly understood. As social scientists, I fear we have raised many questions and supplied disappointingly few answers. . . .*"

He drained the bourbon. "What is it with you and your father? What's this perpetual gripe you've got against him?"

"Tom, what's the use of explaining it to you? I don't dislike Hall *actively*. I just—well, just as you seem to think he's wise to everything going on in the world, I think I'm wise to him. I know him too well."

"Like how?"

"I'll tell you how. He's a professional primitive-lover. He isn't a force for social reform, as you seem to think. He likes his

Indians and Africans for their *own* sake, as a means to glorify himself. He was always running off to some Pacific Island or some filthy Indian reservation. Any excuse to get out of our house. And what does all his work prove? Not a damn thing."

She appeared grave and distracted. "I think Hall is dragging you into this. Do you really want to struggle along like a damned pauper for six or seven years, Tom? Living on government handouts and fellowships? I wonder if you do."

"Why should your old man be so hot for me?"

"He's always prowling around for strong young types to bolster his department. Leaders. Football players with brains. He had his eye on some big Swede two years ago, and the fellow was killed when a munitions dump exploded in South Carolina. Then it was a Canadian boy who had done some work with the Eskimo. You know the kind—a snowshoer, right out of Jack London. Now you."

"Hey, I saw the guy who's his assistant now. Benny Peltz from the Bronnix. A wire-haired terrorist who figured me right off for a fascist beast. He doesn't fit your cockeyed notion."

"That's the point. Peltz is what he's inundated with. He claims that graduate school is filled with Peltzes—misfits, the walking dead. He'd like his graduate students to be able to stand up and tell the Chamber of Commerce to go to hell, and get away with it."

"Wants they should meet a payroll, hah?"

"Don't ask me to explain. It's all part of Hall's crazy notions about society. He's written something about it—the give and take, the constant ebbing and flowing of forces, the increasing intermingling of caste, status and role. One of his heroes is that insurance executive who writes poetry."

"Wallace Stevens. A good man."

"You'll get along fine with Hall, I can see that. He'll have you chewing betel nut in a few weeks."

"I might like it."

He sounded surly and oppressed. She moved closer to him, inviting a kiss, and he obliged, with a gentle grace that spoke of long hours together. Their bodies knew each other well enough to be casual and sweet—ferocity had evanesced after their initial matings.

"Tom, are you sure you want to do this? Bury yourself?"

"It's a decent burial."

"There isn't anything you can't do, if you really make your

mind up. I wish you'd think about it. I know a lot about newspaper and magazine people—you're brighter and more original than any of them. Why don't you give it a try? It's rough at first, the pay is meagre . . . but you could work your way up. Or free-lance for magazines. And there's radio and pretty soon television. Why, for anybody with *any* flair for writing this is the time to get into it! I just wish *I* was more aggressive. I'd be at some ad agency now earning twice what I get."

"No. I can't. I want to catch my breath. I don't want to be another Harlan Goon. First he was for Chancre Jack, then the Nips, then the Reds. Anyone who'd pay the way. To hell with that. I've proved my loyalty to Alma Mater and country. Now I want to start learning something."

"Aren't you noble!" she cried. "I just hope you don't deceive yourself. You may be terribly let down when you find out how unproductive and pointless University work is."

"I told you—I can always bug out. You want me to try writing, I can still do that while I go to school. In five years, I could write my life history—on *lasagna* noodles with a ball-point pen."

They ordered another round, and for a while they sat in silence, watching a sad tableau of elderly fairies in narrow suits, old Irish ladies in basketball sneakers and dignified Negro porters.

"Tom," Marty said, "are you sure you aren't going back to the University as an escape?"

"I'm sure I *am*."

"But isn't that wrong? Just to immerse yourself in that easy life because you *think* it's what you want? Because the government will pay? You'll be over thirty before you're earning any kind of money, and it'll be damn little money." She stopped. "Why am I acting so wifely and motherly?"

"I like it, baby," Tom said. "Talk more like that."

"But it is true, isn't it? All you fellows scurrying back to school —for what? To remind yourselves of how dandy it was before you went off?"

"I figure I'm entitled to some indulgence after putting my heroic life on the line. Be patient. Besides I always figured we were in no hurry to get married. It's too much fun this way. Isn't it?"

She rested her head on his shoulder. "It's marvelous. It's the best time I've ever had."

"We get married, we might not like it so well. That's what my married buddies tell me."

"I'm happy to keep it this way, Tom. I like my job and—"

"But you ain't going to England. Not to be no female Harlan Goon."

Later, the thrustings and thrashings of love allayed all argument. Each chapter of passion seemed to elevate and sensitize Tom. He wondered if he had best cultivate a nonchalance about their loving. The joy was so overwhelming, the impressions on brain and body so exquisite that he feared his capacity to experience *other* pleasures would atrophy. Unburdened by the trivia of domesticity and the strains of family, they indulged their bodies fully; and Tom, pausing sometimes in passion, would whisper: "It's too good. It's the best thing I ever knew. How can anything be as good after this?" And she would laugh, slightly on her guard, still nurturing her abhorrence of excess, except in the crashing seconds of climax, when all that had been hoarded and minimized was shatteringly unleashed.

That night, long after they had exhausted themselves, they lay awake in the narrow bed, fulfilled. It pleased Tom that her apartment was so bare and utilitarian. They needed nothing beyond their bodies, the aching mutual need that sometimes made him wince when he was away from her. He felt a mild guilt for his harsh words to his mother about his sister's forthcoming marriage to the neighbor's boy. Perhaps this was all that he and Marty really sought; he owed Rita and Georgie Schultheis an apology.

"Tom," she said quietly. "Let's not worry about what you're going to do or where I'm going. It's so good now. Why should we make ambitious plans? I don't care for those classmates of yours who had their lives all figured out—the girl, the job, the apartment—any more than you do."

"Right," he yawned. "Why spoil it with marriage? When we want to get hitched, we can. In the Criminal Courts Building by Judge d'Ambrosio."

"He sounds fine."

"On second thought, he probably wouldn't do it. No Italian Cath'lic judge would want to get in trouble with his constituents by conducting a mixed marriage. We'd have to get a Protestant or a Jewish judge."

"Are there any Protestant judges in New York City? I sometimes think Newbold Morris is the only Protestant in town."

"A few. They get elected in off-years." Tom stretched, turned, and embraced her. "My mother started to give me a bad time today," he said. "Neapolitan mamas—they're real terrors with their sons. She finally was generous about it. Anything I wanted to do was fine."

"I don't want to hurt her. I know you're her treasure—"

"Yes. A delicate child with weak ankles. I wish I had a little of my old lady's stubbornness. She's a medium tank. Know how she votes? She goes into that booth and she stomps down every lever over a name ending in a vowel. Parties—platforms—issues—what are they? Just get all the *paisans* in office! I trapped her one day. She admitted to me she voted for a guy named Shapiro, by mistake. He was the only Jew ever elected to the state assembly from our district."

She hugged him. "Cruel boy. Why'd you have to disillusion her about Assemblyman-elect Shapiro?"

"She deserved it. What kind of way is that to vote?"

"She was being loyal. It's something she understood."

They lay quietly, listening to early-morning street noises—a car protesting as its driver attempted to wedge it into too small a space; the blurred inanities of a drunk being ejected from a First Avenue saloon; a superintendent's Cerberus barking warnings to scurrying rats.

"You're good for me, Tom," she said. "You don't make any demands."

"I demanded you into the sack."

"Not that. You don't make demands on *life*—on the world. You're like me. You're burying yourself in school when you could have the world. And me—I'm content to flop around on night-side rewrite. I wouldn't know what to say if they offered me the overseas job tomorrow. Is it good to be that way? So negative?"

"It helps."

"It's so easy to be involved—to force yourself to be everything and try everything and earn everything and buy everything. I can't do it. I get confused in Macy's. When I'm with you, I have an ally."

"Once more," he whispered.

"You weren't even listening to me."

The following spring Marty was offered the foreign job. In fashion typical of the barbaric organization, she was advised that a minor job in the London bureau was hers—provided she accepted *five dollars less per week* than her current salary of eighty dollars and provided *she pay her own transportation* to England. This was a common *modus operandi* at the wire service. Hundreds of bright, talented young people—in and out of the organization—hungered for the glory of a foreign correspondent's job, little knowing that it consisted largely of monitoring a Reuters machine and refiling trivia. In their mind's eye they envisioned themselves in trench coats and Homburgs, young Ainsworths, dining with the Prime Minister in order to get a beat on the new treaty. The dream persisted and the labor supply was endless. Marty, luckier than she could imagine, was of the super-elect in being tapped for the honor. The notion that she accept less money and pay her way seemed perfectly logical to the executives of WNA. When she turned them down they were aghast at her ingratitude. "Something screwy about that broad," Ed Hoag confided, suppressing a whisky belch. "Here's her biggest chance and she blows it. She'd knock 'em dead with that face."

And yet, in turning it down, Marty could not help feeling a sense of loss. The excuse that she used—to herself and to WNA—was that the terms were ludicrous. It was the kind of offer you made to an untalented journalism-school graduate with rich parents. But at the time—and for many years afterward—she was bothered by the feeling that WNA's stinginess had been a convenient rationalization. She wanted the job. She wanted to live in London. She wanted to lunch with F. M. Ainsworth and spend week ends at Stratford-on-Avon. In analyzing her rejection she always came back to the University and the lurching figure of her father. He had been the magnet that had drawn Tom out of the competitive world into the academic fairyland. Tom, in opting to join the ragged ranks, had drawn her along. They had never argued about the London job; she had merely followed his lead in condemning WNA for their niggardly nastiness. At times, that spring, rejoinders formed in her mind: *they'll raise my salary as soon as I prove myself . . . I can borrow money for transportation . . . the opportunity, darling, how can I miss out on it . . . you can continue your studies there . . . the University of London or . . .* She never articulated them. Tom was finishing his first year of graduate school. He was just getting into things, having mastered the factual intricacies of geology, botany and zoology. It was unthinkable that he leave Maitland.

She never held her decision against Tom. At times when she found herself regretting it, it was easier to make her father the villain. Nor did she nurture any antagonism toward Tom's career. If penurious anthropologist he wished to be, let him be one. The harsh reality of economics did not concern them. They would get married when they were good and ready, and they waited until Tom was a year shy of his doctorate. Marty continued working: she was making top minimum by then, one hundred and thirty dollars a week and was the regular dayside rewrite "man." She never once revived the question of the foreign assignment; never again criticized Tom's apprenticeship to Maitland. Occasionally, in those early childless years of marriage, she would prod him on his writing. When she did, he barely knew what she was talking about. He had too much to learn, too much to catch up with to fiddle around with a skill he doubted he possessed. One night in their tiny apartment on the Heights, she watched him sweating and puzzling over his thesis—*Santa Rosa: A Study of Acculturation in Modern Meso-American Society,* and she could not help wondering, with a pang of despair, how much money might accrue to them if the thick stack of typed white onionskins on his desk represented a potential best-selling manuscript, or a screenplay, or anything that related to the *other* world.

PART III

1 *A Defection*

THE memories agitated him with their clear outlines and primary colors. They were like comic strips. He almost saw white balloons crammed with neat lettering emanating from the characters' cartoonish mouths. He did not mind the loss of sleep. In service he had learned how little of it was needed. Staring at the moon-splashed walls, he heard voices rising from the quarters below. He could hear Ballard whispering—the words unintelligible through the plasterboard—and then Peltz, his Bronx whine growing louder as he engaged in angry pleading. He heard the thump of boxes or luggage being manipulated. He got out of bed and put on his shorts.

"What the devil's going on there?" Marty asked.

"Go to sleep. I'm going to find out."

He walked around the splintery balcony, down the steps. As he approached the rear entrance to the boathouse, Ballard's figure appeared in the doorway. He was carrying a cardboard box of notes and books and he gripped a rope-bound suitcase lightly with one hand. As he stepped down, Peltz followed him. Dave halted when he saw Tom.

"Sorry I woke you up, Tom," he said.

"What is this? Moving Day?" Tom asked. "Where you going?"

"I been telling him he's nuts," Peltz whined. "He's runnin' out. He's going in with that Hilltown crowd. He'll get himself killed."

"Is that right, Dave?" Tom asked.

The tropic moon turned Ballard's skin a deep burgundy. Tom noticed there was a fresh bandage on his forearm.

"I'm sorry, Tom. They made a Christian out of me."

"I'm telling him he's crazy!" Peltz cried. "They'll murder him! A smart New York coon sticking his two cents in where it ain't welcome. They don't stand a chance. I can tell him. I know all about this. It never works!"

Ballard laughed. "Benny can't bear the thought of me going into battle."

Two tremulous faces appeared in the doorway. The Burleys eavesdropped, terrified. Peltz spun around furiously. "You two get back in! This is none of your business!" They whisked their heads inside.

"They bombed Harkey's church tonight," Ballard said. "He's

waiting up on the highway for me. I left the pickup for you near Mr. Ellenbogen's driveway."

"They bombed the church?" Tom asked. "Did anyone get hurt?"

"Only Jesus."

Tom's mouth opened, and he took a step back. He could understand Dave's enlistment in the battle, but he was unprepared for what sounded like recidivism. Was this Dave Ballard, the scientist, the calm man, dusting and washing bits of pottery?

Dave noted Tom's aggrieved look. "I meant it *literally,* Tom," he laughed. "They ruined the façade of the church. The statue of Jesus was knocked down. A couple of people were hit with glass fragments. Harkey thinks they're deliberately using dinky bombs to start with. They'll work their way up when the boycott starts."

"I'll miss you," Tom said. "We're just getting hot. Maitland says we should find the rest of that court, or other signs of the Arawak village. Don't you want to be in on it?"

Dave shook his head. "I'm past that. I left my notes on your table. You can reach me at Harkey's if you have any questions about them. I still haven't doped out the stratification."

"You might get hurt. You sure you want to do this?" Having posed the obvious dissuader, Tom was sorry as soon as he asked the question.

"That's what I'm telling him!" Peltz cried. "He's dead! He's licked and he won't admit it!"

"Pipe down, Benny," Tom said. "How about it? And what about the teaching job Maitland promised you?"

Ballard shook his melonlike head. "I'm no hero. I'm the biggest coward you ever saw." He shifted his enormous body. In the selenial glow he looked like some ancient stone menhir come to life. Druid priests should have been dancing around him in the ghostly light. "I have to tell you this, Tom. I'm leaving you because I think they'll be on *your* neck soon. Harkey thinks we were followed out here tonight. A car stopped in back of us on the causeway and a couple of guys got out and looked where I was headed. Then they swung around back to the city. That cop—Fry. He's been questioning a lot of Harkey's people about me—and the dig. So I guess the sooner I disaffiliate, like John L. Lewis says, the better for all of us."

"See? See?" Peltz cried. "It's always that way—you can't win! They got all the strength! Good for him, Tom, good for him—let the dumb bastard go out and get his head kicked in!" Peltz's voice verged on womanish hysteria. "And now he's got *you* tarred! Oh boy, isn't he great! Ballard, he's gonna change the world! He's gonna put love in their hearts with that minister! Well, I got news for you, Ballard, nobody wants love down here! They *like* hate. They feed on it. It keeps them in business, buddy!" Peltz appeared to be crying—a tearless, frenzied crying, the wail of a man trapped by his own failings.

"Shut up, Ben," Tom said tersely.

At the head of the steps, Marty, in flimsy nightdress, awakened by Peltz's outcries, had appeared. Her voice was heavy with sleep and annoyance. She called down: "What are you all screaming about?"

Tom looked up. "It's okay, Marty. Dave is leaving us. Benny got a little excited."

"Don't you people ever grow up?" she yawned.

"I'm sorry, Marty," Ballard stage-whispered. "My fault. Give my best to the kids."

She waved at him as she left. "I will, Dave."

"So long, Tom," Ballard said. He gripped Sorrento's hand. "Tell Maitland how sorry I am. I'd like to be in on the find. I know it's there." He looked up the slope at the precious trenches, the gaping exploratory incisions into the corpus of the past that he had helped plan, dig, interpret. In Ballard's mind the unfinished work recalled painfully his graduation from high school. He remembered touring the biology classroom where he had worked on a project with Cecropia moths—nurturing them from egg, to fat larvae, to chrysalis. He would miss seeing them emerge as handsome, red-brown imagos, and he almost regretted going on to the state university without his beloved moths in full wing.

"You can drop by from time to time," Tom said, as Ballard began plodding up the incline.

Dave shook his head. "I better not. I just hope my misadventures don't hurt you. Maybe I'll call you in a couple of weeks."

Sorrento watched him trudge up the sandy incline—his oversized feet leaving elephantine spoor on the soft earth. In one mahogany arm he cradled his box of papers and textbooks; with the other he lugged the tramp's suitcase. At the crest of the rise he paused for a moment to look at the trench where the mysterious white stones lay embedded, appeared to make some silent farewell to them, then proceeded toward the gate, beyond which the hypnotic Harkey waited for him. His departure had an unreal and disturbing quality to it. Tom had once seen a movie in which

Boris Karloff, a religious nut, went loony in the last reel—wandering out in the desert with a makeshift cross to be cut down by Bedouin bullets. Any minute he expected a fusillade of enfilading fire to blast Ballard, and topple him into the trenches. If he insisted in being a clay pigeon, Tom told himself, he surely would be the hugest target in the state. And then he halted his cynical musings, realizing that he wished he could assist Ballard, comfort him, assure him everything would be fine. The Negro crime rate in Philadelphia would go down; the schools would be integrated; the disfranchisement of Hilltown would be repealed. Ballard vanished around the protective fencing. They heard a decrepit motor spit and cough, then the sound of tires screeching off.

"That's the end-a *him,*" Peltz pronounced shakily.

"Don't be so sure, Ben. If he gets burned, it'll be for the right reasons."

"Hah! Ask me, I'm an expert. Black and White, Unite and Fight! I been there, Tom."

"You didn't learn much, Benny. You think because you landed on your can everybody does? You got in with bad companions. When they made you suffer, you decided *nothing* was any good. Nothing was worth the trouble. Anybody who tries is doomed, and trying is no good anyway, because it's not in our hands. Don't worry about Dave. He'll manage."

"That's what you think. He's red meat for them. A smart New York nigger with an education, living here with white folks. That Lieutenant Fry—he's a sissy compared to some of the customers Dave's gonna have to explain it to."

Tom looked at him with mild disgust. "Know something, Benny? You're scared stiff."

"I'm a realist. How much good you think Dave is gonna do anybody? He'll make it worse for the colored people. He'll get the crackers on his back. Besides, nobody wants any improvement for the handkerchief-heads. Nobody *anywhere* really wants to do 'em good. Up North. The Middle West. Sure, if a guy's a great halfback or outfielder and he's black they love 'em. But what about the whole mob of miserable dinges in Strawberry Mansion or Harlem or Chicago, hah? Who likes them? Who wantsta help them? Maybe a couple of leftover social workers who didn't have the brains to go into advertising. That's who. I tell you the truth, Tom, *nobody* likes them. You and me and Maitland, we told the world there isn't anything called race. Race is myth. But race is *everything,* no matter what you and Maitland say. To hell with what Ruth Benedict wrote. You go tell some Hunky steel worker in Gary, Indiana, who pays union dues, whether he thinks a stove-lid is as good as him. What? Some dirty nigger as good as him? You'll find out about race, buddy. And Ballard'll find out, too. In the showdown, there ain't *anyone* on his side."

"Benny, what's happened to you."

"You know something? I ain't so sure I like Ballard myself. Why was Maitland gonna get him the faculty spot in Vermont?" Peltz's voice wavered. "What about *me?* What about all the years I been hanging around?"

"Go to bed, Ben," Tom said. "If you hadn't been planning the world revolution and then explaining to the committees why you were so horrible, maybe you'd have the Ph.D. by now."

"Sure, you can talk. Father-in-law to look after you."

Tom walked away from him. Ben was his cross and he would bear him—up to a point. The more you attempted to make Peltz analyze himself, to come to terms with his self-inflicted torments, the more obstinate and suicidal he became. If he could not understand that Ballard had been one of his best friends, that the Negro's act in leaving them was as gallant as anything he would ever witness, then he was beyond redemption. As Peltz vanished into the house, Tom heard him issue a rude reprimand to Wilma and Oran. Even in mortification, a touch of the commissar remained.

2 *The Committee of Seventy-five*

FROM his suite's balcony, Ira deKay looked down with disguised revulsion at the loggia. Kitty Schmitt was staging a fashion show. She raced around in glandular fervor, dragging and pushing Barney, the photographer winding and focusing his sixteen-millimeter Filmo with hateful vigor. Ten nubile models, Beach high school girls, comported themselves with self-conscious dignity in authentic Riviera beachwear, moving with writhe of buttock and quiver of thigh among the torpid guests. Mr. Banjo was there, scurrying about at the end of his leash, sipping this man's screwdriver, nipping this lady's ankle. The orangutan wore a teal-blue cabana suit and an Italian straw hat. His shanks, furred with long ruddy strands, were a trifle shocking. They protruded obscenely from the baggy shorts and destroyed the illusion that he was a little boy with a round, red face and too much upper lip. The project, noisily strawbossed by Kitty, was part of Ira's plot for enticing *Our Heritage* to the resort city. The newsreel would be given, gratis, to the network—along with several dozen swimsuits and sports outfits for various key personnel. It would be telecast to *Our Heritage's* nationwide audience, publicizing the Beach, the Peruviana, Mr. Banjo and La Mode Sportswear, a local manufacturer who would then be permitted to contribute to the fund to bring the program to the Beach. It was not merely a case of one hand washing the other. Ira's manipulations assumed the nature of an acrobat in the bathtub, scrubbing and laving each separate member with another. Feet washed hands, arms washed belly, head washed groin, the whole corpus writhing and giggling and working up bubbly lathers in Ira's warm bath of pleasure.

But the prospect of deal and counterdeal, of payoff, tie-in and loot failed to stimulate him. On this cloudless, hot morning, he felt listless, as if the perpetual juggling was draining his energies. The panorama below—the sunlit brown models, the happy guests, the chattering ape, the lusty, prancing figure of Miss Schmitt—all these seemed irrelevant. Ira was a man rarely engloomed; but so thick was his malaise at that moment that he was incapable of savoring the tawny limbs and breasts of the young promenaders. Normally, he would be engaged in "casting" for his evening's frolics. Now, he found only dismay in their hard young behinds and upturned boobies. Kitty Schmitt was not much of a help, either.

"Zotz!" she shrieked at Ira. "Zile kai! *Yaaah*. Hey, everybody, look at deKay!" A selection of guests, eager to be "in" on some apparent byplay between the Girl from Television and that Funny Fellow with the Jokes, turned anointed heads upward to see the grinning man on the balcony.

It distressed Ira that she had so swiftly adopted his expressions, his rhythms of speech, his mannerisms. She was that kind of bedmate. One session in the sack, and she aggressively assumed the traits of her partner. Ira had worked hard and long at his role and he resented anyone filching bits of it, particularly as the result of one unsatisfactory romp. He would have to wind up affairs with

Miss Schmitt, nail down *Our Heritage* and send her back on a luxury flight, with the requisite amount of graft.

In the inner office he found Si and Cleo sitting mopily at their desks. Mermelstein had just returned his phone to its hook. He had a stack of opened letters in front of him, and he toyed with them nervously.

"We just got another protest on the peyote ritual," he said unhappily. "That makes fourteen calls and twenty-two letters. I told you we shouldna got mixed up in that. Ira, no matter what Maitland says, people think that stuff is *dope*. Narcotics. And why we had to send the film out to the networks and the newsreel syndicates—the whole country knows now, and they're mad at us."

Ira sprawled on the gold-flecked couch. "Run me down on the letters, sweetie," he said. "Maybe there's a way out."

"There isn't, Ira. Except we drop the nutty idea and send John Throws Knife back to Oklahoma. Most of the letters are from missionaries. They think the True American Church is a front for dope addicts. Not a real religion at all. Listen to this one, from a minister in Sioux Falls. . . . 'I have seen at first hand what havoc peyote eating can do to an Indian village. The men of the tribe became mindless addicts, thinking only of their next bean. Attendance at my mission church, the Middle Brethren, fell to a record low as the practice of this noxious habit grew. How you can dare to include such bestial savagery in an exhibit aimed at exalting man's highest aspirations confounds me. I suspect you have been sold a false bill of goods by Hall Maitland, a notorious corrupter of Indians. It may please you to know that Maitland has been barred by state law from many reservations because of his espousal of peyote.' "

Si stopped and wiped his eyeglasses on his tie.

"It goes on like this. Some are worse. That last call was from the head of the State Society of Naturopaths. He says peyote has been known to cause blindness and cancer." Si's features seemed to converge around his babyish mouth. "So far I've been holding the newspapers off. But I can't forever, Ira. They want to run a big piece on peyote. A pro-and-con thing. They want a statement from you or Ellenbogen on whether you're going ahead with this peyote deal."

Ira barely heard him. In an hour or so, Martha Maitland would be in his cabana, changing from her street clothes to one of his high-fashion swimsuits. For a few moments she would be naked and alone inside the striped chamber. What was wrong with him? Was he fourteen years old and back in Moriah Center, North Dakota, waiting behind the barn for Celia Underdahl?

"Ira, we oughta plead for time. Give 'em an evasive answer. Like the announcement on peyote was premature and we are now taking the matter under consideration, consulting ecclesiastical experts on the matter. At the moment there is no plan to include a peyote tepee in *The Spirit of Man.* Okay?"

"Reet. You write it, Si baby. Check Erwin before you send it to them."

"We better. Ellenbogen's furious. They been calling him also, but he got so mad, he had all the calls switched to me."

Cleo looked up from her desk. It was the cleanest desk in the world. The immaculate Remington had never been touched, except to address personal mail; the rubberoid surface was unscratched; the spring-controlled fluorescent lamp, capable of assuming any angle and all positions, had the look of just having been unpacked and assembled.

"Serves us right, if you ask me," Cleo said. "Fooling around with those New York creeps. Honest, Ira, from the day you started with those creeps digging over on the island, you've been in trouble. Maybe it isn't my part to say, but you been neglecting the business."

Ira shut his eyes.

"Cleo's right, Ira," Si said. He chewed nervously on his pipe. "The bank balance is the lowest it's been. I tell you, if Ellenbogen hadn't taken over this project, we'd be in trouble. The Peruviana is hollering they aren't getting enough in return for the rooms they let us have. I told Helene not to pay any bills this month until we review our expenses. I mean it, Ira, we have to pay some attention to the other accounts. *La Mode* is sore they were left out of the *Life* spread, after you promised them—"

Cleo tilted her fine nose upward. The premonition of rejection was eating at her again. She had just enrolled Robin in an expensive private school. She had outfitted him as splendidly as if he were a millionaire's child. The darling boy was no cheap item, and without Ira's one hundred and fifty dollars a week, plus extracurricular fees and fringe benefits, what would she do?

"Ira, Si and me are worried about you," she said. "If you'd give us more to do—more responsibility. The clients all want you, and you're never around. You're out at Ellenbogen's, or down at the pool all day with—"

"Slack off, baby," Ira said. He began to pace the office. "We'll tie down some loose ends right now. Si, take care of the papers on that Indian hassle. What *about* the new clients?"

Si took a manila folder from his desk. "Well right off, there's the Beach University. They want action."

The Beach University, as startling as any of the luxury hotels, was hell-bent for academic honors. A series of *gaffes* had rendered it suspect among its older, more austere sisters. There had been marked abuse of the normal prerogatives of any large college to recruit and pay athletes. Its peers had deemed it malodorous even by their lights, when the university's football coach attended the funeral of a rival colleague and handed out prospectuses. Its faculty was meagre, its curriculum slightly more advanced than that of Great Neck High School, and its student body was fanatically preoccupied with water skiing. It was the kind of school that would inevitably turn to Ira deKay to improve its public face and render it more acceptable to the severe bluenoses who sat in judgment on such matters.

"Hmmm. Zile University, Zotzville, USA. They ain't much help," Ira said. "Their idea of publicity is coeds in motorboats. The football team practicing in the surf. Si, colleges are your baby. What do you suggest?"

Si shuffled some papers. "Well—the main idea is they want prestige. You know, they're a laughing stock with all that water skiing." He looked at various mimeo'd handouts and glossy photos from a brochure issued by the Beach University.

"Hey," Si said. "Here's something gives me an idea. They started something new. An annual award for Humanitarian Contributions to Latin American Progress. The ceremony is Friday afternoon." He squinted at the page. "The guy getting the plaque is General Enrico Avilas, President of Santa Rosa."

"A banana-republic chappie? Who cares?"

"Well, they'll expect some help from us. The Latin American bit is very big today. Everybody runs down there to make a goodwill speech whenever we cut the imports on lead and zinc."

"Si, baby, you're so *up* on the news."

Si got up and leaned against his desk. "Here's the thing. What they need more than anything else is *recognition*. When you say Beach University anywhere, people think of water skiers. They want academic standing. And all the local hotshots will be there —editors, publishers, a couple of ex-governors. That's fine. But we can offer 'em one more added attraction—to really make people notice. The kinda thing that'll get people to respect them."

"What you gonna do, baby? Send Mr. Banjo over in cap and gown?" Ira asked.

"He'd be adorable!" Cleo offered.

"Nope. We can give 'em *Maitland.*"

Ira frowned. "Doc Maitland? Marty's old man?"

"Yup. He'd make them take notice. You may not realize it, Ira, but he's one of the biggest names in American education. No question about it. The average newspaper reader wouldn't know him, but you can bet your last nickel, college officials will—all over the country. When they read that Professor Hall Maitland has participated in the first award for, ah"—He turned to the mimeographed release again—"Humanitarian Contributions to Latin American Progress, they'll know about it. And they'll respect the Beach University! Not everybody can land a name like that! Maitland just doesn't go around making appearances, I can tell you."

Ira nodded. "Mellow, Si. Set it up."

Si was transported. He clapped his pudgy hands. "We'll save Doc Maitland for *last.* We'll have him make an address of *response,* after the General speaks. You know—to wind the whole affair up."

"Do it!" Ira cried. *"Do it baby!* Don't sit there like you earned your money already!"

When word reached Erwin Ellenbogen that Hall Maitland had been invited to deliver a "response" to General Avilas, and that the anthropologist had accepted, it came as a pleasant late-afternoon advisory to what had been an irritating day.

The morning had started with his secretary calling him from *The Spirit of Man* offices to read the angry letters concerning the peyote matter. Then had come a flurry of calls on the same distressing subject. These he had referred to Mermelstein, who was no help at all. Erwin thought about calling Maitland or Sorrento, to ask them to assist him in drawing up a scientific, rational answer to the cranks. Didn't they assure him that peyote was *not* a narcotic, was *not* habit-forming, that the True American Church was a legitimate religion? But the two of them, along with his own beloved wife, and a half-dozen colored laborers, were again attacking the land with pick-axe and shovel, with trowel and hoe, looking for the southern wall. Erwin felt it wiser to let them proceed: the sooner they concluded, the sooner he could get the architects to work. Temporary stands would have to go up, a program arranged, invitations sent out for the ground-breaking. If Sorrento and his diggers did not find their precious wall (Ellenbogen by now regarded their frantic search as ludicrous—although he dared not express such sentiments to Lila) he would have no choice but to terminate their work. The hour of decision was approaching.

Looking out of his study window, he could see them at their labors. The giant round pit in which the skeletons had been unearthed was almost thirty feet in diameter now. There was no end to the bodies that had been buried there. Erwin found the whole business of opening up graves distasteful in the extreme, but Sorrento and his father-in-law (and now Lila!) went at it with a ghoulish delight that frightened him.

It was true the old bones were odorless and as dry and brittle as eggshells, but still. . . . By now they had excavated more than fifty dead Indians—men, women and children, all in the curious embryonic position which Lila advised him was "fully flexed" burial. All day long, the little redheaded man, Peltz, scurried about with his tape measure, his flit gun and his camera, positioning his tripod, changing plates, recording the remains of the old inhabitants of the islet. The rest of the site was being probed for indications of the south wall. Of course, Lila admitted to him, there was a good chance they'd *never* find it—it might be under the asphalt highway, or across the road. Or worse yet, there might be *no wall at all.* The whole postulation about the ball court and the Arawak settlement would then be unproven. (Erwin dared not tell her, but he had reached the point where he wanted to say "Arawak-Shmarawak, who cares?" He was bored stiff with old Indian cultures, especially when it meant his wife was out there swinging a shovel, getting blisters and calluses on her soft hands, and letting her lovely skin turn a splotchy brown, so that even her customary skill with unguents and powders failed to transform her into the beauty of his bed.) Every now and then Erwin permitted his antagonism to show, and she made him regret it. She had come hurrying in for lunch one day with the news that they had found postholes. "Postholes!" Lila had cried. "We found postholes! Erwin—you should see them—perfect black marks in the earth—with the outline showing! Dr. Maitland says it's very unusual for Glades—more proof that this might be a Caribbean settlement!" And Erwin had looked at her blankly, unable to share her exhilaration, and had commented: "So much excitement over some marks in the ground?" To which Lila had answered scathingly: "If I have to explain its value to you, you'll never understand it anyway. Just forget it." She bit the last three words off with a frigid finality that made him shudder.

The worst of a nagging day was yet to come. Erwin had left for the factory, eager for the familiar sight of the production line, the completely understandable problems of shipments, sales, inventories and backlogs. The rituals of business were too easy for Erwin, and in the summer months, the plant only operated at one-third capacity. He spent most of the afternoon in his office, catching up on correspondence and devising a new method of crating, based on a time-and-motion study he had undertaken himself. His preoccupation with the satisfying rows of digits, the neat diagrams, the meticulously plotted routine, all laid out on a geometric curve, was interrupted by two unexpected callers. Erwin was a friendly and courteous man, and he did not hesitate to let his secretary usher in the visitors. They were both local men, middle-aged and lean, representing themselves as officers of the Committee of Seventy-five. And what was the Committee of Seventy-five? It was a group of leading citizens aimed at maintaining the Southern way of life. Erwin remained civil. He had marginal dealings with such groups, and so long as they deplored violence (and the visitors assured him they did) he found it easy to humor them, nod agreeably and then maintain his fully integrated shop and his interest in improving Negro schools. He had argued the integrated shop with local intransigents long ago and they had succumbed, largely because he paid higher wages than the average factory in that area. No, that was not why the gentlemen had called on Mist' Ellenbogen. They knew Mist' Ellenbogen was a leading citizen and had done a heckova lot for local innustry. They came to him as friends to tell him somethin' he oughta know, and they hoped Mist' Ellenbogen would unnerstan'. Their manner was direct, polite and edged with a full awareness of rank and caste. While Erwin was an outsider and a Jew, he was also rich. And their Southern way of life, along with its emphasis on the perpetuation of racial fraud to enhance economic and social position, also contained in its bushido a good deal of old-fashioned respect for money.

As Erwin studied the two messengers—lean, white-faced men in chain-store suits and cheap ties, their hands freckled and tufted with red hairs—he sensed the delicate balance that existed between them and himself. They were clearly not of the Beach.

They represented an older, harder tradition, one that despite the incursion of New York mores and money, asserted itself periodically, and in so doing advertised to the invaders that the real centers of power lay elsewhere—not in their hotels or factories.

That was it: there was an aura of *power* about the callers, of legions unsummoned, of secret arsenals and spiritual strength that grew out of an old, warped knowledge of defeat. The strength had survived as hatred. And for all its protestations of reasonableness, of moderation and culture, it was based on greed and fear, and Erwin could smell the menace in his air-conditioned office, although the only odor hovering about the two callers was that of Vitalis.

And so they gently advised him of the purpose of their errand. Mist' Ellenbogen must have read in the papers about the nigra boycott of white stores, all growing outa the new bill to redraw lines of voting districts. He surely knew what havoc this would cause in the business life of the community, and what wrong ideas it would give the nigras. They knew Mist' Ellenbogen was a Northerner and hired colored people, and that was surely his right and privilege, and they were all grateful for the business he had brought to the community. On the other hand, they did b'leeve he'd unnerstan' that there were problems that only Southerners appreciated and knew how to handle. Certain extreme elements in the community—white and black—were spoilin' for a fight and those two bombings of that nigra minister were proof that the whole thing might get outa hand unless reasonable people like the Committee of Seventy-five stepped in and halted the whole mess before there was blood spilled.

Erwin halted them. How did this concern him? He was neutral in the affair. He respected their views. He would like to see the colored people aided, their lot improved. But he realized this took years of doing, of education and understanding. He appreciated their concern. They were coming to that, the emissaries told him. Back of this boycott, they said, there was a concentrated, extremist plot by certain radical and maybe Communistic groups in New York. They had proof of it, and they wanted Mist' Ellenbogen to know about it, because it concerned him directly. Without these Northern agitators, the nigras in Hilltown would never have thought up that boycott or be holding these meetings and creatin' scenes on the buses and in the department stores like they now were. Why, the Hilltown people loved the whites and liked being segregated. They never knew anything else. They wouldn't know what to do if all of them got to vote, anyway.

Erwin again interrupted, this time more firmly. If the pale, gray-suited men in his office represented a residue of real power, he was not exactly a weakling. His annual taxes were probably in excess of the gross earnings of the entire Committee of Seventy-five and Erwin knew that counted for something—in the South or anywhere else. He wished they would get to the point—what had all this to do with him?

They illuminated him. Did Mist' Ellenbogen know that those arkologists on his property, those people digging on the island were actually professional agitators sent down from New York? That the committee had the goods on them? That they had been attending nigra meetings in Hilltown and working with that extremist Harkey to stir up the peaceable colored people? No, before Mist' Ellenbogen started to protest, they'd better enlighten him. Ballard, that so-called nigra arkologist, had even dropped the disguise. He'd left the excavation and had taken up with Harkey as a member of his boycott committee—the Hilltown Betterment Association, they were calling it. And there was a man named Benjamin Peltz on the dig, who was an admitted, confessed Communist who had testified before committees. They had nothing *yet*—the word was stressed—on the others, but they were investigating their backgrounds thoroughly. Now what had Mist' Ellenbogen to say to that? They were sure that he had been taken in—that the people on his land had sold him a pig in a poke. They didn't know how they had wormed their way into his confidence, but they sure had done a good job. The proof was that Ballard had already discarded his disguise. Peltz would be next, and then the others, including that Italian fellah in charge, would be agitating and propagandizing the nigras, causing all kinds of riots and bloodshed.

Erwin protested vigorously. He did not know that Ballard had left the dig, although he would take their word for it. The fact was, he did not see him at the site that morning, so their information was in all likelihood accurate. But wasn't it possible he had gotten involved in the boycott movement *after* he came down? As for Peltz, he was well aware of his background, but he had been fully cleared by the committees and had informed liberally on his colleagues. Besides, Dr. Sorrento, who was in charge of the project, had vouched for everyone. If they were suggesting that he, Erwin Ellenbogen, was in any way connected with the alleged nefarious activities of Dr. Sorrento's people, they were very wrong, indeed. Moreover, he doubted that the doctor (Erwin used Tom's professional title with marked emphasis: like Europeans, his callers respected official designations) would countenance any such behavior on the part of his staff. Ballard's defection, if true, was no doubt the Negro's own doing, and his departure consequently absolved the archaeologists of any complicity.

His spirited rejoinder, delivered patiently yet firmly, gave them pause. They agreed on several points, but their agreement seemed qualified. At length, one of them voiced the true reason for their concern. Did not, he asked, did not the fact that this big nigra buck was living in the same house with *two white women* arouse Mist' Ellenbogen's suspicions? Wasn't that the kind of thing one could expect from atheistical nigra-loving agitators? They were curious why Mist' Ellenbogen had permitted this arrangement. They knew for a fact that in his very own boathouse, where the arkologists were supposed to have their office, there were *two white women* living—the wife of this Dr. Sorrento and a young one named Burpee or Bailey. They had checked all of this out. Mist' Ellenbogen should have known, to begin with, there were state laws against this sort of thing, but beyond that, it was the sort of setup that should have made him suspect that these people weren't just down South to dig. . . .

Erwin cut them short. Their insinuations regarding the members of Dr. Sorrento's group were discourteous and unfounded. The aspersions cast on the women were inadmissible, and he would advise them to keep quiet about their suspicions. To suggest that Dr. Sorrento's wife, who, as a matter of fact, occupied the upper part of the building, along with their young children—well it was just too idiotic and utterly repugnant to any decent mind. The other woman was a Miss Burley, if they cared to know, a minister's daughter, who had her own bedroom upstairs and whose brother was a member of the group. Why, the whole notion was vicious, and frankly, he expected better of two such obviously intelligent and well-meaning fellows. Was that all they had to tell him?

His stiffness unsettled them. Beneath their gentle advisories there rested the deep conviction that in the long run their power would prevail. Ellenbogen was an alien in their midst. His vulnerability, though never referred to, was something they all understood. The fact that there were local Jewish citizens in the Committee of Seventy-five only proved their point. He, as a transplanted New Yorker, did not comprehend the race question and never could. Now that he had dismissed their well-meaning visit so coldly, it remained to establish the focus of power once again. They reminded him that he knew very little of the magnitude of the race problem, that they were headed for dark and evil days, and that his arkologists would be held accountable. Unless he publicly disavowed them and their works, and *threw them off his property at once,* sending them back North where they came from, he might be implicated. The whole story was going to break wide open one of these days, and he would be implicated. And boycotts were funny things. They worked several ways. Lots of white merchants throughout the South would know about his support of agitating elements, and might reconsider stocking his line of furniture. Of course, they weren't threat'nin' him, but these things had a way of catchin' on, and Mist' Ellenbogen was a businessman who understood these matters. All he had to do was disavow them people on his site, kick 'em out, and admit he'd been taken in by them. . . .

It was out of the question, Erwin advised them, and if that was all they had to tell him, they could consider the meeting ended, since he had other matters to occupy him that afternoon. He reiterated that Ballard's departure was his own notion, and besides he was no longer associated with Dr. Sorrento. As for the others, they were winding up their excavating and would be leaving in four or five days. Any attempt to blacken his reputation or to frighten him with threats of a boycott was pointless, since he was guilty of nothing, and besides, two such understanding gentlemen as themselves, reared in the truest tradition of Southern courtesy and fairness, would never stoop to such foul means simply to prove something that was unprovable. . . .

They shook hands warmly and departed, two drab men, in baggy gray suits, cheap white shirts and ties that failed to knot neatly. They were as faceless and devoid of character as the Indian skeletons Tom Sorrento was digging out of his bayfront land, and yet they had brought into Erwin's office a depressing vision of some ancient ugliness, a wickedness that would not die. For a long time Erwin sat silent and thoughtful at his desk, wondering how much you were expected to do in one lifetime to prove that you were decent. He obliterated the memory of his two visitors with pleasing thoughts about *The Spirit of Man*—an endeavor which might do much to change them into better people.

The call from Mermelstein late in the afternoon—that Maitland had accepted the invitation to the ceremonies at the University—also gratified him. If the polite callers, with their pious deplorings of violence, had come to vilify and condemn his guests from New York, Maitland's participation in the University ceremony would be splendid proof that the diggers were men of good will.

3 *Homage to Avilas*

SOMEWHAT toxic from overindulgence (when would he learn?) in Lila Ellenbogen's table of delights, Maitland sat like an Anglo-Saxon Buddha on the high piazza in front of the new library at the Beach University. Higher learning, he knew, wore a hundred guises, but surely none as grotesque as the one that now confronted him. Beneath the burning sky, the startling modern structures, ziggurats in primary colors, leaped and spired around him. The library itself was constructed over a man-made lagoon, afloat with tropical water lilies and other exotic herbiage. Giant palms bordered the walks of the campus, and around the quadrangle below—now filled with guests and visitors sweating on camp chairs—rose sparkling flagpoles, each bearing the national ensigns of "our sister republics to the south."

Inside Maitland's enormous gut, a dyspeptic struggle raged. Last night's brisket-of-beef with horseradish sauce, served with tiny pearly onions baked in cheese, gurgled and bubbled with disquieting vigor. He shifted his legs, trying to ease the rumblings that were the price of gluttony, listening to the drone of the speaker—a local newspaper publisher who regarded it his life's work to "improve relations" with Latin America. The man's flat, Midwestern voice was a soporific to Maitland, and he found himself dozing in the heat. The speaker, he had been advised, was the motivating force behind the university's award for promoting understanding between the Southern Hemisphere and the resort community. He had given the money for the award and seen to it that full press coverage would be given the rather unexciting event—he not only owned both daily newspapers, but controlled a local television station and several radio outlets. His address followed predictable lines: Maitland kept waiting for an appeal to lower the price of newsprint and to keep union demands sufficiently low so that the press might remain free, but these standard items of executive utterance were overlooked.

Beneath the array of distinguished guests and University officials, a crowd of several hundred people sat drowsily on folding chairs. Maitland, his eyes half closed behind sunglasses, discerned in a front row his daughter, his son-in-law, his grandchildren, the Ellenbogens and the improbable man who had invited him to honor General Avilas, Ira deKay.

As the publisher droned on, mouthing generalities about our friends in our sister republics, the children grew fidgety. DeKay had supplied them with balloons and toy monkey on canes, and it seemed to Maitland they were admirably equipped for the academic circus to which they had been brought. They were scrubbed and trig in white summery clothing, and for a fleeting moment the anthropologist regretted his inability to be a true Grampa. They were as dark and as adorably furtive as Arab children or the cheeky little devils he had known among the Pima-Papagos.

It upset him that Tom looked drawn and bleak. He was slumped in the cruel chair, no doubt ruminating about the problems of the dig. Maitland had suggested they take the day off to join in the tribute to the Latin American dignitary. Tom found the hiatus intolerable, but he reluctantly left Peltz in charge of the workmen and got into his seersucker suit when it appeared that it was expected of him. Lila, who sat on the university's fund-raising committee, insisted that he attend. After all, she told him, *he* was a name in American social science also.

Tom had been against the whole project: he knew General Avilas from way back and knew him to be a son-of-a-bitch who had his hand in the till and who specialized in shooting fractious students. "He was Minister of the Interior when I was in Santa Rosa," Tom said bitterly, "and he was the kind of oily bastard who agreed how terrible it was the Indians were dying, and then ordered their manioc burned."

Lila and Erwin objected strenuously; that was eight or nine years ago when Tom worked with the Indians in Santa Rosa—the country had changed. Avilas had raised the standard of living (so they were told) and suppressed Communism. Besides, the university and the publisher had carefully combed the governments of Latin America to find a real democrat, a forward-looking liberal who was genuinely interested in the people. Sorrento felt otherwise, but Maitland appeared more than willing to be convinced and finally he agreed to make a brief speech of tribute.

"What can you say?" Tom grumbled. "That you're glad he isn't using the chute in his office to dump students to the sharks any more?"

Maitland explained it this way to him: the simple process of telling intransigents that they are nice people often works, through sheer repetition. He cited the current trend among right-wing groups outside the South to foster desegregation, racial tolerance and all the constructive attitudes that for decades had been the especial domain of the left-winger. "What happened," Maitland said wearily, "was that editorial writers and commentators kept *telling* the various chambers of commerce and high churches that they really were liberal, tolerant and decent chaps. In time they started believing it. Today, no member of the NAM dares make a speech without saying a few good words for Marian Anderson. The grumpy guardians of caste have become convinced—through insidious repetition—that they should like everybody. And oddly enough, some of them are true converts. Perhaps if I work on General Avilas in this manner, he'll go back to Santa Rosa a little better disposed toward your vanishing Indians."

In any case, the humid afternoon found them all seated in front of the englassed library, listening to the publisher's recital, watching the lazy overhead maneuvers of blimps advertising the dog track and airplane streamers extolling a new night club. Distantly, on the bay beyond the campus, a sailboat scudding under full canvas advised them:

VISIT CHANG'S: CANTONESE COOKING

There was polite applause as the publisher concluded his address of welcome. The chancellor of the university now rose to say a few words and to present General Avilas with his plaque. Chancellor Mainwaring was a friendly, rosy man, a former professor of business law whose skill at fund raising had elevated him to his current post. He had all but swooned on welcoming Maitland, pumping his hand energetically and quoting freely from the anthopologist's textbook, *Man's Rise*. Now, at the lectern, he exuded good will and respectable scholarship. His doctoral gown, draped around his round, Rotarian body, signified a happy union of intellect and commerce. Maitland noted that the faculty was out in full academic regalia and he regretted that his costume was limited to his oatmeal suit. Back in New York, he had a magnificent collection of gowns, caps, hoods and mantles, the accumulated wardrobe of honorary degrees from scores of colleges and universities. At commencement time, he usually chose the most exotic, if only to irk the president of the University, who favored a red velvet pillow on his head and a flowing scarlet gown, the honoraria of a Belgian academy. The president clearly felt that these trappings gave him the edge over the dean of engineering, for example, who sported a kind of fringed green lampshade, emblematic of an honorary degree from the University of Barcelona. Maitland, however, was able to top them all. Some years ago he had received an honorary Ph.D. from the University of Brazzaville, French West Africa. With the degree came a magnificent orphreyed mitre, as breath-taking as the Pope's, with two braided infulae dangling at its rear. The Brazzaville gown was an emetic orange, trimmed with black serpentine braid. Holders of the degree were permitted to carry an ivory wand. The costume had a Halloweenish quality that delighted Maitland, and invariably evoked snide comments from the president, whose red velvet pillow appeared to droop and falter as the afternoon wore on.

Thinking it over, Maitland was just as happy to be bereft of his regalia. It was damnably hot, and the speeches were interminable. The chancellor spoke in glowing terms of the General's furtherance of Pan-American understanding. Particular mention was made of a new school of journalism which he had started in his native country, to be administered in part by the Beach University. At length the honored guest was called forth, and the assemblage rose to applaud him. Maitland, rising dutifully and suffering new painful rumblings in his viscera, glanced at his son-in-law, and fancied he saw Tom mutter: *Throw the bum out.* DeKay, he noticed, was leading the cheering and whistling shrilly, index fingers thrust in his mouth. The cheers and applause subsided and the President of Santa Rosa stood at the lectern, surveying the *Yanqui* gathering. He was a small, compact man, with a pointed, vulpine face. His skin was remarkably white and his oiled black hair was deftly parted in the middle. There was no Indian in him, Maitland concluded—a purebred Hispanic type, the offspring of exclusive matings. In black double-breasted suit, white shirt and navy blue tie he suggested the manager of an export-import firm, not the assassin and the corrupt pol that he was. Maitland sat down, sighing, resigning himself to one more lecture on anti-Communism from the kind of fellow whose abhorrent behavior did more to bring on Communism than a million translations of *Das Kapital.* When the President of Santa Rosa began to speak, however, his remarks were of a far different order. Indeed, they succeeded in rousing the anthropologist to the extent that his dyspepsia ceased, his somnolence gave way to an alertness that defied the heat, and he found himself cupping one ear to catch each precious word uttered by the guest.

"Eet iss no longer ha subject for debate among ceevilized pipple," General Avilas was saying, "eet is agreed upon by all pipples. The poor have rights. The demands of the poor and downtrodden are not rilly demands—but are a summons to duty for dose of us in responsible positions. Een my own small contry of Santa Rosa we respond to these summons—we well not rest huntil every person is clothed and fed and housed; until free education is avilable for all, until joostice and fridom triumph. . . ."

Maitland cocked his head. There it was again: the damned invasive liberal ethos, making a mockery of every battle for social improvement. The litany was too easy; any number could play. General Avilas had learned the trick with charming ease. In spite of his heavy accent, the message got across. Here was the New Look in despots—the believer in *joostice and fridom;* the friend of the poor; the forceful champion of unlimited free education; all the hoary war cries of the liberals and the left wing, now overtaken and embellished by the old enemies, the deceitful perpetuators of greed and force and myth. Where once they employed the rack and the garrote to prolong their power, now the liberals had given them a more subtle weapon: *the word.* They could hold on forever now, merely by utilizing the word. He listened in amazement to the assassin's recital. The words, after a while, ceased to hang together in meaningful combinations, but were oozed out in a bland, white blob, rather like frozen custard being squeezed from a rotary dispenser. To Maitland's ears, they were more offensive than any rock-headed, eighteenth-century defense of avarice. Where were all the reactionaries hiding? Was everybody—including General Avilas—a disciple of Arthur Schlesinger, Jr.? The passionate right had vanished; in its place was the more subtle figure of the President of Santa Rosa, genuflecting in the direction of John Maynard Keynes. The anthropologist listened intently; the words drifted out to the drowsy audience, over radio and television, and for the newsreel cameras, in liquid monotony. Only the speaker's total cynicism, his complete lack of belief in anything he was uttering, relieved the tiresome spectacle. To Maitland, the address soon dissolved into a dull hum of liberal sentiments, as undistinguished as the keynote speech at a League of Women Voters meeting in Chappaqua, New York, and less well phrased. After a while Maitland was only able to clutch at a phrase here and a word there.

"... mumble mumble ... fridom of the press ... mumble, mumble ... good will and brotherhood ... mumble mumble ... full support of the United Nations ... mumble mumble ... cheap housing and slum clearance ... mumble mumble ... the universal desire for piss ... mumble mumble ... friendly relations with all neighbor states ... mumble ... democratic strivings of our neighbors ... mumble mumble ... free elections ... mumble ... where all citizens may vote as they weesh and feel free of reprisals ... mumble ... the right to hold unpopular views ... mumble ... the dignity of man ... mumble mumble ... full program of health insurance and medical aid ... mumble ... respect for all minority groups and understanding of their problems ... mumble ... fridom of religion ... mumble ... mumble ... piss ... fridom ... joostice."

When General Avilas had concluded his peroration—to thunderous applause and a second rendition of his national anthem, a frisky tune suggesting a mambo—Maitland found himself heavy with despair. For one thing, the little murderer had stolen Maitland's speech. As he had explained to Tom and the Ellenbogens, it had been his scheme to lecture the honored guest on his own fictitious virtues, assuring him that he was liberal, progressive, honest and tolerant, in the hope that perhaps the President would go home and benefit fractionally by the moral suasion. Maitland was convinced that this strategy often worked—how else explain the bumptious vigor with which right-wing publishers now served on committees to improve education or erect cheap housing? Now he was trapped: Avilas' pre-emption of the liberal dogma had left him denuded—all that was left him was the truth.

"We are indeed fortunate this day," the chancellor was saying, "to have visiting us one of America's great educators and scholars. These two words hardly do justice to our guest. He is an author, world traveler, anthropologist—a man whose textbooks are standard in thousands of American universities, whose theories of society and culture have enriched man's ever-growing knowledge of himself. He has kindly consented to respond to the inspiring words just delivered by our guest. His interest in Pan-American relations goes back many years, and even now, I am told, he is working on an archaeological mystery which may indicate ancient ties between our own state and our neighbors to the east and south. Ladies and gentlemen—Professor Hall Maitland."

The band struck up the football fight song of Maitland's university—a dubious tribute in that their team had won three games in the past five seasons. There was indifferent applause as the anthropologist, unsteady of gait and unclear of eye, marched to the lectern. He had buttoned the jacket of his oatmeal suit incorrectly, and it hung over his great abdomen in an irregular fold. He needed a haircut and his shoes were unshined, and as the perfunctory applause died down, he fumbled in his pocket for some notes he had made. Of all the people on the piazza, only the newspaper publisher scented the enemy; he leaned forward, his iron jaw slightly atilt. He knew nothing about Maitland; but with the sensitive nose of an old police reporter he had divined that the bloated man in the ghastly suit was up to no good.

Maitland placed a few slips of scratch-pad paper on the lectern, adjusted his sunglasses and began to speak. His high, dry voice was barely audible at first, and a sound engineer, squatting at one side of the steps, was required to twist a few knobs to raise the volume.

"I am honored to participate in this academic ritual," he began. "I feel that those of us in the drab business of learning need more rituals. Dr. Mainwaring—you have contributed notably to brightening the dull academic processes. I, myself, for many years, have advocated weekly rites on this order, possibly with close-order drill by graduate students, or massed card tricks by the doctoral candidates—all to no avail."

There was a mild appreciative snickering; the chancellor managed a throaty chuckle and dug the publisher in the ribs. General Avilas smiled; an uncomprehending, flat lengthening of his mouth. Under the searing sky he was sweatless. The fact of the matter was, he understood almost no English. His speech had been spelled out for him in phonetic Spanish; in conversation he leaned on interpreters.

"Two days ago," Maitland said, "when I was invited to address this convocation, I accepted with eagerness. Santa Rosa summoned up vivid memories for me. Some eight years ago, an ethnological study of that country's Indian problem was made under my supervision. Several colleagues of mine lived in the republic for almost a half-year and I myself spent some weeks among its citizens. So this call to honor General Avilas, exemplar of the new, progressive government of Santa Rosa, was a source of deep gratification to me."

Maitland turned from the lectern and nodded graciously at the guest. The general sprang to his feet with military precision, clicked his heels and executed a snappy half-bow.

"In preparing the few comments I have to make today," Maitland continued, "I am guided by the magnificent speech delivered by the man we honor. I am indebted to General Avilas. He has made my speech for me. We are both devotees of the liberal ethic, that dull hum of good intentions that obviates the need for good deeds. He speaks the new *lingua franca* with rare grace and skill. His glowing tributes to freedom, justice and peace are exceeded only by similar sentiments I heard expressed recently by a visiting Arab oil king, a man who keeps slaves and beheads dissidents. He brings to mind, too, the clever usage of the words, 'People's Democracy' by the monolithic tyrants of the left. That is the beauty of the liberal creed. It is the new elasticized stretchable dogma, snugly fitting all systems, rulers, states. As I listened to the General looting the collected works of John Peter Altgeld, I found myself marveling at his dualism. He is a man to be admired, for he has found the key—the damned liberal doctrine, phrased so cunningly, appealing to all, warm and loving and encompassing—a key that admits its bearer to the treasure of security, stability, perpetuation of his own kind and his own private creed, which I assure you, is neither benevolent nor egalitarian nor humanistic."

By now a small murmuration of horror was agitating the gathering. The newspaper publisher had edged forward on his folding chair; he appeared ready to spring at Maitland's defenseless, ample rear and claw him into silence. His face crimsoned, and the chancellor, sitting next to him, touched his mohair arm lightly. The publisher leaned back, whispered something to the chancellor and folded his arms grimly. He was, after all, a King Dispenser of Words, and he would take care of that sonavabitching professor on his own time. Now both publisher and chancellor glanced covertly at the guest. The President of Santa Rosa, stonily ignorant of the language, and lulled by Maitland's pleasant voice, was grinning at what he imagined was one more *norteamericano* eulogy. His interpreter, politely awaiting the conclusion of the address, had turned a clayish gray underneath his Indian tan. The audience itself seemed uncertain of what Maitland was saying. In a sense, they were as ignorant of his address as was the General. Maitland knew from years of academic rites that audiences rarely heard what was being said. A commencement speaker, he often felt, could publicly demand the burning down of the Supreme Court, the scrapping of the Constitution and the abolition of the Presidency in favor of a Politburo and get away with it.

If the bulk of the gathering in front of the library were unaware of Maitland's evisceration of the guest, his daughter and son-in-law sensed the surgical nature of his address immediately.

"Go get him, Hall," Sorrento said, half aloud. "Eat him up!"

Marty cautioned him. "Tom! Lower your voice!"

"Why?" he said. "I haven't enjoyed anything so much since the freshman beer party."

"You make me sick," she whispered. "Both of you. Can't you see what he's doing? He's going to get all of you in trouble. You may think he's clever and daring—but he's behaving like the boor he is."

"He's telling the truth, isn't he?" Tom asked.

"What's that got to do with anything?" She turned to Ira, expecting to find him distraught over the dirty trick her father was playing on all of them. But the blond man seemed half asleep. He had his smooth brown face upturned, enjoying the sunbath.

"Ira," Marty whispered. "You've asked for it and you've gotten it. Don't you hear what he's saying? They'll blame it on you."

She had touched his arm in speaking to him, and to Ira, it was almost as good as having her disrobe in front of him. She had effectively blotted from his mind all thoughts of business transactions, deal, loot and payoff. If her old man was figuring on goofing up the detail as far as the University was concerned, why should he worry? He never liked the University account anyway—what kind of payola could he work out with them? A free course in Theory and Practice of Motorboating?

On the opposite side of Ira, the Ellenbogens sat in troubled silence. Erwin knew there were times when no comment helped, when no words relieved inner torment. Maitland—his guest and the boss of the dig—would be as welcome as a tropical hurricane by the time the newspapers were out that evening. The faster he dissociated himself from the anthropologist, the better for *The Spirit of Man*. Bland, diffident, behind his hexagonal glasses, he fooled everyone but his wife. Lila nudged him with hard strength;

the digging had endowed her with a muscularity that no amount of canasta could have.

"Smile, Erwin, smile," she whispered. "It isn't *that* bad."

"He's being a little extreme, don't you think?" Erwin asked.

Maitland was reading now from some notations he had made. "I took the opportunity, on learning of my call to duty here, of contacting the Commission for Meso-American Affairs, a governmental agency which puts out a kind of *Sporting News* regarding our neighbors. Their bulletins provided me with some memorable statistics concerning President Avilas' country, particularly during his stewardship of the last four years. Or is it five years since he had the prior dictator assassinated and his cabinet hanged? Ah, well—"

At this juncture the murmuration in the crowd became a shudder, the publisher leaped to his feet and began haranguing the chancellor, and the general's interpreter, seeing his duty, bent over and began whispering to *el Jefe.*

"Per capita income in Santa Rosa has declined from four hundred dollars per annum prior to the Avilas regime to a new low of three hundred and seventy dollars per annum. Expenditures for low-cost housing have been cut from two hundred thousand dollars per annum to less than twenty thousand dollars—ah, I am using the current exchange rate between the peso and the American dollar—and the average daily wage of all workers, agricultural and industrial, had declined to thirty cents, the lowest for any Meso-American country. To depart from dry statistics for a moment—all newspapers in Santa Rosa are now government-controlled. The Students Association for Democracy has been made illegal as have all trade unions except the government-sponsored SOM. As a result of these measures, enrollment in the Communist party has *increased,* obviously as a reaction to his enlightened program. The party, while officially illegal, proselytizes and recruits members—"

The publisher could stand no more. He yanked the chancellor to his feet. The harassed administrator walked tentatively toward the lectern, touching Maitland's back.

Maitland turned. "Yes?" he asked. "Am I running on?"

"Ah—perhaps—there are two other speakers..."

"I'll wind up at once," Maitland said. "Now the point I'd like to conclude with is that General Avilas is no villain. He is guilty of nothing other than carrying on the splendid tradition of his society. He has superb guides—Cortes, Pizarro, Valdivia—and a singleness of purpose that one cannot help but admire. That he is fighting a rearguard action against me and my kind makes his efforts even more admirable. No, my friends, one cannot fault so dedicated a man. Rather it is the damned liberal ethic, the notion that man can help himself, solve his own problems, the invasive do-good, uplift, progressive dogma that is to be abhorred—for it has supplied the General and his colleagues of darkness with the wherewithal to perpetuate themselves forever. All he has to do is quote the New York *Post* editorial page, and he is eligible for one more award, and another term in office. He need never *act* on saving the Indians or raising the basic wage of the rubber workers, he—"

The General, his grin transmuted to an icy mask, had risen and was stalking off the library steps, followed by his interpreter and two sinister young men in tan uniforms, much bedecked with fourragères and fringed epaulets. Unfortunately, there was no exit from the veranda at either end, and having reached what he imagined was an escape route, *el Presidente* and his party were forced to execute an about-face and parade across the landing once more. The crowd was getting to its feet, and the publisher, bursting with choler, raced to the microphone and edged Maitland's paunchy body away. The anthropologist blinked at him. "Thank you. Thank you, sir. I was all but finished." He returned to his seat. General Avilas, having reached the opposite end of the piazza, again found egress blocked. His retinue now included a dozen of his nationals, and he led them back once more, through the ranks of distinguished guests, to the giant glass portals of the library—his last hope.

By now the entire audience was on its feet, most of them uncertain of the plot of the clumsy drama unfolding beneath the palms, not quite sure of what the fat man in the oatmeal suit had been mumbling about into the microphones or why the honored guest was marching around like a man sunstruck. The chancellor skipped to the edge of the promenade and called firmly to the bandmaster: "Play the national anthem."

The bandmaster roused his drowsy musicians; sunlight sparkled on tubas and euphoniums. A glockenspiel jangled as its uniformed custodian rose. The bandmaster raised his baton, then turned around. "Which one?" he asked the chancellor.

"Theirs."

After a few halting notes, the marching band struck up *Arriba Santa Rosa* for the third time. The unfortunate President, trapped as he and his entourage were about to escape through the library doors froze in their steps, did a *volte-face* and saluted.

"A lovely tune," Maitland whispered to the publisher. "I'm no ethno-musicologist, but it suggests Afro-Cuban influence. *Dum-di-di-dum-di-di dum-di-di-dum . . .*"

4 A Famous Victory

DE KAY had left a morning newspaper at the cabana. Attached to it was a note.

> MARTY—
>
> Your old man really did me in. You should have warned me.
>
> IRA

She wondered, reading the accounts of the disaster at the university, how Ira could walk the streets of the Beach again. A banner headline proclaimed:

VISITING PROFESSOR INSULTS AVILAS;
STATE DEPARTMENT SHOCKED

The glib journalese barely concealed the reporter's wrath. The fact of the matter was that the publisher himself had edited the copy; he didn't want the straight news account of the dreadful affair to be *too* violent—he was saving that for the editorial page.

> A ceremony honoring President Carlos Avilas of Santa Rosa became the scene of an international incident yesterday when a guest speaker took the occasion to deliver a scathing denunciation of the Latin American statesman.
>
> One thousand stunned guests of the University, which was honoring General Avilas with its Latin American award, looked on in horror as Professor Hall Maitland of New York attacked the head of Santa Rosa in an ad lib address.
>
> Maitland, visiting the beach to inspect some archaeological work, had been invited . . .

Marty should have enjoyed the spectacle; but as she read on, the whole affair filled her only with a numbing despair. It was not that she disagreed with her father's position or really resented Tom's idolatrous approval. It was rather her picture of them as schoolboys playing a prank. Their protests were meaningless and outside the functioning, practical engines of society. A few years ago she might have laughed at Hall's impudence; today she found him tiresome, irrelevant. That was it. That was the word for him, and, she told herself, the nonsensical work he had euchred Tom into. They were practitioners of the *irrelevant:* their boasts about studying human behavior, of understanding man and his culture, were really cover-ups for eccentricity, for a preoccupation with dirty Indians and old bones. What harm would have been done in letting General Avilas get his plaque and go home happy? She suspected his subjects *liked* his tyranny; that was the story behind most tyrants—they stayed in power because they were wanted. And what business was it of Hall's anyway? All that windy explaining as to how he had to change his remarks at the last minute because the general had stolen his speech, the sly and somewhat cowardly denigration of modern liberalism (which he believed in implicitly) in order to camouflage his insults.

The ride back to the islet in Erwin's Cadillac had been like the return from a cemetery. Erwin had fallen into a frigid silence; when Lila had nervously tried to joke about Maitland's speech he had halted her with one hard look. Apparently she ran him—up to a point. Wearied from the heat, Maitland had slumped in the rear seat, mopping his face with a handkerchief. Marty, eager to ameliorate the sticky situation, had tried to console Erwin—he had indicated before they had left the campus that the incident would be bound, in some way, to hurt *The Spirit of Man*. She had seen Ira sprinting for the press table as soon as *Arriba Santa Rosa* had been concluded and the general had vanished through the library portals. With him was Charlie Rasmussen, the deputy mayor. The two of them fluttered and scurried around the reporters, trying to set things aright. But Erwin refused to accept any balm, and the reportage of the incident in the morning paper which Ira had thoughtfully left for her, had borne him out. The front-page headline was just a warm-up. Inside, Marty found an editorial.

A SHAMEFUL INCIDENT

Yesterday's disgraceful occurrence at Beach University calls for a full, fearless investigation. The embarrassing facts can be read in their hideous detail elsewhere in today's *Register.* A distinguished foreign visitor about to be honored by the Beach, was insulted and abused in public at the very ceremony at which he was to be applauded. Several strong measures are indicated, but before these are undertaken the *Register,* on behalf of all right-thinking Beach residents, extends its deepest apologies to General Avilas. We trust he will understand that the lies and calumnies addressed to him by a New York City transient, mistakenly invited to the rites, are in no way indicative of our sentiments. We dissociate ourselves from everything Hall Maitland said, indeed we cannot find language strong enough to denounce his depraved utterances. It is our fervent hope that in the interest of Pan-American friendship, General Avilas will reconsider and visit us in the near future.

Now, as for Hall Maitland, we can make only these suggestions: First, he had best get out of town as soon as possible. Secondly, we call for a full probe of how he came to be invited to the ceremony. The *Register* has learned that a Beach public-relations firm, one with a good reputation, was instrumental in arranging for the New York professor to participate. We should like to know what motivated them. Was any effort made to request an advance of Maitland's speech? Did he indicate to anyone what the tenor of his remarks would be? Why were not University officials, notably Chancellor Mainwaring, more careful in their selection of a speaker? It would have been interesting, for example, to make a study of Maitland's background and ascertain his political leanings . . . what organizations had he supported . . . where he stands on the question of Red China . . .

There was another column of the same, and Marty marveled at one curious omission. Miraculously, the name of Ira deKay, the prime mover in the affair, had been left out. There had been no qualms about naming the hapless Chancellor. But the magic of Ira deKay, some spell he had cast over the nobles of the press, had saved him from the wrath of the editorial page. He had hinted as much before racing off for the press table; Marty seemed to recall him muttering *Ooops. Got to keep it kosher for our side.* And so he had done; Ira and his firm remained unnamed and strangely untouched by the dreadful business. It was almost as if the fire-breathing publisher refused to believe that a great guy like Ira, so quick with the broads and the booze, could be party to such a foul exhibition.

She noticed, returning to the lead article's jump, that a short two-stick piece had been appended explaining Hall's presence at the Beach.

Maitland refused to comment last night on his attack on General Avilas. He is staying at the home of Mr. and Mrs. Erwin Ellenbogen, on Bay Islet, where an archaeological excavation conducted by some of his associates is taking place. The phone at the Ellenbogen home was disconnected and reporters who sought to see Maitland were told by a servant that he would talk to no one.

Ira's frantic search to tie things together, to relate the unrelated, to demand the public eye and ear with meaningless associations, had never envisioned this kind of disaster. The fact that deKay might be burned by his own incendiary inanities—and would get Erwin scorched—failed to amuse her.

She anointed herself with aromatic oils from the cabana, then settled back for her morning dosage of sun. Usually, she was the first one at poolside, depositing the browned, happy children with the counselor and luxuriating in the vista of ocean and sand. (She found it comforting to turn her back on the glassy geometric balconies of the Peruviana). She was cocooned, insulated, a woman serene in a clear plastic paperweight. Even the presence of Fenton Braud, his blonds and his interminable gin rummy game did not intrude on her solitary, lassitudinous indulgence. At lunch—always served in the cabana by an efficient waiter, on sparkling silver and snowy napery—Ira would join her, and she found herself, with an embarrassed twinge, looking forward to his prattling and jesting.

At least, she assured herself, the atmosphere was relaxing and salubrious. Whenever the old guilts and fears smoldered, the old hatred of excess and ease, she thought of the sweltering boathouse and the insane air that the dig had assumed in the past few days—since her father's arrival. She had left them that morning sweating and gasping on the slope, hacking away at the earth like demented grave-diggers. Tom had started a new trench—every day found them unearthing another area, frantically heaping earth on top of earth, further scarifying Ellenbogen's golden property—a trench that had yielded an odd cluster of postholes. Maitland had found the first one, probing expertly with his trowel, in his comic-opera prospector's outfit, and now Tom and Lila had joined him. The dark stains on the sandy subsoil had followed no pattern—there was no indication of a walled structure, but he felt one might be present if they cleared more land. He explained that weather and wind and shifting tides could have altered the arrangement of the posts, resulting in the haphazard pattern. More digging might reveal something more profitable. And meanwhile, the Negro workmen kept systematically digging pits perpendicular to the expanding row of white boulders, in search of the southern wall. The ball court had become an obsession with them, to the extent that one night, returning from her day at the Peruviana, she found Tom with Sheldon Ellenbogen's inflated beachball demonstrating how the game was played. *Only with the knees, shoulders and behind,* he called out, and with remarkable agility considering his gimpy leg, had proceeded to bounce the ball up and down the Ellenbogen driveway. *No hands, no feets, no head,* Tom shouted—and Lila guffawed, trying to return the ball with a wrench of her rear end, a gesture more sexual than athletic. She had her fill of Lila, too. Her proprietary concern with Tom disturbed her less than the disdain Lila now evinced for Marty's pilgrimages to Ira's haunts. She knew what Lila was thinking: that their roles were slyly and subtly being reversed through some alchemy of sun and circumstances. When she had said her goodbye to Tom that morning he had barely answered. He and Maitland and Lila were too busy hacking at the earth. Walking with the children to the blacktop, where Ira's chariot, driven by Si Mermelstein, obediently awaited them, she heard Tom singing to the tune of "Tammany":

A-ra-wak, A-ra-wak
The Indians with lots of class
Always went around bare-ass
A-ra-wak, A-ra-wak
How they loved co-habitation,
A-ra-wak!

Tom seemed to be regressing into a kind of undergraduate silliness; seizures of high spirits like this one (usually when Lila was around) alternated with a morosity such as he had exhibited the night they had met Jimmy Nudo. She found him difficult to talk to, increasingly brusque. Her inability to aid him rankled. He had always possessed a plodding, heavy strength: his athlete's back was capable of bearing many burdens. It was no accident that the Ben Peltzes and the Burleys turned to him; that in the Marine Corps he was the perpetual friend of maligned Jews, of gawky farm boys who could not keep cadence, of a dim-witted Mandan Indian who could barely learn the manual of arms. Now that a strain of uncertainty was developing in him, she had begun to worry—for him and for herself and for the children.

Her musings were interrupted by the ringing of the cabana phone.

She rose from the chaise, drawing the requisite number of stares and comments, and went into the hut. It was Ira.

"Marty, baby," he said huskily. "Sorry I'm not down to hold your hand this morning. But I got the miseries."

"I would imagine you have."

"What your old man did to us! I'm bleeding and fractured. The mayor had me on the phone all morning, and he was eatin' ass like it was steak. I can't hardly sit down."

She laughed; Ira *in precarium* was almost lovable. "It serves you right, Ira. You should never tangle with intellectuals. I could have told you my father wasn't to be trusted. He's got some nutty idea he can force a postponement of your ground-breaking so Tom can finish the dig. At least I think that's what he's up to. First, trapping you into that peyote business and then that speech yesterday."

"He's rough as a cob. Well, I'm not dead yet. I have to get up a report in triplicate for the University and then Si is gonna draft a formal apology to General Avilas, that greaseball. Ellenbogen is screaming for space and he's no help, because he hasn't chased your husband away yet. I think he's afraid Lila will close the store if he does."

Marty laughed out loud this time. "Oh, no! Don't tell me—"

"Sure. It's the truth. Erwin thinks his wife has the only one in the world." His small mouth seemed to envelop the phone as he added: "But we know different—don't we, Marty?"

"Come down and join me for lunch," she said. "I miss insulting you. I'm sitting here feeling sorry for myself."

"I can't, lover. I got too many phone calls to make. I've been goofing off and Si is swamped. Whyn't you come up and hold my hand? We'll have lunch here."

"In your office?"

"Down the hall. Room 1007. I use it when I want to get away from the office. I know, *I know* it sounds suspicious. Listen, baby, I've just about given up on you."

"All right. But lunch only."

"Zetz. Come as you are. It's that kind of party."

She advised Florrie, the muscular counselor, that she would be in Mr. deKay's office if the children wanted anything. Florrie assured her they would be well taken care of; the youngsters were being taken to Chimpville for an afternoon's fun. Abby and Nicky barely noticed her. They were engrossed with a green water mattress, wrestling each other on and off in the wading pool. A fat seven-year-old girl with yellow hair was Abby's ally against her brother. "This is Carla, Mother," Abby said tensely. "She's the best friend I ever had." Marty smiled at Carla; that was Abby at the peak of her form. Her life was a quest for best friends, alliances, intrigue, searing relationships that carried the germ of inevitable tears and torment. One day Carla would leave her and Abby would wallow in misery.

She sought Ira's lair and rang the bell. He answered the door, wearing only a pair of Jamaica shorts; the vertical stripings seemed part of his natural coloration.

"I didn't expect you so formal," she said.

"I'll stick a shirt on if it bothers you. How many times you see me nekkid like this at the pool?"

"Well, it just seems a little indecent—in this room. Or maybe it's my own guilt feelings."

"Guilt? For what? The only one I know who gets less than you is Si Mermelstein."

He led her through a small foyer into a luxurious sitting room. Through an opened door, she could see a bedroom—curtains and blinds drawn, a dusky haze blunting the bright colors of free-form lamp, silver-flecked bedspread, overstuffed lounge chair. She knew that just out of the field of vision was an immaculate, antiseptic john. The drinking glasses, sparkling like crystal, were encased in cellophane jackets, the toilet had a paper riband stretched across the chasm, bearing the legend: *This seat has been purified and rendered germ-free* and the dazzling tiled wall held a cunning plastic dispenser for the ubiquitous paper tissues. It was a room magnificently accessoried for the aftermath of sex, the washings and dryings and medical duties, and she shuddered, fully aware why the notion had occurred to her, annoyed with herself for lingering on it.

She had no sooner sat down, crossing her browned legs, disturbed by their nudity—there was a considerable difference between the pool and this lush trap—than the buzzer sounded. Ira bounded to the door. A hotel waiter, another surly servitor reduced to smiles, winks and jokes by Ira's magic, wheeled in an ornate wine bucket, loaded with ice and a bottle of champagne. He settled it near the glass doors facing the ocean and placed two stemmed glasses on a serving table.

"Open it now, Mr. deKay?" he asked.

"No, Dickie. I'll do it later. I like the *pop*."

"Right-o. Be real cold in a few minutes. I got the best, like you asked."

"You're a dream, Dickie. Did you get the free pass to the dog races? Helene was supposed to have it for you."

"I sure did, Mr. deKay. Tanks."

When the waiter left, Marty doubled her legs underneath her on the couch.

"You said *lunch,*" she said.

"That's coming," Ira yawned. "You never do the afternoon champagne bit? Ah, what you miss. When I was at the network, that was on my schedule at least once a week. Bubbly is best at noon. It makes the rest of the lousy day worth while."

"I don't think I'll join you. I don't like the connotation."

"Who said anything? I'm entitled to champagne. After what I've been through these last few days. That old man of yours. What a help."

"You've learned something, Ira. Never get too chummy with eggheads. They're sinister. You knew my father was a big name in American university life, so you figured he'd fit in. Why do you have that urge to keep relating things? I suppose I should have warned you, but you wouldn't have listened anyway."

Ira sat opposite her on the couch. He stretched his legs and covered his eyes. *"Ai.* Do I have troubles? *Dunt esk.* You should have heard that hotel manager complain when I asked for this suite for the day. Why the bum gets more publicity from my li'l operation in a week than that New York outfit gets him in a year. Mr. Banjo's had this joint in the papers every day for two weeks already. And he—"

"You asked him for this room? Just for today? You gave me the impression you use it all the time."

"Did I?"

"You're getting sloppy, Ira. You can't even keep track of your lies. I guessed this production had one end in view."

"Yaaah. I can see a little of it now, peeking through the bottom of that bathing suit." He moved nearer. "How can you look so great all the time? And be so nasty about it?"

"It's the fresh air and sun and water. I have you to thank." She tried to get an edge of cynicism in her voice, but failed; she felt honestly grateful to him. He had taken the tenseness out of her neck, the harshness out of her voice. At the Peruviana, around him, she was mindlessly at rest. Only at the boathouse, in the presence of Tom, and around her intrusive father, did she find herself taut and restless. If Ira deKay were an opiate, at least he wasn't habit-forming or weakening. She had never felt healthier, more energetic, more atingle.

"See? See how easy it is? Now all you have to do is agree to Big Casino."

"No, Ira. The trouble is you bragged too much about how great you are. How could you ever live up to all that boasting?"

"Maybe I did yack too much. But what else could I do? You're brand new to me. Nothing worked."

"And today it's champagne?" she asked. "Tomorrow a free pass to the dog track?"

"Ah, come on, Marty. I thought you were friends with me."

"That's just what we are, Ira. Friends. Buddies."

He crooned comically: *"My buddeee ... My buddeee ... Your buddee misses you ..."* He rubbed his eyes. "How come there were no songs out of World War II? My old man was very big with the Legion. Boy, could he sing those World War I songs at Legion Hall. *She's the Rose of Noooooo-Man's Land ...*"

Ira spread his arms wide (he was little Ira Detzler performing at the school again) and closed his eyes. As he dragged the last notes out, his mouth pursed in mimicry of a professional singer, he descended on Marty. He got his rubbery arms around her waist and rested his head in her lap. Her semi-nudity seemed to minimize rather than heighten his strategic move. Moreover, his behavior was comical rather than passionate, and she made no attempt to dissuade him.

"All right, Ira," she said gently, patting the blond fuzz of his head. "Time out. I'll try the champagne now."

"Who needs champagne?" he asked softly.

He moved his silken head a few inches, pressing his face against her bare thighs—just below the termination of her bathing suit. Breathily and lovingly, he kissed the skin with a hundred fast flutterings of his mouth; every few seconds—like an internal rhythm—he darted his quick tongue against her flesh. She tried to pry his head away, but he hung on grimly—a hot and hairy limpet—pecking more voraciously, gripping her waist with strong hands. When at last he disengaged—she was still pressing against his skull to no avail—it was *his* choice, not her strength that forced the break. She moved away. Ira lay the back of his head in her naked lap and looked up at her, a fraudulent look of injury on his face.

"I wish you'd move," she said.

"Naah. It's a democracy. I can stay here. You want to go, go."

"I won't go if you stop being a fool. I'll be happy to stay." She added, almost in conciliation, "You know I enjoy your company. You're like a tranquilizer. You're so brainless."

"Doll. You're putting me on again."

"No, I mean it. I've enjoyed the use of the cabana." She stroked the golden fuzz. "But it ends there."

"I couldn't help it. I was flying. You smell so good. Taste good, too."

"I'm not a free lunch counter. Go open the champagne."

"This beats champagne." He turned his head quickly; his face nested against her knitted belly. "Don't hang me. I asked you to fall up to my pad because I need you. I'm bugged."

"Poor Ira. All fed up with the world at thirty-eight. Serves you right for never reading a book or a newspaper. Why don't you take some courses at the university? Try improving your mind."

"Yeah. I sure see what all that education did for you and your husband."

"Really?"

"When'd he last give you a good time?"

"None of your business."

"Well, that's an admission if ever I heard one." He raised himself on one elbow and became terribly earnest. "That's what it's all about, Marty. If that isn't good, to hell with the rest of the marriage. You know it. You hang on like a punchy fighter. You're gonna shrivel up."

"Ira, if I had the vaguest desire to give in to you, I wouldn't be able to because of your disgusting language. Are you really able to count coup with that kind of approach?"

"Who got a contract? Whazzat about cooze?"

"Counting coup. That's American Plains Indian for making a score. Any act of bravery or daring. I'm sorry I'm so educated. You see how hopeless it is?"

Ira seemed delighted with the notion. "*Counting cooze.* Yeah, that's what my life has been. But I got no regrets. It beats reading books and it's a lot less tiring than digging for bones."

He shut his eyes and let his head lie quietly on her thighs. After a few silent moments his left arm snaked up her side and his hand grasped the back of her neck. Firmly, he pushed her head down to his roseate face; she offered less than token resistance. He kissed her mouth, working his serpentine tongue over the small, upturned lips, delighted by her soft, prim gasping —a sound that, to him, spoke of the triumph of lust over propriety.

"No. No, Ira. That's enough. Get off."

She braced her hands against his shoulder and shoved. He bounced from the couch, hitched his striped shorts and walked to the champagne. He manipulated the bottle with a proprietary air that hinted at long, intimate association with champagne. It occurred to Marty, watching him handle the bucket, the bottle, its cunning wire cage and cork stopper, the snowy towel, that in all matters sensual and sybaritic, Ira possessed a rare, sure-footedness, a familiarity that transcended the connoisseur's. One got the feeling that he not only understood vintage champagne and aged steaks, but possessed esoteric knowledge of the growing of the grapes and the feeding of the steers. When his exotic fondling of the bottle concluded with the orgasmic *pop!* he sampled the wine and rolled his eyes in approbation. He poured a glass for Marty. She got up from the couch and joined him at the ceiling-high window.

"Here's to honor," Ira said. "Once honor, stay honor."

"Must you turn the wine sour?"

"Not this stuff. This is too good for the cloakies. The wine steward keeps a few bottles just for me."

On her starved stomach, the champagne acted first as an abrasive, then as an anesthetic. Almost immediately she was pleasantly dizzy and numb. She glanced at the bottle's label. It was a rare and expensive brand, not the kind of wine served at cozy University dinners on the Heights.

"When you go with Ira, you go first class," he said. "See how easy it is?"

"What is?" She drained the glass—drinking it a lot faster than she knew was good for her. Outside the sparkling glass, beyond the tile balcony, stretched the blue-green Atlantic. High above the noisy and cluttered pool area, it was all that was visible—ocean and hot sky.

"Doing things right," Ira said. "Getting your share." He set his glass down and came at her again, grasping her waist and pulling her against him.

"Stop. You'll spill this expensive champagne."

"It's loot. Who cares?"

The glass fell from her hand as he stroked, probed, pressed and manipulated her—with the same expert's touch, the sure deft movements, the graceful combinations he had used on the champagne. She tried half-heartedly to thwart him, but it was useless. He seemed to effuse a dry, comforting heat and his skin was aromatic with musky scent. Now, with artful hands, he began peeling her bathing suit.

"No. I don't want you to, Ira."

"The hell you say," he said. "It's my bathing suit. And my room and my champagne."

Naked, she felt no shame, no sense of strangeness. There was an undercurrent of the ludicrous in Ira; it made the prospect of adultery something less than sinful and much closer to a prank or a lapse of judgment. In the darkened, muted bedroom, she was a trifle unnerved to see how prepared for her he was. Beside her on the bed, he kept talking—a low, throaty mumble that she imagined was supposed to denote extreme passion.

"Ira," she said. "Just be quiet. Go ahead and make love to me—but I don't need the running commentary. You've won your point."

"Always with the needle. You'll feel different in a few days. You won't care if I play the clarinet when we're in the hay."

"Be still."

He took her with a swiftness that startled her. On the first twinge of sensation, she sighed deeply and, looking at his narcotized face, she uttered the monosyllabic, faintly nasal greeting of the Eastern Seaboard coed: *"Hi."*

The salutation delighted him. It was the kind of embellishment he perpetually sought in his mates. Once before he had heard a woman murmur "hi" at that moment: a well-born daughter of wealth, educated at Vassar or Bryn Mawr or one of those fancy places. The sublime notion dawned on him: that this intoned, formal mode of address, this signaling that all was well, that the essential had been consummated, was a kind of secret carried around by these women. Marty was of the same cut as that partner past; infinitely more lovely and harder to subdue, but similarly bred, educated, indoctrinated. Ira pondered the marvelous idea: was the "hi" something they learned from seniors when they were freshmen?

A few seconds after it had ended, he was off the bed and she could see him in the sitting room, brandishing his limber body in front of the glass portal—and drinking champagne from the bottle as if it were orange soda. He had his round head tilted back and was letting the wine trickle down his arched throat.

He was incorrigible, vulgar and illiterate—and he had excited and stimulated her more than any man she had ever slept with. He had been inventive, considerate, a man so enamored with his work, so dedicated to the job at hand that he transformed love into a perfect mechanical ritual. Her body had never responded so frenetically. The stereotyped leads on fire stories she had written at WNA darted idiotically across her mind . . . *Fire officials said the conflagration was still out of control and spreading early this morning and that residents in the area have been warned to . . .*

He slouched in the doorway, cradling the icy bottle. "Want a shot?" he asked softly.

"No. Come back here."

"Did I lie?"

"No. You lived up to your promises." She turned her head away. Each small motion of her body sent new sensations darting. If she moved a foot, her leg suddenly sparked and buzzed.

"First nice thing you've said to me since we met."

"Come back here."

"Want more?"

"Yes."

He quaffed some more wine. "That's what the bubbly is good for."

Hours passed; she lay half asleep, drugged and soothed with the athletics of the afternoon. He had kept asking her: *Is it good? Is it making you happy?*—like a small boy seeking the approval of adults. She said nothing. Now, her tumescence vanished, she rested in the kind of dreamlike torpor she imagined one felt coming out of deep sedation after surgery. Indeed, the medical qualities of the afternoon's sport had not been lost on her—the efficient tiled bathroom, the nude, scrubbed bodies, ready for the knife, the antiseptic cleanliness...

He was talking to her, mumbling words in her ear, and she barely heard him—it required an effort on her part to dissociate the inane chatter of the man from the marvelous lithe body and its maneuverings.

"I mean it, Marty. I mean it. I love you. I want you to leave the fellah digging the bones. I'm ready for the final act. The marriage of Ira deKay. I never got anything by being backward about it, so why stumble now? Listen . . . I have the whole plot. A divorce is easy down here. No sweat. I've got to have you. And give yourself a break. Live a little. Get the kids off your back. Buy clothes. Drink. Get a big car. You liked what I did this afternoon? Want it all the time? And look at me—big ole Ira, with all the broads he needs. I must love you to make that sacrifice. The skinny legs and the flat rear end . . . and the voice and the face. Come on, sweetie . . . "

"Shut up, Ira. How could I marry you? What would we talk about after we made love?"

"I'm doing pretty good now, ain't I?" He raised himself on one elbow and looked down at her. Her smudged face was as elusive as ever. "I made you sing all over, didn't I? When did you have so much fun?"

"Ira don't talk about us getting married. You become ludicrous again."

"Okay. I'll give you something else to laugh at. How'd you like to go to work for me?"

"Work?"

"You heard it. A job. A position. A profession. I get a message from you—the domestic bit is boring you crazy, aside from the fact you don't get made love to. That newspaper job you had—you miss it."

"Suppose I do."

"You'd be the greatest in my racket. I'll put you on the payroll. Old Cleo has had it. I'm getting ready to lose her anyway. The threads are wearing out."

She jerked her torso to a sitting position. "Isn't it enough you've made the conquest? Am I expected to be your utility infielder, as you call Miss Cooke? Make me available for Fenton Braud and those other dinosaurs?"

"Nah," he laughed. "You'd be mine alone. I mean—with your background you'd fit into the business. I need more brains. Si is overworked. The girls are no help. I've been looking for a new boy. Why not a new girl? You'd knock 'em dead down here. The face. The snotty attitude. They'd slobber over you. I got some big new accounts lined up—real money stuff, not just small change. You could—"

"And what am I supposed to do? Divorce my husband and start a career as a public-relations executive? Just because I've been stupid and selfish enough to have an affair with you? Keep this in mind, Ira—this afternoon's fun is the *absolute* end. It won't happen again."

"It will. So long as you're here it'll happen. The little girl tasted whipped cream for the first time. Try 'n' keep her away from it now."

"Oh, you're repulsive."

"It's perfect. It would be the greatest for both of us. A gasser. A crazy scene." He bounced off the bed and began to pace the room. "You get the divorce. Old Tommy will scream and lose his temper—but so what? He hasn't been able to keep you happy. He's too busy getting mad at those rocks. Or following that screwy old man of yours around. And *that's* some story—"

"And none of your affair."

"Well, he isn't right for you. Guy marries a dame with what you have, he should be prepared to fight off the competitors. The wonder is he's held on to you this long. No kidding, Marty, this is the way I see the plot. You leave Doc Sorrento. I'll set you up. A beach apartment, maid service, a car. And we try it. We don't have to get married. You're going into business with me. DeKay and Maitland, Public Relations Counselors. You'd be so busy you'd forget him in a day. The Beach may not be the Museum of Natural History, but it's *great* for kids. The sun and the swimming. Hell, they'd be better off here than where some boogie can beat them up in Riverside Park. . . ."

"You make it sound so nice. And all this time I'm your mistress?"

"Let's say we're trying it on for size. I'd marry you the day the divorce is final. If you want to give it a whirl single-o, okay. But you'd come around. I'm about ready for the domestic scene. I've been ready since that morning I saw you out at Ellenbogen's land."

"I'd be sick of your jokes in a week."

"But not of this, hey?" He sat at the side of the bed. "When have you felt so good? When did you have so much fun? You'll go back to New York and go nuts. You'll sit in that dusty kitchenette in that dirty apartment and think about the Peruviana and the air-conditioning and the way the kids are taken care of."

"Ira, you are appalling. Hasn't it occurred to you I love my husband? That I owe him something? That the children need both of us?"

He frowned. "Can't I be in love also? Where's the law that

says I have no claims on you? Those kids—they'd be better off with their old lady working and some slick governess herding 'em around."

"You don't love me. You've got some insane notion that I represent a kind of step up for you. You're like my husband's Italian classmates—the football players—who refuse to have anything to do with Italian girls. It gives them some extra kind of pleasure, some little edge, to marry a blond who can't cook. My mother-in-law's on to *them*. And you're just as bad. You keep using the word "class." You think I'd raise your standing. You're wrong, Ira. I'm not nearly as well educated as you think, and I'm not nearly as beautiful as you keep telling me—"

"I'll settle for whatever you got." He lowered his head to her breasts and rested there. "Give it some thought. I don't make offers like this every day. Take advantage now—building coming down. . . ."

He began to caress her, and his clever hands, as expert as a cellist's, forced her to react. Why did someone so skilled and satisfying have to be such a boor?

5 *The Ring*

THE day of Ira's triumph, Si Mermelstein had been assigned two delicate tasks, neither of which appealed to him. He was ordered by Ira to get rid of John Throws Knife, and he had been instructed to enlist Maitland in an attempt to minimize the Avilas affair. Driving out to the dig, he had given the Kiowa Indian an official questionnaire from *The Spirt of Man,* advising him to fill it out when he was back in Oklahoma and mail it to Mr. Ellenbogen. Perhaps in time the peyote tepee would be welcome; at the moment, Mr. Knife would have to understand that his mescaline faith was not entirely in accord with what the exhibit's promoters had in mind. The official of the True American Church looked with furry brown eyes at the papers and pronounced: "Every time an Indian signs something he loses something." But he stuffed it into his blood-colored folder and chewed blissfully on a bean. His coppery face was not dimly aware of the glory that rose about him. He was participant in an older, deeper joy.

Si was astounded by the size of the excavation. Ellenbogen's land had been carved, sectioned off and layed open with what seemed purposeless fury. There were innumerable rows of stakes driven into the soft earth, and there were pits—wide, narrow and circular—almost to the water's edge. The deep trench in which nested the white boulders was almost one hundred and fifty feet long. Si was glad to see that no more had been stolen. A high blue-and-white sign had been erected above the plank fence.

ON THIS SITE WILL RISE

THE SPIRIT OF MAN

The diggers were taking a lunch break. Lila Ellenbogen and her butler were stacking mammoth sandwiches on a bridge table. A plaid cooler stuffed with iced beer cans rested in the hot sand, and alongside it, Maitland sat lumpily in a canvas field chair fanning himself with a dust brush. Beyond, the two hick kids and Peltz were poking in the shell heap, and near the beach a few colored workmen were digging. Sorrento, wielding a long-handled spade, was working in a circular pit south of the boulders. He was stripped to the waist and was sweating violently. His hairy body was blackened and dirt-smudged, and Mermelstein suddenly had a vivid memory of him as the high school hero who had run seventy-five yards for the winning touchdown against James Monroe.

Maitland accepted the news of his Indian friend's fall from grace with good humor. The anthropologist and the Kiowa appeared almost pleased by the repudiation of the True American Church. John Throws Knife advised Maitland that he had already done some missionary work among the Seminole Creeks. He had spent the previous day proselytizing them with hortatory literature and a supply of mescal beans. "I think they'll have a chapter there pretty soon," he told Maitland. "Wait till they chew a few beans."

Mermelstein then got to the point of his call. Ira had come up with a unique notion for unruffling local feathers in re the Avilas matter. To begin with, Si explained, Dr. Maitland had no idea what his attack on the General had started. The State Department's Latin American desk had been on the phone with the mayor; the publisher was planning an exposé of the local university; Ira's own business was in a serious way because of the embarrassing incident. This latter circumstance was the only one that frightened Mermelstein: he knew that without Ira he could never run a successful PR firm. He had no intention of returning to P.S. 178, there to explain *Daniel Deronda* to the Socialistic Gents and other predatory galoots.

And what was Ira's solution? It seemed there was a local radio program—the *Travis Dean Show*—that originated in the lounge of the Blue Paradise Bar. It was a late-night discussion-type show, in which Travis Dean, a brilliant commentator, took on controversial guests for protracted disputation on crucial issues. Everyone in the Beach listened to it. It was an intellectual oasis in the vacation city, Si explained. The anthropologist appeared puzzled. Why did these high-level inquiries take place in a saloon? Lila Ellenbogen, skeptical of anything proffered by deKay, explained that it was the fashion nowadays. Maitland ingested this and approved of the notion. "On the order of Dr. Johnson and his coffee-house conversations, I imagine," he said. "That's it!" Si cried. "That's it exactly!" Mermelstein went on to explain that Ira didn't expect him to exactly apologize for what he said about Avilas, but maybe he could soften it a little. At least, he could explain it was his own idea, that Ira and the University and the Beach were not involved. In fact, he might even mention some nice things about the General. Si's small, worried face quivered behind his outsized glasses, and the misery of this harassed purveyor of trivia softened Maitland. He agreed to appear on the *Travis Dean Show*. "That's swell, Dr. Maitland!" Mermelstein cried. "We'll do it on Saturday night when he gets the biggest audience! I'll get advance word in all the papers!" He plodded back to the car, buoyant.

John Throws Knife bade them all goodbye, leaving a stack of mimeo'd papers on the bridge table. As he walked to join Mermelstein for the drive to the airport, Maitland studied the literature. The flyer was headed: *Articles of Incorporation: True American Church,* and he began to read in his high voice:

> " 'This church is formed to foster and promote religious believers in Almighty God and the customs of the various native tribes in the United States in the worship of a Heavenly Father and to promote morality, sobriety, industry, charity and right living and to cultivate a spirit of brotherly love and union . . .' "

He paused, looking up to wave a last farewell to the Indian, and saw Lila Ellenbogen, busy with the grand lunch, eyeing him oddly.

"Have I done something wrong, my dear?" he asked.

"Oh, not at all, Dr. Maitland. It's just that—well, the Blue Paradise Bar! It's owned by a gangster and they have a floorshow with fairies."

"Splendid!" Maitland cried. "I'm looking forward to it! I really feel I must do something to soothe local feeling about me. I had no idea I'd stir up this kind of brouhaha with my speech."

She opened a fresh can of beer for him and spooned a dollop of potato salad on a cardboard plate set before him. In his faded field uniform, his girth inflating the canvas chair, he suggested a retired white hunter, an alcoholic tropical tramp, living out his years with a native wife and memories of *simba*.

"I think you enjoy doing it," she said. "Am I right? I mean—you love to shock people and make them take notice."

"I suppose I am becoming a show-off in my old age. That's the trouble with academicians. We suffer secretly the outside world's snubs, making believe we don't need their approbation, and then in the autumn of our lives we become exhibitionists to make up for all the lost years. We're victims of the celebrity complex as much as our friend Mr. deKay. Why else would I be reduced to telling stories about foreskins?"

"I can see where Tom gets that talent for minimizing everything he does," Lila said. "You and he would never admit it, but every single constructive social change of the past fifty years originated in a university. And probably in a department like anthropology or sociology."

"How sweet of you," Maitland said, "and how naïve. I won't argue that our notions are slowly working their way into the fabric of modern life—for better or worse, I'm not sure—but the fact is, we're there only by sufferance."

"I'm not sure I follow you." The Burleys and Ben Peltz lined up apologetically at the bridge table, availed themselves of the rich lady's foodstuffs, and retreated to a hot patch of sand where they squatted and ate. Only Tom continued digging. He had dropped to his knees and was troweling. His black head would bob over the rim of the pit every few seconds.

"Well—as an example, take our friend Dave Ballard and his current preoccupation," Maitland said.

"But that's just the point! Dave's education is what's made him join the crusade for his people!" Lila cried.

"Quite the contrary. It is the *crusade,* as you call it, with its mystic connotations that has sucked him into its vortex. It's quite true that the Benedicts and the Boases proved the fallacy of race, the viciousness of prejudice, the resultant chaos in human relationships. But who really cared? Who listened to them? No one but their students, and I assure you, many of them slept through the lectures and passed their examinations with crib notes. The organized battle against racial prejudice, against lingering Gobineau-ism, will succeed only when it is taken over by older and more dedicated forces. Appeals for integration of the races base themselves on two ancient precepts, more powerful than dusty reason and tiresome truth: *money and faith.* It is good *business* to integrate. It is also *good for the soul.* With the trader and the priest on the side of Ballard's friends, they must win their fight eventually. Armed only with truth, with the cold logic of the university, they would not succeed in desegregating a single rest room."

"But that makes your work so much more admirable!" Lila said. "You and your friends proved that it was wrong to have race prejudice! What do you care who puts it into practice?"

"I don't really. If the chambers of commerce and the World Council of Churches seek to steal my academic thunder, let them. They're better equipped for the long haul than I am."

Tom's dusty head rose above the trench; his hairy chest was soaked. He rested against the wall of the pit and squinted at the bottom where he had been troweling.

"Hey, Hall," he gasped. "Look at this before I dig it out." He turned his head. "Benny! Get the camera!"

Maitland waddled to the pit. The others followed. The trench had been started as a test pit; when it had yielded a half-dozen postholes, Tom had decided to enlarge it. Maitland had hoped that more digging might reveal additional holes, possibly in a pattern. When they reached the trench they saw that the new find was not in the nature of the familiar dark stains, but was a large artifact. Tom had troweled neatly around it, and it rested on its matrix of muck, about a yard south of the stake-marked postholes. The object was of gray-brown stone, considerably larger and heavier than any of the small pieces of pottery and tools that had been found previously. It resembled a giant's doughnut—the diameter of the hole about eighteen inches, the over-all diameter about two and one-half feet. Although cunningly hewn to almost perfect geometric roundness, some eight or nine inches had been broken off, so that the circle was incomplete.

"Well I'll be damned," Maitland said softly. He hopped into

the pit and knelt, over the mysterious stone wheel. "This may be the *ring*."

Tom loosened some earth around its edges. "You sure, Hall?"

"I don't know. I've seen Mayan rings and the dimensions are about the same."

Sorrento looked up at Peltz. "You see this, Ben? You could shoot fouls through it all day."

Peltz frowned and said nothing. Since Ballard's departure he tended to lapse into sullen silences—his old readiness to snarl seemed to have vanished.

"You mean it was like *basketball?*" Lila asked. "I thought it was more like soccer. You know—the way Tom showed us the other day—using the rear end and the knees."

"It had several variations," Maitland explained. He ran his hand lovingly over the pitted surface of the stone ring. "The Mayans had the most advanced form of the ball game. The rings were permanently affixed by mortar and masonry into the high walls of the arena. But prior to this, the game was played on simpler courts that weren't enclosed. So the ring was mounted on a high stone pillar, or tenon. Now there's also evidence that before *this* stage, there was an even more modest version of the game, in which portable rings were used. They were lashed to high wooden poles and removed when the game was over. Now if I were to hazard a guess, I'd say this ring might be in the latter category." He indicated the missing section. "It's quite possible that this missing section contained an aperture, or a notch of some kind to facilitate fastening it to the shaft."

"Yeah," Tom said. "It was like a Sunday game in Van Cortlandt Park. You brought along home plate and the bases and then took 'em home at night because the kids from Morris Avenue might steal them."

Maitland chuckled. "Not quite that simple, Tom. The rings had religious significance, and it's not unlikely that they were stored in the homes of the priests when they weren't in use. As a matter of fact, the Mayans carved the likenesses of their gods into the ring. There was a monkey-god, for example, who ruled the game—a sort of combination of Babe Ruth and St. Francis."

"I guess it was a big deal when a guy knocked the ball through," Tom said. "Imagine batting that heavy lump of rubber through a hole—just using your *tuchas* and your knees? They must have declared a national holiday when anyone made a bucket."

"Just about," said Maitland. "A player who scored a goal was honored and feted for days. He won a variety of valuable prizes and generally had his pick of the women."

Peltz had set his camera on its tripod and was photographing the unearthed ring. He had set a metal measuring tape alongside it, to indicate its size. A few of the Negro workmen had drifted over to the site, and having satisfied themselves that the excitement over another old rock was hardly worth it, returned to their excavations.

"If I might hypothesize further," Maitland said, "these surrounding postholes may have supported a platform on which the ring-pole was erected. I think it would be advantageous to extend this trench."

When the Burleys had returned to work, when Benny had concluded his photographing and Lila had trudged back to the field commissary, Maitland, whose physical contributions to the work had been marginal, seized a spade and began to extend the pit that had just yielded the ring. Sweat poured in jagged rills down his liquored face and he grunted with each thrust of the shovel.

"Go easy, Hall," Tom said. "I'll do this."

"No, no!" the anthropologist protested. "Every hand is needed. I tell you, Tom, I suspect we're standing on the *only known Arawak* settlement on the North American mainland. We've *got* to clean this whole area. If I had my way, I'd hack through that causeway to the other side of the road."

Sorrento snorted. "I got a feeling the rent is due any day."

Maitland thrust his spade into the soft earth: the labor was almost therapeutic. "Has Ellenbogen broached the matter to you?"

"No, but it's in the air. Especially since the Avilas business." Tom relit his black cigar stub and knelt again.

"I'm sorry, Tom," Maitland said. "Perhaps we can make it up to them. I'll let myself be interviewed by this truth-seeker and explain it was a misunderstanding."

He resumed digging. "Fancy that. Seminars in saloon."

6 *An Honorary Member*

HAVING assured herself that her entrapment by deKay was but a freakish lapse of judgment, Marty now proceeded to enjoy his skills on a daily basis. She found herself anticipating the meetings with hidden shiverings and a sweet terror, sentiments that aroused her as much as the repetitive disrobings and couplings that now followed a meticulous schedule. Sometimes she went directly to the suite, sometimes to the cabana, there to await his summons. After the first encounter, she returned to the patio convinced that everyone was studying her, that the guests around the pool knew. But when she had settled again in the comforting chaise, facing the embalming sun, she realized that no one knew, and if they did, nobody cared. Did she look different? Smell different? Was there a large red splotch on her face or on a thigh to indicate she had sinned? The assurance that her appearance had not altered comforted her on a more important level. Tom would never know, would never guess. That was the intriguing aspect of an adulterous relationship; it did not alter your exterior, nor did it involve much beyond certain simple physical acts that were no more complex than getting into a tight girdle or doing calisthenics in the morning. Did the primitive liaison of flesh and flesh make her less of a wife or mother? *It did not,* she advised herself. The culmination of the adulterous process was almost comic; how could it infringe on the truer love, the older loyalty?

And yet as the first week of their pairing drew to a close, she knew she was deceiving herself. She looked forward to the meetings with increasing anticipation; when she was away from the Peruviana, she thought about it constantly. At the boathouse, at the Ellenbogens', shopping in town, her mind seemed incapable of any other concentration than the crude burning sensations of Ira's bed, his soft hypocrite's words, his exquisite skills, his energies. In the evenings, Tom—sullen and clouded with smoke from his cigars—would sit with her father and discuss the day's work, the prospect of winding up the dig. She would join them, silent, disinterested, pretending to read a book, or sewing, or offering an occasional comment on their pursuit of the vanished culture. On these occasions, her mind brimming with recollection and envisioning the next day's sport, she almost experienced a secret malicious delight in their ignorance. *If only they knew*—she found herself saying. The secrecy lent it zest. One afternoon when a light rain fell, Ira came to the cabana and they made love behind the locked doors on a still-damp chaise, listening to the happy sound of the drops, secure and warm and alone in the candy-striped interior. She fancied she enjoyed that one best of all; the whole world was outside the cabana door—unknowing, unaware of their pleasures, plagued with frustrations and problems and unfulfilled desires while they—Martha Maitland Sorrento and friend—indulged their heightened senses in the private cell.

With each session, Ira argued his case more persuasively. There was not the faintest doubt in his mind that he would have her—if not as wife, then as professional associate. With her newspaper training, her intelligence, her beauty, she would be an enormous success at PR; the two of them divested of Cleo's bland whorishness, could "murder 'em" at the Beach. He could tell she craved work, a challenge, that the domestic life had palled on her and that Tom's penuriousness, tough as it sounded, was no help to a staggering marriage. He made his points again and again, varying the theme slightly, always interspersing it with the bouts of passion he knew she could not resist, the acts he had forced her to admit gave her more pleasure than she had ever known. Withal, she managed marvelously to maintain some small distance between them. *If only you weren't such an ignoramus, Ira*—and he would abandon the sales talk for the time being and resort to techniques he knew were infallible.

As the affair progressed, each meeting acting as a goad toward the next, she found herself summoning up mental images of what Ira's proffered new life would be like. Apart from the fact that she expected the children would suffer—and the whole idea was impossible anyway because Ira was Ira—she discovered she rather liked the notion. The modern, maid-kept apartment, the children under the care of some watchful guardian, the return to the office routine, writing, telephoning, the desk crammed with impedimenta. . . .

She permitted her daydreaming in this area to take her only so far; it seemed to Marty that these thoughts were infinitely more sinful than her submission to deKay's ineluctable body. She told herself (often while Tom, the innocent, and Hall, the indifferent, sat arguing about stratification on the balcony, five feet from her) that what she was engaged in with Ira was a lapse, an imprudence, a self-indulgence, that *had* to be trivial and temporary because Ira was everything she was *against.* A dirty trick of physicality, a concatenation of events had thrust them upon each other, and had caused her surrender. But it was capitulation on the lowest of levels, an animal coupling of two disparate people. Once she rid herself of the impulse to bed down with him, to abandon her limbs to his wild virility, the world would be set right again. Back in New York, once more into the routine of a University wife, her excursion into Ira's extravagant world of champagne-in-the-afternoon and Chinese beach coats would be all ended. Her better nature, that side of her that was cognizant of eternal truths and responsibilities, would be not a whit affected by the frantic perspirings, the agonized gasps and moans of the Peruviana. Ira deKay and his diaphanous world would be gone forever from her life. And so advising herself, she would set out once more for the hotel, her steps quickened and her eyes preternaturally bright, in search of the conquerer, barely able to suppress the tremulous longings that heralded the afternoon's joys.

Of all the people at the site, only Lila Ellenbogen—in some dark, racial manner—sniffed at conspiracy. She blurted out her instinctive suspicions, barely aware of what she was saying. "Marty!" she cried one day from her pit. "Off to the cabana again? What's deKay got going there for you? A three-ring circus?" And she had smiled back tolerantly: "I'm awful, I guess. I've become a regular beach bum."

And she would settle into the front seat of Ira's chariot, alongside the former teacher of English literature, and speed off. Behind her, the innocent children lounged in bored lassitude. They had grown increasingly docile and lumpish since their enrollment at the Peruviana's day camp. The hot sun and the salty sea appeared to have blunted their sharp little personalities, covering them with a healthy brown coating of sloth and happiness, as sweetly bland as mass-produced milk chocolate.

As the shops and hotels sped by, she was momentarily unsettled by a sense of *belonging,* a kind of honorary membership that permitted her to enjoy the fruits of indolence, but at the same time endowed her with an untouchable, unchangeable essence. As such, she was the moral and intellectual superior of the Ira deKays and the Cleo Cookes: there was no harm in her sipping at the fountain of joy since she was too clever to get drunk. These rationalizations, arrived at with much painstaking logic, could not wholly dispel the growing sense that she *wanted* the life of the

Beach, that her submission to deKay, to his hotel rooms and his loot champagne, were deep and true cracks in her once inviolate armor.

7 *Return to Blue Paradise*

When Maitland, Tom and Si arrived at the Blue Paradise Bar, Mr. Banjo and his manager, Walt Kapustka, had just concluded their radio interview with Travis Dean. The radio program, which was heard from midnight to three in the morning, was conducted from the "lounge bar" of the night club, a dim, cavernous room set apart from the main arena where the Blue Paradise floor show, a snappy review featuring transvestites and pederasts, was held.

The bar was semicircular in shape, frightfully crowded and alarmingly noisy. Tom did not understand the mysteries of radio, but he wondered how the program of controversial interviews—conducted from a long table on a raised dais only twenty feet from the bar—could possibly be audible amid the din. There were three microphones on the table, and behind one of them, Travis Dean, a youngish, dark man with mobile features and a spongy voice, was reading a commercial for a credit company. He read with love and care; his was the soft sell imbued with deep personal conviction. Despite the guffawing and loud liquored chatter at the bar, he made himself heard. Shutting his eyes, Tom realized where he had heard similar determined, relentless voices: Travis Dean had the drive and concentration of a demonstrator of spot remover in Woolworth's. No amount of heckling, of teen-age crudities, of women shoppers' febrile babble, could deter him.

Charlie Rasmussen, who also served as part-time leg man for Dean, materialized in the gloom and guided them to a table. An ill-tempered engineer in a two-dollar sport shirt (automatic pencils decorating his floral pocket like cartridges in a Cossack's *kaputta*) bent bitterly over a control board, pressing an ancient headset to his skull. Dean concluded his recommendations regarding the credit company, introduced a record and got up, as the engineer cued in the first few bars of a hymn recorded by three actresses. The interviewer walked briskly to Maitland's table and introduced himself to the anthropologist and to Tom.

"Mighty glad you came aboard, Doc," Travis Dean said. "There's no holds barred on this li'l ole show. You say what's eating you."

Si Mermelstein cleared his throat. "Well, Travis, the idea—the thing Charlie and I mentioned to you the other day—is that Dr. Maitland explain some of the things he said about General Avilas."

"Oh?" Dean asked. "Oh, yeah. I remember. Ira deKay's bit. Sure, Doc—however you want. I'll just kinda noodle along and ask you about the General, and integration and Red China. It's what I call the high-level, deep-thinker-type interview." He slouched off to the men's room.

Charlie Rasmussen scowled. "Big jerk. He useta do the station breaks for coffee and. Now he's a thinker. We had to issue the bum a working-press card. He speaks at journalism schools."

"I'm afraid I'm lost," Maitland said. "Is this a new development in contemporary journalism? The interview on current affairs—from the lounge of a night club? Is there any significance to it?"

Rasmussen shrugged. "I guess it started down here. Dean was probably the first to do it. I tell you what keeps people listening. You see them phones?"

Tom and Maitland peered toward the long table. There were a half-dozen telephones on it, each equipped with a red beacon that blinked in lieu of buzzing.

"People call in to argue with him, insult him, threaten him. And he insults them back. That's the whole appeal. Because he thought up that gimmick he thinks he's Walter Lippmann now."

A waiter took their orders and returned in a few seconds with doubles—on orders, Tom imagined, from his *goombar*. Mr. Nudo, who lurked hazily in the background. Mr. Banjo and his proprietor, having concluded their interview, noticed Si Mermelstein and left their table to join, uninvited, the Maitland group. As soon as the owner and the ape were seated, Si apologized to Maitland.

"I really hope you don't mind, Dr. Maitland," Mermelstein said. "You know—being seen in public with an ape."

"Not at all," Maitland said. "I like animals. My friend Hooton would have loved this chap." He tickled Mr. Banjo's red whiskers, but the orang slept stonily in his master's arms. The late hours were too much for his little body, and being of low metabolism, he was given to long slumbers.

Walt addressed himself to Mermelstein. "How come Mr. Banjo didn't make *Look* magazine this week? We took all the pictures of him judging the baton-twirling contest and Ira promised they'd be in *Look*."

Rasmussen frowned at the manager and the dormant ape in the smoky gloom. "Whyn'cha go home? People are gettin' sick of that dumb monkey."

"I don't hafta take that," Walt whined. "Mr. Banjo doesn't have to be insulted. I'm tellin' Ira what you said. Why isn't he here?"

Walt started to rise, a difficult feat with the hairy weight in his arms, and Maitland deterred him.

"Do stay, young man," Maitland said. "I like your friend. I've never seen an orangutan so well trained. It's remarkable."

The manager sat, mollified. "It's the tranquilizers. Vitamin B-complex and big shots of tranquilizers. Once a week, I give him an enema."

Maitland nodded approvingly. He turned to Tom. "A lovely specimen. *Pongo pygmaeus*—"the man of the forest." Notice the nice round cranium and the absence of the supraorbital ridge. He must be rather young—I don't see any of the typical flattening of the cheeks."

"He's just a baby," the manager said with a maternal flutter in his voice. "The dealer I bought him from said maybe he was a midget. You know—like he'd never get much bigger. I certainly hope so."

Tom edged aside, to permit the solicitous waiter to bring them a second round of doubles. Maitland was drinking hundred-proof bourbon—clear amberous liquor. He would cradle the whisky in his mouth briefly and then down it, neat.

"You wouldn't have such a big clothing bill if he stayed a shrimp, is that it?" Tom asked.

Si giggled. "Oh, heck, Tom, that doesn't bother him. Mr. Banjo gets—what is it now?—a thousand bucks a week?"

"Eleven fifty. We got an escalator clause in the new contract."

Maitland drained his bourbon. "I had no idea he was that famous. What does he do?"

"Oh, he don't do much of anything," the manager said. "He kind of fools around on the TV. You know—eats the script and makes everybody laugh. He's kind of hard to train. He doesn't do tricks like those chimps you see, but that's why he's so popular."

"It figures," Tom said. "No one's jealous of him."

"That's the idea," the manager said.

Mr. Banjo was clad in a tailored tuxedo. His vestigial feet were encased in black patent-leather pumps.

"Why is he so lumpy around the middle?" Tom asked.

"Diapers," the manager explained. "Around the house, back home, he's clean as can be. He always makes in the toilet and pulls the chain himself. But when we're on the road like this, he gets excited so I have to keep him diapered up."

Eleven hundred and fifty dollars a week. The manager's announcement was like a ritualistic pronouncement in a wizard's unknown tongue: it defied analysis, criticism, examination. In Tom's mind the figures developed a life of their own, a sanctity and a privilege that negated the real world. What was an escalator clause?

Travis Dean returned to his microphone and signaled in the direction of their table. Charlie Rasmussen whispered to Maitland that he was on. The anthropologist got up shakily and Tom realized he had imbibed too freely in too short a space of time. He had downed three double shots of bourbon in less than half an hour; his face was the color of a seed-catalogue dahlia and his skinny shanks seemed unequal to the task of supporting his engorged torso. Guided by Rasmussen, he found his way to the long table and sat puffing alongside Dean. The commentator shuffled a sheaf of yellow papers, found what he wanted, and appeared ready for the interview when a telephone began to blink.

"*Oops*—a live one!" Dean said. He picked up the phone and cradled it on his shoulder, still examining the yellow papers. "Hallo out there," he said. "What's your name and may we put you on the beeper?"

The caller consented and Dean pressed a button. The disembodied voice was now heard, issuant from a small speaker, and intercepted by periodic *beeps*.

"Well, Mr. Dean, this is Fred P. Horton of Cayman Beach, and I'd like to take exception to your comment yesterday about Tito—"

Dean cut him off rudely. "Listen, boy, you should know by now where I stand on Tito. I'm on his list and he's on mine. And you know what that list is."

"But you said last night that he—"

"Just a minute. Just one minute. If you please, I've made myself clear on Tito many, many times. You need not give me lectures on Tito. I kid you not."

The caller tried again. "You stated that Tito—"

"Don't get cute with me, sir. No sir, not with me. My position on Tito is well known. Thank you. Thank you, sir. That will be enough. You're wasting my time." He hung up. "Everybody's in show business," he said with disgust.

Tom noticed that the well-dressed people at the bar were totally unconcerned with him. They chattered and laughed, oblivious to the high-level disputation on the dais. It was as if the Security Council were holding a meeting in the mezzanine of Madison Square Garden during a wrestling match.

"Now then, for our guest," Dean said. He found a page of typewritten notes and proceeded to read. "He's a controversial fellow, to say the least, and you probably read about him in the papers just this week. He's Professor Hall Maitland, who stirred up a little jazz at the ceremonies for General Avilas over at the University. I'm told the prof would like to explain his statements and kind of make up for what he said. The mike's yours, Prof—and remember—anything goes on the *Travis Dean Show*."

Maitland sighed. "Thank you, young man. I—ah—I agreed to say a few words here because of the fuss caused by my speech at the University. Let me say that I'm dreadfully sorry to have caused *anyone* any trouble. I did not clear my comments with anyone in advance. Consequently, neither the university, nor the sponsors of the award, nor the public-relations people who engaged my services are to be held accountable. I pulled a surprise on them and I regret it. Moreover, I've been advised that General Avilas himself was never *personally* guilty of assassinating or executing his enemies. I am happy to learn this and I wish him well. The fact of the matter is, I thought I was complimenting him on his brilliant use of liberal dogma."

Maitland looked appealingly at the interviewer. "That is about all I have to say on the Avilas affair. Does it serve the purpose?"

"*So-lid,* Prof," Dean said casually. "Now that the body's buried, let's proceed." He consulted a list of questions. Apparently someone had researched Maitland's background and the details of the dig.

"Prof, what's this digging bit over on Bay Islet? You want to tell us peasants about it?"

"It's been rather well covered in your newspapers," Maitland said cautiously. "It's part of my university's ten-year program to learn something about settlement patterns among the Eastern Amerind cultures."

Dean seemed to delay before getting to his next query. He read it from a sheet secreted beneath the stack. "Prof, there's been some unpleasant noise around town that the excavation bit is a front."

"A front?"

"Well, don't quote me. It's not my idea. But I hear talk. Like isn't it a fact that one of your people quit to work for the Hilltown boycott group?"

"That's quite true. But I assure you, he did it on his own."

"And wasn't another of your fellows a Red? A commola?"

"That's true, too. But he's been cleared. I beg your pardon, they don't like the word *cleared*—it implies they can keep you from working. They prefer to call them *cooperative witnesses*."

"Mmmm-hum." Dean chewed a pencil. His show-biz jargon, his lubricated voice had the tendency to reduce his serious questions, his interrogations about the state of the world and man's fate, to a vaudeville dialogue. Maitland, in his mind's eye, envisioned Travis Dean and John Foster Dulles, both in blackface and top hats, exchanging outrageous puns on the matter of the offshore islands. *Mr. Bones, gimme a sentence wit' deh woid Formosa. Formosa? Formosa deh summer I likes to swim, 'cept when it gets cool . . . yok, yok, yok!*

"Professor Maitland," Dean asked. "what are your own personal views on integrating the races?"

"My views?"

"You're on, pal. Say what you want. Listen—anything goes here. I had the NAACP fellah on last week. Go ahead."

"Well I really have nothing startling to say. You see—from an anthropologist's standpoint, integration has been going on for centuries in the South. Biological integration, that is. It's inevitable that social integration will follow."

"Biological—"

"Yes. A walk through any colored community will convince you of that. The abundance of light-skinned Negroes—redheads, thin noses, pale eyes. Some of the finest blood in the South flows through Negro veins. There was a Pullman porter I met recently who was a dead ringer for J. E. B. Stuart."

"Do I read you right, Professor? Are you saying—"

"I'm saying that sexual license is one of the most attractive aspects of racialism. You won't find this discussed in the learned analyses in the New York *Times Magazine* but it's there—ugly and primordial and terribly true. Naturally, it's a one-way arrangement. Male members of the ascendant group are entitled to unlimited favors from female members of the suppressed group. It's not a new notion. You don't think all those handsome *mestizos* in Latin America were a result of spontaneous generation, do you? The conquistadores knew a good thing when they saw it."

"Doctor, I think maybe—"

"But of course, that's the damnable thing. It's a wonderful advantage for the ascendant males. What they dread more than anything else is a reversal of the roles. What would happen, they shudderingly ask, if the underdogs became top-dog? Would the production of what they call mongrel children be perpetuated—but with the pigmentation of dam and sire now reversed? They should know something about the problem. The white Southern male is probably the world's best expert on mongrelization in this country, being responsible for most of it. I assure you, his vigor and his cleverness have done more to increase the mulatto population than the entire population of Greenwich Village."

Travis Dean managed a hoarse interjectory cough. "I—ah—I—ah—think you've posed a lot of hot questions, Professor Maitland, and I'm sure our listeners realize these are your views and yours alone. And that if they differ in any way, they're free to—"

Maitland, terribly drunk, barely heard him. "Now then, there's the matter of inferior races and so forth. Again, speaking as an anthropologist, I've always contended that the Negro represents a physiological stage further removed from the anthropoid apes than the Caucasian. This may seem odd at first blush. We are all familiar with the usages of the word "gorilla" or "ape" or "monkey" to denote a Negro. May I point out that nothing could be more inaccurate from an anthropologist's standpoint?"

He wobbled to his feet and gestured to Tom. "Oh, Tom! Ask the chap to bring the orangutan here!"

Walt, delighted with a chance to return to the public ear, lugged the sleeping ape to the table. Maitland stretched Mr. Banjo on the white cloth and stood over him. In the dusky light the tableau suggested a Rembrandt medical lecture.

"For the benefit of our friends out there in radio land," Maitland said, "I have before me a male specimen of *Pongo pygmaeus*—the orangutan of Malaya and Borneo, age about seventeen months. Let's note some similarities and differences between our friend the ape and *Homo sapiens*."

All six phones on Travis Dean's table were blinking furiously, and the interviewer was signaling wildly to a pretty female assistant to take the calls. He was in no frame of mind to stand off the Confederacy.

"First of all—the matter of skin color or pigmentation," Maitland said. "Note that beneath the reddish hair, our ape has a ruddy, pinkish skin. Closer to Negro or Caucasian? Well, that was an easy one. If you were to shave this little fellow, he might pass muster in the locker room of an exclusive country club in Mobile, Alabama. That brings up the matter of body hair. The orang, the chimp, the gorilla—they are all quite hairy. But of all the races of man, none are as hirsute as the *white* race. Negroes tend to be free of body hair. The average Anglo-Saxon, by comparison, is a walking thicket. Note too, the thin lips and small nose of the orangutan. A far cry indeed from the full thick lips and broad, large nose of the Negroid race. Much closer to our Alpine and Nordic stocks. I might add that the much-discussed supra-orbital ridges of the chimpanzee and the gorilla—less noticeable in the orangutan—are most evident among certain Balkan and Dalmatian peoples—whites. Most African Negroes have remarkably smooth foreheads, although pronounced ridges are frequent among the Bushmen of Australia. But that of course is another story. I suspect I've made my point."

He sat down. The presence of the ape had caused several of the people at the bar to turn and study the tableau: the prostrate orang, the fat man in a 1930 suit, lecturing in the fine tones of the classroom, the pale troubled face of Travis Dean, the fearless interviewer. While diverted by the scene, the drinkers had heard nothing of Maitland's comments. They gazed at him with the dimly amused, placidly contemptuous stare of the *lumpen* middle class.

"Well, I guess I got a little more than I bargained for," Dean said lamely. "You realize, Prof, lots of our good listeners will disagree with you. And that's one of the nice things about America, is how anyone can stand up and have his say. No matter how unpopular his or her views may be."

"You've been most generous letting me go on like this. Did I talk too much?"

"No—no—not at all." Dean's female assistant, a gamin in pony tail and angular glasses, handed him a slip. She had been manning the frenzied phones and had been desperately writing down questions.

"Ah, before you leave, maybe you'd like to answer a few queries our listeners phoned in," Dean said. "You know, we have a kind of open house here on opinions. . . ."

He squinted at the paper. "A listener wants to know why the Negroes are so backward, with their big crime rate and so forth."

Maitland waited a moment before answering. "I think the answer to that is not an explanation as to how *bad* they are, but a loud cheer for how *good* they are under the circumstances. I never cease to wonder why *all* of them aren't criminals, why *all* of them don't conspire to murder us in our sleep. The miraculous thing is that there are so many law-abiding, intelligent colored citizens, considering the arbitrary rules we've set up about the limits of their lives. What worries me is not the Negro mugger or addict. He'll be effectively reduced as soon as the social picture gives the Negro more breathing space. What does distress me is the growing tendency of the educated Negro to mimic the shabbiest and most vapid aspects of our culture. Beauty queens—fraternal orders favoring the fez—a kind of jolly brainless gathering around barbecues—I wish we could offer them a better model. But maybe they'll come up with a good one of their own. Now that would be novel. Or would it? After all, the slaves of ancient Greece produced some of its finest art and philosophy." Maitland halted abruptly. "I'm afraid I'm rambling, sir. What's the next request?"

The next request was not interrogatory but peremptory. It was an order from the president of the radio station to get that goddamned crazy bastard off the air before someone threw a stick of dynamite at the transmitter. The young woman in the pony tail, taking the message from the executive on one of the telephones, scrawled it hastily on her pad and shoved it under Travis Dean's sweating face. The purveyor of controversy immediately introduced a new arrangement of *Wang Wang Blues* and, with a limp handshake, dismissed the anthropologist.

Maitland walked stiffly off the dais. In the smoky haze, he discerned Tom, Mermelstein and Rasmussen, rising in hushed awe, as if to offer him a standing ovation. He had the feeling that it was the end of the school year; they were three devoted undergraduates about to offer him the academic accolade he loved best of all.

Marty and Ira had listened to the interview in the latter's car. He had called for her unexpectedly, a few minutes after Tom and her father had left. She had dressed hastily, arranged for Wilma to stay with the children, and without protest or anxiety, permitted herself to be driven to a barren stretch of beach, where, at the dead end of a sandy road, he parked the car (convertible top up, doors discreetly locked) and made love to her. When the mechanics became difficult, it was she who suggested they retire to the back seat.

Their labors concluded, Ira sped back to the boathouse. All the way home they listened to Maitland's high-pitched alcoholic voice lecturing "his friends out there in radio land." His use of that phrase was more grating to Marty than the heresy he preached. Maitland had used it not in jest, but in the belief that this was the proper mode of addressing a radio audience. Back in the thirties, she recalled, he had been a member of a radio panel show and the phrase was probably a vestige of that limited contact with the mass media. What seemed to her callow ineptitude on his part, a kind of hick's unease in the new world, negated all his Olympian pronouncements about race.

"Zotz!" Ira complained. "Wait'll I get my mitts on Si. He euchred me into this. Why didn't your old man just apologize and get lost? That muffin-head Travis Dean, getting him started on the stove-lids."

"Can't you go a little faster? Are you sure you'll get me home before Tom gets there?"

"No sweat. You'll be comfy and cozy in your bed long before he is. You'll sleep better, too. You like what just happened?"

"Yes. But don't talk about it."

"I looked at a cooperative apartment up at North Beach yesterday. Beautiful li'l ocean-front job. Two bedrooms and a maid's room and all furnished in Swedish mod-ren. We'll talk to Tom tonight and . . ."

"No. I don't want to discuss it."

"I'm canning Cleo. Got to have room for the new girl."

"It won't be me. I'm going back to New York in a few weeks with my family. I'm acting abominably, I know. To you—and to my husband."

"I'm not complaining. It's the best *I* ever had. And from an expert like me, that's high praise."

True to his timetable, he had her back at the boathouse well before Tom's return. The dutiful Wilma, asking no questions, perceiving no sin (Ira had parked the car on the blacktop and walked to the boathouse), went below to see Oran.

"Where did *she* go?" he whispered.

Wilma's eyes wobbled behind the distorting lenses. "I don't know. She said she had to pay a visit."

Oran frowned. "*He* was here."

"Who?"

"*Him*. The fellow with the big car. I was in here looking for my notebook and I saw him come down the path and go upstairs to see her. Then he came down and went out the gate again."

Wilma gasped. She ducked her head and chewed on a knuckle.

"And then a few minutes later, she came down, all dressed up and walked out the gate also."

"Are you sure? Oran—it doesn't have to mean anything!"

He patted the fall of yellow hair on his protuberant forehead. "Then I walked up and peeked through the wooden fence and I saw her get into his car and they drove away. And just now he drove her back."

"What are you going to do?" Wilma asked fretfully. "Are you going to tell Tom? Should we?"

He grasped her leathery hand. "We better not. We just better not, because Tom might kill him."

They went to their cubicles, doomed to sleeplessness and a night of horrid images. For Oran, it was torment unlike any he had ever known. He had seen Martha Sorrento, in high heels and silk stockings and a pleated skirt, get into the big car that belonged to that crazy fellow who was always hanging around, and they were both laughing and very happy. When she had sat next to him, he had leaned over and kissed her neck and her ear, and she kept smiling and laughing all the time. If he had seen Ira deKay plunge a knife into Tom Sorrento's heart he could not have been more aggrieved.

8 *A Believer in Marginal Gains*

MAITLAND left the next morning. He glanced at the newspaper coverage of his interview and decided he had tarried too long. Guatemala beckoned; he owed it to Tom to clear out. Moreover, the discovery of the curious broken ring augured new thrilling discoveries. The academic honors that loomed were his son-in-law's, and the longer he stayed, the more likely it would be that he, Maitland, would be associated with the historic find. His daughter was right—in his old age, he was becoming an impossible ham, a seeker of the spotlight, an advocate of unpopular notions and extreme opinions for their own sake.

Tom drove him to the airport in the pickup truck. Marty had not bothered awakening to bid him farewell. Of late, she had become a compulsive sleeper, Tom noticed, clinging to the narrow bed with the determination of an Antaeus drawing strength from the earth.

The pickup bounced erratically over the main drag of the sleeping Beach, speeding along the boulevard of palms and hotels. It made a frightful retching noise when Tom shifted gears, and he had the feeling that high in the air-conditioned rooms, love-sated and half-drunk vacationers stirred and farted in answer to the truck's rude alarum.

"I've enjoyed myself down here," Maitland said.

"You roused 'em a little."

"I don't mean those border skirmishes with the True Believers," Maitland said. "Actually, I'm sorry I got poor John Throws Knife involved with them. And I never would have gotten into trouble with Avilas if he hadn't stolen my speech. I had no intention of causing a rift with an ally. What I've really enjoyed is the *atmosphere*."

"Like what? Lila's meals? Hall, I sometimes think you'd do or say anything for a good dinner."

"That's just part of it." He gestured expansively, taking in the lavish stores and dazzling hostelries that rose about them. "The whole grand idea. The sense of warm, dulling pleasure. The appeasement of belly. I used to think it was awful, but I see its virtues now."

"You sure as hell don't see eye to eye with Marty. This place almost had her bedded down with Southern crud."

"Martha is an incurable nay-sayer. In my dotage, I am concerned only with the defanging of man, the reduction and subjugation of his murderous propensities. I think they may have found the answer, or part of it, here. All this emphasis on mindless pleasure—it may yet save us all. Even *The Spirit of Man* moves me. The notion that all faiths are rather decent, that *all* practitioners of *any* faith are good chaps—isn't that a major step forward? Isn't that better than more exhausting *jihads?*"

"They weren't ready to let the True American Church in."

"I suspect they'll have second thoughts. The peyote tepee will find its way to *The Spirit of Man* soon enough."

Sorrento scowled at the anthropologist. "You mean to tell me that this boobish nonsense down here—this obsession with laughs and the fast buck and sloth—that this can possibly help Dave Ballard and those people in Hilltown?"

"By no means. It won't help him, but in its capacity to distract and bemuse, it may spare him a lot of trouble. The Interfaith Bowling League may succeed where the ADA will fail. I tell you, so long as people are not at each other's throats, we are ahead of the game. I have reached the point where I judge all social institutions—governments, religions, fraternal orders, what have you—by one standard. And it's simply this: to what extent do they repress or transmute into something viable, man's capacity to murder and maim? One more speech on brotherhood by that young Episcopalian fellow in New York, and I may join his church. I am all for the new generalized religion. I like it defanged and declawed. I will take my brotherhood from any quarter, applaud all pleas for tolerance and understanding, whether by the Knights of Columbus or the B'nai B'rith or the African M.E. Zion Church. Will a man's church attendance lower his threshold for murder and hate? I am for that church. Will a vacation in this tropic nirvana make him less inclined toward torturing the next man? Then let us have more such vacations. If the feast of good will that *The Spirit of Man* hopes to engender succeeds in causing *one* citizen to think better of his neighbor, I will be the first to buy a ticket of admission and I will stay for the lecture-with-colored-slides of the Holy Land. I turn down no offers, I welcome all comers—from Mr. deKay with his curious concatenary arrangements, to the peddlers of success through faith. I welcome all marginal gains."

"You never should have taken that job with the concentration-camp commission. It's soured you on everything, Hall. Why don't you admit it's all a racket?"

"A good deal of it is. But I prefer these relatively harmless rackets, peddlings of small dogma and propitiation of lesser gods. Better these than the sort of thing that ended with the soap burial."

Tom said nothing. He wheeled the clumsy truck into the airport and headed for the terminal building.

"I suspect," Maitland said, "that there's a point in the life of every well-intentioned Christian when he feels he's had quite enough of Jews. I reached that point some time in 1945. Was it Pope who said

> The Jews, a headstrong, moody murmuring race
> As ever tried the extent and stretch of grace?"

"It was Dryden," said Tom. "And he didn't mean the Jews at all. The poem's an allegory and he was talking about the English."

"He *was*? I'll be damned. I never knew that. The description fits Jews so well. Oh—of course—you were a scholar of English literature before we stole you. Well, as I was saying, I had really had my share of Jews. For years I'd been signing their petitions, addressing their in-groups, fufilling my ancient debts to them in many ways. I had more than done penance for the Crusades. I didn't want to hear another word about anti-Semitism, or pogroms. The trouble with the Jews' cause is the same as Ballard's difficulties. They suffer from an excess of justice. We have to invent monstrous distortions of history to answer their complaints, and the more we invent, the worse we look. So we keep hating them.

"I won't tell you again about our tour of the concentration camps. It was honest, well conducted and sufficiently shocking so that none of us were ever able to write a coherent report on what we saw. It's getting increasingly difficult to read about the camps because we'd rather forget. Most of the books on them don't sell well. It's significant that the most popular writing on the subject has to do with the sufferings of a teen-age girl. We cry for her, and we forget about the stacks of bodies at Auschwitz, the heaps of gold teeth, the mountains of shoes, the sacks of clipped hair.

"We had taken the grand tour of a minor camp in northern Germany. It was in the Bremen Enclave, a community, we were assured, that had no use for the Nazis or Hitler. I had had enough of testicle-squeezers—a peculiarly Teutonic refinement, I suspect—and ice baths, and had skipped the hot lunch provided by our Army hosts, to wander through the fields that surrounded the barracks."

Tom found a parking space and brought the truck to a weary halt. Maitland's plane to Mexico City, where he should then make a connection for Guatemala, was not due to depart for an hour, so they remained in the cab.

"There's nothing quite as bleak as northern Germany in early winter," the anthropologist continued. "Mists and gray-brown fields and a kind of Nordic misery about the land. I had walked for about ten minutes when I saw a group of people congregated about an open pit. As I walked closer, I heard some Hebrew mumblings and knew they were Jews—a handful of survivors, the last people of their kind on earth. For a moment I was furious with them. What right had they to be invoking my pity? Who had asked them to suffer that much—to be tortured and humiliated and asphyxiated without protest? I had the notion that they were holding their funeral service for *my* benefit, that it was staged to enlist my tears—me, a fat, excessively educated Anglo-Saxon American *goy*—a man so well protected and so well ensconced in the pecking order of human society that they had one hell of a nerve entrapping me like that! I walked up to the open pit. They were muttering the Hebrew prayer for the dead, and out of deference to ancient custom I covered my head. Aparently there was no rabbi in the group. The mourners seemed to be on their own, weeping and wailing and beating their breasts in a kind of ad-lib glut of sorrow. Then I peered into the grave. To my shock, there was no coffin in the pit, but a half-dozen wooden crates, efficiently bound with metal taping and neatly lettered in German. I leaned into the trench and then the true nature of the ceremony dawned on me. They were burying *soap*. The boxes boastfully advertised the contents. What could I say to them? What solace could I offer? I left them to their prayers over the six crates of packaged soap, and sat down at a roadside statue of the Virgin. I am not a sentimental man, and I feel I owe the Jews of the world very little. My despair was not with the Germans and my sorrow was not for Jews. It was for all of us. Where have we been for four thousand years? What have we done wrong? What have we failed to learn? I had spent my life studying man and his social mechanisms and I was as unprepared for this as if I had never read a history book or put a single white rat through a maze. What are the limits of human depravity? The answer, I fear, is that *there are no limits*. The arbitrary murder of people who disagree with you—or whom you fancy disagree with you—is not new. I don't think it was particularly new on the scale practiced by the Germans. But to what pit have we descended, what murky depth have we reached when we make soap of their bodies, package, perfume and *advertise* it? Now perhaps you understand why my demands are small. I will settle for anything that diminishes the latent brute. I don't care how it's done or who does it. If the price we pay is bland conformity and high-powered cars, I'll accept that

—provided it aids in the defanging process. *God-O-Rama? Spirit of Man?* Two weeks vacation? Good. Just keep the beast fed and warm and purring. I have done my duty by all oppressed minorities and I want to be left to my ball courts."

Tom looked at him pityingly for a moment. Then he got out of the truck, helped his father-in-law down, and got Maitland's suitcases from the rear. They walked across the parking lot.

"I tell you what, Hall," Tom said. "You let deKay and the rest of them keep at it long enough, and maybe people'll get so doped up they won't care about *anything*. Maybe they'll *laugh* when someone starts stuffing bodies into ovens again. Maybe they're laughing right now—laughing at those funny big bombs. I can't believe that this warm bath we're in is doing any good."

"I guess I've upset you," Maitland said, as they neared the ticket counter. "Of course I don't believe that the kind of half-witted smiling trance that deKay deals in can save civilization. Or for that matter the peyote tepee. Or tauromachy or any of the new obscurantisms. I am merely saying that we may be entering an era of parallel development. On the one hand, we see a society increasingly concerned with fun—sports, games, sex, jokes, liquor, a thousand and one distractions—every man a Nero, glutted with inoffensive television, worshiping lesser gods. On the other hand, there are people like ourselves—hanging on grimly, experimenting, seeking, trying to solve old, old problems, and being warned that all our solutions are doomed and can only bring about greater evils than the wrongs they purport to solve. We must therefore work harder than ever—infiltrate and subvert the old mechanisms, if you will. We're doing a fairly good job, I think, but it must be better. I hold it a high compliment when critics of the Supreme Court charge that their decision against segregated schools was motivated by *sociology* as much as law. All sorts of strange things are occurring. There's a new effort called *applied anthropology*—some prefer *action anthropology*. They tried it in a small farming village in Peru—a group of ethnologists taking over and changing the economic picture. What a surprise! It worked! The people had more to eat—the land produced more. And no one's freedom was impaired!"

"Some guy in the Western Carolines did the same thing," Tom nodded. "An anthropologist. A storm wrecked the island economy and he had to set up a new system. It worked there also, even though he hated what he had done—it ruined his field work."

"Marvelous!" Maitland cried. "Superb! I'm hoping that we can infiltrate the agents of pleasure, cast our spells over the distractors and turn them to our special ends. And don't let anyone tell you we are amoral, or devoid of value judgments, that we're impartial and coolly scientific. The Nazis made it impossible for anyone to remain neutral, and the Soviets and the Red Chinese are convincing us that there's no such thing as detached, impartial judgments. I hate to use the word, considering the fact that it's now the property of General Avilas, but freedom is still very much our concern."

"I'm glad to hear that," Sorrento said sourly. "For a minute I was ready to throw in my shovel."

"We're needed, Tom. More than ever. Nothing human is foreign to us, and isn't that, after all, the nearest thing to a faith that you and I possess? The arts and customs of the Glades Indians are part of the human picture. That's all that matters."

After Maitland had checked in at the counter, they walked through the terminal, through labyrinthine passageways to the runway. At least half the travelers were Hispanic—dark, vivacious people, bright with gold teeth.

"The Arawaks are still coming here," Tom said. "You think any of these guys in gabardine suits and painted ties could have built our ball court?"

"You'll look hard and long to find an Arawak strain anywhere in the Antilles," Maitland said sadly. "I think the last of them died just after the turn of the century. There was a little colony of them up in the hills in western Cuba, and supposedly a handful in Puerto Rico. Why is it that so much of our work has to do with people exterminating each other? No wonder I take refuge in peyote. I could use a bean right now."

The plane—it was a creaking DC-4, a four-engined relic operated by a Latin American line—was being wheeled into position by a yellow tractor. The sight of the old craft reminded Tom of the war years, of all the wobbly, noisy transports he had flown in—drafty and crowded and having about them an aura of imminent disaster. He had a pang of longing for one more trip in one of them—a faceless Marine lieutenant traveling on hastily mimeo'd orders to some nameless airstrip. He missed the loss of identity, the splendid submerging of the war years.

"I suppose I have no right to talk about Martha," Maitland was saying, interrupting Tom's reverie, "but I'm forced to say she's acting a bit odd."

"How do you mean?"

"Well—I sense a kind of feistiness, a sort of nose-thumbing at our work that upsets me. Martha's difficulty is that she lacks a center of gravity. There's nothing in the world she feels strongly about. I've always had my primitives, and I suppose the University has filled most of *your* needs. Some people find it in sex, or religion, or a political life. Martha's never been terribly interested in anything. I suspect she'd have been better off if she had became a professional beauty—an actress or a model or whatever beautiful women do these days. But she's always had a knack for sneering at her good looks and for curling her lip at just about everything else."

Tom frowned. "I guess I haven't been a help. We always seem to be short something."

"It wouldn't matter what her circumstances were. I think she's one of those people who has to feel above the crowd, but really doesn't have the wherewithal to carry the project forward."

"This town depresses her. She can't stand the noise and the carrying-on. Once we're back in New York she'll straighten out."

"I hope so," Maitland said. "You'll think it out of character if I ask whether she's a good mother—but I wonder if she is."

"Marty? The greatest. You saw how good the kids look."

"Yes. Well, as I say, it's really not my business. Martha and I negotiated a nonaggression pact years ago."

He shook hands with Tom and walked unsteadily to the patchwork plane. A loud, gaudy family of Mexicans surrounded him—stumpy, umbrous people, lugging paper bags and snotty children. Maitland had the look of a Baptist missionary leading a pack of converts to prayer.

9 *Lila to the Rescue*

As he was parking the pickup on the dirt path, Freddie, the Ellenbogen's butler, walked toward him.

"Dr. Sorrento, Mr. Ellenbogen would like to see you."

"Is he up already?"

"Yes. He and Mrs. Ellenbogen are in the study."

He climbed out of the truck and looked at the fretwork of ditches and holes that scarred Erwin's priceless acreage—Naboth's vineyard. Only the Burleys were at work, tidying up the outer wall of the ossuary. Even as Oran troweled and brushed, Tom could see the emergence of another fragile skeleton—the spidery metatarsal bones peeking through the yellow wall of the pit.

"I have a message for you," Freddie said.

"Who from?"

"Dr. Ballard."

"You see him?"

"I was at a meeting of the Hilltown Betterment Association last night. He is on the boycott committee. He asked to be remembered to you and to tell you he's fine."

"Thanks. If you see him again, give him my regards."

"I will do that, Doctor. I'll probably be seeing a good deal of him these next few weeks."

As soon as they had entered the house, Freddie's easy conversation halted. He reverted to his normal role—an efficient colored man in a starched white coat. And yet, watching him move about the house with the efficacy cultivated by all good servants, Tom realized that he was several men, and the one he prided himself on most was unquestionably the meeting-goer, the boycotter.

Erwin was sitting at his desk. The shades of the study were drawn, as if to remove from his purview the unsettling vista of the dig. A fluorescent bulb in a student's lamp invested his hexagonal face with harsh purples and greens. Lila, already in digging garb, picking thoughtfully at a cluster of translucent calluses on her right hand, sat in a maroon armchair. They were both surprised to hear that Maitland had left so precipitously. Tom detected a note of relief on Erwin's part.

"I regret to tell you what I have to," Erwin said, "but you'll have to end your work and leave, Tom."

Sorrento leaned forward. "I thought I had another week. In a week's time I can probably clear most of the land. Even if I don't locate the southern wall, I'll have the whole settlement dug up."

"I am sorry," Ellenbogen said, "but I have no choice."

"Erwin, you have lots of time until Labor Day if you still want to have the ground-breaking. How long do you need to fill the holes and put stands up?"

Ellenbogen shook his dark head; it moved with the unvarying timing of a pendulum. "The question of *The Spirit of Man* is secondary in my mind at the moment. I'm concerned about my own good name and reputation. Tom, you know I'm not a selfish man. I'm not frightened of anything. But I'm sorry to say that your father-in-law has done me a disservice."

"I get it. First the Avilas thing, and then last night. But that's got nothing to do with you. Suppose he was your guest? You don't have to agree with him."

Ellenbogen sighed. "I have had six threatening phone calls this morning. The worst elements in the community, and some of the better ones . . . the usual snide references to my background and the fact that I am a Northerner. The whole thing . . . the excavation . . . the boathouse . . . your friends there . . . and now Dr. Maitland's inflammatory comments . . . they're all tying it in with me. I know, Tom, it doesn't matter that Ballard went off on his own, or Peltz is clean, or that you yourself have absolutely nothing to do with these crazy things. I'm being blamed for it. My business will suffer. My reputation. You don't realize it, Tom, but I walk on eggshells every day. I can't jeopardize myself and my family."

"You leave me out of it," Lila snapped. "Tom—*argue with him!* Don't let him chase you off!"

"Erwin, you haven't done anything. You and your factory are the best things that have happened to this town in years. They can't hurt you."

"Can't they? How much do I have to do to prove I am a valid human being? My grandfather ran a sweatshop on Rivington Street and he would lock the doors on Saturday night and stand guard with a broomstick to make the immigrant girls finish the piecework. Do I have to spend my life making amends for him? Haven't I established my credentials?"

Tom got up and raised the blind. The morning sun splashed saffron on the walls of the den. The workmen were arriving in two old cars and were heading for the lower part of the slope, to make one more attempt to find the elusive wall.

"Erwin, I know it sounds dopey to you, but don't you see what we're on the verge of? A new theory of Southeastern settlements! A whole new insight into the Arawak! We've got some evidence now, but if I could clean the whole place out . . . really study it . . . one week is all I need."

"I'm sorry to say this to you, Tom," Erwin intoned, "but I couldn't care less. I know there's supposed to be long-range importance to your work. Frankly, I have never understood your preoccupation with dead Indians. I'm bringing the bulldozers in tomorrow to fill the trenches and grade the land. And I would like you to conclude your work today and make arrangements to leave tomorrow. Every day you stay out there is another day of torment for me. I have had my phone disconnected and I have refused to talk with anyone from the press. I will not be smeared as a party to some crazy plot to stir up colored people."

"But goddammit, Erwin, it's a lie!" Tom cried. "You know it is! You've got nothing to do with it, and neither have I! As for Hall —he's been making screwy speeches for years. He was drunk last night at Nudo's joint. You want to tell the newspapers he was stoned, go ahead. Hall won't mind."

Ellenbogen's head was still shaking, motivated by an inner engine. "None of that will help. You must get out, Tom. Immediately. When the furor has died down, as I hope it will, we will hold the ground-breaking for *The Spirit of Man* and in that way restore the good will that has been so badly shattered. I am adamant about this, Tom."

Tom turned away from the window. Peltz had just come out of the boathouse, scratching and yawning, carting a load of rusted tools on one narrow shoulder.

"You want me to send the workmen home right away?"

Erwin shrugged. "I'll have to pay them for today anyway. They might as well put in a day's work."

As he left, Lila called after him. "I'll be out there in a minute, Tommy."

"Yeah," Tom said. "Getaway day. Last chance to get even."

When he had gone, Lila sat for a moment knotting a green silk kerchief around her head. Her face was streaked with white zinc ointment. Erwin studied her, grieving for his lover of the red lips and glistening black hair, so sensually waved and so tauntingly perfumed. She seemed less and less concerned about her appearance ever since she had joined the diggers. Evenings, she was now given to dispensing with girdles and stockings and making the most of things in bouffant skirts.

She adjusted the rabbit ears of her bandana and looked harshly at her husband. "You will *not* chase Tom away," she said.

"I beg your pardon, dear?"

"I said you will not chase Tom away. You'll let him finish clearing the land. If you don't understand why it's important for him, I do."

Erwin made a half-turn in his swivel chair and faced her with one sombre eye, peeking from behind the rimless glass. "Lila dear, you really don't know what's involved. I am as fond of

Tom as you are. I like Marty. I appreciate the work they are doing and your interest in it. But nothing less than our survival here is at stake. Lila, I will have no bombs thrown against my home, or the factory, or the temple."

"Gutless."

"I don't appreciate that remark. I'm as courageous as anyone. But I'm practical. I've done more for interracial good will and understanding than an army of silly archaeologists. I won't be crucified on their account."

"Do you realize how important this work is to Tom? He'll get his professorship when he writes it up. Aren't you interested in helping someone as worthwhile as Tom?"

Erwin's shoulders inched above his neckline. Turtle-like, he withdrew into the protective shell of his navy blue suit.

"Everything you say is true, dear," he said firmly, "but you fail to move me. Those people have to leave."

Lila bounced out of her chair. "I think you'll let them stay."

"Now, dearest, don't play any games with me."

"This is no game, Erwin. I'm sick and tired of your sure-footedness, the way you have everything figured out in advance. It's about time something ruffled you. I'm tired of watching you operate on advance information, on some kind of forewarning system you've devised. I love you, Erwin. I love you very much. But I wish you wouldn't have the world by the balls so magnificently. Who told you to catch a marlin the first time out?"

"Now—what in the world has that—"

"And who told you to be able to outguess the competition all the time? To figure the market the way you do and to anticipate price changes? How do you *know* so much? Why isn't there any uncertainty in your life, like other people? You poked around West End Avenue and Riverside Drive, you scouted the terrain and you sent up signals, and then by God you found me, virginal and pure and rich enough, and best of all, cultured. So here I am—feeding you book reports and opinions on classical music, and getting fat."

"Lila, sweetie, you're upset. I'll call Dr. Nassaur."

"You'll need medical care for *yourself* in a little while. You're going to let Tommy finish his work. You know why? The minute you chase him off, I won't let you sleep with me. The bed is closed. Not even a pinch or a goose. I'm off limits to you. Is that understood?"

Ellenbogen blinked unemotionally. "You're not feeling well, Lila. Otherwise you would not speak to me like that."

"I feel dandy. And I mean every word I said. No sex. Not a bit. I'll move into my own room and there'll be a bolt on the door. There'll be no accosting me in hallways either. You aren't the raping type. Let's see how long you can stand short rations."

"I won't listen to you. Working out there in that hot sun—it's done something to your brains."

"Ha! That isn't the part of my anatomy you should worry about."

"Lila! Come back here!"

"I'm going out to tell Tom he can work the land as long as he wants, with your kind permission. Are you agreed? You say yes, and I'll be your sweetie tonight. I'll even tell you about the new Camus I read, and I'll discuss the theory of stereophonic sound. I'll put on spiked heels and the black girdle if you like. But if you tell me Tom has to pack up, that's the end, Erwin."

He looked at her, perplexed, his endless capacity to handle problems shriveled and impotent. It was a terrible joke, he realized, to be so desperately involved sexually with your *own* wife, a dreadful joke on him. In his tax bracket, the rules demanded free and easy affairs, a wide choice of mates, a leisurely tasting of the sexual *smorgasbord*. But because he loved his wife dearly, adored her body and its charms, he was now at her mercy, and mercy she would show him none.

"How about it?" Lila called. "You want me tonight?"

"You know I do. You're being unfair. It isn't at all like you, Lila."

"Does Tom stay?"

"Just for one more day."

"One day isn't enough."

"What is this? How dare you bargain with your body! I don't like it, Lila—it's . . . whorish! You're acting as if there's a price on what's so beautiful and satisfying between us!"

"Oh, wake up," she said wearily. "There's always been a price on it. My parents saw to that, and you were the highest bidder. Don't act so horrified. Now, tell me—are you going to let Tom finish his work? I'll get him to hurry it along, to make some short cuts. If you don't, you can look elsewhere for—"

"Stop. I won't hear any more. You tell Tom I'll give him no more than five days. He has to get out."

"You made a deal, darling." She ran around the desk and kissed him passionately, streaking his cheeks with zinc ointment. Her lips evoked immediate response in him and he clutched for her breasts with one hand, reaching for her dungaree'd butt with the other.

"Enough of *that!*" Lila shouted. "You don't get paid until tonight! My wonderful, generous man!"

She sprinted through the door, her hands itching for the trowel.

Lila found Tom in the workroom. The news that she had, miraculously, gotten Erwin to agree to a reprieve buoyed him immensely. In the morning mail he had received the University physics laboratory's report on the charred bone fragments he had sent for radiocarbon dating. The results were in accord with the hypothesis of Arawak-Glades connections he and Maitland had been discussing.

"I sent them four pieces of burned animal bones," he told Lila proudly. "Stuff we found in the midden. They say it's 1200 A.D., give or take two hundred years."

"How do they work that?" she asked.

"Well, let's see. You know what an isotope is, don't you?"

"I think so. You better explain again."

"Different species of the same element. Carbon has one called Carbon 14, and it's radioactive. It's produced by the action of cosmic rays on carbon dioxide. Now, do you remember high school biology? What living things live off carbon dioxide?"

"I'm not *that* dopey," Lila pouted. "Plants."

"Right. So, this atmospheric, radioactive carbon—Carbon 14—is assimilated by plants, and ultimately by animals. However, the assimilation stops at death. Now once the organism is dead—let's say those deer and raccoons that supplied me with those burned hunks of bone—once it's dead, the disintegration of Carbon 14 atoms begins and continues at a fixed rate. Now what they do in the lab is to determine the percentage of Carbon 14 in the total carbon in the specimen. They measure the state of disintegration with a Geiger counter and they can tell when the organism lived."

"It's fantastic."

"The only thing is there's a plus or minus factor of about two hundred years. That's rough when you're dealing in recent dates where a variance of four hundred years can throw you way off. This figure they gave me of 1200 A.D. means it could be as early as 1000 or as late as 1400."

"Is that good or bad?"

Tom laughed. "Pretty good. A date in that span would mean that the adjacent Caribbean culture was what we call Sub-Taino

—a high-level Arawak tradition. Bahamas, Jamaica and Eastern Cuba—close enough for comfort."

"Close enough to *what?*"

"Close enough in space to the coast here. And close enough in time to the Glades Tradition of the Southeastern United States. Actually the Glades Tradition lasted almost a thousand years—from about 700 A.D. right up to the Seminole period, about the middle of the eighteenth century."

"The people who built the ball court could have made the trip over during that period, right?"

"That's one theory. This whole area might have been an Arawak settlement. There's a story in some of the old Spanish chronicles about a group of them migrating here from Cuba, at the end of the fifteenth century, and setting up a town called Abaibo. The old Spaniard who wrote it down claimed they ruled the local Calusa, the Glades people, but kept contacts with the homeland. They might have built the ball court as a reminder of the good old days in Cuba."

"You mean this might be that town?"

"Who knows? That's why I'm convinced we have to clear every bit of land. The other theory would be that the Glades people *themselves,* either through cultural contact or *parallel* development from the same base, evolved the ball game and the *zemis* and all the other Arawak-type traits, on their own. I've had Peltz rechecking all the pottery against typical Sub-Taino patterns. The incised designs are similar—they both use a kind of loop beneath the rim. I know there's a relationship between the two, but just what kind I'm not sure."

She looked at him with admiration. "How can you be so smart? How can you remember so much?"

"It's all in books. That's what they pay me all that money for. Sixty-five hundred bucks a year to remember Abaibo."

"I don't like you to knock yourself."

He picked up an armload of cigar boxes, each laden with precious bits of bone and pottery, handed her the trowels and brushes and started for the door. With an involuntary deftness, he patted her high, projecting buttocks as they exited. This gesture, less sexual than affectionate, made her pause and sway gently toward him. Instead of a tart reprimand, the reaction he anticipated, she seemed about to fall against him.

"Oh," Lila said softly. "You want to also."

In late afternoon, after a fruitless day of digging, they repaired to the upper story of the boathouse, where Tom, whose manual labors with pick and shovel had intruded on his other duties, began transcribing Peltz's surveying notes to a large map of the site. Lila rested on the daybed, watching him.

"You'll die when you find out how I got Erwin to let you keep working," she said archly.

"I can imagine. The land's in your name."

"That isn't very nice."

"I give up." He worked slowly with a steel rule and a protractor, fixing the position of each new excavation on coordinates.

"I really did something terrible. Where I got the nerve, I'll never know. It just wasn't like me."

"I guess I'm supposed to share your guilt—whatever it was you did. You did it for old Tom, right?"

"You could be a little more grateful, dear."

"I am, Lila, I am. I happen to like your husband. He's too decent a guy to have to suffer for me. I don't want the night riders making his life miserable. He doesn't deserve it." He sensed she was about to make some revelation, and he quickly lit a black cigar, retreating behind the safety of its miasmic screen.

"Would you like to know how I got him to let you stay?"

"You'll tell me anyway."

"I told him he couldn't sleep with me if he chased you off. He worships me, you know."

Tom leaped up, knocking over the cardboard map and spilling a bottle of India ink. He knelt and began mopping it frantically with his handkerchief.

"Why did you tell him that? What the hell kind of trick is that to play on Erwin?"

"It's no trick. I meant it. Tom, I know it was an awful thing to do—but there he was, looking so sure of himself, figuring things out in advance and waiting to grab me, just as if it was the first time for him—"

Tom finished cleaning up the ink. He replaced the map and the bottle on the work table but did not resume his plottings. Instead he sat down on the bed alongside her.

"I wish you'd make love to me," Lila said. The words were alarmingly faint. It was as if a shy child were talking for her, a secret speaker hidden in her larynx.

"I wish I had the guts to," Tom said.

"I should feel horrible talking like this," she said. "But I don't at all. I want you."

"No," he said. "The male Clarissa Harlowe, that's me. The biggest strikeout artist with the broads. *The Man Who Got Less.* If I say no, Lila, it's not because I'm virtuous or saintly. It's because I have to keep my record intact."

"Why do you make it sound so ridiculous? What about *me?* Is it every day a good-looking woman asks you?"

He shook his head sadly. "The Jewish women have a curve in them. I used to read that in Thomas Wolfe and get all excited. And here you are. And here I am. I wouldn't do it, Lila, because I'm yellow. Scared stiff. Not because of Marty or the kids, but just because some dim, irrelevant rule, that nobody cares about enforcing any more, tells me it's wrong. It's what I get for being a cop's son—a cop who took everything seriously. He once saw my little sister Rita walking home from school with a boy when she was twelve, and he slapped her face."

"You make me feel as big as a gnat. I never should have opened my mouth."

He patted her knee, and then, as if to neutralize this act, retreated to one of the canvas chairs. "Now how can a man get so little in one lifetime?" he asked. "When I was on furlough from the Marines, after I came back from the Pacific, I went down to Hollywood. A big hero in uniform with medals. My mother's second cousin was working as a film editor at Paramount—Joe Natale—and he invited me out to lunch. Like a dope, I go in civvies. I met all the wheels at the studio, and when lunch is over, some guy asks me if I want a date with a starlet. With the big wink. You know—advising me this is more than just a starlet. Guess what I did."

"Thank goodness. I thought maybe I had BO. Or simply wasn't your type."

"Yeah. But I had to make excuses. I said I didn't want a date because *I was out of uniform.* At this, the whole table of executives gets hysterical, and they tell me they have a building full of uniforms and medals. What do I want to be? An admiral? A contract surgeon? A wing commander in the RCAF? Any kind of uniform I *need,* they'll supply."

She laughed—but not with her customary boisterousness. His recital of past disasters, of errors of omission in the great sexual game, was his way of easing her embarrassment, and justifying his own archaic morality. She joined in the fun.

"What a hero! What did you end up as?"

"Nothing. I thought up more excuses. My leg was bothering me. I had to visit somebody in La Jolla. I went back to my hotel and went to a movie that night. By myself."

She covered her face with her bandaged hands. "We're a great pair, we are. Why is it in all the books and movies and plays everybody's bedding down with everyone else? Can there really be that much of it going on?"

"I guess it's like golf or bridge. You have to do it all the time to be good at it."

"Maybe it would do you good. You know—the way the marriage counselor always recommends a hobby."

"I have enough trouble keeping my head above water. I worry. I'm still a lousy assistant professor, age thirty-seven. It takes me twice as long to prepare my lecture notes and I'm always behind in my reading. I'm an academician by accident, not because I'm bright. I think maybe they tolerate me because I'm the house Italian. You see what I worry about? And why I don't have time to cheat on my wife? Your mind has to be clear and empty to make a hobby out of that."

"You make no sense at all. You're saying all this just to make me laugh at my own humiliation. Here I was ready to immolate myself on the altar of love, and you sit there, with your brooding Neapolitan eyes, telling me stories you probably make up as you go along."

Tom went back to the cardboard map. "I wish Ballard hadn't left us," he said. "Benny could do this, but I need him outside to supervise the digging now."

"Don't change the subject."

He turned around. "There's nothing left to explore, Lila dollink. We wouldn't enjoy it anyway. We aren't the types. We'd be guilt-ridden and miserable. Don't think I wouldn't like to. I get dizzy thinking how you'd look and feel and smell and how you'd act. But to hell with it. When it's over, you wonder what all the sweating was about."

"You don't mean that, I know you don't. You're as sensual as I am."

"And just as confused. You see, Lila—it's lousy of me to say this—but *not* having you is almost as good for the ego as having you. Wow! Gee whiz! A beautiful, rich, intelligent girl wanted to climb into the sack with—"

She got up quickly from the bed. "You're *impossible*." She

squeezed the nape of his neck as she left, then kissed his cheek. "But I'm crazy about you anyway. This is the closest I'll ever come to having an affair, so I might as well enjoy it. Some joke on Erwin! I never even kissed you on the mouth, but you'll serve the same purpose as if we had a hundred secret sessions—motels, cars, apartments—oh, won't I be sinful in my lurid little mind."

He looked up from his work and they kissed—thoroughly, exploringly, warmly—and she gasped and shuddered, and left him.

10 Don't Make Me Suffer

It had been an unsettling day for Ira. The University had dropped his services. The newspapers kept calling about Maitland's latest affront. Even the friendliest of reporters seemed convinced that the diggers were suspect. The anthropologist's hurried departure confirmed the feeling that the excavation was a front for agitation. Had not the Hilltown Betterment Association just announced plans for monster demonstrations to touch off the boycott? It all tied in—and somehow poor Ira, with his jokes and loot and easy access to show biz and broads, was part of it. Si Mermelstein dutifully answered the calls, issued statements, sent gifts. But Si had a pessimist's nose for disaster (reading *The Mill on the Floss* to the illiterates of the Bronx had impaired his optimism forever) and he sensed a cracking and crumbling of Ira's papery superstructure. And then, of course, he had gotten the latest bank statement and he understood that while loot could carry them very far indeed, the cash balance had become piteously emaciated. And what was Ira doing all this time? He was cruising the bay on Fenton Braud's cruiser—just himself and Martha Sorrento—*fishing,* he said.

In late afternoon deKay was back at the office in natty yachting jacket and white flannels, suggesting the young romantic lead in an early Marx Brothers picture. The dismal advices from Si moved him to action: he would fire Cleo. Martha Sorrento had not agreed to his ingenious scheme of business-and-sex; but he suspected she was weakening. Whether she joined the firm or not, Cleo had become an unnecessary adjunct, as useless, Ira confided to Si before summoning her, as tits on a boar.

She sat primly in the inner office, trying desperately to control the spreading stain of fear in her gut. She had dreaded the moment ever since that flat-assed, flat-voiced woman with no make-up had taken over Ira's affections, and now she awaited the pronouncement—a magnificently blond, superbly tanned woman in a white linen dress.

"Cleo, sweetie," Ira said softly—he had his back to her, feet on the window sill. Ira was a soft-hearted man; the business of firing somebody was not pleasant for him. "Cleo, baby, this is awful painful for me. Si gave me some news that rocked me. The money is running out."

She sat primly, iodine-brown legs crossed, her arms folded across her narrow waist—as if to contain the splotchy intestine puddle of dread. "What do you mean, Ira? If you want me to take a cut in salary, I suppose I could manage. But with Robin in that new school..."

"*Baby.* Don't make me suffer."

"Really, Ira, I know that a hundred and fifty dollars a week is pretty good money for what I do. And an expense account. I *could* manage on less. I could put Robin in the regular elementary school."

"Cleo, doll, I can't keep it from you." He spun around and gazed at her mournfully. His round features drooped slightly. "Cleo honey, I have to let you go. I can't afford you any more."

Her scarlet mouth opened—it suggested a beached fluke reaching for air. "Oh. Oh. Oh, I didn't think it was that bad. I mean, is it that bad? I thought if you could keep me on until I landed something else."

Ira's golden head shook negatively. "I can't, lover. The picture is very black. If I could have kept control of the new tourist trap, it might have worked out. But Ellenbogen scrounged it from me. Right now I got only a small piece, and at that, it was you might call a cock-ulated risk. We lost a couple of accounts this week and the Peruviana is hollering that they can't give me the space rent-free much longer."

Cleo inhaled tremulously, the neatly molded nostrils pulsating. She tried to stop the inadvertent fluttering of her lower lip.

"It's because of her," she said sadly.

"Who dat?"

"I know what you've been doing with her. That professor's wife. Why do you have to take it out on me? I can still be of help to the firm. If you'd let me try to write, to help out Si. Ask Si. He thinks I could work out doing other things."

He could not bring himself to insult her. He knew too well the only commodity she had to sell, her only talent. At twenty-six she had used her body well and wisely, but how far could you go in Public Relations, high-type PR, with that sort of thing? Cleo's spelling was as bad as his own, and every time she opened her mouth she gave the game away—the Ivy League haircomb with the gold clip, the SFA dresses, the haughty gaze.

"It's not for you, sweetie," he said wearily. "I'll ask around. The TV stations, the radio people. They owe me a few."

He thought he had concluded his onerous task, but she remained bolted to the chair. Once she touched her hand to her mouth, as if to stop the faltering of the lips. She succeeded partially, and after a gulp of air, tried a new approach.

"But what—what are you doing about her? Does her husband know? I mean—she has kids and everything."

Ira turned sideways—a small boy's furtive pout distorted his mouth. "Baby, don't get personal. I never asked questions about the twenty-two—or was it twenty-three—fellahs you shacked with."

"That was different. I never made no secret of it, Ira. You know that is a fact."

"Right-o-rini. You were a sport, Cleo."

"Is she going to leave him? Divorce him? And come live down here with you? Oh, that's priceless. Ira a papa. With two ready-made children."

"You better go now, Cleo. I told Helene you'd work through next week and we'll dig up a month's pay in advance for you."

"She's laughing at you. She thinks you're dirt."

"I think you better go, sweetie."

"She won't divorce him. I know those types of creeps. They'll torture each other to death all their lives."

"Cleo, doll. When I took you into the firm, we had an agreement. No serious conversations. Non-involvement with you, except for sack time. Since you're still on the payroll for a week, please observe it. I'll make some appointments for you tomorrow."

The tears came in a blinding, distorting gush, blurring the sedate face, disfiguring the thin mouth and the untroubled brow. Ira, ever the gentleman, got up and hugged her dearly.

"There, there, Cleo, baby. It don't hurt long. It never does.

Li'l Robin will like it just as much in public school. Heck, I never went to any private school—and look at me."

She wrenched her heaving body away from him and raced into the bathroom, there to give full throat to her agony.

11 *The Night Riders*

MARTY found her husband in remarkably high spirits that evening. The sullen inturning, the brooding silences had given way to an almost manic elation. She had understood from Ira that the dig would be ending the following day—he importuned her to make her mind up quickly, to break the news to Tom at once. Now she was surprised to learn that Erwin had given them a week's grace. She expressed revulsion at Lila's gambit. The withholding of sex from the put-upon millionaire seemed to her the ultimate in depravity.

"If she went out and had an *affair* with somebody, I'd think better of her," Marty said. "But to use her questionable charms that way—you should be flattered, Tom. All for the social sciences. I think Erwin must be the only man who was ever cuckolded by an excavation."

He found her denigration of Lila amusing. "We got nothing but good news today. I got the Carbon 14 dates for the site. It fits perfectly with Hall's hypothesis. I was going through the literature with him a few days ago, and we figured this might even be the site of Abaibo—the Arawak colony the Spaniards wrote about."

"It sounds like Mu."

"Only it might be real. I didn't want to ask Hall about it, because I know how he feels about popularized anthropolgy. But why couldn't I do a book for general readership on the site? You know—scholarly but without the tables and charts and summaries."

"Why bother asking him? Do it. It would do you a world of good. By the way—did he get off all right?"

He looked at her narrowly. "I thought you'd ask before the week end. He's fine. A little gouty from Lila's food, but otherwise in good shape. They better look out down in Guatemala."

Marty tossed her head back in mild disgust. "Stop worshiping him. He certainly did you a lot of good. That's all everyone was talking about at the Peruviana today—that crazy professor from New York getting everybody in trouble. Ira's office did nothing but answer phone calls because of his brilliant comments last night."

He was buoyant—no amount of goading could antagonize him. "Hey—how is old deKay? The zile and zotz man. I wonder you haven't picked up his lingo. What's he selling now?"

"I hardly ever see him," she said.

"You mean you just lay around the pool all day, getting browned up? You look like a *bracciole.*"

"Oh, I read and rest and walk along the beach. He drops by occasionally—usually with some woman on his arm."

"Has he made a pass at you yet?"

"Tom. I think even he knows better than to try that. He's really just an illiterate country boy. I try not to be cruel to him."

"I know the type. In the Marines they were the ones who couldn't read or write, but knew how to cheat at craps. Well, so long as everyone's happy."

She left the porch and entered the house. Her casual lying, rather than unsettling her, had filled her with a lascivious exhilaration and she felt the need to leave his innocent, troubling presence. The pleasures of sin, she reflected (and in an age of relativism, who really knew what was sinful?) derived as much from ancillary matters—the lie, the precious secret, the masquerade—as they did from the practice itself.

Abby and Nicky, as brown as Yap Islanders, were playing on the floor with a stack of silver pesos that Ira had given them. They had grown as docile as spayed cats and the rich diet of lunches at the hotel had fattened their bony bodies.

"Why don't you ask Daddy to read you a story?" Marty asked. She busied herself with the dinner dishes—what she called Lila's Goodwill Industries selection.

"Yeah," Nicky said. "Deh gingerbread man." He found the ragged book and carried it out to his father. Abby, complaining that it was a baby story, followed.

Marty watched them through the patched screen door, climbing onto their father's lap. She waited for a pang of guilt, the *pro forma* stab of conscience, and when none was forthcoming, she understood that the wild joys of adultery were heightened and sharpened *simply because she was* a good mother and a good wife. She was having the best of both worlds and was enjoying it. She had once heard the wife of one of Tom's more successful classmates—a television executive with a propensity for young actresses—declare poignantly: *he's so much easier to live with when he's having an affair.* It was quite possible that the same was true of her own predicament. From Ira's perfumed bedroom and antiseptic bathroom to the homely duties of the house and the children was a big journey; but it was the constant comparisons of the two—not necessarily invidious ones—that had transmuted her original morosity into a good approximation of comfort and joy. And of course she had no intention of joining forces with deKay or abandoning Tom. Still, the involvement was exceedingly pleasurable. New York was only four hours from the Beach. Perhaps he would come in quest of her when she left; there would be a reunion in some curtained, darkened hotel suite at mid-afternoon. In time—if the drabness of the University resumed its depressing effect on her—she might make the vital step. But for the moment, her splendid eclecticism intrigued her. She peeked at the porch, saw a cloud of cigar smoke rising around her husband's black, coarse head and heard the children's squeals as he began reading his own ethnicized version of *The Gingerbread Man.*

"Once upon-a time," Tom told them, "there was two old people named Salvatore and Angelina Bevilaqua. They lived in the back of an old pizzeria on East 114th Street and they didn't have any children. So one day the old lady, Mrs. Bevilaqua, decided to make a gingerbread man in the pizza oven. She mixed up pizza dough and flavored it with ginger. Then she made the eyes out of *pignole* and the nose out of a cherry pepper and the mouth out of a hot sausage. The buttons were ravioli and the shoes were two manicotti. Then she covered the whole thing with tomato paste and let it bake for a whole day. When she opened the oven, out jumped the gingerbread man and ran right out the door of the pizzeria, on the East 114th Street where the boys were playing stickball, past the *bocce* alley, past Colavito's Bar where they sell the numbers and down First Avenue..."

When the bomb went off, Sorrento had been having one of those baffling dreams which seem to continue, in marvelous clarity, for hours, and then culminate by merging with a true external circumstance. He had been dreaming about the Iwo landing. He was crouched against a burning am-track, screaming at some idiots in B company down the beach who were tossing mortar shells on his decimated platoon. He could remember cursing, crying, shouting: *The other way, you bastards! The other way!* The dream was alarming in detail—he had forgotten that the side of the wrecked am-track bore the name *No Sweat* and that a scorched arm protruded from the cab. It seemed, when the explosion jarred him awake, that he had been dreaming about Iwo for hours, for most of the night. How did the dream anticipate reality—mesh itself so perfectly with the bombing? As he jumped from the bed, the hangover was so complete that he found himself yelling: *The other way, you bastards!*

Marty was up with him and they raced into the children's room. Both of the youngsters were awake—Nicky crying and Abby bright-eyed and alert—but unharmed. Two rear windows had been shattered, but the force of the explosion had not been strong enough to throw glass fragments across the room. Tom picked up Abby, and Marty grabbed the boy. They ran to the balcony and down the steps. At the rear of the house, Oran, Wilma and Ben were coughing and staggering through a pall of smoke and dusty sand. The charge had evidently been a light one and had been tossed a few feet from the rear steps, which had been splintered and smashed. The screen door, which had been left open, was wrecked. Worst of all, Tom's precious cigar boxes and the skulls and limbs of the ossuary, piled at the door, had been blown willy-nilly around the landscape. Under moonglow, shards and fluted points, crania and ulnas, dotted the sand like the leavings of a cannibal feast.

"Anybody hurt?" Tom called. He cautioned Marty to take the children away from the house on the chance that some of the charge had not exploded. Wilma and Oran, in workhouse pajamas, jumped from the door sill—both of them coughing—and walked toward Tom. They appeared uninjured. Peltz followed.

"I knew it," Ben muttered. "I knew they hadda do it."

"Any of you hear or see anything before this went off?" Tom asked.

They had heard nothing. A giant beam of light made its way through the cyclone fence. It was Erwin, bearing an enormous battery-operated lantern. In brocade dressing gown he double-timed across his land, weaving his way around the pits and trenches, negotiating the obstacle course with surprising speed.

"What happened?" he cried. "What did they do?"

"A small bomb," Tom called back. "The lousy cowardly bastards. With two kids in the house."

"Is anyone hurt?" Erwin ran up to Tom. He was by no means out of breath. Tennis and workouts with weights and pulleys kept him in trim.

"No. The people downstairs got shook up a little."

The Burleys and Peltz huddled together for mutual solace—only now it seemed that Ben had shrunk in size and ferocity. He seemed to be using them as shields against the world of bigots' bombs. The roles were reversed.

"Oh, my God," Erwin moaned. "Oh my God. I was sure this was bound to happen. Tom—can't you see how right I was? How I knew something like this would occur? I hope it teaches Lila her lesson. I wouldn't even let her come out to see what has taken place here. I better call the police."

Tom tried to console him. "Ah hell, Erwin, it isn't that bad. It might have been some screwy kids. Look—they didn't even try hard. The damn thing was tossed from up on the height and it landed short of the house. It couldn't have been a big one—the house is hardly hurt. Just my pottery and bones got tossed around."

"Tom, you have very narrow vision for a man of your intelligence," Erwin said coldly. "Just a small bomb. Just my old boathouse. And next my home. And next the temple. And then my factory. And my wife and child. Is that what I have to look forward to?"

He started to quickstep back to his house, then stopped.

"Marty—you and the children had best spend the rest of the night in my house. I'll have Freddie fix up some beds."

"Thanks, Erwin," Marty said. "I think that's a good idea." She guided the yawning children toward the cone of yellow light and the reassuring figure of the industrialist. Apparently, Erwin had despaired of reasoning with Tom. He turned to Marty as they walked toward the mansion.

"Tom will have to suspend work at once. The boathouse must be vacated and the site leveled. You will all have to move immediately. Am I being unreasonable, Marty?"

"Of course not, Erwin," she said. "You shouldn't be subjected to this. You've done more than your share for everybody."

"I keep telling Lila that," he said poignantly.

At the cyclone fence, as two uniformed policemen walked toward them, Marty and Erwin turned to look at the damaged rear of the boathouse. Tom Sorrento, nude except for skivvy shorts, was on his hands and knees hunting for his precious bits of pottery, his assorted skulls and arms and legs. He was like the crazed Nebuchadnezzar, scratching for the shattered remains of dead Indians by the light of the moon. Suddenly he looked up fiercely at his numb aides—Wilma, Oran and Ben.

"What are you people standing there for?" he shouted. "You going to be scared by a stick of cheap dynamite? Come on! Help me find these pieces! Benny—get the cigar boxes! Police the area or you'll have rifle calisthenics tomorrow!"

They joined him on all fours, a quartet of survivors, digging for clams in primordial ooze. For a puzzled moment, Marty and Erwin watched them, then turned to greet the officers.

Ben Peltz left them during the night.

Evidently he had packed up and vanished after they had finished combing the sand for the find. Tom had returned to the upper story to try to steal a few hours' sleep. No sooner had he dozed off than his old friend of the Hilltown station house, Lieutenant Fry, awakened him, with profuse apologies, to question him about the shocking incident. ("I deplore violence," Fry assured him.) Policemen and detectives had searched the house and the surrounding area for several hours—recovering a few shards and bones that Tom and his diggers had missed—and had finally left at about four in the morning. Tom fell into a fogged sleep, awaking to yellow sunlight and morning heat, and the sight of Oran standing hesitantly on the porch waiting for him.

"What do you want, Oran?" he asked thickly.

The boy shifted from one leg to another. "May I come in?"

"Yeah. Everything okay downstairs? No more bombs?"

"No. We slept fine after the policemen left. They kept taking photographs and shining lights in the window. That fellow you knew—Mr. Fry—talked to me and Wilma for about an hour."

"What did he want to know?"

"Oh—how we felt about China and the right-to-work laws. Wilma and I were very cooperative. He was surprised that our Daddy is a minister, but he was friendlier after I told him."

"Did he talk to Ben?" Tom asked.

"No. He just looked at him kind of funny and said 'I know all about you, buster.'"

"That's all?"

"Yes." Oran edged forward. He seemed to walk through an involuntary locomotive process in which one foot nudged the other. At the bedside, he held out a sealed envelope.

"This is for you," Oran said. "I found it on your desk downstairs when I woke up."

Tom tore it open. Inside was a single sheet of graph paper—the kind Peltz used for his surevying notes. Tom rubbed his eyes, and turning away from the fierce sun, read it.

DEAR TOM:

I am leaving you. I am no good to you or anyone else. You never should have taken me along. If Ballard hadn't started in with that crowd, maybe it would be all right. But he double-crossed you, and I am in trouble again because of him. I hate to run out on the work, but now that they are after you, the dig is over anyway. I am quitting anthropology and archaeology and all this social science crap. It can't do any good anyway. The rats are winning everywhere. Nothing helps.

Remember I told you about those two relatives of mine? An aunt and an uncle. I am going to live with them. Don't come looking for me.

BEN

Oran blinked his eyes and patted his silken hair.

"It's from Ben, isn't it? I knew he would run off. He was packing after the policemen left."

"That's right, kid. It's just you and me and Wilma against the world now. You ready to knock 'em dead, Muscles?"

"Yes! Yes! Who needs them? Wilma and me—and you—we'll dig the whole place up!"

Tom bounded out of bed and punched Oran playfully on one narrow forearm. "You better start digging right now. Keep widening the ossuary for grave goods. This is our last day, Oran."

The boy's face became grave. "Why? We haven't found the wall yet."

"Kid, after last night's raid by the *Camorra,* Erwin isn't going to let us stay here another hour. Not even if Lila turns off the water supply and the electric. Get out there—you and your big sister and your shovels!"

They were out probing in the grave in a matter of minutes. If the search for Arawak-Glades contacts did nothing else, it would help Wilma and Oran Burley come of age. Tom joined them at the pit, hiding his heartsickness with a tirade of harmless insults aimed at his loyal aides.

12 She Said She Knows You

WHEN the Peruviana's manager, a genial fellow normally most appreciative of Ira's jokes, failed to laugh at the one about the old man who smelled the strudel, deKay sensed impending tragedy. The fact was, the manager said sadly, the hotel's owners could no longer see their way clear to letting Ira operate rent-free. The suite of rooms he utilized permanently—not to mention the occasional rooms he took for parties and so forth—represented a tidy outlay of money for them. Rented year-round, it might amount to fifteen or sixteen thousand dollars—a very big bite for public relations, especially since the syndicate had a New York firm working for them in addition to Ira's "special services."

"We realize all you done for us, Ira," the manager said slowly. He was an elderly man with a history of coronaries and bad feet. "But the boys feel for the kinda free space you get, not to mention your regular fee, it ain't worth it. Remember, Ira, you promised us *Life* magazine and we never made it. The competition, the Parthenon, they got in last month."

"Didn't you tell them about the plot to get *Our Heritage* down here? With Hal Justice and everything?"

The manager frowned. "Frankly, we're not convinced all that television mishmash does any good. You know, like that monkey. He was very funny when he first arrived and there was a lot of stuff written in the papers. But really, is he worth a two-room suite, free? He crapped on the carpeting twice and an old lady fainted in the elevator when she saw him naked. You ask me, he's a little horrible."

Ira pursed his lips. *Our Heritage* was a dead issue, but there was no harm in using it to spar for time. Miss Kitty Schmitt had been despatched to New York a few days ago, heavy with loot and Ira's love, but for all the laughs and booze, she had not yet been able to deliver the program. It seemed the network was wary of Ira deKay. Every few months some sharp-nosed accountant would dig up another festering corpse left behind by the promoter. It had gotten so that you couldn't mention Ira's name in the broadcasting offices.

"Of course, we're ready to give you the reg'lar professional rate—thirty per cent off," the manager wheezed. "Same as for newspaper people. But the free ride has got to end, Ira. No one hates to tell you this more than me. But the partners are hollering—with the bad winters and the competition from Vegas and Havana."

His liverish hand fussed with some papers. Like many older men in important jobs in the Beach, he gave the impression of utter incompetence, as if the complex, intricate task of managing the lavish hotel with its infinite rooms and multiform eating places and bars would inevitably cause his death. "And the food and liquor bills, Ira," he said painfully. "They would like some recompense on that."

"*Sweetie.* That was our deal."

"But, Ira, I imagined that meant occasional drinks or entertainment. Not whole cases of Haig and Haig, and whole boxes of Upmanns."

Ira favored the older man with his loose grin. To hell with him and the Peruviana, Ira thought. Soon he would have Martha Maitland Sorrento working for him and that would mean a new kind of client—new prestige and new money. He would not be reduced to stuttering pleas in front of hotel managers.

"All right, Sol baby, all right. We'll work it out. Won't we?" He untangled himself from the chair and started for the door.

"I'm awful sorry, Ira. I'll draw up an estimate of some kind. Maybe we can figure out a way of billing where we can both deduct it."

Ira ambled out of the manager's office into the cavernous lobby. He walked toward the elevator, passing between giant false boulders and spurious tapestries. Near the cigar stand, seated strategically on a mammoth couch, he saw Karger, the disgruntled expelled partner, whose wrath Ira had assuaged. The management's ingratitude piqued Ira. They didn't mind his running up the liquor bills back in the days when Karger was threatening to have them murdered! He recalled the frenzied terror that had gripped the other owners of the Peruviana after Karger, ousted, began calling his gunsel friends. How they had pleaded with Ira to solve their dilemma! And solve it he had—there was Karger, still not owning a penny of the hotel, but nevertheless permitted to buttonhole guests and inform them he was an owner. Ira looked at his pitted, bestial face. Karger had trapped two middle-aged lady guests and was advising them of his plans for expansion. For a moment Ira pondered an appeal to him; Karger had always liked him, had approved of his adjudication of the dispute.

"Frack that," Ira said half aloud. "I still got a little pride." He would not get on his knees before the treacherous lobby sitter. He would work out his own salvation.

At the elevator, the bell captain approached him. "Mr. deKay, you got a minute?" he asked.

"Any time, lover. You get them fight tickets?"

"You bet. Thanks. Listen. Two creeps came in before, asking for you. A dame and a guy. They drove up on a motorcycle. I couldn't lose 'em. They're in the bar now, waiting for you. Want me to get rid of 'em?"

"They say who they were?" asked Ira.

"Nope. The guy didn't say nothing. One of them black-leather-jacket boys. The dame did the talking. She kept saying you'd be glad to see her. She said she knows you."

Ira hesitated. The elevator boy waited for him, asking, with sly smirk: "We going up, Mr. deKay?"

"Huh? No, not this time, Willie boy. Gets tougher and tougher for me to go up. *Hah!*"

Still, he waited outside the Cuzco Bar, his rosy face darkening. "Didn't say what her name was, hey?" he asked the bell captain.

"Nope. She was wearing one of them white crash helmets those jokers wear—she and the guy both—and on hers it said 'Midge.' "

" 'Midge'?"

"Yeah. In rhinestones."

Ira inhaled deeply, thanked the captain, and, with a purposeful hitch of his lavender slacks walked into the Cuzco Bar. Even in mid-afternoon it was icy cold and morbidly dark. The Peruviana did not draw a crowd of daytime drinkers and the only customers were the pair who had come in search of Ira on a motorcycle.

They were seated on bar stools, their leathery backs to him, and he could tell immediately from the arrogant, hard tilt to the woman's butt that it was *his* Midge. She had taken her crash helmet off and it rested on the adjacent stool, a gleaming white mitre. She wore black drill pants, scuffed and dirty, and they were tucked into studded leather boots. The man was clad identically: he had kept his helmet on, and his hunched black-leather shoulders, crowned by the plastic dome, gave him the look of a dingy spaceman. On both black backs were the words, in gleaming aluminum beads: SENECA DEMOCRATS.

Ira walked casually to the bar, lifted the woman's hat off the stool and sat down.

He spoke to the bartender. "George, baby, these folks are my guests. Put it all on my tab."

The woman jerked her head around. "Honest-to-Pete," she said. "It's good old Ira Detzler."

"Midge, *honey*. What a dicty surprise. Why'nchoo tell me you were going to pay Ira a visit?"

She smiled crookedly, displaying the irregular teeth of an impoverished childhood. Her features were small, pert and Anglo-Saxon. What had once been a variety of rural cuteness, a buttony farm-girl quality, had been transmuted, via wind and sand and thousands of motorcycle miles, into a scaly hardness. Her forehead was oddly compartmented with an eroding windburn that gave it the look of an alligator purse. Her hair, once dyed a melted-butter blond, was now shot with muddy brown. In her black highway garb, attended by her silent equerry, she was as truly native American as Ira. About her hovered an aura of dusty county fairs and ragged midways, of kisses stolen behind the tractor exhibits, of corn whisky imbibed neat from the unlabeled bottle in back of the high school stadium. She had sprung from the same rich soil as Ira, and in the guarded informality they now displayed toward one another, these common origins were discernible. What was apparent too, was that somewhere there had been a divergence, that in the febrile quest for pleasure, Ira had found a rewarding high road, but that Midge, unable to employ her corn-fed charms properly, had stumbled ever downward, to the abraded seat of a Harley-Davidson.

"You look great, Ira."

"Oh, I get along. I have worries, but I've made out." He indicated the woman's companion—a beefy slab, adorned with a wispy red mustache and burnsides. He was perhaps ten years younger than Midge. "Your friend?"

"My *partner*, Harvey Hess. Harve—this is my husband."

Harvey nodded his ponderous head. He was still wearing his black gloves, Ira noticed. When he reached for the double shot glass with one leathery hand, he suggested a trained black bear. Ira nodded at him and ordered another round.

"Anything for you, Mr. deKay?" the bartender asked.

Ira smiled. "No thanks, George. I have a big afternoon."

Midge studied him with ungrudging admiration. "That your new handle—deKay? It's very classy. You always had a knack for class. Isn't he just like I told you, Harve?"

Harvey blinked hooded eyes. "Where's the head?" he asked the bartender. "I been on that bike all the way from Daytona and my kidneys is screaming."

The bartender showed him where, and he eased himself off the stool and left.

"How'd you find me, Midgely?" Ira asked.

"The newspapers. Harve and me were doing a little act in Marietta, Georgia. Oh—I guess I didn't tell you—we do a little turn on the bikes—trick riding, and through hoops of fire and that sort of thing. The yokels eat it up."

"Gee, I'm glad you stayed in show biz. You loved it so much."

"Huh? Oh, yeah. One night I'm readin' a newspaper and there's this story about a tourist trap of some kind goin' up in the Beach. Oh, I forget exactly—but some people were digging on this guy's land—and the place was goin' to have these exhibits. And there's a pitcher of the backers and one is a fellah named Ira deKay. Well, I damn near popped a blood vessel. I looked—and I looked—and I *looked*—and I said to myself, Midge baby, that is your hubby, Ira Detzler, who was once a lieutenant in the Army Ordnance at old Camp Santa Anita whom you married in Tijuana in nineteen hundred and forty-three."

Ira leaned over and kissed her hard cheek tenderly. "Aren't you sweet? Isn't that the sweetest thing I ever heard? Coming all the way down from Georgia to see *me*. Why, Midge, baby, it's fifteen years."

"You damn said it, Ira."

"*Listen.* Listen—you and old Harve have to be my guests. We'll get you a suite of rooms and you can do the town. On me. I'll set it up—the clubs, the restaurants, the dog track. Now where'd you like to start? Wanna see the water-skiing tournament?"

Midge shook her head. "Ira, you know I don't like this kind of thing. I'm a county-fair girl. You said so yourself." Her shrewd blue eyes took in the tapestry-hung bar and a glimpse of the soaring stone lobby and dismissed them rudely, with that confident finality with which the lowest and meanest can cancel out anything that smacks of wealth and power. Watching her destroy the Peruviana and his own rich world, Ira was reminded of a squat delivery boy, who one Christmas in New York had brought a case of the finest Scotch to his office. When Ira had expressed his delight at the breath-taking gift—twelve bucks a bottle, he guessed—the man had snarled at him: *Who'd drink dat piss?* Ira shuddered at the memory. He was glad so many of them, crawling and creeping at the bottom, didn't have his tastes and needs. It was one of the reasons that he and Midge had to go their separate ways.

"Well—if you do, sweetie, say the word," Ira continued. "You could at least have dinner with me. We could do the stone-crab bit."

Midge drained her bourbon with the ease of a woman accustomed to more violent beverages. "Ira, we didn't come all the way down here for no crabs."

DeKay shifted his legs and turned on the stool. The trouble was, Ira knew, as he studied Midge Detzler's scaly face, he was unarmed in front of her. She was of his blood and bone, bred on the same baking plain, possessing the same shrewdness, and a lot tougher than he was. In crisis, Ira had always been able to fall back on a few laughs, a promise of gifts, a hint at pleasures unsavored. When they had confronted him with his double life at the network, the evidence that he had his hand in the till, he had won the hearts of his superiors by grinning boyishly and murmuring: "Looks like you chaps have me by the short and curlys, don't it?" Such appeals would not budge her. In space, time and tradition they had been too close.

"I can't guess why you made that big trip, after all these years. If you want some bookings for the act, Midgely, I can call my office. I know all the action around here."

"I bet you do, Ira. I can tell you're a big man."

"Not really, sweetie. I live good, but I work hard for it."

Harvey came back from the men's room and settled on the stool alongside Midge. He still wore his crash helmet, and he spent a few seconds studying his muted reflection in the bar mirror, lovingly adjusting the white crown. The Seneca Democrats (Who were they? What did the name signify?) would have been proud of him, sitting there in a swanky hotel bar drinking free bourbon.

"Ira," Midge said casually, "you are still my husband."

DeKay winked at her. "Come off it, Midgely. We were both drunk and we gave phony names and it was some greaseball Mexican who performed the wedding. Besides, when we woke up the next day, we agreed to have it annulled. Hell, we no more wanted to be married than I'd want to get on a bike with you."

"We never did have it annulled, Ira."

"*Baby*. You wrote me you realized it was all a mistake. You felt so rotten about the whole deal, you didn't even want any maintenance from me."

"I was a good-hearted slob, Ira. I learned plenty since then."

She had indeed. He had met Midge when she was doing a little acrobatic-tap turn at a cellar night club at the ragged end of Hollywood Boulevard. She had the most intriguing body Ira had ever seen—all twists and wild curves and unexpected dips. After a frantic week of bedding down, they had gone off to Mexico for a week end and Ira, heavy with tequila, had found himself a married man when they got back to Santa Anita. Confronted the next day with the evidence of the marriage certificate duly issued by the state of Baja California, they laughed it off and agreed that it was something both of them would willingly forget. Midge had a career—there was this fellow named Leon, a talent scout for Paramount, who had promised her a test, and her dancing was improving all the time, and she fully understood that Lieutenant Ira Detzler, with his big plans for after-the-war, could not be burdened with a wife. They talked it over, two innocents from the corn states, and decided to have it annulled, when and if they got around to it. That had been in 1943, and now, in the harsh, clear light of 1957, they found themselves recalling that untroubled interlude of their youth.

"Sweetie, we can still make the arrangements to cancel the deal. I got this lawyer who knows how to do it—"

"Ira—suppose you was paying me alimony all these years. You realize what it would amount to by now?"

He looked at her vacuously. "You're not on my wave length, Midge. I hear you but I don't read you."

"You're still so cute, aren't you? All those jokes and funny cracks and the nutty things you used to do in the hotel rooms. I knew you'd go far."

"Midge, let's you and me and Harve get into my car, if you don't mind leaving the motorcycle for a few minutes, and we'll go see the lawyer. I bet you in twenty minutes we can draw up an agreement and everyone'll be happy."

Harvey nudged her black behind. "Ast him about the money," he said. He had a shrill, high voice. The words were formed without benefit of labial movement.

"Harve and me figured—I been with Harve these last three years—just business partners, Ira, so don't get any ideas I've remarried or anything—and Harve and me got up this little act. We met on the bikes. When Harvey was racin' with the Seneca Democrats in Shawnee. We do all right, playin' fairs and expositions. Not the way you do, Ira, but I have no complaints. I always liked the outa doors and the crowds and I'm still a farm girl in my heart."

"A shame you quit dancing, sweetie. You sure could wiggle them sequins."

"Ast him," Harvey persisted.

"Ira, when I saw this pitcher of you in the paper, how you were a sportsman and publicist down here, I figured you could help me and Harve out. We need some cash to build up the act. Harve wants to build a little arena in Shawnee where we could stage the shows. He needs new bikes and a couple extra riders and fancy uniforms—you know, in that shiny pink cloth that shows up at night. It would be a big hit. Harve is the best trick rider anywhere, except he's never gotten the breaks."

Ira smiled generously. "Baby, I'll do what I can. I know some wealthy chaps down here who might be interested in investing a skin or two. I can't promise—but I'll get you some introductions."

"No, Ira, that isn't the idea," Midge said. "What I said before about alimony. Suppose it was only a hundred a month. Twelve hundred bucks a year. Well, gee, in fourteen years, you'd owe me close to seventeen thousand dollars."

"Midgely, you got the wrong man. I owe you nothing. Not cent one. This marriage was dissolved by mutual agreement. Why, for every dollar you figure I owe you, you've probably slept with a different man. We've gone our ways."

"Says you. I got the marriage certificate photostated. After we tore up the original I pasted the pieces together. I got letters from you. I got witnesses who swore that the phony names we gave was really us."

"How dumb could we be?" Ira asked.

"I was dumb then, Ira, but I learned plenty. I learned from you. Ira, me and Harve will let you go free and clear—forgetting about that seventeen grand and how you ran out on me and all I went through over you, provided you help us out with the bike show."

Ira started to order another round but Midge stopped him. "The thing is this"—her nasal voice wavered slightly—"the thing is Harve and me need ten thousand bucks to get organized. If you hand that over to me, I'll sign anything you want, and let you out. I'll say anything you want, if our lawyer says okay. But if you get chinchy on us, and try to claim we was never man and wife, I'll hang around here till everyone in the Beach knows. In a town like this, they'll love it. Remember that big movie star and what happened when that fat old wife turned up after all those years? Remember, Ira, I am still bound to you in holy wedlock. For ten grand you can get off the hook. You'll never see me again. It'll be in writing."

Ira slouched onto the bar, resting his golden head in the crook of one arm. He stuck his tongue out at Midge.

"Yah. You don't scare me."

"You'll find out, Ira. Harve and me intend to go through with this."

"I don't think you will, Midgely, because you're too sweet and I think maybe you really loved me once, just like I loved you."

"Hah! You couldn't love anyone, Ira. Even back in the Ordnance Department you were too busy promoting. They ever catch up with you for selling those Army automobile parts to private dealers?"

Harvey assembled his enleathered form and climbed off the stool.

"Tell him how long he's got," Harvey said. He shuffled about the carpeted floor with the true contempt of the *Lumpenproletariat.* His hatred of the rich hangings and carved chairs was a hatred deeper than ordinary class jealousy. Harvey Hess and Midge Detzler were not meanly antagonistic to the exotic surroundings. Rather, as representatives of an old, hard tradition, they hated it simply for what it was. They were veterans of a hundred dusty roads, of midways baking beneath the plains sun, of a thousand crumbling diners and sagging roadside motels. They were frustrated pioneers; divested of the frontier they raced madly back and forth within the civilized nation, seeking lost gods and vanished rites....

"We figured until tomorra afternoon, say one o'clock," Midge said. "If you don't pay us off—in cash, no checks—we'll go back to the lawyer and start the lawsuit for nonsupport and a few other things."

She hopped nimbly off the stool, and in the half-light of the bar, Ira could see the muscular thighs, the contracted waist of the acrobatic dancer. She was probably wilder than ever in bed—

bouncing around on the motorcycle was undoubtedly a sex kick.

"How do I get in touch with you?" Ira asked. "I mean—I might want to discuss this with you a little more. You got to give me time to see my people. Besides—I may look rich to you, but I'm a businessman. My cash is tied up."

"We're at the Twin Palms Motel," Midge said. "We'll wait till tomorrow one o'clock to hear, then we start the action."

At the threshold, their sinister figures sharp against the bright interior of the lobby, Midge paused.

"I must say, Ira, you haven't changed one bit. You don't seem to *age* like everyone else. I guess it's 'cause you never worry. You were always like that."

He blinked his eyes and grinned. "I keep my troubles inside me, Midge honey."

"I'm really sorry to do it this way," she said. "But, Ira, you have to admit, you owe me something."

Harvey took her elbow and ushered her into the lobby. Ira sat quietly at the bar for a few minutes. He heard the arrogant burst as the motorcycle blasted off, shivering the self-conscious Continentals and Cadillacs always in evidence at the entrance to the hotel. Then he turned thoughtfully to the bartender.

"George, you think you could scare me up a cup of coffee from the kitchen without bringing the manager in here screaming?"

"Any time, Mr. deKay." George was a handsome Syrian, a much-decorated paratroop hero. He loved his work and ran an immaculate, efficient bar. He made, Ira told his friends, the best frozen Daiquiri outside of Trader Vic's.

DeKay sat brooding over his coffee, scratching the splotchy rash that had bloomed on one cheek and was expanding into a ruddy edematous lump. He had grasped the essential of his problem at once: *Martha Sorrento*. He knew she was ready to join him. It was inevitable. But if Midge Detzler and her chaperone were to start blabbing, his cause would be lost forever. Without the complication of Marty, he would fight the motorcyclists on their own terms—let them make public their story, let Midge present her claims, and then go to the mat with them. In the Beach, no court would find against him. He was too well known, too much part of the fabric of life. Those two county-fair grifters in their black windbreakers would never last.

But his pursuit of Marty eliminated that solution. It was imperative that he dispense with the motorcyclists swiftly. Martha Sorrento would laugh in his face if the facts of his first marriage were revealed to her. One look at Midge, in her black pants, shiny in the reinforced seat, and all his efforts at creating a new Ira deKay, a version that the professor's wife would find acceptable, would be shattered. Ira, in his innermost heart, was honest with himself, and he understood that Midge was his truest sister, a pursuer of sensuality, a purveyor of the shallow and cheap, a member of the threadbare fringe of American life. It had been his good luck to find firmer footing than she had; the time and the place had been right for his kind of inanity. He had learned, too, that people of wealth and power secretly wanted to be like him, to emulate his brainless existence, to be touched with the wand of everlasting laughter. Midge and her companion would never understand his success: they had preferred sleeping in haystacks and performing in dusty livestock rings for the beneficiaries of parity.

Yet they were smart enough to appreciate his vulnerability, and he knew he would have to accede to their demands. There was also the possibility that a prolonged sojourn by them in the Beach might lead to *their* learning about his association with Marty. Midge would double the ante. The whole prospect was dreadful. He scratched the flowering red patch on his cheek, realizing as he did that he feared Midge Detzler and her friend Harvey. They were not only holding him up, intruding on the painstaking plans he had drawn for his future, they were reminders of the tiresome, cheap things he hoped he had escaped forever. They had come to him wafting odors of the treeless, gray-green miles of bleak land, the sterile, baking towns, the appalling sameness that he had hated so thoroughly as little Ira Detzler.

The telephone in the bar rang and George called him. It was Marty, phoning from the cabana. She wondered why he hadn't summoned her yet: the children were getting water-skiing lessons and she was being bored to death by Fenton Braud, telling her all about his newest product—a reducing aid that one could inhale through a vaporizer while sleeping. There was a cozy quality to their conversation, a mentioning of trivial relationships that delighted Ira. Even in his sorrow of the moment, he found comfort in the small talk: it was as if they were already married, their matings formalized and sanctified.

"I guess you know all about the bombing last night," she said.

"Yeah. A bad scene. I'm glad nobody got hurt."

"It was dreadful. We were lucky it was a small bomb . . .

and not a very good one. That young cop, Fry, seemed to think some high school kids may have done it, just as a prank. The only damage was to the back of Erwin's boathouse and some of Tom's precious bones."

"I checked Chief Ennis on the bit," Ira said generously. "He thinks maybe the leftos did it themselves—you know, just to stir people up."

"That's unlikely."

"Well, I talked to all the papers and radio stations this morning. Si is seeing to it that Tommy doesn't come out bad on the deal. Anyway, the whole thing is over. I hear Erwin's sending in the bulldozers."

"That's right. We'll probably be leaving in a few days."

"*We?*"

"Of course, Ira. I've had a marvelous time, but I told you as firmly as I could—this was a temporary thing. I have to go back to New York and resume my duties as a University wife."

"You'll change your mind. Listen—you don't have to marry me. I canned Cleo already to make room for you."

"You shouldn't have done that. What's she going to do?"

"Peddle it, like she always did."

"Am I going to see you today?" Her voice seemed to drop—and without her being aware of it—became soft and breathy. He could see her in the striped interior of the cabana, slim and private and attempting, with enforced casual banter, to hide her need for his agile body. This conceit buoyed and strengthened him. It would fortify him for the desperate mission confronting him.

"I got some calls to make, sweetie," Ira said. "So let's make it a little later. Like four o'clock?"

"Where?"

"The conference room."

She laughed gently and they said their goodbyes. There would be one more engagement with Ira and then she would cut off their relationship. She looked forward to an afternoon of sun and ocean and the ultimate ecstasy. For the first time she felt a little sorry for Ira, knowing that she would have to frustrate his grand plan.

13 *In the Hall of the Mountain King*

As he drove out to Jimmy Nudo's home in North Beach, Ira had a disquieting sense of inevitability. In the six years he had known Nudo, their contacts had been tangential, yet Ira had a recurrent notion that one day he would find himself crucially involved with the little man. Both of them were agents of pleasure. The only difference, as far as Ira could see, was that Nudo operated outside the law, with the law's forbearance. He, deKay, remained inside the law. Nudo's rewards, naturally, were infinitely greater. He was a rich man, an extremely, secretively, rich man. And Ira, for all his gyrations, was virtually bankrupt. That now, *in extremis,* he was forced to turn to Nudo for succor seemed to Ira appropriate. He wondered if Nudo understood this also. When Ira had called him (after learning from Mermelstein that they had less than two thousand dollars in the account) Nudo's comment was: *I figured you'd come to me.* What Jimmy probably referred to were the ceremonies dedicating *The Spirit of Man*—from which the hoodlum had been surgically separated by Ellenbogen. But that problem, it occurred to Ira, was part of a broader scheme. Nudo appeared to have some special strength, some inner light that beckoned to Ira and that Ira dared not ignore. *I figured you'd come to me.* Ira feared very little and respected nothing. But he knew when he turned to Nudo he would do so with less of his usual bravura and few jokes. On the other hand, he would not be a miller moth dancing around sooty candlelight. There would be a kind of mutual respect: two smart operators, working in different levels, but men who appreciated each other's motives and deeds.

Nudo's house was modest. It was a gray stucco, as colorless as its proprietor, surrounded by a curious arrangement of hedge and fencing. Three feet of clipped privet bordered the outer perimeter, and immediately in back of the bushes, an institutional wire fence, cold and grim, rose an additional four feet. One of Nudo's associates had had his head blown off from good cover in a high, thick hedge five years ago. Jimmy promptly called in gardeners and ordered his own bushes trimmed. The next day, up went the wire fencing, a barrier behind which no assassin might hide.

The gate was locked from the inside. Ira saw no buzzer, so he jiggled the latch and called out: "Hallo! Hallo out there!"

In answer, he heard a dog's murderous barking. A sleek Doberman, its feral head pointing for blood, careened around the side of the house and hurled itself against the gate. Standing upright, baring white killer's teeth, it had a demonic quality that unsettled Ira.

"Nice puppy," deKay said. "Nice doggy. Go make poo-poo in your owner's hat, you big black son-of-a-bitch."

The dog snarled and slavered, hurling its muscled body against the gate. Ira moved back toward the car. "Frack this noise," he grumbled. "I'm too young and handsome to make hamburger for some hood's mutt."

He was about to enter his car and try phoning Nudo, when a teen-age boy in yellow satin bathing trunks slouched around the side of the house and called the dog. "Guido!" he shouted. "Shaddap and come here!"

The Doberman romped away, hurling an occasional bark for the record, and the boy grabbed the link chain around its neck. Then he walked to the gate and unlatched it for Ira.

"You Mr. deKay? My daddy is in back."

The boy was undersized and slender. His face was pointed and smoky, like his father's, but there seemed no cunning in him. He had the vacant look of the ungifted fourteen-year-old: a boy no good at athletics, behind in his studies, unpopular with girls. Ira followed him around the sprawling gray house. It had been arbitrarily enlarged—a wing here, a porch there, a patio in the rear. It had neither style nor charm, and its adornments horrified Ira with their oppressive middle-class dreariness. The lawn—pocketed with brown bald spots—was decorated with atrocious plaster statuary: a green gnome on an orange toadstool, a flaking mother duck and three beakless ducklings, a spotted fawn, balanced on three and a half legs. A choking odor of unmoved garbage and oily cooking filtered through a kitchen window.

Under a fringed blue umbrella, reclining on a matching blue chaise, he found Nudo. In the debilitating heat, he wore a white terry-cloth robe, wrapped tightly around his shriveled body. His skinny ankles and cadaverous feet protruded, reminding Ira of a mummy he had seen in a sideshow many years ago. Nudo's eyes were half shut, gazing blankly across his rear lawn, at a small swimming pool, where a porcine woman in a tight black bathing suit splashed and played with an infant. The woman wore no bathing cap, and her black hair fell in snaky ropes on either side of her coarse face. The ugliness of the setting and of the inhabitants distressed Ira; he felt that if in his dire need he was forced to come to the likes of these for rescue, he had failed somewhere. He did not mind Nudo's being a hoodlum. But why couldn't he live like any decent hoodlum with that much money *should* live? Ira knew about the 400,000-dollar mansions in Chicago and the high-walled estates in New Jersey. Why did Jimmy Nudo—his own peculiar savior—have to live like a second-rate junkyard operator?

"Daddy," the boy whined. "C'n I go to the show today?"

Nudo looked at the starveling child with what passed for a smile on his own shrunken face. "How can you? Ain't Mr. Shapiro coming today for the lessons?"

The boy ducked his head. "I mean after. When we're t'roo."

"Why don't you talk better than that?" Nudo asked him. "How you gonna get into Annapolis if you talk so bad?"

"Ah, come on, Daddy. Lemme go to the show."

"I'll see. If Mr. Shapiro says you did good on the lessons, okay. So you better pay attention to him." The boy danced off, the horrid dog nipping at his side and then braking himself frantically when the youth plunged into the pool. Nudo followed their flight with joy, then looked at Ira.

"He flunked algebra, so I got this teacher from the high school comes out twicet a week to teach him. I want him to go to Annapolis."

"He's a darling boy," Ira said. Nudo had offered neither greeting nor an invitation to sit down. Ira settled into a webbed chair.

"The kid's got it too easy," Nudo said. "I thought maybe if this teacher don't help I'll send him to a military school next year. You know anything about them?"

"No, but I bet I can help. I did a little PR for the State Prep School Association and I could find out what's the best ones. You name it, Jimmy boy, I'll handle it. I often wondered why you don't let ole Ira give you a helping hand on these personal family-type affairs."

Nudo, who had been watching the fat woman and the children during this colloquy, turned suddenly. "You talk too much," he said flatly. "I guess you're all right, deKay, but you gas too much. Shut up about the family."

"Sure, Jimmy baby. Just trying to help out."

Nudo's face darkened. The corrupt power in him discolored it for a second. "What you want to see me about?" he asked impatiently.

"You get right to the ole point, don't you, Jimbo?"

"What do you want?"

"Jimmy, I need some instant money. I'm tapped out. Some woman trouble turned up in my life and I got to get some cash."

"How much?"

"Ten grand."

"What happened?" Nudo lowered his voice. "You knock a broad up? What could be worth ten grand? You ain't married."

Ira patted his forehead with a crisp initialed handkerchief. "Ah, that's the big laugh, Jimmy boy. I had me a wife a long way back. One of them war-type marriages. I made the mistake of never getting a for-real divorce. So this broad turns up today and she's going to make it very unpleasant for me if I don't pay the money."

Nudo looked at him with contemptuous eyes. "All you fast-talking guys. What do you know about marriage? Marriage is kids and a wife. Like my wife, over there." He pointed to the pool, and now it dawned on Ira that the hideous, blowzy woman with the oily hair was *Mrs.* Nudo, mother of his children, light of his life.

"Well, some of us aren't as smart as you, Jimmy."

Nudo squinted at him suspiciously. "There must be a nangle, deKay. You can't need no ten grand just to shut up a broad."

"No angle, James. Just a lotta trouble."

"And you want me to lend you ten thousand dollars? Who are you to me? Why should I do you a favor?"

Ira nodded his head in too-fast agreement. "Right-o, James. Why should you? I guess you feel this has to be a kind of two-way street, right? And who can blame you? That's business, isn't it? You wouldn't be the big business entrepreneur you are if that wasn't your credo. Hah! That's a neat one. Nudo's credo. *Nudo's credo says no-dough.* Well, I guess I'm rambling a little, Jimmy. The thing is I might be able to help you. If I can't I'll settle for a fair innarest rate...."

Nudo's eyes had locked during Ira's appeal. Ira, noting his inattention, let his voice dribble away. It was not the kind of thing that happened to Ira. He prided himself on his talent for talking effortlessly, entertainingly, holding his listeners. But he had no status with Nudo. The racketeer conceived of him as inutile and supernumerary—a small-time conniver and fool whose prattle did not relate to him. Ira remembered hearing on a radio news program a recording of a tapped phone conversation between a fearsome hoodlum and a shyster who had done some fixing for him. The shyster's voice came through loud, clear and febrile on the tape, a voice cajoling, pleading, advising, intimate one minute, detached the next. He kept referring to the hoodlum, with distressing servility, as *Tone*—an unlikely diminutive for Anthony. *Tone,* for his part, responded with an occasional grunt or a "yeah." He did not have to converse, he did not have to observe formalities with the lawyer, and Ira knew why. He held the power of death in his fat hands. He was the ultimate denier. He would, like Jimmy Nudo, have no hesitation about destroying life or altering it in some horrifying manner to achieve his aims. The cringing, talkative attorney of the tape recording with his *Tones* and excessive verbalizing, understood this, just as Ira understood it as he sat on the mangy lawn in back of Nudo's ungainly home, watching the ugly people in the pool.

"You mean-a tell me a noperator like you can't get up ten thousand dollars?" Nudo finally asked.

"Things are rough," Ira said. "You see, Jamey, in my line I get a lot of my income through loot—deals—rather than cashola. I just lost a coupla accounts. But once that big tourist deal on Ellenbogen's place gets going, I'll be flush again. Fat as a hog. I'll pay you back real quick. This broad caught me with the shorts. I got some personal business at hand which requires I lose her fast."

He had slipped in the reference to *The Spirit of Man* casually and gracefully, knowing that this would give Nudo the opening he sought. The little man, his dessicated face finely dotted with sweat, patted his temples. His coal-colored hair was lovingly waved.

"They shafted me on that," Nudo said sorrowfully.

"Beg pardon, Jimmy?"

"Shafted me. You invited me to be a partner and I said okay. I had the money ready. And then this guy Ellenbogen shafted me. I musta called him six times and he wouldn't even talk to me. What right's he got to treat me like that? I gotta right to be legitimate."

"Jimmy sweetie, I tried my darndest. I begged Erwin to let you stay."

"What do you guys know? What's wrong if I want to be legitimate? There's nothing like a legitimate business. You know half my businesses are legitimate? In five years I'll dump the others. I'll just be in legit enterprises. The toy factory. Vending machines. Loan association. There's no percentage in not being legitimate. And I have to think of my kiddies. Vincent wants to go to Annapolis."

"He'll be a credit to the Navy," Ira observed.

Nudo cocked his glittering head. "You still in on this religious-museum deal? I read in the paper they're having the ceremony on Labor Day. All the officials and television stars. You still in on that?"

"Why yes, Jim. As a matter of fact my office is handling the guest list, the program, and so forth. *Yes indeedy*. Mr. Ellenbogen is having the land fixed up tomorrow. Landscaping, the grandstands, the whole thing. It should be very impressive."

"I tell you what, deKay," Nudo said. He swung his spindly body around. "You get me back on the boarda directors of that. I want to sit on the platform with the important people. Why should they say no? You tell Ellenbogen that. You still work with him, tell it to him. You talk very good. Too much, but very good. You do that for me, and I'll lend you ten grand. I woulden even charge interest. What's a lousy ten thousand dollars? You take your time paying me. Like a year, two years. But I hafta sit on that platform. I want people to see that Vincent's daddy is not what that Congressman said I was."

He had never testified, Ira recalled. The Committee had come to the Beach, and had run the usual cross-section of strong-arm men and minor hoods through the investigatorial wringer. But not Jimmy Nudo. Maddeningly middleclass, protected and powerful, he remained inviolate, apart from a few denunciatory comments by an obscure Representative from Illinois.

"Well, I think we've got us a deal-a-rino, Jimmy. I know if I put it to Erwin fair and square, I can get the okay. There's no reason *at-all* why you shouldn't be there on the platform. You were one of the first people I went to, right?"

"Okay. You ask him, then call me back here."

"Ah—how do I get the long green, Jamey? It's got to be in hard cash money."

"I said call me *here*. I'll arrange it."

The savage dog and the undersized boy went streaking by them, around the house to the front gate. In a few seconds they reappeared, followed by a stout mustached man in a wrinkled gray suit. He carried a book and a manila envelope.

"Good afternoon, Mr. Nudo," the man said. "Enjoying the sun?"

"Yeah. Go in and start in on him, Mr. Shapiro. I wanna talk to you about him."

The algebra teacher nodded and entered the house. The boy and the dog followed him.

"He better learn his algebra," Nudo said darkly.

"He sure better," Ira agreed. "His daddy wants to be proud of him, I can see that." Ira looked, with disguised revulsion, at the bloated woman splashing in the water with the child. Nudo had made no effort to introduce his wife to him and Ira knew why. The hoodlum was not ashamed of the ugly woman. Rather, deKay realized, he esteemed his mate and his children so highly that no introductions to servitors like the public-relations man were demanded. The Nudos were aristocracy, Ira realized, and he was just a common fellow coming to beg a favor.

"Swell family you've got, Jimmy," Ira said. "Makes a chappie like me kind of think about what he's missed."

Nudo wanted no more of him. He had turned his back on the promoter and was calling sweetly to the woman. "Don't bounce him so hard, Millie. Don't *bounce* him. He's only twenny months. Just a baby."

Ira left them. He sensed a helpless kinship with Mr. Shapiro, both of them manfully engaged in legitimizing the Nudos.

Back at the Peruviana, he waited a discreet hour and a half, then called the racketeer, advising him that Erwin Ellenbogen had agreed to reinstating him on the board. The invitation would go out that night. *Yes, indeedy, Jimmy,* Ira lied, *I spoke to Erwin a few minutes ago and he realized he was darn unfair to you. After all, I told him, if this is the big religious bit, isn't forgiveness part of the scene? I mean, everyone knows Jimmy is straight as can be with the charities and the nice family....*

The money would be waiting for him at the Blue Paradise Bar that evening. Ira would have to sign a note, but that was all. He had a liberal two years to pay it back, no interest, no strings attached. Ira hung up, breathing heavily. He had been forced to play it by ear. Erwin would have turned him down if he had appealed to him. And he could never explain to Ellenbogen *why* he needed Nudo's favors so urgently. Inviting Nudo was no problem—Si was handling the arrangements. At the ground-breaking itself, Ira felt certain, Nudo's appearance would catch Erwin by surprise. Rather than precipitate a scene, he would let the hood have his seat on the platform. And really—what was so terrible? Nudo had his picture taken with the actors and businessmen and "sportsmen." It was working out better than he had hoped. He would dispense with Midge and her friend tomorrow morning at his lawyer's office. The road to Martha Sorrento would be clear and straight.

Sprawled on the golden couch in his inner office, even the notion that he would soon have to pay rent for the suite failed to deaden his exhilaration. He buzzed Helene Schwenk in the outer office. It was not quite four in the afternoon.

"Helene, doll," Ira said wearily. "Call Mrs. Sorrento at the pool and ask her could she come up. And you and Lucille knock off for the day."

"Right-o, Mr. deKay."

"Where's Si?"

"He's been at Mr. Ellenbogen's office all day. They're setting up the program for the ground-breaking. He's been in conference since this morning. Shall I get him for you?"

"No, doll. Just leave word for Si not to bother coming back. I'll get him tomorrow."

He started removing his clothes. The burdensome day would not be without its rewards.

14 *Oran's Protest*

SORRENTO had climbed to the boathouse roof to take a last overall photograph of the site. The roof was treacherously pitched and the old shingles were hard and scabby. He picked his way gingerly to the highest point, balancing the tripod and the camera on his shoulder, and favoring his atrophied leg. At the zenith, he set up his gear, attached the wide-angle lens, and sighted through the aperture, limning the scarred and pitted land through a morning haze. He was just in time. The wire gate had been removed a few minutes earlier to permit the grumbling entry of two yellow bulldozers. Erwin was losing not a second: an endless flatbed, hooked to a mammoth tractor, had parked on the access road. It was stacked with a variety of fresh white lumber and old gray planking, the kind used to erect prefabricated grandstands. The new lumber, Tom imagined, would be used to build the officials' platform. Maneuvering the handle to get the widest view of the area, he realized he was not nearly high enough to record a decent picture. Actually, a helicopter shot was called for; with another week's grace, he might have gotten one—either through some Marine contacts or through one of deKay's promotions. A chopper would have been perfect: it would have afforded him a beautiful panorama of the field. As it was, he was too low to get a true reproduction of the dig's scope.

The bulldozers stopped and the drivers climbed down. In a few seconds, Erwin emerged from his home with a man in a white sports shirt, bearing an armload of blueprints. He was evidently an architect or a planner—one of the many technical experts who would now go to work on *The Spirit of Man.* Erwin and the man with the blueprints talked briefly to the drivers. They were soon joined by a half-dozen men in work clothes—apparently the carpenters who would begin setting up the stands and the platform as soon as the land was filled in and graded.

Tom took two views of the area, knowing that the pictures would not be very good, and sensing a new annoyance with Peltz, whose task it would have been to get the photographs. Peltz would have done a better job. He was a superb photographer: now he was hiding somewhere in the Beach, living with two old people. What would become of Ben? Where would he work? He thought of the aching years Peltz had spent haunting the graduate schools; the perpetual frustrations; the slow accretion of bitterness and futile anger. Not that it mattered any longer—but Benny might have gotten his doctorate if he had hung on one more year. The thought depressed Sorrento, and he squatted cross-legged on the hard crown of the roof and lit a black cigar.

Naboth's vineyard, where for two months he had hacked and dug and troweled, was peaceful, almost as if anticipating its serene future. If only he had been able to clear the whole thing! The settlement had been taking shape with each new spadeful of earth. There was the mystic row of white boulders—the hypothetical wall of Maitland's ball court; the ominous burial ground where the naked inhabitants of the Glades interred the dead; the refuse heap—the village dump; the curious haphazard arrangement of postholes, each one now bearing a short wooden marker. When he and the Burleys had cleaned up the previous night, he told them to leave the stakes in—a dollar's worth of lumber wouldn't break the University. When the dozers rolled over the land, they would be the last things to go under—like Tashtego's sea bird nailed to the *Pequod's* bowsprit.

A sense of incompleteness, of failure, irritated him. All his report would show would be a hypothesis. They had a handful of culture traits, not a firm tradition. If the southern wall of the court had been unearthed, or if additional clearing would have revealed a *pattern* of postholes... he would have done a superb paper. A book. Two books. One, a scholarly text, the other a popularized version. *Abaibo: The Ball Court Village,* by Thomas V. Sorrento. He jerked his head self-consciously, annoyed with his daydreaming. It was a luxury he no longer permitted himself. *Big jerk. Go back to school and write something so they'll make you an associate professor finally and you'll get seven grand a year. Almost as much as a milkman with a bad route. . . .*

Could Marty be right? Had football and Engstrom and the Marines taken the fight out of him? Or was it just his stupid luck to be incapable of finishing anything? And why did he owe anything to the Ballards and the Peltzes of the world? They had served him poorly on the excavation; only the Burleys had remained loyal. He envisioned their future. He would be babying them and shepherding them for years to come. Perhaps he would send them back to Missouri, where they could help their old man with the soup kitchen for migrant workers....

A deadening sense of inutility in a world that had little need for him, gnawed at him. Yesterday, his mother, phoning frantically from the Bronx after reading about the explosion, had done nothing to buoy him. Her shrieks over the telephone unnerved him; he found himself yelling back, while Marty shook her head impatiently. Serafina appeared concerned only with her beloved grandchildren. Her proprietary screaming angered Tom, and he turned the phone over to Marty for additional reassurances. *Yes, Mother,* he remembered Marty saying, *yes Mother, Abby and Nicky are fine... the explosion wasn't anywhere near them... they're staying at the Ellenbogen house with me . . . no, there's no danger and we'll be home in a few days....*

Mother. Who ever called Serafina *Mother*? She was *Ma* or *Mama* or *Mom*. In his dyspeptic mood these nuances of upbringing heightened his malaise. Serafina was not through with him, by any means, even if it meant another three minutes of long-distance phone call. Assured that her grandchildren were well, she then wanted to set a firm, unbreakable date for all of them to come for dinner. Also, Georgie Schultheis, his brother-in-law, was quitting his job at the bank and she thought maybe Tom could ask around the University to see if there was a nice administrative job open. Georgie was very smart and ambitious. He found it hard to be patient with Serafina. At length he agreed to everything, marveling at the steadiness of her vision, the grim dedication she had to two overpowering things: the family and food.

Moodily, he envisioned the return to New York as a series of new demands to be made on him, new hints by his father that they go into business together (a fellow he knew had this bar and grill off Westchester Avenue) and worst of all, their failure to realize that he was really not much help. He would not be able to get Rita's husband Georgie a job at the University; he had not the faintest desire to go into business with Frank or anyone else; he still found it impossible to bridge the chasm between his wife and the people of his blood. He would bury his nose in his work, write up the dig and mind his business.

"Hey Daddy, what you dooning?"

Nicky was calling to him from the balcony.

"Hi, Nicky. I just took some pictures with Uncle Benny's camera."

"Uncle Benny come home?"

"No. He went to live with some friends. Just like Uncle Davey."

Nicky, incapable of digesting that much information, sucked vigorously on his bottle. He sat on a deck chair, and noting the bulldozers, cried happily: "Deh tractor! Tractor!" Abby joined him a moment later, tense and silent.

Marty came out of the house—trim and fresh in a new white playsuit. At least, Sorrento mused, his family looked healthy. Wife and children were brown and firm-fleshed. Marty's hair was streaked with sun-gold and the youngster's black polls were shot with touches of deep red. The Beach had burned away the apartment pallor, the shadowy quality that followed a winter of steam heat and overshoes and thick slush along Riverside Drive.

"I guess the big show is about to go on," Marty said.

"Yeah. The end of an era."

"You feel badly about it?" she asked.

"I'm not singing 'Baby Shoes.' One week's work would have made a difference. I can see the wiseguys shooting holes in our theory. No one'll ever get to dig again in this area. Everything's excavated, built up, paved. You have to go thirty miles north to find sites worth digging, and by then you're out of any possible Arawak-influenced area."

"That's progress, dear."

The drivers left Erwin and the man with the blueprints and mounted their yellow monsters. Tom clambered down the inclined roof, handed the camera and tripod to Marty and lowered himself to the balcony.

"I guess you'll be glad to get back," he said. "You had your fill of the easy life?"

Her eyes were bright and relaxed. "It wasn't too hard to take." She laughed lightly. "I guess I was a little intolerant at first."

Tom scowled. "I was no help. I don't know, Marty, in the long run this place hit me worse than it did you. It gave me a nice awareness of my own uselessness. Who needs us? Hall gave me a pep talk at the airport. The usual, the endless search for the evidence. Future of Applied Anthropology. I guess he saw I needed a shot in the arm. Maybe Erwin's right. Who really cares about old Indians? Is this what I'm dedicated to? Trouble is, I know I am. Can't quit now, Jack."

"I wish you wouldn't torment yourself with these self-examinations. You'll *always* be dissatisfied."

"All those holes we dug. All the things I've learned. Geology. Surveying. Map-making. Anatomy. Radioactive Carbon Dating. Time and Space Perspective in North American Archaeology. Who's listening?"

She sighed. "I wouldn't dream of trying to stop you from this kind of analysis. You'll be doing it every day of your life."

With deafening, racking coughs, the bulldozers started their mighty Diesels, the drivers adjusted the giant blades and the two tractors moved off in parallel lines, piling up dunes as they rumbled across the site. At the edge of the nearest test pits, the first monster reversed and skedaddled, executed a fancy do-se-do, sashayed and promenaded, almost in hillbilly rhythms. In a matter of seconds the trench was refilled with its adjacent pile of sand. The other, eager to outdo its mate, sped for the long pit filled with the white boulders. It gathered speed as it climbed the slope, and at the edge of the trench, it maneuvered itself into an oblique position, so that with one mighty run along the flank of the excavation, it would bury forever the enigmatic wall left by the ancient dwellers of the Beach. The tractor backed away, suggesting a fighting bull pawing the earth before a charge; there was almost a little hesitancy in its obscene shifting and snorting, an unwillingness to obliterate in a matter of seconds, the uncovered evidence of a civilization seven hundred years dead. Finally, satisfied that the angle and the approach were perfect, the bulldozer belched and farted, dug its mammoth blade into the nearest pile of fill and commenced the burial. The sand spilled into the pit, and three of the white stones disappeared from view.

Tom and Marty heard the screaming—an inchoate, one-note screech—before they saw Oran hurl himself out of the boathouse and race toward the long trench. The boy was waving his undernourished arms, and his white head bobbed and shook in rhythms independent of his flying body.

"Nooo! Nooooo!" he was shrieking. *"Nooo!"*

Reaching the trench of boulders, his pale face encrimsoned by the uphill sprint he leaped into the pit, and in the manner of a theatrical Eliza skipping across wobbly ice floes, hopped erratically from stone to stone, shouting and waving his arms as he raced toward the yellow monster.

"Noooo! Nooo! Oran cried.

The driver saw him bouncing toward him—a crazy boy in a faded green fatigue suit—and tried to halt the grinding forward surge of the machine. He managed to brake the dozer, but not the pile of sand it had just shoved toward the trench. Oran hurled himself toward the blade as if to halt it with his feeble body.

Tom screamed at him from the balcony. "Oran! Oran! Get out of the trench!"

"He'll be killed!" Marty cried.

The great fall of loose dirt, perhaps a ton of it, descended over his blond head like a breaking wave, hesitating gracefully at its crest and then roaring into the pit, burying the graduate student upon a large white stone. Where Oran had been, a puffy halo of fine dust rose lazily upward. Erwin and his architect were sprinting toward the trench. Tom vaulted the balcony, grabbing a shovel as he sped toward the most recent of his disasters. He could hear Ellenbogen shouting: "When? When will they leave me alone?"

Both drivers had unlimbered shovels from their tractors and were digging feverishly. Tom joined them.

"Get him out!" Erwin shrieked. "Get him out and go home, please!"

Tom looked up at his honest, hexagonal face. "You were right, Erwin. We should have quit long ago." He bent to his labors, delighted that, professor though he was, he could outdig the two surly custodians of the bulldozers.

"I hope to God he isn't hurt," Erwin said. "What kind of goofy people are they? Am I wrong? Tell me, Tom—"

Like the skeleton they had unearthed six weeks ago, Ballard's "old-timer," Oran came to them in segments—first the silky head, then a starved arm, then his undersized torso. He seemed no worse for his interment. The sand had formed little patches of mud on his eyes, where it had adhered to his tears. The boy was weeping softly.

Wilma was waiting for him. She put a strong arm around her brother and helped him back to the boathouse. Tom followed them. Halfway down, Wilma turned around and looked ruefully at him. Her eyes seemed unusually distorted.

"*You* shouldn't have let them," she said tremulously. "You never should have let them in. Why did you give in to them?"

What could he say to them? How could he explain to these worshipful devotees that in the pleasurable, sunny milieu of the Beach his powers were limited? That he was a man castrated and nullified? He had lost Peltz and Ballard, and now he had lost the respect of the Burleys. It served him right for staffing his digs with what Marty called the League of Lame and Halt. Sorrento's Raggedy-Ass Marines. Next time, he would go to the University Appointments Office, which always had an oversupply of athletes, and hire five dumb football players.

15 *All I Wanted Was the Job*

BECAUSE of the holiday, Tom was unable to get reservations for their return flight until the Wednesday morning after Labor Day. Learning this, Marty took the children off for a week end of sight-seeing at the Glades National Park to the north. DeKay (was there no end to the man's generosity?) got her a car, and she left several hours after Oran Burley's brief interment. She did not find the incident as amusing as did her husband. To her, it was one more manifestation of their isolation. She was not arguing for head-bowing and genuflection before Ira deKay and Erwin Ellenbogen, she told Tom—far from it. She was still the daughter of an academic family, heiress to a tradition of skepticism. But there were limits to protest; one didn't have to sneer and scoff at the Peruviana or *The Spirit of Man* to prove one's superiority. Indeed, she advised Tom triumphantly, these attempts to snipe at the Outside World were invariably self-defeating. "Don't you realize," she taunted him, "that Hall ruined your dig? If he hadn't insisted on behaving like a bad comedian at the University and on that radio program—you'd still be digging out there. How can you be so blind? He came down here and insisted on hogging the show—and you suffered for it."

Tom frowned and studied his master map of the site. The surface justice of her attitude was undeniable. But what was Maitland supposed to do? Live *in vacuo?* If his application of social science to the follies and miseries of the world resulted in knocks and bruises for the home team, did that make his protest less valid? He was too busy to pursue the argument with her. With Peltz and Ballard gone he had more than enough to keep him busy until their departure. He wanted to visit the local archaeological society and check their records; he still had a batch of photographs being developed; and there was a day's work of cleaning and classifying the last of the find.

En route to the airlines office, he stopped to talk to Erwin. More than anything, he wanted to assure Ellenbogen he bore him no ill will. The feeling was more than mutual, the industrialist advised him. He bustled about the site with the architect and the carpenters, displaying an overwhelming knowledge of construction, material, landscaping and various other matters. Tom realized that his comments were not the bragging of a know-it-all. Erwin really did understand how to build grandstands and platforms, how to set up a loudspeaker system, how to grade for a parking field.

He confided to Tom that the ground-breaking ceremony was moving along splendidly. Tom was invited, in fact. All sorts of dignitaries had accepted, in spite of the rather short notice. Charlie Rasmussen and Si Mermelstein were working overtime getting the event publicized. They had been unable to "go network" as Erwin put it, but the local television stations were covering the event on a "pool" basis, and all national media—magazines, newspapers, newsreels, photo services—were sending representatives. He did not have much use for people like Ira deKay, Erwin said, but the son of a gun really rated with the press. When Ira asked a favor, they responded.

Clergymen representing the major faiths would attend, and a variety of educators, business executives, professional people and some respected show-biz names would sit on the platform. Travis Dean, the commentator, would be the master of ceremonies.

Tom had never seen Erwin so excited, so loquacious. All the harassment of the past weeks, the dreadful phone calls, the threatening atmosphere that had clouded his sunny view of life, all this had been dissipated by the new enterprise. *The Spirit of Man* would bind the community together. Erwin did not even care if it were commercially successful. He would gladly take a loss on it for a few years; he would buy out J. J. Campion and Fenton Braud and the other backers if they complained. He told Tom of some of their plans: The Schweitzer Room, The Story of the Dead Sea Scrolls, The Cyclorama of Faith. Tom was tempted to ask him if he would reconsider the peyote tepee, but thought better of it. He remembered Maitland's admonition: better Bingo than the Christian Front; better the New England Regional Baton Twirling Competition than witch trials.

"How's Lila feeling?" Tom asked.

Erwin walked with him toward the gate where the pickup truck was parked. The sight of the battered vehicle reminded Tom how much they owed to the Ellenbogens. He and Maitland had served them badly.

"Oh, better, I guess. I don't know what's got into her. She's reconciled to your work ending, of course. But why does she blame me for it?"

"She's not being fair to you, Erwin. Maybe if I talked to her—"

"Yes! By all means! She respects you. If you explained to her how I feel about this." He took in the busy area. It was now level and barren. The trenches and pits had vanished, the stakes were crushed into the sandy earth. A dozen diligent carpenters labored around kegs of nails, giant planks, saw horses.

"I think she should be a little more tolerant," Tom said. "What the hell, the dig was partially successful. Those crazy breaks—Ballard running off like that, and then Maitland getting drunk at that interview."

Thus consoling Ellenbogen, he realized that he did so out of some idiotic notion that he had seduced the man's wife. He had abstained where no other man with strong sexual urges would have; he had stolen one kiss and a pat, and had manfully repressed his eagerness for Lila. He would have enjoyed an affair immensely. Now, in his asinine nobility, he wallowed in guilt. The fact that he had done nothing at all, that his sexual adventure had been a comedy of omissions and frustrations, did not make him less culpable. The smothered desire, the recurrent clear and detailed mental images rendered him the evil mechanic of Erwin's cuckoldry.

"I know it seems odd for me to say this—after the way I kicked you out," Erwin said generously, "but I'm going to miss you folks."

"Erwin, you'll have me bawling."

"No, no, I mean every word of it. I understand what Lila means about other values and other truths besides my talents for making money. But all of us can't be pure."

He assured the manufacturer that he was as pure as any of them, as pure as Oran Burley, and a lot more useful to society. Erwin was appreciative of the tribute. He expressed his happiness that Tom would be present for the ceremonies and hurried off for a conference on the loudspeaker setup.

At the airlines office, on the main street, Tom purchased six coach tickets to New York. Three of them—his own and the Burleys—he paid for with the last of the expedition's funds. His bookkeeping had been excellent and the last check he wrote left a balance of eight dollars and twenty-two cents in the account. He was conscious again of the enormous debt he owed Erwin and Lila. Without their generous donations of housing, transportation, laborers, and considerable extracurricular favors, the dig would not have lasted much beyond the beginning of August.

Then he purchased, with his own check, tickets for Marty and the children.

The redheaded girl behind the counter (she had that unique duality—sterile and sexy—so prevalent among uniformed women) studied his name and looked at him quizzically.

"Oh. Yo'ah the archaeologist."

"Wrong. I'm the *linguini* king of East Harlem."

"Y'all pullin' my leg. I read all about you in the *Register.* I think it's awful the way they bombed you. They's a editorial in the paper today deplorin' vah-lence."

"No kidding? Let's see—does it say extremism on both sides must at all costs be avoided?"

"*Why*—you read it!"

"Honest I haven't. The only things I read are the sports page and Major Hoople."

"Funny boy. You must be a rah-it in the claysroom."

She busied herself with the interminable phoning and scribbling necessary to expedite six tickets. Her curiosity about him was a normal outgrowth of the increasing publicity the dig was receiving—first as a deKay-produced vehicle for publicizing the tourist attraction, and secondly as a focus of racial tensions. His indifference to his notoriety bothered him a little—perhaps it was another symptom of his academic insularity. Even the bombing, aside from angering him at the moment, had not excited him terribly. The shattering and scattering of his precious shards and crania had agitated him more than the prospect of death and maiming. *I have become a University Boob in a Tweed Suit,* he mused. Maitland's assurances about the search for evidence, no matter how trifling, seemed to him rationalizations for a sheltered and enisled existence.

"Y'all leave on Wednesday you should be just in time for Agnes," the clerk said cheerfully.

"Who's Agnes?"

"Say—you really don't read the papers, do you, Professor? That's the storm kickin' up in the Caribbean. First of the season, the weather bureau says. We maht catch a little of it next week."

He thanked her, gathered up the sheaf of tickets and walked out of the frigid office into the glare and swarm of the street.

He shaded his eyes from the intolerant sun and started toward the parking lot where he had left the pickup. As he did, a slender blond woman called his name. She had evidently been waiting for him, for she seemed to come at him from a standing start near the curb. He turned and recognized her as Ira deKay's assistant. She was pretty and straight-backed in a pleated white shirtwaist. A white cashmere sweater that hinted at membership in the Young Matrons' Hospital League of Old Westbury, covered her shoulders.

"Hi," she piped nasally. "You remember me?"

"Sure. Stefanowski."

"Beg pardon?"

"I'm sorry. A private joke. You're Miss Cooke. I guess you and deKay and Si are really hopping these days."

"They're quite busy, I imagine." She smiled bravely—with what she imagined to be the courage of high breeding—and lifted her fragile chin. "I been fired, you know." Her mouth dropped, and harsh lines of whorishness asserted themselves around patrician lips.

"I'm sorry," Tom said. "I'd imagine deKay would need you—now that the tourist deal is going up on schedule."

It was apparent she had sought him out and wanted something from him. But there seemed nothing for them to communicate. Her fleshly pride, her capacity for self-adoration made it impossible for Tom to feel sympathy for her. Like Stefanowski, she had gone as far as she could with her body. Tom recalled that the great halfback was a storm-window salesman in Tennessee.

"May I talk with you a while? I'll be glad to buy you a drink—if you won't be offended."

"Let me be the big sport," Tom said. "I have eight dollars left in the kitty. They won't mind an expenditure for entertainment."

There was a narrow enshadowed bar jammed between a store selling fruit baskets and a jewelry shop. Inside, a pair of ill-shaven men slouched over the bar, studying a Green Sheet with occult dedication. Cleo's alluring whited figure did not stir them from their concentration.

Dark draperies and muted lights did little to efface the dinginess of the saloon. He guided Cleo to a booth at the rear—the spurious leather seats were cracked—and they ordered Cokes.

"You were waiting for me, weren't you?" Tom asked.

"Yes, as a matter of fact. I went down to the boathouse and the boy there told me you had gone to get plane tickets."

"What can I help you with? I don't have much influence around here."

"Oh . . . I just wanted to talk. Is your wife going back home with you?"

"Of course. She's taken the kids to the National Park for the week end, but we're all clearing out Wednesday."

Cleo sipped her drink daintily. Tom imagined she wanted sympathy; they all did. Who was he—Father Divine? What was this talent he had for acting as a staff and a rod to the emotionally and spiritually displaced? Cleo Cooke, he feared, would find small comfort in his presence. He disliked her. Her tanned limbs and lovely face reminded him of all his sexual misadventures, his knack for not making out, his trembling, guilt-ridden, left-footed helplessness in pursuit of the prize.

"I know something you ought to know." The nasal quality had vanished; her voice was raspish.

"Stefanowski, you lose me. You've seen me two or three times. You don't even know me. What are you talking about?"

She opened her lovely mouth once, shut it, forming again the lush crimson bow, then found voice. *To what interesting usages and on how many males have those artful lips been put to use?* Sorrento mused. He was a hopeless, unreasoning moralist: getting furious with Jimmy Nudo and condemning Cleo Cooke for sleeping around. Weren't they products of the society? And wasn't society (who dat?) to blame?

"Your wife has been having an affair with Ira."

He knew the truth of it almost as soon as she uttered the words. Disbelief lasted for just a fractional second, as when a surgeon pronounces to a waiting relative: *it is malignant.* There was a fragile moment of rejection in Sorrento's mind, a sliver of hopeful light, and then the darkness of truth closed in: the knowledge that this woman had no reason to lie, the fitting together of bits and pieces of his experience of the past weeks, of conversations and attitudes and expressions, a mosaic of evidence that could not be denied or disproved.

"That's why I was fired," Cleo continued. "Ira had no use for me no more."

"Why should he fire you?" The idiocy of his concern for her appalled him, even as he asked the question.

"To make room for her." Her voice wavered and broke. "It's been going on for weeks. He asked her to marry him. Or else to leave you and come into the firm as a partner."

"And?"

"She wouldn't agree, but he thinks she will sooner or later.

He had an apartment picked out for her and the children, a private school for them. He thinks if she turns him down here, New York isn't that far away. I know Ira. He won't quit. I never seen him stirred up like this. She's wrong for him. That's why I'm telling you. I knew *she* wouldn't tell you, so I thought it was my duty to."

"Where did . . . where did all . . . all of this take place?"

"Where *didn't* it. The hotel. The cabana. Ira's boat. Well, it isn't his, but he borrows it from the Yacht Club. Listen, don't look so grumpy . . . I'm telling you this for your own good. Oh, I have to laugh at you people with your education, how little you know about life."

He hunched his shoulders as if a damp wind were blowing at his back, whistling up the raggedly clipped sleeves of his sweatshirt.

"Get out of here. Don't tell me anything else."

"Aren't you smart! Big college professor. You and that wife." Twin rills streaked down her face. "Bitch. Lousy bitch, going after Ira like that."

"Go. Get out."

"All I wanted was the job," she sobbed. "Listen. You make your wife tell Ira she'll never, never see him. That she can't possibly leave you. I have to have my job back, don't you see? I have a son. He's six years old. I have to buy new clothes for him and pay his tuition."

He tossed some coins on the cold table top and got up, walking past the two acolytes of form, into the sun-smeared street.

He drove the truck slowly through heavy traffic. The intelligence he had just received was so monstrously preposterous that for a few minutes he could only think of it in comic terms. Ira deKay. The zile kai man. Zotz. *Are you putting me on?* The notion of Marty, contemptuous and unreachable, mating with him was something to evoke rude jests. But the comic mood did not survive; soon he was envisioning them together. A remembrance of the night they had gone to Nudo's bar came to mind—something about a man who had been jailed for owning textiles with different positions imprinted on them. DeKay probably knew all of them. An involuntary cry broke from his lips, and, halted at a traffic light, he looked around self-consciously to make sure no one had observed his erratic outburst.

He tried to be detached, analytic. He had not been the completely attentive mate, he realized. But Marty had never been a demanding wife. Theirs had been a marriage of tacit understanding and appreciation. They had avoided displays of sentiment and long, passionate expositions—he in rebellion against his upbringing, and she in accord with it. And now supine and naked she had invited the enemy to take her. *Now, there,* Sorrento thought, *there is part of my difficulty.* It was all so easy for the likes of Ira deKay. It was as easy for him as it was for Tom to trowel out a skull. The mechanics are simple: contact can be made almost immediately; no particular skills are needed. For all the interdicts against adultery, one would imagine it extremely difficult of execution. It was as easy, as Leo Mazzochi would say, as catching a porgy. It was easy. And she found deKay attractive. (There he paused in his analysis and frowned: a disgust with all women agitated him. It was always an Ira deKay who rang the bell.) And something about the hothouse air, the lush, mindless environment, the feeling that none of them had rights or functions in the Beach, all these had plunged her into his perfumed arms. The comic intruded again; in his mind's eye he saw deKay splashing fruity cologne under shaved armpits. According to Cleo she had strung Ira along, through afternoons of hot joinings and stroking, encouraging him with the hope of a permanent alliance, of marriage, or at least, a business association.

He imagined he was now required to purchase a gun, seek out deKay and shoot him full of bullets. How would he proceed? Where do you buy a gun? What do you tell the man? Sir, I want to shoot the gentleman who cuckolded me right in the *colonies....*

He was a big Marine hero. He knew all about guns. That should be easy for him. The truth was, he detested them. He never was any good at field-stripping the Garand blindfolded and he regularly turned down invitations from his father's friends to go hunting for rabbits in Putnam County. He even disliked the plastic six-shooters Nicky wore around the house. *A penile indulgence, guns ... emphasis on hunting and shooting in the South ... perhaps explains why so many Southern writers are fags ... revolt against predominant male fetish....*

So he would shoot Ira right through the head. He laughed out loud. He had enough trouble keeping up on his professional reading and worrying about how he would ever afford to send his kids to good colleges to go around taking target practice at deKay. And with his luck, he would miss. *Try something else.*

Beat deKay up. You can beat him up. You are still a hard-headed dago who could back up the line. Engstrom couldn't run FT-23 through you. The trouble was, all the solutions, all the modes of action open to a man whose wife has cheated, had a faintly laughable quality. He could see himself squaring off with Ira, and a glib ring announcer explaining: *DeKay has the reach but Sorrento keeps boring in, keeping that lethal right cocked....*

At the boathouse he walked up to the liquid heat on the upper story and, stripping to his shorts, lay on the bed, wondering why his wife had done this to him. He concluded that deKay was a master at this sort of thing; he had taken her once and she had found it pleasurable. The absence of a moral censor in her character, of a defense or an antidote, seemed irrelevant to him. Popular literature, all the mass media, had, through repetition alone, made the act acceptable. Only dopes like himself insisted on observing some vestigial standard.

Lying there in the hellish heat, listening to the busy hammering and sawing outside, it occurred to him that he differed from Marty less in moral stature than in *nerve*. He had wanted, with painful longing, to sleep with Lila, to affect that easy fleshly union for which Ira deKay lived and to which he dedicated his frothy life. He had abstained from Lila less through ethics than through *fear*—fear of his own ineptitude, fear of hurting Erwin, fear of harming his relationship with Marty. After the fact of omission, he could be noble: like the time he had refused to date the "starlet" because "he had no uniform." But the irritating truth was that he still desired Lila, that he would spend the rest of his life meditating cruelly on what he had missed. His wife, succumbing to deKay, had at least been daring enough to indulge herself. His own nobility was based on fright and guilt-before-the-fact; in terms of the culture, she had been more to the point. A professor of his had said once (a misanthropic man who went off to live in the piney woods of Georgia) that our civilization is rapidly becoming one in which only two values are recognized: *power and amusement*. Ira deKay represented both—a curious kind of power and endless exuberant amusement. It was a horrid joke—on everyone—that Marty had paid him her respects.

For a long time he lay staring at the mottled ceiling. Then he got up slowly and walked out to the balcony. A sailboat race was under way on the dazzling bay; blimps bearing messages of joy hovered overhead; on the leveled earth a grandstand was rising in skeletal rows.

He did not look forward to the confrontation with Marty. The tacit, unspoken love they had practiced (and which Lila had so admired) was all right as far as it went. But in minimizing emotion, it made communication difficult. In his own family, shouts and agonized cries were a part of daily relationships; when a major issue had to be faced, it could be dealt with in those terms, and somehow it made the resolution of the problem easier. If by screaming and crying one could solve the matter of who got the car tonight, similar expressions generally worked toward resolving the question of a marriage.

With Marty, he had no such weapons. She had disarmed and changed him, robbing him of his familial propensity for violence, for display of temper and unabashed, egregious outbursts. He had allowed himself to be transmuted willingly and helplessly. Thinking back to his days of courtship, the free and endless lovemaking before marriage, the shared exalted movements and the breathy exchanges, he became giddy. He steadied himself against the balcony railing, shuddering at the improbable, ineradicable images of Ira deKay making love to his wife, bringing her back again and again to his mindless hot embraces.

He had no choice. He would choose to terminate their marriage. She was welcome to the Beach and deKay's world, whether she wanted it or not. He had a classmate who was a lawyer with an affluent New York firm. He would call him after he talked to Marty. Walking down the wooden steps, he sensed his fragile kinship with his wards, Wilma and Oran.

PART IV

1 The Return of Dr. Ballard

BALLARD came back in the night. He seemed blacker and huger and more solemn, poking his bowling-ball head through the shattered rear door, studying the splintered threshold and the twisted hinges. A nimbus of night bugs circled his face, as if drawn by some aromatic light. In the glow cast by the bulb within the office, Tom could see three other Negroes standing in Ballard's craterous shadow. Wilma and Oran leaped from the work table and raced for the door.

"Dave! Oh, Dave! You've come back!"

"Hello, kids," Ballard said softly. "How's the King and Queen of the midden?"

Having pumped his hand energetically, they retired, burying their tortured eyes in the *American Anthropologist.* They had an unnerving habit of reading from the same publication, signaling to each other by some occult method when the page might be turned.

Ballard appeared hesitant about entering. Tom got up from the table and walked to the door.

"You're still in one fat piece," he said. "I guess the crusade becomes you."

"I'm okay. I'm sorry about this." He indicated the shattered threshold and the ruined hinges. "It's my fault. I thought my getting out would take the curse off you."

The three colored men standing in his shade edged closer. Oddly, Tom noticed, the insect aureole was missing around their heads. Only Ballard seemed high enough to draw flies. "Tom, you know Spots. And Mr. McIsaac." He recognized his two original workmen.

"Sure. How are you, men?"

They nodded, smiling. All except Ballard wore suits, white shirts and ties. "And this is Dr. Harkey," Ballard said. "*Reverend* Harkey. He's the evil genius behind all this folly. Franklin—Tom Sorrento."

He shook Harkey's hand. The minister struck Tom as determinedly nondescript. He was medium brown and of moderate stature. An enigmatic smile played delicately around his purplish lips.

"I'm glad to meet you, Dr. Sorrento. Dave talks about you all the time. I think you supplied some kind of need in his life."

Was a man ever left alone? Would they all show up and fasten themselves once more to his neck? He fully expected Scharfstein, the inept Jewish boy from Cincinnati whom he had dragged through boot camp, rolling his field pack, shining his messkit, guiding him out of swamps and through gunfire, to turn up, grinning flabbily and asking him to shove his lard-ass up the hill. He reminded himself that Scharfstein had survived three landings and the loss of a leg to become a big man in wholesale groceries in Cincinnati.

"Dave's got some exaggerated ideas about me," Tom said. "I took him on this dig because he's a good field man."

"I'm sure you did," Harkey said. "You make me feel a little guilty stealing him from you."

"He's a big boy. He made up his own mind."

Ballard flicked a few venomous bugs away from his head. "Tom—could we go in the back? We'd like to talk a little and it's uncomfortable out here. We may have been followed."

Tom wished they would go. The old joke—*ain't I got enough trouble being colored?*—flitted through his mind. Didn't he have enough trouble being cuckolded, underpaid, frustrated in his work? Was he now required to take up the white man's burden? Thus pitying himself, he suggested they go upstairs—Marty and the children were away and they could plot their plots privately.

The delegation from Hilltown settled themselves uneasily in the upstairs room. Ballard suggested they keep the room dark. The furtiveness bothered Tom. Then he realized that their struggle could be viewed only in those desperate terms.

"I saw Ben," Ballard said. "He sends you his best."

"You saw Benny?" Tom asked. He was eager to hear about his other defector. "What's he up to?"

Ballard laughed. "He's taken a job. He's living with his aunt and his uncle down in South Beach in the Orthodox Jewish section. He said you shouldn't laugh at him when I tell you what he's doing."

"Me? Me laugh at Peltz? I've spent a good part of the last ten years *weeping* over him. What's he doing? Running a handbook?"

"He's a *shamus*." The Yiddish word, rich with humorous connotations, sounded doubly ludicrous uttered by the colored man. *The Last of the Falasha Jews,* Tom mused . . . *Savage Ethiop Warriors Revealed to Be Lost Tribe of Israel. . . .*

"A *shamus?* That's a cop, isn't it? No—that can't be right. Not Benny Peltz. I know what it means—a sexton! A handyman at a synagogue—a kind of high-class manager. Allie Cooperstein told me once. A little higher than the janitor, but lower than the rabbi."

"That's the ticket," Dave chuckled. "Imagine Benny locking up the Torah and bawling out the women for talking too loud? You should see it—a real old-fashioned *shul*—with the balcony for the girls upstairs, and no ventilation. Ben says he's happy. They can't find him there. They can't scare him any more."

"I hope he's right," Tom said.

"He's going to classes, too. They have these study periods—all the old guys with long beards sit around and discuss the Talmud. Did you know Ben could read and write Hebrew?"

"Well," said Tom, "if it keeps him out of trouble, I'm in favor of it. I wouldn't deny him his happiness."

Tom meant it sincerely; he knew Maitland would have approved. There was nothing wrong with an orthodoxy provided its practitioners did not ram it down the next chap's throat. Indeed, for the gathering of evidence to continue, it was essential that a wide variety of orthodoxies flourish. It lent spice to the work, Maitland insisted. Better a hundred beliefs than one overwhelming, crushing one. Tom recalled, in this connection, that when he was a freshman, the undergraduate magazine had been staffed by a coterie of bearded, slovenly seniors who listened to obscure jazz and read Kafka. One of their number, a poet of singular talent, had become a Buddhist monk. From a reading of his later works, it was apparent that the hot sinful memory of staying awake all night in the men's dormitory and listening to King Oliver records while eating Rice Krispies dry from the box, was what had impelled him into Oriental religion. He had converted a few aficionados of Buddy Bolden to his new faith—unsettled Jewish boys given to medievalism. They had all made the perilous journey from Marx to Bix to Kix to Zen. Try as he might, Tom could never find fault with their pilgrimages. Ben Peltz's journey, similarly, was not a subject for scorn or ridicule. So long as they did not straddle Tom's chest and try to force their dogma on him, what right had he to be churlish about their especial roads to inner peace?

"You know about the ground-breaking?" Ballard asked.

"That's what did me in."

"The Hilltown Betterment Association," Dave said. "will hold its first nonviolent demonstration at the ceremony. We will march and pray for everyone."

Was there a note of sourness in Dave's voice? In the darkness, Tom could not see whether Ballard's face betrayed cynicism.

"You got a permit?" Tom asked. "Don't misunderstand me, Reverend, but I'm a policeman's son. That's the first thing that occurred to me."

"There is none necessary," the minister said. "The prayer meeting and march is under the sponsorship of my church, and the city charter is explicit in affording all religious organizations rights to the use of municipal streets for public prayer."

"I'm missing something," Tom said. "Why don't you make your prayer *part* of *The Spirit of Man?* It's a kind of Open Pro-Amateur Event, the way I get it from Mr. Ellenbogen."

Harkey edged forward. A coppery glow illumined the edge of his prognathous face. "No colored churches were invited. There will be a colored *section* in the grandstand, we are told, open to us. We aren't interested in it."

Tom scratched his head. "I tell you, Reverend, I'm not sure I'm with you. I believe in small gains in areas where they're most needed. It would seem to me the last possible place you'd want integrated is some tourist trap with a bunch of windy boobs making speeches nobody will listen to. Why don't you worry about lynchings and beatings? *Then* jobs. *Then* schools. *Then* the vote. *Then* tourist places and hotels. When Dave told me this boycott hinges on being deprived of the vote, I was a little surprised. You can only vote for local people anyway, and you know they won't be running Eleanor Roosevelt."

"Dr. Sorrento, you haven't been well briefed by David. We take our religion seriously. We are perhaps the last stronghold of the truest faith. Our faith is a working religion, battling for man's dignity and decency. Not just our own. That is incidental. But the dignity of *all* men. Our prayers at *The Spirit of Man* will be as a loving illustration to our white brothers—"

"Rubbing their noses in it a little, hey Reverend?"

Harkey was not offended. "If you wish to view it that way. But you're a social scientist, Doctor. I gather you are not a church member. You would look upon our efforts with misgivings."

"Misgivings? Listen—I'm on your side. That should be obvious. In fact, that's one of your troubles. There's too much justice on your side. You're so right, it hurts. The people like me, who know you're right, we assume justice will be done, since it's inconceivable that this kind of stupidity can possibly continue. So we sit back and *assume*. Not that I'm apologizing. If you must know, it's taken me a lot of growing up to get over the gang fights we had with colored kids in Van Cortlandt Park. Why did they have to steal Allie Cooperstein's football? And then come back and use it right in front of us the next day? Can you guess who waded in and got it back and got the bloody nose? Me. I was big for my age. But that's another story. Okay, so any well-meaning American *assumes* the right will prevail because it's *right*—and we sit back and applaud Willie Mays, while the voting lists get butchered down here. Now the *others*—your enemies—they know all about the excess of justice on your side, so it only heightens their guilt and makes them more determined to do you in. It almost sounds to me like you can't win—at least not in our lifetime. I wish I could see something better for you. I've gotten over those kids who stole Allie's football long ago."

Ballard sighed. He let the wind through his inflated lips slowly and it fluttered them noisily. "Tom, you talk the way I used to talk. Before the Reverend got to me."

"I can't help feeling I'm right," Tom said. "I don't want to upset you, and besides I'm just a lousy assistant professor. But I think it's a losing game. Each time you people boycott or demonstrate or parade you just dig the knife of guilt further into the white people. You remind them how disgusting they are and they hate you the more for it. Suppose you stage your big parade on Labor Day? You join the ceremonies—uninvited—put on your own floor show. What will it do? Free Willie McGee?"

"Willie McGee is dead, Doctor Sorrento," Harkey said firmly. "And we are the living. I know we have found the path."

"I hope you have. I hope so with all my heart." Tom halted, embarrassed. "You see—I had trouble getting that out. The truth on your side is so damned pervasive, so overwhelming, we feel ashamed when it confronts us."

Ballard raised his great body out of a deck chair and moved uneasily about the room. "Tom—we came here to ask you to march with us tomorrow."

"Me? What good will I do?"

"I had the idea," Dave said, "that this should not be solely a Negro demonstration. That white people should join us. We asked around town—you know—the unions, the liberals, the educators. So far nobody wants to be—to be—"

"Tarred with the brush?" Tom asked.

"Exactly. They couldn't sympathize more, they know we're right. But they think the time and place is wrong. We should hold our prayer meeting in Hilltown, not at *The Spirit of Man* dedication. We've drawn a blank."

"Not entirely," Harkey laughed. "A few Indians are joining us."

"Indians?" Tom asked, incredulous.

"Seminoles. You know, most of them are heavily inbred with Negroes." Harkey laughed again. "I was really amazed when they called me. They tend to be professional primitives, glorying in their alligator wrestling and curios. Why am I telling you this? You're the anthropologist."

"Then I thought about you," Ballard said. "Old Tom, he'll be a white face in that sea of black men. Dr. Sorrento, successor to Dr. Livingston. We've got a great program prepared. A bible reading. Hymns. Franklin—tell Tom about Samantha Bates."

Tom felt giddy. The damned fools—the poor, damned, doomed fools. Maybe Peltz was right. Maybe they were all headed for violent death and obliteration. They sounded as if they were staging a church social. *Auxiliary Ladies' Booths at the Rear. Fried Chicken and Burned Niggers.*

"You've heard of Samantha Bates, haven't you, Dr. Sorrento?" asked Harkey.

"Isn't she a blues singer?"

"Gospel. She's a remarkable personality. She's sung in London, Paris, Rome. An extremely wealthy woman and an extremely talented one, she's got a voice—well it can't be described. She used to worship in our church when she was a little girl in Hilltown—before she went on to New York and became a great recording artist. Well, Miss Bates has volunteered to lead our singing. We've rigged up a loudspeaker system on a truck. She should create quite a bit of attention when our service starts."

"I hope I won't insult you," Tom said, "but isn't that dirty pool?"

"How so?" asked Ballard.

"I mean hauling in a ringer like that. A pro. You know, it's like the Dodgers using movie stars to brainwash people into voting for them in Los Angeles. Or an ex-king endorsing cigarettes."

"I suggest our cause is a better one," Harkey said firmly. "I have no objection to utilizing the techniques of commerce and advertising."

"It's your show," Tom said.

"You going to march with us?" Ballard insisted.

"Why me?" asked Tom.

"Because you're crucial, man. You are crucial ever since you saw me cleaning pottery in the Detering lab."

He had an impulse to usher them all out. To wish them well in their public and publicized devotions and get some sleep. *Gentlemen, I would like to help you, but I have problems of my own. For one thing, my wife, whom I love very much, has been sleeping with another man, and I am preparing to divorce her. Moreover, I have been on the verge of a major archaeological discovery, and have had it pulled from under me. Now I bow to no man in my guilt obsessions where you chaps are concerned, but please, get another boy. Am I being unreasonable when I suggest that I have my own personal worries and that as much as I . . .*

Instead, he said to Harkey: "All right. You convince me that what you're doing is going to do some good, and I'll show up, I'm blacker than some of your parishioners, so no one will know the difference in the newsreels, anyway. Talk me into it."

"I'll be happy to," Harkey said eagerly.

"I mean *really* do some talking. You have to excuse me, Reverend, but as you said, I'm a social scientist. I want evidence."

"You have every right to demand that," the minister said.

"Be careful, Tom," Ballard said. "He's a sharp one."

"Let me make a few prefacing remarks about my religion," Harkey began. "I make no apologies for regarding religion—*any* religion—as a social weapon. A colleague of mine has said that any faith that professes concern over the souls of men but is not concerned about the social and economic conditions that ravage the soul, is a dying religion, awaiting its own burial. I'm talking not about my own church—or any Negro church for that matter. I mean all of them. It's taken some of the churches a long time, but they're on the side of social progress. Liberalism, humanism—however you want to call it."

"If you can't lick 'em, imitate 'em," Tom said bitterly.

"What's the difference what the motivation is?" Harkey asked. "The fact that the Catholics are looking for conversions in opposing segregation is of no concern to me. Or that the increasing interest of churches in the labor movement *followed* the growth of unionism."

"I guess it's all right," Tom conceded, "but it's a little unfair. The *Times* gave the front page some time ago to those announcements on the same day by the Catholic and Methodist bishops—segregation was evil and they were against it. I remember when I was in college the people who did the hollering about desegregation and slum clearance were mostly dirty Jews. You know—greasy Communist types. Some of 'em *were* Communists, I guess. And other kinds of ratty radicals. *They* never got the front page of the *Times* for being against segregation. Why should I stand up and cheer because the True Believers have decided it isn't nice to beat up or humiliate or degrade anyone? Where were they when the lights went out? Hey, Ballard—just don't stand there with your big sweaty face—didn't you tell me that eleven o'clock Sunday morning is the most segregated hour in American life?"

"I sure did. But it's changing." Dave sounded defensive.

"But, Doctor—why begrudge them their new humanism?" Harkey said. "Why not welcome them? You're cynical because people like Ruth Benedict spent an unrecognized lifetime proving that racism is mendacious and malevolent. Can't you be generous about it—and look upon the church as a *convert* to your social prophets? And you must admit—ethical concepts are not new in our religions. It's the *application* of them that is."

"I could, if I felt generous."

"And remember this. Many, many millions more people will be swayed to these sentiments by our bishops and priests than you and your anthropologists could ever hope to persuade. I'm afraid that's the truth."

"You haven't won me yet. How's this going to get you back on the voting registers?"

"By uniting us in *love* with our white friends. We do not want to be the white man's brother-in-law. We want to be his *brother*. It is he who needs us. Segregation scars his soul and damns him more surely than it degrades any colored man. We do not seek to humiliate our enemies. We want his understanding. We direct our campaign against no individuals. Not against the people who bombed my church and your boathouse. We are fighting only the abstract notion of injustice. The love of God in our hearts will be turned on our haters and detractors. Can they resist that?"

"They've done a pretty good job. They don't seem to be swooning over you in Alabama and Arkansas."

"They will in time, Dr. Sorrento. You see—they'll have to."

"Why? They got their hog's ass and hominy grits. That and college football should keep 'em happy forever."

"Not forever. They need our love. They need it to destroy their own fears."

"I'm sorry. I haven't noticed it."

"Doesn't that make our crusade more inevitable? Booker T. Washington said, 'Let no man pull you down so low as to make you hate him.' *Perfect love casteth out fear,* Doctor."

Sorrento's eyes had grown accustomed to the darkness. He could see Harkey's smooth face, the features calm and pensive, the mouth in that odd perpetual smile. Did the man honestly believe that prayer and love and a lot of theological rigmarole would integrate the schools? That his surly adversaries would succumb to his feast of faith? Or was he playing a hard, practical game—a game that used economic boycotts, public embarrassment of his enemies and a shrewd capitalization on the new obscurantism, the notion that it was *nice* to be religious? The same doubts that had troubled Dave Ballard two weeks ago now bothered Tom. Yet, as he reclined on the bed, studying Harkey's enigmatic face, then squinting at the towering figure of Ballard and the two workmen who had said nothing but seemed, in some uncanny manner, to be uttering "Amens" to the preacher's exegesis, he realized that the minister's methodology was immaterial.

"I wonder," Tom said, "if this love affair doesn't quite make it, whether you've got some aces up your sleeve. Like economic pressure or political pressure. Could that be as effective as love?"

"How can I deny that?" Harkey asked. "The way of nonviolent resistance is not a coward's way. In boycotting white stores, in refusing to ride segregated buses, we are manifesting our *love* for white people—in a way that may be hard for you to understand, but it's love nevertheless."

"Yes. There's nothing like a drop in sales to bring out the noblest in man."

"You may be cynical about it if you wish. But we have no apologies to make for applying pressure—any kind. Political, economic, social. It's part of the game in our free-wheeling democracy, Doctor. Political leaders have a tendency to react to pressure. Our hope is that this pressure will make itself felt and understood."

"Particularly if you call it love?"

"I don't think you want to be convinced." Harkey sounded a little disturbed—for the first time.

"I'm convinced. I told you before I'm on your side. How can I be anywhere else? How can any reasonable human being be anywhere else? I don't mind you using every weapon you can lay your hands on. Testimonials—prayers—boycotts. Just don't try to sell me on the basis of love."

"But you see—I believe that. I see nothing exclusive between a deep love of my detractors and the use of material pressures to *convince* them of that love."

"And you think this will get you what you want?" Tom asked.

"I am sure it will. You said something, Doctor, about these changes not taking place in our lifetime. Maybe you're right. Maybe the resistance is hardening in some areas. But it's diminishing in others."

"For different reasons, Reverend. Because the Negro is a *consumer*. Because white schools get closed down altogether and white parents get upset. Because the notion has gotten around that economic progress is impeded—you remember, something called *money*—as a result of racism. So far, I don't notice any schools being integrated because of love or prayer."

Harkey sighed. "So much of what you say is true. I just know that our path is the right one. The battle is fought with divers weapons. The one I think most effective is the undying truth that we are all one in Christ Jesus."

They sat silently for a while. In the darkness, a tropic wind had risen, slapping the shutters of the boathouse and whistling across the graded land where the ceremonies would take place the following afternoon. Tom imagined the disturbance was a warning from Agnes—the tropical storm the airline girl had mentioned. But outside the skies were clear and star-heavy.

"There's one final thing you must understand, Doctor Sorrento," Harkey said, after a while. "As a student of man, this should interest you. Let's assume the worst. That our program of nonviolent resistance comes to nothing. I still feel that the work will not have been in vain."

"Why do you say that?" Tom asked.

"I say that because of the change in the Negro himself that must come about. He is learning that the day of acquiescence is over. That it is in his hands to take direct action over injustice. The day of the moaning blues singer will be ended. The day of passive acceptance of evil will be ended. If I can stiffen the spine of one Georgia field hand, raise up the head of a single millhand in Alabama, or open the eyes of a mugger in Harlem, I will have done some of the Lord's work. When I started the Hilltown Betterment Association, I was a voice crying alone. I was shunned and looked upon as an agitator. Today, the community is behind me—including the nonrespectable elements who would trade their dignity for access to cheap pleasure and vice. I take no special credit for this feat. You may laugh at my—what do you call it?—obscurantism, Doctor. But perhaps it will be the Negro who leads us to a new morality, a new faith. In the meantime, like you, I will settle for marginal gains if that's all that the times will permit. I want to see Negroes walk straighter. I want to see their children grow up with dignity and with hope. I don't delude myself on the difficulty of the task. We'll be in and out of the courts, and we'll be bombed and humiliated and strong-armed. But we will do God's work and do it because we spread the gospel of love. *Be strong and of good courage; be not afraid, neither be thou dismayed. For the Lord thy God is with thee wherever thou goest.*"

Harkey got up. He had delivered his sermon in a low, calm voice, never falling into the holy tones of the pulpit. He was like an affable young salesman, an honest fellow who gave you a fair shake.

"All right," Tom said, getting up from the bed, "where do I meet you people tomorrow? Anything special I should bring? Like brass knucks? Or my rosary? Come to think of it, Reverend, I better get clearance from Father Colangelo on Tutwiler Avenue. . . ."

Ballard shook his hand. "That's my crucial friend," Dave said. "We'll come by 'bout one o'clock. You can't miss us—we'll be the ones in blackface."

"Thanks very much, Doctor," Harkey said.

"You bet," Tom said. "We'll love 'em crazy."

2 *The Spirit of Man*

IRA prepared his toilet with the sensual concentration of a middle-aged woman, aware that each pat and lubrication of flesh added subtly to a thrilling unblemished end product. He spent almost a half-hour shaving, lavishing dollops of snowy cream on his cheeks, chin and neck, manipulating his straight razor gracefully around the ruddy eczematous patch. He had imagined that after paying off Midge with Jimmy Nudo's crisp, new money (he could still see the little bitch counting it on the unmade bed in the motel) and getting her to sign a full release from all marital obligations, that his skin would clear. That had been two days ago, and still the itchy, turgid splotches remained. He began to fear he would bear the adolescent rash until Martha Sorrento came around. An expert at cosmeticization, he daubed a flesh-colored cream on the stain and approved of the results. He dressed in monogrammed silk underwear and chose a Swiss voile shirt of remarkable fineness, a pale blue jacquard tie, and solid gold cufflinks—cunning replicas of the Rosetta stone. Ira was drawing on his midnight blue trousers, knife-creased and form-fitting, guiding them lovingly over pointed black suede shoes, when Si Mermelstein walked in. Si, too, sported dark blue—a sedate, natural-shoulder garment —for the august ceremonial, and the sight of his gloomy assistant moved Ira to a raucous cackle.

"Hah! Look at you! The birthday boy!"

"I just hope we aren't dressed for a funeral," Si grumbled. "You hear that wind howling?"

As the morning progressed, Agnes' winds had increased from a moderate fifteen miles per hour to a strong twenty-five. However, the skies had remained bright and were only intermittently shadowed by fat opalescent clouds which the winds whipped inland.

"You're always so *downbeat,* Si," Ira said soothingly. He donned the inky jacket. It was cut curiously—strange little points on the lapels, artfully form-fitting. Ira turned several ways in the three-view mirror, tugging at a suspender here, a handkerchief there.

"The last advisory said the winds might hit gale force by tonight—maybe forty miles per hour. They don't think we'll get much rain, because the eye of the storm is moving north. But who knows this early in the season?" Ira did not seem to hear him, so he continued: "Seventy-five or more is hurricane."

"*Sweetie!* How did you get so smart?"

"You remember the piece I did on the hurricane-warning system. It made every wire service."

Ira shot his cuffs, grinned at his Rosetta stones and began collecting wallet, money clip, key chain and other accessories from his dresser. These appurtenances had the look of tribute purchased by a nervous agent for an actor on whose talents he fed.

"It sure did, baby. Is everything all set at the bay?"

Si pulled a pad from his pocket. "Yep. Charlie Rasmussen is out there now checking the setup. Loudspeakers, PA, full mikes for live TV and radio, plus newsreels and tapes for the networks, press table with typewriters—Ira, Banks Typewriter Rental wants a plug for the free machines and I told 'em okay, but not on this particular show. Walt called again about Mr. Banjo but I told him absolutely not. No apes. I told him he could watch it on television in his hotel room."

"Erwin is happy?"

"He's delirious. He paid us a compliment. He said after all he's gone through on this, it's really worth it, considering the great coverage we got him."

"Good-o. We must keep The Ellenbogen happy. It's his zile kai."

Driving through the Beach toward the islet, gusts of wind battered them mercilessly in the open convertible. Ira was forced to stop, and after much yanking and pounding, he and Si raised the canvas top and locked it.

Under way again, Si seemed troubled. "Did I hear you talking to Nudo this morning?"

"You did, baby."

"Ira—you invited him to the ceremony, didn't you? To be on the platform with the guests?"

"Yah. Ole Jimmy can't wait."

"But you never cleared it with Erwin. What's he gonna say?"

Ira frowned impatiently, turning his aromatic face on Mermelstein. "Erwin is so happy today, he'll kiss him. We can always stick an extra chair up there for Jimmy. With this howler, there'll be a few no-shows."

He plunged the car into the wrong lane, hooted at a surprised traffic cop—who recognized the car and waved back—and sped toward the causeway. He wished suddenly he had called Marty at the Park. She was staying at a lodge with the children and he missed her. She had planned on returning the following morning, to avoid the week end traffic. Perhaps he would surprise her by running up that night. He scratched his inflamed cheek vigorously; his life had become a series of breathy, anticipatory intervals—stretches of blandness in between the time he spent with her. As much as her body and her style delighted him, his growing dependence on her was a source of some unease. This was not the old Ira deKay, the old zile kai man, the Man from Temple, Texas, who had three girls in the air and one on the bed all night. It could be, Ira mused, that this was the nearest thing to real love he would ever know.

When Ira and Si arrived, parking the car in the hastily creosoted area that had been set aside for automobiles, Erwin was already at work. The high wooden fence had been removed, so that traffic on the causeway might witness the spectacle. As Ira and Si walked through the parking area, they could see Erwin talking with a man from the newsreel "pool." The argument had to do with setting cameras in the grandstand—the man contending that the camera positions assigned to him were too low. Ira hurried toward them, eager to earn his percentage of the anticipated profits, but Ellenbogen seemed more than ready to accommodate the newsreel man. If the grandstand he wished, he would have it. Erwin was obviously in a charitable mood. His black mohair suit, whipped and billowed by the wicked wind, gave him more than ever the look of an Oriental potentate, a proprietor of eunuchs and odalisques. This effect was heightened by the magnificent landscaping that surrounded the site—row upon row of palms, hastily deracinated from a local nursery and now arrayed like lissome sentinels. Alternating with the trees were aluminum flagstaffs, each bearing the national emblem of a Latin American republic. The university had the flags left over from the Avilas debacle, and it was Si's idea to borrow them, since they were gathering mold in the basement of the home-economics lab, and nobody could guess when the institution would be sufficiently composed to honor another South American friend.

The high platform was draped with bunting, and a half-dozen carpenters were kept busy tacking and retacking it as the wind snapped at the tricolored cloth. Myriad wires snaked away from a bank of microphones. In front of the platform was a square of gleaming white sand, marked off by four gold pegs and a gold rope. A half-dozen long-handled shovels, the handles stained mahogany and the spades a burnished bronze, were plunged into the earth awaiting the first thrusts. To one side was a press table, where Charlie Rasmussen, his bald head looking more creased and tortured than ever, worried a corporal's guard of early arrivals. Among them were a homely girl from the University journalism school; a Cuban stringer who represented a half-dozen Caribbean newspapers; and an elderly lady from a Fundamentalist monthly. None of the reporters from the wire services or dailies had arrived and Rasmussen busied himself cranking up a field telephone to raise them.

A chartered bus halted on the blacktop and the University's marching band, in palm green and gold, emerged gingerly, gripping their peaked caps in the stiffening wind. A wild gust smacked a sousaphone head-on, and its tenant was hurled against the bus.

Erwin shaded his eyes and looked at the band. "I hope you advised the baton twirlers to stay away," he said to Si. "Did you?"

"Oh, sure, Erwin," Si said. "They complained a little, when they found out it was going to be on TV, but I explained to them the bare legs wouldn't be in the best of taste."

Ellenbogen nodded. "Good." He turned to Ira. "As I told Si, you and your people are to be complimented—thus far."

"*Baby*. We aim to pu-leeze." Ira crinkled his nose.

Fifteen minutes later the band had assembled, the press was in full force, the grandstand was about half filled. On the platform, the honored guests arrived and were duly welcomed by Erwin and by Charlie Rasmussen (acting now in his capacity as deputy mayor, the mayor himself attending a city-managment convention in Los Angeles) and took seats. Prominent in the first row were Chancellor Mainwaring of the university—still wary of platforms and ceremonies since his brush with Maitland; the newspaper publisher who regarded Latin America as his private good-will area; J. J. Campion, Fenton Braud and the other general partners; and three clergymen, representing the major faiths. Si Mermelstein, taking over at the press table, knew how Erwin had settled on the three attendant divines for so weighty an event. Lila had chosen them. Si knew a little about each of the Reverends—their names and denominations of course but also the fact that all were *auslanders*. Back in the formative days of the *God-O-Rama,* Si had interviewed a cross-section of the local clergy, and he remembered the trio. The young rabbi, for example, was a reader of *Commentary* and *Foreign Affairs*. The Protestant minister, an older, white-haired man, had an air about him of Discussion Groups and Clinical Psychology and was a subscriber to the *Reporter*. But it was the priest who intrigued Mermelstein the most. His name was Father Jaretzki and he was originally from Shamokin, Pennsylvania. What his reading matter was, beyond the breviary in which he had now riveted his tiny eyes, Si did not know. But he did know that during the cold and hungry thirties, Father Jaretzki had illegally operated a bootleg breaker for unemployed miners. He had rolled up his sleeves, hitched his cassock, and in the cold Pennsylvania night, set up a cooperative coal breaker to handle tons of unlawfully dug fuel, the difference between a livelihood and shameful government relief for thousands of miserable Polacks and Hunkies. Si could see him now—his round, bulgy face, its nose suggesting something out of a root cellar, smeared with black dust—wielding a Pennsylvania banjo and unloading a truckful of anthracite stolen from some mine owner's boarded-up pits. Enough of the old YPSL remained in Si to experience a surge of admiration for the lumpish, round-shouldered shepherd. There seemed to be less and less people around worth admiring, Si had felt for a long time, and he was gratified to pay silent tribute to Father Jaretzki.

Now the crowd was stirring, apprehensive. It was fifteen minutes until air time. Travis Dean, in apostolic white, was to MC the program. He checked his agenda with Erwin, with Ira, with Charlie Rasmussen. The publisher would be the first speaker, introduced by Erwin in his capacity as chairman of *The Spirit of Man* committee. He would be followed by Rasmussen, speaking for the mayor. Next would come successive benedictions by the three clergymen. Interspersing each, the band would render appropriate musical selections. A small choral group in palm-green gowns had assembled next to the band. Erwin surveyed the gathering, and even the shrill wind, now whipping up whitecaps on the bay and slapping peevishly at the shoreline, failed to diminish his ardor. That the stands were only half filled did not trouble him, although it seemed odd to him that the ten or fifteen rows roped off for colored persons were empty.

Erwin walked up the platform steps with Travis Dean. The commentator was checking the assignment of shovels—one for Erwin, one for Charlie, one for the publishing giant, the remaining three for the clerics—when Ellenbogen noticed Jimmy Nudo walking down the aisle between the two banks of skeletal seats. The gangster, obscured behind mammoth smoked glasses, minced on elevated black shoes. He seemed a trifle self-conscious, cracking his knuckles and keeping his shrunken face directly on the platform of honor. Behind him trailed his family: a fat, dark woman in an electric-blue satin dress with high puffed shoulders that gave her the appearance of a jungle moth, and his son, in a black tailored suit on the order of Dad's. Mrs. Nudo bore in her arms a stupefied baby sucking a plastic pacifier that resembled a misplaced external organ.

Erwin halted his ascent and walked down the steps. Ira, busying himself at the press section, saw the impending meeting and flew from the newspapermen's table to the platform. He got there as Erwin confronted Nudo.

"How do, Mr. Nudo," Erwin said. "May I help you?"

"Hia," Nudo said dully. "Where's deKay?"

"*Jimola!*" Ira cried. "With the whole family!"

"Where's my seat?" Nudo asked.

"Why sure, baby!" Ira cried. He winked broadly at Erwin, but the industrialist's face was an olive mask. Behind the hexagonal glasses an icy film was crystallizing.

"Erwin, sweetie," Ira said, "I forgot the whole thing! I had a little chat with Jimmy the other day and since he was in on the starting of this undertaking, he figured he could sit on the platform with the rest of our friends! I said okay. Now Jimmy, you just go up in back of the *padre* there, and I'll take the missus and the kids to some first-row seats in the grandstand—"

"One moment," Erwin said firmly. "I have made no such promise. There is no place for Mr. Nudo on the platform."

"*Erwin!*" Ira cried. "*Doll!* Just let the man sit down!" He grabbed Ellenbogen's mohair lapel and moved him up a step. "Erwin—I was in a big jam. I needed some help from him, so I promised. What's one seat more or less? The President of Calibur Frozen Fruits won't show, so we'll give Jimmy his place."

Erwin, with the firm arm that had upended middleweights in Juarez, shoved him aside. "There has been a misunderstanding, Mr. Nudo," Ellenbogen said. "I have made no commitment to you. Mr. deKay never told me of this arrangement. Since this is a public exhibition without admission, you and your family are free to sit in the grandstand with everyone else. You are more than welcome, in fact. But not on the platform."

Ira felt a twinge of vertigo. The wind seemed to be looking for him alone, shrieking into his ears, smacking against his inflamed face and running frigidly up his billowing blue pants. "What's one chair, Erwin?" he cried. But Ellenbogen, with a final frigid look at Nudo, had turned his back and begun the ascent, once more to confer with Travis Dean. There was no fear in Erwin. He had had marginal dealings with the underworld and he knew that unless you accept their favors they will not attack. Their venom was reserved for those whom they could buy and control and from whom they expected a return. He had not the slightest tremor of fright in imposing his will on the gutter spawn standing on the sand below. Nudo, watching Erwin's broad back, understood this.

"Now look, Jamey, he's got it all wrong," deKay cried. "You and the lady go take a coupla front-row seats! Erwin didn't understand me, *that's* all!"

"Why'd you lie to me?" Nudo sounded plaintive—a man of honor betrayed.

"I *didn't!*" Ira, towering a head over the small, sad figure of the hoodlum, held his arms out wide and beamed. "He *forgot!* He forgot the whole bit! Hey, Jamesie—after the big deal here, I'll get your picture took—you and the family—with some of the guests—I'll—"

Nudo, unhearing, turned on one elevated heel and grasping his wife's dimpled elbow, guided his people through the buzzing rows of wind-whipped spectators toward the parking lot. He never looked back at Ira's supplicant figure, but hustled his wife and children into an immense black car and blasted his way noisily onto the highway.

One mile from the Ellenbogen site, where the causeway met the city's business sector, the Labor Day Parade and Prayer Meeting of the Hilltown Betterment Association assembled. They came in car pools and on segregated buses, on foot and on bicycles. A thousand colored people, coming to glory through the graces of the Reverend Harkey and modern sociology. At the head of the procession marched the minister. In his neutral gray suit, hatless, he might have been a Negro FBI man. He was flanked by other officers of the Association—Spots and McIsaac, Dr. Emerson, Mrs. Defore. Behind them were some fifty flag-waving school children of various ages (*Lookit them adorable pickaninnies,* a white matron cried, imagining that the revolutionary army was headed for a holiday fish fry.) Behind the children an ancient panel truck wheezed and coughed in low gear. On its newly painted bed was a spinet, a microphone, and in a red plush chair, the regal figure of Sister Samantha Bates. The gospel singer wore a royal blue velvet robe, tasseled and pleated. She was a big woman, her girth and height suggesting neither grossness nor gluttony but charismatic inflation, an enormity caused by mystic inspiration, not calories. Somnolent and queenly, her hair piled high in lustrous waves, she possessed true command presence. Tom Sorrento saw the grandeur, and whether it derived from Harkey's Christ Jesus, or from the fact that she was a very rich and very famous woman, earning over a quarter of a million dollars a year, he knew that the high power was in her. She demanded respect. She had, through miraculous gifts of voice and personality, become a lofty member of the celebrity complex, combining the reigning values of amusement and power—and adding to it the sure-fire contemporary ingredient, faith. Sorrento marveled at her.

He walked with Ballard at the rear of the truck, humming snatches of "Faccemm' Amore" while the crusaders chanted "Jacob's Ladder" and "The Old Ship of Zion." Behind him were two willing dupes of betterment—Wilma and Oran Burley. In their clouded minds, they reasoned that a show of strength with Ballard's people would be a good way of getting back at the men who ran the bulldozer over Tom's trenches. If they were to end up in jail, jail held no terrors for them. Their Daddy had shown them the way. Even as they marched he was being sentenced to overnight incarceration for agitating in behalf of a persecuted colony of Hutterites.

"Who got Miss Bates into this?" Tom asked Ballard. They were both carrying placards. Ballard's read: JESUS LOVES ALL WHY NOT LET US VOTE? Tom's bore the warning: THE KINGDOM OF GOD IS NOT GERRYMANDERED.

"Harkey—who else?" Ballard asked. "That woman's taking a big chance getting involved in this. She'd be almost as big a target as me if something happened."

"And her career. She's show biz."

"It doesn't bother Sister Samantha," Ballard said. "I've been talking to her. She's *above* everything. She does a lot of big television shows with white people. Now there's nothing unusual about colored artists on TV. But usually there's a flurry of ridge-runner letters insulting the network. Never when Samantha sings. Everybody's sort of agreed she's special. Wait'll you hear the voice —it makes you believe in the supernatural."

"Some scientist you turned out to be. You mean she is the chosen instrument?"

"Amen. The Lord speaketh through her. Don't look at me like that. And hold your sign higher, soldier."

"I don't like the message," Sorento said. "Why couldn't I get something more in keeping with my origins? Like 'Elect Marcantonio—Vote Every Star'?"

If, in Sister Samantha Bates, Harkey had enlisted an agent of

Yahweh, then surely the driver of her truck could have been considered the walking delegate of the Other Party. At the wheel of the creaky chariot was Mr. Shorty Freese, proprietor of the Green Dot Grill and the banker of Hilltown's bigger crap games. His supra-orbital ridges glistened and his jeweled black hands gripped the cracked steering wheel with proprietary tenacity. To Harkey, he was a prize beyond the dreams of ministerial avarice. Snatched from the bosom of Lucifer, he had come, burning with sin, to the Hilltown Betterment Association, willing to forsake evil so that six hundred of his neighbors might get their names back on the voting registers. He had brought not only his own scarred, black person, but several dozen of his nonrespectable adherents. These acolytes marched at the rear of the processional, considerably gaudier and noisier than Harkey's church members, but nonetheless infused with new love.

But of all the practitioners of nonviolent resistance, none intrigued Tom more than the Indians. A few paces behind the nonrespectables—as if to underscore the special nature of their errand—a dozen Seminole Creeks, in traditional ruffled shirts and skirts, as varicolored as gypsies, marched resolutely, holding high crude placards. The messages indicated that they were less concerned with disfranchisement than with a new vision that had come to them.

TRUE AMERICAN CHURCH
SEMINOLE CREEK CHAPTER

WHY NO PEYOTE TEPEE?

UNFAIR TO EXCLUDE US
PEYOTE IS GOOD

HE GIVETH MAN
THE GREEN HERB

Their archaic brown faces (somewhat muddied by Negro blood) seemed blissful and detached. John Throws Knife had left his mark on them. No doubt, Tom surmised, they were all chewing mescal beans, summoning up new wonders, heightening their powers of concentration. Would Maitland have classified their conversion as another marginal gain? It was hard to say. In any case, the orthodoxy of the bean was endowing the ragged Indians with new determination and dignity. Their marching hitherto had been limited to opening day at the race track. Now they were enlisted in a cause, devotees of *Lophophora williamsii.*

The processional reached the site of the ground-breaking. As the front rank neared, there was a collective turning of heads in the grandstand. Several dozen police officers had been stationed along the blacktop to assist in directing traffic. Now, as the seemingly endless line of Negroes appeared—three and four abreast, singing "When I Wake up in Glory" and gripping their hand-lettered placards against the bruising wind—the cops readied themselves. Some mounted motorcycles (one of them bore scars on his forehead—he was the officer who a month earlier had ridden shotgun for Mr. Banjo) and others, on foot, deployed across the highway. Their lieutenant dog-trotted to the platform for a conference with Erwin and Charlie Rasmussen.

"Look like they comin' for trouble," the lieutenant said shrilly. "Y'all want us to shoo 'em off?"

Charlie scowled and cursed. The mayor had left instructions that peaceable prayer meetings by the colored people were not to be interfered with. The mayor was, after all, a former resident of Middletown, New York, and he understood the peculiar nature of the Beach as an enclave of liberalism.

"Erwin, whaddya think?" Charlie asked. "We could get rid of 'em easy enough."

Ira edged in on the discussion. "Zotz," he offered. "Man, they got all of 125th Street and Lenox Avenue out there. I could get Max to send over some pork chops and watermelon and they'd all go home—"

"Shut up, Ira," Erwin said coldly. It was not the Jimmy Nudos of the world who frightened Erwin Ellenbogen; it was the moral crises that all men of good will faced daily. "What is the mayor's feeling, Charlie? You are his deputy."

"His Honor said leave 'em alone if they don't break no laws."

"Mist' Ellenbogen, I could clear all them burrheads out in ten minutes with the bikes." The lieutenant seemed pleased by the prospect.

"Air time in three minutes, Erwin sweetie," Ira said. "We should all be up there on the platform for the Star-Spangled Banner."

"Let them stay," Erwin said. "They mean no harm. I can't help it if *other* people are depriving them of the vote. I can't help it if the state laws won't permit integrated seating at public events. Lieutenant, let them join us."

"You'll excuse me, Mist' Ellenbogen, but them people don't want to join, they wanna embarrass you and provoke something. I wish you'd let me clear the road. There's half a dozen city ordinances I can invoke, includin' impedin' police officers in the carrying out of their duties."

Erwin looked at the gathering swarm. The Negroes had lined up on either side of their truck, three and four deep at the edge of the blacktop, and were now facing the platform. There was a loudspeaker setup on the truck, and a fat colored lady seated on a red chair. In the quiet, chanting skirmish line of black faces, most of them waving posters, Erwin, stunned, realized he was looking at Tom Sorrento. The anthropologist was holding a huge sign and was standing next to Dave Ballard and they appeared to be joking with each other. *A fine joke,* Erwin thought. And those two crazy kids—the one who had thrown himself in front of the bulldozer, and his sister—they were also there. Erwin, who saw life largely in terms of contest, envisioned the matter as a moral duel with Sorrento for Lila's approval. His wife, taciturn and withdrawn since the destruction of the dig, had refused to attend the ground-breaking, claiming a psychosomatic catarrh. But Erwin knew she was standing at the study window, looking down hostilely at the ceremony. It seemed to him that he could do no less than let the Negroes stay—especially now that Sorrento, his putative moral rival, had thrown in with them. Although her bed was now available to him, much of the spice and zest had gone. Lila had taken to reading the *Annals of the American Academy of Political and Social Science* after their love-making, and had rejected his pleas for brief summations.

"No, no, Lieutenant," Ellenbogen said. "They won't cause any trouble. In fact *I'll* invite them to stay."

"Let's get with it, Erwin!" Ira called. "It's Howdy Doody time!"

"Do what Mr. Ellenbogen says," Rasmussen snarled at the officer. "There won't be no trouble."

The lieutenant nodded and ran up the aisle toward the highway to relay the information to his men. A television camera blinked red and focused on Travis Dean. In a second they were on.

"Good afternoon," Dean said. "The Public Affairs Department of stations KMG-TV and KMG radio, AM and FM, bring you a special event as a public service. We are assembled here on Bay Islet for ceremonies dedicating a new concept in human relations —the ground-breaking ceremony for *The Spirit of Man.* Our program will begin with the national anthem, played by the

Beach University marching band under the baton of Captain P. J. Crain. Will you all join in the singing?"

The celebrants rose—the surly members of the press, the guests on the platform (their ranks unsullied by Jimmy Nudo), the sparse audience seated on the splintery grandstand. The wind howled and whistled around them, garbling and liquefying the words of the anthem. Only after a few bars did it emerge loud and clear, and the reason was apparent: the assembled members of the Hilltown Betterment Association were singing, too. And over *their* loudspeaker issued the soaring voice of Sister Samantha Bates. No winds of gale force could subdue those rude, rich notes. She closed her eyes, clasped hands on her mighty chest and gave throat.

And this be our motto
In God is our Trust . . .

Even the glockenspiels and the sousaphones sounded tinny by the time the last stirring note was played.

On the platform, Dean turned hesitantly toward Erwin. He cupped the microphone with one hand. "Mr. Ellenbogen—do you think an announcement—or an invitation—I mean—in the newsreel and on the TV—the way they're just standing up there kind of isolated—"

Erwin bounded up to the microphone. "Yes," he said. "A good idea, Travis." He cleared his throat. "You folks up there on the highway," Ellenbogen said over the loudspeaker. "You folks up there are welcome to come down and join this ceremony. It is open to the public. There are rows of seats vacant in the stands where you may sit."

Harkey had climbed into the truck and he answered Erwin over the windy plain. "Thank you. But those rows are segregated. There is no segregation in the Kingdom Beyond Caste."

"Well—then—just stand around if you'd like," Erwin said.

Newsreel cameras hummed; the wind-whipped reporters bent to their machines. Some photographers had already clambered up to the blacktop to get pictures of the marchers, notably of Samantha Bates.

"Thank you," Harkey said. "We would merely like to pray with you."

"Yes, of course," Erwin said. "There's a regular program of prayer arranged, but we only have so much time. Now, if Mr. Dean would introduce our first speaker—"

Dean returned to the microphone, fumbling with his notes, looking for the laudatory résumé of the publisher that Si Mermelstein had written for him.

"Oh my brothers," Harkey suddenly cried, impassioned. "Pray with us! We love you with God's love! The love of God in us is directed at you! We hate no one! We seek no revenge! Why do you bomb us and humiliate us? What is a gerrymander in the eyes of the Lord? If you take one colored man's name off your voting lists, you offend Christ Jesus! Let us pray!"

The marchers, on signal, fell to their knees. Only Ballard, Tom and the Burleys remained standing.

"Come on," Ballard said, kneeling. "Go for broke."

Tom joined him. The Burleys followed.

It had been growing increasingly dark. Now the skies were layered with bellying clouds, ranging in hue from pale amethyst to a deep blue-black. They seemed to boil up from some distant oceanic cauldron, pushing each other along with bumpy speed.

Harkey's voice rose high and clear: "Though I have all faith, so that I could remove mountains, and have not love, I am nothing . . . love suffereth long and is kind . . ."

Amen, cried the kneeling flock.

"The wind bloweth where it listeth, and thou hearest the sound thereof," Harkey cried out, "but canst not tell whence it cometh, and whither it goeth; so is every one that is born of the Spirit!"

Amen, the members called.

Tom glowered at Dave. "Some ad-libber. He's got a bit for the wind prepared. I tell you, Ballard, he shouldn't do this to Erwin."

Harkey concluded his invocation with one more appeal for universal love. The words *love, God, spirit, faith, light, hope* jumbled together in a blurred cascade, as if the minister had lost his reason. Yet the total effect was thrilling.

"*Damn you,* Ballard," Tom said. He turned on Dave. The giant's eyes were closed and he rocked back and forth, a Nubian slave making obeisances before his Egyptian master. He opened one orb and winked at Tom.

"Damn you, Ballard," Tom said, "I defy you to parse those last few utterances by your leader. What is he talking about? *What did he say?* He's incapable of parsing. Unparsable. Mumbles. How can I follow his banner when he refuses to talk sentences?

You tell *me* what that outgushing of unrelated words means, buddy. And stop making believe you're praying."

Harkey's sermon concluded, Travis Dean tried again to get the ground-breaking under way. The six burnished shovels rested in the white sand. They seemed determinedly irrelevant; there was a growing feeling that they never would be used that day. The rain began to fall—fat, swollen drops, plopping silently into the combed sand and pitting it with tiny depressions.

"Thank you, sir, for your—unscheduled prayer—now, if we may, let's proceed." Dean had lost his schedule of events. They had been sucked from his hand by a vicious gust and were airborne over the bay. He looked helplessly at Erwin.

What happened next was the subject of considerable speculation in the newspaper accounts. Under lowering skies, with the savage wind clouting spectators and participants relentlessly, it was admittedly difficult to establish a logical sequence of events. Most observers agreed that some inadvertent jostling involving the police and some of Mr. Shorty Freese's nonrespectable friends at the left flank of the skirmish line touched off the confusion. Later, Mr. Freese claimed that a policeman's insulting remark had been overheard by several of his adherents and they had reacted. A *black burrhead bastard,* was the way one of Mr. Freese's associates recalled the phraseology. The marcher had swung on the officer, taken a hefty wallop from the policeman's billy, and tumbled, bloodied, to the blacktop. Soon the pushing and shoving became general. The Seminoles, untroubled in their mescaline euphoria, plunged into the melee and in a matter of seconds a surging mob was agglutinizing around the police. An Indian woman's dress was ripped and she shrieked. There was a fearful moment when it seemed that the nonviolent demonstration would inflame into the kind of public horror Harkey so desperately sought to avoid. At that perilous juncture, Sister Samantha Bates, regal and inspired, stepped to the microphone and hurled her message into the wind.

Out of the depths of my soul I cry
Jesus draw nigh
Jesus draw nigh
Lord draw near to my honest cry
Jesus draw nearer to me.

It was, as Ballard had advised Tom, a voice like no other voice in the world. It cut through the unnerving scream of the gale, defying the dark sky and the downpour, finding its melodic, rich way into the hearts of her audience—stunning even those who would have preferred not to listen. To Ira deKay, seated disconsolately on the platform, and knowing that the ball game was over, it was a particularly rotten trick. He leaned over and tugged Charlie Rasmussen's sleeve.

"The sneaks," he said. "They've outprogrammed me. How did I know that broad was in town and they had her signed up? If Erwin had given me a few more days to get talent maybe I could have landed her for *our* side."

It was the painful truth. All *The Spirit of Man* had to offer were some minor local people and amateur talent from the University. Harkey, on the other hand, had in his legions a woman who had recorded five gold-label discs. Ira had indeed been outprogrammed. His world of deals, favors and quick, happy association with celebrities had failed him. He began to worry again that he was losing his touch.

The voice rose and hung in the moist air—a powerful, floating presence that demanded attention and awe. The singer, aloof from the shoving police, the frustrated people on the platform, the damp, puzzled spectators, seemed guided by some mystic inner light, some charismatic force that was her secret. Her voice dipped and soared, broke unexpectedly, quavered and trilled, sometimes evocative of a field hand's country blues, sometimes grandly operatic.

> Oh, Lord I want to lay down
> Faithful each day
> Tell your true way
> Tell this old world what a Savior I've found
> Spreading the gospel around!

At what exact point, on what note of exaltation Father Jaretzki, the labor priest, left the platform to trudge through the wet sand to the Negro ranks, there was some argument later on. Si Mermelstein, who helped the reporters put the story together, seemed to recall that the Roman Catholic ambassador to *The Spirit of Man* made his crucial move along about Sister Samantha's second chorus, when she was ad-libbing wildly, in what Ira described as "holy scat singing." In any case, Father Jaretzki, a man who accepted literally the Vatican's dictum on integration, a shepherd who understood that the flock is never big enough and new members are always welcome, was taking his stand with the Hilltown Betterment Association.

This unilateral decision was to be the *coup de grâce* to the ground-breaking. In his steps, of necessity, followed the young rabbi and the white-haired minister. It occurred to Mermelstein, observing this interfaith solidarity in behalf of man's dignity and against the gerrymander, that Harkey had been extremely lucky. It was, after all, Lila Ellenbogen's shrewd selection of divines that had won the day for him. The bald truth was that by and large the various white ministerial associations in the state had abstained admirably from Harkey's crusade. But for Lila's insistence on prelates who, like Jaretzki, believed in the social church and believed in it deeply, the prayer demonstration might have been, in Ira's words, a bomb-a-roo.

The procession moved off in the rain. The three clergymen walked with Harkey. No words were exchanged. Their public support of the Betterment Association, Tom realized, was one more of Maitland's beloved marginal gains. They marched now—Father Jaretzki's lumpish, bowed figure to the fore—three apostles of the social church, putting into practice an old and viable morality that had rarely been given a chance. Sorrento, peeking over his shoulder, extended silent congratulations to them. What would happen, he mused, if the next morning every religious in the country awakened and announced for Harkey?

As they passed the boathouse, Tom excused himself. "Congratulations, Ballard," he said. "You won the whole game. The point spread and everything."

"Yeah," Dave said. "It was almost too easy. But it isn't easy at all. It's going to be worse. You didn't see the real enemy today. This was a piece of cake. Everything worked for us—Bates, the weather, that priest. The enemy was hiding, waiting to catch us off guard."

"Good luck," Tom said.

"Thanks, buddy."

"What did I do? Besides looking stupid and not knowing the words." Tom lingered at the edge of the highway. "I did you a favor. Now you do me one. Come down and finish the mapping for me. I'm a punk cartographer. Come on—you don't have to parade any more. You're out of camera range."

"Okay," Ballard said. "A last good deed for Dr. Sorrento."

They walked off the highway, down the slope to the boathouse.

In the semi-darkness, they could see a flurry of confused motion on the platform.

It was decided that the ground-breaking had best be postponed. The Hilltown Betterment Association had carried the day. Erwin suggested to Si that he invite all the gentlemen of the press into his home for hot coffee and for some new information on the future of *The Spirit of Man*. The rain and wind having intensified, the crowd departed the rickety grandstand. The newsreel cameras were disassembled and the truckloads of gear loaded. Soon the site was barren save for the wooden skeletons soaking in the downpour and shivering in the blast.

Ira advised Si to write some snappy lines for Erwin for the reporters. Charlie Rasmussen would help him.

"It would help if *you* were there, Ira," Si pleaded. "You know how they respect you. They'd print anything you want."

"Sweetie," Ira said wearily, "I got some urgent calls to make. I'll check you tomorrow afternoon at the office."

Si shook his head and plodded through the littered sand to Erwin's mansion. He had a dread premonition that Ira deKay Associates was moribund, and he shuddered. There was no money in the bank, no more free-loading at the Peruviana, and now the giant tourist attraction had evaporated. Come what may, he assured himself, he would never teach school again.

Ira, unmindful of the gale, watched them troop off to Erwin's house. A few of the reporters were whining their complaints and one, a corrupt old wreck from a press association, turned around to yell at Ira. "Hey deKay—this another one of your cons? Where's the loot?" And Ira, aware that something rare and precious was being lost, howled back at him: "Pat, sweetie—it's all there—your own special brand of Scotch!" The reporter was a notorious "taker" even by Beach standards, and Ira made a mental note to propitiate him with liquor in the morning. But even as he plodded across the sand toward his car, a chilling sense of powers waning and strength diminished grew in him. As a general in the great national army of dullers and deadeners of the human spirit, he was beginning to have the worrisome notion that perhaps not everything could be dulled and deadened; that loot had its limits; that the pleasure bath was not sufficiently soapy or warm to comfort everyone and that there were areas where his everything-for-laughs view of life were as nonfunctional as Doc Sorrento's search for arrowheads. *That crazy ginzo!* He had seen Tom kneeling on the highway next to Big Stuff, the dinge who had put him on the first day he had come to the site. Every man to his own particular kick, Ira thought. And yet, seeing Sorrento out there with those praying eight-balls (and then watching the curious defection of the cloth to Harkey's army) he wondered if he didn't envy him a little. Ira was, after all, a show-biz liberal, an admirer of colored musicians and singers, a man so intent on *everyone* having a good time, that he found it hard to begrudge it to Negroes. Perhaps, he mused, that was what was missing in his operation. A little high-level uplift. He knew that all the big PR firms in New York always took on one *free* client—a kind of do-good job, like the Society for the United Nations Charter, the Foundation for All Nationalities, The Geriatric Improvement Fund. He would consult Si on finding such a worthy client whom they would service gratis. Perhaps a modest start would be the Negro Orphanage in Hilltown. All them cute little nigger babies, Ira reasoned, who could resist running pictures of them?

He climbed into the comforting leather interior of his convertible and turned the heater on full blast. He was drenched—the artfully cut blue suit, the silk underwear, his own adored skin. Speeding back to the Peruviana, he convinced himself that Martha Sorrento would be vital to his new plans for the firm. It was now imperative that she leave her husband. He ached for her, trying to curb a shivering, sinking, agitation in his loins as he thought of her responsive flesh. He would get into some dry clothes and make the trip to the Glades that night.

3 *The Man Who Rolled Scharfstein's Field Pack*

THE storm never reached hurricane force. It stayed at what the weather bureau called gale strength, knocking down palm trees and smashing windows, and causing flooding in the bay area, where the waters were perilously close to the lavish homes. In the course of the wet, wild night, the bay, roiled and fattened by the storm, splashed over the sea wall guarding Erwin's home and flooded the rear lawn. Along the unprotected shore of the digging site, the waters had risen almost three feet. By morning, a stubborn surf was slapping at the littoral, carving a peculiar eroded pattern in the sand.

During the night there had been some seepage of water through the lower story of the boathouse, into the room where the Burleys slept. Tom had invited them up to sleep in the children's beds, and in the morning, when he arose, he saw that they had brewed coffee for him on the midget stove and vanished to the damp office below.

He walked to the balcony. The rain had changed to a diffuse spray, suggesting the frantic haphazard movements of gaseous molecules, but the wind was adamant. Tom was amazed to see the shoreline—the battering of the waves had etched out an irregular cliff, almost a yard high at some points. Even now, with the winds reduced, the surf pounded against the beach and every now and then would break off a chunk of yellow earth.

The grandstand and the wooden platform were wrecked. A few dismal strips of bunting fluttered in the wind. About half the transplanted palms and all the aluminum flagpoles had been upended. They lay in crazy patterns like a giant's game of jackstraws. Tom looked at the desolation and felt a deep sadness for Erwin. He had visited the Ellenbogens last night after the debacle. Tom wanted to assure Erwin that he had not been an instigator of the Negro march, that he was sorry it had turned out the way it did. Erwin advised him that it was just as well. Perhaps the time was not right for *The Spirit of Man*. He was still getting crank calls and threats; he had turned off the telephones and could keep in touch with people only via an answering service. Lila understood Erwin's sorrows and comforted him; Tom was glad. They played scrabble until after the eleven o'clock news on television (Erwin won all three games) and then Tom staggered through the gale back to the boathouse, where he had found the Burleys almost awash downstairs and had moved them.

A man was plodding through the half-flooded sand, down the slope toward the boathouse. He wore floppy black boots and a black slicker and his face was hidden beneath an official-looking black umbrella. At the rear of the house, he peered inside, then climbed the stairs and walked toward Tom.

As he lowered his umbrella and attempted to close it, a gust inverted it, and he battled with it for a few seconds, turning his back to the wind. Sorrento recognized the neat head. It was Lieutenant Fry.

"Those things always do that," Fry said peevishly. "Wonder why no one's invented a better one?"

They exchanged greetings and Tom invited him in.

"I thought you'd be around," Tom said. "I guess you saw me in the line of march yesterday. I did it as a favor to Ballard. I can't tell you a thing about this boycott. I've never been to his meetings. Besides, we're all clearing out tomorrow morning—me, my family, the kids downstairs."

"Oh heck," Fry said. "I know all about why you marched. Harkey and that bunch came to see you the night before. You're not really involved with them."

"You don't miss anything, do you?"

Fry shrugged. "Modern police methods. We have 'em down here in the backward South, Dr. Sorrento."

"See—you're starting it again—imagining things. I didn't say a word about the South. *You* did. But since we're on the subject, how's the boycott going?"

"It's going to be rough, mighty rough. There'll be blood spilled and bad feeling engendered. It's a shame those people can't be convinced they're wrong."

"How about those jerks throwing bombs? You think maybe *they're* wrong?"

"I deplore that kind of thing. I have a hunch that some outside groups may be responsible. The very fact that the bombs are so weak and nobody's been hurt makes me think they're just for propaganda. However, that isn't why I'm here—although I do enjoy chatting with you about the race problem. I always get the feeling you want to agree with me, but you're afraid to."

Fry whipped out a shorthand pad and a ball-point pen. He leaned back, fingering the leather sheaths attached to his belt.

"Dr. Sorrento, I'd like you to give me an accounting of where you were and what you did after the ceremonies broke up yesterday."

"Why?"

"Why don't you tell me, and *then* I'll tell you. Look—I can't force you to do it. I can bring you in, but I prefer not to. I happen to trust you and I wish you'd trust me."

He was clearly the new look in detectives; Frank Sorrento would have been aghast at his friendliness.

"Okay, if you want to be secretive." Tom rested his forehead in his hands. "Let's see. When the free-for-all broke up here—what time was that? About three o'clock? Four?"

"Three thirty-seven."

"You been doing some checking already, hey? Come on—what's the plot? Somebody steal the free whisky Ira had for the reporters?"

Fry laughed. "I promise you I'll tell you."

"Well—I dropped out of the parade with Ballard. I asked him to finish some work he had abandoned when he threw in with the Hilltown crowd. Dave agreed, and he was here till about seven-thirty."

"What sort of work?"

"Cartography. Mapping. I was making a master map of the site, filling in the details, but I'm not very good at it." He pointed to the giant white cardboard resting against the wall. "That's it over there—the big round circle is the ossuary; the thing that looks like a snake, that's the wall; the other circle is—"

"Fine, fine, Doctor. Was Ballard the only one with you?"

"No. The kids were with us—Oran and Wilma. You know them, don't you?"

"Oh, yes. I met them after the bombing."

"Well, we ate some canned corned beef and some cherry peppers at around seven-thirty and Dave beat it. About eight o'clock I started feeling guilty about what happened to Mr. Ellenbogen, so I walked over and stayed with them for a few hours."

"Yes. I know. I spoke to them this morning."

"Why you bothering me then?"

Fry smiled. "I'm thorough." He looked at his pad. "You called your wife at the Glades and you advised her you'd all be leaving Wednesday morning, and told her to wait till the rain let up before driving back. Is that right?"

Scowling, Tom said: "Who won the scrabble game later?"

"And then you stayed till eleven-fifteen and came back here."

"And went beddy-bye listening to the raindrops."

Fry made a notation in his book and looked up. "Thanks very much, Doctor. It's pretty much as I guessed it would be."

"What the hell are you talking about?"

The officer crossed his legs and leaned back, looking gravely at Tom with synthetic blue eyes. "Ira deKay was murdered last night."

Almost involuntarily, Tom sucked his breath in. He hunched forward and stared at the lieutenant. The news, horrifying in itself, was doubly hideous, in that it was apparent that Fry had suspected him of some connection with it. The notion that he might even be *thought* a murderer seemed as dreadful as the possibiltiy of actually committing murder.

"Oh, Jesus," Tom said softly. "You sure? I mean—there's no doubt he was murdered?"

"No. No question about it."

"And I suppose I was a suspect?"

"As I said, I have to be thorough."

"Because of my wife. And deKay."

"I didn't want to mention it. I'm sorry about what went on between them. I found out last night when we questioned that woman he had fired. Miss Cooke."

"She could have been lying," Tom said, almost hoping that Fry, the all-seeing and prescient, had checked out Cleo's story and found it false.

"I'm afraid not. We talked to hotel employees, and so on. There's no doubt deKay was having an affair with your wife, and had asked her to leave you. Frankly, I never could imagine you doing something like this to him but I had to make sure."

"What—what happened to him? Where?"

"Well, the way we figure it, he went back to the Peruviana after the ceremony was canceled. About an hour later he left and started heading north." He stopped abruptly.

"To the Glades?" Tom asked.

"Yes, that's what we imagine. Anyway, he never made it. Someone must have been waiting for him outside the hotel and followed him. His car was forced off the road about twenty-five miles north of here. There's a stretch of pine barrens above Boca Largo—nothing on the roadside but empty land for maybe three or four miles. Whoever it was, they made sure they'd killed him. He was forced out of the car and shot eight times—from two different guns, we think. Then they stripped him and—you have a strong stomach?"

He was numb and chilled. Nothing he heard could heighten the cold misery that had enveloped him. "I'll hear about it anyway."

"Well they cut off his genitals and stuffed them in his mouth."

"Aaaagh. Poor miserable bastard."

Fry got up and put on his slicker. "You see, that's what

puzzles me. The pattern is a *mob* pattern. That kind of surgery is usually reserved for traitors to the mob. It's their own way of taking care of their own. Or occasionally to welshers—big welshers. I've checked deKay's operations, and I can't find anything illegal or sub rosa. He's never been involved with professional criminals, except for some minor dealings he had with Jimmy Nudo over this tourist exhibition."

"Why don't you ask Nudo? You seem to have gotten around to everyone else."

"Oh, we'll get to him," Fry said. "Mr. Ellenbogen told me about the scene they had yesterday—how he turned Nudo away after deKay tried to get him seated. But that's certainly not reason enough to commit murder."

"Beats me, Lieutenant." He thought suddenly of Marty—learning about deKay's death, the savage maiming. "Is the story out yet? I mean—the papers and the radio. I thought I might call my wife—"

"We told her last night. I hope you don't mind, but we had to move quickly. She's being escorted back this afternoon by one of my men."

"How'd she take it?" Tom asked. "She say anything?"

Fry looked at him curiously, with an amalgam of disbelief, admiration and what almost seemed to Tom, pity.

"I'm sorry," Fry said. "I didn't ask. You can talk to her yourself in a few hours." He turned and walked through the door and called in to Tom: "You come back and see us again, *hyeah?*" It was, Tom reflected, the first Southernism that had crept into the man's speech, and he knew it was intended to convey kindness.

When Fry had left, he sat immobile at his desk for several minutes, listening to the slapping of the bay against the beach. It seemed as if the calm waters, delighted by their new-found savagery, were determined to prolong their assault against the shore as long as possible, with or without the help of the dying wind.

He shivered, trying to reconstruct in his mind the horrifying final scene of Ira's life: the assassins yanking him from the safe shell, the two-toned leather interior that was Ira's castle, and then emptying their guns into the smooth body on which deKay had lavished so much self-love. All the heady potions and imported soaps, the fine male powders and the silk cloth, all of these had been powerless to insulate the well-nourished torso. And the final, nauseating indignity: the stripping of the organs that to Ira were his wand and his magic, symbols of his infinite capacity to amuse and divert, the bases of his not inconsiderable power. Tom suddenly recalled the night Ira had secured the release of Ballard and Peltz—he still marveled at the way deKay had manipulated the chief of police.

Sorrento was not given to reading portents and omens into events, but he could not help feeling some arcane inevitability about the manner of deKay's death. Assuming it had been Nudo or his employees (the latter was more likely the case since Jimmy had long ago pulled his last trigger and wielded his last ice pick) Tom could almost see a fiery rightness about their ultimate meeting. If the wages of sin were death, what were the wages of endless pleasure? Were there not two parallel roads—Nudo's road of violence and the worst in human behavior, and Ira's road of brainless joy, of abandonment to nonsense and comfort? Was it not possible that the two roads crossed somewhere, and when they did, Ira's way either *became* Nudo's way—or was destroyed by it? He wished he were a better logician; he felt he had his finger on something, but the moral eluded him. Was it proper to believe that a man who dedicated his life to the mysteries of aged steaks and knew where to get French cologne free, inevitably lost all moral values, all respect for life, all the hard, immutable values that the species had set up in some five thousand years of trial-and-error? Did this loss—the substituting of endless orgasms and soaring horsepower for the old rules—point the way to oblivion? He thought of Maitland's cynical optimism—the notion that deKay and his legions, the great army of distractors, performing a valued function, making it possible for the search to continue. *A breathing period,* Maitland had called it. Now, with Ira's mutilated body in a morgue, he wondered whether Maitland was right.

He could not suppress compassion for deKay—not only because of the brutal manner in which he had been extirpated, but because of some vacancy, some great gap, in the man's life. Thus summoning up pity, he was immediately annoyed with himself. DeKay loved his manner of living; he enjoyed a ball of his own making. Still, the effrontery of death made Tom wince. He could not be impartial—even where deKay was concerned. The flaw of uncritical compassion unsettled him—that, and a pointless sense of the just and the unjust, influenced by years of listening to his father's tirades against the arbitrary evils of which men are capable. It made him furious one minute, sorry the next. He could recall in detail the day he had flushed the Koreans from the last dugout on Saipan. They had staggered out of the smoking hole—burned and bleeding ghosts, alarmingly small men, none of them armed, although it was no secret that they had been fighting alongside their Japanese masters and killing Marines. *Any one of those gooks gives you trouble,* Tom's captain told him, *shoot the bastard—we just threw the rule book away. Anyone disobeys an order—like to march, or stand up, or lay down—kill the bastard.* Tom could not blame the man. He was twenty-three years old, a graduate of Holy Cross, a decent skinny boy from Haverhill, Massachusetts, and he and Tom were the only officers in the battalion who had been neither killed nor wounded. The beach stank of their own dead. When the last of the Koreans had crawled from between the felled palm trunks, they were ordered off to a compound. One man refused to march. He sat down on a fallen tree and lowered his head on his shrunken chest. There was a raw red hole the size of an orange on his upper right arm. A bone splinter peeked through the seared flesh. Tom prodded him and shouted at him in Japanese; he refused to budge. The captain, at the head of the line of prisoners, raced back to the dugout. *Shoot the bastard,* he screamed. *What the hell are you waiting for, Sorrento? They killed your men. They murdered your buddies. They shot them in the back.* And Tom stood there, hypnotized, smeared with dirt and sweat, and shook his head dumbly, saying nothing, having the nutty sensation that the bloody hole on the laborer's arm was spreading. And then the captain, in a single move so swift and coordinated that it might never have happened, yanked his .45 from an under-arm holster and blew the man's head off. Tom said nothing and turned away, and that night, bivouacked on the beach, the captain had come to him and said: *You think that was terrible, don't you? Well I don't. That's where you and I are different. What right have you got to be so kind to everyone?* And the more he talked, the more Tom understood that he, too, wanted compassion. Years later the captain, then in Harvard law school, had written Tom a long, self-examining letter explaining, with forceful argument, why he had murdered the Korean. *I understand,* Tom wrote back to him. *It was my fault. I should have obeyed orders. . . .*

His musings seemed designed to lead him away from Marty, and yet she seemed part of his cruel self-examination. There was no question now of her leaving him for Ira deKay. The decision was his to make. He would postpone the decision—until he spoke to her. He had found that procrastination was sometimes a solution in itself.

The news of Ira's death was more than shocking to Erwin; it endowed him with a sense of guilt. His shrewd mind could not help feeling that somewhere Ira had run afoul of Nudo. How, or for what reasons, he could not guess. Like Fry, he dismissed the scene at the ground-breaking as only symptomatic of some grander scheme involving the two men.

Tom had gone over to the Ellenbogens to discuss Ira's death and to await Marty. He listened to Erwin's attempt to unravel the sordid affair, and he realized that it was less respect for deKay that moved them to these examinations, than a recoiling from the bestial reminder of old horrors that the murder had evoked in them. Si Mermelstein joined them later and they sat in the cavernous, bedraped living room, feeling the chill of some ancient amorality. Hot coffee and buttery cake could not dispel a sense of the abyss.

"There's three detectives going through Ira's books," Si said sorrowfully. "But they'll never find anything."

"You mean something that would tie him up with Nudo?" Erwin asked.

"That's what they're after," Si said. "The thing is—the thing is if Ira *did* have a deal going with Jimmy, he'd never have anything in writing. And you can bet Nudo wouldn't. In fact, nobody would probably know about it except the two of them."

"But what could it have been?" Lila asked. "Maybe Nudo wanted to buy his way onto the platform and paid Ira off. He wants to be respectable so badly, I bet he'd commit murder for it!"

She said it with a comic intonation and they all smiled: the notion was so ridiculous that no one would dare entertain it.

Si blinked. "One of the detectives told me the reason they think Nudo's involved is that the job must have been done by hired hoods—guys who were just passing through town and did it for cash. You see—they dumped Ira's body only a coupla hundred feet from a public campsite. That's why it was found so fast. The cops think if it were local hoods, they'd have hid it better. Nudo would operate that way, getting out-of-town guys and then getting rid of them in a hurry. That's why the police think they'll never pin anything on him."

"I guess we'll never know," Erwin said solemnly.

"Does Ira have any family?" Lila asked. "Has anyone been contacted?" She sounded solicitous and genuinely worried. In times of crisis she would naturally think of family.

"It's funny," Si said, shoving his droopy glasses up his nose, "I worked all these years with Ira and I hardly knew anything about him. I found out his real name was Detzler, but that's about all. He told me once his parents were both dead. They lived in North Dakota—some little town where his father had a store. I know he didn't have any brothers or sisters and I don't think he was ever married." Si permitted himself an ironic laugh. "It's as if—as if—Ira was a kind of happy spirit that walked among us. You know—came out of nowhere and went back there." Mermelstein got up. "I better go. The cops aren't through with me and I have to set up the funeral."

He thanked them all—and advised Erwin he would have some new statements on the future of *The Spirit of Man*. However, the firm would be dissolved as soon as Si had paid off a few outstanding debts, and then he would be looking for work. Erwin, aware that Si had intended no plea for aid, nevertheless felt impelled to cheer him. Erwin always had the feeling that Si was a kind of ineffective kid brother—smart enough, but without the necessary hardness to succeed.

"Si," he said, "please feel free to drop by and talk to me when you've cleared up the business. Maybe we can work something out."

Si thanked him again, wished Tom a happy trip, and left. It seemed to Tom that he was administering the post-mortem rites with a sorrowful relish. It was hard for Tom to believe that Mermelstein had ever had any use for deKay.

In the course of his visit, Mermelstein had omitted one phase of the previous evening's nightmare. He was the first person to be notified of Ira's murder. Si had an extension of the office phone in his apartment, and Lieutenant Fry, ringing the suite at the Peruviana, had gotten Mermelstein, drying out and exhausted after the debacle at the ground-breaking. A half-hour later they were at his apartment, questioning him. Later that night, he took them to the office where they began combing Ira's records.

At about eleven at night he began thinking about Cleo. He felt it his duty to inform her of Ira's death. He would be noble and kind and reassuring. And she would show her gratitude by letting him make love to her. The notion dizzied him with its lustful perfection. He would rehire her that night, ensure her future, permit her to provide for Robin, heal the spiritual wounds that Ira had left on her maddening body. And she would give herself to him; their love-making would be a requiem for Ira, one that the dead promoter would understand.

With the detectives' permission, he left the Peruviana and drove to the beach-front apartment where Cleo lived. He had dreamed of her little flat a thousand times, envisioning himself as a welcome caller, a user of its bed, bath and kitchen, a participant in Cleo's marvelously self-contained world. By the time he reached her door, shaking raindrops from his trench coat, he was fluttering with ecstasies verging on fulfillment.

Even the act of pressing her doorbell seemed sexually provocative. When no one answered, his excitation flagged and he decided that perhaps it was just as well. He buzzed again, waited, and was about to leave, when the door opened fractionally, and he saw Cleo's fine nose and one bright eye peering at him over the chain.

"You have one awful nerve coming here in the middle of the night," she said. "Go away."

"Cleo, you have to let me in. Ira—"

"I know all about Ira and I am not concerned. The cops called me already. I have no interest in him, dead or alive."

Si got one pudgy hand inside the door and tried to shove it ajar. He managed to open it the length of the chain. Her face seemed overlaid with a white patina. Her breath smelled fruitily alcoholic and she wore a filmy beige peignoir.

"How can you say that?" Si pleaded. "Aren't you sorry about what happened to him? After all he did for you?"

She tried slamming the door on his intrusive arm, but by now he had a cordovan foot wedged on the threshold. "Go away," she said. "Don't bother me."

"Cleo," he whined. "I have to talk to you. You know what I want—you know what you mean to me—I want to hire you back—make you a partner—"

"You *jerk,*" she muttered. "Get out of the doorway." She turned her blond head as if appealing to someone in the room for assistance. Behind her materialized the hunched, corrupted figure of Fenton Braud. He wore a green velvet dressing gown and was still chewing some invisible crumbly cracker. A tuft of chest hair protruding over the convergence of lapels hinted that he wore nothing beneath the robe.

"Be a nice boy, Mermelstein," Braud croaked. "Go home. We

all know about deKay. It's terrible, but what can any of us do?"

Si retreated from the door; Cleo shut it. The former teacher of English literature adjusted his trench coat and walked away. Outside the apartment house, bending in the gale, he began to laugh. There had indeed been a kind of perfection, an inevitability about his mercy errand—not the kind he had anticipated, but one appropriate and predictable.

Lieutenant Fry's emissary to Marty proved to be another Christian Endeavor type, much like his boss. He was most solicitous of Marty, did magic tricks with a half-dollar for the children, and insisted on driving Ira's courtesy car on the return trip. "Y'all been through enough, Miz Sorrenta," he advised her, "y'all let me drahv." In his cursory questions of her, he had tried to skirt references to their affair with a clumsy prissiness that exasperated her. "Now Ah hardly know how to phrase this, Miz Sorrenta," he had begun, "but we are advahs'd that theah was somethin' goin' awn 'tween you and Mistah d'Kay . . ."

She had cut short his attempts at gentleness, answered his questions and lapsed into a morose silence. The children had overheard that Ira was dead, and she explained to them that Uncle Ira "had an accident"—his car had skidded on the wet road and they would not see him again. The appalling inhumanity of the young rendered them unmoved, except for some morbid curiosity on Abby's part. *Was he crushed? Did he die right away, Mother?*

It did not occur to her until they had passed the site of the murder that her own feelings were almost identical. The detective slowed the car down as they approached a stretch of pine barrens. The rain had stopped and the sun was drying out the sand; wisps of steam rose from the ground.

"Right around heah," he said. "I guess they moved the automobile this mornin'." He pointed to a patch of scrubby pines and thicket just beyond a public campsite sign. "Ah'm sorry, Ma'am. I guess I shouldna mentioned it."

"That's all right, Officer," she said.

And the chilling truth was that it was *all right.* She had almost been filled with relief to learn that he was dead. The total absence of warmth, of emotion, in their relationship—all these omissions made Ira's death not only acceptable but in a sense welcome.

He had functioned in her life as a mechanical agent of pleasure;

her involvement with him had been in terms of flesh, motion and sensation. What sense of loss could one feel for a wrecked sports car? An expensive bottle of perfume emptied into the sewer?

Dehumanized and compulsive, he had been nothing to her beyond the bed. That was the true horror of what they had done. She felt no revulsion concerning him—in life, or now in death. The horror was reserved for herself and what she had done so effortlessly.

When she arrived at the Ellenbogen house, she could see a small tractor hauling a pump and generator toward the rear of the mansion. Apparently there had been a good deal of flooding around the islet. She was surprised to see, too, that the bay had eaten away a few feet of shoreline.

In the house, she and Tom kissed perfunctorily. There were gloomy exchanges of greetings with the Ellenbogens. Nicky and Abby, Tom noticed, were heavy with gifts—final acts of generosity by deKay. Abby had a rubber snake and an Indian doll and Nicky carried a monkey in a glass snowstorm and a rubber raccoon whose eyes lit up in the dark. Seeing his children thus endowed with Ira's largesse, Tom shuddered. It seemed to him the kind of petty corrupting (were not the presents payment for their mother's favors?) that, inflated to monstrous, giant fraud, had caused his death.

"Have they found anything out about Ira?" Marty asked shakily. She was gray and drawn; the lustrous tan she had acquired in her afternoons at the hotel had waned.

"No," Lila said. "They think it has to do with Nudo. But no one's sure. They'll never find out."

Marty lit a cigarette; her hands trembled. "It's unbelievable," she said. "Not that he was *close* to any of us. But he did seem to insinuate himself into people's lives—forcing himself on you—trying to make a big joke out of everything."

Lila licked her lips tentatively. "I guess you got to know him fairly well—all that time you spent at the hotel."

"Me?" Marty asked. "I hardly ever talked to him. Oh, he'd come by and try some of his dreadful jokes on me, but we found it hard to communicate."

Tom said nothing. It seemed to him he was in training again; sparing energies of body and mind for a contest not of his choosing. He was studying his wife—as beautiful as ever, poised in spite of the racking fears inside her—and marveling that she could lie so fluidly. At length he suggested they go to the boathouse and pack. They were on an early-morning flight, and it would be best to get everything organized before going to bed. At Lila's urging, the children stayed. Sheldon was on his way home from nursery school and would want to play with them once more before their departure.

In the boathouse Marty stripped quickly, taking off her suit and high heels. She walked about the room in a white slip, and the sight of her undulant body, barely concealed by the garment, made him dizzy. It was less his own resurgent passion, he knew, than the stabbing knowledge that this was how deKay had seen her and known her. He could stand it no longer—watching her opening suitcases, throwing in their clothes, collecting the odds and ends of their sojourn in the pleasure land. He grasped her wrist and told her to stop.

"Sit down," he said. She complied—tucking her bare feet beneath her. He could not imagine her more wrenchingly desirable; she had been too grand a prize.

"What do you want?" she asked. "You look like you're going to be sick."

"I'd have reason to." He tried to be firm—angry—bitter. It was useless. In the Corps he had always had a terrible time making himself sound fierce to the enlisted men. "I know about you and deKay," he said. "I have the whole story."

She shut her eyes. "How did you find out?" Her voice was dim and disembodied.

"Cleo told me."

Marty nodded—or was it a tiny convulsion that agitated her head?

"I suppose you would have found out—somehow." She opened her eyes and looked at him vacantly. "You have me at more of a disadvantage than you know. You see, Tom—you're noble—under the worst of circumstances. I'm more disgusting than you can imagine."

"Yes, you are. Did you ever see cats make love? That's what I kept thinking about. Dogs are dogs—dopey and out in the open. But cats are like depraved people. They think nobody's watching. You get the feeling if they knew you saw them, they'd skitter away. *Cats*. You and Ira deKay."

"Stop. Just tell me what you want."

"I wish I knew."

"Do you want a divorce? Some arrangement for the children?

Would you like to beat me—or kill me? I know it sounds childishly dramatic, but there's nothing else I can say."

"I guess I'm supposed to hate you," he said. "But I don't. If you could tell me *why*. If you could explain it. I can't help it if I have a pictorial mind. That's the worst part. I see the details. The bits and pieces. I feel I have to ask you *how many times, and how many places, and how many different*—"

She sobbed out her protest. "Stop! I'll tell you if you want to hear. I know you don't. For God's sake, stop torturing yourself. I suppose it was inevitable that I do this to you."

"Why did you go to bed with him?"

She rested her head in her hands. "I don't know. I'll get away from you. I'll take a job somewhere. You won't have to support me."

"I'll decide that. Now I want to know why you did it. Considering I'll spend the rest of my life thinking about it, you owe it to me. What did I do wrong?"

"Nothing—nothing, Tom." She gasped, trying to control the calm voice she had always used to such advantage. "It was an indulgence. My own selfishness. That really makes it more horrible, doesn't it? I didn't for a minute love him. Or even respect him. Oh—he was funny and he seemed to have a knack for solving problems, for making everything easy. Even something as ridiculous as stopping Abby from having hysterics in public. He had control—"

"That's a great excuse for adultery. He stopped the kid from bawling, so you give in."

"You have too much justice on your side—like Ballard and his friends."

"What's this nonsense about his having control? I still don't see how this gives you the right to kick me. To wreck what little we've got left of this marriage."

"It didn't. How can I explain it? I kept getting the feeling we were useless, unimportant. You and me and our children. Yes, and Hall and his friends at the University. There was something about this town—and Ira was the *essence* of it—that crushed me. None of my defenses were any good. It just seemed to me that the deKays were winning. That we had to join them—"

"You sure did. All things human are subject to deKay. I don't buy that nonsense."

"Well—it's the truth." Streaks of unhealthy color splotched her face; she gripped the sides of the deck chair. "At least it was the truth the first time."

"Yeah. He won you over with a Chinese coat and a nurse to look after the kids."

"That was part of it. He seemed to be in charge—of everything. What everyone wants—fun, comfort, no worries. You must believe me I resisted for some time. But, Tom, he's not like us—"

"Not like *me*."

"All right. What I mean is—he works at it full time. He's compulsive about sex. He's good at it because he won't let anything else clutter his brain."

"And that was the first time. Then what? How did this develop into a marathon?" He slumped deep in the chair—trying to strangle the horror.

"I—I enjoyed it. It excited me. Why do you make me tell you this? Why don't you just shut up—divorce me—and hate me—the way any other man would?"

"What else?"

"I wanted him. It had nothing to do with who he was, or whether you loved me, or whether it was wrong. It had no relation to anything—except our bodies and what he did to mine. I was greedy for him."

"And you were greedy enough to leave me for him—is that right? Cleo says you were encouraging him. Good thing our man Nudo worked him over. He'd be drawing up the partnership papers right now."

"No. That isn't true. I didn't want to leave you."

"Just maybe have a few reprises in New York, hey? Or something to think about on cold winter nights?"

"Why are you insisting on this? I know I'm filthy, and disgusting. There should be a huge suppurating sore on my face to signify my guilt. But what can I tell you? If I say I'm sorry it won't make anything right again. I can't kill myself. I did it for the worst reasons—for pleasure, for excitement. If the circumstances were different, I might have eaten myself sick and gotten fat down here. Or become an alcoholic."

"Don't blame it on the Beach," he said firmly. "I'm tired of behaviorism. I'm sick of the inclusive environmental excuse. There are no bad parents, just bad boys."

He did not expect her to cry. In twelve years of marriage and several years of courtship, he could not recall Marty ever surrendering to tears. Her placidity at times astounded him. But now she was weeping—decorously and silently, making no effort to hide her face, holding her exquisite head erect, the eyes closed, the mouth only fractionally distorted.

"Don't pay any attention to me," she said. "I'm not worth it. I can't even be brave."

"Listen. Listen to me. Stop your goddam crying."

"Forgive me, Tom. I told you once I have no strength."

"I know. Hall says you have no center of gravity. He says what I've always believed. You should have used your good looks as a club. Look how far it got Cleo."

"I deserve it. If you'd scream at me it would help."

"I can't Marty. I want you."

"I don't want your pity, Tom. It's what gets you into trouble all the time. You'll pity me—and how do you know I won't do this again?"

"I don't know. I'm simple-minded. If you don't mind not having a monopoly on it, I'm being selfish. I don't want my old lady bringing up the children. I want you to. She isn't their mother, although she'd like to be. You'll come back with us tomorrow. And you'll move back into the apartment. And you'll sweat out the next promotion with me. I'm sorry, but that's how it is. I love you."

"There's something unfair—unfair," she stammered. "There should be a way for me to be punished—"

"To hell with it," he said gruffly. "You know my theory about a marriage. With all the bitchery and misery around us, it's the one thing that *better* work. I have enough trouble as it is. We're expected to be heroes, successes, civic pillars, friends of minorities and labor. Every day I worry why I'm standing still, and why I can't earn more, and how the kids are turning out. If what you've got with your wife is no good, you might as well quit. It's the anchor. It isn't always great, but it's all you have. There were months when my father wouldn't talk to my mother. He used to come home two nights a week. Sometimes we'd hear them shrieking at each other in the bedroom. But they managed to keep it going—because of the children, and because they realized there wasn't much else. I hate to sound so negative, but what do you expect? The wild romantic notions of success and fame went out of this marriage when I decided to stay with Hall in graduate school. You've got to stop thinking how great it was in 1945 when you were going to be a famous newspaperwoman and I was going to be a rich writer."

"I have," she said raggedly. "I just wish—I wish I could be good for you—in *ordinary* ways. Are you sure you want me?"

He walked to her and kneeling, rested his head in her silken lap. The musky-sweet odor made him giddy. He put his arms around her waist.

"You'll do the best you can," he said. "That's all I ever do. I could say I forgive you, but what sense would that make? Forgiveness is a fraud—especially when you're full of anger inside. I could say we're back in love, and love is everything and love, love, love, like Harkey does. But that's an even bigger fraud. Who knows what love is? Nobody loved me, so I went wrong. Love—or no-love—its an excuse for irresponsibility. I hate to sound trivial, but I am a trivial man."

She hugged his coarse head. "No—you're not, Tom. Davey told me, a long time ago, before we were married. You're crucial. You *matter*. That's what makes this wretched repentance of mine so dreadful—worse than anything I've done. I can only feel bad in terms of what I owe *you*—not because of my own corruption."

They kissed—a long and thoughtful meeting of their faces. "I'll let you be like everyone else," he said. "Blame what you did on someone else. Blame it on the Beach, or deKay, if you like. We'll know different, but that's our secret."

"Will you wake me some night and tell me I'm forgiven? I know what you said about it . . . it's a fraud. But I don't believe what you said about love. You've lived your life giving it to people. To all your misfits and your enlisted men and your family and your students. You won't admit it, but that's why you're crucial—as Dave says."

"You and Ballard should write a book. If I didn't roll Scharfstein's field pack—who would have?"

She kissed his forehead, his ears, his flat, tanned cheeks, the crushed and reshaped nose. "Lieutenant Scharfstein and Dave and Ben and the Burleys—and your wife."

He would settle for that. A believer in marginal gains, he would have found no joy in beating her, humiliating her, denying her. Nor did he tell her that he, too, had all but succumbed to the pleasure bath, that the joys of Lila Ellenbogen's round body had almost been his—that only his archaic, self-inflicted righteousness had kept him from the thrilling union. Virtue, he told himself, now holding his wife's body and resting his head on her breasts, was usually the *ex post facto* cognomen for fear. Knowing he had craved Lila, he could not summon up total anger regarding his wife's behavior. She would have to work out her own salvation. He could be neither more nor less of a mate than he had been. Inflammatory, encompassing love he had never believed in; the giant heaving intimacies and revelations were myths. The best you could hope for in a world where the maintenance of sanity was a perpetual problem was—the barrenness of the words upset him—respect and affection and understanding. Beyond these there was the perpetuation of the species in the best possible manner—the care and keeping of children. They had given each other this much in the past and there was reason to hope they could continue to do so.

4 *The Southern Wall*

In late afternoon he walked across the site to bring back Nicky and Abby. He could see them, with Sheldon Ellenbogen, racing wildly around the throbbing pump, still clearing Erwin's lawn of water. The children seemed happy, unperturbed by the knowledge that deKay was dead. It could not mean anything to them; they were blessed with the hard selfishness of the very young. Abby's shrill voice came to him loud and clear. *Sheldon! Give me that ball this instant or I won't play with you in New York!* Erwin's son was shy and delicate and Abby's yeasty effervescence had overwhelmed him. He worshipped her crashing voice and Lila assured Tom that this kind of contact was very good for him. Tom wondered whether she meant it; if she did, he was at least glad his family had been able to do *something* for the Ellenbogens.

It was almost five o'clock. The sky was hot and clear, and the sand, except for a few pools that had settled above some of the filled-in pits, was virtually dry. The bay, boiling with waves early that morning, had settled into its familiar placidity. Tom had read somewhere that under certain climatic conditions inland waters can often be agitated more fiercely than an ocean because of their lack of depth. The bay was artificially dredged to form the ocean-front beaches. Its shallowness perhaps explained its ferocity under the whip of the gale. The erosion of the littoral was more apparent to him now that the waters had receded. He walked down to the sloping beach, studying the Lilliputian cliffs and gullies that the waves had carved in the embankment.

He was halfway across the site, hearing the children's voices and the arterial pumping of the generator, when he saw the white stone. His first reaction was that it was a practical joke, and he associated it with Ira. Even in death, Tom imagined for an instant, that nutty deKay is trying to promote. He half expected the stone to be inscribed: *Dine at the Blue Paradise.* But it was not; and it was genuine. It was half exposed, squatting in its bed at the base of the little cliff that the waves had eaten into the shore. And there was no mistaking its kinship with the now reburied northern wall of the ball court. Tom flew at it. He dug with his hands, scooping away the damp sand with fanatic exertion. Soon he had the top exposed—a flat white boulder, almost a yard in diameter. Immediately, he began digging adjacent to it. In a few minutes his hands struck the unyielding surface of a companion stone. He dug no more but leaped to his feet and shrieked at the boathouse: "Wilma! Oran! Marty! The ball court! The wall, goddammit! *The southern wall!* I found it! Bring the shovels!"

Marty appeared on the balcony. The Burleys edged hesitantly out of the house.

"Don't stand there! We found the wall! The *water* uncovered it! Come on! Bring the shovels!"

The children and the Ellenbogens also heard his hoarse screaming. Abby and Sheldon Ellenbogen had a race across the beach—she won. Nicky galumphed after them; he would never be an athlete. The Burleys sprinted toward him, each bearing a long-handled shovel and a trowel, and Marty came down to witness the event. Erwin and Lila joined them, and even Freddie—discreet, smiling, stood on the hallowed ground, nodding approvingly, as if registering his delight. His joy was perhaps of a different order than the sense of fulfillment that the others shared: Dr. Sorrento had marched with his people.

"*Dig! Dig!*" Tom shrieked. "Give me the shovel, Oran! Work, you little rat! Wilma—use the trowel—stand back everybody!"

The three of them fell upon the stones with febrile violence. The sand flew, forming small tan pyramids; the stones emerged.

"Oh, what a thrill!" Lila cried. "Isn't it marvelous?"

Erwin smiled. He stood a step or two behind his wife, moving his knowing head in small, disbelieving arcs. His manner suggested a Venetian patron acknowledging a new triptych. The

Burleys said nothing. They flanked their leader and worked the digging tools with a fury that belied their starved bodies.

"Dig!" Tom shouted. "You two goldbricks! You wanna come with me next year? To Guatemala? *Dig*—or I'll trade you to the Theological Seminary for a Talmudist!"

Tom was coated with sweat. His black head and brown skin were drenched—as if a final wave had arisen from the shoal bay and inundated him.

"You see?" he said, gasping between thrusts at the earth. "We didn't bring the test trenches down *far enough!* This line here—it's underwater at high tide—where the waves dug away the sand. No wonder we missed it! Look—there's the line of our last test trench! What a break! *The whole ball court!*"

Erwin cleared his throat. "Tom—I would like to suggest—perhaps you can stay another few weeks. Finish the job. I realize we've wrecked the stratification with the grading, and all your stakes have been destroyed, and so on—but you could at least dig out the wall—or some new trenches—"

"Yes!" Lila shouted. "Yes! He'll stay! And we'll do it"

The Burleys rested their shovels, staring at their chief.

Tom stopped his assault on the sand. He leaned on the wooden haft and daubed at his forehead. The temptation was there: he merely had to arrange to have his classes covered. He stared at the white boulders. They had partially uncovered two of them—stolid pale twins, mute, immovable, evidence of the vanished people of the Glades. From some long-dried riverbed the Indians had dragged the ashlars through pine barren and swamp to the shore. Within the stony boundaries they had played their feverish games with clever wrenchings of buttocks and graceful knee-bends. The mystery of the savage past hovered over the southern wall. It intoxicated Sorrento, filling him with the romantic thrill that had been such a source of distress to Maitland. Yet who could deny the romance? Who could not be moved by the discovery—the fragile union with the past? Even if the evidence was useless and repetitious, was it not beautiful simply because it was another scrap of knowledge, another pinpoint of truth about the species? Looking, half hypnotized at his boulders, ruminating on Erwin's offer, he understood more vividly than ever what had drawn him into what his wife had once called the department of mud huts.

But he knew that the sealed box that was the Beach and the dig had closed forever. One more chamber of experience had been closed and he could not reopen it. These intervals of life, he told himself, had arbitrary limits, but they were limits nonetheless. Sorrento knew that the closure of the compartment had taken place a few hours earlier when he had talked with his wife about Ira. Or perhaps the box had been shut forever when the bulldozers had moved in. In any case, he could not stay.

"Thanks, Erwin," he said. "But we've had it. I can't stay. I'll unearth a few more tonight—to make sure they're not isolated rocks, and I'll get some photographs."

"No!" Lila cried. "You have to dig out the whole wall! The whole site! All the things you talked about—"

"Come on, Lila," he said wearily. "It's too much work. The dozers wrecked the levels. We'd never get a true picture now. But I tell you what. I'll call the State Archaeological Society and let them send some amateurs around to dig out the wall. They might find some interesting stuff at the east and west ends. Can I put them in touch with you, Erwin?"

"By all means." Ellenbogen beamed. This would delight Lila, and that mattered a great deal to him.

"It's very kind of you, Erwin," Marty said. "But Tom is right. We really have outstayed our welcome."

Lila frowned petulantly. "Well, I don't intend to lose track of you people *that* easily. When your paper is finished, Tom, you'll come down and read it to my women's club. And of course, we'll see you in New York this winter anyway."

"You bet, Lila," Tom said. "We'll all eat *scungilli* at Sally's First Avenue Bella Napoli Bar and Grill."

He permitted himself the luxury of an acrid cigar and resumed digging. The Burleys also bent to their work. Marty took the children to the boathouse—they needed baths in preparation for the departure. The Ellenbogens and Freddie left. At the water's edge, Sorrento and the young people worked until dusk, unearthing two more of the flat rocks, unmistakable evidence of the venerable arena. Lights winked in the soaring hotels on the ocean front and the summer air was weighted with tropic blossoms.

"Knock off, team," he told Wilma and Oran.

Obedient, the Burleys plodded toward the boathouse. Tom rested a moment on his shovel, noticing Sheldon Ellenbogen's beachball on the sand. He picked it up and tossed it a few times. For a fleeting moment he wished it were a football—fat and hard and tautly laced. A memory of autumn afternoons twenty years ago saddened him—crunch of leather and flesh and the wet turf beneath cleated shoes. Then he tossed the varicolored ball high, and as it descended, twisted his body, and with a vigorous wrench of his behind, thwacked it and sent it arcing high over the beach. The Burleys stared at him with solemn love.

"That's the way they did it, kids," Sorrento said gravely. "Can't you see them out here? All of them? Running bare-ass in the moonlight and knocking the big rubber ball through the ring? Can you see them? The Arawak people of the coast—*right here—right here* on Mr. Ellenbogen's land?"

He walked up the slope with them. "And there was the burial ground and the refuse heap and the huts, probably in a wide circle around everything—and the big old ball court in the middle, right down to the edge of the water!"

They walked ahead of him, smiling with childish self-satisfaction.

"Hey, you two—I asked you something!" he called. "Can you see the village? Can you see the people?"

They turned and nodded their wobbly heads. They saw them.

5 *Leave-Taking*

THEY were waiting at the gate for the plane to start loading when Ballard came lumbering down the passageway. He was excited about the discovery of the southern wall and he demanded to read Tom's manuscript before publication.

"I want to make sure you don't go fiction-crazy, boy," Ballard said. "You'll need the firm hand of a dull fellow like myself. You make sure he sends it to me, Marty."

"I will, Dave. It was sweet of you to see us off."

"Least I could do." He squatted and kissed the children. Abby, about half as brown as Dave, squinted at her father.

"Daddy—why is Dave staying down here? Doesn't he work at the University any more?" she asked.

"No, honey," Tom said. "Uncle Dave has a big job down here. He's running a revolution." Sorrento looked at the ogreish face. Ballard was like China—enormous, enigmatic, misunderstood. "How's the campaign coming?" he asked him. "Got any more marches in the works?"

"I'll let you know," Dave said. "You can fly down and parade with us again."

A handful of white passengers—well-dressed vacationers, bearing cameras and small bags—were looking curiously at the black giant who appeared to be on such intimate terms with the white family.

"Yeah, we've got our work cut out," Ballard said. "Harkey's in jail."

"In jail?" Tom asked.

"Just for a day or so. Until we raise the bail. They got him on some old law forbidding boycotts. But we'll have some news for *them* in a few days. We're going to sue the state."

"You *what?*" Tom asked. "How much nerve can you have?"

"Why not? We're asking the federal district court to force the legislature to abandon the gerrymander on the grounds that it denies us rights, privileges and immunities. It's going to be fun. I'm on the legal committee."

The plane had been eased into position; the wheeled stairs had been affixed to the door. An attendant was beginning to check tickets.

"You're going to be in the history books," Tom said.

"Or the obituary page," Ballard said.

"So long, Dave," Tom said. "We have to get on board." Ballard shook his hand and said his goodbyes—to the children, to Marty, to the Burleys. Wilma and Oran, dressed for travel in their Salvation Army best, had the look of wards of the state. Ballard started to walk away. His hulking figure seemed to bulge the roof and walls of the corrugated tin arcade. Suddenly he turned and walked toward Tom again, and kissed him on the top of the head. There was a purity in the gesture that forbade embarrassment. No one said anything and Ballard resumed his journey down the passageway toward the terminal.

As Tom's group edged toward the gate, a redheaded middle-aged woman in country-club clothing affixed him with shriveling eye. She said nothing to Tom, but addressed herself in stage whisper to another passenger, a woman similarly garbed. "Did you see *that?*"

"It's all right, lady," Sorrento said gently. "He was my Nigger Mammy when I was a baby."

When the admonition FASTEN SEAT BELTS had been blacked out, the children demanded their freedom. Marty extricated them from their window seats and they proceeded to explore the plane. In a few seconds they returned, breathless with excitement.

"Daddy!" Abby cried. "Guess who's on the plane! The *monkey!"*

"Which one?" Tom asked.

"The funny red one! With the long hair!" Abby pointed to the rear of the plane. "He's there—*fast asleep.* Oh, he's a darling!"

"He got a bottle," Nicky said. "Deh man change his diaper."

"Yes!" Abby cried. "And there was a man who said he knew you!"

Tom got up. "I guess I should pay my respects," he said to Marty. "You want to join me?"

"No thanks, dear."

He did not press the point. There had been an obscene intimacy between deKay and the orangutan. He was obliged to spare his wife any hurtful memories.

Following the children, he walked down the aisle, returning the mechanized smile of the stewardess, and entered the circular lounge in the tail. Mr. Banjo was indeed aboard. He slept in foetal bliss in the arms of his manager, Walter. A baby's bottle was clutched in his haired fingers and his flaccid mouth was glued to the nipple. The manager was distrait and pale. A month's vacation in the sun had done nothing for his chalky face. In the adjacent seat sat Si Mermelstein, in sedate Eastern campus clothing, thumbing through a leather-bound magazine.

"Si!" Tom called. "You leaving town?"

Mermelstein greeted him with morose weariness. "Oh—Tom. I thought you might be on the morning flight. I'm going to New York to settle a few of Ira's deals. Then I got to find me a job." He laughed uneasily. "Everything sort of fell apart when Ira died."

He went on to explain that Ira was being buried that day. He doubted that anyone would attend the burial except the office girls, Helene and Lucille. Si admitted a pang of guilt over not attending, but he assured himself that Ira would have forgiven him. It was strange, Si told Tom, how everybody had been Ira's pal but nobody had really been his friend. When the jerry-built structure of loot and deals had begun to collapse, it was as if Ira had been denuded and shamed. In the last few days preceding his death, Mermelstein explained—blinking his small scholarly eyes and biting his lips—people had stopped calling, stopped asking for favors, stopped listening to Ira's jokes.

Tom did not want to pursue the funerary analysis. He pointed to the sleeping ape.

"How about him?" he asked. "Is he well rested?"

The manager said nothing; his face was heavy with sorrow. Mermelstein leaned forward. "That's what I *mean,*" he said to Tom. "Mr. Banjo was fired yesterday."

"Him? Fired? I thought he was one of the nation's leading TV personalities. Didn't I hear that more people could identify him than the cabinet members?"

The manager opened his mouth, then shut it, gulping back his misery.

"It's spooky," Si said. "Just about when Ira got into all this trouble—the network decided Mr. Banjo wasn't dignified enough for *Our Heritage.* They canceled his contract—paid him off for thirteen weeks and dropped him. That's one of the reasons I'm going to New York. You see, Ira—the firm, that is—still owns a piece of him."

Tom nodded. How marvelously complex were the ways of modern culture! Maitland would have been intrigued. The rise and fall of Mr. Banjo—the exaltation of the orangutan, the cult of *Pongo pygmaeus,* the dying god—all these were matters that future archaeologists would ponder and interpret. A ruddy ape earning *eleven hundred and fifty dollars a week,* enough money to have fed the entire Tapapa Indian tribe for two years, perhaps to have saved them from extinction. Sorrento realized he was being unfair to the orangutan. Like Ira deKay, the ape was of the laughing, orgasmic army of distractors, perpetually in motion, clotting the increasingly radioactive air with inanities and irrelevancies. One *had* to believe with Maitland that this great congeries of deadeners and blunters had their unwitting function in the complex contemporary scheme. They were, one hoped, a buffer, an insulatory mechanism, diluting ancient evils, affording precious time so that all those ridiculous people—the humanist, the liberal, the social scientist—might pursue their insidious experimentation more urgently, more thoroughly.

The pilot had taken the plane on a wide circling movement, winging south and west a few miles to reach flight pattern. Now its shark's nose soared over the Ellenbogen land, the bay islet where once the dark dwellers of the Glades played their ritual ball game. Tom peered from the window and caught a last sunbright view of the old village site. He could see his newly unearthed white stones, the final, irrefutable evidence of the court, sparkling in the morning sun. He was surprised, too, by the dark streaks that his buried trenches manifested from the height. Some disturbance of stratification, perhaps the rapid in-filling of the pits with soil from lower layers, had preserved the pattern of excavations. He would have liked to have hovered over the site a bit longer; he might have learned something new from his lofty viewpoint. He made a mental note to read up on aerial archaeology: British diggers had long employed the technique to locate old Roman walls, roads and structures, but it had never been used with any precision in America. It might offer some intriguing possibilities for his next dig.

He left his children goggling at Mr. Banjo and walked back to the forward compartment. He had brought some notes with him regarding the Arawak-Glades hypothesis and he would use the four-hour trip to study them. To the north, the University awaited him and he longed for the severe, green-crowned piles, as eternal as truth. He was grateful that he had been allowed to become a minor member of it, that he might offer his microscopic tithe to the immortality of ideas.